PETER CORRIS

A CLIFF HARDY COLLECTION

THE DYING TRADE

THE MARVELLOUS BOY

WHITE MEAT

GW00730175

PICADOR

PUBLISHED BY PAN BOOKS
Sydney and London

The Dying Trade
First published by McGraw-Hill Book Company Australia Pty Limited July 1980
First Pan Books (Australia) Pty Limited edition published in 1982
© Peter Corris

The Marvellous Boy
First published by Pan Books (Australia) Pty Limited in 1982
© Peter Corris

White Meat
First published by Pan Books (Australia) Pty Limited in 1981
© Peter Corris

This Picador combined edition published 1986
by Pan Books (Australia) Pty Limited
68 Moncur Street, Woollahra, New Souh Wales
9 8 7 6 5 4 3 2

© Peter Corris 1986

National Library of Australia
Cataloguing in Publication Data
Corris, Peter, 1942-
A Cliff Hardy collection.
ISBN 0 330 27073 7
1. Detective and mystery stories, Australian.
I. Title. II. Title: The dying trade. III. Title:
The marvellous boy. IV. Title: White meat.
A823'.3

Printed and bound in Australia by
The Book Printer, Maryborough, Victoria

CONTENTS

THE DYING TRADE

5

THE MARVELLOUS BOY

237

WHITE MEAT

409

THE DYING TRADE

I was feeling fresh as a rose that Monday at 9.30 a.m. My booze supply had run out on Saturday night. I had no way of replenishing it on the Sabbath because we still had Sunday prohibition in Sydney then. I didn't have a club; that'd gone a while before, along with my job as an insurance investigator. I also didn't have a wife — not any more — or friends with well-filled refrigerators. Unless I could be bothered driving twenty-five miles to become a bona fide traveller, Sunday could be as dry as a Mormon meeting hall. I didn't travel. I spent the day on Bondi beach and the evening with tonic water and Le Carré, so I was clear-headed and clean-shaven, doodling on the desk blotter, when the phone rang.

"Hardy Investigations?"

"Yes, Cliff Hardy speaking."

"Good. Mr Hardy, I need your help. You've been recommended."

I could think of perhaps ten people who'd mildly recommend me. None of them would know the owner of this voice — eight hundred dollars a term, plenty of ordering people about and international travel.

"Yeah, who by?"

He named a name and I heard a faint bell ring. An insurance area boss or something, a hundred years ago. Still, it was a better start than the faded wives whose husbands had taken a walk or the small businessmen with payroll panic.

"Who am I talking to?"

"My name is Gutteridge, Bryn Gutteridge."

That didn't mean anything to me. There are three million people in Sydney, maybe a hundred are named Gutteridge and I didn't know any of them.

"What can I do for you, Mr Gutteridge?"

Mr Gutteridge didn't want to say too much on the phone. The matter was delicate, urgent and not for the police. He said he wanted advice and possibly action and asked if I could come out to see him that morning. Maybe he wanted to see if I was the advising or the active type. I felt active.

"I ask for a retainer of two hundred dollars, my fees are sixty dollars a day and expenses. The retainer's returnable if nothing works out, the daily rate starts now."

He spoke as if he hadn't heard me.

"I'm glad you're free. The address is 10 Peninsula Road, Vaucluse. I'll expect you in an hour."

"The money's OK then?"

"Oh yes, fine."

He hung up. I leaned back in my chair and dropped the receiver onto the handset. I traced a dollar sign with my little finger in the dust beside the dial. Money would be no object to that voice; it came from a world of Bible-fat cheque books and credit cards that would get you anything, anytime.

I left the office, went down two flights of stairs and out into St Peters Street. It was hot already, and a dry wind was pushing the exhaust fumes and chemical particles down the throats of the people in the street. I went round the corner, down a lane and into the backyard behind the tattoo parlour. The tattooist lets me park my car there for ten bucks a week. I backed the Falcon out into the lane and headed north.

Gutteridge's address fitted his voice. Vaucluse is several million tons of sandstone sticking out into Port Jackson. The sun always shines on it and the residents think it vulgar to talk about the view. I permitted myself a few vulgar thoughts as I pushed my old Falcon along the sculptured divided highway which wound up to the tasteful mansions and shaven lawns. Mercs and Jags slipped out of driveways. The only other under-ten-thousand-dollar drivers I saw were in a police Holden and they were probably there to see that the white lines on the road weren't getting dirty.

Bryn Gutteridge's house was a steel, glass and timber fantasy poised on the very point of a Vaucluse headland. It stretched its sundeck out over the sandstone cliff as if rebuking Nature for lack of imagination. The Falcon coughed its way through the twenty-foot high iron gates which were standing open and I stopped in front of the house wondering what they'd think about the oil on the drive after I'd gone.

I walked up a long wood-block path to the house. A gardener working on a rose bed looked at me as if I was spoiling the landscaping. I went up fifty or sixty oregon timber steps to the porch. You could have subdivided the porch for house lots and marched six wide-shouldered men abreast through the front door. I stabbed the bell with a finger and a wide-shouldered man opened the door while the soft chimes were still echoing about in the house. He was about six feet two, which gave him an inch on me, and he looked like he'd been the stroke of the first rowing eight maybe ten years before when the school had won the Head of the River. His suit had cost five times as much as my lightweight grey model, but he still wasn't the real money.

"Mr Gutteridge is expecting me." I passed a card across into his perfectly manicured hand and waited. He opened the door with a piece of body language which stamped him as a man of breeding but a servant nonetheless. His voice was a deep, musical throb, like a finely played bass.

"Mr Gutteridge is on the east balcony." He handed the card back. "If you wouldn't mind following me?"

"I'd never find it on my own."

He let go a smile as thin as a surgeon's glove and we set off to discover the east balcony. The rich always have lots of mirrors in their houses because they like what they see in them. We passed at least six full-length jobs on the trek which put expensive frames around a thinnish man with dark wiry hair, scuffed suede shoes and an air of not much money being spent on upkeep.

The rowing Blue led me into the library cum billiard room cum bar. He stepped behind the bar and did neat, fast things with bottles, ice and glasses. He handed me two tall glasses filled with tinkling amber liquid and nodded towards a green tinted glass door. "Mr Gutteridge is through there sir," he said. "The door will open automatically."

That was nice. Perhaps I could have both drinks and take the glasses home with me if I asked. The oarsman shot his cuffs and went off somewhere, no doubt to fold up some untidy money. The door slid apart and I went out into the harsh sun. The balcony was got up like the deck of a ship with railings and ropes and bits of canvas draped about. I started to walk towards a man sitting by the railing in a deck-chair about twenty feet away. Abruptly I stopped. He was a picture of concentration, resting his arm on the railing and taking careful sight along it and the barrel of an air pistol. His target was a seagull, fat and white, sitting on a coil of rope ten yards from his chair. He squeezed the trigger, there was a sound like a knuckle cracking and the seagull's black-rimmed eye exploded into a scarlet blotch. The bird flopped down onto the deck and the man got up quickly from his chair. He took a dozen long, gliding strides and kicked the corpse under the rail out into the bushes below.

I felt sick and nearly spilled the drinks as I moved forward.

"That's a shitty thing to do," I said. "You Gutteridge?"

"Yes. Do you think so, why?"

Despite myself I handed him the drink — there didn't seem to be anything else to do with it.

"They're harmless, attractive, too easy to hit. There's no sport in it."

"I don't do it for sport. I hate them. They all look the same and they intrude on me."

I had no answer to that. I look like a lot of other people myself, and I've been known to be intrusive. I took a pull on the drink — Scotch, the best. Mr Gutteridge didn't look as if he'd be nice to work for, but I felt sure I could reach an understanding with his money.

Gutteridge stabbed a block of ice in his glass with a long finger and sent it bubbling to the bottom. "Sit down Mr Hardy and don't look so disapproving." He pointed to a deck-chair, folded up and propped against the railing. "A seagull or two more or less can't matter to a sensible man and I'm told you are sensible."

I thought about that while I set down my drink and unfolded the deck-chair. It could mean a lot of things, including dishonest. I tried to look at ease in a deck-chair, which I wasn't, and intelligent.

"What's your trouble, Mr Gutteridge?"

He put the pistol down and sipped his drink. He was one of those people you describe as painfully thin. He had a small, pointed blonde-thatched head on top of shoulders so narrow they scarcely deserved the name. His bony torso and limbs swum about inside his beautifully cut linen clothes. He was deeply suntanned but didn't look healthy. Under the tan there was something wrong with his skin and his eyes were muddy. He didn't seem particularly interested in his drink so the cause of his poor condition might not be that. He was somewhere in his late thirties and he looked sick of life.

"My sister is being harassed and threatened," he said. "She's being goaded into killing herself — in strange ways."

"What ways?"

"Phone calls and letters. The caller and the writer seem to know a lot about her. Everything about her."

"Like what?"

"People she knows, things she does or has done, the perfume she wears. That sort of thing."

"Has she done anything special with anyone in particular?"

"I resent that Hardy, the implication…"

I cut in on him, "Resent away. You're being vague. Is this private information coming through damaging to your sister's reputation?"

He clenched his teeth and the skin stretched tight over the fine bones of his face. Letting my roughness pass exasperated him. He gave a thin sniff and took a tiny sip of his Scotch. "No, it's quite innocent — innocent meetings, conversations reported back to her. Very upsetting, almost eerie, but not what you're getting at. Why do you take this line?"

"She might be a blackmail prospect, the harassment could be a softening up process."

He thought about it. The outward signs were that he had good thinking equipment. He didn't ape the appearance of a mind at work by scratching things or screwing up his eyes. I rolled a cigarette and put my own tired brain into gear. I find that people are very reluctant to tell you the nub of their worries. Perhaps they think the detecting should start early, as early as detecting what they really have on their minds. The trick was to hit them with the right question, the one to open them up, but Bryn Gutteridge looked like a man who could keep his guard up and slip punches indefinitely.

"How's your drink, Hardy?"

"Like yours, barely touched."

"You're direct, that's good. I'll be direct too. My father committed suicide four years ago. He shot himself. We don't know why. He was prosperous, healthy, the original sound mind in the sound body." He looked down at his cadaverous frame. He was saying he wasn't sound himself, underlining the verbal picture of his father. There was something disembodied about him, fragile almost. I thought I had my question.

"How was his love life?"

He paid serious attention to his drink for the first time before he answered. He looked like Tony Perkins playing a suffering Christ.

"You mean how's mine," he said. "Or you mean that as well. You're an uncomfortable man, Hardy."

"I have to be. If I'm comfortable for you I'm comfortable all round and nothing gets done."

"That sounds right, glib perhaps, but right. Very well. *His* love life was fine so far as I know. He'd married Ailsa only about two years before he died. They seemed happy."

"Ailsa?"

"My stepmother. Ridiculous concept for grown people — my father's second wife. My mother and Susan's died when we were children. We're twins by the way, although we're not alike. Susan's dark like our father." I nodded to show that I was following him.

"My father was fifty-nine when he remarried. Ailsa was in her mid-thirties I suppose. As I say, they seemed happy." He jerked a thumb at the house. "He bought this to live in after he was married and he bought another place down there for Susan and me." He pointed down into the expensive air over the balcony. "He wanted us all to be close but independent."

It sounded about as independent to me as the pubs and breweries but Gutteridge didn't need telling. He finished his drink in a gulp and set the glass down. A real drinker, even if he paced himself, likes to have them end to end, gets nervous in the gaps. I knew the signs from personal experience and it was comforting to observe that Gutteridge wasn't a drunk. He ignored the glass and went on with his story without the support of liquor, another sign. He crossed his skinny ankles which were bare and black haired above long, narrow feet in leather sandals.

"Mark made a lot of money. He was a millionaire a few times over. Death duties took a lot of it, but there was still plenty left over for Susan and me. And Ailsa. I don't know why I'm telling you all this, we seem to be getting away from the matter at hand."

"I don't agree." I said. My drink was finished now and the tobacco between my fingers wasn't burning. I felt fidgety and ill at ease. Gutteridge's personality had had a strange effect on me, his words were hard and economical. He'd be a terror in the board-room when he was trying to get his way. He made me feel flabby and self-indulgent, this in spite of what I'd seen of his failings and the fact that it was he who had the million dollars. Or more. I felt about for the words.

"Things are connected," I said. "It sounds obvious but some-times the connections are extraordinary. I don't mean to sound Freudian, but I've known men who've beaten the life out of other people because of what happened to them when they were ten years old. There's a background, a connection to something else always. This trouble of your sister's, you can't expect to cut it out of your life, clean and simple. I'll have to look around, look back..."

"You're a voyeur," he snapped.

We were way back. He was feeling intruded upon and that, with him, was dangerous as I'd seen already. I tried to slip sideways.

"Tell me how your father made his money," I said. "And you could try thinking how it might link up with what's happening to your sister."

"Mark's was real estate money, of course," he said, sounding a bit too pat, as if he'd rehearsed the answer. "This place should tell you that. It's the ultimate development, the ultimate spiel. He sold people on this sort of thing and he believed in it himself."

"He was a developer then. Did he build houses himself?"

"Yes hundreds, thousands."

"Good ones?"

"Fair, they didn't wash away in the first rain."

"He sounds like par for the course. What else did you know about his business?"

"I can't see what you're driving at."

"Enemies, people with grudges, visiting the sins of the father and all that."

"I see. Well, I don't think Mark had enemies. He didn't have many friends come to that, mostly business acquaintances, lawyers, a couple of politicians, senior administrative people, you know."

"I get the idea. Pocket friends, just as good as enemies any day."

"I don't think you do get the idea." He emphasised the words snakily. "My father was a warm and eloquent man, he won people to his point of view. He almost invariably got what he wanted. He pulled off some remarkable deals, some colossal gambles."

"You liked him?"

He looked down at the deck, the first evasive gesture he'd made.

"Yes," he said softly.

It was beginning to look to me as if Mark Gutteridge and his manner of departing this life were more interesting than his children's problems, but that wouldn't pay the bills, so I just nodded, rolled another cigarette and snuck a look at my glass.

"Would you like another drink?"

"After you tell me some more about your sister's problem. When it began and your ideas on it."

"About a month ago Susan got a phone call. It was from a woman with a foreign accent — French possibly. She talked to Susan about her underwear, what brands she bought and how much it cost."

"No heavy breathing?" I asked.

"Nothing like that at all. She said things that upset Susan very much. Mostly about the money Susan spends on clothes and things. It's rather a lot I suppose. Susan likes nice things, nice things cost money."

14

His silver spoon was shining; some nice things don't cost money and some things that cost money aren't nice.

"It doesn't sound particularly sinister to me," I said. "It could almost be funny. Why was your sister so upset?" I could guess at what was coming next, but I wanted to hear how he put it.

"Susan has a strong social conscience. She's involved on Community Aid Abroad, Amnesty International, Freedom from Hunger. She's very busy and devoted to these causes."

I could just bet she was. The sweat from all that devotion and business was probably running down into her crepe-de-chine knickers so fast that she had to change them three times a day. I was having trouble getting interested in Susan Gutteridge's troubles and beginning to suspect that this investigation wasn't going to bring out the best in me.

"There was more than one phone call? And you mentioned letters?"

"Yes, calls have come at all hours of the day and night. The Voice — that's what Susan calls it — goes on and on about her private life, tells her how useless and parasitic she is, how meaningless her life is. It ... she ... refers to our father and tells Susan to do the same thing, tells her that she's cursed and her suicide is ordained."

I felt more interested and asked again about the letters.

"I only have one to show you," he said. "Susan tore up another five or six, she's not sure how many." He stood up, six feet of bony, moribund elegance and took a folded sheet of paper from his hip pocket. He handed it to me and reached down for his air pistol.

"Please don't do that," I said.

He sneered at me. "You mentioned your fee and your terms on the telephone. You didn't say anything about your sensibilities." He slid back a lever on the pistol and checked a pencil-thin magazine of lead pellets. "Have another drink, Mr Hardy, and turn your attention to what you'll be paid for." He rammed home the lever. "Or piss off!"

I shrugged. Big men were raping little girls, fanatics were torturing each other and people were going mad in cells all over the world. A protest here and now seemed a vain and futile thing.

15

"I'll take the drink," I said.

"I thought you might." He moved along the deck to where it took a right-angle bend into what I supposed was the south balcony. His hand came up sharply and he squeezed the trigger six times. Fifty yards away the pellets rattled like hailstones against metal and glass.

"The drink's on its way." He weighed the pistol in his hand.

"This is the most fun I have," he said. He waved the thing at me like a conductor's baton, signalling me on. "Get on with it!"

I got on. The paper could have been hand-rolled or beaten out with steam hammers for all I knew. It was a bit smaller all round than quarto and the words on it were in red ballpoint ink, printed in capitals like things of this kind usually are:

SUSAN GUTTERIDGE
YOU DESERVE TO DIE

Gutteridge hadn't fired his pistol while I was studying the note. He moved back to where I was sitting. He was tense, stretched tight.

"What do you think?"

"I don't know. I wish she'd kept the other notes. Did any of them mention money?"

He put the pistol down on the deck again and slumped down into the canvas chair. He was about to speak when the rower came out onto the deck carrying a tray with the drinks aboard. Gutteridge nodded at him in the first friendly gesture I'd seen him produce. He took one of the glasses and sipped it. "Just right, Giles," he said. Giles looked pleased in a well bred way and extended the tray to me. I took the glass and put it down beside me. I thought Giles was all right but Gutteridge seemed to think he was something more than that. He picked up the threads.

"Money, no I don't think so. Susan didn't say and I think she would have. I think the other notes were in the same vein as this, getting more savage."

"In what way more savage?"

He spread his hands and took a deep, tired breath. "I didn't see them all. One I did see said that Susan was sick. Another one said she was rotten. That's what I meant, sickness, rottenness, death."

"I see, yes. I still think this could be connected with your father's death in some way. But I suppose you've thought of that too?"

"No, I hadn't, but you've had experience of this sort of thing I presume, and I can see why the thought suggests itself. I don't think it's likely though."

This was better. He was beginning to afford me some field of expertise and it looked as if I might get enough cooperation from him to allow me to do the job. The sister was an unknown quantity at this point and my prejudiced snap judgment about her on the basis of the little I'd been told might be inaccurate.

"What do you think is likely then?" I asked.

"A crank I suppose, someone who gets kicks from baiting the rich."

"Maybe. Any political angle?"

"I shouldn't think so, we're not at all politically-minded, Susan and I."

Of course not, with their money you don't have to be. You win with heads and you win with tails, one way or another. But it would be easy enough to check whether or not Susan's actions had offended some part of the lunatic fringe.

"I have to know more about your sister, obviously," I said, "I'll have to talk to her. Where is she now?"

"She's in a clinic at Longueville. I suppose I could arrange for you to see her if you think it's essential."

"I do. She took all this so badly that she had to go into a clinic?"

"Partly this business," he said slowly. "Partly that, but there are other things involved. My sister is a diabetic and as I said she keeps very busy. She neglects her diet and regimen and her health suffers. She spends a week or so in Dr Brave's clinic a few times a year to recover her balance."

I nodded. I was thinking that my mother was a diabetic and she often went off the rails, but she didn't go into clinics, just ate apples and drank milk instead of beer for a while. But then, she died at forty-five. Money helps. "A diabetic clinic doesn't sound too formidable," I said. "No reason why I shouldn't see her if they had some notice."

He looked uneasy. "Dr Brave's clinic isn't exclusively for diabetics. It's for people who need care in different ways. Some of them need mental care. I'm not wholly in favour of the place but Susan won't hear a word against the doctor. She always seems rested and secure when she comes out so I go along with it."

He didn't like going along with anything that wasn't his idea, but his sister was his weak spot apparently. She was responsible for my being here talking to him and he didn't altogether like it. He seemed anxious for our talk to end.

"I'll give you the address of the clinic and telephone to let them know you're coming. When will I say?"

"This evening, about seven or eight."

"Why not this afternoon? What will you be doing then?"

They're all the same, rich or not rich, when they're paying for your time they want to see you running. Perhaps he thought I'd spend the day knocking down his retainer in a pub and doctoring the odometer on my car. I had a feeling that there was more to learn from him, perhaps just a point or two but they could be important. To get them I had to sting him.

"I'll be checking on things," I told him, "including you. It's standard procedure. Perhaps you could save me time and you money by telling me some more."

He bristled. "Like what?"

"Like how do you keep this going? Like what share in it does your sister have? Like where can I find your ... stepmother?"

"Her? Why in hell do you want to know?"

"The connections, that's where they might lead."

He looked straight at me with all the hardness back in his face. He was a capricious bird, intelligent, resentful of something and charming in a grim way, and these qualities washed across him alternately like intermittent rainstorms across a desert. He held up three skeletal fingers. "I'll answer your questions. One," he touched the tip of the first finger to his mouth and pulled it away, "Mark left his money well invested, it brings in now much more than he ever had. I sit on some boards, I own a couple of concerns outright and have interests in quite a few others. Two," he made the same gesture with the next finger, "Susan's interests are quite separate from mine. She *has* business dealings of course, here and in New Zealand and the Pacific. She did a tour of some of the places where her firms operated a couple of years ago. She's got a good business head, like me. Three," the finger flicked, "Ailsa lives in Mosman. She sold this house to me and bought one over there. I can give you the address."

He did and I clinched the arrangement by accepting his cheque for the retainer and three days at the rate I'd quoted. I was convinced that he had the money in the bank to cover the cheque, but even if I hadn't been, I'd still have taken the cheque because it's nice to have your client's name on a piece of paper if you have to yell for help. I agreed to keep him regularly informed and not to worry Susan unduly. The only thing he said about his father's second wife was that I was on no account to bring her to his house. I agreed. Giles showed me out through the corridors and ballrooms saying just what he'd said on the trip in, which was nothing.

I'd been in the house for over an hour so the gardener looked at me with new respect. I tried to look as if I always spent my Monday mornings with millionaires but I didn't quite bring it off. My car betrayed me by refusing to start. It caught just as the gardener was sauntering over with a supercilious smile on his face to give me a push. I sprayed a little gravel over him and took off on the long drive to the front gate. I didn't have to move over an inch to allow a white Bentley to go through the gate in the opposite direction at the same time as I did. The car was driven by a guy in a cap and through the grey tinted glass I caught a glimpse of a man whose face must have been paper-white in the sunlight, if he ever went out in it.

2

My first stop was the Public Library. I parked the car over near Mrs Macquarie's chair and walked through the Gardens. There were people in shorts, shirt sleeves and light cotton dresses sprawling on the grass and eating lunches. Flights of gulls came wheeling down when they spotted bits of thrown and discarded bread. I felt like telling them to stick to the public parks, they were safer there than at millionaires' mansions although the pickings mightn't be so good.

Who's Who and *Who Was Who* confirmed the outlines of the Gutteridge family picture as Bryn had given it to me. His father had been self-made, no old school ties and titled antecedents to back him up. He had remained a very private individual; there were few entries under the categories of clubs and interests. Horse-racing was his only spotlight activity. The only thing to cross-reference him under was "money". My researches turned up only two points of interest. One, Ailsa Gutteridge, nee Sleeman, had been married previously to James Bercer (deceased) who had been a tycoon on much the same scale and in much the same area of business as Gutteridge. Two, no Dr Brave was listed in the medical directory.

I walked back through the park. The rubbish of scores of lunches was being picked over by the birds and made me feel hungry. I drove home to Glebe, stopping only to pick up a flagon of white wine. I was thinking about Ailsa Gutteridge. I had a feeling that she might be a key to it all. If I was wrong I was prepared to try a new tack, but it's nice to get off on the right foot once in a while.

My place in Glebe is a small, two-storey sandstone terrace close to the dog track. I put most of the severance money I got from the insurance company down on it and in good months I can make the payments. The dog track is a convenient meeting-place for some transactions in my trade and, as they say, Glebe is one of those places where if you can't see a pub by looking both ways down the street then you must be standing outside one. The Falcon just squeezes into the back courtyard of the house which has two rooms up and three down. I cook, after a fashion, and listen to music on the bottom floor and sleep and read on the top.

I showered in the outhouse two feet away from the toilet and wolfed down a curried egg sandwich and several glasses of the wine. I put Nina Simone on the stereo partly for pleasure and partly to annoy my neighbour on the left. She sings the songs other people write better than they do, but for Dr Harry Soames, my neighbour, Dylan is king and Mitchell is queen so that Nina's versions of their stuff drives him beserk. Soames is an economist and when he isn't on sabbatical he spends his time under earphones or bitching about my not repairing the iron lace on the front of my house. Word is that he wants to buy me out to raise the tone of the street.

Three o'clock seemed as good a time as any to call on Ailsa Gutteridge. There wasn't anything useful I could say over the phone and if she wasn't home I could at least look her place over, ask around a bit about her and maybe wait a while. I eased the Falcon out of the courtyard by backing and filling. I find this relaxing, though Soames thinks it adds to the air pollution.

Sydney was sweltering. The roads were bubbling asphalt cauldrons and white-hot concrete paths to hell. Most people had managed to stay inside or find some shade, but there were several thousand of us who had to cook slowly inside mobile glass and steel ovens. The crawl through the city seemed endless and the traffic only began to move when it got onto the harbour bridge. Off the freeway into the precipitous harbourside streets, the drive became less of a military manoeuvre and more of a social occasion, with the big cars deferring to each other according to a fine, dollar-determined etiquette of their own.

Mosman looks nice from across the harbour and just as good up close. Mrs Gutteridge's house wasn't quite on top of the highest hill around but there was nothing blocking her view. The house was a gracious old brick job, very broad and deep with plenty of fresh paint on the woodwork and iron. A three-car garage at the side held a white Porsche sports car, a black Alfa Romeo sedan and a boat that looked eager to be off to Monte Carlo and quite capable of getting there.

I parked at a forty-five degree angle outside the house and was walking towards the front steps when I heard a scream. I ran in its direction between the Porsche and the Alfa. Glare from the swimming pool hit me and turned the world momentarily white, but I kept moving towards the two shapes at the far end of the pool. They were struggling and looked like frames from an undeveloped film. As my eyes and brain got back into cooperation I could see a tall, heavy built man trying to hold a woman by the strap of her halter top. He was taking swinging roundhouse slaps at her at the same time. The woman was past her first youth but she wasn't doing so bad; she was ducking some of the swings and getting in a few of her own. But he had the weight and reach on her and he must have landed a hard one to cause her to scream. I moved in behind him and shouted something. He let go and turned. He was hopelessly off balance and I hit him hard and low in the midsection. All the breath went out of him and he collapsed on his knees by the side of the pool. The woman recovered fast. She stepped in neatly and tumbled him into the water with a half kick, half push to the shoulder. The water was shallow but he went under once and sprawled, spluttering for a minute before pulling himself half over the tiled edge.

The woman was trying to light a cigarette with hands that were shaking like a tall mast in a high wind. She got there, drew smoke deep and blew it out. Her breasts rose firm and full under the halter top and her kicking-men-into-the-pool leg and its partner were pretty nice too.

"You'd better go Ross" she said evenly. "Take the Alfa and leave it and the keys at the office." Ross was big but my punch and the ducking had knocked the fight out of him. His silk and gabardine slacks were going to need some expert laundry work and his suede shoes were probably beyond repair. Water dripped from his thick black hair down over a face that was still handsome despite a badly set broken nose and a criss-cross of scars around the eyes and mouth. His look suggested that he might try to laugh it off, but the woman's face was stony, so he turned away muttering under his breath and squelched off towards the garage. An engine roared a few seconds later. There was a crunch of metal on metal, then a screech of tyres on concrete. The engine noise rose then receded.

"Jesus Christ!" The woman shut her eyes and flicked viciously at her cigarette.

"Who was that?" I said.

"Nobody. Who the hell are you?"

I explained who I was as she poured us both tall glasses of lemon juice and tonic from the fixings on a slat table beside the pool. So far the Gutteridges I'd met seemed to be good at not drinking and kicking things into oblivion. I'd have preferred a bit more drinking and a bit more concern for the lower forms of life.

We sat down in garden chairs and I took a good look while I was talking. She was cool but exciting; there was a lot of work left in her but she looked as if she'd be very choosy about who got the job.

"Have you got any identification?" Her voice was breathy and there wasn't a lot of power in it. She sounded tired and she didn't look very interested in me as she handed back the documents.

"What can I do for you, Mr Hardy?" There was an ironic, unencouraging edge to the standard words. I put the papers away and took a sip of the drink. It quenched the thirst.

"This concerns your stepson and stepdaughter, Mrs. Gutteridge."

"Sleeman!" she rapped out.

"Mrs Sleeman," I said quickly.

"Miss!"

"All right, Miss, but I'm still here to talk about the Gutteridges."

"That'd be right, private detectives are just about their style."

"What do you mean, Miss Sleeman? Have they used private inquiry agents before?"

She put out her cigarette, lit another immediately and looked at me through the fresh, blue smoke.

"I wouldn't know. Tell me what you want."

I rolled a cigarette and got it going before I answered. She was hard to fathom, she seemed uninterested but it might just have been that she was gathering the energy to be really antagonistic.

"Your stepdaughter's life has been threatened, your stepson wants to find out by whom."

"Let's call them Susan and Bryn, that step this and that routine makes me feel sick. Bryn wants to find out who and why, I presume?"

"The 'why' is my problem at the moment. 'Why' will tell me 'who', I hope."

"Perhaps not," she snapped, "I can think of lots of reasons to do down that little silvertail but they wouldn't necessarily have names attached."

"That's interesting," I said. "Give me some reasons."

She flexed her back, emphasising her best features, and stretched out her long brown legs. It was hard to guess her age; the heavily tinted outsized sunglasses hid some of the signs, her cheekbones were high with the skin smooth and taut across them and her mouth was full of even, white teeth — but the rich can do a lot in those departments. Her figure was full, but firm looking, and if Ross had been taking liberties with her I could easily see why.

"I'm not very interested in this, Mr Hardy," she underlined the statement with a sigh and took in some cigarette smoke. "I don't like the Gutteridge children — that is Mark's children — I appreciate that they're grown-ups in the obvious way at least — for a lot of reasons that I don't care to go into with you. You'd better tell me something to capture my interest or you'll have to go. To be frank, you're boring me."

She pulled over a bottle of suntan lotion which had a $5.50 sticker on it and began rubbing it into her thighs. I gave her a brief version of what Bryn Gutteridge had told me which she listened to with enough attention to call me a dirty name for using the word "stepson" again. She snorted and choked on her third cigarette when I asked her if her late husband had had enemies.

"Hundreds," she said. "He swindled dozens of people, defrauded scores."

"What about you, Miss Sleeman, were you his enemy?"

She flicked the cigarette butt into the swimming pool and waved a hand back at the house.

"What do you think?"

I said I didn't know. She yawned and turned her head away to look at the twenty foot high greenery which separated her swimming pool from her neighbour's. I had a feeling that she was working hard at her tough act but if so she was succeeding well enough.

"Go away, Mr Hardy. I have nothing to say to you. I'm just not interested."

"What are you interested in?"

"Not very much. Making more money, up to a point, and I read a lot."

"I bet you do."

She sneered at me very effectively which is an unusual thing for a woman to be able to do. "Don't try your hard-case masculine stuff on me, Mr Hardy." She lifted her head so that I could see her smooth, brown neck. "I'm forty, just about, I don't look it but I am and I haven't time to waste on men who are busy, busy at their little jobs."

I couldn't afford to let it go at that. I had too little to work on and I didn't want to be thrashing about in the dark when I spoke to Susan Gutteridge that evening. I looked her over again; heavy smoking but not drinking, at least not in the mid-afternoon. She wore a brief but not ridiculous swim-suit that looked as if it'd been wet and dry a few times. At the other end of the pool was a medium high diving board, with well-worn fibre matting. It looked like she dived, swam in the pool and watched her weight. A lot of pool owners dangle their feet in the water while knocking back gin and sailing little boats made of their chocolate wrappers across it.

"You're the best forty I've ever seen," I said. "Who's your doctor? Dr Brave?"

She dropped the bored display of the goods pose. Off came the shades and a pair of hard eyes bored into me. She had a strong-boned face that had never been beautiful but which must always have been arresting, as it was now. A few wrinkles around her eyes put her out of her twenties, but I'd meant what I said. She looked like one of those tennis playing women you see on local courts on the weekends, not aping youth but actually retaining it in the planes of her face and body.

"Why did you say that?"

"About Dr Brave? I don't know. You look like someone who takes good care of yourself, possibly under medical advice. Bryn Gutteridge mentioned Brave this morning, his sister is at his clinic. Bryn's not too happy about it. It just came into my head that as you dislike Mark Gutteridge's son so much you might have a different taste in doctors."

Her hard shell was beginning to split a little. She lit another cigarette with trembling hands and dropped the gold lighter onto the paving. She scrambled for a bit with one hand before giving up and working hard on the cigarette. She looked up at me as if I might just possibly be worth a minute's thought. Her voice was raw with something more than tobacco smoke affecting it. "You're right and wrong at the same time. Bryn's been lying to you. He and Brave are as thick as thieves. Brave's his head-shrinker, hand-holder and I don't know what else. I detest him."

"Why?"

"I've said all I'm going to say. I don't care if I never see Mark's children again and that goes double for Brave. I want to be rid of the whole bloody crew of them." She stood up, tall and struggling for her natural composure which I'd somehow shattered. "Off you go, Mr Hardy. I'm going to try to have a sleep and forget you ever happened."

I took out one of my cards and put it on the arm of my chair. She didn't look at it and turned towards the house. I stood up, stiff and tense from the pressure exerted by her abrasive personality. I started to walk towards the garage, then I turned towards her.

"One last question, Miss Sleeman." The distance between us was widening.

"Yes?"

"Why isn't Dr Brave listed in the medical register?"

She turned her face towards me and howled, "Go away!" She

jerked off her sunglasses and threw them blindly away fom her. They sailed through the air, spiralling down like a disabled fighter plane and dropped into the pool.

"Why?" I shouted.

She clenched her fists by her sides and the face she lifted up was a mask of pain. She spoke harshly, grittily. "He's not a medical doctor, he's a psychologist from somewhere . . . Canada . . . somewhere. Now will you please go!"

She marched into the house and I went.

3

I drove across to The Rocks and bought a paper from a barefoot kid in the public bar of the Eight Bells. The pub is tucked away in a crevice of the sandstone and claims to be directly descended from the first inn built by the waterside in Sydney and maybe it is. Its other main claim to fame is that Griffo drank and fought there, and since Griffo drank and fought in every pub in The Rocks this is incontestable. Seekers after authenticity are starting to discover the pub and pose a threat to its integrity, but for the moment it's holding its own against the pressure to become another unisex, unidrink playground. The counter tea, served early, was steak, salad and chips and I ordered it along with a litre carafe of the house plonk. This made me an eccentric in the saloon bar where workers in singlets were putting down beer with their food and a scattering of executives and trendies were drinking wine from bottles with theirs. They gave me a beer glass with the carafe which suited me fine.

The paper was full of the usual drivel — the Pope pronouncing on sex and politicians claiming to speak for the common man. The lead story was about Rory Costello — standover man and armed robbery expert, who'd been sentenced to twenty years in Long Bay. He'd escaped ten days ago and had been sighted simultaneously in Perth and Cairns. The steak was good and the wine fair. I ate and drank slowly and tried to make some sense of the information I had on the Gutteridge case so far.

I hadn't established any clear connection between the threats to Susan Gutteridge and the suicide of her father, if it was suicide. Bryn Gutteridge hadn't provided any connections out of his picture of his father — an honest, if forceful, businessman. Gutteridge's ex-wife had a different picture of him — unscrupulous and dishonest, with a thousand enemies, any one of whom could be taking it out on the daughter. This view of the late Gutteridge appealed to me most, but that could have been my bank balance and prejudices speaking. Against Bryn's story in general was that he had lied about his attitude to Dr Brave, or a lie was implied in what he'd told me. That is, if Ailsa Sleeman was telling the truth. She was a complex woman who'd seen two tycoon husbands off, but she had no obvious reason to lie on this point. It was easily checked, but that went for Bryn's story too. He seemed to be in dubious control of his cool. Maybe he lied about everything. Maybe he was an eccentric millionaire who liked to send private detectives on wild goose chases. Suddenly, that seemed like a clean, uncomplicated thing to do — to chase wild geese in northern Canada. I ate, drank, smoked and thought until it was time to go and meet the stricken sister.

Leafy Longueville features trees and water glimpses. There's some big money and a lot of middle-sized money around; the middling people are working to keep up with the big people who are looking across the Lane Cove river towards Hunters Hill, where everybody has big money, and wondering if they can afford the move. The people work outside the area, send their kids out of it to school and don't talk to each other. They spend their time cultivating high, privacy-making hedges and looking the other way.

At 7.15 Longueville is quiet. Hoses sprinkle on lawns and the big cars are all sitting in their garages. Nobody and nothing moves in the front grounds of the houses. The terraces and swimming pools out back could be awash with gin and naked women, but you'd never know from the street. The clinic was a block from the suburb's main road. That put it close to the river, and into the heart of the Hunters Hill envy zone. I didn't lock the Falcon because there are no car thieves in Longueville and I didn't take my gun because there are no muggings either. Longuevillians do their thieving in the city five days a week, nine to five, and they get away from it all at home. The Brave clinic was an assemblage of white brick buildings with tinted glass standing in an acre or two of lawn and trees. There were no fountains or benches of the kind that are supposed to soothe troubled minds. Rather the air was of tight security. There was a high cyclone fence with concrete-embedded posts and a glassed-in reception booth which looked a bit too well equipped electrically for the sort of place the clinic was supposed to be. Since my commando days I've always been tempted by cyclone fences — the sadistic instructors must have sent us over hundreds of the bastards at terrific risks to our virility — but not this one. It was wired up to blazes and looked as if sirens would wail if you touched it, while relaying TV pictures of your blackheads to the main block.

I walked up to the booth. Some distance from it a metallic voice bounced off my chest.

"Please state your business."

The guy in the booth leaned forward to look at me through the glass. He wore a white shirt, grey jacket and black tie. Through the thick glass his face was a pale, distorted blob. No microphones were visible. He just spoke in my general direction and I heard him loud and clear. I had to assume he could hear me.

"I have an appointment to see one of Dr Brave's patients at 7.30. My name is Hardy."

He pressed a button, a pane of glass slid back. He put his right hand through and snapped fingers tightly gloved in black leather.

"Identification please."

I fished in my pocket and pulled out the licence card. It looks like a student ID card and would get me into Robert Redford movies half-price if I looked twenty years younger and could stand Robert Redford. I handed the card over. More glass slid back and the guard looked me over critically like a Russian customs officer who can be satisfied as to your identification but is pretty unhappy that you exist at all. He nodded, handed back the card and pressed a button; a gate beside the booth swung open.

"Please walk up to the largest building ahead of you, Mr Hardy. Stay on the path all the way please."

I went through. There were a few lights up on poles and some in hatches at ground level. They focused on the wide, intricately laid brick path. There was no excuse for slipping off it onto the velvet grass but I dawdled off to the left and took a couple of steps on the sward just for the hell of it. Closed circuit security TV is even more boring than the public kind, and I might just have made someone's day.

Close up all the buildings had a severe practical look. The main block had heavyweight glass and timber doors at the top of a dozen steps. I went up, pushed them open with a featherlight touch and went into a cool, navy-carpeted lobby with a reception desk set at an artful angle. No blondes. A tall burly guy who looked like an Italian eased himself off the desk and stepped towards me. He was wearing a denim suit with knife edge creases and white shoes. His white silk shirt was open far enough to show a gold medallion nestling in a thatch of thick, black hair. His waist was slim, there was no flab on him and only a slight thickening of his features betrayed how many fights he'd been in. He looked as if he'd won most of them.

"Please come with me, Mr Hardy. Dr Brave is waiting for you."

He inclined his black pompadour towards a teak door at the end of the room. He'd said it before, more or less, but he was still having trouble wrapping his western suburbs Italian accent around the polite words. He was built for action and it was a pity to make him talk. He ushered me through the door and down a long corridor done up in the same style as the lobby. Glass-panelled doors opened off it at frequent intervals and the Italian plucked at my sleeve when I slowed down to take a look through one. The place was getting to me — it looked like a jail for people who were very rich and very sorry for what they'd done. I passed him on the left and pulled open the next door on that side.

"Interesting place this," I said, sticking my head into the room. Empty, sterile, with bars on the windows. A hand fell down on my shoulder and the fingers closed vice-like around the bone. He pulled me back as easy as a kid pulling on a wad of gum.

"Don't do that again, Mr Hardy."

"I'm sorry," I said. "Just curious." I had a feeling that he was trying to hurry me through this part of the building. I wondered why.

"Don't be."

We were side by side when we reached the next door on the

right. I hunched myself and cannoned into him blasting him against the wall. I opened the door and stepped in. He recovered fast and moved towards me. When he was half-way through the opening, I swung the door back full into him. He took some of it in the face, some at the knee and the handle in the solar plexus. He collapsed like a skyscraper in an earthquake. I turned around to look at the room. I caught a glimpse of a man with a bandaged face sitting on a bed before I felt like I'd been dumped by a gigantic wave: a ton of metal tried to tear my head from my shoulders and sandbags crashed into my belly and knees. I went down into deep, dark water watching a pin-point of light which dimmed, dimmed and died.

Everything hurt when I swam up out of the dark. I tried to slide down into it again but I was slapped hard across the face and pulled up into a sitting position on a short, hard couch. I turned my head painfully and saw the Italian dusting off his hands. He looked bad — one side of his face was a purple smear and he stood awkwardly, favouring one leg. But he was on his feet and in better shape therefore than me. Sitting behind a table in the middle of the room was the man I'd seen pulling into Gutteridge's driveway in the Bentley. His face had the colour and texture of chalk. His hair was jet black and there was black hair on the backs of his hands. His eyebrows were thick, black bars that met in the middle; he looked like a chessboard come to life. His voice was soft with a burr that could have been Scots but might have been the echoes and rings inside my head.

"You have been very foolish, Mr Hardy. You were asked to observe certain civilities. May I ask why you did not?"

"I wasn't asked, I was told." My voice seemed to come from somewhere behind me but it would have hurt too much to turn and look. "This place made me feel rebellious."

"Interesting. It's supposed to have the opposite effect. But never mind. The question is, should you be allowed to see the person you've come to see after this behaviour? I have my doubts."

I swung my legs off the couch and wrestled myself into a less invalid position. I felt in my pocket for my tobacco, then I noticed that Brave had the contents of all my pockets neatly arranged in front of him. He waved a hand at the Italian who reached over to the desk top, picked up my tobacco and matches and tossed them into my lap. I rolled a cigarette, lit it and drew the smoke deep. It caught halfway down where everything felt loose from the moorings and I gasped for breath and spluttered. The Italian clouted me hard enough on the back to clear the smoke and rearrange some organs.

"Gently Bruno," said Brave, "Mr Hardy's had a nasty fall."

My voice was wheezy and thin. "You can't stop me seeing her," I said, "not when her brother's OK'd it."

Brave smiled. "Her brother's not her keeper," he said.

"Who is? You?"

"In a way, but not as you may think. Miss Gutteridge is in poor health physically, and she has been under severe strain. Being questioned by a roughneck detective could do her great damage."

Bruno cracked his knuckles to remind me that I wasn't the only roughneck around. I had been out-muscled and now I was having professional rank pulled on me. It seemed time to fight back.

"You're not a medical doctor. I checked the register. What are you, a PhD? They're drip-dry on the hook I hear, at some places."

It upset him. He lifted a hand to his ear and pulled the lobe gently down. He dropped the hand to push my things contemptuously around on the desk.

"Your qualifications are here," he said. "Sleazy and sordid. And your physical powers seem ordinary. What point are you trying to make by insulting me"

"At the most," I said, "you're a psychologist. You may not even be that, reputably. You're not a psychiatrist, that needs a medical degree. I question your professional and legal right to prevent me seeing anyone at all, especially someone who's nearest of kin has endorsed me."

He gave it some thought, then spoke rapidly, the accent now twanging angrily in his voice. "Who told you that I was a psychologist?"

"I could have worked it out myself," I said, "but since you ask, Ailsa Sleeman."

"I see. Did she know you were coming here?"

"Yes," I lied.

"Who else?"

I kept lying. "A guy named Ross, Miss Sleeman's boyfriend; my answering service; a petrol station attendant I asked directions from; maybe Giles, Gutteridge's man."

Brave looked like the subtle type. I didn't think he really intended to have me dumped in the harbour and he knew I didn't think it, but if he found the threat worth implying I could find it worth countering. But I was getting impatient and didn't want to lose the initiative, if that's what I had.

"How about it, doctor? Do I see her now or come back with a court order?"

"You're being foolish again. Bryn wouldn't take out a court order against me. He wouldn't go against my advice on this."

"You've convinced yourself, you haven't convinced me."

He ignored me. His eyes were as dark as an arctic night under the heavy brows and they seemed not to be registering my presence in front of him at all. I didn't look much. My hair was matted around a wound on the back of my head that was seeping blood and I had the general look of a man who'd been sick for a week and hadn't changed his clothes, but to be looked through quite so devastatingly was disconcerting. He spoke slowly as if talking to himself. "However, they've all been through a lot and it might be best for you to do your clumsy act and run along."

He got up, tall and spare and snapped his fingers at Bruno. "Take him through to Room 38. I'll be along in a minute. He's not to see her until I'm there. Fifteen minutes Hardy!"

"For now," I said.

Bruno opened the door and I followed him shakily out into the corridor. We walked warily, taking a couple of turns to right and left, not chatting. Bruno stopped outside a bolted door which had 38 painted in gold on its smooth black surface. He put his back against the door.

"We wait," he said.

I didn't argue. Balanced and braced like that he was about as movable as Gibraltar and I wasn't feeling rebellious any more. I needed time to think out an approach to the woman whose problems had brought me here, and my condition for thinking wasn't good. I'd come up with exactly nothing when Brave came round the corner. He'd put a fresh white jacket on over his white shirt and dark trousers. His eyes were dark, shining obsidian spheres and he seemed to be carrying himself very stiffly. He might walk and look lit up like that all the time, but there seemed a better than even chance that he'd given himself a shot of something. Bruno stepped aside, Brave drew the bolt, pushed the door open and I followed him into the room.

Room 38 was an expensively appointed sick room; there was a big low bed with a mountain of pillows and acres of white covers, assorted bottles on a bedside table, fruit in a beaten metal bowl, a streamlined portable TV set and a smell of money cloying the air. A woman, on the right side of forty but not by much, was sitting up in bed reading a paperback — *Family and Kinship in East London*. Her hair was dark brown, cut severely, her face was pale, puffy around the eyes. Bryn Gutteridge was right when he'd said that he and his sister weren't look alike twins. This woman didn't resemble him at any point. Reading, concentrating, she wasn't bad looking, but she wasn't interesting. When she looked up to see Brave standing at the end of her bed her face transformed. She swept her hand over her hair making it careless, pretty. She smiled a good wide smile and something like beauty flowed into the bones of her face. She held out her hands.

"Doctor, I didn't expect to see you again today."

Brave moved around the bed. He took her hands, pressed them, laid them on the bed, not quite giving them back to her. "I'm sorry to disturb you, Susan," he said. "This is Mr Clifford Hardy, he's a private investigator."

Her eyes flew open in alarm, she went rigid for a second then grabbed for Brave's hand. She got it and calmed down, but she was strung up and stretched out and I doubted my ability to get anything out of her without having it filtered through Brave first. And he was making a lot of very strange moves. But I had to try. I stepped past Bruno and went up to the bed, facing Brave across it. I tried to keep roughneckedness out of my voice.

"Miss Gutteridge, your brother hired me ..."

"Bryn!" Her hands shot up to her face and lines appeared around her mouth and neck which made her look fifty. She'd sweat and twitch if you said Santa Claus too loudly. Like Freud's, most of my clients are middle-class neurotics, but some of them have real problems in a real, hostile world. Some don't have any problem but themselves and I couldn't be sure which category Susan Gutteridge fell into. Brave did some more hand-squeezing.

"Susan, you don't have to talk to him if you don't want, but he has been persistent and I judge that you should see him now, once and for all. I'll stay right here and I promise I won't let him upset you."

Whatever he judged and promised would be fine with her. She relaxed and turned a scaled-down version of the smile on me.

"I'm sorry, Mr Harvey?"

"Hardy."

"Hardy. I'm overwrought, one thing and another. If my brother and Dr Brave think it wise for me to talk to you then I'm sure it is. I've never met a detective before. It's about the threats I suppose?"

"Yes," I said, "and other things."

"Other things?" She looked nervous. Susan Gutteridge's rails were long and narrow and she had to summon all her strength to stay on them for very long. Maybe it was the surroundings — clinics, psychologists, threats — maybe a slight physical resemblance, but I found myself thinking of Cyn, my ex-wife. Cyn, beds, breakdowns, lovers, lawyers: I pushed myself back from it.

"I mean related things, Miss Gutteridge, family things mostly which might throw some light on the problem. Give me something to go on, you understand."

Brave's snort of derision underlined my own awareness of the cliched cant I was spouting, but cops have to say "it is my duty to warn you", and doctors have to say "put out your tongue".

"I'd like to hear your account of the threats," I went on, "and your ideas and reactions. You're a sensitive woman. The threats came from a woman and you might have picked out something that a man would miss."

She looked blank. Wrong tack. I buttered her on the other side. "You have experience of people in need, social problems. Maybe you can guess at the disturbance in this woman's mind, what she wants, what lies behind it." That was better. Smugness crept into her face. She moved her hands away from Brave's for the first time. She smoothed down the covers. It was hard not to dislike her.

"You are acute in your own way, Mr Hardy," she said. "Of course, one of the worst things about this, for me, is the thought of how disturbed that woman must be to be saying those things. The person speaking to me on the telephone was emotionally disturbed. As you say, I have some experience in this area. The language was frightful."

I suppressed an impulse to laugh. "Do you mean it was obscene?"

"Yes, horribly so. I had to burn the letters."

"Were they obscene too?"

She started to look nervous again. "No, not at all, just awful."

"Why did you have to burn them then?"

She plucked at the bedcover, shredding some of the raised nap and balling it in her fingers. "I meant that, well, the filthy language and the letters came from the same person. So I burned the letters."

"You think the phone calls and letters came from the same source do you?"

"Yes, of course."

"Why, of course?"

"They must have."

"Tell me one, just one, of the objectionable phrases in the phone calls."

"I can't, I couldn't say it."

"What were the letters about? The same thing?"

"No — sickness, decay, death."

"Come on Miss Gutteridge, one phrase from the calls."

She glared at me, bunched her fists and hammered them on the snowy bedcover. "Fucking capitalist!" she screamed in my face.

There was a silence that seemed to let the words hang in the air forever. Then she started sobbing and Brave moved in with all systems go. He took her hands and clasped them inside his while murmuring comforting, animal-like sounds in her ear. He swayed above her like a mesmerised snake putting the music back into the pipe. She regained control very quickly. I knew that this kind of command over another person was extremely difficult to obtain and incredibly costly to bring about in time and effort. There was no short cut to it and I wondered why Brave had made an investment of this order in this pathetic woman. There was no time for on-the-spot investigation. At a nod from Brave, Bruno moved forward and took my arm just above the elbow. His grip hurt like a dentist's drill on a nerve.

"You've had your time, Hardy," Brave said, "I hope you're satisfied with what you've done."

If that was supposed to make me feel sorry for the woman it didn't work. Her problems were mine only in a strictly professional sense, but I had to stay with them. At this point I had to assume that Bryn had hired me for reasons other than those he'd stated. That isn't unusual, but you have to sort the real reasons out fairly quickly if you don't want to be the meat in the sandwich all the way. I had to fire a shot in my own war.

"Goodbye, Miss Gutteridge," I said, "I hope you know what you're doing."

"Out," Brave hissed the word like a jet of venom and Bruno swung me round and we trotted out of the room like big Siamese twins joined at the shoulder.

We made the same turns in reverse and Bruno shooed me into the room I'd surfaced in before. I sat down on a chair near the desk and started scooping my things up and putting them in my pockets. Bruno stepped forward and a puzzled look spread over his face as he tried to work out whether he was supposed to stop me or not. He couldn't tell and he couldn't think and hit at the same time. Not many muscle men can and it gives the weaklings a fractional edge sometimes. I made a cigarette as the Italian hovered in the middle of the room looking like a discus thrower turned to stone in the middle of his wind-up.

"Don't worry, Bruno," I said. "I'll wait here for your master and in a little while you'll be able to go off and do something about your face." That gave him something to think of. He put a hand up to his face and pressed gently. "Harder," I said, "maybe there's something broken." He worked his jaw and grimaced. I might have been able to get him to give himself a karate chop but there was no challenge in it. The door swung open and Brave walked in. He sat down primly behind his desk and the first colour I'd seen in his face appeared — high red spots in his cheeks like daubings on a clown.

"You've been very troublesome, Hardy," he said, "and achieved very little, I should imagine."

"Why should you imagine that?"

"I won't fence with you. You are a nuisance, plain and simple. A blunderer into delicate situations. The question is, how to be rid of you."

I wanted to bring his dislike of me up as high as it would go.

"A blunderbuss," I said.

He registered it like a deep internal pain.

"As I understand it," he said slowly, "a private detective is without any authority and credibility if he is without a client."

"You've read too much Chandler," I said.

He looked puzzled for a second but didn't let it stop him. "I think that's so," he went on, "and therefore you represent no problem at all Mr Hardy, none at all. Show him out Bruno."

Bruno and I did our dancing bears act down corridors and through doors and in five minutes I was walking down the path towards the gate. The night air hit me hard and I gave my attention to finding a chemist for my head and a bottle shop for me.

4

The Green Man and Joe Barassi's All Day All Nite Pharmacy at Drummoyne put me back together. I washed down two red Codrals with a couple of hefty slugs from a half bottle of Haig. I looked at the wound on my head in the mirror of the Green Man's washroom. It didn't look too bad, the blood had stopped seeping and I managed to clean the area up with damp paper towels. Whoever had hit me had known his business and had chosen to give me a purple heart rather than a posthumous medal of honour. I felt vaguely grateful to him and had another nip out of the Scotch bottle for him.

The traffic flowed easily over the Iron Cove bridge. People were all in the cinemas and pubs and there was little competition for me on the drive home to Glebe. I wasn't up to shuttling the car into the courtyard so I left it outside the house with a steering lock on the gearshift which would hold up a good Glebe car thief for about two minutes. My head throbbed and a little laser of pain stabbed over the right eyebrow but I decided to try and make some sense of the night's play before I let another Codral and some more whisky sing me to sleep. I sat in a bean bag with a tall Scotch and soda on the floor beside me. I rolled three cigarettes and set them in the grooves of the ashtray the way Uncle Ted used to. Uncle Ted had a good war, sent back hundreds from the Tobruk two-up games and survived. I'd survived high school, two erratic years at university and Malaya to become an insurance investigator — long hours, high mileage and pathetic incendiarists. The work had coated my fingers with nicotine, scuttled my marriage and put fat around my waistline and wits. The deals and hush-money made divorce work seem clean as riding a wave and bodyguarding noble and manly. Suicides and Svengalis were a different thing though, and I wasn't sure that I was up to coping with them. I was on the third cigarette without having any inspiration, when the phone rang.

I heaved myself out of the bean bag and put the receiver somewhere near my face.

"Mr Hardy?" A woman's voice, drunk or panicky.

"Yes, who's this?"

"It's Ailsa Sleeman, I found your card. I didn't know what else to do. I'm frightened."

"What's happened?"

"It's horrible. Bryn just called me, I don't know why me, I suppose he just doesn't know anyone else . . ."

"What's happened?"

'It's Giles. He's been shot. He's dead."

"When was this?"

"I don't know. Bryn rang me about an hour ago. I've been trying to reach you since then."

"You sound frightened Miss Sleeman. Why?"

"It's hard to explain. Impossible over the phone. It's to do with Dr Brave who you seemed interested in this afternoon. I'm afraid of him. I need help, perhaps protection. I'm willing to employ you."

That was a switch. A few hours ago she was willing to forget me like a bad dream. This would give me two clients on the same case. I wasn't sure it was ethical, it had never happened to me before. But if Bryn meant me to proceed with the investigation maybe I could work out a package deal. If Brave could carry through with his threat, I'd lose Bryn as a client so it would be convenient to stay with it on La Sleeman's behalf. I was hooked on the Gutteridge's now, and I felt that I'd got into some kind of conflict with Brave that had to be seen through. I needed a bit more to go on though.

"I'm interested Miss Sleeman," I said in my deliberate voice, "but I need a little more information. Did Mr Gutteridge mention Dr Brave?"

"Yes, they've had a quarrel."

"OK. Can you come in to my office in the morning?"

"Tomorrow?" The panicky note was back, "I thought tonight . . ."

"Miss Sleeman, I've driven a hundred miles today, been lied to, had two fights and lost one badly. I'm out of action until 9 a.m. tomorrow."

All true enough, but what I really wanted to know was whether she was serious about her proposition and alarm, or was just feeling lonely for the night. She could be one of those rich people who think they have everything they need behind their high walls but occasionally have to send out for some help. Or she might still be in touch with the world outside. I also felt a need to do some talking on my own territory after the lies I'd been told so far. There's something truth-inducing about a hard chair and a smell of phenol in the hall.

"All right," she said. Her voice was steadier, no drink in it. "I'll be in at 9 o'clock. You will help, Mr Hardy?"

I told her I would, made sure she had the address right, made a few reassuring noises and she rang off. The phone rang again almost as soon as I'd put it down. I let it ring a few times while I visited my drink and finished my cigarette. I took Bryn's cheque out of my wallet and spread it out in front of me. It was one of those big, friendly cheques from a big, friendly chequebook. I'd hoped to collect a few more. I picked up the phone.

"Hardy? This is Bryn Gutteridge."

"Yes?"

"A dreadful thing has happened Hardy."

I had to decide quickly whether to let him tell it or to tell him I knew what was up and judge his reaction. The first way seemed to leave me more cards.

"You sound upset. Take it quietly and tell me."

"Giles has been shot. He was in the car, going on an errand for me . . . and someone shot him in the head. He's gone."

"I'm sorry Mr Gutteridge. You've called the police?"

"Yes of course. They've been and gone. They were very considerate. I was surprised."

I knew what he meant but I wasn't surprised. The Commissioner would have got in on this quickly and he'd have kept the public lavatory prowl squad well out of it. "Do you want me in on this?"

"No!" Sacking people was second nature stuff to him. He did it with no embarrassment.

"The police will be prying into my affairs. That's enough. When this is over I'm going away, perhaps for a few years."

"I see. What about your sister?"

"I'll take her with me. We'll get out of this. Drop the investigation Mr Hardy. Thank you for . . ."

"For what? Just for interest, when did you decide to let the investigation drop, before or after Giles' death?"

"Oh God, I don't know. Before, I think. I'm not sure. Why does it matter?"

"It matters to me. What did Dr Brave say to you when you saw him this evening?"

"I didn't see him, he rang." He broke off confused and annoyed with himself for replying. "This is no longer your affair, Hardy."

I didn't have much of his time left. "Did he threaten you?" I said quickly.

"I'm hanging up Hardy. Send a bill."

"You've overpaid me. Have this for free — Giles' murder and the threats to your sister are connected. You can't run away from it." He hung up.

That left me with Ailsa. I took another pill and finished my drink.

I went to bed. The street was quiet, no dog races so my head was spared the roar of punters' Holdens and the purr of the bookmakers' limousines. It was too hot for the street fighters and gutter drinkers to be out lending the area colour and Soames must have had the music down low. I drifted off to the quiet hum of my fan. I slid into a dream in which Ailsa Sleeman, standing tall, reached down for my hands and lifted them up onto her massive breasts.

5

I woke with a headache that was partly due to the crack I'd taken the night before. I looked out of the window across the rusting roofs of Glebe. The sky had a dull, leaden look — the day was going to be hot. A Sahara wind was already whipping the ice-cream wrappers and other crap along the gutters. I made coffee but it was bitter and I swilled it down the sink. About the only good thing I've ever heard of Mick Jagger is that he likes scrambled eggs and white wine for breakfast. I made my version of scrambled eggs, piled a glass up with ice and topped it up with hock and soda. I put the drink down fast, made another, and took it, the food and *The News* out to the courtyard, feeling better every minute.

The paper headlined the hunt for Costello, the police expected a breakthrough hourly, and there were pictures of beefy guys in shirt sleeves heavying honest citizens. Giles' departure from this vale of tears didn't get a mention. I ran my eye hopelessly over the cryptic crossword and consoled myself with the meteorological report — hot, high winds ahead of a thunderstorm. I skimmed the paper again and was surprised to find an idea forming in my mind. I let it take shape for a few minutes and then gave it another drink in case it went away hurt.

I shaved, took a shower and put on my other suit which is said to be lightweight but always makes me sweat like a pig if I move at a pace above a royal stroll. I was already hot when I slipped into the car. The radio aerial had been broken off just above the mounting and was lying in three pieces across the bonnet in the shape of the mark of Zorro. I swore and swept the pieces into the gutter. Insurance was supposed to cover things like that, but how do you insure yourself against insurance premiums? The car started cheerfully and I moved off towards the city.

I reached my office, two floors up above St Peters Street, close to 9.00. The Cross, or what's left of it after the developers had their way, is just a block north. The whores were already at work, not doing any business among the winos squatting on the pub steps, but keeping in practice. My office opens straight into the corridor, no ante-rooms for people to wait or die in. I inherited it from a clairvoyant who fell under a train. The desk was covered with astrological signs and cabbalistic symbols in inks of various colours — I never had the nerve to rub them out and confined my own doodling to the blotter.

The knock came at exactly 9 o'clock. I sang out that the door was open and she came in slowly and tentatively like a schoolboy coming into the head's study. She wore a light blue mottled smock over tight flared white trousers. Her fine breasts complemented the tailoring of the smock and that length of lean thigh in white denim was something to see. Her low-heeled sandals vaguely matched her tooled leather shoulder bag and there wouldn't have been much change out of three hundred dollars for the set. Yesterday she'd been wearing a scarf or something over her head. Now I could see that her dark, reddish hair was cut short, almost cropped. It lay on her sleek head like a burnished metal cap. She wore yesterday's sunglasses, or maybe she had a few pairs the same. A cigarette came out of her bag almost before she hit the chair and she was one of the fastest people with a lighter I've seen.

She took a quick look around the office which in colour scheme and layout is more like a railway waiting room than anything else. She didn't react to it one way or the other, which probably meant that she'd been in worse places, maybe much worse. She drew hard on the cigarette.

"It must have seemed strange to you," she said, "telephoning like that last night."

"It did, but when people need help they do strange things."

"Can I take up some of your time, Mr Hardy? I have a long story to tell. I'll pay you of course, starting from now."

"Before you start spending money I'd like to know why you've changed your mind about me. I was a fly on the wall to you yesterday."

45

"That's a fair question. Yesterday I was having a bad time with the man you saw. I'm sorry, it made me testy. Today I need help and I've been thinking. I don't like Bryn Gutteridge, but he's a good judge of people. If you're good enough for him you're good enough for me."

She acted on the "if you have to ask the price you can't afford it" plan and that was all right with me. I nodded reassurance on the point, rolled a cigarette and settled back to listen.

"Today is close enough to fifteen years to the day since I gave up being a dancer. I wasn't bad, I can still do a bit. I'm pretty fit."

"Yes," I said, "you look fine. Put 90% of people to shame."

"Well, I gave up dancing and that sort of life, theatre and so on to get married. I married a man named Bercer. I was twenty-four, he was fifty-nine, I was poor, he was rich. It's an old story and there was nothing very different about it except that it worked out all right. He was nice to me. I liked him and for about three years I thought I'd done the right thing. I read a lot, went to plays I wouldn't have given a thought to before. I improved myself."

"You did a good job," I said, "but then …?"

"But then I met a man more or less my own age. I fell for him and we had an affair, a pretty hot one. He was married and I handled it all very badly. I got upset when I couldn't have it all my own way when things went wrong. James, my husband, didn't suspect that I was being unfaithful but he was worried about me and sent me to see a doctor, a counsellor …"

"Brave."

"Yes. He was helpful at first, encouraging. I'd lost track of the friends I'd had when I was dancing and they weren't much anyway, pretty wild. I had no one to confide in. Brave was sympathetic and available day and night. I came to rely on him absolutely and I told him about my lover. That was a terrible mistake."

"He blackmailed you?"

"No, not me. He blackmailed James. He told James that there were things about me that would ruin him financially and socially."

"What was Bercer's business?" I knew but I wanted to know whether or not she did and what she felt about it.

"Property development, building, and he did big stock exchange deals. It all hinged on the people he knew, politicians, lawyers, top public servants, even a few military men. We went to hundreds of parties, had dinner engagements six nights a week, sometimes seven. There were lots of smoke evenings, the gentlemen with their cigars and the ladies talking trivia."

I looked down at the frayed end of my cigarette and teased it with my thumbnail. "It sounds terrible."

"It was, a lot of the time. But there were some good holidays, good trips, and the men weren't all oafs and the women weren't all vacuous. It wasn't so bad. I went to a good school, my accent's all right and I could hold my own. But James had to be absolutely clean for his deals to come through, no dubious connections."

"Your lover was a dubious connection."

"He certainly was, the worst. If it got out that he was my lover those important people would drop James cold."

"Why didn't James drop you?"

"He loved me for one thing, but that wasn't all. Brave's line was that James mustn't drop me or he'd spread word about Carl."

"Carl who?"

"It doesn't matter. The important thing is that Brave was bleeding James dry. I found out later that he got over a hundred thousand from him, maybe two hundred thousand, maybe more."

I whistled. "That's big. What does Brave do with the money?"

She set her teeth in a grimace like that of a firing squad commander who has to administer a coup de grace.

"He has expensive tastes in ... erotica. He gambles like a madman. But we're talking about me, not him."

"Sorry, he's of interest. So are you of course."

She looked impatient and ran a hand over that fine, glowing pelt.

"Right. I'm jumping ahead in telling it this way because at the time I didn't know what Brave was doing. I just saw James getting more and more tense and felt more and more guilty myself."

"Bercer didn't front up to you with it?"

"Never. He just broke under the strain. He started taking bottles to bed and gorging himself on rich food. He blew up like a balloon and had a heart attack. He had two, actually in a few days and he died."

"How did that leave you?"

She was so used to the idea that she didn't even pause to knock the ash off her cigarette — the second since she'd started talking.

"Comfortable, if I'd been careful. I wasn't."

I raised an eyebrow, a stagey trick I'd learned from my drunken, diabetic mother who'd pounded a vampy piano in London pubs and queened it up on the Oronsay on the £10 scheme.

"Brave dropped out of the picture when James died. I gave up my lover, unpleasantly, and went a bit wild. Not here — in the States and Europe. I worked through a lot of money and came home a good bit harder. I'd seen a lot, I was too old for dancing and too smart for whoring, so I thought I'd better have another try at what I'd succeeded at before."

She'd gone through it in her mind a hundred times and had made her own role tougher with each run through, but she had intelligence, directness and an awareness of the reality of other people — something real gold-diggers don't have. And her men hadn't been soft-cocked sugar daddies: Bercer sounded like a shrewd operator in a high-powered world and Gutteridge had been smart and tough. But she was telling the story and this was the part she'd assigned herself. I wanted to hear more.

"You did all right again," I said.

"No," she shook her head, "I was getting nowhere for going on a year until I got help. Guess who?"

"Brave again."

"Yes. I met him at a party. I think I'd tried to find him when I first got back but he'd vanished. Remember that I didn't have anything against him except perhaps a bit of resentment that he'd gone off so soon after James died. He said he'd had to go back to Canada. OK, I was pleased to see him and pretty soon I was confiding in him again. He talked to me about needing an anchor in my life, a strong man. He introduced me to Mark Gutteridge."

She was moving steadily through her packet of cigarettes and the room was smoky and heating up fast. My watch put the time at a little past ten which meant that the pubs would be open.

She agreed that it was hot and that a drink would be a good idea. We went down the stairs and I felt my stocks in the building go up several points in the eyes of a dentist with a quiet practice, a hairdresser with big blanks in her appointment book and a guitar teacher whose rooms were smoky and sweet smelling. They hovered about in their doorways as I followed Ailsa's firm white-denimed buttocks down the corridors of their dreams.

The heat hit us like a jet engine blast when we reached the street. Ailsa had slipped the Porsche I'd seen the day before into an illegal but unobtrusive place behind the building. It was unlocked and she stepped in and reached into the glove compartment, also unlocked, for the keys. I wondered if she ignored security the same way in her house. As she pulled out from the kerb I noticed a red Volkswagen pull away half a block behind. I watched it in the rear vision mirror for a mile or so till it turned off or fell a long way behind. I couldn't see the driver. The light wouldn't fall right for me to get a look at him even when the car was close. I directed Ailsa out to Watson's Bay where the big pub on the beach serves the best fish in Sydney. If Ailsa was only half-way through her story it looked as though we could string it out through lunch, and I was on expenses. She didn't talk much. She drove fast and well using the Porsche's power when it was needed and not for show. We reached the pub just before eleven and she slid the car into a patch of shade where a tree hung over the parking bay. She reached over to drop the keys into the glove box.

"Lock it," I said.

She gave me a sharp, unfriendly look and shook her head.

"For me," I said. "Your security's lousy, it's time to start improving it."

She shrugged and locked the car putting the keys in her shoulder bag. We went through the cool lounge, up some stairs and into the dining room which has a view of the boats and the water that puts twenty-five per cent on the price of the food and drink.

"What will you drink?"

"Tonic and a slice of lemon. I hardly drink at all these days."

I gave the waiter the order. I had the same with gin. Out came the cigarettes and she took up her story again without preamble.

"It was all different with Mark. We had a good sexual relationship at the start and he was a very different proposition to James."

"No playing around?"

She shook her head. "Out of the question. It was all much more complicated. Brave can judge people. He'd picked me and Mark as a good fit and he was right. But the fit wasn't all that comfortable."

"The children?"

"Right. Mark doted on them and they were as suspicious as hell of me. He doted, but kept a tight rein on them. He seemed to have them scared. He scared me too at times."

"Where was Brave in this scene?"

"I'm coming to it."

The drinks arrived and I tried not to show an indecent interest in mine. She gave hers only the attention it deserved.

"Brave seemed to be a friend of Mark's in a low-key way. Mark advised him in business matters and helped him to get the land the clinic's built on. You've seen it?"

"Yeah, must have been quite a deal."

"It was. Some old houses came down. Mark had people in his pocket as I told you. I was interested in Mark's business. I thought I'd been wrong not to pay more attention to what James did, it might have kept me closer to him. Well, I talked business to Mark quite a bit. In bed mostly, and he gave me the gist of what it was all about. He was involved in land and property speculation. He got tips from people in high positions and he profited from them. He paid off the people who gave him information, in cash sometimes, more often in land and shares. Sometimes the payments came years after the deal, sometimes the kick-backs went to the wives, you understand?"

I did. If I'd got any kick-backs when I'd had a wife I'd definitely have seen that they went into her Swiss account. But the only kick-backs I've ever had have been of the in-the-teeth variety. I finished my drink and signalled for another. Ailsa's had scarcely lost a drop.

She went on: "Sometimes he told me names, but not often. Sometimes it was obvious to me who he was talking about even if names weren't mentioned. It became a bit of a game with us, a sort of Mata Hari thing, a bedroom game. I'd probe and he'd be indiscreet."

"It sounds like a bloody dangerous game to me," I said.

"It turned out to be. Mark roasted me a couple of times when I let a name slip in company, when I'd had a bit to drink. I watched myself after that. Mark would say that he had things on everyone, there was no one who had anything on him that he didn't have something on in turn. When he was low he even told me that he had something on his children, he never said what, and something on me. I didn't understand and I didn't want to. I used to try to pass it off as a joke. That was hard because Mark didn't have much of a sense of humour, like Susan. He had a dramatic sense, our bedroom spy games showed that, but that's about it. Jokes for him were visible, practical things. You know what I mean?"

I nodded. "Yes. I'd say Bryn's a bit that way too. Speaking of the practical-minded, did Gutteridge keep records of his deals?"

"I'm not certain but I think so. I'll get to that."

She drank down the tonic and lemon peel in a few gulps and refused another. I accepted the wine list, a little early perhaps, but busy people often eat early lunch I'm told. Ailsa sent the waiter for cigarettes and tore them open untidily as soon as they arrived. When she had one lit she went on.

"I used to see Ian Brave occasionally, have a drink with him. I didn't need him as I had before, but he was a confidant of sorts and I still didn't have any friends to speak of. I had problems with Mark's children and occasional bouts of depression. I went to the theatre with Brave twice. The second time he doped me." She sucked in her cigarette and blew the smoke out in a thin, vicious jet. "He took me back to his place — not the clinic, a house he has on the beach. He put needles into me, he questioned me for hours and hours. You can guess what about."

"Yeah. Where was your husband then?"

"Away on business, interstate. He often was. When I came out of it, some time early the next morning, Brave told me what I'd told him. That is, he gave me some snippets, about big names. He thanked me and told me to forget what happened. He said he'd leave me alone."

"I don't follow."

She stubbed the cigarette like it was her last and she was giving it up for life. Except that she lit another straight away.

"Oh shit. He had some pictures. Are you with me?"

"Photographs?"

"Right. He used them to keep me quiet and he used the information I'd given him to blackmail Mark to glory."

"Did your husband suspect that you were the source of Brave's information?"

She fiddled with the cigarette and lined up a napkin, an ashtray and her lighter on the table. "I'm not sure," she said, "I suppose so. He became morose and withdrawn. I couldn't reach him, no one could. My feeling is that Brave had him so cold he didn't care anymore."

"His whole approach to things had been turned round on him?"

"Something like that."

"Did he still see Brave? Socially I mean?"

"No, not to my knowledge. But they hadn't met regularly anyway."

I was interested but there were lots of loose ends. I played with the menu while I considered them. The story had a ring of truth but it was a bit too close to the first episode of husband and betrayal for comfort. Her innocence looked to be stretched a bit thin. I tried to keep the scepticism out of my voice as I asked the question. "How do you know all this happened? You said you weren't aware of what Brave had done in the case of your first husband. Why are you so sure about all this now?"

The question was important. If she slid about on it the whole thing could be a pack of lies. Dancers can be actresses. Only another good serve of her directness would incline me to believe her. She was direct.

"Brave told me himself," she said, "I went to him one day when Mark was black-minded and told him that I thought he was driving Mark crazy. I threatened to go to the police and accuse him of drugging and molesting me. I said I'd finish him professionally and in every other way."

"What did he say?" It wasn't hard to guess.

"He laughed at me. He said there were good reasons why I wouldn't do what I'd said. He threatened to name me as an accomplice in the blackmailing of James. He said he had so much on Mark that he could play with him, just as he pleased and that he could ruin him and put me on the streets. He didn't want to. Mark was making him rich and he was happy with things as they were. If I left him alone, he'd leave me alone. He said he'd ease up on Mark, but I guess he couldn't. He's a greedy bastard."

"How's that?"

"He pushed Mark past the limit, he must have done. Mark was dead about ten days after I had this talk with Brave."

"Are you sure he killed himself?"

"No, I'm not. But he was in a tortured state in the last few days and a gun was found near his body. The coroner's verdict was suicide but I'm sure such things can be arranged."

She stopped when the waiter arrived to take the order. I called for half a dozen oysters naturelle and some grilled whiting. She said she'd have the same and took about half a glass of hock when that arrived. Waiters were hovering about and she smoked and made some small talk until we had privacy again. The golden brown fish fillets and potato chips hid among the salad like Dyaks in the jungle.We pushed them about and sipped the wine. I tried to fill her glass but she glared at me. I munched a few decent mouthfuls of fish and got on with it.

"You think the police didn't pursue the matter satisfactorily?"

She mashed up some fish and salad and pushed the mess aside. She hadn't eaten a single potato chip and I had to keep myself from reaching over and spearing them. I drained my glass instead and filled it from the bottle which was still healthy. She lit a cigarette and more smoke drifted into my face than seemed necessary.

"What are you so cautious about, Hardy?" she asked. "Your licence?"

I shrugged and took in a bit more wine. "You were talking about your husband's death," I said. She nodded and did her cigarette flicking act again. The ash sprayed into the plates and I pushed mine aside.

"Look, this gets back to your question about Mark's records, if you're still interested. Mark died at his desk, in his study. The police found a secret safe in the study, one I didn't know about. It had been opened. It was empty. Maybe Mark kept the records there."

I nodded. "That sounds like a lead for the police, didn't they take it up?"

"No, they didn't take anything up. They rushed on to the inquest and let it go at that. I don't have to spell out what I think?"

"No, you think Brave has the records, maybe killed your husband to get them. Maybe not. In any case he was on the scene pretty quick I assume?"

She nodded, "Very quickly."

"You think he used the records to bring the shutters down on the case?"

She spread her hands quizzically and drew a deep breath. The coffee arrived and she dropped as many grains of sugar into it as you could balance on the head of a nail. I took a gulp of wine and popped the question.

"Your husband's been dead for four years and you've suspected Brave's hand in it all along. Why are you frightened enough to want to do something? To hire me? Brave hasn't threatened you directly has he?"

"Not yet," she said, "But it's only a matter of time. I've done something with the money Mark left me — invested it, got a couple of companies going. I told you this?"

I couldn't remember, I looked non-committal. She went on: "I'm a worthy target for Brave now. He's a leech. But it's more than that." She leaned foward. She had fine broad shoulders and her movements were athletic without being masculine. Her lips were a sculptured counterpoint to the vertical lines of her face. "I think Brave killed Giles. I think he's insane and obssessed with the Gutteridges. I think he's behind the threats to Susan and after Bryn now."

"Bryn's certainly afraid of something, or somebody. I think it connects back to his father's death but I don't know how."

"He's afraid of Brave I tell you. And if Bryn's afraid of him I'm bloody terrified." She slapped down the coffee spoon she'd been playing with and jerked off her sunglasses. There seemed to me to be as much resolution as fear in her face. Her voice was unemotional, businesslike. "You drink too much, but you're intelligent and capable in your own field. I want you to do two things — investigate Brave's affairs and put him out of business, for good. And protect me!"

"It's tough doing two things at once."

"They're two sides of the same thing. I'm sure of it."

She smiled for the first or second time since I'd met her. It was a nice smile but under careful control. "I don't know why you wanted to come out here. The food isn't that good and the view is rather corny. I've been here before."

"Why did you agree to come then?"

"To show anyone who might be interested that I've got protection."

"I guess you hired me a couple of hours ago then."

"Well, yes, I did in a sense. But are you interested in the complete job now you know what's involved?"

I gave it about half a second's thought. Handled right it would keep me clean of guard duty and the cheap rooms and caravan parks for weeks. I had too much good wine inside me to think of much else. I believed at least half of Ailsa's story and that was enough. I told her my rates and conditions of work. She pulled a chequebook from her bag and wrote words and digits on it with a gold pen. I put it in my wallet, not too far from Bryn's cheque so that the two of them could debate the ethics of it.

I had just enough cash to cover the bill and I was feeling clever and successful when we walked out into the parking lot. The sun was beating down hard and the shade had retreated from the Porsche leaving its rear bumper shimmering and reflecting like a white hot steel mirror. Ailsa stepped up to the driver's door, pressed the button in and pulled the door free. She had it three inches open before my half-stewed brain got the message. I took two rabbity leaps across the melting asphalt and swept her off in a diving football tackle. Her bag came adrift from her shoulder and flicked the car door full open as we hit the ground. The Porsche burst into flame like a Molotov cocktail on impact, the bonnet lifted and the windows cracked in quick succession like rifle shots. Hellish heat surged towards us as I rolled Ailsa over three more times in the gravel and tar.

"You should always lock your car," I ground into her ear as we came to rest twenty feet away from the inferno.

6

We were both shaking as we brushed the grit of the parking bay off our clothes. Ailsa's white pants were a ruin and her smock was smeared and torn. My trousers had a great three-cornered tear in the knee and blood from a bad graze was seeping into the ragged edges of the tear. The car was burning fiercely, the tyres were bubbling like lava and the vehicle was sinking slowly, lopsidedly onto the rims. There was a stench of burning rubber and vinyl and a cloud of dark smoke had settled in the still hot air over the parking area. I put my arm around Ailsa's shoulders and helped her across to the steps in front of the hotel. Staff from the place were thronging about and Ailsa accepted a woman's offer of help to a toilet where she could clean up.

The manager came out and mumbled about calling the police. I told him I'd do it myself if he could show me to the phone and produce some brandy. He seemed relieved to escape the job and took me into an office which contained a desk, chair, a telephone, a pot plant and a bar. I'd always wondered what hotel managers did in their offices. This one must have twiddled his thumbs and drank. He left me in the room telling me to help myself. I mixed a strong Hennessy and soda, sat down with it behind the desk and dialled a number. The voice at the other end was tired and unsympathetic. It had answered ten thousand telephone rings and never once heard good news.

"Police, Evans speaking."

"Grant, this is Cliff Hardy."

"Oh good, you're going to pay me the money you owe me and take me on a holiday to Coolangatta."

"This is serious, I need your help. And I might be able to help you with something you've got on your plate."

"Yeah? What would that be?"

"I can't tell you just now."

"That's terrific. Well I'll just drop everything here. It's nothing much, a couple of murders and a multi-million dollar extradition job and hurry on over to your place. What shall I wear?"

"Stop joking, I've been bombed."

"You're always bombed, tell me something new."

"I mean really bombed, detonator, gelignite, explosion, flames. I'm OK and my client's OK but a Porsche is dead."

"You've got a client and he's got a Porsche? Maybe you will pay me what you owe me."

"She has one. It's dead now, but she'll have another tomorrow."

"You sound more or less sober. Are you dinkum, Cliff?"

"Yes, blood oath I am. Here's what I'm asking. If you've got some cars that aren't busy picking up the take, send them over to the pub at Watson's Bay. The sightseers will need dispersing, the car will need towing to your forensic parlour, Miss Sleeman will be requiring a lift to Mosman and I'd like to come down and see you."

"Charmed. Consider it done, anything else?"

"No. See you soon Grant."

"Yeah. I don't like that crack about the take, Cliff."

"That's because none of it ever reaches you, mate. You've got to put yourself forward, make friends."

I hung up on his stream of obscenities. Grant Evans was ex-army, ex-Malaya, like me. His sense of humour wasn't his strongest point, but he was fairly honest like me. That made us mavericks in our respective professions and useful to each other. We were also old friends who'd been under fire and under the weather together too many times to count.

The manager was hovering outside the door. I told him the police were on their way and that I'd probably be able to see that the matter was kept pretty quiet. He looked pleased and showed me through to where Ailsa was sitting in a private room. She doused her cigarette and came up out of her chair to meet me. We put our arms around each other and stood together, not moving. It felt like the most natural thing in the world to do — coming that near to death seemed to draw us close.

"The police are coming," I said after a minute or so, "they'll take you home."

"You saved my life," she said.

"And mine don't forget."

She didn't move away. "The tough guy's tough guy."

"Not really. I nearly spilt the brandy they forced me to drink."

"You're a drunk, but you seem to be lucky for me. Will you stay with it? This doesn't change anything?"

I told her I would and it didn't and we were still patting each other like timid middleweights in a clinch when the manager came in to let us know that the Rose Bay cops had arrived. Ailsa continued not to do silly things. We walked out to the parking lot and she barely gave the burnt out wreck a glance. She answered a few basic questions from the senior uniformed man and then turned things over to me. Grant had clued the men up and they were willing for her to go home and for me to go down town and give a detailed account of the bombing. A cop picked up Ailsa's bag from where it had landed after being blown clear by the explosion of the petrol tank. He handed it to her and ushered her into the back of one of the patrol cars. She mouthed "Tonight" at me and I nodded. The cop slammed the door and the car took off. I was surprised to find that I wished I was going with her, but it was time to start earning her money by playing the "bumping pitch and blinding light" stuff with the law.

On the ride I tried to work out how to play the cards I had, or thought I had, but I found myself spending more time admiring the driving of the young detective at the wheel. He whipped the big Holden Kingswood through impossible gaps and caught every light from Watson's Bay to East Sydney. He didn't say a word on the journey.

"Great driving," I said as I got out in front of the central police building. He looked at me and jerked his head at the steps. A specialist.

I went into the building and gave my name to the desk sergeant. He lifted a phone and spoke briefly to someone in Grant's inner sanctum. The sergeant lifted old, tired cocker spaniel eyes to me.

"You know the way?"

"Yeah. OK to go up now?"

He nodded wearily and turned his attention back to the stolen car sheet. He read it like a form guide maybe hoping that if he spotted a few on the way home he could get out from behind the desk. Then again, maybe it was just a stunt the police PR boys put him up to as something that would impress the public. I went up three flights in the creaking lift. The view from the corridor windows was dull, out across the commercial buildings of East Sydney. The park on the other side was a better eyeful. Grant was still on the dull side but I knew he hoped to go up a floor and cross over. I might be able to help him if I could persuade him at this point with nothing. I pushed open the door and went into the office he shared with two other senior men.

Grant was alone. He was sitting at a desk which was untidy with papers, coffee cups and full ashtrays. He pushed himself back from the desk and waved me into a chair. He took hold of his spare tyre and pinched it.

"I'm getting fat, Cliff, not enough action. Are you going to give me some?"

I sat down. "Could be Grant, could be. I'd better fill you in."

I told him the tale, an edited version which left some things out and under-played others — especially the events at Brave's clinic. Grant listened closely, making occasional notes. He ran his hand ruefully across the thinning dark hair on his skull. He was one of those men who took the disintegration of his body hard. His wife still appeared to think of him as the twenty-five-year-old parat-rooper she'd married and his three daughters thought the sun shone out of him, but he bemoaned each lost hair and extra ounce. He'd been a superb fighting machine in Malaya and he'd killed three men on active duty as a cop, three hard men. He'd saved my life once in the jungle and kept me out of jail a few times since then. I usually played court jester to his gloomy king.

"Well, you seem to have yourself a nice case," he said when I'd finished talking. "Well-heeled client, real Lew Archer stuff. What do you want from me?"

"Can you sit on the bombing for a while, keep it quiet?"

"Yeah, I think so. No one really wants to know about car

bombings. Everyone assumes they're about crims and punters welshing on debts. Mostly they're right. No reporters there?"

"No, not that I saw. The management won't talk, that's for sure."

"Naturally. All right, quiet it is. What's in it for me?"

I rolled a cigarette and offered him the makings. He hesitated then took them and expertly made a cigarette. We both blew smoke at the stained, cracked ceiling.

"I want to know something about the Gutteridge case. Four years ago, remember it?"

"Yep, I was on it for a while."

"Did it get sat on? I hear there were some loose ends — an open safe for one."

"That's right. He killed himself though. I was the first to see him and it looked real to me. I've seen a lot of dead men who got dead in different ways. I'd say this was an auto."

"Or set up by an expert."

"Maybe. Unlikely."

"What about the safe?"

"Puzzling."

"Look, was it a bloody cover-up?"

He stubbed the cigarette out and dusted his hands. It looked as if he was trying to stop smoking again. He'd tried it a dozen times to my knowledge and it always made him mean. His face set in one of its tough, bloody-minded official masks.

"You're asking everything and giving nothing. If you want to offer me something juicy out of the Gutteridge case forget it. I don't want to know."

"No, it's not that. I'm working on something connected with the Gutteridge case and I want to know all there is to know about it. It might give me some leverage. I'm pretty confident I can put your name in lights over something which has nothing to do with Mark Gutteridge's death."

"Give me a clue."

"I can't. You wouldn't buy it at this stage."

Grant sighed. He reached into his pockets, pulled the hands out empty and did an isometric exercise against the edge of the desk.

"You weren't in Sydney when this thing came up?"

"No, I was on a country job, Broken Hill and Melbourne after that. I had a holiday in Fiji on the proceeds, I must have missed it all."

Grant looked sour, I shouldn't have mentioned the holiday, but he went on: "OK, well it made a fair splash in the papers. The open safe was hinted at in one of the papers, but that was as far as it went."

"Who called you?"

"Servant, an old one, she'd been with the Gutteridge guy for years, nothing there. Nothing much for her in the will."

"Who else was around?"

"The lot, from memory, a driver, two gardeners as well as the old housekeeper — that's the underlings. Then there was the wife and a son and daughter. Probably ran out of places to spend their money in and had to stay home."

"Now Grant, don't be bitter. They have their troubles just like you and I. The fix came in, did it?"

"Yeah, the photographer arrived fast and fired off a few but the support squad had some heavies in it and they took over — OK Cliff, you've got the inside dope. Make me feel good about it within twenty-four hours," he said, "or I'll call it all square, all round."

The pressure of his job was getting to him, or maybe it was some other trouble. Whatever the case, now wasn't the time to sketch out my suspicions. Just now he'd rather fight than think.

"I think I can promise you that," I said.

"Lovely," he gave me a tired smile. "Now, I got something off my chest and I've got your promise, my day is made. Shoot through Cliff. I'll be expecting to hear from you." I got up and patted him on the shoulder. He faked a collapse into his chair and picked up the top file in his IN tray.

I walked down the corridor and took the lift again. From the noise it made I might just have caught it on its last journey. The desk sergeant called me over and handed me the phone. It was Grant.

"I forgot to tell you to take care of yourself," he said.

"Why do you say it now?"

"I keep up with what's going on. Bryn Gutteridge's chum was shot once, close in but very neat. Whoever did it had done it before."

"I'll sniff every hand I shake and watch for bulges under jackets."

"If you meet him you probably won't have time for one wisecrack." The phone went dead. I hung on to it for a second listening to nothing.

7

I realised how beat up I looked when I hit the street and how ill-equipped I was for the weather. The storm that had been brewing broke when I was in the police building. Rain sheeted down bringing clouds of steam up from the pavements. The water soaked into my torn pants and dirty shirt which was pinkish from diluted blood. I had a change of clothes back in my office and I decided to complete the picture of ruin by taking the short walk there despite the rain.

I started out and caught sight in an oddly angled shop window of a red Volkswagen. It was well back and crawling along in the thick traffic. I took a turn and walked slowly down the street. A look in a parked car's side mirror showed that the VW had stopped at the top of the street after making the turn. I still couldn't get a glimpse of the driver.

I walked back to St Peters Street the most direct way, cleaned up, changed my clothes and came down after checking that there hadn't been any calls. The rain had stopped, the air was moist and clean-tasting and all the city's photochemical sludge was running down the gutters to the sea. I got the Falcon out of the tatooist's backyard and took off going south-east. The VW picked me up and stayed with me through Taylor Square, Moore Park and Kensington. He was doing it quite nicely, like a pacer, one out and one back, and then letting me get away a little. I cruised past the University and took the turn to Maroubra.

The used car yards cuddled up against each other on both sides of the road over a short stretch of ugly Australia. I made a late turn left, a quick one right and pulled up under a heavily over-growing row of plane trees the council pruners must have missed. I pulled the Smith & Wesson out of its clip under the dashboard and jumped out of the car onto the road. The Volkswagen came round the corner and I faced it fifty yards ahead with the gun up. I counted on the element of surprise to bring the car to a stop but I was wrong. The driver slowed a fraction, then accelerated and came straight on like the Light Brigade. I swore, jumped aside, hit the Falcon hip and thigh and dropped the gun. The little red car roared to the end of the street, brakes screaming, then it slewed around in a full turn taking some of the sidewalk to do it, and came belting back towards me. Dead end street. That gave me a chance to reverse the roles. I picked up the gun as the VW passed me and had my car turning before its tail whipped around out of what had been a quiet little street twenty seconds ago.

The Volkswagen was new and the Falcon was old, but the horsepower was all on my side. I had the car in sight as it turned onto the highway and kept with it through thick and thin. The traffic thinned as we got into Maroubra and I moved up closer. The driver appeared to be small with frizzy dark hair and I saw the flash of light on wrap-around sunglasses on one of the turns. From his driving I assumed that he was worried, it was jerky and he wasn't timing things well.

We moved on down towards the beach and then turned right up a steep hill flanked by tall apartment blocks with names like "Nevada" and "San Bernadino".

I crowded the VW near the crown of the hill opposite "Reno", but the driver found a little more speed and went into a cheeky slalom down the other side. I took evasive action, conscious of my lack of insurance, but I was hard on its twin exhausts when we turned into a long, flat run parallel to the beach. A mistake, I'd surfed along this beach for ten years and knew its geography like the back of my hand. It was deserted now, dark clouds were boiling up out over the sea and the road was slick with oily rainbow patches showing between the puddles.

I closed up behind the VW, timed the move and brought my black paintwork up alongside the red. I pulled my door handle down and held the door ajar. I blared my horn and gave the little car a quick flick with the door. It slewed away and shot through the only gap available — into a fenced parking lot which reached down to a toilet block and changing sheds on the beachfront. The VW driver struggled for control and then had to pull up within twenty yards. He made it, just. I ran in after it and brought the Falcon skidding in on an angle that closed off all exits.

I killed the engine, grabbed the .38 and moved around my car. The other driver was sitting quietly, hands on the wheel, crying softly and shaking. The frizzy hair was short and black as pitch, the thin shoulders in the dark T-shirt were heaving and her face when she turned it up to me was dark as chocolate and beautiful as a rose. I put my hand on her shoulder and gave it a gentle shake. The flesh under my hand was soft and the bone felt like a fine steel rod.

"Take it easy," I said, "I'm not going to hurt you. Calm down and tell me why you were following me."

She kept on shaking and sobbing and she dropped her head, the crisp hair curled on the nape of her neck like black metal filings. I wanted to touch them and moved my hand up.

"Don't! Don't touch me!" Her voice was lilting with an accent, not American. I stepped back and rubbed my tired face with the hand holding the gun. She jack-knifed from the car and sprinted for the beach bent low and balanced, legs pumping. I yelled and brought the gun up but she was too fast. She rounded the changing shed and was into the scrub before I'd taken a step. I lumbered after her but the day had taken its toll; there was no one in sight on the sodden beach and the flickers in the scrub a hundred yards away could easily have been branches in the wind.

I gave the car a quick once-over. It was a recent model which had been well kept. The clean vinyl and interior paintwork probably carried hundreds of fingerprints but I couldn't see any point in collecting them. There was a service book in the glove box and a street directory in the driver's side pocket. A folded copy of *The News* lay on the back seat open at the international news page. There was a pair of pliers and a roll of insulating tape in the passenger side door pocket; no cigarette butts, no night club matches, no soil obviously from the lower eastern slopes of the Great Dividing Range. For no special reason I wiped off places I'd touched in the car and wrote down the licence number. There were no keys in the ignition. That could mean one of two things — the car was stolen or the crying had been an act put on after she'd had the presence of mind to take the keys out of the lock. I pulled the bonnet release, yanked back the cardboard housing and looked in at the panel — nothing across the ignition terminals. Fooled again, Hardy.

It was after six and a warm drizzle had settled in when I got back into my car and started the motor. The Falcon protested the change in the weather by coughing and it flooded before I got it running reasonably. I swung her around, pulled out of the parking lot and took the road back to town. I stopped at a hamburger place and picked up one with all the trimmings. I got a six-pack of beer from a pub full of used car salesmen working on late afternoon marks and tired-looking men putting off going home to their wives.

8

I ate the hamburger and swigged the beer as I drove. The traffic was light and I made good time to Longueville. Lights were on in the front rooms and the colour TV sets were semaphoring comforting messages to each other across the deep gardens and quiet, damp streets. I parked about a hundred yards from the entrance to the clinic on the opposite side of the road, and focused my night glasses on the relevant point. I could see cars approaching and turning into the reception booth from the other direction and I had a good view of the ones that passed me to get there. I figured I had about an hour at most before someone inside might tally up comments about the tone of the street and come out to investigate.

So I gave myself an hour with the thought that I might sneak an extra fifteen minutes if nothing happened. I was pretty sure something would happen — enough shit had been hitting the fan over the last twenty-four hours or so to produce some reaction in this area. I risked a cigarette or two, drank the beer, now heating up a bit but not too bad, and waited. The first car came about ten minutes after I arrived. It was a Rover, nice car.

The street light caught its number plate nicely as it made a purring turn to the reception booth. I had the glasses on it and wrote the number down. I was too far away to be sure, but I thought there was a driver in front and one passenger behind. Fifteen minutes later a car came up from behind, moving fast. I hunched down in the seat but it roared past. I sat up and then went down again as another car came from the same direction. A light coloured Fairlane swished past me and took the turn, too fast and not quite steady, into the clinic. The light didn't hit this one as well as before, but he had to back out and take another run at the drive so I got the number with no trouble.

Ten minutes went by to the whisper of the falling rain. The Rover slid out onto the road and went back to where it came from. I checked my reading of the number plate and found I had it right. The second car left and the third arrived almost simultaneously. The Fairlane lurched out onto the road, collected the kerb and almost collided with an Italianate sports model which was gliding up towards the clinic and me. The driver flicked out of the path of the Ford and neatly whipped around to stop perfectly aligned with the gates. The number plate was a blur through all this. I swore and settled down to wait for the car's reappearance. I felt edgy and exposed, I was pushing my luck.

After eight minutes lights went on in the compound and I heard a dog bark. Warning bells rang in my head and the name of every prison I'd ever heard of flashed through my mind. I didn't have all the information I wanted but I had enough.

The Falcon threatened to flood but relented. I revved it firmly, did a tight U turn and got the hell out of Longueville.

Mosman seemed a hundred miles away and all of it uphill. I washed down a few caffeine tablets with a swill of beer and concentrated on navigating the greasy roads. I was tired or I would have noticed it at least ten minutes sooner — an unchanging pair of headlights centred in my rear vision mirror like bright, sparkling diamonds. The driver knew nothing about tailing, which was comforting, but I felt I'd had enough of that scene for one day. He would have followed me down a sewer and it was child's play to fake a right turn and then run him into the kerb. When he stopped his left front wheel was up on the concrete and the genteel, muted neon lights of the Waterson & Sons funeral parlour were flashing in his eyes.

I got out cautiously and kept the gun down in my jacket pocket. The car was an old FB Holden and the driver was not all that much older than it was. He had damp blond hair, pretty long, but there wasn't enough of it to be worth spending much time on. There wasn't much of him all round — he looked almost childlike sitting in the car with his sports jacket collar turned up. I could see a tight grin on his face and he was fumbling inside his breast pocket as I approached the car — he was so amateurish it was almost funny.

I leaned on the car and rapped on the driver's window. A wallet and some papers spilled out on his lap as he pulled his hand out to wind down the window. He leaned forward to recover the papers presenting me with a thin, clean neck that I could have broken between my thumb and forefinger.

"I have identification." His voice squeaked a bit and was young and educated.

"Let's not worry about who you are first off," I said. "Everybody has identification, everyone is someone if you get what I mean. Why were you following me?"

"That's connected with who I am."

He seemed determined to tell me and I thought I'd better sit down to receive the impact. I walked round the back of the car and climbed in on the passenger's side at the front.

"Right. This is cosy. Now, who are you and why were you following me?"

He pushed the wallet over. Tucked in one of its compartments was a press identification card with photograph. The name on the card was Harry Tickener and it was him all right on the photograph; he had to be the only one of his kind in captivity.

"OK, you're an artist. Let's have the answers."

"I work on *The News*. I just got up to the political reporting team last week, from sports, you might have seen the byline?"

"I don't follow the volleyball all that closely. Come on, get to the point."

"I haven't done much yet in the political line. I've mostly run errands for Joe Barrett."

Now that *was* a name with clout. Barrett was by way of being a crime-busting political reporter and he'd made some fat faces very red in his time. *The News* occasionally gave him his head on a story and he was very good for circulation when they did. He went a bit wild sometimes so they used him sparingly. Tickener pulled out some thick plain American cigarettes and got one lit after a struggle. He puffed, didn't draw back and the Holden turned into a fair imitation of a second class smoking compartment on the New South Wales railways. I reached across, pulled the cigarette out of his mouth and threw it out the window.

"If you want me to say 'Quit stalling' I will. I'll pull a rod and do a Cagney impression if you insist, but how about just telling me in plain and simple English what you're up to."

He nodded and the words tumbled fast. "I took a call for Joe. She must have thought she had got on to him direct, anyway I didn't get time to say who I was. She said she had a tip on a big story and if I . . . if Joe wanted to get in on it he should start taking an interest in Dr Ian Brave. She said she'd call again if she saw any signs of interest at our end."

"So you took the job on?"

"Yes, there didn't seem to be any harm in it. Joe's in Canberra for a few days. I thought I could do the initial poking around and let Joe take it from there. Or maybe he'd let me follow it through, I don't know. Anyway, it sounded interesting so I went out tonight to have a look at Brave's place. I saw you parked and watching the clinic, so when you left I followed you. I thought you might lead me to someone, maybe the woman who rang."

"Where were you?"

"My car was two blocks away. I watched you from the garden of the house on the corner of the street you were in."

He looked wet enough for it to be true and the story sounded straight.

"Tell me about the woman's voice."

"It was nice, educated, with an accent."

"What sort of accent?"

"European, not Italian, maybe French."

It checked. The net was getting thrown wider all the time and it seemed like the moment to bring in some keen, unpaid help. I was thinking how to put it to him when I caught sight of my face in his rear vision mirror. It looked like it had been made out of a kerosene drum; my skin was pale and creased and my nose and jaw were sharp and cruel. I tried to produce a smile out of this unsuitable material and to get a half-way human tone into my voice.

"Look Tickener, we could get together on this. I think there is a story in it and you could have it. If I call you in it's your story, not Barrett's. That tip was incidental, get it?"

He nodded slowly. "It isn't quite ethical, but . . ."

I broke in. "Ethical is what doesn't keep you awake. It's different from one person to another, that's what's interesting about it. Do you want to hear more?"

"Yes."

I gave him some of the details, stressed the political implications and the likelihood of high level police involvement, hence the need for security at the investigative end. He came in like a well hooked trout. He was eager to do anything, he'd go anywhere, meet me anytime. I almost regretted the impulse to use him, faithful dogs can get in the way, but I felt that events to come would justify co-opting him. I gave him the licence numbers — of the Volkswagen and the cars that had visited the clinic that night — and told him his first assignment was to get the names and addresses of the people to whom they were registered. He said he had a contact in the right place for this dating from the days when he used to follow football players to get a line on what clubs they might defect to. I felt better about him. We agreed to be at our respective phone numbers at a certain time the next day. We shook hands. I got out of the car and he drove off, probably with dreams of Watergate in his head. I eased myself back into the traffic and headed for Mosman where the drizzle would look romantic falling on the lapping waves and the mansions.

9

The Alfa was looking racey and the boat toey when I arrived at Ailsa's place. I parked the Falcon next to the boat and took the steps two at a time to test my wind. It seemed to take ten minutes to reach the top and I wondered how Ailsa made out on fifty smokes a day. The door was made of oregon pine with glass panels. The curtains inside drew across what looked like a hundred yards of glass on each side. I gave the handle an experimental turn. It was locked, as befitted the front door of a lady whose car has been booby trapped with gelignite. I pressed the bell and waited. Ailsa's voice came from inside, back a bit and to one side. Good.

"Who is it?"

"Cliff Hardy."

To judge from the sound she was drawing a bolt and undoing a chain. She said "Come in", and I opened the door and pushed aside a section of the heavy curtains. Ailsa was standing well inside the room, with one hand up to the electric light switch and the other full of a big, black gun pointing at my navel. We looked at each other for a full quarter minute.

"That's good security," I said. "Congratulations."

"Thank you." She lowered the gun to her side and took a step towards me. I took three or four and put my arms around her. She pressed in close and we kissed expertly and carefully. She pushed me away gently and handed me the gun.

"Put it down please, I hate it."

I thumbed forward the safety catch and put the big automatic down on a chair.

"You looked like business."

"I've never fired it, I don't think I could."

We circled around each other for a while in the kitchen and

living room while she made me a drink and tea for herself. She'd spent the afternoon in bed and had taken it quietly in the evening, fixing herself a meal and watching TV. She was wearing a silk chinese-looking robe, all red and black with wide sleeves. It suited her, she looked rested and good. We sat side by side on the floor of her den which was book-lined and comfortable. The wind whipped some branches against the window. The soft, warm rain pattered down and I sipped my drink while telling her about my comings and goings in her service. Some kissing spun the story out and after two drinks, with her head on my shoulder and my hand on her breast inside her robe, I was feeling miles away from coffee coloured girls in red Volkswagens and rainy vigils outside hospitals. She brought me back to it with the big question, or one of them.

"Who do you think the woman with the French accent could be?" I stroked her breast drowsily, it seemed the right thing to do when considering French-accented women and was very nice for its own sake too.

"Brave has Canadian connections you tell me. Maybe that's the answer, some French Canadian woman. But since talking to Tickener I'm not so sure. She put him on to Brave. They could have fallen out I suppose, but I'm not wild about the whole theory."

"Why not?"

"Brave and bombing don't go together, he's more subtle. Still, there's Giles' death to consider. Can't rule Brave out on that and therefore he could be involved in the bombing."

"It's getting very complicated, isn't it?"

"It is, that's why you need a specialist in complicated criminal cases."

"Like you?"

"Like me."

Her breast was warm under my hand and her fingers on my thigh reminded me that it had been a long, long time. I pulled her to her feet and we did some more kissing and eye gazing. She broke away and led me off by the hand — it felt like the fifth or sixth time, when you know enough to take it slowly and be touched by it. We undressed each other in her timber-beamed, white-bricked bedroom and closed like tired but healthy and experienced animals. She finished before me and opened up warmly beneath me. I went down and around and moaned out my gratitude.

She seemed to feel the same thing — a gratitude and release and we each smoked a cigarette and made mildly dirty remarks in each other's ears. It was an exchange of needs, strengths and weaknesses and both of us knew that was all it was for now. She rolled away from me and slipped her hand between my legs.

"Go to sleep." Her hand soothed me beyond the power of food, drink or money. "I might catch you again before morning."

We woke soon after first light and moved in on each other urgently and hard. It was a different event, less tender, more athletic and she got out of bed almost as soon as we'd finished.

"Tea or coffee?"

She wrapped a cheesecloth cloak around her and ran her hand over her hair. I wanted to pull her back into the bed but the look on her face told me she wouldn't be playing. She looked preoccupied, withdrawn and anxious to get on with some task to divert her from the reality of a man in her bed.

"Coffee, black please."

"Do you want anything to eat?"

I pulled the sheet up over my head. She snorted and went out. I unsheeted and looked around the room. It was austere with built-in wardrobes, a low camphorwood chest with a lamp on it and some paperbacks, and a full length mirror. The outlines were muzzy in the early half-light, softening down the lines of the neat, not self-indulgent decor. It was a fine room to wake up in. I got up and pulled back a little of the curtain. The pool was immediately outside — you could dive into it from the decking if you were good enough or drunk enough. I wandered around the room and into the compact ensuite bathroom. There was a man's shirt, several sizes too big for Ailsa, hanging on the back of the door. It was slightly soiled and monogrammed RH on the breast pocket. It was silk, very expensive. I took my empty bladder and the little puzzle back into the bedroom.

Ailsa came in with the coffee on a tray as I was riffling through one of her books — *The Day of the Jackal*, good stuff by a guy who wrote passably and had something good to write about. She kept the cloak on and sat down on the bed away from me. She handed me the coffee which was strong and hot.

"I suppose you want brandy in it?"

"It has been known. What is the H in RH for?"

She put down her cup and looked away from me, at the mirror.

"That's it," she said, "I was waiting for the thing you'd say that would be all wrong, and you come out with that."

She reached for her cigarettes but I checked the movement and pulled her down beside me. She didn't resist, didn't comply. I stroked her hair.

"I'm sorry," I said, "That was a question to ask a suspect at midnight. I'm sorry love, I'm off on this case again. I didn't think."

"It's all right, you don't have to soothe me. I'm not going to cry or anything like that. But you're not being completely truthful. You saw Ross' shirt, right?"

"Right."

"Well, what does it mean to you?"

"Jesus! Not a 'what does it mean session' this early."

She pushed herself up and away from me angrily.

"You're a ripe bastard this morning, aren't you? Is this your usual style? Do you fuck your clients and piss them off in the morning and keep the retainer? Nice work."

She got the cigarettes this time and lit one shakily. I recovered my coffee and drank some trying to work out how to calm the storm. Maybe she was right, I'd woken up with clients before and worked my way out by the shortest route. But I wasn't feeling like that this time.

"Ailsa, it isn't like that. There's loose threads hanging everywhere in this case. I saw your fight with this guy Ross. I just want to fit him into the picture a bit more clearly. If he's in the picture."

She tapped ash off her cigarette and drank some coffee, not looking at me.

"Very well," she said tightly. "Yes I suppose Ross is in the picture, or was. He's been my occasional lover for a year or so.

Mostly we fight, sometimes it's nice...was nice. I don't expect it to be any good again. That fight was beyond the limit."

"What was it about?"

She drew on the cigarette and looked at me, her head nodding slightly.

"You know men aren't all that attractive in the morning," she said. "Bristly, stinking a bit of tobacco and bad teeth. You're no major exception Cliff Hardy. You'll have to warm up a bit to get anything more out of me. Would you admit to being jealous?"

"Under pentothal."

She finished her cigarette and coffee, dropped the butt in the dregs and slung herself down on the bed beside me. She put her hands behind her head and drew her knees up until she was sitting in a sort of yoga posture.

"OK, the full story, for your files. Ross came to me a few months after Mark's death. He had some references, pretty impressive ones. I was just getting around to thinking I'd have to do something with the money Mark left me. Ross had ideas."

"Like what?"

"He knew about setting up companies and minimising taxes and quite a bit about the share market. He made some nice killings for me there, early on. I've got a fashion business, manufacturing and retail, I've even gone international with it in a small way. I've got a vineyard — that'd interest you — and some outlets for the wine. I've got a company to co-ordinate things and Ross is second in charge."

"Who's in charge, you?"

"No, only nominally. The real boss is a man called Chalmers. He's a chartered accountant and the dullest man in the world. He's ultra-cautious and he's never lost me a penny. That's why he's in charge."

"Ross has lost you pennies?"

"A few. A couple of times, that's why he hasn't got the job. I work on old Sophie Tucker's dictum, 'I been rich and I been poor...,' you know it?"

"Yes."

"Most people just take it on faith. I know it's true. But I'm not a

77

maniac about it. I just like being rich and I don't intend to get poor by going into wildcat schemes."

"That's Ross' style?"

"Yes, it is now. He wants to be in charge of everything or failing that to play a few hands without Chalmers' interference. I don't feel like staking him."

"And that's what the fight was about?"

"Yes. He's been getting very pushy lately. He was pressing me to go into a mining deal and I'm not interested. He got nasty and started putting me down. I'm a lot older than him and he pointed it out. You saw how it went."

"You were doing pretty well, you might have won it on your own. How's it going to be, business-wise, if you break with him?"

"He'll just have to accept it or move out. He hasn't got a contract and I know he's not short of women. He gets a good salary and the usual perks. He's useful, he knows people. I think he'll stay."

"The silver spoon?"

"I don't think so. I'm not sure. He's never told me anything much about his background."

We'd got over the hump and she relaxed letting her long legs slide down the bed. We kissed for the sheer pleasure of it. She rubbed her hand over my face.

"Bristly, black-bearded bastard."

"Virility," I said. "Tell me about Chalmers."

"Christ, you like your work don't you. What do you want to know?"

"Just one thing, was he connected in any way with Mark Gutteridge?"

"Yes," she spoke slowly, beating her hand in time to the words on the bed. "He was Mark's chief accountant for many years."

I did the same. "And how did he come to work for you?"

"He approached me. I don't know exactly why he picked on me. I do know that he couldn't get on with Bryn."

"In what way?"

"I don't know. Ross once said something about Walter being a repressed homosexual, that could have something to do with it. But Ross isn't reliable on the subject of Chalmers."

I thought about it. There were more connections back to the Gutteridge trouble for Ailsa than I'd realised. I still felt that the car bombing related back to the harassment of Susan Gutteridge, but I didn't know how. Ailsa had given me some more people with possible motives, but Brave was still out in front and my main concern as well as hers. He was Harry Tickener's concern too.

"I'm going to be very busy on your behalf today love," I said, planting a firm kiss on her shoulder.

"And your own. Your rates are moderate verging on extortionate. Do you make a lot of money?"

"No. Overheads are high and I have long slack periods. Most of what I makes goes on booze and books anyway."

"I can imagine. And on women?"

I disengaged myself and rolled off the bed. "Very little on women. Use your shower?" she nodded. "Are you married Hardy?" she said. "Was. Tell you about it sometime." I started for the shower and turned back. She was sitting up again and lighting a cigarette. With the cream coloured fabric draped around her she looked like a young, scared Christian about to go to the lions. I walked back and put my fingers in the hair at the nape of her neck. I massaged her neck gently.

"We'll have lots of time to talk," I said. "Today I've got ten men to see and six houses to break into. Can you write me down the addresses of Chalmers and Ross...what's his other name?"

She rotated her head cat-like under my fingers. "That's nice. All right. Ross' other name is Haines." She got up, crossed to the wardrobe and got out a thick towel. She tossed it to me and I caught it and went into the bathroom. When I came back into the room she handed me a page torn from a notebook. The names and addresses were written in neat capitals. She made a grab at the towel around my waist and I backed off. She looked amused and got out another cigarette. I pulled on my clothes, bent down over the bed and kissed her on the head.

"You could have typed it out," I said.

"Can't type, never learned."

I nodded. "What are you going to do today?" She blew smoke at the mirror. "Since I evidently can't stay here with you," she said,

"I'll go into the office and check a few things. I might go to the library. Where's my protection by the way?"

"You should be safe enough if you stick to doing what you say. Take taxis and stay with other people. You can do it all the time if you try."

"Taxis, OK. That reminds me, what about the police and my car? Will I have to talk to them again do you think?"

"I don't think so, I've squared it for the time being."

"Fully insured, I'll get someone in the office onto it today. Good car, I think I'll get another one the same."

"You do that," I said.

She flared. "Don't be supercilious with me. I employ a lot of people, I spend my money. I do the best I can and I'm not hypocritical about it."

"Like Susan Gutteridge?"

"Yes."

"You've got a point. I'll call you about six, maybe we could have dinner, then I'll have some things to do."

"Tonight?"

"Yeah, it could be all over tonight if things go right."

"You're being mysterious."

"Not really, if I told you all about it you'd think it was so simple you wouldn't feel like paying me."

She laughed and came up to me. I pulled her in and we kissed and rubbed together for a minute or two. I promised to call her at six, come what may, and left the house.

10

I took the first drink of the day in an early opening pub at the Quay. My companions in sin ranged from a tattooed youth, who was playing at looking tough and doing pretty well at it, to a grizzled wreck who was mumbling about the Burns-Johnson fight at Rushcutters Bay in 1908. He claimed to have been the timekeeper and maybe he was. I bought him a schooner and he switched to Sullivan-Corbett which was a bit unlikely. A scotch would probably have got me Sayers and Heenan. I had a middy of old and tried to anticipate the results of Tickener's inquiries. The smell of toasted sandwiches interrupted this train of thought and I put the matter aside in their favour. I ate two cheese sandwiches and had a second beer. The rain had cleared and the day was going to be warm. Students and the unemployed would be on the beaches, accountants would be at their desks, private detectives would be peeling secrets off people like layers of sunburnt skin.

I got a shave in the Cross at a barber shop where I'd once seen Gough Whitlam, before he became Prime Minister — I figured he'd know where to get a good shave. The Italian razor man was neat and economical and let me read the paper while he worked. He was coming on strong with garlic and aftershave but I fought back with beer and I guess the honours were about even. *The News* had put Costello on the second page and had splashed a government statement about unions across the front. There was a front page picture of a cricket player kissing a paraplegic girl to remind everyone that God lives and life is still all fun and games.

I got to to the office, checked the mail and the incoming calls with the answering service. There nothing of interest in either. I rang the number which Harry Tickener, newshound and wordsmith, had given me the night before. He must have been sitting on top of the phone because it was snatched up the second it rang.

We established identities, confirmed that we were both in sound health and got down to business. The records branch of the motor registry never shuts down to accredited people and Tickener's contact had got what we wanted during the night. In a voice as thin and reedy as himself, Tickener recited the facts: "The Rover is registered to Dr William Clyde, 232 Sackville Drive, Hunters Hill, the Fairlane to Charles Jackson, 114 Langdon Street, Edgecliff, the VW to Naumeta Pali, Flat 6, 29 Rose Street, Drummoyne."

"Good. Do you know anything about these people?"

"Not a thing. The only Charles Jackson I know of is a cop, Detective Inspector, CID. I don't know where he lives or what he drives. Never heard of the others, could find out though."

"Right, you take Clyde, call me in an hour."

I tidied my desk, throwing away bills and advertisements, and paid a couple of modest accounts with cheques I could cover by lodging Gutteridge money. I phoned Grant Evans at home. It was delicate but I was getting more confident.

"Grant? Cliff, I'm getting closer but I need a piece of information."

"How big a piece? I'm feeling weak."

"Not big, but close to home. You have a colleague by the name of Charles Jackson?"

"Yeah, what about him?"

"Your assessment."

"No comment."

"What does he drive and where does he live?"

"A Fairlane, he lives in Edgecliff somewhere."

That spoke volumes. Evans trusted me but not enough to give out information on anyone for whom he had any regard. I had a character sketch of Jackson from those seven words.

"Anything else Cliff?"

"Not until tonight. You on duty?"

"Yeah, seven to three."

"Good men with you?"

"Good enough."

"I'll call you at eight."

"You'd better come through on this, Cliff. There's a bit of flak about the car bombing and some bright boy has got on to the Gutteridge connection. I'm not sure how long I can sit on it."

"Just hold the lid on until tonight. What I've got will be big enough to make you smell like a rose."

He rang off without saying any more. Grant's position in the force was secure, but it would add to his troubles if the promotions didn't keep coming. If he got stuck on a rung too long he'd dry up with frustration and snap like a dead branch. He needed to get up to the top and get there soon. I hoped I could help him make it. Tickener's call came through at 10.00 precisely. It tied things up.

"Dr Clyde's a plastic surgeon," he said without too much interest. "What about Jackson?"

"He's the cop you've heard of."

"Yeah?" He sounded keener. "What's it all about?"

Suddenly I had doubts about telling him, not about his honesty but about his control of his tongue. If he went around talking to the wrong people for a day, word could get about and the whole thing could be blown. If Gutteridge's files existed and were being put to use there could be prominent people in all sorts of places treading the high wire and alert to anything in the breeze about Brave and the Gutteridges. I decided not to risk it.

"It hasn't quite come together yet," I said, "but I expect it to tonight. I'll call you at eight and you can be in on it from the start. Meanwhile I'd dig up all I could on Brave's background if I were you. You're going to need that sort of stuff for your story. And keep quiet about Jackson, he's a small fish. How are you fixed in there? Is Barrett around?"

"No, still in the ACT."

"Good, do you know Colin Jones, the photographer?"

"Yeah, a bit."

"Line him up and be there at eight."

He said okay and for his ego I told him to be sober and to have a full tank of petrol in the FB. That wrapped things up in that direction as far as I could see. I was sure that Costello was at Brave's clinic. Jackson was covering the police inquiry end and Dr

Clyde was doing the face job. They'd been alarmed when I'd blundered into the clinic and seemed to have held some sort of conference the following night. But they hadn't moved Costello yet and perhaps they couldn't. It mightn't be medically advisable. If they were going to move him it would almost certainly happen at night and I had plans to head that off. I wished I had a man to watch the clinic in the daytime but I didn't and there was no use lamenting it.

All this planning was thirsty work and I left the office to repair the damage. Before I took off I put a handful of shells for the Smith & Wesson in my pocket and added a plastic wallet of easily assembled burglar's tools. I had a licence for the gun but no one has a licence for skeleton keys and lock slides.

11

I drove to a pub near the University where you can sit in the shade, drink old beer and eat passable rissole sandwiches. I took my street directory into the pub and looked up the addresses of Haines, Pali and Chalmers while I worked on the food and drink. Students around the place were talking in their derivative argot and preparing themselves to fall asleep in the afternoon lectures. One hairy intellectual studied me for a while and then announced that I was obviously in real estate — so much for higher education.

The addresses were more or less on the same side of the city. Geography determined the order of my visits — Pali, Haines, Chalmers. I finished my drink and got up. The pub was emptying but the vocation spotter seemed to be putting off the evil hour. He was rolling a cigarette from makings he'd bludged from one of his fellow seekers after truth. I caught his eye as I stood up and pressed a finger to my lips. As I passed his table I dropped one of my cards, face up, into the beer puddles.

Naumeta Pali's flat was in a six storey red brick building which was a wound in a wide street flanked by neat terrace houses. The flats were built over car parking space and there was a wide expanse of those smooth white stones that are supposed to replace grass around them. The whole set-up was modern, tasteless and medium expensive. The parking area was divided into bays of white lines; each bay had a flat number painted on it and there were a couple of signs around warning the public that this was private space. The space allotted for flat 6 was empty. I went into one of the lobbies in the building and located the flat. It was three floors up. In Glebe there'd have been milk bottles and cats on every landing and you'd have to fight a gang of kids for every inch of territory. Here there was nothing.

I knocked on the door of flat 6 and heard the sound echo about emptily inside. After a second try a woman put her head outside the door opposite.

"She ain't in," she said.

The voice jarred with everything around and I turned around to take a good look at its owner. She was fortyish, fat and a good advertisement for cosmetics — black circled eyes, rouged cheeks and fire engine red lips. She'd had a few drinks but not enough for her to forget that she had to hold herself together. She had some help from corsets and a bra that pushed her breasts up out of the tight floral dress towards her loose chin. She wore gold, high heeled sandals. I looked closely for a cigarette holder but she didn't seem to have one just then.

"If you're looking for the darkie she ain't there." Her voice was city slummy with a touch of country slowness.

"Do you happen to know when she'll be back Mrs . . .?"

"Williams, Gladys Williams. Who're you? Is she in trouble?"

"Why do you ask that?"

"Well, you know them. She comes an' goes, all hours like. Must be doin' something shady."

"I see. Do you mind if I ask what you do Mrs Williams?"

"Nothin', not any more."

I raised an eyebrow and she gave a lopsided grin. "Nah, not that either, not for years. Married now."

I nodded. "Husband's a bookie," she went on, "in Lithgow. That's where we live. He comes to the bloody city meetings once a week, bloody dumps me here."

"Why don't you go with him?"

She shook her head, the frizzy red tendrils danced about like the Gorgon's snakes. "Sick of 'em, rather stay here. Might go out tonight. Hey, why're you askin' all these questions, wanna drink?"

I'd only asked three that I was aware of, but she was ready to open up like a sardine can and her qualifications as an observer of her neighbours were impeccable. I produced a card from the insurance days.

"A drink would be very nice," I said, moving towards her so she couldn't renege on the offer. "I'm an insurance investigator. Miss

Pali isn't in trouble exactly, but any information you could give me might help to clear things up a little."

She wanted it to be trouble. "Fiddlin' a claim is she?" We moved through the door straight into the living room. It was over-furnished and over-cleaned, the blinds were drawn to enhance the television viewing — the real day closed off to allow the fantasy one fuller rein.

"I'd rather not say Mrs Williams. It's rather unsavoury in some ways."

That was better. She nodded conspiratorially and went off into the kitchen. She made noises out there and came back with two hefty gin-and-tonics. She handed me one, sat down in a quilted armchair and waved me into another. She tucked her legs up under her and took a long pull at her drink.

"I understand," she said throatily, "how can I help youse?"

I sipped the drink. It was something to take in slowly over half an hour with a novel.

"What can you tell me about Miss Pali? I understand she drives a red Volkswagen, is that right?"

"Yeah, like I said she comes in at all hours of the day and night. Makes a bloody awful noise that thing."

"What does she do for a living?" She wasn't stupid, she gave me a suspicious look. "Don't you know?" I cleared my throat and took another sip trying to look guarded. "Well, we're not sure, that is . . ."

"Umm, well I dunno. Seems to have plenty of money to judge by her clothes, not my taste of course but they aren't cheap — slack suits and that. Could be some sorta secretary, 'cept not in an office. She's home a lot an' types for hours. A couple of blokes come and bring . . ." she made a vague gesture with her hand. "Files," I suggested, "papers?"

"Yeah, somethin' like that. Folders and that."

"I see. How many men?"

"Couple."

"Can you describe them?"

"One's a big bloke, bigger 'n you and younger. Other one's dark, not a boong, more dagoey looking, sharp dresser."

"All business is it?"

She looked sly, "No way, young man stays the night sometimes."

I took out a notebook and pretended to write in it. "You keep your eyes open, Mrs Williams."

"Bugger all else to do here. I stay down sometimes see, go to a show and go up to Lithgow at the weekend. Got a coupla relations in Sydney."

I wrote some more gibberish. "Can you describe them more closely, her visitors?"

"Nah, never looked that close. Both wear good clothes, better 'n Bert's."

"Bert?"

"Me husband. Bert wears old fashioned clothes, he reckons bettors don't like trendy bookies. I reckon they don't like bookies full stop, but you can't tell Bert a thing."

The gin was getting to her and she was wandering into the dreary deserts of her own life. I only wanted the spin-off from that — the fruits of her boozy, envious snooping.

"I see. What else can you tell me? Does she have other visitors?"

"Yeah, course she does, other darkies mostly, but they piss off when the white blokes arrive."

It was time to wind it up. "When did you last see her, Mrs Williams?"

"Yestiddy mornin', didn't come home last night don't think. No sign of her this mornin'."

"Is that usual?"

"No, always comes home sometime, *he* comes there, see. I dunno, suppose it's all right, black and white and that. She's a funny sort of blackie anyway, not an Abo', comes from some funny place, New ... somethin', saw the stamp."

The gin had hit her, she was coming apart and I pressed in for just this last scrap.

"New Guinea?" I prompted.

"No, I heard of New Guinea, Bert was there in the war. Never heard of this place, New..."

"Hebrides?"

"No, don't think so."

"Caledonia?"

"Yeah, that's it, New Caledonia. Where's that?"

I told her, thanked her for the drink and eased my way out. She slumped down in her chair muttering about a cruise.

Strictly speaking, it was a little too late for me to be making another call. I'd meant to give the Pali flat a quick once-over and be on my way, not get stuck drinking gin with a lady whose best days were behind her. Still, I'd learned a bit and this encouraged me to stick to my schedule and tackle Haines next. The traffic would hold him away from home for at least an hour after office hours, if he observed them. If he didn't, then one time was about as good as another for what I had to do. It was a short drive but my shirt was sticking to my back and my throat was oily with the humidity and the almost neat gin when I turned into Haines' street. It was a migrant and black neighbourhood which surprised me a little from what I'd heard of Haines, but perhaps he liked slumming. His flat was in a big Victorian town house, free standing with massive bay windows on both levels. Someone enterprising had made the building over into flats about thirty years ago and it was now in a fair way to return a thousand dollars a month. There was a small overgrown garden in front of the house and a narrow strip of bricked walkway down each side. At the back the yard had been whittled away to nothing to allow four cars to cuddle up against each other under a flat roofed carport. There were no cars at home.

I took this in from a slow cruise around the block formed by the street onto which the house fronted, two side streets and a lane at the back. I parked across the street and a hundred yards down, took the Smith & Wesson from its clip, dropped the keys under the driver's seat and walked up towards the house. My car blended in nicely with the other bombs parked around it. Two black kids were thumping a tennis ball against a brick wall. I gave them a grin and they waited sceptically for me to pass. The iron gate was off its hinges and leaning against the fence just inside the garden. I went in and took the left hand path to the back of the house. It turned out to be the correct side; a set of concrete steps ran up to a landing and an art nouveau door with slanted wooden strips across it and a swan etched into the ripple glass. I coaxed the door open with a pick lock and slid inside leaving the door slightly ajar.

It was what the advertisements call a studio apartment — one big room with a kitchenette and a small bathroom off to one side. A three-quarter bed was tucked into the bay-window recess, and a couch and a couple of heavy armchairs were lined up against one wall with a big oak wardrobe facing them across the room. A low coffee table and a few cushions filled in some of the space and an old wooden filing cabinet stood in a corner away from the light. The rug left a border of polished wood around the room; it had been good and expensive fifty years ago and still had much of its charm.

In the kitchenette were the usual bachelor things and there was no one dead in the bathroom. There were no papers in the filing cabinet, just socks, underwear and folded shirts, all high quality. The drawers of the wardrobe held tie pins, cuff links, a couple of cigarette lighters and some dusty stationery. I flicked through the suits hanging in the long cupboards, four of them with custom labels, nothing in the pockets. Nothing either in the bathrobe, trench coat, duffel jacket or two sports coats. The shoes were in the bottom of one of the cupboards, formally aligned like waiters at a wedding breakfast. There were no bathing suits, no tennis sneakers, no camera, no records or cassettes. There was a small transistor radio, but no television and there wasn't a book in the place.

I found the personal papers in a drawer in the base of the bed — on the side turned to the wall. They occupied one large manila envelope and it took me about two seconds to spread them out on the coffee table. They didn't amount to much: five photographs and five pieces of paper. Unless he carried them around strapped to his thigh, this guy had made a point of not accumulating the usual pieces of plastic and paper that signpost our lives from the cradle to the grave. That in itself was interesting.

If they haven't been kept with any special care, a collection of photographs is fairly easy to arrange from the earliest to the latest and so it was with this batch. The earliest picture, yellowed and a bit creased, was of a building I'd never seen before to my knowledge — a nasty red brick Victorian affair with a wall around it and the look of a women's prison. Next oldest was a muzzy snapshot of a woman in the fashions of twenty years before. A young woman with flared skirts and plenty of lipstick — she looked vaguely familiar but it might just have been the clothes; my sister had looked much the same at the time. Number three, according to my layout, was a careful shot, taken with a good camera, of a land-scaped garden — a beautiful job with rockeries and tiled paths and garden beds spreading out over what could have been an acre or more. The fourth picture was a booth print, passport size, of Ross Haines taken about five years ago. He had a dark bushy beard and was slimmer than he now looked; he was wearing a department store shirt and tie and a suit which, to judge from the cut of the shoulders and the lapels, had come off a fairly cheap hook. Haines wasn't smiling or scowling or pulling any kind of face, just present-ing his puss neutrally to the camera. The most recent of the photos could have been taken yesterday — it showed Ailsa Bercer Gut-teridge, nee Sleeman. She wore light coloured slacks and a denim smock and her eyes were slightly crinkled up against smoke from a cigarette which she was holding rather stiffly in front of her. She looked a bit surprised, a bit off guard, but she wasn't doing anything she shouldn't unless you disapprove of smoking.

The documents, all but one, dated themselves. There was an extract of birth to the effect that Ross Haines had been born on 8 May 1953 in Adelaide, South Australia. It was only an extract so no parents' names appeared. There were two references from employers dated October 1970 and November 1971, both let-terheads were of plant nurseries and garden suppliers and land-scapers in Adelaide. They established the solid credentials and serviceable talents of Ross Haines in this line of work. The other dated document was a diploma from a Sydney business college. It detailed the creditable performances of Haines at typing, short-hand and commercial principles and practice. A map of the Pacific Ocean completed the personal papers of Ross Haines. It folded four times, down to the size of a ladies' handkerchief. I opened it out. There were no marks, no circles, no pin-pricks; at that scale most of the islands were dots or straggly shapes like ink-blots in a vast and trackless sea.

I couldn't make much of this very selective preservation of the past. I studied the photographs of the building and the women closely so as to recognise the originals if I ever saw them and then put the whole lot back in the envelope and the drawer just as I'd found them.

This piece of illegality had taken longer than I'd expected, over half an hour, and I felt an itch at the back of my neck that told me it was high time to go. I went out onto the landing and pulled the door shut behind me. I froze as I heard a car engine being cut under the car port twenty feet away. A door slammed and leather-soled shoes started hitting the bricks. I risked a look down and saw a short, heavy-set man with a head as bald as an egg move briskly down the path and turn into the doorway of the front flat on the ground floor. I let out a stale, sour breath and went down the steps and out through the spaces in the car port. Flat 1's space was taken up by a red MG sports model with wire wheels and kerb feelers. I sneered at it and walked through the lane and up the street to where the Falcon stood with its rust patches and bald tyres gleaming in the late afternoon light.

I had just enough time to try a long shot which would round off the day's work. I drove against the flow of traffic, which was thick and moving as slow as a senile snail, across to the University. I arrived when the day students were pulling out and just before the evening sloggers took up all the space. I got a parking place near the east gates and strolled across the lawn to the main library. I had once done a little research into architecture when I was investigating an insurance fraud on a fire in a Victorian hotel and I remembered where the architecture section was in the library. I looked along the rows until I found Chiswick's two volumes on *The Public Buildings of South Australia*. The book had been very expensive when it was published thirty years before and the quality of its photographs was excellent. It was meticulously indexed and it only took a few minutes to find out that the building of which Haines had kept a picture wasn't a prison. Another few minutes showed that it wasn't a school. Perhaps it was a combination of the two though: I found it on page 215 of the second volume, the picture was taken from a slightly different angle but it was undoubtedly the same forbidding edifice — St Christopher's Boys Orphanage. The short history of the building wasn't interesting but I read it through just the same. I put the books back and left the library.

12

The part-timers, looking tired already, were getting out of their cars as I got into mine. I decided to make for a pub and have a few drinks before calling Ailsa. I'd been hired to help a woman I found I cordially disliked and had ended up working for one about whom I had quite different feelings. It was a big changeabout in a short space of time and I wondered what effect it was having on my judgment. I wonder better over a glass of something, so I put off the effort until I had the conditions right. After a scotch in a place near the dog track, I picked the right money out of my change and put it into the red phone at the corner of the bar. The wall was scarred with a hundred telephone numbers and the names and numbers of innumerable horses and dogs. The directory was a tattered ruin. I read the record of losing favourites and one-leg doubles as I waited for Ailsa to answer her phone. It rang and rang hopelessly and I hung up, checked the number and rang again. The result was the same and the repeated buzz on the line chilled and sobered me like a bucket of ice water in the face.

I ran to the Falcon and unparked it regardless of duco and chrome. I ripped my way through the late afternoon traffic towards Mosman.

There were no cops about and I set records through the winding roads towards the Bridge. I hit the Harbour Bridge approach and pushed the Falcon to the limit cursing it for its sluggishness and refusal to steer straight.

I ran into Ailsa's drive too fast and nearly spun the car around full circle in bringing it to a stop in front of the house. I unshipped my gun and went up the steps at a gallop. I hammered on the door and wrenched at the handle but it was locked so I kicked in the glass pane next to it. The thick glass shattered and splintered where my foot hit it and the rest of the pane came crashing down like a guillotine. I went in through the jagged hole and raced through the house, poking the gun into each room and calling Ailsa's name. I found her in the bedroom. She was naked and her clothes had been torn in strips to truss her up and tie her to the frame of the bed. She was breathing harshly through puffed, split lips and her body was criss-crossed with long, heavily bleeding scratches. There were round, white-flaked burn marks on her forearms and the room smelled of singed hair and skin. I grabbed the bedroom phone and called for an ambulance, then I untied the strips of fabric and lifted her up onto the bed. I tucked a pillow under her head, her pulse was strong but she was rigid and sweating and there were now lines in her face that looked like they would stay there forever.

I got some water from the kitchen, went back to the bedroom and lifted her head a little to the rim of the glass. She opened her eyes and lapped at the water. Her eyes showed that her body was a package of pain. She looked at me reproachfully.

"Some protector," she croaked through her battered lips.

"Ailsa, I'm sorry," my voice sounded like grit in ball bearings. "Who did it love, why?"

"Bryn . . . and another man. I let them in. Other man slapped me and stripped me. Bryn just watched."

The effort of speaking was doing her no good, she was in deep shock and her face was pale and waxy, but I had to know a little more.

"Listen love, just answer in one word or shake your head, understand?"

She nodded.

"What did Bryn want?"

"Files."

"Gutteridge's files?"

A nod.

"Did Bryn touch you?"

A shake, no.

"Just the other guy. Was Bryn there all the time?"

A shake.

"Why did he leave? What did you tell him?'"

"Brave."

"You told him Brave had the files. Is that true?"

She closed her eyes and I eased her back down onto the pillow.

"You don't know," I said almost under my breath. "Good girl, that was smart." There was one last thing I needed to know. I smoothed down the cap of hair which was sweaty and sticking up in spikes. "Ailsa, I have to know this. When did Bryn leave, can you tell me?'"

"You rang," she whispered, "he left."

That made it half an hour or so, a little more. If he went to Brave's place directly he'd be there within an hour. Maybe he wasn't there yet and perhaps I could still spring the trap. Ailsa seemed to have lost consciousness, I checked her pulse again, still strong, I pulled a sheet up over her body and was just watching the blood ooze through it when I heard the sirens.

"Where?" the shout came from the front of the house.

"Back bedroom," I bellowed.

Two ambulance men charged into the room carrying a stretcher. The young fresh-faced one stopped short, he hadn't done much in this line of work before. The older man took a glance then busied himself preparing the stretcher. His face was an expressionless mask.

"Anything broke?"

"I don't think so."

He pulled the sheet aside carefully and gently lifted her arms and legs an inch or so; he put his ear to her chest.

"Think you're right. Has to be moved anyway, needs treatment fast. OK Snowy, stop gawking. On the stretcher."

The boy did his share smartly enough.

"Who did this?" he said as they were fastening the straps.

"A friend."

"God, I'm sorry."

"Thanks, he's going to be sorrier."

While this was going on I found Ailsa's address book and the name and number of her doctor. I wrote them on the back of my card and tucked it into the older guy's overall pocket.

"I'm admitting her. Her doctor's name and number are on the card, it's my card. Her name's Ailsa Sleeman, double e. Where will she be?"

He raised an eyebrow and seemed to be going to protest until he got a good look at my face. "St Bede's," he said nervously. "You should admit her personally, but I guess you're going to be busy."

"That's right."

I told him I'd contact the police and he offered no argument to that. They carried her gingerly out of the house, down the steps and put her in the ambulance. The siren screamed and the vehicle wailed off towards the city.

It was early for my calls to Evans and Tickener, but perhaps too late. A packet of Ailsa's cigarettes was lying on the floor near the bed and I took one out mechanically and put it in my mouth. Then I looked at the floor again. Three long butts had been squashed out into the deep pile of the carpet making charred holes as big as five cent pieces. I spat the cigarette out, grabbed the phone and dialled. Tickener's voice was flat, bored, he wasn't expecting me yet.

"This is Hardy," I said, "things are breaking. Here's what I want you to do . . ." He interrupted me. "Listen Hardy, I've been looking into this Brave. He's weird, he . . ."

I cut in. "Yeah, I know. Tell me later. I want you to get out to the clinic as fast as you can. Colin Jones around, is he?"

"Yes, matter of fact he's right here now. I had a word with him, mate of yours I understand . . ."

I cut him off again. "Bring him! The cops won't be far behind you and I won't be far behind them. Give the place a bit of air the way you did before, OK?"

"OK Hardy. We're busting Brave?"

"Wide open," I said, "and you're an A grade from tomorrow if you handle it right."

I rang off and dialled Evans' number. He answered testily.

"You're early, you're never early, it can't be you."

"It's me, I was pushed. My client's been cut and burned and our men aren't standing about. Can you move now?"

"Yeah, but give me something for the sheet."

"Put what you like on it, but don't put this — Costello."

97

"Shit!"

"Right. I think Brave has him at his clinic in Longueville. Your mate Jackson is running interference and a Dr Clyde is doing the remodelling of Costello's dial. I want Brave. Costello's just a by-product to me but I haven't got any time for him anyway. Suit you?"

"And how!" I could hear the scratch of his writing across the line. I gave him the address and a few other details. I was praying that Bryn's trip to Longueville would delay things out there enough so that all the principals wouldn't be on planes to Rio by the time the law, the press and I got there.

I got up off the floor with creaking knee joints and needles of pain in my skull. I looked around the room, at the bloody sheets, the cigarette ends and the ripped clothes. Some light was coming in from an opening in the curtains and I could see the swimming pool still reflecting light challengingly close, but I doubted that Ailsa would ever feel like reading her novels, smoking her cigarettes and being warm and loving in that room again. It was a room I'd liked more than most, and it made me sad to know how it'd been used by the worst sort of human being to create the worst sort of pain.

There was a small clutch of neighbours across the road standing on a second level balcony exhibiting well bred interest in the proceedings. They had glasses in their hands as if they were toasting the most excitement seen in that part of the world in years. I gave them a rude gesture and drove off leaving them twittering and fluttering like birds who've been thrown a handful of seed.

I was getting to know the route out to Longueville well enough to drive it in my sleep. I pushed the Falcon flat-out. A few solid citizens shook their heads disapprovingly as I passed them and two bikies gave me an outrider escort for a mile for the hell of it. The day was dying and a soft, limp night settling down on the suburbs and hills when I reached Longueville but I was thinking of Ailsa and wailing sirens and it seemed to be raining blood to me.

13

Tickener's Holden was standing around the corner from the clinic and half a block back along the street. Across from it were two unmarked cars carrying four men who could only have been cops. I pulled up behind Tickener. Grant Evans got out of his car and walked across to the Holden. He got on the front seat and I got in the back. I sat down next to a small, relaxed looking guy who wore a Zapata moustache and an intelligent expression. Evans spoke first.

"You didn't tell me that the press were in on it, Cliff, I could get my arse kicked for this."

"You won't," I assured him. "The fish are too big and too many people are going to be scared shitless to worry about you. You'll do yourself a lot of good. Oh, by the way, Harry Tickener, Inspector Grant Evans." They shook hands warily. Tickener half-turned and nodded at the photographer sitting next to me who was fiddling with what looked like twenty different camera attachments. "Colin Jones," he said. Evans stuck out his hand and Colin gave it a quick shake and went back to his cameras. He'd been a man of few words when I'd met him as a reconnaissance cameraman in Malaya, and he hadn't changed a bit.

"This should be right up your street, Colin," I said. "Here's how it stands. I think Rory Costello's in there getting a face job. There are legitimate patients in there too which poses a bit of a problem and there's plenty of muscle. A boy named Bruno who can handle himself and at least two others who can dish it out. And Costello of course, but I imagine he's out of action. He was bandaged up like a mummy when I saw him, if it was him."

"It better be," Evans growled. "Weapons?"

"Didn't see any but sure to be some. The guy on the gate is

almost certainly armed and he's our first problem."

"That booth looks like a fortress," said Tickener.

"It's pretty formidable," I agreed, "but the problem is that it relays pictures and alarms to the main building. The fence is electrified and there are TV cameras about."

"So it's no go to divert the guard and go over the fence?" Evans leered at me. "What are we going to do, parachute in?"

Jones spoke up. "Have you been inside the fence and the building, Cliff?"

I said I had. "Did you hear any constant background noise of any kind?" All I'd heard was a lot of talk and a lot of ringing inside my head after I'd been hit. I tried to remember the feeling of being inside the place, lobby, corridors and rooms. "No," I said, "No background noise." "Any flickering in the lights?" Jones asked. I thought about it. "No."

"Then it's no problem." He slung a camera around his neck. "No generator, they're working off the mains supply — amateurs. You knock out the supply lines temporarily or permanently and in you go."

"Is it hard to do?" I asked.

"No, a cinch, I can do it."

"Can you now?" said Evans thoughtfully.

The cameraman smiled at him. "I was trained in Her Majesty's armed service, Inspector. It's easy if you know how, I'd need a hammer and a couple of big nails and a screwdriver."

"I'd have them over the back," said Tickener. "I'm building a shack up the Hawkesbury."

"All right for some," Evans muttered as the reporter got out of the car, went round the back, dropped the hatch and started a few seconds of noisy rummaging. My nerves screamed at the clanking of metal on metal and I was anxious to be moving. Evans sat there shaking his head gently and looking resignedly out into the night. Tickener came up with the nails and tools and put them on the bonnet of the car.

"Assuming we get in OK," Evans said, "how do you read it from there, Cliff? No warrant, no nothing."

"They'll react. They'll shoot, I think. That lets you in."

"True, true. Shooting's illegal." Evans began to enjoy himself. "Right, I'll leave two men in a car outside to mop up or follow us in if need be. The rest of us will go in — you, me, Varson, Tickener and Jones. The objective is Costello, right?"

"Right," I said, "and Brave if he's there. I think he will be."

I had my own thoughts about others who might be there and it probably wasn't fair not to tell Grant about them, but I had plans about what to do if Bryn and his mate got within pistol distance and I didn't want any interference.

Jones spoke again. "Do you want the blackout permanent or temporary?"

"Temporary," said Evans, "I want to see who I'm arresting."

"OK." The photographer deposited his equipment carefully on the seat and got out of the car. "Let's find the power line. Oh, I forgot to tell you, if it's right outside the front gate we're stuffed."

Evans, Tickener and I got out of the car and followed Colin. Evans beckoned to the car behind, a man got out and jogged to catch up with us. He had a quick confab with Evans, ran back to the car to fill his colleagues in, and was out of breath when he caught up with us again. We set off to pick up the perimeter of the clinic at the north end. Evans' offsider was a big, bald-headed man with a bald man's look of hostility at the world. From the bulge under his coat I guessed he was carrying a fair sized gun and I was glad that he was on my side. I assumed that Grant was adequately armed, I had my .38, fully loaded, in my jacket pocket.

We walked around the fence with Jones looking up and down every few yards. After walking the full length of one side of the block and half of the next, Jones stopped and clicked his tongue softly.

"This is it, a cinch."

He pulled his belt from his pants, took off his jacket, put the nails and screwdriver in his pants pocket and shoved the hammer inside his waistband. He buckled the belt on the first hole and looped it over his shoulder. The lamp post stood about twelve feet back from the fence and it was a good twenty feet up to the cross beam. Jones whistled to himself as he shimmied up the post using hands, knees and feet like a south sea islander after coconuts. He reached the cross beam and slung the belt over it. He steadied himself by hanging onto the strap and began to hammer and probe the electrical equipment. Two minutes later he slid down the pole. He was carefully holding a piece of wire in his hand when he hit the ground.

"Always plenty of spare wire up there," he said cheerfully. "This is all set up. One pull and the lights go out all over Europe, another tug and they go on again. You trip a switch and untrip it, see?"

"I believe him," I said to Evans who grunted. The other cop spoke for the first time since he'd joined us. "How do we handle it? Do we go through the fence or the gate?" It was a pretty good question. Evans looked at Jones. "You're the one with all the ideas at the moment, what d'you think?" Jones paused, he was probably thinking of his compound-storming in Malaya and he'd been in on some tough ones.

"The gate's the easiest. The guard's going to be as blind as a bat when the lights blow. Should be easy to grab him and keep him quiet. We can get the gates open and drive in. Of course, someone'll have to stay here and do the pulling."

"That'll be you, Ron," Evans said to the cop, then he waved a hand at us. "Sorry, Hardy, Jones, Tickener — Ron Varson, rough as guts."

We nodded at him. Varson didn't look happy with his second fiddle job but he took Evans' description of him as a compliment and looked grimly determined. Evans was in control of it now. He issued his instructions briskly and authoritatively. We checked our watches and agreed on lights-out time and three of us headed back towards the gate. Varson stood holding the wire and looking up to where it connected with the switches. He still looked a bit unhappy with the job, as though he was about to flush himself down a giant lavatory.

We proceeded in a huddle as close as we could to the main gate without being noticed. We decided to take Tickener's car because that meant the reporter and photographer could go in with a maximum of cover. Maybe Evans was hedging his bet a little, but no one argued. Jones huddled down in the back of the FB,

Tickener hunched over the wheel. We waited. The clinic grounds and the reception booth were almost floodlit, very bright. Evans eased a black automatic out of his holster and checked it. I patted my gun. There was no traffic within earshot and the quiet of Longueville at that moment was just the sort of quiet the residents had paid all that money for.

The clinic blacked out suddenly as if it had been covered by an old-time photographer's cloth. Evans and I sprinted for the reception booth. By the little moonlight and the street light we could see the guard flailing around pushing buttons. Evans fronted the glass cage and pointed his automatic at the guard's nose. He reached for a sawn-off shotgun which rested against the wall of the booth but he was too slow. I had the side door open and my gun in his earhole before he could grab the weapon.

"Easy does it friend, you don't want to die for five hundred a month."

He saw the wisdom of it and let go the shotgun. Evans came into the booth and prodded the guard out. The guard walked towards the car, moonlight glinted on the barrel of a pistol which one of the detectives held out of the car window trained on his chest.

The light came on again and Grant pushed a couple of buttons on the instrument panel in the box. The wide gates swung open. I grabbed the shotgun and went out and through the gates at a run. Evans took a swipe at the control panel and followed me. Tickener came burning up to the gate and we ran along beside him as the FB roared up to the clinic. He wavered on and off the brick path and the wheels churned furrows up in the smooth green grass on either side. There were three cars parked near the main entrance and I was shouting at Tickener to block them when a red and blue flash came from a window in the main block. Glass shattered in the car and I heard a yelp from Jones. Tickener stalled the motor and we crouched down behind the car. Another flash and a bullet whined off the Holden's bonnet. I peeked around and snapped two shots at the window. Evans crouched double and ran for the porch. He went up the steps, fired twice into the glass doors and jumped aside. A bullet from inside splintered a panel on the door and I made it to the other side of the porch in six heart-in-the-mouth strides. Footsteps pounded up the path and the gun behind the window opened up and Varson dropped like a stone. I couldn't tell if he'd been hit or not. Evans kicked the shattered door in and we both went into the lobby, almost on our bellies. It was empty. Then the door at the end of the room opened and Bruno fired a quick shot at Evans before ducking back. He missed and Grant took a chance. He rushed through the door and flattened himself against the wall. I went through and pasted myself against the other side. Bruno was half way down the corridor and his next shot whistled between us. Evans dropped to one knee, sighted quickly and fired. Bruno screeched and went down like the last pin in the lane and his gun skittered crazily along the polished floor.

Two men came out of a door on the right. One of them snapped a shot at me and they jumped over Bruno and rounded the bend at the end of the passage. I was vaguely conscious of movement and sound behind me and took a quick look. Tickener was crouched down near Evans and slightly hampering his attempt to take a shot, his face white and his eyes wide and scared. Jones was standing up behind Evans, snapping and flashing. A man lumbered out of the door the other two had come from. He was big, dark hair spilled through the unbuttoned top of his pyjamas coat and he was groping at the tie of the pants. His face was heavily bandaged and the pistol he carried was pointed nowhere in particular.

Evans shook Tickener away and bellowed. "Costello, police, let go the gun."

The blind-looking bandaged face turned slowly towards the sound of the voice. Jones stepped foward and snapped. The bulb went off and Grant threw up his hand to ward off the glare. Costello lined him up like an Olympic shooter with 20/20 vision. I swung the shotgun on him and fired. The charge hit him in the chest, lifted him up and slammed him against the white wall. He slid slowly down it, leaving a bloody trail behind him like a wolf shot high up in the snow country coming down the slope to die. Jones walked up and took a careful picture. His hands were as still and steady as Costello's corpse.

I put the shotgun down. Evans was leaning against the wall. His gun was pointing at the floor and his lips were moving silently. He knew how close he'd come.

"There's more of them, Grant," I said quietly.

As I spoke the door behind us opened and Varson came through it sideways, propping it open with his back. He waved a man through with a quick gesture of his enormous, gun-filled right hand. Dr Ian Brave strolled into the passage.

"I got him outside," said Varson, "he was leaving."

"He stays," Evans said.

Brave looked at the crumpled, bloody ruin on the floor. His face had a vacant, other-worldly look — for my money he was floating high and free somewhere a long way off. Along the corridor Bruno groaned and tried to pull himself up against the wall; everyone had forgotten him.

14

The quiet tableau broke up after a minute or two. Jones backed off down the passage and took a quick picture of Brave with Varson looming over his shoulder. Brave was Varson's prize, all he had to show for the night, and he kept close to him like a nervous spouse at a party. Evans, Tickener and I went into the room which Costello had come out of to die. The window leading out into the shrubbery at the side of the building gaped open.

"He had two goons with him the other day," I said, "one of them socked me but I guess they weren't shooters."

Tickener scribbled on a pad and Evans grunted. "Looks that way."

"Two hopped it just after I shot the Italian. That makes four on the loose. I hope the boys at the gate got them, but it's a lot to handle." He brooded on this for a moment and then shrugged. "You didn't quite level with me about the strength of the troops, did you Cliff?" I opened my hands apologetically. "Never mind," he said, "we done OK." Varson called his name and he went out into the corridor. Tickener looked at me inquiringly but I turned away from him and looked out through the window thinking my own murderous thoughts. Tickener walked out. I rolled a cigarette, lit it and followed him.

Susan Gutteridge was standing in the corridor along with a woman with wild hair and eyes. They both wore severe calico nightdresses. Brave was trying to do his hand-holding act with Susan but Varson was shouldering him aside. Jones had left the scene and Bruno had passed out. The other patient was staring at the body on the floor. Suddenly she collapsed to her knees and pitched forward over it. Blood soaked into her nightdress and she daubed it over her face and body.

"Sally," she moaned, "oh Sally, Sally."

Evans started pushing the buttons. He told Varson to take Brave in and book him for harbouring an escapee. He pointed at Tickener who was still scribbling and poking his long thin nose into rooms off the passage. "OK, Tickener," he roared, "you've had your ringside seat, now do something useful. Get on the first phone you see and call an ambulance. Call police headquarters and tell them I want a police doctor out here right away."

Tickener turned away obediently and Evans rapped out a few more words. "And a nurse or two, tell them about the women." I was next. "So you know these ladies?" he snapped.

"Take it easy, Grant. Yes, I know the younger one, she's Susan Gutteridge." He rubbed his hand over his eyes, then looked down surprised to see that the hand was still holding a gun.

"OK, OK," he said tightly. "Get her away somewhere. Jesus what a mess!" The older woman was still embracing the corpse and sobbing. I took the Gutteridge woman's arm and led her down the passage.

I didn't remember where her room was, so I let her lead me. She plodded on not saying anything until we came to room 38. I pushed the door open and she walked in ahead of me. She still hadn't spoken a word. I had nothing I wanted to say to her, but I felt an impulse to stir her from her trance if I could. Perhaps I didn't want her to have the luxury of a cotton wool wrapping while people were dying around her.

"Do you remember me, Miss Gutteridge?"

"Of course I do," she snapped, "do you think I'm crazy like Grace?"

"Grace?"

"Grace Heron, back there." She jerked her head at the door.

"No, no I don't. But you've had a shock, I thought..."

"I'm all right I tell you," she cut in, "what's been happening here? I heard shots."

I was surprised at her composure. When I'd last seen her she was as fragile as a spider web, ready to be torn apart and dismembered by the slightest harshness, now she seemed to have put together a tough, no-nonsense personality. But it was hard to tell how real it was or how enduring it would be. She sat quietly on the bed while I gave her an outline of events as they related to what she'd seen in the hall. She nodded occasionally and once smoothed down the rough material over her thighs — they weren't bad thighs — otherwise she kept still and attentive. I didn't mention Ailsa in this explanation, but when she asked me directly who I was working for now, I told her, including what had happened to Ailsa that night. I didn't bring Bryn into it. She said something reassuring and patted my arm so there must have been some indication of how I felt in what I said. It might have been the automatic, professional touch of the social worker, but it felt sincere.

"Well, Mr Hardy," she said, "you've really got yourself tangled up with the Gutteridges, haven't you? Have you any idea yet who was threatening me and did these other things, I mean to Giles and Ailsa?"

"I don't even know if the same people are involved," I said, "Ailsa thought Brave was behind it all." I waited for her reaction to that. She bit her lip and pondered it so I decided to go on. I wanted a drink badly, but it seemed possible that this new woman with the mind of her own might help me do some reappraising of the case at this point. "That could be," I continued, "if he's fallen out with an accomplice. You saw a ferrety-looking guy out there?"

She nodded. "Yes."

"He's a reporter. A woman phoned him at his paper and tipped him off about Brave. She had an accent that sounded French. It could be the woman who phoned you."

Her face screwed up in distaste. "Yes, I suppose so, her voice could have had a French sound to it. I'm not much good at that sort of thing. I was rotten at languages at school."

I was liking her more. "Me too," I said. "Then again, your brother might fit. He could have killed Giles himself and put the frighteners on you and arranged for the bomb in Ailsa's car. But there's one thing wrong with that line of theory."

"What's that?"

"Why would he call me in in the first place?"

She gave it some thought. "It seems to me that in books, you know, detective stories, the guilty person sometimes hires the detective. Doesn't it ever happen in real life?"

"Yeah, sometimes it does, it can be a good blind. But Bryn seemed to be genuinely distressed about Giles, it didn't look like an act to me. It's still a possibility though, if he was tied in to some deal with someone else and they fell out."

"What someone else?" she asked.

"God knows. I'm just trying the idea out. Brave maybe? But I get conflicting reports on Bryn and Brave's relationship. I just don't have any firm candidates."

"Well, I can fill you in a little there, on Brave and Bryn. God, it sounds like a stage act, doesn't it? What do you want to know?"

"For a start whether Bryn and the doctor were on good terms and whether Bryn trusted him. And secondly, who really advised you to come to this place and put yourself under Brave's care?"

The cigarette I'd lit fifteen minutes before was dead between my fingers. I fumbled for a match and lit it, it tasted bitter and stale and I crushed it out into an ashtray on the night table beside the bed. I rolled a new one and fiddled with it. She watched me with a look of concentration on her face. I lit the cigarette.

"Bryn and Dr Brave became very close after my father died," she said, "Bryn saw a lot of him socially and professionally. You know what Bryn's like, his . . . orientation?" I nodded. "Well, he's got it sorted out most of the time and Giles is . . . was good for him. He functions in business life very effectively and in private life pretty well. He's been doing better at it in the last two years, but he does know some terrible people, vicious, depraved people. Dr Brave helped him a lot, trying to get Bryn to control and channel his impulses. Bryn can be very cruel. I'd be very surprised if there was any rift between them."

"Bryn told me there was," I said, "and he also said that he was against you going into the clinic."

"That's just not true." She frowned and spoke quickly. "Ever since my diabetes started playing up and I began having these bad spells Bryn has urged me to rely on Dr Brave."

"When did this trouble start?"

"Oh, fairly soon after my father died. Diabetes can be affected by emotional upset. I just couldn't seem to stabilise myself again, and I'd been stabilised for years."

"When did the diabetes set in?"

A shadow seemed to pass over her face which surprised me, but I was adjusting to the new personality and forgetting about the old, fragmented one.

"I was sixteen when it started," she said shortly. "After Mark died I started working harder and harder for charity and other causes. Dr Brave encouraged that too, but I got very tired and I came here more frequently."

She seemed now to have a completely different attitude to Brave from the one I'd seen before and it puzzled me. At the risk of breaking up her present helpful mood I decided to ask her about it.

"You seem able to talk pretty objectively about Brave now," I said. "Do you feel differently about him?"

She nodded. "Yes, yes I do. I seem to recall thinking you were a perceptive man when I met you before." I tried to look modest. "You are," she went on. "I felt differently about him the minute I saw him in the passage with all that blood and that man standing next to him. Is he a policeman?"

"Yes."

"I thought so. Dr Brave doesn't control him. He controls everyone here you see and he was controlling everyone at home — me, certainly, and Bryn to a large extent. I suppose not having the treatments for a few days might have something to do with it."

"What are the treatments?"

"I've been on a course of injections, hormones. And I have hypnotherapy sessions with Dr Brave."

"What goes on in them?"

"I don't remember very clearly. They seem to be mainly about the day Mark died. I was the first one in the family to see him. Dr Brave seems to think my trouble is psychosomatic, stemming from finding my father like that. I had a sort of memory lapse, a breakdown, you know."

I knew. "And Brave questions you about this under hypnosis?"

"Yes, at least I think so, it's hard to remember when I come out of it."

"Does it do you any good do you think?"

She wrinkled her forehead and drew a deep, slow breath; she

was treating the question as if it contained a mint fresh idea she'd never heard before.

"I thought it did at the time," she said, "now I'm not so sure. No, that's not true, now I don't think it did. On and on about safes and things..."

"Safes? Brave asked you about safes?"

"I think so, yes. But I don't know anything about safes. He said they were symbolic, the womb and all that. I couldn't ever seem to satisfy him about it."

She was getting tired and all this forced recall was making her edgy. She still looked a lot better than she had when Brave was doing his Svengali bit all over her though. I told her to get into bed and she did it.

"There'll be a nurse here soon. You might as well spend the night. Then in the morning, if you feel up to it, I think you should check yourself out and go see a good doctor. Get the diabetes straightened out. Will you?"

She sniffed and wrinkled her nose before answering me.

"What's that smell?" she said.

I lifted my hands. "Cordite, I've just fired a shotgun."

"Did you kill him, the man with the bandaged face?"

"Yeah."

"He looked blind."

"He was meant to, he wasn't though."

She nodded, then glanced across at the dressing table, on it was a white plastic case, about four inches tall, with a screw top, and a roll of cotton wool. She gave the kit a look I'd seen before — it was her lifeline and her cross.

"Do you inject yourself?" I asked.

"Mostly, not in here though. Do you know anything about diabetes?"

"Not much. My mother was one, but she was a drinker. When she was on a binge it used to go all wrong and she'd get in a bad way."

"I'm not a drinker," she snapped.

"No, but you've got a problem with your condition just the same. Will you see another doctor?"

She lifted the sides of her hair up and let her fingers slip through the soft waves. She still looked tired, older than she should, but there was some shine in her eyes that could just possibly be hope.

"I don't know why I should let you tell me what to do," she said. "But yes, I will. I'm still interested in your investigations. Will you let me know how they proceed?" I said I would. "And I'd like to see Ailsa in hospital," she went on, "if I can be of any help I will."

I had some red Codrals from the night before in my pocket and I offered them to her as a sedative. I thought she might need them to get to sleep in a building where a man had died the hard way. She took them.

"Thank you, Mr Hardy. Dr Brave would never allow any kind of sedative. I'd lie here for hours some nights. Thank you."

"Good night Miss Gutteridge." She swallowed the tablets with some water and let herself slide down the bank of pillows. "Susan," she said. "Goodnight, Mr Hardy."

I'd been dimly conscious of some car noise and other flak from outside while I'd been talking to Susan, so I wasn't surprised when I found only Tickener's FB and one other car outside the building. There were lights flashing at the end of the drive and a certain amount of shouting and hurrying about. I started towards the gate and had covered about half the distance when a figure loomed up in front of me and pointed a pistol at my hairline which is low and just in front of some pretty vital parts of my brain.

"Put your hands on your head slowly," the shadow said. He took a flashlight from his pocket and shone it in my face.

I raised my hands. "I killed Cock Robin," I said, "take me to your leader." The flashlight beam wavered and the gun muzzle looked a fraction less eager.

"You Hardy?" he growled.

"Yeah. Is Grant Evans still around and can I put my hands down?"

"You can. Have to be very careful, Mr Hardy. One of the heavies who was with Costello is still loose, we got the other one."

"Dead?"

"No, my partner winged him and he's talking a blue streak already."

"Good," I said. "What about the other two?"

"They got away. There's another way out around the back. We reckon they lay low while the shooting was going on, then hopped in one of the cars at the front and scooted out. They went over garden beds and all. We had other men coming and they reported a car moving fast on the road but they didn't know the score and let it go. Bad luck. Anyway, Inspector Evans is down there."

He jerked his chin at the gate and went off to shut the stable door a bit tighter. I was thinking that it was partly my fault, I hadn't noticed another exit. I reached the gate where Evans was in a huddle with some cops in uniform and some men in plain clothes. Tickener was looking serious and about ten years older. Jones was photographing two white-overalled men sliding a long, white-wrapped bundle into the back of an ambulance. Bruno was lying on a stretcher which had little fold-out legs to keep it up off the ground. I jolted it a bit as I came up.

"Careful," he groaned and turned his head to look at me. I grinned down at him. His elegant flared trousers had been slit to the crotch and there was a large dressing around his knee. He didn't look happy.

"How's it going Rocky?" I said. "I bet the police surgeon'll do a great job on that knee. You'll be back kicking old ladies to death in no time."

"Get fucked," he snarled.

I tut-tutted him and walked over to Evans.

"Back exit, Cliff," he said, "it'd never have done for Malaya."

"True," I said. "What car did they take?"

"Fiat, sports model."

"That'd be right," I said wearily.

"How's that?"

"Never mind, Grant. What's the drill now? Headquarters, statements and such?" He nodded. "OK," I said, "see you there."

I trudged over to the Falcon, climbed in and turned the key. The engine leapt into life as if it had thrived on the action.

15

I was at police HQ for over four hours. It would have been longer and tougher if Grant Evans hadn't been on side. I made statements about my earlier call on Brave. Evans allowed me to leave the Gutteridges with a very low profile in the whole thing. The Costello affair was what he was interested in and what Tickener's readers were interested in as well. They were both happy for me and my involvements to take a back seat. I told Grant that I might have something soon on the Giles killing and he said that would be nice in an uninterested way. I read on a message sheet on his desk that "attempts to contact Senior Detective Charles Jackson and Dr William Clyde had been unsuccessful". Bulletins were out on them. In a break from the recording and questioning, I got on a phone and called Bryn Gutteridge's number. There was no answer. The same ten cents bought me a call to St Bede's hospital and the information that Miss Sleeman had responded well to transfusions and a saline drip and was sleeping peacefully. When I gave my name the desk attendant said that the police were anxious to contact me in connection with Miss Gutteridge's injuries. I told her where I was calling from and she seemed satisfied. I hadn't heard anything about it at headquarters and I didn't want to if I wasn't going to be there until mid-day.

Brave, Bruno and the thug who'd been picked up in the grounds were securely booked. The third man had sung like a bird and there was a bulletin out on his mate, a long-time hood with an impressive record and a history of association with Rory Costello. Nobody put pressure on me to identify the two men who'd escaped in the Fiat and I kept quiet about it. Evans prepared a statement for the press and went into a huddle with Tickener and Jones about their respective rights to the glamour and gore of the evening. They sorted it out and the pressmen, looking pretty pleased with themselves, came over to shake my hand before leaving.

"Lucky I followed you, Hardy," said Tickener. "Instinct, eh?"

We shook. "I guess so," I said. He hadn't handled himself too badly and he'd be well clear of the sports page and Joe Barrett's errands now. Also, he now owed me something and it's handy in my game to have a pressman in your debt. Colin Jones looked like he needed some sleep, but if he was going to get his pictures into the morning editions he probably wouldn't get it. He let go my hand and slapped one of his cameras.

"Miles to go before I sleep," he said.

"You're the only educated cameraman in the west, Colin."

"Yeah, it gets in the way. Thanks for letting me in, Cliff, it made a change." They wandered off to put the final touches on the thrills in store for their readers over the yoghurt and crispies.

I'd exhausted my packet of Drum and drunk all the autovend coffee I could stand. It was 2 a.m. and I felt like I needed a new skin, a new throat and quite a few other accessories. I had an Irish thirst and the image of the wine in my refrigerator beckoned me like the damasked arm of the lady in the lake. Evans started slipping papers into folders and his telephone had finally stopped ringing hot. I was sitting across from his self-satisfied look. He reached into a drawer of the scarred and battered pine desk and fished out two cigars in cellophane wrappers. He offered me one.

"Keeping 'em since Jenny was born. Thought it might be a son. This is the next best thing, have one?"

I shook my head. "Wouldn't have a cold beer would you?"

He smiled, lit his cigar and leaned back blowing a thin stream of the rich, creamy smoke at the ceiling. "Piss artist," he said indulgently. "Case closed, Cliff?"

"Yours or mine?"

"Mine is like a fish's arsehole. I mean yours."

"I don't know yet." I was lying, I suspected it was just beginning and that there were many little corners of it still unexplored and a great highway of truth still to put through the lives of the people concerned.

"Well, anything I can do, just let me know." He looked at his watch and I took the point. We shook hands and I trudged down the corridor and took yet another chance on the lift. We made a nice couple as we wheezed down to ground level and I closed its wire grille gently; with care and kind treatment we might both just last out the decade.

I picked up my car which was looking sheepish and barely roadworthy among the powder blues in the police parking lot, and drove home through the back streets and quietest roads. I tried to think of Ailsa battling with her pain in hospital, and Susan Gutteridge coming out of a long slide, and Bryn cruising and cruel like a harbour shark, but all the pictures blurred and the people receded far off into the distance. A truck backfired when I was within fifty yards of home, and as I sidled the Falcon into the yard my ears were ringing with the noise and I could smell the smoke and feel the shotgun heavy and deadly in my hands. I went into the house, drank a long glass of wine and made coffee, but I went to sleep in a chair while waiting for the cup I'd poured to cool. I swilled it down cold and went to bed.

Tickener made a good job of it. His headline was lurid but his story was sharp and clear. Evans got a splash verbally and photographically and there were lots of adjectives scattered through the writing like "fearless" and "masterly". I got a few mentions and anyone reading between the lines would come away with the knowledge that I had killed Costello, but who reads between the lines any more? The name Gutteridge didn't figure in the story and it seemed that a combination of brilliant investigatory journalism and enterprising police work had delivered the goods. That suited me. The last thing I wanted was pictures of myself in the papers and my name a household word — it might feel good, but it would play hell with business if kids came up to ask you for your autograph while you were staking out a love nest.

I read most of this sitting on the lavatory while a warm, soft Sydney rain darkened the courtyard bricks. Back in the kitchen I made coffee and welsh rarebit. Ordinarily, I'd have been at least semi-relaxed. I was on a case, on expenses and earning them and hadn't had any bones broken in the past twenty-four hours. But

116

this one was different, my client was special and she was in hospital and I was partly to blame. The villain was in custody as they say, but villains were coming out of the woodwork and the past was sending out tentacles which were winding around the necks of people living and dying in the present. It's a dying trade I'm in.

I called the hospital and was told that I could visit Miss Sleeman at 10 a.m., seeing that I was the one who'd admitted her. I took a long, hot then cold shower, which made me feel virtuous. I capitalised on this by taking the flagon and a glass out onto the bricks along with my electric razor and my razor sharp mind. I sipped the wine and ran the tiny, whirring blades over my face. The sun climbed up over the top of the biscuit factory and beamed heat down into the courtyard. The bricks started to steam and sweat began to roll off my chest down into the thin layers of fat around my waist. I resolved again to walk more and to cut out beer and that was as far as my thinking took me. I towelled off the sweat, dressed in cotton slacks, shirt and sandals and played inch by inch with the Falcon out onto the street. There was a sweet, malty biscuit smell in the air as I drove past the front of my house. Soames had just put on his first record of the day. Pretty soon he'd take a peek over the fence, shake his head at the empty flagon and roll his apres-muesli joint.

I don't like hospitals. My mother and father and Uncle Ted died in them. They all smell and look the same, all polished glass and lino and reek of disinfectant. Ailsa was on the fourth floor in a ward past the maternity unit. It was crammed full of rosy cheeked mothers smothering babies, black, white and brindle, against their chests. It made me feel my childlessness like a burden and I wondered if Ailsa felt the same way. Perhaps she didn't need to. She hadn't mentioned any children, but then I had only got a pretty episodic biography of her, perhaps she had twins being finished in Switzerland. Dangerous thoughts for someone for whom marriage was a busted flush and kids were something not to shoot when out on business. I had wanted kids but Cyn hadn't unless I was going to be home at six o'clock every night and I couldn't give her that guarantee. I was in an intensely self-critical mood when I arrived at Ailsa's ward. A roly-poly matron who hadn't heard how dragon-like she should be showed me to the door and told me I could have an hour. I went in.

Ailsa was sitting up in bed wearing a white cheesecloth nightgown. She had no make-up on and had lost a lot of colour in her face, her eyes were shadowed and huge so that she looked pale and fragile like a French mime. The bronze hair was newly washed and a bit curly and she had a scrubbed clean look as if she was about to be delivered somewhere. Her face and lips were still puffy and bruised, but when she looked up from her book she managed to work her features into a smile.

"Hardy," she said, "the great protector."

I moved up, took the book away and grabbed her hands. She winced with pain and I swore and let her go. She reached out slowly and stiffly and put her hand on my forearm, it rested there light and feathery like a silk stocking across a chair.

"You're hopeless," she said, "no fruit, no magazines. How'll we fill in the time?"

I gave her a leer and she smiled before shaking her head. "Not for weeks," she said. "But when I can you'll be the first man I call."

I was relieved. We'd seemed to be plunging into something very heavy and I wasn't sure I could handle it yet, or ever. Her version of the way we stood, even though it was determined by her injuries, accorded with my feelings and relaxed me. I patted her hand and we sat there quietly for a minute or two feeling something like trust and understanding flow between us. I eased back the loose sleeves of her nightdress and saw that her forearms were bandaged. I told her again that I was sorry I hadn't been there.

"Don't be silly, Cliff," she said, "how could you have known what was going to happen. The whole thing has got out of control. I don't understand it properly, do you?"

"No, I can't make the connections. It's all hooked up. Brave, Bryn, the files and the threats, but I don't know how they're linked exactly. That makes it hard to take the next step with any confidence."

"What are you going to do then?"

I looked at her and ran my finger lightly across her high, sharp

118

cheekbone. The skin was stretched thin and tight across it like a rubber membrane over a specimen bottle. "I haven't finished checking all the possibilities I was working on yesterday. Brave is out of circulation of course." I nodded at the newspapers lying on a bedside chair.

"Yes," she said, "thank God for that." She was looking tired already and spoke slowly. "But I want it seen through, you'll stay with it won't you? Bryn's dangerous, he's got to be put away, and the bomb...!"

"I'll stay with it," I said. "I was hoping you'd want me to."

"You should have known."

I nodded and we did some more quiet sitting. After a while her eyelids flickered and she said she was tired. It was partly that and partly the dope they were giving her. I got up from the bed but she motioned me closer, she patted her chest with one hand.

"Touch me here, Cliff."

I did, she felt warm and firm. She reached up with both hands, grabbed my hands and pressed them hard against her breasts, her face contorted.

"Cliff, the pale one, he was going to...to do something there next."

I felt a rush of atavistic rage. I gently freed my hands, smoothed her hair and kissed her forehead.

"Don't worry love," I said harshly, "it'll be all right, it'll be over soon."

I promised to call the hospital twice a day and to visit whenever I could. She smiled and nodded and slid down into a deep sleep that the dope was calling her to.

When I left the hospital I intended to finish yesterday's job by checking on the residence of Mr Walter Chalmers, but sitting in the car with the engine running and the street directory beside me, I changed my mind. It suddenly seemed a hundred times more important to track down Bryn and his inquisitorial mate. Bryn was my starting point for this twisting, turning affair and it seemed like the right moment to check back to the beginning. And I was looking forward to a meeting with the man with the cigarette butts and the razor blades. I turned off the engine and reflected. Men like Bryn, with money like his, have houses scattered about the countryside — mood houses, hobby houses. I'd known one millionaire who kept a $50 000 hunting lodge on land which cost him $5000 a year to lease because he liked to go deer shooting about once every three years. He got shot to death up there on one of his rare visits but that's another story. It was a sure bet that Bryn had hideouts on the sea and in the mountains, but they wouldn't be public knowledge. How to find out about them? Easy. Susan Gutteridge, the lady on the mend. I tried to remember whether I'd mentioned a particular diabetes doctor or not and decided I hadn't. But there was no doubt as to who was the best diabetes man in Australia, Dr Alfred Pincus. He charged like the six hundred, but there was more information about diabetes in that polished, clever dome of his than in a shelf of textbooks. I'd seen him on the subject on television and he was so interesting about it he almost made you wish you were a sufferer. Susan Gutteridge would contact him as sure as her bank balance was in the black.

I walked back to the hospital lobby and looked Pincus up in the directory. His rooms were in Macquarie Street naturally, a half mile away. I went back and locked the car. This was as close as I could expect to park to the address anyway. I tramped down the street which was lined with coffee bars and chemist shops the way streets around hospitals and medical offices are. I found the three storey sandstone building which Pincus shared with a dozen or so other top-flight men on top of the hill which gave it a commanding view of the water. The brass nameplates told me that several of Pincus' co-occupants were knights. The lift was ancient like the one in the police building, but it had been better serviced and it slid up its cable like a python up a tree. I got out at the second floor and fronted up to a door which had Pincus' name and degrees and memberships of this and that engraved on it in a prince's ransom of gold leaf. I pushed the door open and looked straight into the eyes of the secretary. She was worth a look, a Semite with raven dark hair and a pale golden face like the image on a Mesopotamian coin. Her nose jutted and her brow sloped back to where the sleek mane of her hair began. Her voice was deep and sweet coming up from well below a pair of heavy, firm breasts.

"Are you Mr Lawrence?"

"No," I said, "I'm Hardy, who's Lawrence?"

She smiled to show she understood but withheld approval. "He telephoned, he's been referred to Dr Pincus. Have you been referred?"

"No, I don't want to see the doctor, at least, not yet. I want some information." She picked up a pencil and tapped it against her big, strong white teeth. "About what?" she said.

"I want to know whether a Miss Susan Gutteridge has contacted Dr Pincus and whether she gave her address." There'd been no number listed for her in the directory.

"I can't possibly tell you that."

"Then she *has* contacted him?"

"I didn't say that."

"You as good as did. Look, I referred her to Dr Pincus. She was having trouble with her diabetes, I knew he was good, the best."

She unbent a little. "I still can't help you, Mr Hardy," she said, "I can't give out information about patients."

I took out my wallet and showed her my card. I found Bryn's cheque with his name stencilled on it to establish my connection with the family. She was inclined to help but a tough professionalism held her back. I noticed a copy of *The News* tucked into a basket beside her chair.

"Look, Miss...?"

"Steiner, Mrs."

"Mrs Steiner, this is a serious business, it's connected with things that happened last night. The story's in your paper. I'm mentioned. Take a look."

She pulled out the paper and ran her eyes over the story. She looked up at me with huge dark eyes that seemed to invite you in for a swim.

"I haven't time to explain," I said. "Miss Gutteridge was at that place last night, I saw her. I advised her to see the best diabetes man in Sydney and now I need to see her again. I don't know where she lives."

She gave a convinced nod. "I believe you Mr Hardy." She flicked over the pages of an appointment book. Pincus looked to be booked solid until the end of the century. "Miss Gutteridge has an appointment for tomorrow," she said, "she gave her address as 276 Cypress Drive, Vaucluse. She called from a private phone so I assume she was at home."

I thanked her and took back my licence folder. I gave her a smile and a half-bow as I left, but she was too busy re-reading the story in the paper to notice.

I went back to the car and drove out to Vaucluse again. Life went on out there as it always would, the traffic flowed smoothly as traffic does in places where no one has to get anywhere at a particular time. Cypress Drive was a notch down from Bryn's lofty eminence, but it was still nothing to be ashamed of. The house was on a rise and the grass, shrubs and trees had never lacked fertiliser. A concrete driveway led up to the house like a stairway to paradise. There was no way the Falcon could have coped with the grade, so I parked it outside the wrought iron gates and took my exercise for the day — keeping my promise to myself to do more walking.

I was short of breath and sweating when I reached the top of the drive. The house had too many arches and white-painted, sculptured pillars and railings. It looked like a wedding cake by a baker who'd let his passion for decoration run away with him. I sat on a set of marble steps to catch my breath and then went up two more flights of marble to the door. The bell was the eye of a tightly curled, plaster moulded snake. I shuddered and pushed it waiting to hear the William Tell Overture inside. In fact a few clear, plain notes sounded inside. It was loud and audible even through a house of twenty squares, but it got no response. I tried again with the same result. I pushed at the door but it didn't give an inch. I went down the steps and around the house on the right side; pebble-strewn garden beds bordered the house from front to back and the windows were at least fifteen feet from the ground all around. There was a slight look of neglect about the lawn edges and shrubs as if they were feeling embarrassed to be caught in such a state.

The back door of the house was reached by a railed set of concrete steps that lead to a tiled patio, but the garage took my attention first. It would hold four cars but there were signs of frequent occupation — tyre marks and oil stains — in only two of the bays. A third bay had a very slight tyre mark and a small grease spot. Above the garage was a long, low structure which looked like quarters for the staff.

I went up the steps to the flat and pushed the door open. I stepped straight into a neat kitchen and announced my presence by rapping on the wall. There was no answer. I went through to the next room which was pleasantly furnished with a good timber table, a serviceable divan and some built-in cupboards. A man was lying on his back on the divan, snoring quietly. There was a two-thirds empty brandy bottle and a sticky glass on the floor beside the couch. The sleeping man was short and spare, beak-nosed like a jockey, with thin, sandy hair and bad teeth. His mouth was open and he smelled like the Rose and Crown on a Saturday night. There was a rinsed glass on the kitchen sink indicating that someone had helped him on his way to oblivion.

I went out fast and took the steps to the back of the house three at a time. The back door was locked, it looked solid but wasn't, it sprung open at my third kick. The house was an exercise in total comfort, total push button luxury, total soullessness. It was intended to be clean and tidy at all times but it wasn't now; the bed in one of the large bedrooms was a tangled mess, the mattress was slewed off the base and there were clothes, books and make-up strewn about. A sleeve ripped out of a satin nightgown lay on the floor in a passageway and objects had been knocked and spilled from tables through the house. Susan Gutteridge had given whoever had carried her off quite a fight, but it appeared to have been a fight with rules because I didn't see any blood.

I went back into the bedroom and began a search of Susan's belongings. One thing was clear — whoever had taken her wasn't interested in her papers or possible hiding places. Nothing was disturbed in the dressing table drawers, there were no edges lifted, no seams ripped, no books disembowelled. It wasn't money either. Susan's purse was on a sideboard in the living room; it had all her personal tickets in it as well as four hundred dollars in cash. It also had what I was looking for — an address book. There were four addresses for Bryn listed along with telephone numbers — one in the city, Vaucluse, one near Cooma in the snow country and one at Cooper Beach on the Central Coast. I slipped the book into my pocket and wandered across to a window. There was a harbour view of course. The early rain had cleared and the day had turned into the sort of Sydney special that persuades Melburnians to give up their football and settle. I saw in a series of mind-made movie stills images of Bryn Gutteridge sitting on his sun deck potting at sea birds with his air pistol. His skin was saddlebag brown and he was a heliophile if ever I've seen one. He'd be at Cooper Beach. The scene around me screamed for a telephone call to the police, but I'd had enough of desks and blotters and forms in triplicate for a while. The guy in the flat should wake up in a few hours and would probably call the cops. That left me with a fairly clear conscience and about as much of a start as I needed.

I was congratulating myself on having thought this out when a slight sound made me turn. I couldn't tell at first whether it was a man or a woman. There were flared purple slacks and a flowered shirt, shoes with metal buckles and a stiff brimmed black hat on top of a head as pale and fair as a lily in a snow field. I decided that it all belonged to a man, and that the man was holding a gun. He was almost albino, slightly pink around the eyes and he spoke with a high voice, lisping a bit.

"Hold your hands out like this." He fluttered a hand at full arm stretch. "If I do, can we be friends?" I said. He didn't move a muscle in his face and the gun was steady on my navel.

"Just do it!"

I did it.

"Now turn around."

"Oh, don't take advantage of me."

He'd heard it all before and it didn't touch him. I felt as if I was digging my grave with my teeth. I knew I should stop riding him, but the words seemed to come out wrong.

"I might have what you want," I said.

Still no reaction.

"Just turn, I'll let you know when to stop."

I had nothing to lose. He looked as if he'd enjoy killing me and his only problem would be where to put the bullet for maximum enjoyment. I reached into my pocket. He did none of the things an amateur would do. He didn't clutch at the trigger or move back; he knew he had me cold and maybe he just wanted to see what sort of gun he was up against. I flicked the address book out of my pocket and threw it at him with a jerky movement as I dived for his legs. The book missed him by a mile. He sidestepped a fraction and swept the side of his gun down onto my perfect target of a skull. The blow hit the same spot as before and the blood must have flowed like Texas oil. I blacked out for a second and when I came to I couldn't breathe and my heart seemed to be missing three beats for every one it caught. I heard the paleface say, "Shit, he's dead." I thought for a minute that I was but that was quickly replaced by fear. If he thought I was dead that was fine with me, even an animal like him wouldn't want to kill me twice. Through half-shut eyes I saw him pick up the address book and go off towards the back of the house. I tried to pull myself up but my arms and shoulders couldn't take the strain. I went down hard and blacked out again.

17

I was out for about ten minutes. I was rubbery legged like an unfit businessman pushed through a three mile run when I came to. I had flickering vision and the hemispheres of my brain seemed to be competing for the space. I propped myself up against the nearest wall, wiped blood out of my eyes and debated whether to look for whisky or die. I opted for the whisky and found some in a small room got up like a cocktail lounge. I had a choice of nearly full bottles of four different brands and decided on Teachers. I took a long, breath-cutting swig of it. The liquor fused my double-sided headache into one which was slightly less painful overall. My hair was matted with blood and an external clean-up seemed to be the next thing indicated after the internal treatment. I staggered off to find a bathroom, dimly aware of what sort of figure I'd cut before a policeman, a judge and twelve citizens good and true.

I lapped water up into my face and eyes and waited for the snowstorm vision and morse code heartbeats to stop. I lowered myself gently down onto the edge of the bath, soaked a face towel in water and mopped carefully at my scalp. After a few painful minutes of this and a close look in the mirror I decided that the experience hadn't aged me much more than ten years and that I was up to doing some thinking. It didn't take much — the albino was Bryn's offsider, the torturer; Bryn had sent him back for something, probably the address book. He was going to catch Bryn up somewhere or maybe Bryn was waiting for him. It didn't matter because he thought I was dead. I closed my eyes and brought the writing on the page of Susan's notebook back and up into focus. I got it — 24 Seaspray Drive. I dried my face and ten minutes later I was in my car heading for Cooper Beach.

I stopped in North Sydney for petrol and water for the car and tobacco for me. I pelted through the north shore suburbs up to where the Pacific Highway joins the Newcastle tollway. The old road holds close to the hills. Driving it you call in at a couple of pleasant little towns. It's nice but slow and Bryn wouldn't have taken it. The tollway rips through the country defiantly, it sits on huge concrete pylons over valleys and it passes through thirty-metre-high rock cuttings that look as if they've been carved by the hand of God. You get a different picture of the country from this route. The Hawkesbury looks a mile wide, and little beach towns look like pretty fishing villages instead of the take-away horrors they are.

The car coughed a little on the hills and I felt a bit unsteady on the bends, but I used some more of Susan's whisky which I'd brought with me and that helped. It took three hours from the Harbour Bridge to the rickety wooden affair that crossed Cooper Creek. Seaspray Drive was on the beachfront at the northern end of the town. Bryn's house was a modest two-storey timber and brick hideaway that probably had solar heating and an indoor pool. The Fiat I'd seen before and a Land Rover were parked in the driveway, the gates were shut and there was no air of imminent departure. I drove past quickly. It was after three o'clock and I felt light-headed from the beating, the whisky and the lack of food. I went into one of the town's two pubs and persuaded the stringy, faded barman to get me a toasted sandwich although the food went off at 3.00. I got a beer from him first, breaking my promise of the morning, and he went grumbling off to the kitchen.

He came back with two great steaming chunks of toasted bread, meat and tomato that had been prepared by an artist. He accepted my offer of a beer.

"Wife made' em," he said, pointing to the food.

"They're great." I couldn't see why he was so woebegone. The beer seemed to lift his spirits a bit though, and I thought he might be good for a few questions.

"Do you know a Mr Gutteridge, Seaspray Drive?"

He took a deep pull on the middy. "Yeah, rich bloke."

"That's him, see much of him?"

"Not much. Now 'n' then. Doesn't come in here but, sends for some grog occasionally. Why d'y wanna know?"

"I've got some business with him, just want to get him sized up a bit. What do you make of him?"

"Well, I don't know him properly like, just talked to him on the phone a coupla times and seen him up the house when I've been delivering the grog. He's a homo."

I nodded. He finished the beer and I fished out the money for two more. He pulled them, looking closely at what he was doing. He put mine in front of me and lifted his own.

"Thanks, cheers. Well, we get plenty of them up here, their business I suppose. Gutteridge himself seems all right to me, but there's some funny jokers up there with him sometimes."

I finished the second sandwich, terrible for the waistline and for getting shot on, but good for morale.

"Have you ever seen a very pale man up there, white hair, just about albino?"

"Yeah, he's the one I had in mind. Something off about him."

"Like what?"

"I dunno. Partly just the weird bloody look of him, but I seen him shoot a seagull once, pointblank with a .22. Bloody cruel. I reckon he's not the full quid."

I left the pub with the brisk step of a man on business although I was very unsure of my next move. The beer had fuzzed me up a bit so I decided to take a walk along the beach to clear my head. I took off my sandals, rolled up my pants and walked along in the shallows for a mile or so until the rocks running down in sharp spines to the beach turned me back. The beach was clean and white with a light scattering of driftwood on the squeaky, powdery sand above the tideline. Like everyone who lives in the city and draws their bread and butter and stimulation from it, I indulged in some dreams of a seaside hideaway where I could cut down on my drinking and be free of pollution, mortgages and everything else. But mortgage was the native tongue in the hills above this beach and on the walk back I consoled myself with the thought that many of the residents of Cooper Beach were deeper in debt than I was.

It was five o'clock. I sat on the sea wall while a little of the daytime warmth seeped out of the air, but not much. I put on my sandals, glanced over towards the pub and saw a man in white denims and a pale blue shirt going into the bottle shop. His hair was silver white and among the expensive sun tans and liquor complexions on the street he stood out like a bishop in a brothel. The Land Rover I'd seen in Bryn's driveway was parked across the street from the hotel. Getting the grog in was a good sign, it meant they didn't intend going anywhere in a great hurry. You don't send your minions down to the inn for Campari if your next move is a dash to the airport and a plane to Paris. My car was parked under trees around the corner from the Land Rover and it was unlikely that Pinkey would see it. I was congratulating myself on this when he came out of the pub. The barman I'd been talking to was with him, carrying a carton and nattering away. Pinkey was nodding his head and looking up and down the street like a circling hawk watching for chickens. He pointed across to the Land Rover and went back into the pub, maybe for a drink, maybe to phone, no way to tell. In any case it seemed like London to a brick that my presence in Cooper Beach was soon going to be known about in all the wrong quarters. I'd been careless and slow and the thought came to me, not for the first time, that I might be getting too old for this line of work.

I ran across the street and came up on the Land Rover from the other side. I got in the driver's door and climbed over into the back. There was the usual mess of tools, rope and groundsheets that every four wheel drive freak collects, and I huddled down in a corner behind the passenger seat and pulled a light tarpaulin over me. The door opened, glass clinked and cardboard scraped on vinyl. The door closed. I wished like hell that I had a gun and that made me think of Bryn and his guns and the possibility that he might keep one right here. I risked a quick peep out of the window. No sign of the albino. I rummaged about quickly and found lengths of pipe, two fishing rods, a pump and a .22 rifle. The rifle was in a waxed paper sheath and there was a box of bullets taped to the side of the sheath. I pulled out the magazine, put six shells into it and worked one up into the breech; I put the safety catch on and laid the gun down on the floor parallel with the seat. I pulled the tarp up again and waited. Sweat rolled off me and I wanted to scratch in ten places, the tarp was damp with sea water and I felt as if I was slowly pickling like a joint of meat.

He moved like a cat, as I'd seen before. He was in the driver's seat and starting the motor in one smooth motion and hadn't made any noise outside that I could detect. His driving was also smooth and efficient and we'd made a few turns and were heading for home before I'd had time to plan the next move fully. The car wouldn't be visible at the gates I decided, and it wouldn't be audible, what with the Pacific crashing in a hundred yards away and the breeze roaring through the Norfolk Island pines. I had to hope that the gates were closed. They were. He pulled up a car's length from them and as he set the handbrake I came up and poked the end of the rifle barrel into the nape of his neck.

"Put your hands on the wheel," I said.

He did it.

"This is a rifle, feel the sight." I slid the end of the gun round and rubbed the front sight into the back of his ear, not gently.

"Convinced?"

He didn't answer, he was thinking and I didn't want him to. I jabbed the sight into the ear hard, it made a ragged tear in the flesh and blood seeped out.

"OK," he said, "it's a rifle."

The voice was still thin and lilting, there was no fear in it and I realised that I sounded shakier than he did and that I was afraid of him. I started gabbling even though I knew I shouldn't.

"You hurt a lady I like and you hurt me. I wouldn't mind killing you, so be careful."

He let out a light, reedy laugh. "You're talking too much, you're scared shitless."

His voice had a hypnotic quality and I felt a little mesmerised. He was right. I hadn't done anything positive apart from putting the gun on him. His calmness was getting to me. If it went on like this he'd have me presenting him with the rifle and opening my mouth for him to shoot into. It was no time for subtlety and I was losing at badinage. I reached out my left hand and grabbed one of

130

the lengths of pipe. He made his move — a grab into the door pocket on the right side. But before he got there I hit him left and right with the pipe and the barrel of the rifle. The rifle smacked into his ear and the pipe landed lower down and further back on his skull and he slumped forward and slammed his forehead into the stem of the steering wheel.

I climbed into the front seat and pushed him aside. He slumped against the cardboard box. The motor was still running and I crunched the vehicle into a gear of some sort and kangaroo hopped the thing around to the right of the gates. It stalled close enough up to the fence to be hidden from the house and not at such an unnatural angle to attract attention from the road. That just left me and him. I got some wire out of the back and trussed him up as tight as I could without paying too much attention to his circulation. The gun in the door pocket was a beautiful old Colt automatic. I pushed it into the waistband of my trousers and got out of the Land Rover. I took another look at the albino. He was tied up tight but he could still make a noise so I stuffed a piece of stinking oily rag into his mouth. I grabbed the rifle and set off along the fence to pick an entry point that would give me cover and easy access to the house.

I went over the fence at a point where a gum tree conveniently dripped some branches over it and approached the house from the rear through a few thickets of shrubs and one great maze of a privet hedge. By hopping between the outbuildings I was able to get up close to the back door without breaking cover for more than a few seconds. I sidled round the corner of the house and listened at the kitchen window. I could hear voices but it was hard to tell where they were coming from. There didn't seem to be anyone in the two rear rooms on the ground floor so I decided to go in. I parked the rifle by the back door, checked the pistol and inched open the fly wire door. It came easily, the door handle turned smoothly and I moved into a glassed-in porch. The kitchen was well-gadgeted, but plain. It was about six o'clock and I thought nervously about the possibility of someone coming into the kitchen to get the drinks, then I remembered that you didn't go to the kitchen to get the drinks in a house like this, the booze had a room of its own.

I went through a door into a dining room and through that into a hallway dominated by a carved staircase, painted white. From near the front of the place I could hear Bryn Gutteridge's voice. I moved forward and flattened myself against the wall outside the room. This was the den or something such, ice was tinkling in glasses and I heard the soft hiss of the springs giving in an armchair when Bryn got up. I could hear every word spoken. Bryn sounded nervy, impatient.

"I just don't believe you," he was saying, "it doesn't make sense, you have to know something."

"If I do, I don't know what it is." It was his sister's voice, fairly calm and even. "I know it sounds like nonsense," she went on, "I almost believe that I do know what you want me to know. But I can't remember..."

"That's bullshit, Susan. Brave says you didn't forget anything important, and this is important."

"Brave! What would he know? He isn't a doctor. He's in jail now and serve him bloody right. God, how you two have put me through it. What the hell do you think you're doing now?" There was strength in her voice. She hadn't gone back to the vegetable kingdom where they'd been keeping her and she seemed to be standing up to Bryn nicely. That took some doing because, along with the edginess, there was a menacing quality in his voice which was pretty telling in combination with the usual authority.

"You know very well what I'm doing, Susan. I'm going to force you to tell me where those files are. It has to be you, no one else could have got them. You always were a sly bitch, Susan. You found out the combination to that safe somehow, you took the files when you found Mark dead."

"I didn't! You can talk till you're blue in the face. I didn't know there was a safe, let alone the combination."

"You're lying, Susan. Brave knew you were lying but he was too gentle with you. You'll tell me here and now!"

"You're mad, Bryn. How do you know there were any files? I just don't know what you're talking about. You've got everything screwed up, you need help."

"Know what I'll do sister dear, just to prove to you that I mean what I say? I'll tell you something. Someone's been using those files. Someone knows a hell of a lot they shouldn't know about some very big people. They wouldn't be able to put the pressure on they have unless they had Mark's own brain inside their heads. So it *has* to be his files. There are some very scared people about, some politicians, a judge, a couple of lawyers and developers. They're very scared and they're getting at me. They think I'm the one and I'm not. It has to be you or someone with you."

"It isn't, I swear it isn't. I've been ill for so long . . ."

"Well, you would be," said Bryn with sneer in his voice.

"What do you mean?"

The springs creaked again. I guessed that Bryn was leaning forward trying to impose physical as well as emotional pressure on her. There was heavy silence in the room like when old lovers go over the ground and discover how hopeless it all was from the beginning. My scalp was crawling and I sneaked a look behind me, but it wasn't a threat from outside that had produced the sensation, it was some kind of inbuilt resistance to hearing people expressing their deepest hostilities and antagonisms with no holds barred.

"I've been doctoring your insulin for ages, Susan, or having it done. You've been eating yourself up, literally."

"You bastard!" They were twins alright. Susan had exactly the same kind of venom in her voice now. "I wouldn't tell you anything even if I could. Christ, I've felt so rotten, so weak, and Brave nagging away at me, all that stuff about clearing my mind and starting afresh. Well your man Hardy put a rocket under him!"

"Hardy," Bryn said slowly, "yes, that was a mistake."

"Why did you hire him?"

"I thought he might stir Brave up, I didn't think he'd bust him. But let's get back to you."

"Yes, let's. At least I understand it now, that's a relief. I was doing everything right, the shots, the diet, the exercise and it wouldn't come good. You're a sadistic bastard Bryn."

"I had to do it, Susan, I . . ."

She cut him off. "Like hell you did. I thought I was mad in that place sometimes. Now I know I'm not. Thanks Bryn, thanks for telling me. I despised myself for being such a dishrag, I'd rather be normally dead than what I was. I don't know a damn thing about Mark's files and I don't give a damn what you think or do."

Gutteridge was coming apart, I could hear him sloshing his drink about and fidgeting in his chair. When he spoke his voice was a low moan. "Susan, I'm about at the end. They killed Giles, God knows how many of them are after me. You must help me."

"I can't, and I wouldn't anyway."

"Don't say that, you'd have done anything for me at one time . . ."

Susan let out her breath in a long hiss and a glass crashed to the floor. Her voice was so different in tone and quality that it sounded as if a third person had materialised in the room.

"You rotten little queer," she said, "I hope they kill you slowly."

Chair springs, a slap and a scream and I was in the room with the Colt gripped tightly in my hand. Bryn had his sister by the hair and was reaching back for another slap. Susan's knees had buckled and she was falling, trying to cover her face and keep him back. I chopped him in the ribs with my left hand but he seemed bent on scalping her, so I slashed the sight of the pistol across his wrist. He yelled, freed the hair and collapsed on the floor. Susan twisted away and fell back into a chair sobbing and scrabbling her fingers in her tortured hair.

When she'd recovered a little she held out a hand to me. I fended her off. "He's still dangerous," I said, "and he might have some help around."

She pulled back and composed herself in the chair.

"I don't think so," she said. "There was just Bryn and the albino man from the beginning." A look of panic appeared in her face. "Where's he?" she said quickly. "I'm afraid of him, he's terrible."

"I don't care for him much either," I said, "but he's out of action for a while. I surprised him, he's tied up down at the gates."

She breathed out noisily. "That's good. I hope you tied him tightly. I hope it hurts."

"It does."

Bryn was crouched on the floor listening and not moving. I couldn't tell how badly I'd hurt him but I guessed it wasn't much. He was strangely resilient.

"Into the chair, Mr Gutteridge," I said, "you've got some talking to do."

"Mr Gutteridge." His voice was heavily ironic and he'd recovered his breath fast. "Are you always so polite to people you pistol whip, Mr Hardy?"

"Only to ex-employers and you never can tell when it'll stop in your case. Why did you bomb Ailsa's car?"

Confidence and control were flooding back into him. He looked bored and just slightly puzzled.

"I didn't."

It was my turn to look puzzled, I believed him and my attention must have wavered for a split second because he came up out of the chair and launched a flying kick at my head. It isn't supposed to work against a well prepared man with a gun but it did. I took it on the shoulder and went down clumsily against a chair. I dropped the gun, scrambled for it and by the time I got it Bryn had rolled over neatly and was out the door moving fast. I got up and started after him. Susan moved in all the wrong directions and I cannoned into her. We both went down and I lost time extricating myself and apologising.

18

Susan held me by the arm longer than seemed necessary — some instinct to protect such close flesh and blood I suppose — and by the time I'd shaken her free Bryn was out of the house. I craned my neck up over the foliage from the back step and thought I saw him moving through the shrubs, already half-way to the road, but I wasn't sure. I ran across to the Fiat, the keys were in it but I lost some time figuring out how to drive it. When I got the right buttons pressed it roared down the drive in great style. I lost more time opening the gate and when I got out I saw the tail end of the Land Rover disappearing behind a corner a hundred yards ahead. I followed fast, thinking that if he stuck to the roads he didn't have a chance and if he took to the bush I didn't have a chance — a nice even money bet. I also tried to remember whether the rifle had been still leaning against the house where I'd left it. I couldn't remember and it was important to the odds in a showdown between Bryn and me.

. The road from Cooper Beach north is all ups and downs with a long drop to the sea on one side and high, densely timbered slopes on the other. It's a place for closely concentrated driving at the best of times. Bryn handled the four-wheel-drive job like an expert; it looked new and must have been in top condition because it touched seventy when the grade permitted and it whipped around the bends like it was on rails. The Fiat was almost too fast for me; it was so long since I'd driven a good car that I had trouble controlling it. Bryn couldn't get off the road and as I got the hang of driving the sports car I drew closer to him and I could see a shape swaying about in the front seat — the albino. Bryn wouldn't have had time to untie him, which was a point or two for me.

We screamed along in tandem, thirty feet apart for about five miles. The narrow, winding road was empty both ways and we burned down the middle towards the long, twisting descent to the salt-flat and lake country. If he reached the bottom first, Bryn could pull off into the salt pans and ti-tree and take all the points. I hadn't driven the road for fifteen years, but it hadn't changed much and I remembered the tight, cruel turns and bad cambering we were entering. Bryn was using all his power and all the road he needed to stay ahead and get a break on the flat. I lost a fraction of time and an inch of speed correcting a slide but I was in command of the car when a timber truck came lumbering up around a bend. The Land Rover swung desperately into the shoulder and missed the truck by the thickness of a coat of paint. I slid past easily and when I rounded the bend I saw Bryn's vehicle sliding and fish-tailing down the road fifty yards ahead. The road coiled into a wicked S bend and he didn't make it — the Land Rover shot over the edge and began scything down saplings. I hit the brakes; the Fiat stopped straight and true. I set the lights flashing and ran to where Bryn had gone over. A hundred feet down the vehicle was wrapped around a tree and before I could move an inch it exploded with a roar and a yellow and blue flash like an incendiary bomb.

I sat on the edge of the drop waiting for the truck driver to come back and compel me to become an honest citizen. There were going to be a few questions about this accident — a brand new Land Rover goes over a cliff with a healthy young man at the wheel, beside him is another man who was unhealthy before he got dead. The fire would do incredible damage to them both, but there was no mistaking baling wire and it wouldn't take long to trace the car to Gutteridge. A bomb, a murder, a raid, a torturing and a fatal crash all with the name Gutteridge included — Grant Evans wasn't going to sit on that too long.

The truckie didn't come back and no one else happened along. I was left to make my own moral decisions.

I scooted back to the Fiat, pressed my luck by making a three-point turn and drove back to Cooper Beach as fast as Italian engineering could take me. I sneaked a few looks in the rear vision mirror and from the high points on the road I could see an orange glow from Bryn's funeral pyre. The penalties for leaving an accident scene in this state were tough and my investigator's licence was forfeit from the second I'd got back into the car. But the truck driver, who must have heard the explosion, was the only one who could tie the Fiat to the Land Rover, and he wasn't playing. The odds on getting back to the house unspotted and gaining a breathing space seemed pretty good. I could use the breathing space to get Susan back to town, report to Ailsa and keep my credentials on the case good and tight. The thought occurred to me that there was a reason to bring Susan and Ailsa together at this point, but I couldn't quite clinch it. I was thinking about how to handle the bright lights and sleeplessness of a police interrogation when I swung the Fiat into the late Mr Gutteridge's immaculate concrete driveway.

I put the Fiat back where I found it, reluctantly. It would have done wonders for my professional and neighbourhood image, but I wouldn't have been able to afford to have its oil changed. I wiped it clean and gave its bonnet a pat reflecting that probate on it alone would be six months' earnings for me. Pity the rich. The rifle wasn't where I'd left it. I went through the porch and kitchen and was heading for the den when I froze like an ice-trapped mammoth — Susan Gutteridge was sitting on the staircase about ten steps up and she had the rifle trained directly on my middle shirt button. Her face was dead white and her mouth was set in a hard, concentrated line. She looked more determined than nervous and I wasn't sure that she recognised me.

"Miss Gutteridge." It came out as half-croak, half-giggle. "It's Hardy, put the rifle down please." Nothing moved in her face or hands. Some people say a .22 is a toy. Don't believe it — at that range and with a bit of luck it can be just as final for you as a .357 magnum. I drew a breath and tried again in a more confidence-inspiring tone.

"Put the rifle down, Susan. I'm here to help you, just put it down slowly."

"I thought you were Bryn." Her voice was calm and detached, as if it belonged to no one in particular.

"No."

138

"Bryn or the other one. I was going to kill you."

"There's no need. I'm a friend."

She looked at me for the first time. I must have looked a pretty unlikely object for a friend in her circle, but she got the message. She stood the gun up, not inexpertly, and handed it to me with the muzzle pointing safely away. She'd had it cocked and the safety catch was off. I wouldn't have fancied Bryn's chances if he'd come into view. I worked the action and shook a shell out of the breech.

"Come and sit down." I held out my hand to her. She took it and we moved towards the den.

"You said something strange just then," she said.

I thought I'd been making good, solid sense, but she pressed it.

"It was odd I said I was going to kill Bryn and you said there was no need."

"That's right. It was just an expression though."

"But he's dead already?"

I nodded. "His car went over a cliff, it burned."

We sat down in one of the den's deep chairs, then she jumped out of it and moved across to another chair. I went to the bar and hunted for whiskey. I found an empty decanter and held it up to Susan inquiringly. She pointed to a long cupboard, like a broom cupboard, in the corner of the room. I opened it. A supersize bottle of Johnny Walker swung inside a teak frame; it looked like it held ten litres or more of the stuff and it was still half full. I filled the decanter and poured two stiff ones over ice. I sat down in the chair Susan had deserted and took a few restorative gulps. She did the same and in a strange way we seemed to be toasting her dead brother.

"Have you reported this to the police?" she asked.

"No." She asked me why and I tried to explain stressing that I didn't know how she wanted her kidnapping handled, but I also pointed out how deeply I was involved and how being held by the police would hamstring me. She saw it.

"Well it's not going to matter to Bryn," she said, "in a way it might please him, the end of it all. He had a sort of Byronic . . . no, satanic streak, he cultivated it. You might have noticed?"

Byronic was closer I thought. "Yes, I did."

She was quiet for a minute, thinking God knows what. I let the good liquor work on me and sat being soothed by the sound of the waves on the beach and the feel of the deep piled carpet under my feet. There was a hell of a lot Bryn hadn't been able to take with him. I wondered if Susan was his heir and what she'd do with all the loot if she was. I wondered about everything except the essential point — what to do next. Susan broke up the reverie by asking me exactly that. I had a few smaller questions of my own, like was Bryn telling the truth when he denied all knowledge of the bombing of Ailsa's car, and did Susan really know nothing about the files? But I was too tired to pursue them or to come up with any plans for interstate flights, midnight meetings on lonely airstrips or hard drinking, incognito, in low-life taverns.

"Let's get back to town," I said, "we can talk a bit on the way."

It was a mundane suggestion, but she sloshed down her drink and took a quick look around the place. A trifle proprietorial and previous, but who could blame her? I'd have been making an inventory and marking the levels in the bottles. We turned out the lights as we went through the house and I pulled the back door locked. I gave it a test tug but Susan waved me on.

"Don't worry about the house, or the car. Someone from the town comes up to look after it."

I hadn't liked her when she had no personality at all and I wasn't too keen on this one emerging. I snapped my fingers.

"Of course, silly of me," I said.

Her head jerked sharply round to look at me. She grinned, then tossed her head back and laughed. "Fair enough Hardy," she said when she finished laughing. "Don't like rich bitches, eh?"

We were tramping down the drive now and it didn't seem to occur to her to ask why. Maybe she trusted me, in any case her stocks with me were climbing a bit.

"Not much," I said. "I feel awkward around large amounts of money, I don't get enough myself to practise on."

"That's a pity, we must see to that."

We went through the gate, she stopped and looked around.

"Where's the car?" she said.

"What car?"

"Your car!"

"It's parked back in town, I caught a ride with the albino. We're walking."

She shook her head. "No way, it's too far."

I was getting a bit tired of her and my voice wasn't gentle.

"Look Susan, you have three choices, walk, wait here for me to drive back from town or go up to the house again and call a cab. It's late but you might just get one to take you to Sydney, if you do he'll ask why you're not using the Fiat. You'll have to lie, later you'll have to explain to the cops why you lied. You can wait here if you want to, but who knows when things are going to break. I think you'd better walk."

She nodded and we started out. It was dark, the road was rough and Susan's thin-soled slippers weren't ideal for the job but she didn't complain for the whole forty-five minutes. She didn't talk except to confirm the direction a couple of times. I tried to draw her out about the house and the family connection with Cooper Beach, since she obviously knew the area pretty well, but she wasn't responsive.

Bryn had gone over the high side closer to the next town, Sussman's Wharf, than to Cooper Beach, and I was hoping that the police and ambulance action would come from there when the wreck was discovered. That's the way it happened; when we trudged into the little township the streets were as quiet as a Trappist prayer meeting. One milk bar cum eatery was open at the far end of the main street and the pubs were still serving a thin scattering of hard cases. My car was where I'd left it and the keys were where I'd left them. There was no obvious sign that anyone had taken any interest in it, but I prowled around it a bit just to be sure. Susan obviously thought I'd lost my mind, she sat on the grass looking beat but not downhearted until I was satisfied. She got in looking dismayed at the peeling vinyl and the general air of ruin. It was probably the oldest car she'd ever been in apart from vintage models in rallies with some of the chaps from her brother's school.

"Why were you crawling about in the dark just then?" she asked after we'd got moving and she'd found that the passenger side seat belt didn't fasten. I told her about the bombing of Ailsa's car again and asked her if she'd forgotten.

"Stop trying to trip me up Hardy," she snapped. "I'm not crazy."

"You're cool, I'll say that."

"What do you mean?"

"Your twin brother's dead and you're here exchanging insults with me."

We were on the winding road up to the tollway and I couldn't get a look at her until we made the highway. When I got on it and could glance across I could see that she was gripping the sides of her seat and weeping silently.

"I'm sorry," I said, "that was cruel, you've got the right to feel whatever you feel."

"That's the trouble," she said, "I don't think I feel anything. I think that's why I'm crying." She brushed her hand across her face and made an effort to steady her voice. "I've got some questions for you, Mr Hardy."

"I have some for you," I said.

"Well, let's try a few as far as we're each prepared to answer."

"OK, you first."

"Do you think Bryn and Dr Brave were behind everything that's been happening, the bombing, Giles and so on?"

"No."

"Who then?"

"Someone else, or others, plural."

"Who?"

"I don't know, I have suspects, just that."

"Are you going to try and find out for sure?"

"Yes."

"Can I hire you to do that?"

That conflict of interest seemed infinite. "No," I said, "afraid not. Thanks just the same for the compliment."

"Why not?"

"I'm already retained on the job."

"By Ailsa?"

"That's right."

"And just how do you feel about her?"

"You just reached the end of your questions, my turn."

She rummaged about in the glove box among the odds and ends and spent Drum packets and slammed it all back in frustration.

"Haven't you got anything to smoke except this vile tobacco?"

"No. Do you know anything about the files?"

"Not a thing, I wish I did."

I let that pass to avoid side-tracking her. "What did Bryn mean when he said you would once have done anything for him? You reacted very strongly." She jerked up in her seat. "Nothing, nothing at all," she said quickly, "we were once very close that's all."

"I see. This may or may not be related. What did your father have on you and Bryn that kept you in line?"

"Who told you that he had something?"

"Never mind, what was it?"

"No." She slumped down and ran her fingers through her hair, lifting and dropping the wings, her voice was old and thin as it had been back in the clinic. "No more questions."

"One more, do you remember exactly who was around the night your father died?"

"I could, I have an excellent memory when conditions are right. I'd have to sit down and think about it."

That brought it back to me, the reason I'd had a flash about bringing Ailsa and Susan together. The key to all this was somewhere back four years ago when Mark Gutteridge had killed himself. I needed to know all I could about that night. It didn't seem like the right time to put this to Susan, so I let her answer stand and we drove on together in silence towards the smoggy lights of Sydney.

Susan gave me the address of a friend she could stay with for the night and I took her there. I stopped the car outside the place, a tizzed-up terrace in Paddington, got out and went around the car to open her door. She stepped out and put her hand on my arm.

"Thank you, I'm going to see Dr Pincus tomorrow," she said.

"I know," I said. Then an idea hit me. "Try for St Bede's."

"What?" She looked at me, puzzled and deeply tired.

"If he wants to put you in hospital, ask to go to St Bede's."

"Why?"

"I hear it's the best anyway, so you'll probably go there as a matter of course. But as well as that it might help me if you're there."

She was too tired to pursue it, she shrugged her shoulders, pushed open the stained wood and iron gate, and climbed the steps to the house. I saw light flood out from the open door and heard a woman's voice say Susan's name in startled but welcoming tones. The light went out.

19

It was after midnight and I was low on everything — energy, alertness, courage, the lot. I drove mechanically away from Paddington towards Glebe. The car felt as tired as me, unresponsive to the pedals, resistant to the wheel, dull as lead. I needed rest very badly and I couldn't think of anywhere to get it except at home. I vaguely considered crashing at Evans' house but rejected the idea. Motels were out for psychological reasons — I'd lie awake all night thinking of death.

I turned into my street and killed the engine and lights outside my house. I was fumbling about with the key in the front door lock when a beam of light hit me in the eyes and a hundredweight of hand fell on my shoulder. Another hand reached out, took the keys and dropped them into my jacket pocket. I tried to shield my eyes from the light to get a look at them but they weren't co-operative. One twisted my arm up behind my back just short of breaking point and the other jammed his torch into the end of my nose. The torchcarrier's voice was like rocks rumbling about in an empty oil drum.

"We hear you're tough Hardy, care to prove it?"

"Not just now," I said, "I'm short on sleep. I'll be tough again tomorrow."

The other one laughed. "You won't be tough tomorrow mate," he said. "You'll be soft, soft as jelly." He emphasised the prediction by putting another fraction of an inch strain on my arm.

"Whatever you say. How about easing down on the lighting and the strong arm stuff and telling me what this's all about?"

I was getting used to the light and was able to make out the general shape and size of them. Even under these imperfect conditions they were obviously cops, the kind that start off as slim, eager youths on traffic duty and end up as big, beery corrupt bastards shoving the citizenry around for kicks. The bulk of one of them looked vaguely familiar, the one with the torch.

"Is it yourself, O'Brien?" I said, all mock bog and peat.

"Don't be a smart arse, Hardy, just come along quietly and you won't get hurt unnecessarily."

"I haven't said I wouldn't. Who's the half-nelson expert?"

"The name's Collins, Hardy," he said, "and I'd really like to break your arm, know that?"

"I can sense that you love your work, yes."

O'Brien switched off the torch and turned me around by the shoulder. Collins wasn't quite ready for it and it turned me partly out of his grip, I stumbled and my clumsy foot came up sharply into his shin.

"Oh, sorry Collins," I said. He swore and reached for me like a bear in a bad mood. O'Brien pushed him back.

"Leave it, Colly," he said, "this guy's a fancy prick and he'll have us doing something we'll regret later if he gets to us."

"He's fuckin' got to me already," Collins ground out, "why's he got to arrive spick and span?"

"If you can't figure it out for yourself there's no point in telling you," O'Brien said with an air of tolerance for weaker intellects. "Let's just take him in as we found him, he doesn't look in such good shape anyway."

He was right, I wasn't. A little adrenalin had flowed over the past few minutes, but all the guns and king hits and karate kicks of the past twelve hours had worn me down and left me in good condition to be leaned on. I still felt cheeky though.

"Do as he says sport," I said. "Grant Evans will explain it all to you just before they cut you down to Constable Colly."

O'Brien gave out with his basso laugh again and Collins chuckled along in chorus.

"That's where you're wrong, Hardy," O'Brien said, "Evans is on leave, sort of a reward for his good work handed down from above. Someone up there isn't too happy so there's a bit of shit coming down all round. Inspector Mills is copping it and he wants to unload some on you. Let's go down town and talk about it."

They eased me down the path and into the car. It's a pity Soames wasn't watching, it would have made his day. I slumped down in the car and tried to think but nothing came. I was in a very bad spot without Evans to protect me even if they hadn't placed me at all the scenes I'd visited that day. If they had, and they didn't want explanations, it was going to be some time before Hardy walked proud and free again.

Collins got behind the wheel and O'Brien sat in the back with me. I'd left my .38 and the albino's Colt in my car which was lucky, but I didn't like the air of confidence hanging around the two of them.

I tried pumping O'Brien for some information so I'd know what to expect at Headquarters but he just told me to shut up and sweat it out. I did. Collins drove like a maniac, jumping lights and bullying everyone on the road. O'Brien shook his head at a couple of the more flagrant breaches of road decency but in general he seemed to regard his partner as beyond redemption. I was almost glad when we arrived at the Police Building. Collins slammed the tyres into the kerb and cut the ignition just as he gave the motor a last, lead-footed rev. The engine shuddered protestingly into silence. Collins yanked open his door as if he meant to take it with him and, after O'Brien had sat still long enough for him to get the idea, he pulled open the back door in the same style. It might have been a subtle intimidation ploy but somehow I thought it was just that Collins didn't know any other way to behave.

We went up the steps and into the building. There was a different sergeant on the desk but he looked just as pissed-off with the job as his predecessor. I suppose the old lift was still running but I didn't get a chance to find out. We went down a set of steps following a sign which said Interrogation Rooms 1 to 6. Room 1 was long and narrow, painted cream and the only furniture was a table and two straight-backed chairs. There was a small shade over the light but not enough to make it comfortable and there was something very disconcerting about the washstand and towel in the far corner. It made the room feel like a fourth-rate hotel hole-up which you take when you're running low on money and aren't expecting any glamorous company. I sat down in one of the chairs and began feeling in my pockets for tobacco. O'Brien took the chair opposite, put a cigarette in his mouth, lit it and blew the smoke into my face.

"No smoking," he said.

I forced a laugh. "You aren't really going to pull all this interrogation stuff are you? Doing it in relays with your handsome mate, no smoking, no sleep?"

"Depends on you, Hardy, makes no difference to me. I can go out for a drink or a nap any time. You're on the spot."

"Well, that's a start. What have you got on me?"

O'Brien took a small notebook out and flipped over some pages.

"A whole stack of things, big or small according to how you want to play it. Failures to report felonies and such."

I leaned back and smiled. "Littering, loitering."

O'Brien still looked confident. He grinned and scratched his ear.

"Very droll," he said. "How about murder?"

"I haven't murdered anyone lately that I can recall."

"That so? Try Terrence Cattermole."

"Never heard of him."

"He heard of you, he said you killed him."

"Now how could that be?"

"I'm giving you a chance to do yourself a bit of good. Judges and juries go for voluntary admissions, they go easy on people."

"Judges and juries can laugh cases out of court too. I'd like to help you, O'Brien, but you've got me shot to bits. I don't even understand how a murdered man can name his murderer."

"Have it your way. It seems a Land Rover went over a cliff up the coast a bit. Seems there were two guys in it when it went over. One of them was tied up with wire. You tied him up, Cattermole his name was. He got thrown clear, see? Just before he died he told us about it. He said that he and the other guy had roughed up a woman you're interested in, you followed them, jumped them, knocked the other guy out and put the wire around Cattermole. You put the Land Rover over the cliff. All this happened about five hours ago, that means you've got an accomplice who did some of the driving. Like to tell us who it is?"

"Shit, have you got it screwed up!"

148

"Well, that's the way Inspector Mills put it to me and my guess is that's the way someone put it to him. Now that's the way we can leave it unless you have something to say."

"What about?"

"I hear the name Gutteridge is involved."

"That so?"

"Yeah. And I also hear that the name Gutteridge is of interest in certain quarters. Need I say more?"

"Blood oath you do. What about my phone call at this point?"

"Oh yes, well, we go by the book here. Let's see, we'll need an extension phone. Collins can get one somewhere, can't you, Colly?"

Collins was leaning against the wall near the door. He'd been listening with a slightly puzzled, but relaxed grin on his face. He was enjoying himself. For a horrible second I thought he was going to say "Sure Boss", but he didn't.

"Must be one around somewhere," he said through the grin.

"That's right. Then Hardy could ring Simon Sackville and he'd come running down and get him out on habeus corpus or something. Right Hardy?"

He had me cold and he knew it, or someone had told him. Sy was out of the country, consulting on a constitutional case — independence for some group of islands off to hell and gone. He was the only lawyer whose confidence I'd ever gained. That wasn't surprising as I was a slow payer and lots of trouble.

"Sy's away," I said, more to myself than O'Brien.

"Aaw, that's too bad," O'Brien said, "maybe you could get one of his partners and explain it all to them?"

Sy's partners were as straight as he was strange — they only tolerated him because he was brilliant and almost always successful. They disapproved of me the way a saint disapproves of sin.

"No way," I said wearily, "and you know it."

O'Brien grinned. "How about legal aid?"

"You're holding all the cards, O'Brien," I said. "I wonder how that came about. You're not smart enough to figure all this out for yourself."

Collins levered himself off the wall and moved towards my chair.

"My turn, Paddy?" he said.

"Not yet." O'Brien waved him back and leaned forward towards me over the table.

"Look Hardy, you're a smart guy. You can add two and two. We know this Cattermole was a hood. No one's very worried about him. Maybe the whole thing was an accident. If you've got something to say about Mark Gutteridge I think we can work something out. I've got Inspector Mills' promise that he'll interview you in private himself and that you won't lose by it. He's standing by."

The penny dropped. The Gutteridge files were being used and some top cops were hurting. As long as they thought I knew something about the Gutteridge files I was worth keeping alive. My life wouldn't be worth two bob if I told them a thing, either way.

"How about Jackson?"

"What?" O'Brien was startled and dropped his suave mask for a second.

"Senior Detective Charles Jackson, the crooked cop, bent as buggery."

"He's on suspension," Collins said.

"Shut up Colly!" O'Brien rapped out. "What's Jackson to you Hardy?"

"He's shit to me," I said, "and your Inspector Mills sounds like double shit."

O'Brien slammed his notebook down on the table and banged his fist on top of it. He drew a deep breath and seemed to be internalising some deep moral struggle. Cop training won out. He scooped up the notebook, tucked it away in his pocket and got to his feet.

"OK, Colly," he said, "five minutes, nothing visible." He walked across to the door and went out of the room. Collins leaned across and snibbed the lock. He walked up behind me and took hold of the lobe of my right ear. He pinched it.

"Tell me," he said.

"Get stuffed, you don't even know what you're asking about, you dumb gorilla."

My vision and my breath and my hearing were all cut off by the kidney punch. It knocked me off the chair and left me hunched up on the floor fighting to keep control of my stomach and my bladder. Collins reached down into the waistband of my trousers and put his hand around my balls.

"Let's hear it."

Nothing had changed. I was dead if they found out that I knew nothing worth knowing about the files. I had to pretend that I knew and to take whatever they dished out.

"Get your hand off my balls, you faggot."

He squeezed and I screamed and writhed away from him. He came after me and I lashed out at him with a foot. It caught him on the thigh and made him beserk, he jumped on me and started pummelling me with his fists. Through the mist of red and black I was dimly aware of a hammering on the door. Collins let go of me and I saw the door open, then slid down into an ebbing and flowing sea of pain.

I woke up in a cell and my watch told me it was three hours later in my life. They'd taken my wallet and keys but left me the tobacco and matches. I struggled up to a sitting position on the bench and looked around. I suppose it would have been luxury in Mexico — sleeping bench, large enamel bucket, fairly clean washbasin and dry concrete floor — but I wasn't taken with it. My mouth tasted like a sewer and I rinsed some water around in it and tried to smoke a cigarette. The taste sent me running to the bucket for a monumental heave and I crawled back to the bench and pulled a thin grey blanket over me. My kidney and testicles competed for the major seat of pain award. I curled myself up under the blanket and became aware for the first time that my trousers were wet. I sniffed at my hand and got the unmistakable smell of urine from it.

By experimenting carefully I found a position in which everything didn't hurt at once. I held it until sleep hooked me and reeled me in and away from my bed of pain.

20

Breakfast came at 6.30, a cup of instant coffee and two pieces of soggy toast. I got it down somehow and sat on the bench feeling miserable. A cop came in an hour later and emptied the bucket, the only diversion for the morning. I sat on the bench smoking cigarettes and longing for a drink. I thought of asking if I could telephone the hospital but there were disadvantages in bringing Ailsa's name to the cops' attention just then. Mostly I worried about whether they were going to try to hold me on the charges they could get together and whether I could get anyone to put up the bail. Sy usually arranged such things for me and he'd picked a great time to go off liberating the Third World. Fretting, and a disgusting mess that could just have passed as an omelette, took me into the early part of the afternoon. I'd reconciled myself to several weeks or more of Long Bay jail when Collins unlocked the door and beckoned me out of the cell. Just the sight of him made me ache in all the old familiar places. He didn't look as chipper as he had the night before though. He held the door open.

"Out."

"Where to?"

"It'd be a quick trip to the harbour if it was up to me, but it seems you got friends."

That sounded hopeful. I followed him out of the lock-up to a kind of lounge, a gentle version of the interrogation room. We went in and O'Brien was sitting at a desk talking to another man. I didn't know him and from the look he gave me I decided I didn't want to. I was unravelled and unshaven, he was shaved as smooth as an egg. He looked to be quite tall, a self-satisfied number. He wore a light grey suit that didn't come off the peg, handmade brogues, a pale blue shirt and a tie from one of the good schools or regiments. His hair was thick and dark although he must have been approaching fifty to judge from the tiny wrinkles etched into his suntanned face. His teeth were white and his eyes were blue, he was perfect. O'Brien waved me into a chair and Collins took up his usual position by the door. He'd have done the same in a Bedouin tent.

It was one of those occasions where nobody likes anybody else. I sat down and O'Brien broke the silence.

"This is Mr Urquhart," he said, "he's got a writ for your release Hardy and we're just working out the details."

I looked over at Mr Cool and he gave me a slight nod which would have cost a month's earnings if I'd been paying him.

"Good," I said, "don't let me disturb you, just pretend I'm not here."

"You don't seem surprised," O'Brien grated out angrily.

"Not at all."

When someone hurries in with a writ for your release you don't sit around discussing your good fortune with the cops, you just accept it graciously and hope he'll throw in a drink afterwards. Urquhart reached into his breast pocket, pulled out a wallet that looked as if it had cost more money than I'd ever had in one, and extracted an envelope. He put it on the table in front of O'Brien who prodded it and blinked.

"What's this for?" he said.

Urquhart smiled. "I understand this is how you like to do business, Mr O'Brien. My principal has no objection and I think Mr Hardy hasn't noticed anything untoward."

He inclined his head towards me and I smiled smoothly back. I pointed at the envelope lying alongside the legal document.

"Bit of betting money for you there Paddy," I said, "Collins can help you pick yesterday's winners."

"That will do Hardy," Urquhart snapped. "I'm sure the sergeant knows his business."

O'Brien looked again at the envelope and let out a breath slowly. He glanced up at Collins who had an idiot smile on his face.

"Very well, Mr Urquhart," O'Brien muttered, "all in order I think."

"I should think so," said Urquhart quietly, "I'll see you outside Mr Hardy. I assume you have possessions to collect?"

"Just the gold watch and lighter and the mad money. Lead the way Sergeant."

Collins opened the door and the lawyer walked out purposefully — he was the kind who memorised routes in and out and never got lost no matter how many times you turned him around. When he was gone O'Brien gave me a hard look.

"Don't put a foot wrong Hardy or you'll be back faster than you can fuck."

I shook my head disapprovingly and drew my finger across my throat.

"Cover your tracks, mate," I said, "heads are gonna roll." I walked out with Collins close behind me.

"What are you talking about?" he said anxiously.

"Don't worry Colly, you have a solid asset."

We got to the admission desk and I was given my things back in exchange for a signature in a ledger. I stuffed them into my pockets and headed for the door.

Collins padded after me. "What d'you mean solid asset?" he asked.

I tapped my forefinger against my temple and kept moving.

Urquhart was standing on the pavement propping up a gunmetal Celica that looked fresh from the showroom. When he saw me he went around to the driver's side and got in. He beckoned at me with an imperious forefinger and I got in beside him. He turned a key which apparently started the engine, not that you'd know from the noise level. I pulled the seat belt out slowly to show him that I knew how they worked and settled myself down into the leather.

He didn't smile, he didn't say anything until we were out into the traffic — he was gold plated and platinum tipped. He avoided a truck and rounded a bus with two easy movements.

"I am Miss Gutteridge's solicitor," he said at last.

"Oh yeah, lucky you."

"Don't try to upset me, Mr Hardy, you won't succeed. I'm not interested in you, and your tough guy act doesn't impress me.

People who have to be bailed out of police lock-ups in the sort of condition you are in are obviously stupid and no amount of repartee can redeem them."

"Yeah. I have the same view of people who wear three hundred dollar suits and have to shave every day, so we're even. How did Susan know I was in the can and why did she tell you to get me out?"

"Miss Gutteridge called me late last night and asked me to contact you to discuss a matter she wishes you to pursue. Your telephone didn't answer, your answering service is hopelessly unsatisfactory, so I called at your address and made inquiries. I felt you couldn't do whatever is required of you in jail."

"Very true. Where's Susan, in hospital?"

"I haven't been instructed."

"Of course not, you're a messenger boy, not privy council."

He winced and pulled in to the kerb. "Your jokes are as terrible as your appearance, I think I'll ask you to get out." I opened the door and eased my aching body out slowly. "Here will do," I said. He reached over, closed the door and glided away into the traffic with the air of someone who had won the round. Maybe he had.

I hailed a taxi and got home in ten minutes. Nobody had broken in, nobody was waiting for me behind the door with a cosh. I called the hospital and was told that Mrs Sleeman was sleeping well and taking solid food. I left the message that I'd call that night if possible and the following morning if not. I didn't ask about Susan Gutteridge, but the receptionist sounded just a touch excited when I gave my name. She told me that Miss Gutteridge had a message for me which I was to collect at the hospital. I gripped the handpiece so hard my knuckles cracked.

"Miss Gutteridge is a patient in the hospital?"

"Yes." The receptionist sounded like a willing participant in a high drama.

"For stabilisation of diabetes, under Dr Pincus, right?"

"Yes, and . . ."

"And what?"

"For two broken legs and multiple broken ribs. She was run over just outside the hospital."

"When?"

"At ten o'clock this morning."

"How did she manage to write a message?"

"She insisted, she terrorised the emergency ward and wrote your message before she allowed the doctors to attend to her. She threatened them with lawsuits. She's sedated now. The message must be very urgent, Mr Hardy."

"Can't you give it to me over the phone?"

"No, it's in a sealed envelope. After what she said I daren't open it. You'll have to collect it yourself."

I told her I'd be there within half an hour. I hoped she wasn't going to be too disappointed when she saw me.

The hospital lobby was crowded with departing visitors when I arrived. Most of them looked in good health and glad to be on their way back to the land of the healthy. The receptionist didn't disappoint me. She was dark and fresh looking in crisply starched linen which was fashionably cut. It made her look like someone playing a part in a TV hospital drama. Perhaps she expected me to play with a hat and unlit cigarettes. I didn't, but she had the thrill of looking at my investigator's licence before handing over the envelope. I walked back to my car and got in before ripping the paper open. The writing was shaky as you'd expect and this reinforced the feeling of fright which the short note conveyed: "Mr Hardy — I was deliberately run down. The car was a red Volkswagen. Please help me. One of my solicitors will contact you, name your own fee. Please help."

There was a shaky, scrawled signature at the bottom. I rolled a cigarette and tapped my fingers on the steering wheel as an aid to thought. The Gutteridge Terroriser was still operating and his targets had been narrowed down by one. I wondered how much pressure from how many directions had been put on Bryn to make him crack the way he had, but I knew that the question would never be answered. Bryn had taken the brunt of the danger that lay in association with the files squarely on his chest and it had killed him indirectly. Now the two remaining targets were both asking for protection. Conflicts of interest would have to be sorted out and I intended to get onto that as soon as they were able to stand the strain of each other's company. Right now the straightforward move was to round off some unfinished work by checking on Walter Chalmers.

I drove across to his place via the flats where Naumeta Pali lived. Her place in this was one of the most puzzling aspects of the whole affair. There was no red Volkswagen parked under the building so I kept going. Chalmers' house was in what is called a garden suburb in England. It was a large brick bungalow, built soon after World War I by someone who had money to spend. There was a deep front porch with a low brick wall around it and two massive plaster cast water maidens on top of the porch pillars. The house had a high pitched roof with deep overhanging eaves and nicely carved woodwork around the windows and ventilation ducts. The block it sat on was larger than average for the area, getting on for half an acre and it was crowded with flowers, bushes and shrubs. I saw every kind of flower I can identify, which is four, and dozens of others. The lawn was meticulously cut. Someone spent many hours per week in that garden and knew what he was doing.

I took a run past the house, turned at the top of the quiet street and came back down on the other side. I stopped a few doors further on. There was no activity in the street. There wouldn't be — this was a both-people-working and children-at-creche-or-school zone. I got out of my car after finding a clipboard and some paper amid the rubbish on the back seat. I riffled through the blank sheets of paper, adjusted the clip, tucked the board under my arm and marched up to the gate. I walked briskly to the front door and rang the bell. Behind all that shrubbery I was scarcely visible from the street or the flanking houses. If my entry hadn't attracted any adverse attention I was set. If someone had seen me go in and knew the house was empty I could be in trouble, but I probably had some time to work in before they'd get up the spirit to ring the cops. I gave it a minute. The air was warm and still and full of insect noises. I slipped a skeleton key into the old Yale lock and turned. The door came open as if I was the master returning from a hard day's work.

The door gave onto a hallway with wallpaper that reminded me of my aunt Joan's — men on horseback in pink coats, and dogs and foxes chasing each other from floor to ceiling. To the left were double glass doors which opened onto a large living room with a big handsome fireplace. On the other side of the house there were two large bedrooms and a bathroom and toilet. Behind this the kitchen ran the width of the house and behind that was a glassed-in sun porch with full length sliding doors. A very nice drinking area. The back garden was as well kept and well stocked flora-wise as the front. I went through the porch, down a cement path to the garage. All the usual carpenter's tools hung up above a bench against their silhouettes carefully painted in black on the fibro cement wall. A wide selection of gardening tools stood against the wall lined up like soldiers at attention. There were some oil stains on the concrete floor but no one's perfect.

Back in the house I began a systematic search of drawers and cupboards to see if I could turn up anything which might suggest involvement in Gutteridge affairs beyond what was normal for a loyal employee. Contrary to their image, accountants have a very high rate of criminality — their training and professional habits make them formidable schemers and planners. Chalmers, however, seemed as honest as Baden Powell. His kitchen drawers showed him to be a model of efficiency and tidiness. The household accounts were spiked and filed down to the last detail in the second bedroom which he used as a guest room and study. My keys got me into every drawer and cabinet and revealed a man pretty much as dull as Ailsa had portrayed him. He had plenty of money, from his salary and stock market investments which seemed to be cautious and consistently profitable. His income tax submissions were a joy to see. He practically deducted his shoe leather and they bought it every time.

The main bedroom presented a contrast to the rest of the house where the fittings were austere, almost plain. This room had a softer, sensuous feel. The double bed was low slung and springy, the sheets and pillow cases were black satin under a knotty Peruvian woollen cover. There was a large cedar wardrobe with two full length mirrors and a chest of the same wood which stood five feet high — both thousand dollar antiques. The right hand door on the wardrobe offered the first resistance I'd met with in the house. It had a double lock with the second mechanism low down and concealed by a movable panel. I had to work on it with two keys and a piece of stiff plastic to get it open. The hanging space inside was crammed with full length and street length dresses and nightgowns, they ranged from frilly, frothy affairs to sleek streamlined jobs. A set of shelves in the cupboard was occupied by layers of silk and satin underwear — panties, bras, petticoats, stockings and suspenders. A box on the bottom shelf was full of make-up — lipsticks, false eyelashes, brushes and pencils, eye shadow and other pots and tubes beyond my experience.

The bottom drawer of the set between the two full length doors also put up a struggle. I jiggled it open with a long key and a lot of quiet swearing. Ross Haines couldn't have been more wrong about Chalmers; he was a homosexual alright, but about as repressed as Nero. The drawer was full of photographs, loose and glued into several albums. Many of the pictures were heavy stuff even in these permissive times. They showed a man whom I took to be Chalmers, in woman's clothing, making love, sometimes in pairs, sometimes in threes and fours. Several of the pictures had been taken in the room I was in, some were outdoor shots, others were taken in what looked like motel rooms. One album contained photos of Chalmers taken over about twenty years. He was a medium sized man with a thin face and hair that time was harvesting. One picture was arresting: Chalmers stood, dressed in a suit cut in the style of twenty years before, alongside a woman with a fresh pretty face and a neat figure. From their accessories and the background it was clearly a wedding picture — Chalmers' smile was a death mask grimace. There were a few blank leaves in the album following this picture and signs that others had been torn out. Later leaves held snapshots of men, sitting around tables, standing in streets or sprawling on grass or sand. Chalmers wore white, opennecked shirts in most of the pictures and he looked like the photographs you see of Kim Philby in Russia — not quite relaxed in front of the camera, but obviously having a good time.

I muttered "Good luck to you" under my breath and returned the photographs to their original places as carefully as I could. I looked around to make sure I hadn't disturbed the room and left

159

the house by the front door. Clipboard under my arm I walked to the car. I rolled a cigarette and smoked it down while staring through the windscreen. Walter Chalmers had his own deep secrets and I judged that this made him unlikely to trade in those of other people.

21

I was back in the hospital by five o'clock. The same crowd of
visitors milled about in the lobby waiting to catch lifts up to the
wards. There was a different receptionist at the desk but the same
smell in the corridors. Ailsa was sitting up in her bed. She was
wearing a little make-up and a different nightgown. This one had a
loose tie around the neck, a sort of drawstring, and she was
fiddling with the strings when I walked into the room. She looked
outwardly better but inwardly worse. The hands she held out
tentatively to me were trembling and cold. I held her hands for a
minute and broke the silence clumsily.

"What's wrong love, cigarette withdrawal or morphine addic-
tion?"

"Don't joke, Cliff," she said, "just look at that." She nodded
down at the newspaper which was lying folded up on the bed. I
picked it up and read the lead story. It said that Dr Ian Brave, who
had been held in custody in connection with the sheltering of Rory
Costello, had escaped from the hospital wing of the Long Bay Jail.
Tickener had the byline and he'd made the most of the meagre
facts he'd had to work with. Brave had been taken ill with severe
vomiting and internal pain and had been escorted to the hospital.
He'd been sedated and an armed guard had been set up outside his
room. The room was inspected hourly and Brave had vanished
between eleven o'clock and noon. The guard denied leaving his
post and said he'd heard nothing suspicious from inside the room.
Tickener described Brave as a "consulting psychologist" and mentioned obliquely that he had an intimate knowledge of drugs and
had used hypnotism in the treatment of his patients.

Ailsa was gnawing at her nails as I read and she dug a jagged one
into my arm as I put the paper down.

"I heard about Bryn on the news this morning and now this. What's happening, Cliff? I'm scared, I don't understand it. I don't feel safe even in here with Brave out there somewhere."

I poured her some water and tried to calm her down, but she was close to hysteria. She brushed the glass aside.

"I don't want water. How could he escape from prison? How could he?"

"Easy love, you're safe here. It could have been fixed for him. He's had one cop in his pocket, why not more? The story doesn't say whether it was a police guard or a prison guard. I don't really think he could have used hypnotism on the guard, but it's possible. It gives the guard an out anyway."

"Jesus, it scares me," she said.

"Me too," I said, then mostly to myself, "I suppose he could have fixed it while he was inside."

She jumped at it. "Fixed what?"

She was so edgy that it seemed better to give her something real to bite on rather than let her fantasise herself into nervous collapse. I told her about the attempt to kill Susan Gutteridge and worked back from that through her abduction and my part in Bryn's death. I didn't tell her that Susan wanted to hire me. She listened attentively and reached up to touch my face when I was finished. She seemed calmer. We went into one of our silent communings, looking at each other with foolish smiles on our faces.

I broke the mood by getting up to look at the chart clipped to the end of the bed. It didn't make much sense to me but she told me that it meant that the intervals between them interfering with her were getting longer and that she was gaining strength. I nodded and smiled inanely and began to pace up and down in the narrow room. She let me make a few turns then she reached out for a paperback from the bedside table. It hit me on the chest.

"Will you stop that pacing. It's making me as nervous as hell."

"I'm sorry."

"Don't be sorry, be open, be frank. Talk to me about it."

I sat down on the bed again. "It's hard to talk about," I said, "there's loose ends all over the shop, there are hints of connections but I can't quite make them. Maybe I'm losing the touch."

"Don't be silly and don't be pretentious," she said, "and don't look at me as if you'd like to cosh me. You just need more information. For instance, what do you make of Ross and Chalmers?"

"Haines is Mr Anonymous, orphan. Got where he is by application and a ton of ability, night school and so on. Chalmers is as gay as a goose, do you want the details?"

"No, he does a terrific job for me, I don't care if he fucks sheep."

I grinned. "He doesn't. Do you know anyone who drives a red Volkswagen beetle?"

She thought about it. "Don't think so. I know a girl who drives a red Audi."

"No good, lower division."

"No, why?"

"There was one around the day your car was bombed, one followed me after that and Susan says the car that ran her down was a red VW."

She shook her head. I'd put it that way to see if the Pali girl was part of her world, or maybe I was just being nastily suspicious all down the line. There was no value in it anyway. I started to make a cigarette.

"Have you ever been to New Caledonia?" I asked abruptly.

"No, are you going to take me?"

"You'd have to take me, I can hardly afford the Manly ferry."

"New Caledonia is part of it?"

"Could be."

"You're not going to start pacing again?"

"No, I'm going to act, take control, be masterful."

"You can't be masterful with me for a few weeks, nothing to stop you taking control with someone else of course."

"I might just store it up a bit. I think Hemingway advises it somewhere. No, you're right about needing more information. I want to dig for it. I want to set up a session between you and Susan and sift through the circumstances of Mark Gutteridge's death down to the last grain. Will you be in it?"

She pulled a sour face and plucked at the sheet. "If you say so. I detest her, you know."

"That's no way to talk about someone who's in traction no more than fifty yards away."

"Say traction again."

"You're a bitch."

"You're so right. OK Cliff, I'll be in it. When?"

"I'll need your doctor's permission and hers, the sooner the better."

"You've got my man's permission as of now."

"I think it'll be much the same with her. Could be Monday then."

Bells starting ringing and we did a little gentle kissing. I promised her that I wouldn't go chasing off to New Caledonia and that I'd be in over the weekend. I joined the exodus of the sound in wind and limb.

For a day that had started in jail it hadn't turned out too badly. I bought a flagon of riesling and a few bottles of soda water on the drive home, put the car away with consummate ease and went cautiously into the house. I was pretty sure I hadn't been followed at any time in the day, but if I was wrong and O'Brien had observed my illegal entering then I was in the shit. It would be like him to pounce just as I got the top off the first bottle. But the house was empty. I took a quick look at the mail — bills and invitations to spend money I didn't have on things I didn't need. I was getting the proportions of ice, wine and soda just right when the phone rang. I jumped a mile and spilled the wine. The sudden movement put a shaft of pain through my kidneys and reminded me what a rough twenty-four hours I'd had. I sloshed a drink together and took a big gulp of it before moving creakily to the phone.

"Is that Cliff Hardy?"

"Yeah. Tickener?"

"Right. Did you see my stuff today?"

I grunted.

"What's wrong, you don't sound too good."

I grunted again and drank some more wine.

"Look, I was wondering if you had any ideas about where Brave might hide out."

"Sorry, no idea. I'm still on the same case though and I'll let you know if I turn up on Brave."

"Fair enough."

"What do you hear about the constabulary?"

"I hear that some very high people are very edgy. A retirement is foreshadowed and two guys have gone on their holidays. No sign of Jackson, he could be a lead to Brave. What do you think?"

"I think it's terrible that such a fine band of men should be subject to such morale-lowering pressures, but don't splash it all over the front page."

Tickener's sigh came whispering across the wire. "I suppose that's the price of fame, I get a private eye to wisecrack with over the phone."

"That's right, are they talking A grade yet?"

"Can't be long."

We agreed to stay in touch and rang off simultaneously. I made another drink and put some eggs on to boil. I wandered up into the room where I kept my books and looked through the four volumes of the Naval Intelligence series on the Pacific Islands. I'd once met one of the professors who'd had a hand in writing them in a bar in Canberra. He was a tall, gaunt-faced character who told a good story and liked a drink. He'd told me about his work in intelligence when I told him what I did for a living and he told me where to get the books second-hand in Sydney. I bought them out of curiosity and I'd never been disappointed. The professor was dead now and I often regretted I'd never seen him again and got him to autograph the books. There was a long section on New Caledonia in volume III.

I mashed up the eggs, sprinkled curry powder on them and made them into a couple of bulging sandwiches. I took the food and another drink to the table and read about the islands while I was eating. New Caledonia had been something of a political football between France and the Australian colonies for a time, but it had come firmly under French military rule about the middle of the nineteenth century and had stayed that way for over fifty years. There'd been a couple of native rebellions but they'd been put down firmly in good French colonial fashion. In the end the

165

French had managed to convince the majority of the islanders that the smart thing to do was to become black Frenchmen. The place had settled down, had a fair tourist trade, some extractive industry and was receptive to development capital. The Palis were chiefs in one of the settled areas close to Noumea. They'd seen the light in religion and politics pretty early and had done quite nicely all through. The information was very much out of date and I browsed around looking for something more current. I turned up a two year old copy of *Pacific Islands Monthly* that mentioned concern among New Caledonians at the behaviour of some Australian mining engineers who'd blundered in on a ceremony they shouldn't have seen. There was also a letter from a New Caledonian about the French nuclear tests in the Pacific.

I tidied up the kitchen and worked through a bit more of the wine and soda. Things didn't become any clearer and an hour of television didn't help, and a re-read of two chapters of Louis Golding's *The Bare Knuckle Breed* only reminded me of Cyn who'd bought it for me and made me wish I had someone to spend the night with. I wandered up to the dartboard, pulled out the darts and went round the board in twenty throws. Like hell I did. I went to bed.

22

There was nothing useful to be done on Saturday or Sunday. I paid Bryn's cheque into my TAB account and drew out some money, half of which I lost on the horses within the next four hours. I bought some flowers and went in to see Ailsa in the afternoon. We agreed not to talk about the Gutteridge case and tried to get by on books and other subjects but it didn't work very well. I drank too much wine that night and stayed in bed with my head aching until late the next morning. At two o'clock, as I was thinking of getting up, the phone rang and the hospital informed me that Miss Sleeman wasn't feeling well and didn't want any visitors. Great. I got up and went for a long walk through Annandale and down into Balmain. The sky was low and grey and the discarded race tickets blowing along the pavement increased my bad temper. The water at the end of the peninsula looked like a dark, bottle green swamp, barely rising and falling, and the boats riding on it looked like they were stuck in the ooze. I tramped home, took the dead albino's Colt apart and oiled it. It was a little worn but a fine gun despite its owner. Guns are like that. I assumed it was untraceable, the serial number was filed away; a useful gun.

At 9 a.m. on Monday, wearing my best suit, the grey one again, I was in Dr Pincus' office being told that he wasn't in and that I couldn't see him when he did come in. Mrs Steiner was doing the telling and it was a pleasure to watch her at work. She was wearing a brightly printed kaftan and her hair was tied back in a glossy bun. With the slope of that forehead and nose she could have just stepped off a Phoenician oarship. I stood in front of her desk thinking that if Pincus was keeping his hands off her he must have a wonderful marriage.

"You're just saying that," I told her, "because you think you have to, and you do. But I know it isn't true. In the parking lot beside this building there's a space reserved for a car. The space is full of Rolls Royce and the guy who hoses down the lot and watches over the cars tells me it's Dr Pincus' car. He's in and my business is important."

"He has a patient with him."

"He hasn't. There's no talking going on in there," I pointed to the heavy oak door, "and your appointment book shows he kicks off at 10 o'clock. Half an hour is all I need."

Her eyebrows shot up and she bared her beautiful white teeth at me.

"Half an hour!"

"I know that's probably a couple of hundred dollars' worth of his time but I still need it. A quarter of an hour might do."

Like most people connected with the medical profession, she took umbrage at the mention of money.

"It's not that, he's terribly busy today, he's seeing patients all morning and going to the hospital this afternoon."

"Yeah," I said, "so am I."

That seemed to hold her for a minute and I walked past the desk and knocked on the door. She half rose from her chair but I had the door open and was part of the way through before she could do anything about it.

The television hadn't done him justice. He was of medium height and build and his smooth, olive-skinned face was alight with what you'd have to call piercing intelligence. His white coat was a thing of beauty and had certainly cost more than every stitch I had on. He was bald but he looked like he'd never given it a second's worry. He frowned when I came into the room.

"I'm sorry to intrude doctor, I know you're busy but this is important. My name's Hardy, a patient of yours is a client of mine — Miss Gutteridge."

That was stretching the facts but I wouldn't get time for the niceties.

"Ah yes," he said, "the detective. She mentioned you. She seems to trust you. Please sit down."

I sat. He had everything the top Macquarie Street man should have — voice, looks and a fitness and vitality to him that gave you something to aim for.

"I'll come straight to it, doctor," I said. "I want to arrange a meeting between Miss Gutteridge and her father's widow, a Miss Ailsa Sleeman. She is only a few years older than Susan Gutteridge."

"Why?" he said as I drew breath.

"To discuss the circumstances surrounding Mark Gutteridge's death four years ago. Both women have been threatened and assaulted, the reason why lies back at that point I believe. I think such a meeting would be productive and help me to pursue the case more effectively."

"Can you give me some more details, briefly?"

He wasn't fidgeting or looking at his watch. I had his whole attention and had to make the most of it.

"Not many. The police investigation of the death was less than exhaustive. Some facts are unclear, some things went missing, unexplained. There's blackmail involved and intimidation. Susan Gutteridge's insulin was tampered with for example."

He leaned back in his chair without taking his eyes off my face.

"Yes, she told me that. I find it intriguing, I must say."

"You'll authorise the meeting?"

"Susan Gutteridge is an unstable person. I tell you this in professional confidence of course."

I accepted the compliment.

"Her diabetes is in a mess from what she tells me, she needs a lot of rest and treatment. But a diabetic's condition is affected by the emotions to a great extent. Susan Gutteridge is very worried and frightened. Have you considered the possibility that she is guilty of some crime?"

I said I had and expressed the opinion that it might help if it all came out. He stroked his chin and let his eyes stray off to his bookshelf.

"So they say," he murmured, "so they say."

"There's an old enmity between Susan Gutteridge and Ailsa Sleeman, this meeting might resolve it. Ailsa is an intelligent woman and a strong one, she could become a friend to Susan."

"That's probably better psychology," he said. "Very well Mr Hardy, I'll authorise the meeting. Where and when? Susan Gutteridge is in hospital, you realise."

"I do, so is Ailsa, same place."

He raised an eyebrow. "What for?"

I told him and that seemed to clinch it. He said he was going to the hospital early in the afternoon and would leave messages supporting what I wanted to do. I had no doubt that those messages would be treated like the order of the day. I thanked him and asked if he'd like to be present at the session. He looked ruefully down at his desk calendar.

"I would like to be," he said, "very much, but I simply haven't the time. You must let me know how it works out."

I said I would, we shook hands and I went out. A fat woman in a coat much too warm for the day that was shaping up was sitting in the waiting room. I gave her my hard-boiled look and she squirmed a bit. Mrs Steiner was looking flustered and she pressed the wrong button on the intercom when Pincus buzzed her. She got it right on the second try.

"Mrs Hamersley-Smith is here doctor."

Pincus said something inaudible to me and Mrs Steiner repressed a smile. She raised a finger which boasted a long, blood red fingernail. Mrs Hamersley-Smith waddled past me and reached the door just as Pincus opened it. Beautiful timing. I smiled at Mrs Steiner.

"Can you tell me when Dr Pincus is due at the hospital and how long he'll be there?"

The twenty minutes of the boss's time had done me a power of good in her eyes. She flicked at her desk calendar and ran the crimson nail down a page of the appointments book.

"He's there for an hour and a half," she said, "from two o'clock until 3.30."

I thanked her and left. I carried the image of her dark, bottomless eyes with me all the way back to the street.

I had a few hours to kill which isn't supposed to happen to a private detective busy on a case but sometimes does. I could have killed it by doing some banking and writing cheques for people who could legitimately expect them, or I could have gone to my dentist for a check-up or I could have put the car in for a service. I didn't. I walked across to the Public Library and ordered a batch of newspapers for the year 1972. They came on microfilm in fifteen minutes. I worked through the papers pretty fast looking at the business news mostly and checking the correspondence columns trying to get a feel for the shape of things as they were then.

Mark Gutteridge got a fair bit of coverage as a canny and successful land developer, but there was nothing out of the ordinary about it — no shady deals hinted at, no subsidiary companies collapsing and ruining shareholders. His death got a big spread and there were follow-up stories over the next few days. I read this stuff closely to brief myself for the meeting later in the day. The reporters were starved of facts from the start. The cops were close-mouthed about their investigations and the coverage soon tailed off into human interest material about Gutteridge and his family. There were a couple of good photos of Ailsa, an indifferent one of Bryn and one of Susan that was so poor that it took imagination to relate it to the person I knew. There was no mention of robbery, no details on the gun or the wound, and the coroner's verdict came in as smooth as silk stockings on shaved legs — "Death by his own hand while of unsound mind". I made a few notes, tucked them away in my pocket and told the attendant that I'd finished with the papers.

I left the library looking for somewhere to have lunch. I approached a cafe in a new chrome, concrete and glass building and a name on a directory board jumped out at me. Sleeman Enterprises' office was on the fourth floor and I took the lift up just for the hell of it. The decor was all plastic, glass and middle-of-the-road wall to wall carpet. There were a few pot plants, not so many as to prevent the employees seeing each other, and a general air of work being done. A desk just outside the lift had a sign reading "Inquiries" hanging above it and a dark-haired girl looked up from her typing when she saw me peering keenly about. A good sign that, a receptionist who can type. She asked if she could help in a voice that suggested she was serious about the offer. I took out my wallet and extracted a card a little guy who'd come to my office a month ago had given me. He gave me the card but he knew I was a lost cause.

"My name is Riddout," I said, "Claude Riddout, I'm from Simon's Office Furniture and Decor."

"Yes Mr Riddout?"

"Well, I was just visiting a client on another floor and I thought I'd glance in on a few other establishments just to see if our services might be required."

"I don't think . . ."

I waved both hands in the air. "No, no, I can see that everything is very nice here, very tasteful indeed, I compliment you, it must be very pleasant to work in such surroundings, very pleasant indeed. You wouldn't believe the drabness I see in some places."

I'd succeeded in boring her silly in half a minute which is good going.

"Yes, it's fine, now uhmm . . . is there anything . . .?"

"No, no, if I could just look about a little, take a wander down a corridor or two? I promise I won't intrude on anyone. I'd hate to interrupt the workings of such a smooth running organisation. Just a peep, just a professional peep."

She grabbed the out although she had to cover herself. "Well, I really shouldn't allow you to, but if you make it brief I suppose it'll be all right. The stairs are at the end of that corridor."

She pointed, I ducked my head at her and set off down the passage. There were three offices off to the left along one passage, one on each side of a short connecting corridor and a further three or four on both sides of another passage. Some of the offices had names on the door, some didn't. Some were partitioned to permit a secretary to work away out of sight of her master but within beck and call. Along one wall was a large map of Australia and the Pacific islands. Little pins with red heads were stuck in at various points — all the mainland capital cities as well as places like Geelong and Wollongong, and here and there among the islands — Port Moresby, Suva, Noumea, Pago Pago.

The biggest office had Walter Chalmers' name on the door. The next biggest was occupied by Ross Haines. I opened the door to Haines' secretary's cubicle and said "Oh sorry" to a startled blonde. I did the same to Chalmers' secretary and got an ice cold look from a middle aged woman wearing violently dyed red hair and a Chanel suit. I went back to the lifts past the receptionist who saw me coming, put her head down and kept it there like Anne Boleyn on the block.

I grabbed some fruit from a street stand and made do with that for lunch.

At 3.45 I was at the hospital and as unpopular as a bikini in a nudist camp. I'd been shunted about from reception desk to waiting room and back again, but, given the size of the place, I'd made it fairly fast into the hospital director's office. He had a couple of medical degrees, Harvard business administration ticket, a hyphenated name and he didn't like me. He looked clean-cut like an American lawyer and he spoke in a clipped upper class voice like an English doctor.

"This is all extremely irregular, Mr Hardy. Hospital routines are delicate things, not to be tampered with lightly."

I didn't say anything, the fact that I was there meant that I was going to get what I wanted and if I had to take a little crap from him along the way I would. He ran his hand over his greying crewcut and riffled through some papers on his desk.

"However, the two ladies are not dangerously ill, private patients of course so no one will be disturbed."

What he meant was that the two ladies were rich and rich people who've been well treated in hospital sometimes remember that when they've got their chequebooks out. I nodded.

"Dr Pincus and Sir John concur in the matter," he went on, "so I think it can be arranged."

I don't know how hospital directors are fixed for status and prospects, but this one had elected to keep two medical heavies very firmly on side. That was fine with me. I grinned at him infuriatingly. He levelled up his papers and plonked a solid silver paperweight in the shape of a kidney on top of them. It was my day for making people glad to get me out of their sight. He flipped an intercom switch.

"Are we ready for Mr Hardy?"

He looked relieved at the reply and even more relieved when the door opened and a male nurse presented himself. The boss said, "Nurse Mahony will attend to you, Mr Hardy." I said, "Thank you" and he pretended not to hear me.

The nurse was tall and brawny; anyone who made jokes about him might very soon be attended by him in his professional capacity. I had trouble keeping up with him as he strode down the corridor. I broke into an undignified trot, then checked myself.

"Slow down nurse," I panted, "and tell me where we're going."

"Sorry sir," he slowed imperceptibly, but he called me sir. "We're going to the conference room on the fourth floor. It's a sort of VIP room. We get business executives and politicians in here from time to time. In for check-ups and so on. They sometimes need facilities like telex machines, computers and tape recorders. We've got them here, got a computer terminal and all."

"Great, what about the ones who have to stay in bed?"

"It's a big room, the beds can be wheeled in and arranged with writing tables and so on alongside. The room will hold ten beds. The hospital can provide a stenographer."

"I don't think I'll need that, but it sounds like a good set-up. You sound proud of it."

He gave me a sideways look and grinned. "It's interesting," he said. "One gentleman died in there when he got some bad news on the telex. Very wealthy gentleman he was."

"Serve him right," I said.

"That's what I say. Here we are."

The room was all he'd promised. It looked like a boardroom except for some of the chromium fittings and it smelled antiseptic instead of cigars and good booze. There was a long table with slots in for the beds. When in place the person in bed was within reach of a cassette tape recorder, a set of earphones, a telex keyboard, a fresh writing pad and a row of sharpened pencils. A chair was drawn up to one of the slots, two others were occupied. Ailsa sat propped up by pillows, her arms were bare and her hair was shining like a burnished helmet. She smiled at me as I came into the room in the shadow of Nurse Mahony, it looked as if all was forgiven. Susan was opposite her slumped down in her bed. There was a huge lump under the bedclothes from the waist down which made her look like a victim of Dr Moreau. She looked peeved and anxious.

It wasn't going to be easy.

23

Susan started on me right away.

"Hello Hardy," she jeered. "What are we having here, a seminar? Professor Hardy is it?"

Her old self was showing as it always would. I knew I could expect to see a deal more of it before we'd done our business. It would abort the whole exercise if it got out of hand, so I had to be careful not to provoke her too early. I nodded to the nurse who gave a you-rather-than-me look and closed the door behind him. I checked my watch, sat down in the chair and tried hard not to be pompous.

"Hello Susan, Ailsa," I said calmly. "It's a bit much isn't it? We could probably go somewhere less formal, but they think they're doing the right thing. It's in deference to your millions I gather."

"Oh, it's all right," Susan snapped, "though God knows what good it'll do. Why aren't you out looking for whoever ran me down?" She jerked her head at Ailsa. "And bombed her."

At least she was acknowledging Ailsa's existence, that was encouraging for something coming of the session.

"I am in a way," I said quietly, "I'll be surprised if we don't work most of it right here."

"How, will we play charades? We're a bit disadvantaged."

I looked across at Ailsa who hadn't spoken.

"Ailsa's employing me. Maybe this is not such a good idea after all. She can call it off if she likes, or you can pull out Susan."

She came to the hook like a hungry fish, the last thing she wanted in her starved, unhappy soul was to miss this show.

"No, no, you could be right Hardy. I'm sorry, I do have faith in you. I'm in pain, I feel so wretched . . ."

Ailsa had sat there looking interested in Susan's emotional

swoops and amused at my role as MC. Now she displayed her tact.

"We're neither of us very well, Cliff," she said, "I tire very easily and I expect it's the same with Susan. Shouldn't we get on with it?"

"I think so," I said. "Susan?"

"Yes, I've been thinking back. I know what I know. The police weren't interested from the beginning."

I didn't want her to have it all down pat. It was time to stop being bland and agreeable.

"Yeah, so you told me. I want to cover a bit more ground than that. I've got a few questions for you both that could be uncomfortable, but first I've got to deliver a monologue of sorts. I'm sorry."

Ailsa winced at the pomposity of it, but nothing showed in Susan's face that I could interpret. She looked old and strained, the actual relationship between the two women could have been reversed to judge from their appearance.

"Neither of you has been quite frank with me," I began. "Perhaps you haven't been honest with yourselves. This affair has reached a crisis point, you've both put some trust in me and I know a lot more about you and your affairs than anyone else. But we've got to go a bit further. Bryn knew a lot about you but he's dead. Someone else knows a lot too and he, or she, is the person we have to identify. It could be Ian Brave, I don't think so, but he's a candidate. If we're going to pin this person down you're both going to have to come clean about some things. You know what I mean. It might be painful for you, but you're both under some sort of threat of death, so the pain is relative to that. I want undertakings from you that you'll be honest, to the limits of your knowledge."

"And sanity," said Susan. She was wrecking a fingernail with her teeth.

"Of course." I smiled at her trying to lighten the mood a bit. "I don't want either of you going back to Nanny and the wielded slipper, but short of that, can I have your word that you'll tell it like it is, or was?"

They both nodded, Susan slowly and painfully, Ailsa with a neutral, sceptical smile.

"Right, Ailsa you told me that you thought Mark Gutteridge had been hounded to death, if not exactly murdered."

"Yes, that's right."

"You believed Brave to be behind it. If it wasn't Brave, or if it wasn't *only* Brave, does that give you any other ideas? Is there anything else you remember as relevant? I mean about your husband's conduct, his state of mind, apart from what you knew Brave was doing to him?"

Ailsa massaged her temples and drew her palms down the side of her face.

"God, I wish I had a cigarette," she said, "but I'm giving them up. Yes, there is something. I didn't mention it before because I thought Brave was all that mattered." She looked across at the other woman. "It's going to be hard on her," she said.

"That's inevitable," I said, "let's hear it."

"Let me get the sequence right." She paused for a full minute. Susan kept her eyes on Ailsa's face and not a muscle moved in her own. Flesh seemed to be falling away from her bones, she wanted to hear it and at the same time she wanted to be far away.

"About a month before he died," Ailsa began slowly, "Mark found out that Bryn was queer. An anonymous letter gave him all the details, so he said. I never saw the letter. Bryn hadn't given Mark the slightest ground for suspicion, he acted very straight, macho even if you can imagine it. But he told Mark that he'd been queer since he was sixteen. Mark was devastated by it. He became impotent, at least he was with me and I don't think there was anyone else. He was distraught about it, it was total. He'd been pretty active before, not a stud or anything, but enthusiastic. Well, he started reading about impotence and he came across the Don Juan complex thing, latent homosexuality and so on, you know it?"

"Yes."

"Mark became convinced that he was tainted and responsible for Bryn being the way he is, was."

"Is that all? Did he see a doctor?" I knew the answer before I asked the question — he wouldn't, couldn't, not Mark Gutteridge.

"No, he didn't. I'm quite sure he only talked about it to me, and then only because he had to. But that isn't all, there's one thing more. About a week before he died Mark was involved in a fight, he had very badly skinned knuckles and he'd dislocated two fingers. He wasn't marked on the face. I think he must have hurt the other person very badly. Mark was a powerful man."

"You don't know who he fought with?"

"No, he wouldn't tell me. The way he said 'he' and 'him' made me think it was someone he knew, not a stranger. But that was just an impression, I could be wrong."

"You could be right. Is that all?"

"That's all. He couldn't make love for the last month of his life. But I never heard him sounding suicidal about it. If he did kill himself it could have contributed, but I still think Brave put the real pressure on."

"Maybe. No unusual letters found after his death?"

She considered it. "No, the executors took all the business correspondence of course. I looked through the personal letters, photographs and things. It all harked back a long way, before my time mostly. I turned it over to Bryn."

"Why?"

"Oh, you know, father and son and all that. It seemed like the right thing to do."

"Yeah, I suppose so. It all ties in with some of my ideas. Not easy stuff to talk about."

"It's not easy to listen to either." Susan spat her words out as if they had a bad taste. "God, what muck! It's probably true though, we're a degenerate lot."

"What do you mean, Susan?" I said softly.

"You're the detective, you work it out."

She was going to get full mileage from the situation, I was going to have to play her very carefully. She had to have an atmosphere of intrigue and trauma to work in if she wasn't going to hold back.

I made a cigarette and Ailsa asked me for one and I made another and gave it to her. I lit the cigarettes and pulled the heavy crystal ashtray over to within Ailsa's reach. Susan jeered again.

"Love is it? Scarcely young though."

"What would you know about it?" Ailsa said icily.

"You'll see. What are you going to ask me, Hardy? What's your first probing question?"

"I think we'll switch for a minute to the more straightforward stuff. I want to know who was living within the grounds of the Gutteridge house on the night he died. You were both there?"

"Yes, I was there," Susan said. "I'd come up to visit my father, Bryn was there too, I don't remember why. Anyway, we stayed for a meal and then I felt a bit ill. I stayed the night, so did Bryn."

"Why? Was that unusual?"

"No, we did it fairly often. Mark liked us to stay and see him at breakfast before he went to work. Plenty of room in the house of course."

"Bryn got drunk that night," said Ailsa.

I was surprised. "He seemed a pretty careful drinker to me."

"He was," Ailsa replied. She looked at Susan for confirmation and got a slight nod. "So was Mark, but they both went at it a bit that night. After dinner they got on the whisky. I don't drink so I went to bed."

"To read?" I asked.

"Yes."

"What, what did you read?"

She played with the ties on her nightgown. The cigarette had gone out, she hadn't enjoyed it so maybe she was on the way to beating them.

"I can't remember," she said.

"Good," I said. "Now, I want you to write down on the pads the names of all the people you recollect as being on the spot that night. Include yourselves."

"Oh Hardy," Susan said, "this is so corny."

"Just do it please, you'll be surprised."

"What are you paying him to set up this nonsense, Ailsa?" Susan asked. Ailsa smiled, stubbed out the half-smoked dead butt and took up her pencil. The two of them switched on their recall apparatus. I pulled my pad towards me and started doodling and writing words that had nothing to do with the matter in hand. I looked up at them a couple of times over the next couple of minutes. Susan looked relaxed, as if the writing exercise was therapeutic for her. Ailsa sucked on the pencil, substituting it for a cigarette. She probably hadn't written anything without smoking in the last twenty years. I wrote down my version of those present

I had only four names and one unnamed servant. I was going on the newspaper reports. The two women looked up more or less simultaneously.

"OK," I said, "let's have a look."

I got up and collected the leaves torn off their pads. Ailsa's sheet read: Ailsa G., Mark G., Susan G., Bryn G., Mrs Berry, Verna, Henry, Willis. Susan's read: Gutteridge — Mark, Bryn, Susan, Ailsa. Cook (Mrs Berry), maid (Verna), driver (Willis), gardener (Henry), assistant.

"Good," I said, "pretty close, one discrepancy. Susan says the assistant gardener was there, Ailsa doesn't list him. Was he or wasn't he, and what was his name?"

"He was around all right," Susan said, "I remember because he was sick, he lived in quarters behind the garage. The light was on there and Bryn mentioned it to Mark. He said the young gardener was sick."

"What else do you know about him?"

"He wasn't interviewed by the police in the house. I suppose they saw him in his room."

Ailsa nodded. "That would be why I didn't list him," she said. "I was going on the order of the police interviews."

"What was his name, Ailsa?" I asked.

"I don't know. Do you, Susan?"

The thing was drawing them together a bit which was good.

"No, he was fairly new, I don't think I ever heard his name."

"What did he look like? He was young?"

Susan thought about it. It was obviously difficult for her to think about servants other than in the abstract.

"He was young I think," she said, "hard to tell, he had a beard."

"That makes sense," said Ailsa. "All men with beards look the same to me, the driver had a beard."

"But Willis had a small beard, a gingery one, pepper and salt sort of. The gardener's beard was fuller and darker, like, like . . ." she giggled, "like Fidel Castro."

Finding Castro funny was just her style, it explained a lot about how the rich are able to carry on merrily being rich. But she'd hit the right note and things came together in my brain and clinched and paid off like a perfectly executed piece of football play. It must have showed in my face because they both straightened themselves up in their beds and took on expectant looks. Ailsa said it.

"He's important, isn't he Cliff, the gardener? And you know who he is. Come on, tell us."

I took a deep breath and pushed the things I'd been fiddling with away. It's a strange feeling when you've worked it out or got close enough, you become reluctant to surrender it. I went to a lecture once given by a guy who was an expert on the Tasmanian Aborigines; his expertise was mostly a matter of word of mouth, he hadn't published very much. He said practically nothing in the lecture, he couldn't bear to yield it up. It's like that.

"I told you it'd get harder," I said. I looked at the woman with her lank hair, the bright eyes and the vast hump where her legs should be, "Where were you in May 1953, Susan?" I said.

24

She took it pretty well, she didn't turn green or any other colour and she didn't scream. Her hands gripped the bed cover a bit harder, but the main expression on her face was that of relief. She'd lived with it a long time until it had become a part of her, but never a comfortable part, never something that augmented her. It was more like a demon to be exorcised except that the exorcism might be too painful, and the hole left by its departure might be too great to bear. There was probably an associated fear, a fear that didn't matter and had never really mattered to anyone but her. A fear that her innermost personal experience didn't matter a damn to the rest of the world. At least now, at whatever the cost, it looked as if it did matter somehow and she felt relief.

She looked at me and spoke through a smile so thin you could slip it through a bank vault door.

"You know where I was, don't you?"

"Yes, I think so."

"Then you tell it. I'd like to hear someone else talk about it. No one has ever referred to it but me for over twenty years and I talk to myself about it every day."

"You're sure you want me to say it? I might get something important wrong."

"That won't matter, go on."

"You were in Adelaide. You gave birth to a child, a boy. He was healthy. You were fifteen or sixteen. The baby went to an orphanage."

"No, he was adopted!"

"Maybe it didn't take, I don't know. He grew up in an orphange though."

She was crying softly now and speaking through the sobs.

"What could I do? What could I do? I couldn't keep him. They sent me away and arranged it all. I kept his birthday every year."

"What do you mean?" I said quickly, then something like an understanding hit me, "no, you don't have to explain, Susan."

"I want to, it's not much to tell. Every year I buy a birthday card and write something on it and seal it in a plain envelope. I post it, just like that."

"Oh Susan." Ailsa stretched out her arms to her, ten feet away across the table.

I got up and went round to her. Her shoulders were heaving and tears were streaming down her face. I tried to touch her hands and put an arm around her but she rejected me with savage, jerky movements of her arms and head. Her mouth was working convulsively and she had her eyes shut tight as if she wanted to blind herself.

"She's had enough Cliff," Ailsa said softly. "Ring for the doctor."

I picked up one of the telephones in the room and got an immediate line to an action point of some kind. I spoke quickly describing Susan's condition, and a doctor and two nurses were in the room within seconds of my replacing the phone. Susan had calmed a little but this was no less disturbing; she stared straight in front of her and her lips moved silently. The doctor gave me a hard disapproving look and slid a needle into her arm. Almost immediately the stiffness went out of her and she relaxed back onto the pillows. Her eyes fluttered and closed. The nurses released the brakes on the bed and wheeled it out of the room. The doctor looked at Ailsa inquiringly but she shook her head.

"I'm all right doctor, I want to talk to Mr Hardy a little longer. I'll have him call when I want to go back to my room."

She said it firmly and that, along with the reminder that she was in a room of her own, was enough to send him off about his business.

I rolled two cigarettes, gave one to Ailsa and lit them. After a few puffs she butted it out.

"I'm going to stop smoking, really! Stop tempting me!"

"You never know how strong you are till you know how weak you are."

"Bullshit!"

"Yes, yes it is."

I sat down on the bed and ran my fingertips down her arm.

"I'm getting better," she said, "I won't break."

I leaned down and kissed her. After a minute she pushed me back. She smoothed down her cap of hair and gave me a look that reminded me that she was paying my hire.

"Well, you certainly broke her up," she said.

"I didn't mean to, but it was bound to happen."

"I suppose so, I've never had any children, you?"

"No."

"They make you vulnerable."

"You're vulnerable anyway."

"Oh, profound."

"That's me."

I meant it though and I was considering how to face her with her own little piece of vulnerability right then. I couldn't think of any subtle way and it probably wasn't necessary.

"Do you want to know who Susan's son is?"

"Yes of course, you've been detecting?"

"Just a little. He's the man you know as Ross Haines." I went on to give her the whole thing in a piece. "I found some records that tie it up. Birth extract, picture of the orphanage. There's a picture of him taken a few years back wearing a dark beard. My guess is that those scars he's got are the result of the beating Mark Gutteridge gave him. They've changed his appearance enough to let him dispense with the beard."

"But why would Mark beat up Ross?"

"I don't know. My guess is that Ross confronted Mark in some way. I'm really guessing now, but I think he found out about Bryn and wrote the letter to Mark. Maybe he tried to blackmail Mark, I don't know."

"He must have hated him."

"He hates all of you."

She took this in painfully, some strain and tiredness was showing in her face and she had to think back over her relationship with a person she never really knew. It's a hard thing to do. I'd done it myself about Cyn a few times and it never failed to leave me feeling wretched and stupid. It's a consolation that you have to be very unlucky to make more than one of these complete misjudgments in your life, but Ailsa had the added problem that the person she now had to totally reconstruct was trying to destroy her.

"Just explain it to me as you see it now, Cliff." She lay back on her pillows and twined the drawstring of her bedgown in her fingers.

I picked up a pad and a pencil and drew a few squares, put names in them, scribbled a few dates and connected the bits and pieces up with arrows and dotted lines. I'm not much of an abstract thinker. I crossed pieces of the diagram out as I spoke.

"Ross Haines grew up in an orphanage. Maybe he was adopted out at first and that's how he got the surname, but something went wrong with the adoption, must have because I think he was in the orphanage for most of his young life. The adoptive parents could have been killed I suppose, I don't know. Maybe he was only fostered out. Anyway, he was bright and he had a lousy time. Orphans don't get any of the system's breaks. He did better than most by becoming a landscape gardener. He was pretty good at it. My guess is that he had no sort of a life at all as an adolescent. To judge from his possessions he had nothing from the time he wanted to remember with affection. OK, he's working away in Adelaide as a landscape gardener, working for rich people and that's important. He's wondering who the hell he is and what he's doing not being dead when somehow he finds out that he is a Gutteridge. I don't know how he does it, gets hold of his actual birth record somehow? Don't know. He has an old, faded photograph of her, you could say there's a resemblance. From that point on his course is straightforward, if insane. He comes to Sydney, gets a job as Mark's gardener, snoops out Bryn, puts the needle into Mark and goes on belting away at every Gutteridge he can find. The files are a bonus. He uses them to squeeze people for things, testimonials, money, God knows what else. He's bent on destroying the family that disowned him and he's doing pretty well. He might have had a hand in Mark's death, Bryn's gone as a result of events he set in train, you and Susan have both come pretty close. It all hangs together, but there are a few things that puzzle me."

"A lot of things puzzle me," Ailsa said. "He could have killed me twenty times, why didn't he?"

"I think the strategy is to do some other sort of damage first. He probably wanted to send you bankrupt."

"I see. What things puzzle you?"

"Quite a few. It's hard to believe that he isn't interested in the Gutteridge money, he's not that mad. But how could he get it after knocking off all the Gutteridges? He might be able to establish a legal claim if he can prove he's Susan's son. But suspicion would fall straight on him. It wouldn't work. Another thing, why didn't he just tell Mark that he was his grandson. He's a well set up lad, not a queer or anything and Bryn was out of favour. He could have done himself some good you'd think. Instead of that he goes sneaking about poisoning minds. Doesn't make sense."

Ailsa shrugged. "Something else," I said.

"What?"

"There's not a scrap of proof. It would take a serious, detailed investigation to establish Haines' movements and actions and there's no way of setting one up. The police wouldn't look at it, and more than that, he's got the files and I think they could get him some high level police protection if he ever needs it. He's pretty safe."

"I'll fire him," she said.

"Let's mull that over for a while first. It might not be a good idea."

"What would be a good idea?"

"We need to know more about him, to get something on him if possible, maybe force him to make some mistakes or get within reach of the law in some way. At present all we have on our side is that he doesn't know we're on to him, that plus you and Susan being safe in here for a while."

Ailsa's concentration was fading. She was interested and involved but tired and drained emotionally. She was still on drugs, there was an artificial quality to her composure and it was starting to crack. She gathered up some strength to see it through for now, but it was obviously an effort.

"What do you want to do now, Cliff?"

"I want to meet this guy again to size him up. Also I think I should go over to Adelaide to check out his background as much as possible, try to get a line on him that will help to explain things. I especially want to know why he's used the search and destroy method lately instead of infiltration and sedition."

"He's done that?"

"Yes, the methods of attack have changed, someone else could be involved of course, in a secondary way maybe."

"You sound like a military man."

"I was."

"You didn't tell me."

"That's true of a lot of things. You don't like military men?"

"Not especially, but I like you. And do you realise you haven't had a drink for two hours?"

"Yeah, I'll have to do something about that soon, my brain has almost seized. I need something from you love."

"What?"

"A note from you introducing me to Haines and instructing him to introduce me to whoever handles your executives' expense accounts, travel warrants and such. There is such a person?"

"Yes, it's a delicate job actually, taxes involved."

"Don't tell me. I think this could throw a scare into Haines as well as being useful for itself."

"It's all right with me, I hope he shits himself."

I gave her a pen and some instructions and she set to work on a pad that carried the hospital's letterhead. The result was a signed note that authoritatively introduced me to Haines, without any reference to our earlier meeting of course, and directed him to arrange an air ticket to any part of Australia and the Pacific and expenses of up to one hundred dollars a day.

"This will make Ross furious," Ailsa said.

"That's too bad, I'm weeping."

I took the note, folded it up and put it away in my breast pocket. The only advantage I've ever found to wearing suits is the number of pockets you get with them, but it still doesn't swing me in their favour. I sat with Ailsa for a while and we said the things you say early on in an affair when the words are new and the feelings are mint fresh and shining bright. She told me to be careful. I said I would be. I called for the nurses and they wheeled her back to her room. I gathered up the bits of paper in the conference room and stuffed them into my pocket. I was desert dry and wrung out from the afternoon's work.

25

I was at the reception desk of Sleeman Enterprises at 9.30 the next morning. The same girl was behind the desk but at first she didn't associate my denims and shirt sleeves with Mr Riddout. When it dawned on her, her face took on a sickly look and she started to cast about her for help.

"Yes Mr Riddout?" she stumbled over the words. She'd giggled about Mr Riddout to her friends and now she was embarrassed to see him again in the flesh.

"Hardy's the name Miss, I want to see Mr Haines."

"But I'm sure you're the man I saw yesterday. You looked around . . . interior decorator."

I made a non-committal gesture and handed her Ailsa's note. She read it quickly despite her agitation and got up from her chair.

"I'll tell his secretary," she said.

I reached over, took the note and eased her back into her chair by the shoulder.

"Calm down," I said. "I'll tell her. I just let you see that so you'd let me go through. That's OK?"

"Oh yes, yes, the door you want is . . ."

"I know where it is."

I gave her a small salute and a grin and went down the passage. I knocked on the door and went in before the blonde answered. She didn't like it and got ready to high hat me. Her hair dominated her, it was fine and yellow and swept up into a beehive arrangement that defied belief. Her voice rasped slightly and I suspected that the hair would be harsh to touch from silicone spray.

"Can I help you? Sir."

The last word just got into the sentence and hung there looking as if it might lose its place. I took out the note, unfolded it and put it on the desk. I put my licence card down on top of it and gave her my strong, silent look. Her reaction to the name Sleeman nearly cracked the mask of make-up on her face and had the same effect as on the other girl. It brought her to her feet, sharp.

"I'll tell Mr Haines, he's in, you can see him . . ." She was practically stammering. God knows what would happen if Ailsa herself walked in. They'd probably start fainting and this one would spill her nail polish all over the copy.

"That's nice," I said, "I'm glad he's in, but couldn't you just buzz him?"

She looked down at the intercom as if she'd never seen one before and didn't know whether to talk into it or put a coin in it. She sucked in a breath and flipped the switch.

"Mr Haines, a gentleman to see you. It appears to be important, he has a letter from Miss Sleeman."

"Five minutes." Haines' voice had a nice timbre and pitch even over the furry intercom.

I collected my papers and walked across to the connecting door. The blonde jumped up and moved towards me with beckoning hands.

"You can't go in," she said breathlessly. "He said five minutes."

"I'm not afraid," I said and opened the door.

Haines got up looking surprised and I looked him over carefully. He wasn't as big as he'd seemed the first time I'd seen him, but he was taller than me and he was noticeably heavier. It was all wrapped up in an expensive linen shirt with epaulettes and the latest thing in gabardine slacks — a high-waisted production with narrow belt loops and deep cuffs. He had thick dark curly hair and even this early in the morning his beard was making his chin blue and shadowy. He looked a bit loud, a bit florid. My mind jumped about trying to register a firm impression of him before giving it up. He bore a close resemblance to a picture I'd seen in the papers of Mark Gutteridge, twenty years back, accepting a racing cup after one of his horses had carried off a major event. Others might have missed the similarity but Mark Gutteridge, who was probably a two shaves a day man like this one, could not have.

It seemed to be everybody's day for getting up abruptly from

191

their chairs. Haines was nearly clear of his when he checked himself and moved back to its padded leather comfort. He was sharp, he'd recognised me immediately I'd stuck my face in and he didn't like it a bit.

"Don't get up," I said, "this won't take long. Your boss has a little chore for you."

I handed him the note, he read while trying to work a big chunk of flesh out of his lower lip. When he finished he put the paper down on the blotter and slid one of its edges under the leather envelope corner that held the blotter in place. I went up to the desk and repossessed the note. He didn't object and I was beginning to wonder if you had to spit in his face to make him act as aggressive as he looked. He made himself comfortable in his chair without looking at me: I thought he might feel he had an edge sitting down so I perched on the end of the desk. That still left quite a space between us. He reached out for a cigarette from the open box in front of him. He flicked one out and lit it with a gold desk lighter.

"What's the nature of your business with Miss Sleeman?"

I was listening for a South Australian accent. I didn't pick any up but maybe there's no such thing.

"Sorry," I said, "didn't catch it."

"What is your business with Miss Sleeman?"

I paused while he blew smoke around and tried to think of something to do with his left hand.

"I don't think you're too bad," I said. "Just much too young for what you're doing and a bit out of your depth. You'll get the hang of it."

"I don't know what you're talking about. I asked you a question."

"It doesn't deserve an answer. The business is private, confidential, that's all you have to know. Now do as you're told."

He opened his mouth to speak but I cut him off. "And don't say 'You can't talk to me like that' because I just did."

"I wasn't going to say that."

"What *were* you going to say?"

"Never mind." His voice was firmer and he seemed to think he was making up some ground. "I can see that you're trying to push me around as much as you can short of hitting me again. I wonder why?"

He *was* making up ground. He let go a smile that crinkled up the fine white scars around his eyes and mouth in a way that was probably very attractive to women.

"How is Ailsa?" he said suddenly. He'd dropped the hurt look and the probing look, now he was mild and charming. He was a chameleon.

"She's OK," I said gruffly. It seemed inadequate.

"Bloody awful business," he said, "I got the gist of it from Sir John Guilford, and I read about Bryn. Dreadful. A chapter of accidents."

"Maybe," I said. "I don't want to sit here exchanging chummy gossip with you, Haines. I don't like you, you don't like me. But since we're at it, did you hear about Susan Gutteridge? She's in hospital too."

He looked and sounded surprised. We were talking about his mother although he didn't know that I knew it. Nothing like filial concern showed in his face but there was no way it would — his feelings about his own flesh and blood were unique to him.

"God, no. What's the matter with her?"

"Hit and run."

"How bad?"

"Broken legs, she'll live."

He shook his head. It was a bad moment for me because, despite myself, I believed what I saw — a man who apparently didn't know a thing about events he was supposed to have engineered. It was time to get on with it before I found myself giving away too much for this stage of the game. I got off the desk and made impatient movements with my feet. He looked at me curiously for a second and then flicked the intercom button. He told the secretary he'd be with Mr Kent for a few minutes and we went out of the office.

Mr Kent looked like just the sort of man for tax dodges, he faded into the background without a trace. He had wispy hair, a grey suit and a general air of not being there at all. Like everyone in the place he was smart and efficient. He read Ailsa's note, reached into his desk for a manila folder and wrote my name on the top of it. He went to pin the note inside the folder but I stopped him and told him I wanted to keep it. He smiled knowingly. "Very wise," he said. He pressed a button and a girl appeared in the open doorway about two seconds later. "Photocopy please," Kent said extending the note to her, "and arrange credit cards for Mr Hardy. The usual things." The secretary nodded a sleekly groomed head and whispered away. Kent busied himself with a ruled form on which he wrote my name and made some entries in a tight, cribbed hand. There was no love lost between him and Haines who straightened his cuffs and looked more or less in my direction.

"Satisfied Hardy?" he said.

"Very. Thank you Mr Haines. Don't fall in any swimming pools."

Kent looked up bemused but Haines' face was a bored, non reacting mask. He inclined his head to Kent and went out, leaving the door open. Kent got up and shut it. I couldn't think of anything to say to him and he seemed to feel the same way about me. We lingered in silence until the girl came back with the papers. She handed them to Kent who dismissed her with the economical nod that seemed to be his speciality before slipping the photostat into the file. He handed the original back to me.

"A credit card valid for the standard airlines for six months will be ready for you at the desk, Mr Hardy," he said. "And now, Cashcard?"

"What's that?"

He unleashed what appeared to be the whole of his personality in the form of a tight, self-satisfied smile. "It's at the desk, you can use it to draw a hundred dollars a day for the next calendar month."

"Wonderful," I said, "what about taxis, call girls and squaring cops?"

"Your problem, Mr Hardy. To me you are a miscellaneous expense."

He scribbled the day's date on the outside of the folder and pulled a bulging, loose leaf file towards him like a long lost lover. I was dismissed, I know a perfectionist when I see one.

194

The girl at the front desk was having a bad day. She held out two cards, one of them similar to a bankcard, the other plainer with a gold edge.

"Please sign these, Mr Hardy."

I signed them. She slipped them into plastic holders and handed them to me.

"Don't worry," I said, "capitalism is doomed."

She gave me a brilliant smile. She'd solved it, I was a madman.

I went home, packed a few things into an overnight bag and phone booked an afternoon flight to Adelaide. The credit card worked like a charm at the first bank I came to. I caught a taxi out to the airport and called the hospital half an hour before my plane was due for boarding. I left messages for Ailsa and Susan telling them not to see anyone except their doctors. After buying the Sydney afternoon and the Adelaide morning papers I went through the ticket collection and seat allocation routines and got on the plane. It was half empty which felt strange until I remembered that it was nearly always that way in first class, I just hadn't had much experience of it.

The plane boomed along for two hours damaging the ozone. I had a couple of gins and tonic because I like the miniature bottles.

Adelaide doesn't rate too highly with me. It's flat and there's no water to speak of. The celebrated hills are too close to the city. It feels as if you could kick a football from the city stadium up into the hills without really trying. When I go there it's always raining and I'm never dressed for it. The plane slewed about a bit on the wet runway and we all scampered for cover in our lightweight ensembles. The rain was more a spit than a shower, but the only happy-looking people at the terminal were those who were flying the hell out of the place.

I went to the Avis desk and hired a Ford Escort for two days after proving beyond all doubt that I was Clifford Hardy, licensed to drive, and handing over enough money to make it not worth my while to steal it. My luggage came down the chute, I slung it into the back of the car and drove in to what they call the city. I tried to cheer myself with the thought that the Athens of the South is a great place for the cheap food and drink, but I only half-succeeded.

The buildings were dribbling water down their grey faces and those damn hills were still much too close. I checked in at the Colonial Hotel across the road from the University and ordered a bottle of Scotch with ice and a soda syphon. I settled down with a tall glass, a map and the telephone directory. The orphanage was listed and I called it. I might as well have saved my breath and money. The woman I spoke to wouldn't confirm that Haines had been an inmate, wouldn't give out information about past directors of the place and wouldn't arrange an interview for me with the present boss. She wasn't interested in sarcasm either, she hung up as I was thanking her. But that was all right. The first dead end in an investigation is a challenge to me, it's only after one or two more that I feel hurt and start sulking.

They couldn't conceal the address of the place from me. I located it on the map, poured out and drank a quick neat one, and tucked the ice and soda away in the miniature fridge. I got the car out of the hotel parking lot and drove off towards the hills. The rain had stopped.

It took me nearly an hour to reach the orphanage which put the time at close to five o'clock. The photographs I'd seen of the place hadn't done it justice. It was straight out of Dickens or maybe even Mervyn Peake; every angle and corner suggested order and discipline. It had no charm; I like old buildings, but I wouldn't have minded if they pulled this one down. It looked in pretty good shape however, and the grounds were well cared for which suggested a groundsman. Groundsmen and caretakers tend to be long-term employees and I was counting on that now. I parked back up the road from the main gates and set off on a circumnavigation of the grounds which covered about ten acres. The main building stood on a rise more or less in the middle of the land which was enclosed by a high fence of cast iron spears. A paved drive ran from the main gates up to the front of the building and down to a smaller set of gates on the other side. There was a football oval and a fair bit of lawn and garden but too much asphalt and government issue cream paint.

I scouted around the fence until I found what I was looking for — a small cottage in the northeast corner of the grounds. It would have been a city trendy's dream, sandstock bricks, double fronted and without obvious signs of later improvements. A man was standing in front of the cottage doing nothing in particular. At that distance he looked old, bent over a bit, and there was a pipe smoking gently in his face. He had his hands and a good part of his arms deep in the pockets of a pair of old khaki overalls. I stuck my head up over the spears.

"Gidday," I shouted.

He stood like stone. I shouted again with the same result. He might have been deep in reverie, but it seemed more likely that he was hard of hearing. I looked around for something to throw and found a piece of rotten branch. I heaved it over the fence and it landed a bit off to one side of him. He took the pipe out of his mouth and looked at it. Then he put the pipe back and looked at it again. I reached down for another piece of wood to throw when he made a slow turn in my direction. I stood there with the wood in my hand feeling foolish. I gave him another hail and he ambled over to the fence, scuffling his feet in the damp leaves. He made it to the fence in pretty good time given that he wasn't in a hurry.

"Didn't mean to startle you," I said.

"You didn't startle me, mate." His voice was the old Australian voice, slow and a bit harsh from rough tobacco and a lifelong habit of barely opening his mouth when he spoke. I handed him one of my cards through the fence and brought a five dollar note out into the light of day.

"I'd like to ask you a few questions if you've got the time. There's a quid in it."

He stuck the pipe back in his mouth. The hair was classical, a brutal short back and sides and his ragged moustache, yellow from tobacco had nothing in common with the modish Zapata model. He was one of the old style of tie-less Australians, one without a collar to his shirt so how could he wear a tie? He inclined one ear towards me, but his faded blue eyes were sceptical.

"How long have you worked here, Mr . . .?" I bellowed.

He shuffled back. "Don't have to shout mate," he said, "I can hear orright. My name's Jenkins, Albie Jenkins and I been here since the war."

He didn't mean Korea.

"Since 1945?"

"Forty-six. I got demobbed at the end of forty-five and this's the first job I took, been here ever since. I went through all of it, unnerstand? Middle East, New Guinea and that."

"I see, like this job do you?"

He appeared to be thinking about it for the first time. He took the pipe out, looked at it and put it back again.

"Dunno," he said slowly. "S'orright, crook pay but a place to live, they leave ya alone. You weren't old enough to be in it, were you?"

"No, I was in Malaya though."

"Where?"

"Malaya."

"Oh yeah, against the Japs?"

"No, later, against the communists."

He shook his head. "Never heard of it." He wasn't interested, the only real wars had been those with the Germans and the Japanese. I asked him if he remembered a dark boy who would have been at the institution in the 1960s, but he didn't have a clue. He explained that he didn't have much to do with the kids. He said that they'd be able to help me up at the office and when I told him they wouldn't he shrugged as if that settled it. I handed him the five dollar note to unsettle it.

"Who's in charge here now?"

"Bloke named Horsfield, soft bugger if you ask me."

"He's new is he? Wasn't here when you came?"

He sparked up and drew hard on the pipe, the smoke surged up into the trees that grew along the fence. Then the pipe died abruptly. He took a pull, found it dead and knocked the ashes out against the fence. He waved it about for a minute to cool it, re-packed it from a leather pouch and got it going again. I waited while he did it.

"No," he chuckled through the spittle, "when I came it was the Brig, tough joker, ex-army, kept everyone in line and they bloody loved him."

"When did Horsfield take over?"

"Five, six years ago."

The big question. "Is the Brig still alive?"

"Yeah, course he is. He'll bloody live for ever, he was out here for something or other last week. Had a yarn with him, 'bout the war."

"What's his full name?"

He scratched his chin. "Jesus, I'm not sure, just think of him as the Brig. Easy find out though." He jerked his thumb back at the cottage. I pulled out another five and it went through the fence. He tucked it along with the other one into the bib pocket of his overall and shuffled off to the cottage. I stood at the fence gripping the iron until it occurred to me that I must look like one of our primate cousins who didn't quite make it to civilisation, suicide and the bomb. I let go the fence and dusted off my hands and tried to think of something else to do with them. As usual, a cigarette seemed the only answer and I rolled one and had it going by the time Albie came back. He looked down at the sheet of paper he was holding and read off it very carefully: "Brigadier Sir Leonard St James Cavendish."

I couldn't see much problem about finding that in the phone book. I reached through the fence to shake his hand, he obliged but he was very out of practice.

"Thanks, Mr Jenkins, you've been a great help."

"Orright, so've you. I'll be able to have a decent drink for change."

He shambled off through the leaves. I finished my cigarette and ground the butt out into the concrete in which the iron spears were embedded.

I stopped at the first phone booth I saw and called the Brig. He lived in Blackwood, not far away, but you don't just drop in on Brigs. A gentle female voice answered and confirmed that I had the right residence. I gave my name as Dr Hardy from the Australian National University and told her I wanted to consult the old soldier on a point of military history. She said she'd ask her husband and I stood with the silent phone in my hand for about five minutes feeling guilty and exposed. She came back and told me that Sir Leonard would be delighted to see me and would ten

199

o'clock the following morning suit. I said it would, got my tongue around "Lady Cavendish", hoping that was right, and thanked her. I drove back to the hotel. The rain had started again. I had a Scotch and wasted the time watching the news on television and watching the rain pissing down on the churches.

I had a shower and went out at 7.30 to look for the laminex cafe where I'd eaten a brilliant steak on my last visit to Adelaide three years ago. I could still taste the steak and the carafe of house red had been like Mouton Rothschild compared with the swill we buy in the east. I found it at the end of one of Adelaide's narrow, quiet, wet main streets. I ordered the same food and drink and experienced that feeling when eating alone — that everyone is looking at you with pity whereas in fact no one gives a damn. I combated the feeling by reading Forsyth's *The Dogs of War* which I'd bought at a newsstand opposite the hotel, and I learned all there is to know about equipping a mercenary force while I worked through the meal. It was better than spreads I'd paid three times as much for in Sydney, but when I got outside the cafe that cool drizzle reminded me that I was a long way from home. I walked fast back to the Colonial and worked on the Forsyth a little more. I went to sleep and had a long, involved dream about Uncle Ted and his two-up games at Tobruk.

26

I skipped breakfast in the hotel's lounge-dining room in favour of a quick research job in the Barr Smith library at the University of Adelaide. Cavendish got a mention in Lean's *Official History of Australia in World War II*. He'd been in on Wavell's North African offensive in 1941, with the Ninth Division at El Alamein and he was there at the capture of Wewak in May 1945. There was one obvious question — why didn't he go on to Borneo? But there was plenty to ask him about the New Guinea campaign and his assessment of MacArthur whose reputation is a bit on the decline at present I gather. The morning drizzle had cleared when I left the library and the traffic was moving quickly along the roads which were drying out by the minute. It took me three quarters of an hour to get to Blackwood.

He either had a private income, or Brigadiers' pensions can't be too bad, or he'd done all right out of flogging off army jeeps for scrap metal, because Sir Leonard St James Cavendish wasn't feeling the pinch. He lived in one of the better houses in a neighbourhood which comprised mostly hundred foot frontages and tennis courts in the back yard. Adelaide doesn't have the same amount of old, gilt-edged money as Melbourne or the new, flashy stuff of Sydney, but there are plenty of people in the city of churches who've put it together at some time and are watching it grow. Cavendish's house stood on a corner block with frontages on three streets so the high, white painted brick wall was enclosing a tidy parcel of prime residential land. The house was a mock Tudor job with lots of stained wood strips, sitting well back from the road in a leafy setting. The whole effect made me wonder why the Brig had taken on the directorship of an orphanage — a multinational oil exploration corporation seemed more the style.

I parked the car on the street outside the house. That still left room for two buses to drive side by side down the middle of the road and not scrape the Jaguars cruising along on either side of them. A high iron gate was hinged to brick pillars with plaster crests on them. Bands and blobs of colour were bright against the faded white background and there was a Latin inscription under the crest. I saluted it all with the manila folder full of blank paper I was carrying. A stroll from the house down to collect the milk and papers at the gate would set you up nicely for breakfast. The house had a long, low verandah in front of it with some sort of thatch on top. I pushed the bell beside the heavy oak door and it opened almost immediately. A small wisp of a woman held the door open. She couldn't have been more than five feet tall and she seemed to be having some trouble keeping control of the door in the draught. Her hair was white and her face was wrinkled and beautiful like an old parchment. Her voice was the one I'd heard on the phone.

"Dr Hardy?"

"Yes."

"Please come in, my husband is on the back terrace reading the newspaper. He's looking forward to your visit. Would you like some tea?"

I thought it might be in character to accept even though I detest the stuff. She showed me down a long passage hung about with paintings which looked pretty good and some interesting Melanesian weapons. We went through a big sun porch lined with books and she opened a wire door out to a flagstoned terrace. A man was sitting on a garden chair positioned so he could get some sun through the tips of the trees. He had the *Advertiser* spread out on the table in front of him and he folded it up and got to his feet as I approached.

"Good morning, Sir Leonard, it's good of you to see me."

We shook hands.

"How do you do, Mr Hardy. Please sit down."

He pointed to a chair on the other side of the table and I took it. He was a bit blimpish, clipped moustache and plenty of colour in his face. His voice was quiet and soothing to judge from the few words he'd spoken, not the snarl a lot of army officers acquire or affect. He had on a white shirt, open at the neck, grey trousers and an old corduroy jacket. He wore slippers but had none of the appurtenances of old age — hearing aid, glasses, walking stick; he looked about sixty although he was actually seventy-one.

"Well sir," he said, "so you're a military historian?"

"No, I'm a private investigator."

"I see."

"You don't sound surprised."

He smiled. "I'm not, except at your coming clean so quickly."

"I had an idea I couldn't fool you."

He smiled again and nodded. "I'm flattered, you were quite right, you didn't fool me. There is no Dr Hardy in History at the ANU. My son's a Fellow there you see, and I have the current calendar in there among my books."

He pointed to the sun room. As he did his wife came out carrying a tray with tea things on it. She put it down on the table, poured milk into three heavy enamel jugs and swilled the stuff about in the pot.

"I'm sorry Dr Hardy, I should have asked, do you take milk?"

I nodded and forced a smile while fighting down nausea.

"And sugar?"

I shook my head.

"You've lost your tongue," she said, "I hope you two haven't fallen out."

The Brig reached across for his tea and cupped his hands around the mug. "No, no. Thank you my dear. No, we haven't fallen out. Mr Hardy isn't a military historian as I told you. It turns out he's a private investigator. Now he's going to drink his tea and tell me all about it."

"How interesting. Drink your tea, Mr Hardy." She pulled a pencil from her apron pocket and reached for the paper. "I think I'll do the crossword while you sort it out. Don't mind me."

She'd known me for a fake before she'd opened the door and she'd played it as cool as Greta Garbo. I sipped the tea. It all tastes the same to me whether you make it in muslin tea bags or boil it up in a five gallon drum. I swallowed a minute amount and kept my hands around the mug as if I might possibly go back for more.

"I'm sorry about the deception," I began. "It was very important that I see you and I wanted to make sure you'd give me a hearing. I thought the military history device would get me in."

"I don't mind about the deception young man, lived with it all my life, in the army and after. I'm mildly interested in military history, not a fanatic though. War's uncivilised. Trouble is, a lot of people enjoy it. I like that remark by the man who *would* be a colleague of yours if you were an historian. 'War is hell, and army life is purgatory to a civilised man'. Good, that. Where did you get the idea I'd take the military history bait?"

"From Mr Jenkins out at the orphanage."

"Talked to Albie did you? Well you got the wrong end of the stick. I yarn to him about the war for his sake, not mine."

"I can see it now. You would have seen me anyway?"

"Probably. See anyone who wants to see me, might be interesting. Which brings us to your business."

He'd handled it pretty well as I guessed he'd handle most situations in his life. The woman worked away at the crossword, the cryptic, making good progress. They looked like a comfortable couple with affection flowing strongly between them. The incongruity between the house and the job he'd held for twenty-five years still puzzled me though.

"Yes, I hope you can help me," I began. "I'm investigating a family matter in Sydney. It's very confidential and complicated. There's at least one murder involved, possibly more. A lot of money too and the happiness of several people who've done nothing wrong. I believe that a young man who grew up in the orphanage here is at the centre of it. I've come over to get more information about him, to help me get on with the case in the best way."

"What sort of information?" There was still no military bark to the voice, but some of the gentleness had gone out of it. He was looking intently at me. I had his attention, his co-operation was still to be won.

"I'm not sure, almost anything, your impressions of his character for one thing. What I really want to understand is how he came to do the things he did."

"You will have a choice about how you proceed in the matter? Your subject didn't actually commit murder?"

"I believe I will have a choice. No, I'm pretty sure he didn't kill anyone and isn't directly responsible for a death."

"Very well, so far so good. You'll understand that I'm reluctant to talk loosely about the St Christopher boys. It's hard for anyone who hasn't spent a lot of time in such a place to understand what a handicap most orphans start out with. First, who are we talking about?"

"I'm sure you're right, Sir Leonard," I said. "The man I'm referring to is named Ross Haines. He's twenty-three and he spent his first fifteen or so years in the orphanage. He found out who his mother was and he's been operating at close quarters to her and her family for the past few years. His grandfather, his uncle and a friend of his uncle are all dead and Haines' activities are some sort of key to their deaths, the causes. His grandfather's widow and his own mother have been harassed and assaulted, attempts have been made on their lives. Haines' motive appears to be revenge on the family that disowned him at birth, or before birth even. The family money may be a consideration, there's a lot of it, but that's a cloudy part of the affair. I'm retained by a Miss Sleeman, Haines' grandfather's widow, a second wife. I have the backing of Haines' mother, but she doesn't know about her son's involvement. It's very delicate as I said. A lot of people have been hurt and some more will be, that's inevitable. My client is in hospital, she was assaulted and tortured. I can show you a letter which establishes my standing with my client. Apart from that and my professional documents, you'll have to take me on faith."

I handed the letter and my licence across to him and he studied them closely for a minute or so. His wife had finished the crossword and was listening intently. Cavendish looked up.

"Don't you like tea?" he said.

"No, I hate it."

He smiled and handed back the papers. "You should have said so. But never mind, you're direct enough and your eyes don't slide around all over the place. Been in the army ever?"

"Malaya."

His nod might have been approving, but remembering the quote he'd spouted before I couldn't be certain.

"I'll help you as far as I can," he said. "Have you any more to add at this point?"

"No. I'll be grateful for all you can tell me about Ross Haines. If you remember him at all."

He leaned back in his chair and let the sun strike his face. The veins were intact and the high colour was healthy. I decided that it probably came from gardening and walking rather than the bottle. He crinkled his eyes a little with the effort of memory. "I do, very well indeed," he said. "And there's a good deal to tell. Haines was in the orphanage for fifteen years or so as you say. He'd been adopted after birth but the parents parted within a year of taking him and he came to us. He also had a slight deformity of the shoulder. It was corrected by an operation when he was three or four, but parents want perfect children so he stayed in the orphanage. He was fostered once but the people returned him after a couple of months. He was uncontrollable. This was when he was about six or seven. He wouldn't go to school and played merry hell when he was dragged there — wild tantrums, totally negative and destructive attitudes. The couple who took him on were pretty rough, they knocked him about a bit, but I expect he gave as good as he got. After he got back to us he was changed, quiet, cooperative, worked well at school. He was very bright. A bit unnerving really, he was glad to be back at the institution."

"Did he ever give you trouble after that?"

"Yes, he did. In two ways. He was very mild and amiable, some of the others would tease him, run him ragged for days. He'd let this go on longer than you'd think flesh and blood could stand then he'd turn on them and thrash hell out of them. He was big for his age and strong. Then he'd go back into his shell."

"How often did this happen?"

"Oh, I suppose half a dozen times. He put one boy in hospital but he'd been unmercifully teased, persecuted really and had shown great restraint. It was impossible to discipline him for it. He was in the right."

"What was the other way he gave trouble?"

"It was strange. Haines was very able in his studies and he excelled in a variety of sports — beautiful cricketer, natural talent. The sporting ability is very important with these lads, get them into teams, have them travel, meet people. Builds up their confidence."

"But Haines wouldn't be in it?"

"That's so, he wouldn't play in teams outside the orphanage grounds. In home matches of football and cricket he'd score goals and runs all over the place, but he wouldn't play the away matches. Dropped him from the teams as discipline, all that, made no difference. He hated stepping outside the place, excursions were a nightmare to him, eventually we stopped taking him. He'd stay behind and read or train for some sport or other. Probably haven't made it clear: he was a great reader, read everything and he retained it. They wanted him for a television children's panel game, brains trust sort of thing, you know?"

"Yes, I think they're ghastly."

"Just so, but some children thrive on them in a way. Haines went white when it was put to him, he refused to consider it. He was violent."

"How did the suggestion come up in the first place?"

"Haines had been entering competitions in newspapers, puzzles and general knowledge things. He was an omnivorous newspaper and magazine reader, devoured the things. Won prizes all the time."

"What sort of prizes?"

"Book vouchers mostly, money too, small sums. It was banked for him. The newspaper people must have talked to the television people, same crowd I expect, and they approached us about him. Well, he reacted as I told you, he threw things, went into one of those rages that he used to display in fights. And he stopped entering competitions, never touched them again. He seemed to ease back on everything, he'd pass his subjects at school and do respectable things with the bat, but all the brilliance was gone. Sometimes it would flash out, so would the ungovernable temper, it was all still there but he kept it completely under control. He could probably have got a scholarship to go on studying but he had a horror of competing. He opted to go to work at fifteen or so, gardening I think it was?"

"That's right."

"He left us when he was sixteen, he was earning a wage, boarding with a respectable family, time to go."

"Did you ever see him after he left, or hear from him?"

"Never."

"What was your relationship with him like?"

"Quite good, as far as he'd let it be. I used to nag him a bit about not trying his best, but I gave that up. He was his own man from a very early age."

"At some time he discovered who his mother was, or became convinced he knew. Could you pin-point a time when that might have happened?"

Cavendish looked across at his wife. "You remember Haines dear," he said, "can you help with this?"

She took off her gold rimmed spectacles and polished them on the sleeve of her cardigan. "Yes," she said quietly, "I believe I can." She replaced the glasses precisely. "Haines was involved in the office incident, wasn't he? About the same time as the television idea came up. He was in a state over that and his part in the affair was never clear."

I sat up, this sounded like it. "Could you please explain, office breaking . . .?"

"There was what I believe is called a sit-in at the orphanage," said Cavendish. "Some of the boys were protesting about being denied access to their personal records. They aren't permitted to see them, that's the law. Right or wrong, that's the law. Some of the older boys broke into the office, barricaded themselves in there and ransacked the filing cabinets."

"Haines was one of them?"

"No, his part in it was curious. He volunteered to act as negotiator. The boys were on hunger strike in the office. Haines went in and talked to them and they came out. He was in there for about an hour. It wasn't a popular act."

"Why not?"

"There was some talk that Haines had put the others up to it. He denied it and it was never confirmed, the accusation was put down to spite. But there were whispers. Some of the boys were eager for a fight, and the intermediary was seen as something of a spoilsport."

"Haines could have seen a file on him when he was in the office?"

"Yes."

"What information would that carry?"

"Date and place of birth, parents' name or names if available, medical details."

"Haines' file, did that have his mother's name on it?"

"I don't know but almost certainly it would. Such records are very precise and very private."

"And a marked change in Haines' behaviour dates from this time?"

Cavendish spread his hands out on the table, there were fine white hairs across the backs and the nails were broad and strong, no nicotine stains, no tremors.

"It does, Mr Hardy. We put it down to the idea of going on television. The impact of that on him seemed more dramatic than the other affair which only lasted a couple of hours. But it could have been due to the discovery of his mother's name." Cavendish paused, then he rapped his knuckles against the table. "No, no, how stupid of me. Those records were all computer coded in the late sixties. Haines couldn't have got a name from his file, just a number. Still, that might have been enough to set him off, certainly the psychologists said he was obsessed with the parentage problem."

I leaned forward grasping at it. "Just a minute sir, two things. How could a number set him off?"

"Some of the files would have had a multiple zero number — parents unknown."

"I see. Now, Haines was examined by psychologists?"

"Yes, several times. A team from the University was working on a study of orphaned children, their psychological problems and so on. They were very interested in Haines and examined him at some length. I can't remember the details, I recall one of the team telling me that Haines was positive that his people were wealthy, substantial citizens, but that's a very common complex I gather."

"Was this examination done before or after the office sit-in?"

He raised his eyes to the sky, then glanced at his wife.

"Dear?"

"After, I think," she said, "soon after."

"I really can't remember, Mr Hardy. I'd trust my wife's recollection though, steel trap mind she has."

I smiled. "I can see that," I said glancing at the blocked in crossword. "It's interesting, and fills in a lot of gaps."

"I don't know whether it will help you much though. Haines was a very complicated boy, an unusual individual in every way. I'm sorry to hear he's in trouble, but I can't say I'm surprised."

I was only half-listening now. "Oh, why's that?"

"Colossal determination combined with a very passive, yielding streak. Very odd combination, unstable elements I'd say. No, I shouldn't say that, that's what the psychologist said."

I nodded. "Were the results of this study ever published?"

"Yes," he said, "in something called *The Canadian Journal of Psychology*. I understand it's a periodical of repute. I've never read the paper, should have I suppose, but it was a full-time job running that place."

"Will you have some coffee, Mr Hardy, or a drink, it's after eleven?" Lady Cavendish obviously thought it was time to wind the show up.

"No thank you, I've taken up enough time and you've been very helpful."

There must have been an inconclusive note in my voice because Cavendish leaned forward with a quiet smile on his face.

"But you haven't finished?"

"No. You might think this impertinent, but I must ask you something else."

"Let me guess," he said. He got up and took a few springy steps across to where the lawn began, he bent down, picked up a pebble and juggled it up and down in his palm. "When we live in such style why did I spend twenty-five years running an orphanage?"

"Right," I said.

"Easy," he looked at his wife and they exchanged smiles, "we've only had this place for a couple of years and we'll only have it a couple more the way the rates are going. I inherited it from an uncle, title too, the old boy lived to ninety-six, still thought of Australia as a colony. When I left the army, Mr Hardy, the deferred pay was negligible and I had a large, bright gaggle of a family to educate. The orphanage directorship was the best thing offering. I tried to do it in an intelligent fashion, it wasn't always easy."

"I'm sure you did," I said. I got up and shook hands with them.

Cavendish flicked the pebble away, he looked sad. "You might drop me a line to let me know how it works out," he said quietly.

I said I would. They walked with me down an overgrown path beside the house and we said our goodbyes near the front veran-dah. I went down the path to the gate and looked around before I opened it; they'd half-turned and he had his arm down across her thin, straight shoulders.

27

I drove back into town and checked out of the Colonial. The Avis people took their car back and gave me enough refund money to pay for a bottle of beer and a sandwich in the airport bar. I killed the waiting time there, pouring the Cooper's ale carefully so as not to get the sediment, and pushing the crumbs of the sandwich around on my plate. I watched the sediment settle in the bottle thinking that the bits and pieces of this case were starting to settle into place, but not satisfactorily. The whole thing needed a violent shake if it was going to be resolved in the Gutteridge woman's favour. I might have to give that shake myself, but I had a feeling that it might be done for me and pretty soon.

I finished the Forsyth book just before we landed at Mascot. I settled back into a taxi seat and almost fell asleep on the ride to Glebe. I kicked an old clothes appeal and several monster sale leaflets out of the doorway and stomped through the kitchen to make some coffee. I dumped the overnight bag under the table knowing that it'd stay there for days and hating myself for it. A newsboy yelled out in the street and I went out to the gate and bought a paper. I read it while I drank the coffee — the election was still in doubt, there was an earthquake in Greece, a cricketer had his shoulder packed in ice and Dr Ian Brave was still being hunted by the police. I finished the coffee and the telephone rang. I grabbed it and got Ailsa's voice, panicky and barely coherent over the wire.

"Cliff, Cliff, thank Christ, I've been ringing for hours and minutes . . . no . . ."

"Hold it, Ailsa, hold it. Where are you?"

"Hospital. I've seen Brave."

"What!" I shouted. "Where?"

"Here, right here. I saw him when I was going to the toilet. He didn't see me, but Jesus I went cold all over. It took me a while to calm down and ring you and you weren't there!" Her voice went up to the panic level again.

"I'm just back from Adelaide. Look, when was this?"

"I don't know, I didn't know the time. Half an hour ago?"

"What was Brave doing?"

"He was leaving, but I know what he *had* been doing."

"What?"

"Seeing Susan."

I let out a breath and my mind went blank.

"Cliff, Cliff!"

I came back and muttered something into the phone. She almost screamed the thing apart.

"What are you going to do?" Her anger and fear pulled me together. I got some control into my voice, told her I was getting a gun and lots of help and that everything would be all right. She wasn't happy but she rang off after I promised to call her as soon as anything happened.

I got the Colt out of the oilskin cloth I'd wrapped it in and pushed the cloth back behind the bookshelf. I grabbed an old army jacket with deep zipped pockets and headed for the back courtyard. Before I reached the door the phone rang again.

"Sweet suffering Jesus," I shouted into it, "what?"

"Hardy, it's Tickener. I've just seen Brave."

"Shit, not again, where? No, don't tell me, at the hospital."

"Right, how did you know?"

"Never mind, how did you get on to him?"

"I've been following that black girl, you know, Pali?"

"Yeah, and . . .?"

"She came streaking out of her flat, first time she's been there in days. I picked her up in Redfern, spotted the car. Then she drove to the hospital and picked up Brave. I've got them both in sight but they're going to split. He's hiring a car. Who should I stay with?"

"What else have they done?"

"She went to a bank."

"Who's holding the money?"

"He is, she handed it over to him."

"Stay with him, he's going for a fix. I know where she's going. See you." I hung up and belted out to the car. In the rear vision mirror I saw a drawn, yellowish face that looked tired and frightened.

A different black kid was playing ball against the same wall when I pulled into Haines' street. I drove around the back and saw that his car slot was occupied by a white Mini. I parked up near the end of the street beside a set of sandstone steps which led up an embankment and ended with an iron railed landing a good thirty feet up from street level. I got the jacket from the back seat of the car and the Colt from under the dashboard. I put the gun in a pocket, slung the jacket over my shoulder and went up the steps. The landing was overhung with shrubs that had rooted in the thin soil of the embankment. It was after six o'clock and the sun was just starting to sneak down to the high points of the building line. I hung the jacket on the railing, rolled and lit a cigarette and waited.

Half an hour and two cigarettes later, a red Volkswagen turned into the street. It did a circuit of the block the way I had and stopped opposite Haines' house. A girl got out. She was wearing pink slacks and shoes and had a lacey, fringed poncho affair over her shoulders. From where I was crouched I could see that her skin was the colour of polished teak and the inky frizz of her wig stood out a foot from her head. I started down the steps as she went through the front gate. I stumbled on a step and my jacket hit the metal rail with a terrific clang. I swore and crouched down but the sound hadn't carried far enough to alarm Naumeta Pali. I crossed the street and went up the side of the house to the back stairs that led up to Haines' door. I heard the door close above me and climbed the stairs quietly taking two at a time. I heard the sound of voices in the flat and then the ringing click of a telephone being lifted. The girl spoke again but what she said was inaudible. I pressed up close to the wall beside the door and tucked my ear into the doorframe. The receiver banged down and I heard the girl speak in her smoky, French accented voice.

"Come on, Rossy," she purred, "we're going to the mountains."

I took the steps four at a time on the way down.

I was down behind a car parked twenty feet away from the Volkswagen when they came out. Haines was walking a little ahead of the girl with his hands in the front pockets of a windcheater jacket. Pali had her arms under her cloak but from the way it bulged out about waist high it was obvious that she was holding a gun on him.

There were a few people in the street but she ignored them. She walked Haines to the driver's door and said something to him, emphasising the words by moving her hands under the poncho. Haines opened the door and got in, another gesture from the girl and he buckled on the seat belt. She moved around the front of the car with the gun held up chest high and levelled at Haines' head through the windscreen. She'd handled a gun before. She opened the passenger door and got in. She sat slightly swivelled round. I heard the engine kick and saw a puff of smoke from the exhaust. The car started off in a series of kangaroo hops. Haines was nervous and who could blame him? I kept low and under the protection of other cars as much as possible and ducked and swerved my way back to the Falcon. I slung the jacket into the front seat, started the engine and was moving up the alley in time to see the VW making a right turn out of the street into the main road.

The mountains were probably the Blue Mountains which meant that we had a couple of hours driving ahead of us. The route the VW took along the roads in this part of the city seemed to confirm that destination. I had plenty of gas and plenty of gun, I should have felt reasonably confident but I didn't. Pali's phone call from Haines' flat nagged at me like a hangnail. I supposed it was to Brave and it was reasonable to assume that he was coming to the party too. I was covered there to some extent, by Tickener, but I couldn't be sure that the reporter would be able to control the junkie psychologist in a tight spot. Then again, Brave and Pali could have agreed on the meeting beforehand and the phone call could have been to a third party who I didn't have covered at all. I couldn't call for police help unless the VW stopped and even then my story was thin and only Grant Evans could help me. I didn't even know if he was back from his enforced leave.

This potentially dangerous loose end kept worrying and distracting me as I drove so that I almost lost the Volkswagen at a three way junction. I pulled myself together and concentrated on keeping back and varying my lanes and position among the other cars in the traffic stream. Haines was driving better now, quite fast and tight and making good use of the gears. We hit the Katoomba road as the last flickers of daylight died in the trees beside the highway.

The easy time to tail cars is at dusk and later. There's not much possibility of them spotting you or of you losing them if you stay alert, but there is a kind of lulling feeling about it which introduces the chance that you might ram your subject up the back number plate while in a hypnotic trance. I fought this feeling as I trailed up the hills and coasted down the "use low gear" grades. The traffic thinned after Penrith but there was enough of it to provide cover and the winding road and glaring oncoming headlights demanded concentration. We passed through Katoomba after eight o'clock; the real estate agents had closed so half of the town's business was under wraps, only the usual pinball places and take-away-food shops kept the neon going in the streets. The pubs emitted a soft, alluring light through the lead-glass windows which reminded me that I hadn't had a drink in hours and was heading away from sources of it fast.

After Katoomba it got harder. There was a little chopping and changing on the highway as cars peeled off to houses in the hills whence their occupants commuted to Sydney at the risk of their sanity. I'd taken a fix on the peculiarity of the VW's tail light which was a bit brighter on the right side than on the left and I clung to it like a mariner to a beacon. I had my doubts about it twice, once after oncoming lights on high beam dazzled me, and again when a lighter coloured Volkswagen surged up in the right hand lane to pass everything in sight and I started to go with it. A truck coming round a bend lit it up as a grey or light blue job and I slipped back and picked up Haines and Pali who weren't doing anything so fancy.

They pottered uncertainly along in the left lane for a while and I had no choice but to dribble along behind them. Cars sped past us and I was starting to feel conspicuous when the VW's left indicator flashed and the car shot off up a steep road that left the highway at a forty-five degree angle. I looked quickly in the rear vision mirror. There was no one behind me so I didn't touch the indicator arm, I just slammed the Falcon down into second, killed the lights and took the turn praying that the road didn't fork three ways or end in a ditch. The lights ahead bobbed and danced in front of me; the road was rutted and lumpy and the Falcon's springs and shockers took a beating as I ground along in second. At one point the road moved back close to the highway except that we were now above it. Cars scuttled along below like phosphorescent ants beating a path to and from their nest.

We were driving through thickly timbered country, still climbing steeply and following wide, looping bends to left and right. The nearly full moon sailed clear of the clouds and illuminated the classic Blue Mountains landscape — tall, arrow-like gums and sheer-faced ridges that had defeated a score of explorers until Blaxland, Lawson and Wentworth had brought a little imagination to the job. The moonlight gave me a look at the road and allowed me to give the other car a bit more leeway. It also increased the risk of being spotted because moonlight can gleam on chrome like sunlight on a steel mirror. Fortunately, the Falcon's chrome was rusted and dull. Then the Volkswagen disappeared. I hit my brakes and pulled up well back from where I'd last seen the lights. If I'd spotted someone tailing me up there in the mountains I'd kill my lights and engine and coast down a bit waiting for the bastard to come blundering through. I had to assume something like that was happening now, at least until I proved otherwise. I turned off the interior light switch that operates when the door is opened, slipped my arms into the service jacket and eased open the driver's door. I dropped out and rolled under the car. Nothing happened so I worked my way back to the wheels, got my feet under me and scooted across to the other side of the road.

People expect other people to get carefully out of cars on the non-traffic side and keep to that side of the road, sometimes people have to break that rule or they get dead. I hunkered down in the grass and scrub beside the road and peered into the blackness ahead of me. Nothing to be seen, but that didn't mean a thing. I took the pistol out and crept forward with it held stiffly in front of me; still nothing visible and not a sound except my breathing and soft scuffling in the bush where some species were doing their best to exterminate others. Very sensitive stuff, I thought, totally in tune with the environment, Hardy. But a waste of talent. Where I'd seen the last flash of the car's lights was a dirt track running off into the scrub. The grass in the middle had been scythed down between the wheel ruts by the underside of cars and back from the road was a tree with the word HAINES painted vertically down it in white.

My flashlight was at home, corroded to blazes, and the moon had decided to play it coy among the clouds. It was close to pitch black when I started up the track to what was evidently Haines' weekender. Judging by the distance from the road to the shack and trying to remember when I'd last seen a house light, it was a fair sized block. The house wasn't much, a fibro and galvanised iron structure with decking around it on three sides. It looked self-built, but Haines had put his main stamp on the place in the garden. When my eyes got used to the dark I could see terraced vegetable beds and trellises with tendrils twining through them. Almost outside the door, hanging over the decking was a huge clump of bamboo, the leaf tips tall and waving just slightly in the night breeze. Water from the roof, a few chickens and a still out the back and the place would be self-sufficient.

I picked my way carefully through the vegetable beds and staked plants and did a circuit of the shack. It had a door in front, one at the back and a single window in each side. The track from the road came up and looped around the house, the Volkswagen was parked on this path at the back. A brick path from the back door led to a fibro dunny and there was a lean-to shed holding what felt like garden tools. An axe was embedded in a chopping block outside the shed. The wood pile was healthy, a big stack of the kind you use in a stove or sealed heater. I crept up to the decking out from the left side window and tested it with my foot. It was solidly built and didn't creak. I eased the Colt back out of my pocket and moved over the boards to the window which was about chest height from the deck level, too low to stand, too high to kneel. I crouched and inched my head up to get half an eyeball's worth of look-in.

28

The room I saw was the whole of the shack. It had a sink at one end flanked by a refrigerator and a small stove. There was seagrass matting on the floor. The girl was sitting in one of the two Chinese saucer chairs and Haines was sitting on the bed which looked like a pile of mattresses, maybe three, with a tartan blanket over them. I couldn't see a telephone so Pali hadn't set anything up here. The girl was nervous and Haines was frightened, they sat like figures in a painting that couldn't move a muscle until the end of time. Haines' mouth moved but I couldn't catch what he said. The girl got up and moved smoothly across the room like a classy feather-weight. She slammed Haines in the face with the gun and hit him again across the hands when he brought them up to shield his eyes. Haines collapsed on the bed and the girl moved back and half-turned away from him. From where I was I could see Haines fumbling behind the mattresses. There seemed like a good chance he was going for a gun and it was time to move if I wanted anybody left to talk to. I smashed the window in with the Colt barrel and made it to the door in two strides. I kicked it in and was inside the room while Haines and the girl were still interested in the broken glass. Haines had a gun in his hands but it was still tangled in the blanket. He'd never have made it. I pointed the Colt at the bridge of the girl's broad, flaring nose.

"Put the guns down," I said harshly.

Haines gave up the struggle with the blanket but the girl held on to her gun. She held it loosely, pointed nowhere in particular. She looked dazed, out of touch with what was happening, but danger-ous. I raised my gun to send a bullet over her head and pulled the trigger. It stuck like a wrong key in a lock and I remembered the clang my jacket had made when it hit the iron railing. I threw the gun at her but I was way too slow, she ducked slightly and brought her pistol up so that the bullet would hit me in the throat.

A thin, high voice shouted my name. I swayed out of Pali's line of fire and she snapped at the trigger as a man appeared in the doorway. The bullet hit him in the eye and he screamed, blood welling out over his face. His hands scrabbled at the broken door jamb but couldn't get hold, he staggered back over the deck and there was a thrashing, snapping noise as he collapsed into the stand of bamboo. The girl stood still, in shock, with her eyes staring, seeing nothing. I took the gun from her and pushed her down into a chair. Haines had blood dribbling down the side of his face from where Pali had hit him and he didn't look like giving trouble. I heard a rustling outside.

"Tickener?"

"Yeah, you all right Hardy?"

"I'm fine, come in."

He came in cautiously through the shattered door. He was even paler than when I'd first seen him and he was shaking as if he needed a drink, a cigarette and a cup of coffee all at the same time. Me standing there with my hands full of guns didn't help his nerves.

"Couldn't you put them down?" he said.

"I will, just for you." I put the pistols on a ledge above the window. I bent down and retrieved my Colt, I freed the action and put it in my pocket. "Thanks Harry, this one was going to shoot me when you sang out." I pointed at the girl who was sitting stiffly in the chair with her knees drawn up.

"So was Brave," Tickener said, "there's some kind of pistol out on the boards. Shit, you can't move for guns around here."

"Is Brave dead?"

"Very."

"You had no trouble keeping up with him?"

"Not much, he went for a fix like you said, then straight up here."

"It was quite a procession," I said.

"I know a bit about the girl," Tickener said, "who's he?"

"Name's Haines — bomber, gunman, hit and run merchant."

Haines snapped out of it and looked across at me.

"What the hell are you talking about? I'm none of those things."

"What about sending anonymous letters, that more in your line? Harassing women?"

He answered slowly, taking the difference in tone and content of my words seriously. "Yes, I've done those things. I had reasons."

"I know you did. What about blackmail? What about Mark Gutteridge's files?"

He looked away and clamped his lips and jaw as if trying to give himself strength of character.

"Look boy," I said sharply, "you've lost control of this. You must be able to see that. This bitch was going to kill you, or at least she wasn't going to cry if it worked out that way."

Haines looked across at Pali, she was still striving for the foetal position and not making it. Her hands were twisted in the strings of the poncho and she was looking intently at the knots and poking her fingers through the holes. I handed Haines a tissue from a box on the floor which had been heavily trampled in the last few minutes. He dabbed at the cut on his face.

"I've got the files," he said slowly. "I didn't use them much, I got some money and I kept my word."

"Who did you squeeze?" Tickener asked.

"Who're you?" said Haines.

"Keep quiet, Harry," I said. "It's all right, Haines, this is all between us, it doesn't go any further. My job is to protect Ailsa and your mother, that's what I'm interested in. I'm not playing God."

"You know." His head jerked up. "How could you?"

"I put it together. You tell me if I'm right. You were hung up on the idea of your family background, you couldn't accept that you were a pleb. You read all the papers and the magazines, you saw pictures of Mark Gutteridge and saw the resemblance. You found out that Gutteridge had a daughter and that she was in Adelaide when you were born, I don't know how you did that, but you concluded that she was your mother and you decided to destroy the Gutteridges."

"That's pretty close," Haines said softly. "I got a picture of her and showed it around the hospitals. I didn't get a positive identification but a few people were pretty sure."

"You got something out of the orphanage file then?"

He looked surprised. "You know a lot don't you? Yes, I worked out that I was born at a hospital, I cracked that code, the rest was easy. You're wrong when you say I wanted to destroy them though. Not at first, I wanted them to, to . . ."

"Accept you?"

"Yes. I tried, he refused to listen. I found out things about his son. I told him."

"Did you kill him?"

"No, I didn't! He killed himself I think, I don't know. I still don't know why he treated me like that. He beat me up." He lifted his hands to the fine scars on his face and fingered his off-centre nose. "I found him dead. I got the files though."

"I don't like to interrupt," Tickener said nervously, "but I don't understand any of this, and there's a dead man outside."

"That's all right, Harry," I said. "You should stick around and learn something and he's not going anywhere."

"I suppose not." Tickener dropped into a saucer chair and I sat on the bed beside Haines. "Is there anything to drink?" he asked. I looked at Haines who nodded at a cupboard over the sink. Tickener went across, opened it and pulled down a bottle of Cutty Sark. He took four glasses from the draining rack on the sink and poured solid slugs into them. He brought them over, I accepted one, so did Haines and in one smooth, snakey movement Pali knocked the one he held out to her to the floor. Tickener shrugged.

"Your loss, Miss," he said.

I took a pull at the whisky. It was good but it burned my dry throat and didn't help a slight headache that was ticking away inside my skull. It was a bad way to feel when there were some sharp distinctions to be made. I rolled a cigarette and accepted a light from Tickener who lit up one of his stinking tailormades. Haines refused his offer of a cigarette and Pali didn't even acknowledge it. She was starting to take an interest in proceedings again though. I drew a breath and started in again.

"What happened after Mark Gutteridge died?"

"I hid the files." Haines took a sip of the whisky and nearly choked on it. He coughed and snorted into a tissue. Pali gave him a look of contempt and reached out her hand to Tickener.

"Cigarette please."

Her voice startled him but he obliged her fairly smoothly. She leaned back in the chair and crossed her legs, the pink denim stretched tight over her thighs and her breasts lifted under the cloak as she lifted the cigarette to her lips.

"Go on, boy," she said, "this is damn interesting."

Haines made a better job of his next go at the Scotch. "I sat it out for a while. I hid the files, I could see what they were worth. I did some night classes, I got a job at Sleeman's. I formed a relationship with Ailsa. I thought I could bankrupt her without any trouble. I used to watch Susan Gutteridge, I hated her and I wanted her dead. She looked very ill most of the time anyway."

"Yeah, that was Bryn's work, Brave's too maybe. You remember Brave, from Adelaide?"

"No."

"You should. He was the psychologist you spilled the beans to in the orphanage. He's been working the other side of the street."

He got that genuine puzzled look again. "What do you mean?"

"Never mind, go on."

"I got some money from the politicians and lawyers, and a couple of policemen; I bought this place. I kept on at Susan Gutteridge, but I wasn't sure what I wanted to do anymore."

"I was!" Pali's voice was like snakeskin rippling through your fingers, beautiful and repellent.

"Shut up you!" I snapped. "You'll get your turn." I looked at Haines. "Do you see it?" I said. "You told Ian Brave about your suspicions that you were a Gutteridge. You did some work on it and squeezed Mark Gutteridge. Brave also had something else on him that concerns you. He had information from Ailsa as well. Maybe he killed Gutteridge, maybe not, we'll never know. That is, if you're telling the truth and you didn't kill him."

"I didn't," said Haines, "I wanted to but I didn't."

"I believe you, well, anyway, Brave misses out on the files. He doesn't know you're around, you've got a beard and keep a low profile. Ailsa he can't approach because he's lost an old hold he had on her but she doesn't seem to fit the bill. He suspects Susan, so does Bryn and they go to work on her. Brave turns up with this one." I nodded at Pali. "She's got political axes to grind, Ailsa and Susan have business interests in her country and Australia didn't do much about the French atom tests. Right?"

Pali sneered at me and blew smoke at the ceiling.

"OK," I went on, "I put it together this way: Bryn didn't know about you Pali, and you started going it alone, making the heavy phone calls and so on. You fell out with Brave and he fell out with Bryn. Bryn panicked a bit, people Haines was squeezing started putting pressure on him. He called me in. Brave went right off, he killed Bryn's boyfriend. Pali blows the whistle on Brave when she finds out he's into mad sidelines like sheltering escaped crims. We raid Brave and he's out of the picture for a while. Bryn goes on the rampage and finishes up dead. Then Brave gets a real line on Haines and the files and he and Pali get back again for one last fling. That brings us all here folks."

"What was all that stuff about bombing?" asked Tickener.

"Ailsa Sleeman's car got bombed and Susan Gutteridge was run down," I replied. "At first I thought it had to be someone working in with Haines or Brave, now it looks as if it was his bird on her own hook. That right?"

There was no getting under her skin. She turned to look at me, her face was beautifully boned and every fold and curve of her skin added up to the sort of beauty you don't often see. She knew it too and her cool smile infuriated me.

"Listen you savage," I said violently, "you might think you're Angela Davis, but you're just another homicidal mess to me." I ticked off the points with a forefinger across the palm of my hand. "One, I've got a gun with your fingerprints on it, that gun killed a man here tonight; two, your car will have signs on it of your running down Susan Gutteridge; three, I've traced where you got the materials for the bomb. You're gone a million girlie, you're in prison or deported if I tell what I know. You might leave Australia under your own steam if you co-operate now."

It didn't touch her, she was a fanatic. She blew more smoke.

"Since this is all so civilised among you nice white people," she said evenly, "could I have that drink now?"

Tickener picked up the glass and poured a generous dose, at a gesture from me he passed the bottle over and we had a little more all round. The girl tossed the whisky off and held out her glass for more, Tickener poured and she sipped a toothful. She looked at me and her mouth split open in a wide, bitter grin.

"If it does your ego any good Hardy, you're pretty right in what you've said. Australian capital is screwing New Caledonia and those bitches you're protecting are up to their twats in it." She let the grin down into the glass for a second and when she looked up her face was a mask, vaguely triumphant and hard as flint. "Australia doesn't care about the nuclear tests as long as the shit comes down on our dirty black hides and not yours."

"Spare us the rave. You're a killer, you can't criticise anyone."

It was a pathetic response, she knew it and I knew it.

"But you'll let me go Hardy," she said softly. "You're a liberal, soft as butter, you haven't got the guts to do anything else. You probably half agree with me."

"You might be right," I said wearily. "Anyway you're not important. It suits me to have you on a plane to New Caledonia tomorrow and that suits you too. You're on your way."

"Jesus, Hardy!" Tickener was up out of his chair spilling his drink down his shirt. "You can't just turn her loose. She killed a man tonight. I don't have a bloody clue what's going on. Look at her, I'm not sure she should be allowed out on her own, she looks like she'd cut off your feet and eat them."

I laughed. "She'll go like a lamb Harry." I picked the bottle up and poured him another drink. "You've got all you need, you can break the Brave story once and for all, final chapter, in about two hours. I'll phone the cops and your story only needs a few touches to it."

"Yeah, like who killed Brave?"

"That's easy, we don't know. I'll phone in that he's dead, I won't identify myself, the cops will think it's a spin-off from the Costello thing. That's easily fixed. You get an anonymous tip. It's simple."

Tickener scratched his chin. "That puts you and me in very

deep. Three people know what really happened. You're clean, why not let it all come out the way it really was?"

"I'm protecting my client." I said. "This way no one gets hurt, no injustice is perpetrated. Do you really think most situations like this get properly aired and resolved down to the last detail? Come on, Harry."

"I guess not. OK, have it your way. What about them?" He pointed to Haines and the girl.

"She's leaving the country tomorrow."

All eyes swung to Haines. He was finishing his drink, his face was white and his big body looked light and fragile. I was reminded of Cavendish's description of him as passive, given to violent outbursts. There didn't seem to be an outburst left in him.

"What about him?" said Tickener.

I looked at Haines again and something clicked in my mind and I felt sorrier for him than I've ever felt for anyone in my life, except myself.

"No worries there," I said softly, "I've just worked the last little piece into place. He'll do whatever I say because I can tell him what he's needed to know all his life."

Haines looked up at me with complete understanding. He'd lived for twenty-odd years for just the moment that was coming and nothing was ever going to be the same for him after it had passed. It was going to be a kind of death.

29

I washed up the glasses and put the liquor away, then I went around retrieving things like used tissues and cigarette ends. I got Haines to drive the VW around the track a few times and had Tickener bring up my car, his, and the hire car Brave had arrived in. We drove them round and by the time we'd finished the track was criss-crossed with tyre marks and skids that no one could make any sense of. I wiped the hire car, a Valiant, clean and left it parked half-way up the track from the road. Pali and Haines did most of the watching, Tickener and I did most of the work. When we'd finished we all congregated, by chance, around the body of Dr Ian Brave. He lay on his back, fully stretched out, with broken bamboo stems jutting up all around him and pushing through his clothes. He was inelegant and lumpy in death, he looked like an old, collapsed scarecrow. One eye looked sightlessly up to the clouds, the other was a dark horror; one half of his face was a smooth, chalky white, the other was crumpled and stained dark — it was a map of heaven and hell. Pali looked down at him and I thought I saw a nerve jump in her ebony mask.

"How did you fall in with him?" I asked gently. She responded to the tone of the question by making a keening movement of her head. She ran her right palm down the inside of her left forearm.

"Drugs," she said.

I nodded and turned away. I didn't touch Brave and cautioned the others to keep well clear. I left the gun where it was. A few footprints wouldn't matter. The cops would figure it the easiest way for them, but there was no point in leaving clues about which might set them doubting. Haines was off in some private world of his own. He sat on the edge of the deck picking at his fingers and only came to life when Tickener suggested firing the shack.

"Why would you want to do that?" he asked nervously.

"To confuse things, cover the tracks a bit more," Tickener said.

"You're ruthless," Haines said shaking his head, "ruthless."

I laughed. "Don't listen to him, Ross," I said, "he'd just like to have a fire to spice up his story a bit."

Tickener grinned and lit a cigarette. "It's not a bad idea," he said. "And speaking of stories, how do I write it just from an anonymous tip-off? Where's the journalistic thoroughness of investigation, not to mention integrity?"

"Where it usually is," I said. "Listen Harry, you're learning fast but you've got a long way to go. You listen to the police radio, they'll send a car, the car will call for an ambulance, you'll get some details that way, not many. Your story is that this confirmed the tip-off, you took the plunge — journalistic flair and derring-do."

"It sounds shaky," he said doubtfully.

"It'll do," I said, "happens all the time. By the way, how's Joe Barrett these days?"

"Not so good," he said happily.

I went back into the shack for a last look around. I collected the guns and took a minute to examine Haines little .32.

"Have you got a licence for this?" I asked him.

"Yes."

"How come?"

"Company executives who sometimes carry large sums of money can get pistol licences."

I tossed it to him and he caught it. "You shouldn't have it up here though," I said, "better shift it. It might get some cop's mind working, miracles do happen."

He put the gun in the pocket of his windcheater, he was as docile as an old, pampered dog.

"OK Ross," I said, "you've been a good boy so far, let's see if you can keep it up. Where are the files?"

He hesitated for just a second, he looked at Tickener who had on his bloodhound face and Pali who was immobile, uninterested. He raised his eyes to mine and if I looked as old and empty and comfortless as I felt it must have been like the last gaze into the mirror before you cut your throat.

"I'll show you." His voice was a hoarse, thin whisper. He went across to the food storing and cooking end of the room and knelt down. He peeled up the sea-grass and prised up three lengths of floorboard with his fingernails. It was a hiding place that an experienced man would have located within five minutes, but Ross was one of life's amateurs and nothing I'd seen of him so far suggested that he'd ever become a pro. He reached into the gap and pulled out a medium sized executive brief case. It was black with lots of shiny metal trim.

"Let's have it," I said. "And put the boards and mat back."

I snapped open the lid, it wasn't even locked, and took a quick look at the contents. The case was full of letters, bank statements and sheets of paper with what looked like bank note serial numbers written on them. Some of the material was in original, some in photostat. There were half a dozen cassette tapes and an envelope full of photographs. I rifled through the stuff. It was a complete blackmailer's kit with applications for development permits neatly stapled to notes about sums of money and times and places of delivery. There were different versions of subdivision plans with names of surveyors and others entered on the back along with information about money paid. There were several newspaper extracts from court proceedings with the names of police witnesses underlined and code numbers entered in the margins; typed lists of the names of municipal councillors had similar entries alongside as many names as not. The numbers bore some relation to digits written on the faces of the cassettes. Handled right it was a meal ticket for life and the only thing that surprised me was the relatively small bulk of it. Mark Gutteridge had been in business a long time and if this was his game he should have collected more dope than was here.

"Is this all?" I asked Haines.

"Yes, I gave the people I contacted the material that affected them. There must originally have been about this much again."

"How much money did you raise?"

"About twenty-five thousand dollars."

I groaned and sat down on the bed. "You must have driven them crazy," I said, "you said you marked some of the cops?"

"Yes, three, the really bad ones, they . . . ."

"Spare me. You hit them for a thousand or so?"

"That's right, roughly."

"A fortnight's takings, a month when things are slack. No wonder there was flurry from on high, they wouldn't understand it. You were dead safe in a way. No copies?"

"No."

"Of course not, wouldn't be fair would it?"

"No."

"You're an idiot." I snapped the case shut and got to my feet.

"Hey can I have a look?" said Tickener.

I fended him off. "Harry this is too hot to handle, I can't let you have it."

"What are you going to do with it?" There was pain in his voice and I remembered that he'd saved my life.

"Tell you what I'll do mate, I'll look through it, get out a crumb that won't be traceable necessarily to this little box of goodies and give it to you. You can use it one quiet Wednesday when nothing's happening."

"What about the rest of it?"

"Burn it and let the bastards sweat."

We went out to the cars. I got in the Falcon and motioned for Pali to sit alongside me. She did it, like a sleepwalker. Haines drove the VW. I locked the briefcase into a compartment under the driver's seat. Tickener followed us along the track in his ancient Holden and we bumped down the road back to the highway. We drove to Katoomba like beads on a string with a set gap between us. I signalled a stop and went into a telephone booth for four minutes. It wasn't a NIDA performance but it was good enough to set the wheels in motion. I walked back to Tickener's car to check a few details of the story with him. We shook hands and agreed to meet soon for a drink. He pulled the Holden out and set off for his typewriter and coffee. It was midnight. We drove back to Sydney; Haines and the girl changed places at Central Railway and she drove off without a word.

I drove to Glebe, took Haines into the house and made some coffee. We talked around it a bit and confusion was the keystone of his attitude. He was a bit in love with Ailsa but too screwed up to know it. Any mention of his mother was like drawing a toenail. He was like a man with every layer of skin off except the last, tender to the touch at a hundred points, bleeding here and there where his obsession obtruded and teetering on a terrible abyss of pain. What I had to tell him pushed him over the edge and he fell, screaming silently inside his lonely, alien shell.

After that we sat quietly for a while drinking the last of the coffee. I called a taxi and he went back to what he had to call home.

30

I crawled out of bed around 10 am. It was one of those bright, cool summer mornings that Sydney specialises in. I made coffee, got the paper in and read it out in the courtyard. Tickener had made the front page again with his account of the discovery of Brave's body. There were no pictures. Haines was mentioned as the owner of the property and I spared him a thought for the yarn he'd have to spin to the police, but we'd worked out an alibi — a phone conversation with his employer which I'd have to confirm with Ailsa today — in case he needed one. My guess was that he wouldn't. The cops had no reason to disbelieve that Haines' place had been picked at random for the revenge killing of Brave and no reason to connect Brave to Haines beyond the Gutteridge connection. I didn't think they'd be very interested in probing that.

I went inside and phoned Ailsa. She sounded well and I told her I'd be in that afternoon.

"Is it over Cliff?" she said.

"It's over."

"Is it all right?"

"It's all right for you."

"And Susan?"

"It'll never be all right for her. I'll tell you all about it this afternoon love, be patient."

"Not my strong suit as they say in the books."

I asked her if the police had approached her and she said they hadn't. I asked her to confirm Haines' alibi and she said she would, but she never had to. I rang off and went back to the paper and another cup of coffee.

Tickener shared the front page with the latest cricket win. That seemed to call for a modest salutation. I hauled the wine and soda and ice out of the fridge, made a bacon sandwich and set myself up out in the yard. The biscuit factory was just tingeing the air with butterscotch.

I got the briefcase out of the car. I scrabbled about for some kindling and paper and stuffed it into the barbecue I'd built out of bricks pinched from here and there at dead of night. I poured a glass of wine and opened the case. After thumbing through the papers for a while I selected and set aside a newspaper clipping, a typed sheet and a photostat of a land title deed. The remainder of the papers I fed into the fire. I put the cassettes across the top of the grill and watched them melt like chocolate. The smell in the air was of plastic, laminated paper and corruption. I drank some wine, ate the sandwich and watched the thin, dark smoke from the fire threaten the unsullied purity of Soames' whitewashed wall. The Gutteridge files were a heap of fine ashes interspersed with blobs of molten plastic when the fire died down. I pushed them about to make sure of the completeness of the destruction and slung the briefcase back into the car.

After a shave and a shower I went out and drew another hundred dollars with the credit card. I drove over to Paddington and rambled through the shops, eventually coming out with a djellaba in blue and white vertical stripes with a hood and drawstrings at the cuffs. I had lunch in a pub and drove over to the hospital.

Ailsa was sitting in a chair beside the bed. She was wearing a long, off-white calico nightgown cut square around the neck. I went up and kissed her on the mouth and then in each of the hollows of her shoulder bones. She smelled of roses.

"You look good, you smell good, you feel good."

She put her arms up around my neck.

"More," she said.

"You're the queen of the world."

I gave her the parcel, she unwrapped it and smoothed the robe out on the bed. She immediately began fiddling with the drawstrings.

She looked up at me. "It's lovely," she said. "Now tell me about it."

I gave her all the details, it took a long time and she listened quietly, tracing patterns in the raised nap of the robe on the bed.

"What was the black girl's motive?" she asked when I finished.

"Partly political. She's some kind of nationalist, anti-British, anti-French, anti-Australian. Anti just about every bloody thing. You have interests in Noumea?"

She nodded.

"So has Susan I suspect. Your people must be stepping on toes over there, maybe it's a genuine grievance, I don't know. Anyway, she was here for a little private terrorism. But Brave got hold of her, something to do with drugs. Brave was an addict. Did you know that?"

"No. I'll have to look into that."

"The Noumea operation?"

"Yes." She drew a deep breath and expelled it slowly. "Well, Mark started it all I suppose by keeping the files. There are a lot of casualties. What about the survivors? What did you mean about Susan never being right again?"

"That connects back to Ross," I said.

"Obviously, what about him?"

I got up off the bed and moved around the room. I picked up one of her books and smiled at the dog ears at fifty page intervals.

"Don't start pacing again Cliff or I'll bloody kill you. No, I just won't pay you. Just tell me about it."

I sat down again. "I was on the wrong track about him for a long time. I thought he was obsessed by his mother, he wasn't. I was misled by the photographs he had. He was hung up about his father. Natural I suppose."

"Yes, yes," she said impatiently, "well, do you know who his father is?"

"Was. Yes, I worked it out eventually."

"How? Who?"

"How first. It was the only thing that fitted. Mark Gutteridge sent Susan away to Adelaide to have her child. OK, he wanted to spare her and everyone else the teenage pregnancy trauma. Fair enough. But a tremendous change in the nervous pattern of the Gutteridges dates from then. It manifests itself in different ways and they never get over it. That's the first point. Secondly, Mark

Gutteridge wasn't a conventional man. He shouldn't have been horrified when his illegitimate grandson turned up with proof of his identity. He'd be more likely to be intrigued, inclined to do something for the boy, like a Renaissance prince, right?"

"Yes, I think so."

"But he doesn't. He flips. He can't handle it and that sets Ross off."

"All right, that's a lot of how. Now, *who* was Ross' father?"

"Bryn," I said.

I sat on the bed and Ailsa rested her head against my thigh and we watched the day dying slowly outside the open window. An ascending jet littered the sky with dirty brown smoke, its boom drowned out something Ailsa murmured and I stroked her hair in reply. Maybe she was thinking about Mark Gutteridge, maybe about the children she'd never have. I was thinking about raw, haunted people who twanged the nerves of everyone they touched — like Bryn, like Haines, like Cyn. They couldn't sloop along in the shallows where the water was warm and the breeze soft, they had to jut up into spray and icy winds with their secrets for sails and the rocks dead ahead.

THE MARVELLOUS BOY

1

The house had an unhurried, gracious air; the grounds were big, a couple of acres, and the three storeys rose up white and serene to a grey slate roof. But the lawn was scruffy and neglected, the garden beds needed weeding and from where I stood on the porch I could see daylight up through holes in the section of guttering above my head. When the house was built the view down to Rushcutters Bay would have been uninterrupted — the green would have flowed down to white shimmering sand with a deep blue beyond that. Now there was a lot of rooftop and highway and bad air between the house and the water.

I stood in front of the doorbell, a no-nonsense black button on a brass plate, feeling ambivalent. I should have felt out of place, a private detective with one phone, one car and no secretary, but the house's down-at-heel character comforted me. Great edifices, like people, could fall on hard times. I hoped Lady Catherine Chatterton's times weren't too hard. I work for money, not for the privilege of dropping the names of my clients.

I rang the bell and straightened my clothes — leather jacket, good but old, clean shirt, clean denim pants, no tie. The door opened soundlessly and a dark-haired woman with a bold, beaky-nosed face stood there looking at me as if I were a rag-and-bone man.

'Yes?' Welcomes weren't her big talent.

'My name's Hardy. Lady Catherine telephoned.'

She stepped forward as if she was going to smell me. 'Ah, the detective.' Her thin lips and small white teeth were contemptuous. 'Yes, she told me to expect you. Usually I do her telephoning.' She made a challenge of it and I decided that a smile might be in order.

'Well, maybe you were busy.'

She sneered at that but stepped back and opened the door just enough for me to go past her. I smelled dust and the temperature dropped suddenly; the hot November morning was somewhere else and so were the bustling, vulgar 1980s. I'd stepped into a reception lobby with parquet flooring and panelled walls. The usual sounds of a modern house — refrigerator hum, air conditioning, talk-back radio — had never penetrated here. There were paintings on the walls, portraits I thought, but my eyes were slow to adjust to the gloom after the bright day. I had an impression of moustaches.

The woman pointed ahead of her with an imperious gesture like a general directing troops.

'This way.'

I followed, trying to keep my feet clear of the legs of carved tables and ornately upholstered chairs. We went down a wide passage and then swung off into a narrower one, dropped down a short flight of stairs and entered a drawing room that reminded me of my school's meeting hall. It was high-ceilinged with oak panelling reaching halfway up walls which were hung about with more paintings — dark, gloomy jobs that evoked memories of those school honour boards on which my name never appeared. A woman was sitting on a straight-backed chair in the middle of the room. A similar chair was placed a few feet in front of her; the woman and the chairs had all the warmth and charm of an executioner with his axe and block. Her arms were stick thin inside tight black velvet sleeves. She raised one dismissively.

'You may go Verna.'

I watched how she took it; she'd been devouring the old woman with her eyes, burning her up and now she cut off the contact with an effort. Her dark hair was pulled back in a tight bun and her thin lips were like a strap keeping the pale, clear flesh on the lower part of her face tight. She was about thirty, handsome in an only-one-of-her-kind-in-captivity way. She looked as if she had a very good opinion of herself and a low one of nearly everyone else. She left the room.

The old woman waved me into the chair in front of her.

'That is Miss Reid,' she said. 'My companion. A tiresome person in many ways but invaluable. You will be dealing with her in future.'

'If I take the job.'

She raised an eyebrow. The gesture caused hundreds of tiny wrinkles to spring into life all over her face. Her skin was old-leaf yellow. She had a thin nose and mouth and all the life in her face was around the eyes. They were dark and still large although flesh had fallen in around them. They looked disconcertingly young in that ancient face.

'I am of course Lady Catherine Chatterton.'

'Of course.'

'Don't be flippant, Mr Hardy. The world is not a flippant place and neither is the situation I am about to confront you with.'

She sounded as if she had thought it all out so I let her have her say. Something about her voice, firm with the stamp of the right breeding and the right schools on it, struck a note in my memory. I'd been in court five or six years before when her late husband had handed down one of his savage judgements. It hadn't worried me, I'd been on the winning side, but the manner and tone of voice of Justice Sir Clive Chatterton had stuck. Making allowance for the sex difference, this was the same stuff — measured, arrogant, utterly self-assured. I couldn't have been flippant to save my life.

'I want you to find my grandson.'

'The police have a missing persons department,' I said. 'They're experts.' You have to tell them that. It's like reading them their constitutional rights. They never listen. What she said in reply sounded like 'Psshaw' and might have been.

'He's been missing for many years. The police would not have the resources or the flexibility the matter needs. Besides, I have been told that you are . . ' she hunted for the word, 'discreet.'

That was nice. Not brave, not clever. Discreet.

'Who told you that?'

She waved the question and everything to do with my professional standing aside.

'I forget. It doesn't matter.'

It did to me, a little. I'm not domineering but I don't like having feet wiped on my face. Besides, it's a bad working relationship. Mutual respect, that's the thing to shoot for. I broke for cover.

'I charge seventy-five dollars a day and expenses. I don't touch political work and I don't beat people up unless they try to beat on me.'

241

Her mouth slid down into a sour arc. 'Ridiculous. That could run into thousands.'

I felt more relaxed, a chink in the armour. 'It seldom does,' I said soothingly. 'Most matters are resolved one way or the other fairly quickly. I reduce the rates for the exceptions, when it's a sort of long-term watching brief.'

I'd made a concession. She looked happier. 'You're in an unsavoury trade, Mr Hardy.'

'It's a living, like any other.'

'No, that's where you're wrong. There are differences. The only honourable money is the sort of money that built and sustained this house.' She looked around the walls. 'Money from the land, money from the professions.'

I shrugged. She was a bit boring. Then it struck me that she burbled on like this because she was lonely, didn't get enough people to talk to. Another chink.

'Tell me about your grandson, Lady Catherine.' I took out a pad and pen. 'What's his name?'

'I don't know.'

That wasn't boring. I tapped the pen on the pad and waited for her to go on. She enjoyed the effect of the statement. I began to warm to her, a little.

'It's a long story, would you care for some tea?'

I wouldn't but said I would and thanked her. I sensed that she'd rehearsed this scene in her mind and that it was important to her that it be played just right. I hate tea, but if tea was part of it I'd go along.

'Good, some should be arriving presently.' She glanced at a tiny gold watch and nodded confirmation; her eyesight was remarkable.

'I must tell you things, Mr Hardy, which ordinarily I wouldn't tell a soul, not even a close member of the family — if such a person existed.'

I nodded and tried to look discreet, my strong point.

'My husband and I had only one child, that was a sadness.' She raised a hand to her pale, dry hair as if saluting the days of her fertility, or infertility. 'Our daughter, Bettina, was born in 1931, she was married very young, at seventeen years of age. The marriage did not last long, a few years only. Bettina's husband was a barrister, a very promising man at

242

the time but he turned out to be weak, a drunkard. He was some years older than Bettina.

'How much older?'

'Oh, twenty years.'

'I see.'

I didn't really. Seventeen-year-old girls don't usually go for men in their late thirties. They tend to regard us as doddering. Some do of course, but I thought I could smell 'arrangement' in this one and her next remark increased the suspicion.

'My husband took steps to terminate the marriage.'

'Divorce?'

'An annulment.'

'Why did your daughter marry so young?'

She shot me a sharp look. 'Not for the reason you may be entertaining. Bettina was . . . well, wild and flighty. She showed an interest in Henry and he seemed steady. We thought marriage might settle her down. She was our only child, we had to protect her.'

'From what?'

'From herself.'

It saddened me. 'From her youth' she might as well have said. I turned a page of the pad.

'Tell me about Henry, the husband. What's his other name?'

'Brain, Henry Brain . . . ah, here's the tea.'

2

Verna Reid wheeled a glass and stainless steel trolley about two feet into the room. Silver pots and jugs gleamed, bone china tinkled. She poured milk and tea, added sugar and brought the cup across.

'I'm going out,' she said.

'You will not!' The old woman strained at the chair's arm rests trying to lift herself. 'Not with that man. I forbid it!'

Verna Reid laughed. She thrust the tea out. Lady Catherine took it and tea slopped into the saucer. Two spots of high colour burned suddenly in her parchment pale cheeks. She slammed the cup down, tea sprayed and bits of thin china skidded across the floor. The dark woman laughed again.

'Get on with your silly chat,' she said and walked out of the room.

The old woman fought for control. She blinked and plucked at her scrawny neck. I got up and pulled the trolley across, poured her more tea and handed it to her.

'Thank you.' She took the tea then reached out and took a buttered scone. Her hand was rock steady. 'I'm hard to work for,' she said. 'You'll find that out.'

'I still haven't said I'll work for you.'

'We won't fence, Mr Hardy,' she said around her scone. She did it without any offensive noise. Breeding. 'I'll pay your seventy-five dollars a day and my accountant will look over your expenses. If they are not too ridiculous they'll be met.'

It had been a lean six months with more going out than coming in. The Falcon's clutch needed overhauling and the stack of bills at home was reaching half way up the spike. I needed every cent of the seventy-five a day and she could see it.

'I'll need a retainer of two hundred and fifty dollars,' I said.

Her tea cup rang against the saucer and she let out a short, high laugh. 'All right, Mr Hardy, all right. The last word is yours, you'll get a cheque when you leave. Now perhaps I can get on with what I have to tell you. Have some tea.'

I shook my head.

'Bettina had a long illness after the marriage ended, she travelled abroad with my husband and myself on one occasion and with a friend on another. I believe her to be unstable, she was a disappointment to us.'

'Does she live in Sydney? Do you see her?'

'Yes to your first question, no to your second. We had a falling-out. I dislike her second husband and her children. Always have. The rift between us has grown.' She looked at a point above and behind my head. 'My husband was a great man, Mr Hardy, a great man. He had the greatest legal mind in this country in this century, but no son, no way to build a legal firm of distinction. I am editing his memoirs, they'll show the world his quality.'

She was talking to herself and there was nothing for me to say. Still I felt there was a connection between all this and the information she had to give me. I was sure of one thing — she blamed herself for not giving the great man a son. The memoirs would be a belated child.

'I share Sir Clive's tragedy, the absence of an heir.'

'I thought you said your daughter had children.'

'They are not suitable,' she flared. 'I have disinherited them. Bettina, too, although she doesn't know it. I am pinning all my hopes on you, Mr Hardy. You see, I have learned of a grandson.'

I struggled not to leer. The armour was cracking like sandy cement.

'Sir Clive had an illegitimate child?'

'Certainly not!' she spat. 'He was the most moral of men, the most scrupulous. No, Henry Brain and Bettina had a son, he must be thirty now.'

'How did you discover this?'

'Henry Brain told me. He wanted money from my husband. He came here. I hadn't seen him for a great many years and I scarcely recognised him. He was a wreck, a ruin from drink. He looked as old as . . .' She stopped herself. 'How he got to the house and inside I don't know. He forced his way in here, almost knocked Verna down. He broke in on me, here.' She waved her hand around indignantly.

245

'What did he say exactly?'

'He raved. He was frightfully drunk. My husband was away in Canberra. When I refused to give him money Henry became abusive. He taunted me by telling me about my grandson whom I've never known.'

'What did he say?'

'He said he wouldn't be surprised if the boy . . . man was on the way to being just like him, a piece of rubbish. It was a terrible thing to say.'

'I mean, what details did he give you of the birth?'

'None, or almost none. He said the child was born during the first year of marriage, that Bettina went away to have it and returned without it. He said Bettina blackmailed him into concealing everything about the child. She hated him and wouldn't bring up his child.'

'Do you remember her being away for long enough at the time?'

She put her hand up to her forehead, a tracery of fine, blue veins was visible through the tight white skin.

'I've tried, I can't remember. They travelled a good deal.'

'How would she have blackmailed him?'

'Henry Brain had a full complement of the human weaknesses, Mr Hardy, it could have been almost anything.'

'You say he was drunk and raving, why did you believe him?'

'I can judge character. Truth has a different quality from falsehood. Henry was telling the truth, I'm sure of it.'

She wanted to believe it. It could have been true, but the story had a wild insubstantiality like the memory of a dream. Even thirty years ago it was hard to evade registering the birth of a child. Not as hard as now but hard enough. I asked her what her daughter had to say about it and got the answer I anticipated.

'She denied it, denied it utterly. I pressed her hard but she said that Henry was a worthless liar and that we should never . . . that she should never have had anything to do with him. She was lying.'

'This was when you and your daughter fell out?'

'Yes.'

'When was it?'

'Two years ago.'

'Two years!'

'Sir Clive was not well at the time,' she said quickly. 'I didn't want to alarm him by taking any steps then. He died a year ago, as you will know.'

'I read about it. Why wait until now to do something about this? Have you been in touch with Brain again?' I added, hoping.

'No, he never troubled us again. He was too addled to follow a fixed purpose. I suppose he just took it into his diseased brain to batten on to us and gave up when the approach failed. I've had time to mull this over, Mr Hardy. My daughter is like a stranger to me. I'm sure I'm doing the right thing. I want that man found and restored to his rightful place in the world.'

'What if Brain was right . . . what if he's . . . unsuitable?'

'I pray that it won't be so. He may be a man of distinction in his own right. It will take delicate handling, Mr Hardy.' The idea of her scheme succeeding took hold of her and shone in her eyes. 'I'll pay you anything you like, a hundred dollars a day. Just find my grandson.'

'That won't be necessary. A hundred a day would warp my style. Seventy-five is fine. It's an intriguing case and I'll take it but you have to be aware of the problems.'

She sat back, tired by her outburst and regretting the slip of control.

'And they are?'

'Basically three. One, Brain may have been lying and there is no grandson, never was. Two, there may have been a child and it could have died. Three, if there was a child it may be impossible to trace. Thirty years is a long time and the trail this end is cold by two years. Brain is the obvious starting point and if he was as far gone as you say, he could be dead by now.'

'I accept those hurdles. I have faith that they can be overcome.'

She was used to getting her own way and I could only hope that her luck would hold. Her luck would be my luck. If the thing fizzled, two weeks on those rates would be a thousand plus change. Handy. Besides, I fancied working for the aristocracy, it'd give me something to put in my memoirs. That train of thought led me back to the judge and his daughter.

'I'll need a number of details, Lady Catherine. Your daughter's name and address, information on everybody in this house.'

She was displeased. She grunted. Suddenly I wanted the case and the thousand, bad. I went on quickly. 'I'll need as many descriptions of Brain as I can gather, others may recall different details. By the way, does anyone other than you know about his claim to have had a son?'

'No one.'

'Not Miss Reid?'

'Certainly not, I sent her away when I recognised Henry.'

'Who else could have seen him then?'

'I really couldn't say. I have no staff now apart from Verna.'

She sounded like Bob Menzies lamenting the Empire.

'Sir Clive had . . . expensive tastes and there is not a great deal of money left. But there are possibilities. The right man could revive our fortunes.'

It was sounding thinner, more fantastic. I felt less sure about my expenses but you have to give of your best.

'Did you have any staff then — when Brain was here?'

She tilted her head back as if it took a physical effort to recall details of menials. 'There may have been a chauffeur then. Yes, I think there was.'

'Would you have some sort of record on him?'

'Verna would. She should be back soon.'

She said it as if she hoped so; I wondered about their relationship. I also wondered about the Judge's tastes. I asked for a description of Henry Brain.

He was a tall, thin man she said, but stooped over. His hair was grey and sparse and he was almost toothless. She said that the only sign that he had once been a gentleman was his hands — they were clean and well kept. His clothes sounded like cast-offs.

'Did he tell you what he'd been doing in the past twenty-odd years?'

She paused. 'I think he said he'd travelled. I don't recall

distinctly. It was easy to see what he'd been doing — drinking. My guess is that he'd been in and out of jail.'

'That could be important. Any evidence?'

She shook her old head, no. But it hadn't stopped her saying it. Her husband had sent enough men inside in his time, perhaps she had an instinct about it.

'He didn't tell you where he lived?'

She shook her head.

'No. But I believe you should look for him on skid row.'

Her hands flew up to her mouth too late to stop the incongruous words. They were totally out of place for a woman so careful in her speech, so mindful to avoid the lurid. They suggested that she could be a closet television watcher and that raised another problem for me — this whole thing could be a bloody fantasy. The moment was awkward and then we were both startled by the sound of a voice screaming. 'No!' and the sound of a door crashing closed. Lady C brushed a scone crumb from her dress.

'Verna,' she said wearily. 'Fraught as usual. Go and see her and get what you need, Mr Hardy. It will give me a respite.'

I got up, said something vague about reporting to her and went out.

The passage outside the room had a big window with a view of the drive up to the house. I took a look and saw a blue car shooting down the gravel; it skidded around a bend in the drive and took off through the gates as if someone was out there with a chequered flag.

3

I found Miss Reid two turns down the passageway. She was leaning against the wall breathing heavily. Her fists were clenched and a few wisps of hair had escaped from her bun. I told her what I wanted, got a short nod and she set off down the passageway which ended at a heavy oak door. I caught up with her and stood close while she unlocked the door. Years of training and field research paid off — her breath smelled of gin.

The room was small with a desk, a straight chair, an easy chair and a couple of filing cabinets. Without speaking she took a cheque book from a drawer in the desk and a pen from a set precisely lined up with the desk blotter. She wrote out a cheque and handed it to me.

'Thanks. Do you sign all her cheques, Miss Reid?'

'Yes,' she snapped. 'For the household and the estate.'

I folded the cheque and put it in my pocket, it restored my confidence; she didn't look like the sort of woman who wrote rubber cheques.

'Good bit of that is there? Estate I mean.'

She bit on the end of the pen and then pulled it away, almost spitting the words out. 'I sized you up in one look. You're going to trade on this poor old fool's weakness and bleed her for whatever you can.' She threw down the pen. 'You make me sick.'

'I didn't see too much weakness.'

'You wouldn't, you're too stupid. She's batty.' She got up, opened the biggest filing cabinet and riffled through until she came upon a single sheet of paper. 'Get out your notebook, detective,' she said.

I did and wrote what she read out to me — 'Albert Logan, 31 View Street, Leichhardt.' She put the paper back and slammed the drawer home. She stood with her back to the cabinet, tight and hostile, still breathing hard and wafting a little gin across to me. She was like no paid companion I'd ever seen; that sort of job dries people out. Being paid for their responses and emotions erodes their personalities, turns them into husks. She was well and truly living and breathing. Her clothes were severe on her lean frame but they suited her. She obviously knew things, had opinions, but there was no way to make her an ally.

I dropped into the easy chair and took out tobacco and papers. She started to protest but I gave her a hard look and she subsided. She sat down behind the desk, scornful again, and watched me get a cigarette going, flip the dead match into a waste paper basket and dirty the air.

'It'd all be easier with your co-operation,' I said.

She gave a short laugh. 'Why should I make it easier for you to snoop on me?'

I was genuinely surprised and nearly choked on the smoke. 'You? I'm not investigating you.'

'What then?'

'I can't tell you,' I said weakly.

She stirred in her chair. 'You're a cheap liar. Snoop away, I've got nothing to hide.'

'Why do you stay here?'

'So that's it,' she snarled. 'You're going to harass me. It won't work. I'm staying until I get what's due to me.' She was short-fused and fierce burning.

'And what's that?' I asked quietly.

'Money. What else? Bonuses and money promised. That old bugger . . .' Her mouth clamped down and she drew in breath as if to recall the words. She glared at me. I put the cigarette out carefully in a glass ashtray.

'I want you to tell me all you can about the man who called here about two years ago, the one who looked like a tramp.'

It was her turn to look surprised. 'Why?'

'Just tell me.'

She thought about it, calculating the odds like a street fighter. 'I remember him,' she said slowly. 'Dreadful smell.'

'Was he violent?'

'A bit. Not too much. He was too drunk to be a danger to anyone except himself.'

'What happened? Did he just walk in? What about this chauffeur — he didn't try to stop him?'

'I assume he was bribed. He was a miserable dishonest wretch. That's why I sacked him.'

'Over this incident?'

'Not specifically. There were a lot of things. Expenses connected with the car, using it himself. He was a cheap crook.' She looked me directly in the eye when she said it so we were back to square one. I grunted.

'Back to this derelict. Can you describe him?'

She did, in terms very similar to the old woman's, but their descriptions didn't sound collusive. Brain had struck these two very different women in much the same way which probably meant that I had a pretty good picture of him.

Miss Reid's dislike of me was bubbling up again; she was anxious to remove my cigarette butt and ashes, all traces of me. I asked for and got the daughter's address, a request which made her look thoughtful again but not friendly. I told her I wanted to look around the grounds and she showed me out through a side door. She didn't say goodbye. A thought niggled at me as I was leaving the house and I trapped it as I walked across a patch of dried-out lawn. If Lady C. had disinherited the daughter and her brood, who was in line for the estate as of now? It was something to check.

The sun had climbed while I'd been in the house and sweat jumped out on my body as I moved. I peeled off my jacket and slung it over my shoulder. The land behind the house was taken up by a tennis court, a swimming pool, plenty of lawn and a two car garage. The garage was empty except for oil stains and some rusted tools; the swimming pool was empty except for leaves, dirt and greenish slime. I looked back at the house and the full force of its elegant shabbiness hit me. There were broken tiles on the roof and discoloured bricks showing through peeling paint. The place looked as if it was waiting for a renovator or a demolition crew. I walked across to the tennis court, recalling my athletic youth and hoping for comfort but the tapes marking the lines were buckled and broken and wind and water had removed a lot of the surface from the court.

I trudged down past the house to my car; its dull paintwork and air of neglect fitted the scene but depressed me. I had a week's money in my pocket and an interesting case on hand and I should have felt better as I turned the car on the gravel and drove off towards the highway.

4

It was midday, too early to go search out bums on skid row. They stand out better at night when the moonlight is shining on the port bottles and their throats are dry and a dollar will buy you everything they know. It was time to deal with the daylight people. I did a mental check on how much money I owed Cy Sackville my lawyer, decided it was a flea bite to him and put through a call.

We exchanged pleasantries and I told him I was on a case which should net me a few bucks. He congratulated me.

'I need some information, Cy.'

'The meter is ticking.'

'Don't be like that. You scratch my back and I scratch yours.'

'When do I get scratched?'

'Sometime. Have you ever heard of a man named Henry Brain, promising barrister in the forties, went on the skids?'

'The forties! Are you kidding, who's still alive from the forties?'

Cy was and is a boy wonder. He refused a chair of law at age twenty-five — no challenge. He despises everyone over thirty-five. It used to be everyone over thirty.

'Could you ask around? There must be some old buffer who'd remember him. He married Judge Chatterton's daughter.'

'It so happens I'm going to a professional dinner tonight. There could be some octogenarian around who'd remember him.'

'Thanks. Do you know who handles the late Judge's estate, legal affairs and so on?'

'Yeah, we've transacted — Booth and Booth. What's your interest?'

'The widow is my client, confidential enquiry.'

He coughed. 'Of course.'

'Thing is, I'd like to know who she's going to leave the loot to. Any chance of finding out?'

'That's a tall order, confidential matter, very, very . . .'

'Quite,' I said, 'but . . .?'

'Possible. Young Booth'll be at the dinner. He might get pissed and we could discuss the earthly rewards of judges. I'll try.'

I thanked him, asked him to find out all he could about the Chattertons and said I'd call again soon.

'Cross all cheques,' he said.

I headed north to have a chat with Bettina. She went by the name of Selby, now having married one Richard Selby, company director. I stopped in the dry belt, where restaurants are many and pubs are few, and bought beer and sandwiches for lunch. It was hot in the car so I wound all the windows down and sat there eating, drinking and thinking.

A full frontal attack on Mrs Selby was out of the question. *'Mrs Selby, did you have a child in 1948? And if so where is it?'* She'd throw me out or call the cops. I didn't expect to get the unassailable truth which she alone knew but she'd be worth a look. If she turned out to be a sober, steady woman of straight eye and piercing honesty I'd have to drop the odds on finding baby. If, on the other hand . . . I screwed up the wrapping and took it and the beer cans to the bin. They're hell on litterers in this part of the world.

The Selbys lived in one of the northern arcadias that developed over the last fifteen years. None of the houses would have sold for under a hundred and twenty thousand dollars but it was remarkable what different things that sort of money could get you. The place was a map of the building fads of the sixties and seventies — quintuple-fronted brick veneers, long ranch houses with flat roofs; grey brick and tinted glass creations hung off steep slopes like downhill skiers ready to let go. There were Spanish arches and Asian pagodas, even a tasteful townhouse or two among native trees.

Chez Selby was one of the worst — a monstrosity in liver-coloured brick with a purplish tiled roof. The whole thing reminded me of a slab of old meat. It was up to scratch in the neighbourhood though, with a half acre of lawn and shrubs. From the street I could see the glint of a pool out back. I pulled up outside another heavy mortgage down the street. I looked at my clothes and decided that I was a journalist. She'd never believe I was from Booth and Booth.

The street was quiet the way such streets are in the early afternoon; the kids are at school, the old man's at work, the wife is playing golf or gardening. The butt of a Honda Accord stuck out of one of the two car ports — Mrs S wasn't on the links. I had my jacket on and I was hot. Up the path past the shrubs to the front door. It was a heavy number with a security screen. The bell was in the navel of a foot-high plaster bas-relief mermaid attached to the bricks. Chinese opera gongs sounded inside the house.

She wasn't the golfing or gardening type, more the bar and bed type. She opened the door, dropped a hip and eyed me off. She was a tall, heavy woman, a redhead with fine dark eyes courtesy of her mother. There the resemblance ended; Bettina Brain Selby nee Chatterton was a chip off the old block. Her colour was high and her shoulders were broad. She carried her bulk as the Judge had done, as if heavy people were still in style.

I looked at her for just a fraction too long. 'Mrs Selby?'

'Yes.' The voice was furry with liquor, sleep, sex? Maybe all three. She might have a lover there. Awkward.

I gave her a grin. 'I'm Peter Kennedy, I'm a journalist doing a feature piece on your late father, Sir Clive Chatterton?' I let my voice go up enquiringly the way the smart young people seem to do these days. I'd shaved close that morning, my shirt was clean, I might make it. She swivelled her hips and made a space in the doorway.

'Come on in, Peter.'

I went past her into a hall with deep shag pile carpet in off-white and oyster walls. It felt like stepping into a bowl of yoghurt. Mrs Selby slid along a wall and opened a door and we went into a big room full of large leather structures to sit in and polished black surfaces to put things on. She picked up a glass and rattled the ice cubes.

'Drink?'

'Not now thanks, perhaps after a few questions?'

She looked bored, sat down and waved me into a chair.

' 'Kay. Up to you.' She sighed and a lot of big bosom under cream silk went up and down and some bacardi fumes drifted gently across towards me.

'You should ask my mother about all this shit,' she slurred. 'She's the one who keeps the shrine, not me.'

'That could be an interesting angle. Was Sir Clive a harsh parent? He had a reputation for severity on the bench.'

'I can believe it.' She sipped. 'Christ yes, he was tough on me. Course, I'm the same with my kids so I can't talk. He used his belt on me plenty of times. Can't print any of this, you know.'

'Why?'

'Can't afford to offend the old girl. She's got the money. We never seem to have enough.'

'What's your husband's business, Mrs Selby?'

'Bettina. He makes weight lifting stuff, gym equipment, all that. He does all right but we eat it up. School's bloody expensive and holidays . . . Christ, I live for those holidays. Ever been to Singapore, Peter?'

I said I had.

'Smart man. Great isn't it? We have a ball.'

'It's marvellous,' I said primly. 'You were saying something about not offending your mother?' I had the pen and pad out again.

'Ah, was I? Well we don't get along. She knows I'd belt that bloody mausoleum down and sell the land for units. But there's the kids to consider. I try to keep on the good side of her but there's that Reid bitch, she's got her eye on the land. Christ, what a miserable place to grow up in. Look, I'm rambling, you don't want to hear any of this crap you can't use. Have a drink.'

'All right, yes.'

'Bacardi okay?'

'Fine.'

Her own glass was lowish, not what you'd call empty but getting that way. Lots of drinkers don't like to see their glasses one-third full, it looks like two-thirds empty. She was in that league and keen enough to haul all that weight to its feet and take it out to where the booze lived. She drifted out, moving like someone who knows how to move; it was part theatrical, part sheer confidence. It made her hard to assess — like a car that looks and goes all right but is a bit too old and exotic for comfort.

She came back with her own glass full and nice big one for me. The rum had been introduced to some tonic but not too closely. On top of my lunch it made the beginnings of a formidably alcoholic afternoon. I took a pull and she knocked back a good slug. I took out tobacco and cocked my head enquiringly. She pushed an ashtray in the shape of a temple at me — a touch of Singapore.

'One vice I don't have,' she giggled. 'I knew a writer once who rolled his own. He lived in Balmain. You live in Balmain?'

'No, Glebe.'

She rolled her glass between her palms. I was sweating despite the air conditioning and started to ease out of my jacket.

'You don't mind?'

'Hell no, it's hot, take if off, take off your pants.'

I grinned. 'Business,' I said firmly, 'business.'

She lay back in her chair. 'You're going to be dull,' she said petulantly. 'You didn't look dull. Everyone's dull except me.' She downed half of her drink to prove it. I didn't want her to turn nasty so I put some away too.

'We haven't talked at all yet,' I said. 'Back to the judge . . .'

'No, not yet — bottoms up. Next drink we'll really talk. C'mon drink up.'

She tipped her head back and drank the stuff like lemonade. I finished mine in two swallows and she picked up the glasses and ambled off again. I tried to remember why I was there as the liquor rose in my blood and started to fuddle me. I got up — keep moving, that's the rule, sit and you're gone — and slid open the doors dividing the drinking room from the next. It turned out to be the eating room; there was a big teak table with six pricey-looking chairs around it and a bowl of flowers in the middle. A couple of nasty prints hung on the pastel walls and a framed photograph stood on a sideboard. I weaved across and picked it up. It showed the lady I was drinking with, a man and two children. Bettina looked a few years younger and a few pounds lighter. I studied the man; he was a heavy character with a round face and receding hair which he wore longish with thick dark sideburns. He was packed into an executive suit with the trimmings and had his arm around Bettina and the girls. But he was smiling as if the camera was on him alone. With him the photographer had failed to achieve the family feel. He was the type to make every post a personal winner. The girls looked to be about ten and twelve, they were round and red like their dad — their mother was right, they'd need the money.

She wandered in and handed me the glass. Her own was full but if she was the drinker I thought she was she'd have sneaked one out by the ice cubes. She stood beside me, close.

'That's us,' she said.

'Nice family.' I put the picture down.

She stayed where she was and I was pinned in a corner. In her high-heeled sandals she wasn't much shorter than me. She tossed back her hair and put her hand on my arm.

'You know Richard and I have an arrangement when we go to Singapore. Want to know what it is?'

'Sure.'

I sipped rum and looked at her eyes. The lids were drooping and the pupils were dilated. She was well on the way to her afternoon nap. She had just one thing in mind now and there was no point in pretending to be a journalist or a gentleman. I took hold of her arm to steady her. It was a nice, firm arm. She leaned into me.

'We give each other two free nights, no questions asked. Understand?'

'I think so.'

'I'm a passionate woman.' She pressed her breasts against me and set her glass down to have both hands free.

'I can see that,' I said. 'No wonder you enjoy your holiday. When's it due?'

She stopped trying to undo my shirt. She grabbed the drink to help her ponder the question.

'Must be soon,' she said slowly. She drank some more and spilled a little down the front of her dress. She wiped at it and the contact with her own body seemed to excite her. I edged back a bit.

She came after me. 'What's the matter? Don't you want me?'

I didn't. I've got nothing against women older than me. I'd

258

just finished a relationship with a woman almost as old as Bettina and it had been good, for a while. But this lady was skidding and disintegrating and I didn't want to be part of the wreck. As well as that, I'd have to see her again as the enquiry developed and a boozy bedding now was no way to start. I tried to deter her by passivity but she came on reaching for my head. I noticed that she had long fingernails, almost colourless. She was in close with her hand on the back of my neck when I heard a noise, like something falling to the floor.

The man in the photograph was in the room, a briefcase was on the floor and he was moving towards me with his fists clenched as I pulled free of his wife. She clung and he got one punch in, a hard swing which I took on the shoulder moving away. He was taller and wider than he looked in the picture, but musclebound. He was slow and I ducked his next swing and slammed him in the ribs. A one-punch fighter who didn't seem to know what to do after that, he lowered his head and blundered forward and I clipped him hard on the ear and let him fall over my foot. He went down heavily and lost his wind. He started to get up and I put my foot on his chest and thumped him down. I was lucky he wasn't a Famechon. I was in no condition to handle anything fancy.

Bettina had stood stock still, breathing heavily. I'd kept a side eye on her in case she decided to take part but she seemed frozen. Selby levered himself up from the floor, I guessed that the flab on him was old weight-lifting muscle. He'd still be dangerous if he could use the weight. I tensed myself but he swung around and belted Bettina across the face. She doubled over and just made it to a chair. She sat and started to giggle. Selby jabbed a finger at me.

'Get out,' he gasped, 'before I call the police.'

I collected my jacket and tobacco and moved towards the door. He rubbed at his ear; I picked up his briefcase and flicked it at him, hard. It took him in the chest and he staggered back. Cheap stuff.

Bettina giggled again and let her head drop; the hair hung across her face like a curtain of blood.

5

It hadn't been my proudest hour. Mrs Selby hadn't passed the sobriety and steadiness test but she wasn't a complete ruin. There was a strength about her, eroded by the booze and other things, but still present. She might be capable of obliterating a child from her life, then again that act might have something to do with the drinking. But Richard looked like the candidate for that role — a hell of a good timer when he was up and a real bastard when he was down. Bettina had no time for mum and dad, that was clear — appeals to uncover the lost grandson would cut no ice with her for the best of reasons. Weighing it all up, as much as the aggressive traffic would let me, I concluded that I hadn't learned a damn thing, hadn't earned a cent of the money in my pocket. The way to start earning it was to find Henry Brain.

The traffic was heavy all the way back to the city and beyond. I picked up Bridge Road and slogged down through Glebe to Leichhardt which has some nice places and some not-so-nice. Logan's address was somewhere in between, veering towards the non-nice. It was a big three-storey terrace with a deep, overgrown garden in front. The place was divided into flatettes and a roughly painted notice on the gate told me that Logan was upstairs front in flat three. The walls had been painted within the last five years, the floor had been cleaned within the last month and the stair carpet was anchored on most steps. I went up; the bright day died on the first landing and a boarding house gloom took over.

I knocked at a plywood door with 3 painted on it. Paint had dribbled down six inches from the tail of the figure. Someone inside swore softly; bedsprings creaked, paper rustled and a drawer opened and closed. I waited. Bare feet squeaked on the floor inside. I had ten dollars in my hand and held it in front of his face when he opened the door. He grinned and grabbed. I whisked it away.

'Albert Logan?'

'That's me, mate. You can leave the money.'

'I might if I hear what I want to hear.'

'I'll try to oblige.' He held the door open and I went in. It wasn't much. Fifteen dollars a week tops. Albie must have been saving his tips. There was the usual mahogany veneer furniture and anonymous lino. There was an old, lumpy looking department store bed with a pair of fifty dollar shoes peeking coyly out. The mirror on the dresser was streaked, the doors leading to the balcony had grimy glass panels — Albie wasn't spending anything on front. He sank back onto the bed and pulled cigarettes towards him.

'Smoke?' he held out the packet.

I shook my head and sniffed the air. Albie watched me like a fire spotter watching a pine forest. The sweet smell of marijuana hung on the air like a promise. Albie lit up and blew smoke around ostentatiously.

'If you're on a bust you're wasting your time.'

'Why?'

'Protection,' he blew a shaky smoke ring. 'I've got protection. You check around, Slim, you'll find out.'

I sat in a tired armchair. 'I'm not on a bust. You can cut heroin with ground-down toenail for all I care. I want some information.'

'Tough guy,' he sneered.

'Don't push me,' I said. 'I've had a hard day in the suburbs. I might throw you off the balcony just to hear the glass break.'

It wasn't much to say and didn't look so hard to do. He was more like a jockey than a driver or a steward, not more than five two and the ball of muscle he'd once been was getting a coating of fat. Still, he could be right for those trades; drivers and stewards work in confined spaces and extra inches get in the way. His hair was thinning across a pink scalp and dark stubble was bristling on his pale cheeks — a night person who slept while the sun shone. I smoothed out the ten dollars.

'You used to work for the Chattertons, driving.'

'Right, no sweat there Slim. I left that job clean as a whistle.'

'Who said you didn't? Put your guilty conscience away, it craps me. Do you remember a tramp coming to see the old lady, a few years back?'

He drew the cigarette down to the filter and squashed it out in a saucer. 'I remember him. What a wreck! You could have bottled his breath.'

'What did he say to you?'

'Not much. He wanted to see the lady.'

'Why'd you give him a hearing?'

He scratched his jaw, remembering. 'Well, it was like this. I was surprised to see a tramp up there. But that's not all. He got out of a cab and I saw him flash some money. He told the cabbie to wait.'

'Did the cab wait?'

'You bet it did. He had a roll like this.' He made a circle of his thumbs and forefingers. 'Well, I'm stretching it a bit but he had some dough, I can tell you.'

'What sort of cab was it?'

'City.'

'You're very sure.'

'Look, it was very unusual, I can see it like yesterday.'

'Did you see the driver?'

'I did, yeah.'

'Remember him like yesterday?'

'When do we start talking money? I think I can help if you're trying to find that guy. That's it isn't it?'

'That's it. What've you got?'

'Five'll get you a whiff of it.'

I pulled out my wallet, peeled off five dollars and gave it to him.

'Thanks.' He put it under the pillow. 'You asked the wrong question Slim.'

'What question?'

'Him. You shoulda said her.'

'Who?'

'The cabbie was a her — blonde, that's all I saw.'

'Good, go on!'

'Well, like I said, he had money, new tens, I got one . . .'

'So I heard, and . . .?'

He'd shot his bolt. He groped around for something to say. 'Ah, let's see, he talked pretty good — educated, you know? But the grog had got to his voice.' He did a fair imitation of a meths drinker's croak on the last words.

I was depressed by what I was doing and hearing. The room depressed me. I wanted to be eating and drinking somewhere light and airy with someone young and optimistic. It made me impatient that I didn't know anyone like that.

'You'll be tap-dancing in a minute,' I snarled. 'Cut out the shit. Did he say anything important? Give you any idea where he lived?'

'No. He lived out mate. Face was buggered, you know the way they get. There was something though . . .'

'His hands?'

'His hands! Right! Most derros, shit you wouldn't let them put their hands down your dunny, but his hands were white and smooth like.'

I handed over the floating ten. 'Do you remember Miss Reid, the companion?'

'Do I what. Hatchet-faced old bitch.'

I wouldn't have called her old or particularly hatchet-faced, but he was talking character, not physiognomy.

'You didn't get on with her?'

'Who could?' He lit a cigarette, needing something to counter the angry memories. 'The judge couldn't stand her and I was with him all the way.'

'What was wrong with her?'

'High and mighty. Humble as shit when the old lady was around and Queen shit when she wasn't.'

He was scrambling his images and running low on vocabulary but the sentiment sounded genuine. 'All servants hate servants', who said that? I couldn't remember. Maybe that was all there was to it but it was worth another question.

'Did Miss Reid have a boyfriend when you were there?'

His answer was a derisive snort and a shake of his head. Then he looked down at his belly and the room and recognised that he wasn't doing so well in the sexual stakes himself. The realisation sobered him.

'She's got one now,' I said.

'That right? Must be a mug.'

Our exchanges were getting aimless but I had a feeling that he was holding something back. The talking and drinking and driving had unravelled me and I couldn't think how to probe for it. I got out a card and put it on the bed.

'That's me,' I said, getting up. 'If you think of anything useful get in touch. There could be some money in it.'

He put the card and the ten where he'd put the five.

'You mean about shit face Reid, Slim?'

'Don't call me that. About her or anything. You've got something more to say about her?'

'I might. Give us another five.'

I moved over to the bed, grabbed the neck of his shirt, twisted and pulled. The cloth cut into his fat neck.

'You know Albie, I don't really like pushers, not really. I don't think I've had good value from you. What will your protection do about a jelly nose?'

He squirmed and tried to pull free. I twisted harder.

'Okay, okay,' he rasped. 'I'll tell you. Let go.'

I dropped him onto the bed, the saucer jumped and spilled ashes and butts across the blanket.

'Shit! I drove Miss Reid to the Botanical Gardens once.'

'Albie, you didn't. What tree did you do it under?'

'Don't joke about it, I'd rather go without. She met a bloke there. I got pissed off waiting and went to take a look. I saw her sitting on a bench talking to a bloke.'

'Describe him.'

'That's hard, I wasn't close.'

'Young or old?'

'Middling. All I remember is he had sideburns,' he sketched in facial hair, 'like Elvis Presley.'

'Maybe that's who it was. How long did they talk?'

'Maybe half an hour.'

'How was she afterwards?'

'Same as always, fuckin' frozen.'

'Funny you don't like her Albie. I got the feeling she thought you were a bit of all right.'

He looked up at me and dug the card out.

'Private detective,' he said.

I nodded.

'Smartarse.'

'Don't push your luck. I could fix it so's you'd be cleaning out the carriages.'

I went out leaving the door open. It slammed when I was halfway down the stairs.

6

It was nearly five o'clock, Friday. I drove to my bank in Glebe, paid in the Chatterton cheque and drew out half of it — my grandfather was a Scot. Then I thought that it could be a busy weekend coming up and a shortage of cash would be inconvenient. I drew another hundred and to hell with my grandfather, what did he ever do for me? I might even have some fun, he'd have hated that.

I bought groceries and wine and went home. The house was quiet as usual, lonely as usual. My ex-wife Cyn had never been there and my ex-woman Ailsa very seldom. It was just a place for sleeping, eating, drinking and thinking. I put on some music, B. B. King, got out my pen and pad and tried to arrange what I'd learned, see what directions it suggested. Nothing came, too early. All I had were male and female signs on bits of paper with names and some bits with signs but no names — like the woman who delivered the baby, if there was a baby. And a bit with a male sign on it and a question mark. I gave up on it, grilled some meat and tossed some salad. The beer and bacardi were old memories and I poured some riesling down on top of them.

After the meal I used the telephone. All organisations present confidential fronts — especially about their personnel — which can be cracked if you know how. It took me three calls to breach the defences of the City Cab Co. Hilda Bourke was the only woman who'd been driving for the Company two years back and she was still with them, on the road just then. I persuaded the base to get her to call at my place by promising to pay for her time — a taxi ride to nowhere.

While I was waiting I got my .38 and ammunition out of their oilcloth wrapping and mated them. I put on a shoulder holster and tucked the gun away. A car horn sounded softly outside. I turned off the lights and went out to the cab. The driver was a stocky woman in her forties; blonde hair gleamed in the car's interior light under her head scarf. She had a strong, tired face devoid of make-up.

'Hilda Bourke?' I opened the front passenger door.

'That's right. Mr Hardy?' Her voice was pure Sydney, a slightly nasal drawl.

I got in. 'I want to ask you a few questions about a fare you handled. I'll pay you. I cleared it with your base.'

'Stuff them, it's a change. I might not remember anyway.'

'You should, it was out of the ordinary — a tramp you took up to a big place in Rushcutters Bay.'

'Jesus, you're going back a bit.'

'Yes, but you do recall it?'

'Mm, pretty well. I waited for him and he gave me a tip — five bucks I think. He was pretty drunk.' She said it apologetically, as if it was against the ethics of the job to take big tips from drunks. 'Poor bugger,' she went on, 'I've thought about him since. I wonder what he wanted up there?'

'I know what he wanted,' I said. 'What I'm interested in is where he came from.'

'That's easy. I took him back to where I picked him up, the Noble Briton pub.'

'At the Cross.'

'Right, little fare and a big tip like I said.'

'He hailed you from the street?'

'No I think there was a call from the pub. He looked pretty rough but had the street right. Sorry, I can't recall it.'

'That's okay. Did he behave himself in the car?'

She shot me a look but she had no vanity. 'Yeah, no chucking or burning smokes. He was a gentleman really, spoke well.'

'He went into the pub when you dropped him?'

'Like a shot.'

I gave her ten dollars.

'Thanks, I hope that old codger's not in trouble.'

'Why d'you say that?'

'You look like trouble to me, Mr Hardy. Hey, can I take you to the pub? You've paid.'

I shook my head, thanked her and got out. She u-turned and drove off. I coaxed the Falcon into life and drove off sedately towards the Cross.

They've gutted it of course, the Cross, stripped away nearly everything that made it a unique place. But coming up from the empty city and the quiet park, the Cross still had some glamour. It still reminded you that not everybody lived tidy and safe. There were still bodies for sale, gambling games older than civilisation, men-women and women-men, phoneys and genuine seekers after truth.

The Noble Briton is a survivor; it's just out of range of the developer's knife and looks defiant. A few tiles had peeled off the front, exposing the grey pitted cement beneath, but the 1930s beer advertisements were intact.

The public bar was like a thousand others. There were a few stools around the bar, a clear space near the wall-mounted TV set and some benches around the tiled walls. Two pool tables were tucked in near a dartboard. I ordered a beer from a thin, pale barmaid with an enormous, teased-up blonde hairdo. I sipped and looked the few early starting customers over. None looked like Henry Brain.

The barmaid teetered up and down behind the bar like a colt in a stall. She had on a see-through blouse, skin-tight black jeans and enormous heels. With the fairy-floss hair she must have topped six feet. I watched her with interest and she caught me watching.

'You want something else, mister?' Her voice was like a noise from a sheet-metal shop. I spun two fifty cent pieces on the bar.

'Have a drink.'

'Ta.' She grabbed one of the coins in mid-spin and dropped it into a glass by the till. I spun the other coin and she plucked that up and dropped it into the Help the Blind tin. Charm having failed I fell back on professionalism. I showed her my licence to investigate.

'I'm looking for a man. I understand he drinks here, or did.'

Her pencil-line eyebrows shot up. 'Ooh, it's like a movie, isn't it?'

'Not really,' I said. 'This is just a legal matter, nothing exciting. But I'm on expenses . . .'

'What's that mean?' She flapped her hand impatiently at a customer at the far end of the bar who was holding up his glass.

'Serve the man,' I said, 'I'll tell you when you get back.'

I put the licence away and drank. The barmaid came back and leaned over me like a crane.

'You was saying?'

'I'm going to describe a man to you. See if it fits anyone you know.'

She nodded, dead keen. The hair flopped dangerously forward and I could see light through the top six inches. I put together the descriptions I'd been given and delineated Henry Brain. She let me finish, then bared her small, even teeth in a triumphant smile.

'Got him, that's Perry.'

'Perry?'

'Perry Mason, you know, the lawyer on TV? That's what he's called in here. He reckons he was a lawyer once and he can do the talk — gentlemen of the jury and all that. Course, the only way he'd get in court now would be to get thirty days. Yeah, Perry Mason, you remember.'

I did, on black and white television, played by Raymond Burr who bought an island in Fiji that I coveted. There was irony in it. Here, where there was a dream in every glass, Henry Brain was given high rank.

'That's the man,' I said. 'He *was* a lawyer. Will he be in tonight?'

'I reckon. I've been here five years and he's never missed except when he's sick. He'll be in around eight.'

I separated ten dollars from the thin roll and pushed it towards her. She made a pushing-back motion.

'Keep it. Give it to Perry. He needs it more than me.'

'I'll have another beer then. You like him — Perry?'

She pulled the middy. 'He's okay. Doesn't get stroppy and goes when it's time. He's okay.'

I sat over the beer and smoked a couple of cigarettes. It was just after eight when Brain came in. It was a warm evening but he was wearing the derelict's overcoat. With some of them it's their cupboards, their shelter, their address. The pub was half-full, with darts and one pool game going. Brain cranked himself up onto a stool and thrust an arm into his overcoat pocket. It disappeared to above the elbow. I went around and stood behind him.

'Good evening Mr Brain. Can I buy you a drink?'

He lurched around and almost fell off the stool. I steadied him. The cloth of the coat was greasy with years of dirt, the arm felt like a broomstick wrapped in rags. I held him until he was firm on the seat.

'Thank you sir, you are a gentleman.' His voice was a ruin, a desecration of what had been a fine instrument. I ordered two double scotches from the barmaid. Brain raised a finger to her skinny back.

'No ice, Eunice.' He got his tongue around the words with difficulty.

'Right Perry.'

Brain winced. 'My nom de bar,' he croaked. I smiled and we examined each other. I saw a gaunt wraith dressed in other people's clothes. There was a feeling of incompleteness about him set up by the thinning hair and missing teeth. The hair had gone in patches giving him a piebald look and a few yellow stumps of teeth still sat stubbornly in his mouth. His faded eyes were watery and there were deep wrinkled pouches like walnuts hanging under them. The skin of his face was leathery and it wrinkled and sagged its way down his slack jaw and grizzled neck into the top of a dirty, collarless shirt.

What he saw didn't seem to interest him and he fidgeted waiting for the liquor. His hands shook violently and attracted my attention. They were long and thin with blue veins showing through translucent skin. Unlike the rest of him they were scrupulously clean; the nails were trimmed and pink as though a scrub with a hard brush was part of his regular toilet. Otherwise he was battling to stay out of the gutter. A struggle was going on. There were signs of attempts at parting the sparse hair and his heavy, broken shoes had been rubbed up to a dull shine. But he was losing the fight, day by day.

Eunice put the drinks on the bar and I paid her. Brain lifted his glass to the light and smacked his lips.

'Neat quality whisky,' he rasped. 'It's the only way to drink. Cheers.' He put half down in one swallow and carefully cupped his hands around the rest.

'I didn't catch your name dear boy.'

'I didn't give it. It's Hardy, Cliff Hardy.'

'Why are you hastening me towards the grave, pray?'

He sipped, still not looking at me. He must have known this day was coming. He'd held out a juicy bait to top people. Maybe he didn't care or perhaps his brain was so eaten out by alcohol that he'd forgotten. Two years is a lot of booze in his league. I spoke quietly and carefully, striving for some intimacy in the noisy bar.

'I want some information you were once prepared to sell, Mr Brain. I might be buying or I might be just asking.'

He looked at me shrewdly as if judging how much drink I'd be good for; nothing else mattered to him, his whole being seemed focused in on the glass in his shaking hands.

'You talk in riddles dear boy.' He took a sip. 'I can't claim to be a busy man, the desk is not littered with briefs, but please come to the point.'

'You were married to Sir Clive Chatterton's daughter Bettina,' I said close to his grimy ear. 'The marriage broke up, childless. Sir Clive's widow claims you called on her two years ago. You spoke of a grandson and requested money . . . I don't hear an objection.'

'Ah.' The sound came out slow and easy, oiled by the whisky. 'So that old piece of carrion has sent you on an errand. You are an operative.'

The old-fashioned word touched me somehow, off-set the impatience I was beginning to feel. I showed the licence.

'I don't want to cause you trouble, Mr Brain, but Lady Catherine has developed an obsession about the child. I mean to find him, if he's real.'

'He may be dead,' Brain said quietly and tossed off his drink. The words were my first firm evidence that the story was true. They had a quality, a substance, that convinced me.

'I want to know, one way or the other.'

'Is the noble lady prepared to be generous?'

'To you? No, I shouldn't think so. She's not a generous or forgiving woman. For the man the sky's the limit.'

He didn't seem interested; he was concerned with his own sentiments and prospects. If the child was dead it wouldn't touch him, nor did the old lady's need. His own life was a tatter and to small rents in other people's lives he was indifferent. Mending them didn't signify.

'Could you make the next an Irish whisky,' Brain was

saying to me. 'I haven't drunk Irish whisky in eons.'

The bar was nearly full. A few people were showing some interest in Brain and me, unwelcome interest.

'I'll buy a bottle of Irish if you like,' I said quickly, 'and we can continue our discussion somewhere else.'

He looked around the bar as if he was seeing it for the first time. Desire for the whisky shone in his reddened, bleary eyes like a beacon through fog.

'I am tempted by your offer, intrigued you might say. I promise nothing however.' He looked squarely at me for practically the first time. 'I don't suppose you could stretch your funds to the extent of two bottles of Australian whisky?'

I signalled to Eunice. She tripped over and took orders while looking down on the old man.

'Is he treating you right Perry?'

'Like a prince, dear Eunice. It's been a long time since a handsome young man paid attention to me.'

'Now, now, none of that. What'll it be?'

'Get me two bottles of Irish whisky,' I said. 'Jameson's.'

She finished pulling the beers and dispensed them, then she leaned close to me. 'I know youse can get them anyway,' she said gratingly, 'but will you do something for me?'

I was impatient: 'What?'

'Buy him some food too, I'll give you a cut on the whisky.'

'All right, all right, I will. Just get the whisky will you?'

She stalked off and came back with the bottles in brown paper. I paid and helped Brain off his stool. He never took his eyes off the bag and followed me like a dog. There was a fast food place a few doors from the pub and I bought him a pie and some roast potatoes. His skin was grey under the neon and he used his beautiful, white hands to shield his ruined face from the light. He eyed the food with distaste.

'Muck, dear boy. You can't expect me to eat that.'

'You'll eat it,' I said grimly. 'We've got talking to do and I don't want you passing out on me.'

'I thought it was altruism,' he muttered.

'No, pragmatism if you like.'

He looked sharply at me. 'Are you intending to be pragmatic here?'

The mild night air was gritty with exhaust fumes and dust.

The Cross was just getting into stride. The footpath was rippling with people, some buyers, some lookers.

'No, we can talk in my car or my office. Both are close by.' Something, some shred of dignity still clinging to him, made me go on: 'Or at your place if you like.'

'It so happens that I have a room, a modest place you understand, but my own. We might be more comfortable there. We will need glasses,' he pointed at the bag. 'Whisky like that needs glasses.'

'Okay, where is it?'

'In Darlinghurst, not far. We could take your car, I haven't ridden in a car for some time.' He scratched at the brown paper. 'Perhaps . . . perhaps a small promise of things to come?'

'No, the car's this way.'

He trudged along beside me with his hands in the pockets of the too-large coat, holding its skirts in to him. The sound of his brogues scuffling the pavement depressed me. The thought of his room depressed me. I was riding a small wave of hope that he could point me to the heir to the Chatterton millions, but it was only a small wave. I was looking forward to the Jameson's, too.

7

He ate the food as we drove. For all his protests he wolfed it and I heard him masticate and swallow every morsel. We were in Palmer Street when he spoke through a mouthful of potato.

'Here, dear boy, just here.'

I pulled up outside a tumble-down terrace. We got out of the car and I locked it. Brain watched me.

'Very wise,' he said drily. 'There's no respect for property around here.'

The gate was missing and a makeshift plywood panel in the front door was flapping loose. The entrance hall stank of cooking and neglect. Brain started up the stairs then stopped and turned. He leaned over me like a gallows.

'Don't let the bottles clink,' he whispered, 'or we'll have every denizen of this low house knocking on the door.'

I took a tighter grip on the bag and followed him. We went up two flights and down a passage to the back of the house. He dug into the coat and produced a key with a safety pin attached. He moved to put it in the lock, then drew back.

'Open,' he said. 'Odd, I could swear I locked it.' He said something in Latin. 'Ovid,' he informed me.

'Open the door,' I said.

He flicked on the light. 'My God!'

The room was a mess; it couldn't have been much to start with but now it was uninhabitable. The mattress on the old iron bed had been ripped apart; bits of stuffing were all over the room and tufts still floated in the air like grey snowflakes showing that the damage was recent. A few hundred books were part of the ruin. They were ripped and torn and strewn over the floor, bed, wash basin and chest of drawers. The drawers were gaping open; a couple had been smashed to matchwood. A wooden box about a foot square and six inches deep was lying upside down on the floor. Brain bent painfully and picked it up; the lock had been broken and the top hung crazily from a fragile hinge. Brain swore and poked around in the mess. He came up with a roll of moth-eaten paper.

'My degree,' he said.

I took a quick look at it. Henry Winston Brain had graduated with honours in Law in 1934 from the University of Sydney. Brain put the document carefully on the bed and began picking up books. He shook his head.

'Ruined,' he muttered, 'ruined . . .'

I looked at some at random. There were legal works but also novels, poetry, drama. A nice old dictionary with a thumb index had been savagely dismembered. The search hadn't been expert but looked ruthless and furious enough to have turned up anything hidden in the obvious places.

'What were they after?'

Brain placed a long, thin finger beside his nose. 'As you said, Mr Hardy, we have talking to do.' He groped among the rubbish by the wash basin. 'The glasses!' He held up two streaked and stained glasses and examined them against the dim light. 'One is cracked,' he observed. 'I shall drink from that, it's only fitting that I should.'

I hauled up one of the bottles, opened it and poured.

'Aren't you going to clean up a bit?'

He accepted the whisky. 'Many thanks. No, I shall move.'

That might have meant the searchers had what they came for or it might not. Perhaps what they wanted was in his head and he could see that they wouldn't ask gently. I picked up the nearest book while I thought about it — an omnibus edition of Conan Doyle bought in the Charing Cross Road. Brain's initials and surname were written inside in flowing purple ink — better days.

Brain raised his glass. 'You bring me ill-luck Mr Hardy, only this compensates.'

'Does anything else matter to you?'

'Not much, not any more.'

'Well it does to me. Your story about the child matters. Is it connected with this, do you think?' I gestured at the mess.

'Bound to be, dear boy. Nothing like this has happened to me for a quarter of a century. I've drunk in peace.'

'You've done a good job of it. Why?'

He finished his drink and held out the glass. 'I lost my

calling, my vocation. I lost everything when I married that slip of a girl.'

'She's no slip now.'

A sound came from him that could have been a laugh. 'Nor was she then. Such strength, such will.' He drank. 'You've seen her recently?'

'Today.'

'How was the dear girl?'

'Drunk.'

He smiled. 'As drunk as me?'

'Not quite, different style, but headed the same way.'

'God help the child.'

The remark struck the same confirming note as before. I leaned forward.

'You're sure there was a child Mr Brain?'

'I'm sure. I have proof.'

I picked up my glass and drank. He watched me hawkishly. Expressions were hard to interpret on that desiccated face but this looked like triumph. There was some cunning in it too, maybe.

'Are you sure you still have it?'

'I'm sure Mr Hardy.'

'What is it, the proof?'

He placed the finger along the nose again. 'Ah no, dear boy. Less haste, we have arrangements to make.'

Maybe it was the whisky or just plain slow thinking. It suddenly struck me that I didn't have a clear run in the game any more. Dully, I considered the angles. For me, interference from other parties unknown was a tough break. For Brain it could represent something much more serious.

'Do you know who did this, Mr Brain?'

'Don't change tack,' he said querulously. 'I'm an old man and I have trouble concentrating. We must talk terms.'

'There might not be any terms. Someone else wants to know what you know. He might not buy you liquor.'

He finished his whisky and I poured some more to underline the point.

'Drink up while you can,' I said.

'Your attempts at intimidation are crude, Mr Hardy. I have little to live for. I'm not afraid to die.'

'It's the manner of dying,' I said quietly.

He gulped some whisky. 'True, true, you have a point. You think I'm in danger?'

'I'm bloody sure of it. If I was you I'd go to Melbourne. Get a train. It's summer, can't be too bad down there.'

He mimed a shiver inside the coat. 'Foul hole, Melbourne, a wasteland. No, I shall rely on you and Lady Catherine for protection.'

'That might be a bit hard to arrange.'

'I confess I can't see why — supply and demand.'

'Not that easy. I need some indication that you're speaking the truth when you talk about proof. Protection is expensive.'

'I know. My need is great. It would cost a fortune to rehabilitate me.'

I wondered what he meant — a drying out farm, hormones? It suggested a will to live, vulnerability, but I couldn't see Lady C. footing the bill without something solid in return.

'The proof will have to be good.'

'It is, I assure you.' He came close, too close; the stink was like standing in the middle of a street with a tannery on one side and a brewery on the other. I pulled back a bit but he grabbed my shoulder.

'Look at this,' he croaked. He pulled a small photograph from the depth of his overcoat pocket. I peered at it, trying to make out the detail. The picture showed two women against an indeterminate background. The photograph was poor quality and it was creased and grubby; the women's features were indistinct. Brain pointed with his trim, clean fingernail.

'That's Bettina. See, she's pregnant.'

It was hard to tell — maybe.

'Who's the other woman?'

'A nurse. Look on the back.'

I turned the picture over. On the back in the same flowing purple hand was written: *B, Nurse Callaghan, Blackman's Bay.* Brain snatched it back as I tried to get my hand around it.

'Took it myself from hiding,' he chuckled. 'What do you think of that eh? Intriguing?'

'Very,' I said. 'Is there more?'

'In here,' he tapped the side of his head. 'Much more.'

'Well . . .' I began.

Brain hitched his trousers and scratched his crotch.

'Nature calls sir, consider the evidence while I appease the gods . . .' He lowered the rest of his drink and walked unsteadily to the door. I heard his feet shuffling on the lino and a stumble when he reached the stairs. I sat and drank. The room was settling back into its old shape. There was a ragged curtain across the window which had dirt and cobwebs in its corners. The ceiling was mildewed and strips of paint hung from it like stalactites. I tidied some books and reached under the bed for a far-flung one. My hand touched something and I pulled it out — a travelling bag. It was slashed and the bottom had been ripped out but it had been new and expensive not so long ago. That set me to poking among the books; some, dated a few years back, were medium-pricey. Brain had had some money and I remembered his bankroll and wanted urgently to know where the money had come from. I went to the door and looked out into the gloom. I called his name and the house swallowed up the sound.

With the .38 out I went down the passage and the stairs; the toilet was off the first landing giving out a dull gleam and smell of stale piss. I pushed the door open.

Henry Brain had had his last drink. He was sitting on the floor with his head resting against the bowl. A dribble of saliva dropped from his open mouth into the murky water. The back of his head was a soggy red pulp that had spread out and matted his hair and run into his ear. I went in, put the gun away, and let the door close behind me. There was barely room to squat on the seat with the knees drawn up, but it was enough space to die in. I bent over the body and went carefully through the pockets of his coat, shirt and trousers. I ran a finger around the lining but there was no photograph. The front of his pants were wet and the smell was strong. I eased away from the body and let it sag back the way it was. One of the clean, pale hands fell in a strange, crooked fashion — a finger seemed to be pointed at me accusingly.

I went back to Brain's room, retrieved the whisky and smeared up my glass and the bag and the books I thought I'd touched. I left the house quietly, not letting the bottles clink.

8

It was trouble, lots of it, and too early. It would take no time at all to trace Brain back to the pub and to me. It was an hour's work for a smart cop or even a dumb one. The question was, when would Brain's body be found? If the Palmer Street house was full of alcoholics he mightn't be missed until Saturday morning — there were probably other toilets in the house and wash basins. I might have twelve hours, I might have twelve minutes.

These profundities came to me as I drove around the streets of Darlinghurst. The comforts of home beckoned but the waves were up and it was no time to be out of the water. I stopped and called the Chatterton residence. Miss Reid answered in a voice full of annoyance but not sleep. I told her I had to speak to Lady C.

'That's impossible, Mr Hardy, quite impossible. She has retired for the night.'

'Tell her who's calling and that I said it was important.'

'I tell you it's out of the question. She takes two sleeping pills at ten o'clock. She'll be sound asleep now.'

'Wake her! A man's dead.'

'It might kill her.' From the way she said it, it sounded as if she was considering the idea. The last thing I needed was for the old girl to peg out now. The phone sputtered.

'Mr Hardy, *Mr Hardy!* Who is dead?'

'No one you'd know.' The words made me do a mental double-take. Maybe, just maybe.

'Miss Reid,' I said urgently, 'do those files on Chatterton employees go right back?'

'Yes, I believe they do. I haven't concerned myself with them recently but my impression is that they go back quite a long way. Why?'

'I'm on my way out there,' I said. 'Wait up for me, I want to go through those records.'

She almost wailed. 'I've been up since six, it's after eleven o'clock. Can't it wait until morning?'

'No, it has to be tonight.'

She was stubborn. 'I'm not sure I'm authorised to let you look at those files,' she said primly.

'Listen lady,' I grated, 'you'll be out on your ear if you don't. I'll take the responsibility. Be there with your bunch of keys.'

'I don't like your tone.'

'That's tough. I have to see those files tonight.'

She muttered something about melodrama and hung up. I skipped out to the car and got moving.

The Friday night revellers were out in fair strength. They came cruising up from the eastern suburbs to spend their money in the dirtier parts of Sydney and then purred back for their beauty sleep. The lights of the Volvos and Jaguars and Mercedes were mocking me as I hammered up to the Chattertons. The cars and their owners were safe and well insured, so were the boats that bobbed in the water gleaming under the moon. A soiled man dead in a slum house seemed remote from all this security and money, but the connections were there.

As I approached the Chattertons' gates a small car swung out onto the road, moving fast. The car looked Japanese, the driver looked big, that was all I got. I drove up to the path that led to the house and got out. A second later I was pressed back against the door with the flesh creeping all over me: a big yellow dog was growling impressively and showing me his white teeth about two inches from my kneecap. Then a voice came from the porch.

'Rusty! Down Rusty!'

Rusty! Carl or Fang surely, but down was where I wanted him.

'Call him, Miss Reid, he makes me nervous.'

She did. The dog went up to her like a poodle; she spoke and it went off into the shadows beside the house.

I went up the steps. 'Good protection.'

'Yes, it's necessary. There are many valuable things in the house.'

'Get many night-time visitors?'

She hesitated a split second. 'No.'

We went into the house and through the passages to the

room I'd seen that morning. She handed me the keys to the filing cabinet.

'I trust you won't disturb anything.'

I looked her over. The tone was still severe, she was one of those people in the habit of saying cautionary things, usually because they've been spoken to themselves in that way often. But she was more obliging, or trying to be. I couldn't smell any gin and her hair was in military order, but she exuded that glow people usually have after some sort of satisfying experience.

'I was having some coffee to help me stay awake, would you care for some?'

'Thank you, yes, black please.'

She nodded, almost approvingly, and went away. I opened one of the cabinets and started working through the files. They weren't well kept — more than one person had done the job over the years and it showed in the arrangement. There were business records and papers relating to the management of earlier houses than this one. Bills paid and receipted went back forty years, so did shopping lists and bank statements. At the bottom of the second cabinet I found a folder which contained information on staff pre-war. The turnover in maids, cooks and gardeners was steady.

Miss Reid came back with the coffee and perched on the edge of the desk. It was an unusual posture for her, almost jaunty. Albie would have been surprised. I kept my finger in the file while I drank the coffee and then went back to it. Miss Reid watched me. I found it among the last few sheets. 'CALLAGHAN, GERTRUDE' was printed in neat capitals and a date, '8/5/33.' This was when she'd come to work for the Chattertons as Bettina's nurse, nanny or whatever. Two hand-written references were pinned to the sheet. One was from the matron of a country hospital testifying to Callaghan's qualifications and competence; the other was from a doctor and expressed unqualified praise for her trustworthiness and abilities with children. Dr Alexander Osborn had a practice in Blackman's Bay. I made notes from these testimonials and from the woman's letter of application. Gertrude Callaghan was a spinster, born in Liverpool, England, in 1905. She left the Chattertons in June 1946 —

her forwarding address was 11 Yancey Street, Blackman's Bay.

I straightened up. Miss Reid was still sitting on the desk. She was looking tired but content.

'Finished?' she said. She let go a small, polite, well-covered yawn.

'Nearly. I need the library.'

The old aggression flooded out. 'You can't go there. Lady Catherine is working on the memoirs in there, nothing must be disturbed.'

'I won't disturb anything. I have to look at a medical register. The Judge must have had it. I have it myself at home but I can't go there.'

'Why not?'

She came off the desk and moved towards the door; I herded her on and she opened it.

'It'll sound melodramatic, Miss Reid,' I whispered, 'but if I go home the police might be there and if they are they'll arrest me.'

She was moving, keeping me at a distance. 'What for?'

'Murder. One I didn't do.'

'Who did?' she gasped. 'I didn't . . . don't believe you.'

I didn't reply, just kept moving her along and we ended up at the library as I'd hoped. Miss Reid pushed open one of the high, heavily carved doors and fumbled for the light. When it came on it showed a big room with a high ceiling; two large windows were covered by heavy curtains. There was a long desk with papers laid out in neat bundles and some freshly sharpened pencils lined up.

Books dominated the room; there were thousands of them in cedar cases from floor to roof and there were two ladders on wheels ready to go. I thought of Henry Brain and his books in piles on the floor.

'Is this catalogued?' I asked.

'Yes.' She pointed to a wooden cabinet in one corner. I went over and thumbed through the cards. The medical directory was listed and numbered. I read the numbers on the shelves and climbed the ladder. The Judge had six copies going back as far as 1930, the most recent was 1975.

Dr Alexander Osborn was listed: born in Edinburgh,

Scotland in 1899, educated in the same city; medical training interrupted by two years in the army; served in France and Africa, rank of Captain. Osborn was a P & O ships' doctor in the twenties and settled in Australia in 1929. Since 1939 he had had a practice in Blackman's Bay. If he was still there what he wouldn't know about the place wouldn't be knowable. I noted the address and put the directories back.

'All ship-shape,' I said to Miss Reid.

'You looked pleased with yourself.'

I was surprised and not pleased. 'Do I? I shouldn't be, this is just the start. But I've started to earn your boss's money.'

'I suppose that means something,' she said acidly. 'I wonder if I could go to bed now?'

I could have said something smart but didn't. I don't always. I wasn't sure how to handle her. She probably didn't know what I'd been hired to do, but there was her park assignation to consider and the half-lie I'd caught her in that night.

It seemed like the right time to do some work on her. She moved to open the door but I took hold of her arm.

'Don't touch me,' she snapped.

'I'd like to know what you plan to do about Rusty.'

'Oh.' There was relief in the sound. 'I'll call him.'

'Is that what you do when your boyfriend visits? I mean the big guy in the blue car, the one Lady Catherine forbids you to see.'

'I see who I like. Get out!' She was a sabre fighter not a fencer; it was all beat-down-the-guard and thump for her. I decided to play the same way.

'What's his game, Miss Reid? Is he a chauffeur, a footman, what?'

The slur got straight to her. 'He's a property developer,' she spat. 'He makes more in a day than you'd scratch in . . .'

She knew it was a mistake and she hated herself, the hand that came up to her mouth almost delivered a slap. I let go her arm and opened the door.

'Thank you Miss Reid,' I said. 'Be sure to call the dog.'

I heard her do some heavy breathing that seemed to characterise her anger; she didn't call the dog and my flesh crept until I had my bum safely on the seat of the car.

I wanted a drink, a shower and a sleep. I had the drink, of Jameson's Irish whisky. I still wanted the shower and sleep. Instead I drove south and stopped at the first open coffee bar. I drank two cups of black coffee and looked at the posters of Greece on the walls. Greece, that'd be nice. I like ouzo and I could run off the fatty food along the beach. I could lie in the sun, find a girl and learn Greek in bed. I pulled myself back to the here and now. For a trail thirty years old and not fresh lately it wasn't so bad. But whoever had taken the photograph from Brain would be on the trail of the Callaghan woman too. If she was still alive. It was time for some night driving.

I paid for the coffee and thought again about a Greek island. Maybe I'd get a bonus if I found young Chatterton. I put my notebook and .38 in the glovebox of the car and locked it. My jacket went on the seat along with three rolled cigarettes and the half-empty bottle. I got petrol and oil and water for the Falcon and told it we were going south and that it'd have a few hills to climb.

9

Blackman's Bay is on the coast, about a hundred and fifty miles south of Sydney. It's at the mouth of a river and was once a whaling port. After that it kept on with deep sea fishing for export, local fishing and tourism. I'd been through the place a few times and liked the look of it. I remembered it as a good-looking little town with a long timber and iron bridge over the river. At a pub a mile or so upstream I'd eaten some memorable oysters. Not a Greek island, but then I wasn't on holiday.

I drove down the Princes Highway and took the freeway that skirts Wollongong and Port Kembla. The steelworks were a glowing, flame-spurting delirium too close for comfort. I hadn't been out of the city in a long time, and south of the smoke and steel I began to feel some benefit from the drive and the sense of space around me. The Falcon coughed and protested on the hills. It was adapted to the harsh, stop and start grind of city driving. I nursed it. The air tasted cleaner by the mile and drunks on the road thinned out the further south I went. I'd smoked the cigarettes and now I took a careful pull on the bottle. The clean air blew into my face sharp and fresh and I felt good.

It was a clear night; the road slid down to the coast and the stars went on forever out to sea. I hit the Blackman's Bay bridge sometime around 3.00 a.m. The planks rattled as I passed over them and I thought I could feel a slight swinging motion in the bridge. The main street was quiet; there were no all-night joints and most of the shops still used ordinary electric light which was switched off. A few neon tubes glowed prophetically in signs and windows. There was an extra service station and a shop or two, otherwise the town didn't seem to have changed much. I drove down to the park near the beach where there was a town map on a board the way there always is in these places.

I located Yancey Street and went back to the car. Call it intuition, call it experience, but I was confident that she still lived there. There was no reason she should but I had a feeling I was dealing with something frozen in time and space. The nurse would still be there and so would the doctor. I realised I'd forgotten to check the doctor's address and I went back to the board. A big wave lifted up and crashed on the beach and I could hear the bridge creaking in the light wind. I took a few steps onto the sand and looked out to sea. I could make out a few lights moving slowly a long way out. Off to the left a cliff dropped sharply down to the water. For no reason I thought of it as a jumping-off place for suicides. Suddenly I didn't want to disturb the old ghosts, didn't want to check on whether people still lived where they had once lived and knew about things that happened thirty years ago. I wanted a future, I didn't want to rake over a painful past. I wished I was on the ship and at sea. I shook the thought off and went back to the car.

The roads threaded up behind the town into the hills. I bore left at a crossroad; Yancey Street was an unpaved track with no town lighting. I crept down it trying to pick up its features in the headlights. There were only a few houses as far as I could tell from gateposts and signboards and they were located well back from the track. Number eleven was identifiable by a sign painted on a handsome gum near a bend in the road. There were no houses opposite and it seemed to be flanked by vacant lots. There was a lot of pampas grass along the front boundary and no welcoming lights winking beyond it. If I'd been an old lady I wouldn't have felt secure there; I was a middle-aged man with a middle-sized gun and I still didn't feel secure.

I got the gun from the glove box and a torch and locked up the note book and the spare ammunition. The trunk of the gum tree was broad and pale and reassuring in the beam of the torch. I put the car keys on top of the offside front wheel and moved towards Nurse Callaghan's abode. It was no time to go calling on an old lady, but I could poke around, get the feel of the place. And some old ladies get up very early in the morning, especially in the country.

The light danced over the springy grass and picked up a straggling track where vehicles had brushed Nature aside. I started up the incline, flicking the light to each side and bringing it back to the rough drive. Away down the hill the sea moved convulsively. Up here the only thing moving was me. Everything thickened in front of me suddenly and I realised that the track had taken a turn. I rounded the bend and was pulled up by a shape looming in front of me. I swung the torch, got an impression of shape, a car, and colour, blue, and then the starry heavens fell in on me. Pain sketched a searing yellow and red diagram in front of my eyes, all zigzags and angles, and then it blacked out and so did I.

When I came out of it a salty seaside dew had settled on me. My clothes and hair were moist and my skin was tacky and cold. It was still dark but the sky was lightening over what had to be the east. It all swam around when I lifted my head and I crunched dirt between aching teeth. Everything ached. I stretched out my hand and felt about in a wide arc. The torch was still there and still working. The car was gone. It had passed over me or around me — I was still in one piece. I pulled myself up and stood swaying, getting my bearings. I began to walk up towards the house which someone hadn't wanted me to visit — not before they'd left, anyhow. It couldn't be good. Daylight was seeping in, a couple of birds started up singing and I swore at them. My head hurt.

The house was a modest fibro-cement job that had been reasonably well looked after. A garden bed running across the front of it had had loving care. It was a showpiece of pruned rose bushes and other flowers that didn't get that way on their own.

The house was on three-foot brick pillars and I looked under at intervals as I skirted round. Nothing moved under the house and I couldn't hear anything moving inside. I went to the front door, knocked quietly and waited. Nothing. The door was locked. I went round to the back; a flywire screen had a tear in it near the door handle. I reached through and turned. I went into a small enclosed porch cluttered with gardening tools and fishing tackle. I went through a kitchen which was tidy and neat into a short passageway with two doors off it. The door on the left let into a sitting room; in the dawn light I could make out a fireplace, some easy chairs, a television set. There was a low table with a pile of plastic-jacketed library books on it.

The other door opened onto a bedroom. An old woman was lying on her back on the big bed, her hands were stretched out on the cover with the palms up. I cleared my throat and knocked on the door jamb. She didn't move. I went closer. The gardening and the fishing and the TV and the reading were all over for her. She was dead.

There was no sign of violence on her face or in the room; the only unnatural thing was the position of her hands. I looked closely at her face but her eyes seemed to have closed naturally and the light beside the bed was soft enough to have been a night light. The bed cover was smooth but not too smooth. I went back to the kitchen and looked at the pile of bills on the spike — they covered the usual things and were made out to Gertrude Callaghan. I looked at the tear in the screen door but if there's a way to tell whether fine plastic mesh has been cut recently I don't know it.

Back in the bedroom I stood at the end of the bed and wondered if she'd died naturally or not. It seemed unlikely that she had and I felt guilty as if I'd brought this on her. It wasn't true of course; totally innocent victims are few, but that's how I felt. She was an impressive-looking old person with snow-white hair and a strong, intelligent face. The signs were around of an active and meaningful old age that should have ended better. I read somewhere about some people — Indians I think — who used to put their problems to the newly dead. I think they arranged the corpse in such a way that its head or arm could move involuntarily and a man with special powers would interpret the movements. I looked down at the old nurse.

'Did Bettina Chatterton have a son?' I asked quietly.

Not a hair stirred.

'Is he still alive?'

Nothing. I'd have to do it the hard way. I searched the place thoroughly — drawers, cupboards, books, floor coverings — for evidence of a connection between the nurse and the Chattertons after 1946. There was nothing. I found the Judge's reference which gave Gertrude a good character and the documentation of her employment, all on the coast, over the following twenty years. There were photographs showing how the Liverpool girl had turned into the nurse and the old gardener and fisherwoman but nothing pointing to a grandson for the late Sir Clive. There were two things of interest: a flock of intimate notes, spanning three decades, from Dr Osborn to Nurse Callaghan and signs that someone had gone through the place before me.

It was almost daylight when I left the house but the sky was overcast and a thin fog was hanging around the tops of the trees. I went down the track and poked around in the grass until I found my gun. Nothing was stirring in Yancey Street except the birds. My head still hurt. I touched the spot and felt dried, caked blood. I was getting less presentable by the hour but there was no one around to notice. Everything was quiet and serene like Nurse Callaghan sleeping the last sleep.

10

When I'd cleared Yancey Street and made a few turns I stopped to take stock of things. The notebook was still in the glove box and the lock was intact. It was more than I could say for myself. My head needed a dressing and I needed a shave. That was what showed; my teeth were scummy from a day's drinking and my body was stiff and sore from lack of sleep — lying like a log for a couple of hours in wet grass doesn't count. My head ached fiercely. I looked at the whisky and shuddered. Then I salvaged a couple of aspirin out of the rubbish on the back seat and swilled them down with the whisky. I almost gagged but I grabbed the steering wheel and hung on to everything. After a minute or two I didn't feel any worse, maybe even better. Time to tackle Dr Osborn.

He was in front of his house, bending to pick up a newspaper. He wore a checked dressing gown and the wide trousers of striped cotton pyjamas flopped around his ankles. He bent like an old man, stiffly and slowly, but he bent. I walked over and called out something polite. He looked in my direction but I had the feeling that he couldn't see me. I reached the gate and called out again.

'Dr Osborn.'

'Yes, wait a minute.' There was still a faint Scots tang in the words despite fifty years of exposure to Australian speech. He moved slowly down the path towards me holding the rolled-up newspaper in his hand. I waited by the gate and watched his face. A certain blankness was in it until he was about ten feet away, then interest came into his eyes. He fished out a pair of spectacles from the dressing gown pocket and hooked them on.

'Yes young man?'

'I have to talk to you doctor, about Gertrude Callaghan.'

'You'll do me the favour of telling me who you are.'

'I'm sorry — my name is Hardy. I'm a private investigator from Sydney. Does the name Chatterton mean anything to you?'

'You'll not be referring to the poet?'

'No, not the poet, the Judge.' I rattled the gate a fraction. 'Can I come in and ask you a few questions?'

'Perhaps. You mentioned Gertrude. What of Gertrude?'

'She's dead, doctor. She died this morning. I came from Sydney to see her but I didn't make it in time. That's why I'm here.'

Emotional control of the kind that is generations deep fell away from him in a split second. He clutched at the gate and the newspaper fell; I held his arm to steady him and we stood there like father and son mourning a wife and mother. I opened the gate with my free hand and helped him up the path towards the house. He was a portly man with a weatherbeaten face. His eye sockets were sunken and surrounded with dark, puckered skin as though a stain was seeping out of the eyes into the tissue. Flesh sagged on his cheeks but his chin and neck were firm; it was as if he'd aged selectively, in patches.

The house was a big, plain weatherboard, painted white with a glassed-in verandah running along three sides. I eased him up three steps and across to a cane chair. He sat down stiffly, like an old horse sinking to its knees for the last time.

'Can I get you something doctor?'

He spoke slowly and remotely, as if from far away. 'I was making coffee.'

'I'll get it.' I went into the house and through a couple of well-ordered rooms to a neat, bright kitchen. I collected mugs, milk and sugar and took the pot off the stove. When I got back to the verandah Osborn had straightened up a little in the chair, lifted his head and seemed to be looking through the window to a far distant point. I poured a black coffee for him and he nodded and took it. I made one for myself and sat down opposite him.

'I'm sorry to hit you with it like that.'

He seemed not to hear me. 'Forty years,' he said. He moved his head and looked directly at me. 'It was her, you're sure?'

'Yancey Street,' I said. 'A handsome old lady, white hair.'

The coffee slopped and he set the mug down before covering his eyes with his hand. I drank some coffee and waited. After a minute or so he made an effort, palmed tears from his face and drank the coffee. He didn't look at me but pulled himself up out of the chair.

'Excuse me,' he said. He walked slowly through into the other room and I heard him lift the phone and dial. There was silence and then the sound of the phone being put down. I poured more coffee and sipped it while he resumed his chair.

'No answer,' he said. 'I can't just leave her there, all alone.'

'I'm sorry doctor, I've got the living to consider.'

'Yes. You're a detective you said? A policeman?'

'No, I'm a private detective. I'm sorry about Nurse Callaghan.'

'Nurse, Sister, Matron,' he said softly. 'The most wonderful woman.' I drank some more coffee and he watched me critically.

'You should put milk and sugar in it,' he said. 'I'd guess you were a drinker, a drinker with an empty stomach. Your metabolism needs something to fuel it.'

'I've also been hit on the head,' I said defensively. I leaned forward to give him a look. He put down his cup and eased the hair gently aside. I brought my head up and he looked directly into my eyes.

'Nasty,' he said. 'A possible concussion. You should be at a hospital. I'm afraid I don't practise any more.'

'You did though, until recently.'

'And how would you know that?'

'From the medical register.'

'You've been researching then. You're right, I retired two years ago. You should go to the hospital, there's a good one here.'

'Maybe later.' I sipped some coffee. 'I want to ask you about Gertrude Callaghan and things that happened here thirty years ago.'

'Do you now? You come here bleeding and smelling of spirits and you ask me that. How do I know you didn't kill Gertrude?'

'Would I have come here and told you about her if I had?'

'Perhaps not,' he said wearily. 'But I doubt I have anything to tell you.'

'I think you do. Thirty years is a long time but I need information and you're the man that knows where the bodies are buried.'

He winced and a sharp breath came out of him; he tried to cover it by lifting his cup to his mouth.

'Just an expression doctor. Why does it startle you?' He didn't answer and I pressed on. 'I'll dig for it doctor. I'll be working in the dark and things will just have to fall out as they may. It doesn't have to be that way though.'

'What are you saying?'

He was good, very good. Without trying he'd got me to say more than I meant to while he hadn't volunteered a damn thing himself. I had to plunge on with my uncertain knowledge and try to flush him out. I had hints, clues and guesses and just one piece of hard information on him — knowledge of his feelings for Gertrude Callaghan.

'I've seen a photograph of Nurse Callaghan with a pregnant woman taken down here. The photograph was authentic and I've identified the locality.' This was a lie but it seemed like a safe one. 'My interest is in that woman specifically and the child, I'm not concerned with the wider issues.' I chose the words carefully but they still sounded thin.

'May I see this photograph?' he said.

'No.'

'And why not?'

'It's a crucial piece of evidence and I don't carry it around with me.'

He leaned back in his chair and drank some coffee. 'You mean you don't have it,' he said confidently.

'The man who had it is dead. He was murdered, probably by the same person who killed Nurse Callaghan.'

The smugness left his face. 'Murdered! You didn't say that before. No, not Gertrude. Did she . . .'

'Tell me anything? I'm not going to answer that doctor, it's time for you to open up a little.'

I finished the coffee, thought about a cigarette and decided against it. It wasn't a time for betraying weaknesses. He sat back further in the chair and his eyes seemed to sink deeper into those cavernous, dark-rimmed sockets. He looked like a man letting his mind run back. I waited. When he spoke it was carefully and slowly with the Scots accent more pronounced.

'I'm going to talk in generalities Mr Hardy, at least to start with. Do you understand? A lot of reputations and lives, good lives, are at stake in this. A lot of harm could be done.'

I nodded.

'Let me say for a start that I know nothing about anyone by the name of Chatterton. I might have had some dealings with a Chatterton but if so I've forgotten. I'm an old man and I have forgotten many names.'

'But you remember some?'

'Aye, and with good reason.' He ran a hand over his head and plucked at the dewlaps on his face. 'This is hard for me. I'm not sure I'm doing the right thing. I know nothing about you.' He groaned. 'Tell me about Gertrude, was she . . . hurt?'

'She was in bed. I didn't see any signs of violence but someone had searched her house, probably the same person that hit me. Something happened up there.'

He suddenly looked every day of his age. Gertrude Callaghan was woven into his past and he wanted to talk about it, but secrecy had become a habit.

'You seem to be having some trouble starting your story doctor,' I said. 'Let me help a little. There was an establishment of some sort down here thirty years ago, a place where women came to have babies. Or not to have them. I assume it was a well-regulated place. I'm not a moralist.'

'I'm glad to hear it. Myself, I'm a radical, a reformer and a radical. I am a moralist you might say.' His eyes, which had been focused on my face, drifted away. It looked like he was going into the mind-cranking stage again. I was impatient but judged it better to let him set the pace. I leaned forward to get some more coffee. He didn't notice.

'I love this place Mr Hardy, these people, I've been here nearly fifty years. Did you know that?'

I nodded, took milk.

'I went back to Edinburgh once, detested it! I found the Scots ungenerous and narrow. Well, that's by the way. Do you know what used to be the single greatest cause of human misery in a place like this?'

I said 'No', which was true.

He leaned forward and tapped me on the knee. 'Unwanted children. Forced marriages and unwanted children. It was behind most of the crime, nearly all the drunkenness, most of the trouble.'

'A problem,' I agreed. 'Still is, I suppose.'

'It's different now, more information, better methods. And there's some support for the girls bringing up the babies.'

'Come down to cases doctor,' I said gently.

'Aye. I ran a clinic here for twenty years, abortions and births, adoptions. Proud of it.'

'It was a secret though.'

'It was. A secret entrusted to a few.'

'Nurse Callaghan?'

'Helped me, the whole time. Wonderful woman, she believed in the work.'

It was more than that and I tried to keep the knowledge out of my response. Unsuccessfully.

'I was unhappily married,' he said simply. 'A daughter died in childbirth with no one to help her.'

It explained a lot but I wasn't happy with the drift of his account. Too much flavour of abortion in it; abortion wasn't what I needed.

'How many abortions did you perform doctor?'

'Hundreds.'

'How many births and . . . adoptions?'

'Fewer.'

'It's the adoptions I'm interested in.'

'Both things were illegal.'

'I don't imagine anyone cares now.'

He misinterpreted me and flared. 'But I must explain what went wrong, how my ideals were perverted.'

The craving overtook the tact; I pulled out my tobacco and made a cigarette. I said 'Go ahead' more roughly than I'd intended.

He glanced at me sharply, annoyed, as though I wasn't worthy to be his confessor. But he was too far into confession to stop. 'I did this community a great service for twenty years. A law-abiding community. Blackman's Bay, very low incidence of violence, disruption. But they wouldn't let me be.'

'They? The locals?'

'No, the others, from Canberra and Sydney. Men and lasses, some terrible stories I can tell you.'

We seemed to be moving into the right area. I blew smoke away from him and juggled the ash.

'What did they do, blackmail you?'

'Aye, and worse. Terrible place Sydney, full of the lowest people.' He looked hard at me and I felt I had the harbour bridge growing out of my head and Kings Cross painted on my face. I knew I had a day's beard and a very dirty shirt.

'How do I know I can trust you?' he said harshly. Some of the power he must have had when younger suddenly seemed to flow back into him. 'You're a man for hire.'

'Aren't we all,' I said, then I corrected quickly. 'I'm only partly for hire. There are things I won't do. I don't cause unnecessary pain.'

'A fine speech,' he sneered. 'Who judges what is necessary, you?'

'Yes.'

'Aye. I thought so. That won't do. What are your standards? What would you know of a lifetime's dedication to an ideal?'

Not much, I thought, and thank God for it. Ideals should change like everything else. But he felt he had got some sort of moral and ethical drop on me and in a funny way I felt it too. Perhaps it was the lack of sleep.

'You come down here out of nowhere,' he went on, 'telling about my oldest friend. You could be lying.'

He was pacing up and down the verandah now; his slippers flapped on the floor and his pyjamas swished around his white, bony shanks. His voice became more vehement as he moved as if the pacing was giving him strength and purpose.

'Nurse Callaghan is dead,' I said dully. 'You'll get news of that soon enough.' I fingered my cut head. 'This is real.'

He snorted, still pacing. 'You could have done it yourself.'

'You're going in circles doctor, a minute ago you accepted that she was dead . . .'

'Don't you dare criticise my logic. I'll thank you to know that I'm in full possession of my senses.'

I doubted it. He was getting more excited by the second

and trying to construct defences against me. I'd lost him, just like that, in a sentence or two.

'I'll say no more Mr Hardy, and I'll be obliged if you'd go. I have nothing to say to you.'

I spoke quietly, trying to calm him down. 'That's not true doctor. I must know more. I know a good deal already. It's vital to my investigation . . .'

'You're threatening me!' His voice rose and cracked. 'I won't stand for it. You come here and threaten me.' He whipped across the floor and through the door into the house. I stood up wondering what my next move should be. He came back and he wasn't alone — he had a double-barrelled shotgun for company and he levelled it at my chest.

'Go Mr Hardy.' He jerked the gun at the door. 'And don't come back.'

I make a point of not arguing with old men waving shotguns. I went.

11

There was a telephone booth on the street three houses along from Osborn's place. I called his number and when he answered I dropped the phone, ran back down the street and jumped over his fence. I sprinted up to the side of the house and then bent low to keep under the windows. Osborn was still holding the phone when I got to the back part of the house. I risked a peep up and saw him put it down, dial, listen and hang up. He moved around for a few minutes and I was wondering how to handle it if I heard paper being torn or smelled it being burned when I heard drawers opening and closing in the room nearest me. I heard him grunt the way men do when they bend over to put on their shoes. Then he left the room and I heard a door at the back of the house slam. I sneaked down and hung an eye around the corner: Dr Osborn, minus his shotgun, was heading for his garage.

I went back the way I'd come. I'd left my car around the nearest corner from the doctor's house out of old habit. I drove back to a point where I could see his gate and watched a green Cortina roll down the drive and head south for the hills. I tailed him from as far back as the traffic would allow. Osborn drove sedately, like a man used to motoring in a more leisurely age. I hung back on the highway which wasn't easy because most cars were passing him. We followed the coast for a few miles and then swung inland. The Cortina toddled along off the bitumen and up an unmade road into the hills. I stopped and let him get well ahead, then I crawled up after him. The road climbed steeply but straight so he couldn't wind round on top of me. I hung back behind the drift of his dust cloud. Suddenly the road got rougher and another track ran into it on the left. I stopped and examined the ground; it looked as if nothing had gone straight on for a while and as if the Cortina had turned left. Hardy of the 5th Maroubra Scout Troop.

I pulled the car off the track, got the gun out of the glove box and started to follow the tyre marks in the dust. The track was steep and I had to stop for breath twice. I stumbled once, jarred my leg, and sent waves of pain curling and dumping inside my skull. The morning was warm, I sweated and the handgrip of the .38 became wet and slippery. Each time the track took a turn I went into the rough at the side and worked through so as to get a look at the road ahead, but each time it was quiet and still except for the noise and movement of the forest birds. After about ten minutes walking the trees thinned out and the ground levelled. I used the cover of the trees to approach a clearing extending over an acre or so on a stretch of flat ground.

In the middle of the clearing, spaced about forty feet apart, were two crumbling brick pillars that would once have been chimneys. Some blackened timber was piled off to one side. I watched from behind a tree as Osborn came into the clearing carrying a pile of branches. He threw them down near the old chimney closest to me, squatted, and began working on the bricks of the old fireplace. He pulled them out and piled them up beside him. Then he reached into the cavity and hauled out a box about the size of a beer carton. He stood up and slapped his pockets. I stepped out and levelled the pistol at him.

'Keep your hands still, doctor. Move towards me slowly.'

He started and stopped the slapping movement. Then he looked down at the box and bent over.

'Don't!'

He was on his knees now by the box. 'It would be hard for you to explain, Mr Hardy, killing an old man. And not a bad solution for me. I think I'll keep on.'

I was almost close enough to kick him. 'I wouldn't kill you doctor, just hurt you a bit. It'd solve nothing. Now get away from that bloody box!'

He straightened up and stood there rock still. I looked over the blackened earth. A couple of the building's stumps still stuck up stubbornly through the weeds. I glanced about for the shotgun but couldn't see it. The branches by the bricks were light with feathery leaves, tinder dry. I nudged the box with my toe.

'Your records doctor?'

'Yes.'

'I'm surprised. Was it discreet to keep them?'

His old face turned up and he looked affectionately around at the ruin and the overgrown land.

'It was my life's work,' he said softly. 'I thought that someday I could write it up, publish it. Opinion has changed, it could be done soon.'

'Maybe so,' I said. 'I'm not going to stop you. I just need some information from those records myself. You can do what you like with it after that.'

'You don't understand.' His voice was thin and strained. Pleading was foreign to him and he was having trouble getting the sound right. 'That would be a violation of my trust. I can't allow it.'

'You can't stop me. I'm the one with the gun now. Move aside doctor, I don't want to hurt you.' I bent down and examined the box; it was metal, heavy, but unlocked. The lid came up stiffly and revealed rows of file cards, neatly packed.

'This was the place? The clinic?' I tried to let a little kindness into my voice and I let the pistol drop a bit, not too far.

'Yes, this is it. This is where I did my life's work. Later the vandals had their fun. All my memories are here . . . Gertrude . . . my daughter . . .' He pointed. 'You can see the ocean from over there. I'll show you.'

He set off for the far edge of the clearing and I followed. We pushed through some undergrowth and went up a steep track which led to a broad, flat rock washed pale and pitted by the weather. I lost sight of him for a second as I moved forward to step up onto the rock. I stopped, peering ahead, and that saved me — a branch of the tree beside the rock came slashing towards my face like a stockwhip. I ducked under it, side-stepped up and moved along the edge of the rock away from the tree. He saw me and threw something. It missed and he stumbled towards the edge of the rock like a sleepwalker. I dropped the box and went after him fast; he was tensed for the jump when I locked my hand around his upper arm and jerked him back and down hard.

I was off balance and fell and he came down half on top of me. I rolled away and he flopped on the rock winded and gasping like a landed fish. I lifted him and carried him across to the tree where I propped him up. Then I recovered the metal box and sat down on it. We looked east: the water was a fair way off but that made it more impressive. The tree tops flowed out towards the band of blue; a light wind was coming off the water and it moved the upper branches about and reached us with a tang of salt water and eucalyptus. He gazed out over the scene possessively — I felt like an intruder at a shrine.

'My daughter's ashes are scattered out there. She loved this place dearly.'

'We have to talk doctor.'

'What is there to talk about? You have the records, took them by force. You'll use them for your own corrupt ends. I'm old and this trouble will kill me. But that's fitting, that my life's work should finish me off. I'm sorry about the branch and the shotgun. I've never harmed anyone.'

He seemed to be raving, losing his grip under the spell of the place and the pressure of events. I wanted him in control, as an ally if possible.

'There are those who would think,' I said softly, 'that you've killed many times.'

He glared at me, his tired old eyes shining out of the beaten flesh around them. 'Fools,' he said coldly. 'Fools and hypocrites. I have evidence that lives are wrecked by unwanted children, and saved by abortion.'

'What do you mean?'

'I followed them through do you see? I kept notes on what people did — those who were forced into marriages they didn't want and those who were free to develop. You'd be surprised, Mr Hardy, if you knew who were some of the fathers of children born and aborted. I know.'

'Jesus. You mean you got all that stuff from the mothers? You've got names and dates?'

'Yes indeed.'

The enormity of it washed over me slowly. The box was a powder keg of secrets. He'd mentioned post-war Canberra and Sydney and hinted at big names. The thought flickered in the back of my mind that the cards would be better burnt but I let that go. I had a job to do and I was very, very curious.

'You appear to be struck dumb, Mr Hardy.'

I was suddenly aware of the gun and stuck it in my belt. It seemed like a ridiculous toy; I wanted the box in my hands.

'Come on doctor, we have to find a way out of this mess.'

He followed me off the rock. 'Mess? What do you mean?'

'You can't be that innocent. Those records are dynamite.'

'Why?'

'Men like to father their own children for one thing. It's a quirk I've noticed. They don't like having it done for them.'

'Yes, well, I know of many . . .'

'Don't tell me.'

'I knew it was . . . sensitive, but that's why I kept it out here, partly why. I used to drive out and do some work on the cards, add things. But I always thought of it as scientific data.'

'I think of blackmail and other things.'

'But it's so long ago, twenty years and more.'

'Memories are longer, suspicion doesn't age.'

'You're a philosopher, Mr Hardy.'

We went down the rutty rabbit track to the clearing. The air was warm and pungent with forest scents. It would be a fine place for a picnic with nice food and cold wine and a good spot for making love on some trodden down bracken. We got clear of the trees and the sight of the stark, lonely chimneys brought me back to the business which had nothing to do with picnics and not much with lovemaking in the bushes. I talked to him and he listened. He did some talking himself and I tried to respond to his descriptions of the clinic, as he called it, and how he and Gertrude Callaghan had handled the work. There was a touch too much of 'moral rehabilitation' in it for my taste, but he was talking of other times, when illegitimacy could be a life-long curse and divorce court judges were like priests of the Inquisition.

He leaned against the Cortina and looked at me through narrowed, sceptical eyes.

'And now?'

'Now you drive me back to my car and we both go back to your house. You help me find what I'm looking for in these cards, if it's here. I make some notes and hand the whole box of tricks back to you, with some advice.'

'And that is?'

'Make up your mind to write up your findings soon or turn the whole lot over to a library or an archive. You can do that doctor. And you can put a time bar on it, say twenty-five years. You leave a key to it all if that's needed and it's off your hands. When the time comes some student will dig into it. Your work will get its due although you'll be dead and gone.' A shiver went through me as I spoke and I wondered whether I'd invoked some god of ill-luck and I might be dead and gone myself in that time, or sooner.

We got in the car. 'I'm inclined to believe that you'll do as you say,' he said.

'Right,' I said. It was time to stop monkeying around. All the talk of by-gone days had distracted me. I'm a sucker for it. But I might have a solid lead to the last of the Chattertons under my arm and I felt a keen professional urge to get on with it.

'Right,' I repeated.

He started the car and trundled down the track just as he'd done many, many times before.

12

Back at his house we settled down into the verandah chairs and I lifted the box. I jiggled it up and down for a minute and then passed it across to him.

'Let's try to keep this on the square, doctor,' I said. 'I'm interested in your records for a period approximately thirty years ago. My information is that a child was born to a young woman at that time. I don't know what name she gave but I do know her married and maiden names — it's unlikely to be one of those.'

'True.' He drummed his fingers on the top of the box. 'The woman was not bearing her husband's child, I take it?'

It hit me then for the first time that she might not have been. But it didn't matter either way. It was the Chatterton blood that was important.

'I'm told that it was her husband's child. It doesn't affect the enquiry. It's the mother who's important.'

'I see.' He dipped into the box and started riffling the cards, plucking them up and stuffing them back. I wanted a cigarette but I didn't want to disturb our uneasy detente. He looked up at me. 'A young woman you said?'

'Yes, very young — late teens.'

He nodded and kept digging. Eventually he held up a batch of cards. 'I terminated the pregnancies of twenty-three such women in those years.' He handed me half the cards. I glanced at them. They were covered with neat, spidery handwriting. I flicked a thumbnail against the cards.

'I don't think the pregnancy was terminated.'

'You mean you hope it wasn't. Can you be sure?'

'I think so,' I said slowly. I was conscious of the thinness of my information, and my ignorance of childbearing. 'The photograph I saw showed a women who looked pregnant. Wouldn't that suggest she was too far advanced to be terminated?'

'Not necessarily. Cases differ.'

'The nurse,' I said desperately. 'The nurse was in the

photograph. They were acquainted. The nurse must have treated her as something special.'

He removed his glasses and rubbed his eyes. 'That is an ignorant remark, Mr Hardy,' he said. 'Gertrude Callaghan was the most warm and loving woman I have ever known. Everyone was special to her.'

I accepted the rout. 'You're right. I'm *hoping* a child was born. May I see the other cards?'

He passed them over, seven in all. I looked at them carefully. At the top of each a name was written, surname first, in capitals. There were dates then statistics. The data didn't mean much to me — medical stuff, drugs used, tests, various readings. Each card contained a few lines describing the birth of a child giving time, weight, other measurements, instruments used and so on. I read through this and handed three cards back to Osborn. He took them in at a glance.

'Females. Only a son will do?'

I nodded.

'I wanted a son myself but it wasn't to be. Do you have any children, Mr Hardy?'

I shook my head, still looking at the cards.

'It's a paradox, parenthood. Children enslave you, but they bring you great joy. My own daughter . . .' He stopped himself. 'What are you doing?'

I had a pen out and was scribbling on the back of an envelope. 'I'm trying out some of these names, trying to see an anagram or something. Most people who assume false names don't just pluck them out of the air.'

He leaned forward. 'I'm good at that, a crossword fiend. What are the names?'

I handed the cards and the envelope over. I hadn't got anywhere.

He examined the cards and wrote the names down vertically on a blank card. Then he wrote Brain and Chatterton opposite the list. He doodled on the card, making scrolls and stick figures and blocking in the letters. I was getting impatient, felt let down, and could sense the tobacco craving sneaking up on me. I shifted in my chair and held out my hand.

'I'll have to do it the hard way, doctor,' I said. 'Check on each one in turn. I just hope they aren't too scattered.' I was edgy and almost snapped my figures for the cards.

'You won't, you know.' He separated out one card and handed it to me. 'I'll wager this is the one.'

I looked at it. Nothing. 'Why?'

'You were on the right track, just a bit off course. It's not an anagram though.'

'What then?'

'Association. The poet Chatterton imitated the works of Sir Thomas Malory. That's the name on the card. You didn't know that, about Chatterton?'

'No. I knew he was a fraud of some sort.'

He sighed. 'You're not as big a cynic as you make out. Malory, Morte d'Arthur. That's a great work, written when English was a real language and not a grab bag of this and that.'

'It was all like French as I recall,' I grunted. He said something else which I didn't catch. I was reminded of Henry Brain's quoting habit but my attention had shifted to the card.

The delicate writing had faded as if such a pack of untruths could not survive the passage of time. Barbara Malory's age was given as 17 years and there was a brief account of her physical condition which was excellent. Doubts were expressed as to her mental stability. On Saturday 3 December at 1.34 p.m. she had given birth to an 8 pound 12 ounce male child. The birth was uncomplicated, the child was without defect. There was no address for Barbara on admission or discharge — she came from nowhere and went nowhere. She had stayed at the clinic for 11 days and paid £5 per day; she had paid £38 for the doctor's services. Okay, that was fine, congratulations all round, now what about the kid? The child had stayed a few days longer than his mother and had been declared 'exceptionally strong and healthy'. This information was followed by a simple one-line entry: Mr and Mrs Gilbert Brudin, 116 Red Oak Road, Forrest, ACT.

I held the card out to Osborn with my thumbnail under the address. The nail was split and full of dirt. I must have clawed the ground when I went down in the night. I suddenly felt weary and in very bad shape but the adrenalin was running. The card was a shower and a shave and a bottle of champagne.

'They took the baby?'

'Yes.'

'Not a formal adoption?'

'No.'

'How were the details arranged, registration and so on?'

'I don't know.'

'That's hard to believe doctor.'

'It's true, nevertheless. These people who took the children were determined folk. They'd been rejected by the official agencies, usually for ridiculous reasons like not being Christians.' He looked as if he would have liked to spit. 'They were prepared to do anything to get a healthy child and they made all the arrangements you speak of themselves.' He read the name aloud. 'Baudin, Baudin, no, I don't recall them. But some of these people had influence, they were all intelligent and responsible, I saw to that.'

'You said you kept a check on the children.'

'In some cases, yes.' He turned the card over. 'Not in this one.'

I wrote down the name and address and returned the card. He balanced the box on his bony knees and deliberately put each card back into place. I stood up and held out my hand.

'Thanks for your co-operation doctor.'

We shook hands. He didn't stand.

'You got what you wanted. You're good at your trade, Mr Hardy.'

'Sometimes,' I said.

He put the box on the floor and eased himself up. One leg protested and buckled and he dropped back into the chair. He breathed heavily.

'I believe I'll do as you suggest with the records. I won't write it up myself, too old.'

'You've got a bit of fight left in you.'

I had the feeling that he didn't want to let me go. It was as if we had some unfinished business. But I didn't know what it might be or what else I could say to him. I moved towards the verandah opening. He looked shrunken and deflated in the cane chair.

'There's not much fight in me. Do you think I'm in danger?'

'From whom?'

'You said Gertrude was murdered . . . something to do with my work.'

'I was theorising a bit,' I said. 'I don't know for certain that she was murdered. There were signs that the house had been searched but she might have died naturally. She was an old woman, and frail I suppose?'

'Yes, and getting more so.'

'Well . . .' I thought of Henry Brain again who certainly hadn't beaten himself to death in the w.c. But whoever had cooled me had been content to leave it at that. Perhaps Brain's death was a sort of accident. In any case I didn't feel that a mindless killer was on the loose and I told Osborn so.

'I won't mention you when the police come to tell me about Gertrude.'

'They might not be involved. She must have friends, someone will find her soon?'

'Yes.'

I said I was sorry and realised that I was repeating myself. I wanted to say more, to indicate that I knew what he was feeling, but I didn't. He was a secrets man. The stain around his eyes was almost black now and spreading. He seemed to be looking through me and down a long, dark tunnel.

'Those records . . .'

'Yes?' It crossed my mind that this case was mostly records so far, cards and files, plus a few deaths. In my mind I was already on the way to Canberra, a whole city of cards and files.

'Those records are honest in a way that most medical records are not. Doctors cover their mistakes, they use hindsight. I've done it myself. But not there.' He looked down at the box. 'That's my real medical career.'

'Then you have something to be proud of.'

'No. I was selfish. My wife . . . I did nothing for her. My daughter died in childbirth.' He was in the grip of it now, wandering painfully in the garden of his memories. 'And Gertrude, Gertrude lost three children. There was nothing I could do. The people I loved and should have loved, my work did nothing for them.'

His voice broke. Tears were running down his worn-out old face. I lifted my hand in a sort of salute and left. I'd hardly been further inside his house than the verandah but I'd been deep, deep inside his life.

13

It was nearly noon. I hadn't slept, I hadn't eaten, I hadn't shaved. I was tired, hungry, dirty and I stank. The day was cloudy but hot and I sweltered inside my sweat-stained clothes. I drove down to the foreshore, dug out a towel, and walked over some grassy dunes to the beach. The tide was out and the sand stretched clean and white in front of me. I walked as far from the other people on the beach as I could; they were a couple necking under an umbrella and two sagging mothers with about ten kids between them. A mile away the bridge looked like a spider's web thrown across the estuary; a collection of small boats tossed up and down in the deep blue water out beyond a line of gentle breakers.

I stripped to my underpants and went into the water. It was cold; I went down under a wave and swam hard for the boats with short, choppy strokes. I got past the breakers but was still a long way short of the boats when my breath ran out. I floated on my back for a while looking up at the sky which was cleaner and closer than in the city. Then a plane ripped across it leaving a thin white streak behind it. I flipped over and swam back. The waves were no good for body surfing but I couldn't have caught them anyway — the speed just wasn't there.

After a walk along the beach and a cold shower in the toilet block I felt revived enough to contemplate the drive to Canberra. I got petrol and some salad rolls in Blackman's Bay. It was still a nice town but my memories of it would never be quite the same. I bought a couple of cans of beer for company; I still looked rough but I felt fine.

From the coast to Canberra isn't the worst drive in the world. The road is good for most of the way, a bit narrow in parts and some of the bends are hairy. I've never done it in a good car; for me, if I make it over the mountain without the radiator boiling, it's a good trip. I made it and pushed on through the flat farming country at a steady fifty-five. The academics and public servants have moved into the cottages in the small towns and the main streets now have restaurants and shops full of pottery and raw wool.

The traffic thickened near Queanbeyan and held me down to a crawl. The city seemed to have its own patch of blue sky resting neatly above it. After the freshness of the hills and farms the air tasted of exhaust fumes and tyre rubber. I found a medium-price motel on the south side and checked in. I washed my shirt in the handbasin, took a swim in the pool and had a nap after asking to be called at 7 p.m. I came out of the sleep fairly fresh and shaved with an old blade and the motel soap. It hurt. I washed my hair with the same soap and thought of Ailsa, my ex-woman, my rich ex-woman, who'd bought me soaps and shampoos and shaving creams and kept me smelling nice. Then I thought of Cyn, my ex-wife who didn't give a damn after a while how I smelt or what I did or thought or said. Funny thing was, I missed them both.

At eight o'clock I was wearing a freshened up shirt and a clean face and was ready to go calling. I got directions to Red Oak Road from the motel office and negotiated the circles and crescents they have in those parts to take the cockiness out of strangers. The neighbourhood looked like Professor and fat-cat territory; the gardens were wide and deep in front and the houses featured a lot of timber and glass and weren't short on stone walls and terraces. The Baudin place didn't let the street down. It had half an acre of garden out front and the trees seemed to have been specially chosen for their cumulative effect of taste and order. I could see a big garage at the end of the drive which held a brace of European cars. A few more of the same were standing out in the street.

I parked and went through the open gates towards the house. It was a well set-up affair in white brick with ivy or something growing on it. Splashing and the strains of jollity from behind the house took my attention and I kept on the drive towards the back. A gate in a white trellis fence gave on to a flag-stoned patio with a low wall around it. Beyond the wall was a swimming pool and a lot of smooth lawn. There was still some light and enough warmth in the air for fun, fun, fun; water splashed up from the pool and glittered like quicksilver. There were about ten people in the pool and three times that many out of it. The dry people were wearing casual clothes and drinking drinks. The sexes seemed to be about equally represented. I took a few steps across the patio and a big man in a dark suit came quickly out of the house and barred my way.

'Private party sir,' he said quietly.

'This is the Baudin residence?'

'A private party,' he repeated. 'By invitation.'

'The night is young. I hope they enjoy it. I'm not here for a party, I want to see Mr and Mrs Baudin.'

'What's your business?'

I handed him a card. He read it and then looked me over carefully; he was poker-faced but his eyes told me he was wondering how anyone could sink so low. I felt resentment.

'Who're you by the way — the caterer?'

'I'm Mr Baudin's personal secretary.'

'And bouncer?'

'If necessary. There's been no call for it so far.'

If it was an invitation I was prepared to pass it up. He had a couple of inches and many pounds on me and none of it looked soft. He held himself well and he'd put the card out of sight so fast I hadn't followed the movement. His hands were free again.

'I don't want any trouble, just a minute or two with the host and I'll be on my way — I won't even dirty a glass.'

Our encounter must have looked intense because it had attracted the attention of some of the drinkers. A couple of them ambled across towards us. The secretary made a motion of his arm that suggested my dismissal, possibly by force, when one of the onlookers spoke up.

'Hey, Cliff Hardy, Cliff.' He lifted his glass. I recognised him as a reporter I'd known in Sydney. I'd heard he'd joined the staff of a cabinet minister. I raised my hand and my mind searched for his name. We shook hands.

'How's tricks Cliff?'

'All right.'

'Do you know Mr . . . Hardy, Mr Rose?'

Tom Rose.

'Yeah sure, from my Sydney days. Still enquiring privately Cliff?'

'Right. Still a fiercely independent voice?'

He laughed. Rose is a short, broad man and his laugh sounds like someone pounding on an oil drum. The laugh did for the secretary. I was in. He leaned forward and dropped a few discreet words between us.

'Mr Baudin has been indisposed. I'll take your card in and mention that you are acquainted with Mr Rose. He might see you.'

'Thanks Jeeves,' I said. He went off athletically into the house and I turned my attention to Rose. 'You carry a little weight in this town, Tom?'

'Just a little. Come and have a drink. Look Cliff I'd like you to meet Richard . . .' He swung around to where his companion had been but the man had drifted away. 'Shit, he's gone. Never mind, come and have a drink, there's gallons of it — the best.' His voice was a bit sloppy. It wasn't his fault there were still gallons. I fell in beside him as he moved towards the throng.

'Who's this Baudin anyway?'

He almost did a skip. 'Captain of industry mate, captain of industry. Least that's what he is now. He was a public servant once, just like me.'

'What was it? Land, rate of the dollar?'

'I wouldn't like to say Cliff. He's big in mining now. Here we are, what'll you have?'

We'd reached a trestle table covered with bottles, ice buckets, siphons and chopped-up lemons.

'Gin and tonic,' I said.

A thin blonde in a pink pantsuit detached herself from a clutch of drinkers by the pool and came over to the table.

'Let me do your bidding,' she said throatily. ' 'Lo Tom. And who do *you* write for?' She got busy with the Gordons Dry gin and the Schweppes tonic and ice as if she knew what she was doing.

'*The New York Times*,' I said.

'Stringer or staff? Do introduce us Tom.'

Rose sighed. 'Cliff Hardy, Billie Harris.'

She smiled and handed me the drink. One of her front teeth was a little yellow but the drink was blue and cold as a good gin and tonic must be. 'You don't sound American Cliff, spent much time there?' Her hands were busy building another drink but her glittering eyes never left me. 'Are you on politics with the NYT, features?' She started to move out and around the table towards me.

'I'm sort of freelance,' I said desperately.

Someone large fell or was pushed into the pool. The displaced water flew up, women shrieked, men swore and Billie Harris turned to look. I moved fast to the right, lurked for a few minutes, and came out on a landscaped higher level. Tom Rose was pouring beer into a schooner glass from a king-sized can.

'Still got your pants on Cliff,' he crowed, 'what's wrong with you?

'Get stuffed, I'm working. Tell me more about the Baudins. What about the wife?'

'No wife, she died a few years back.' He drank some beer and dropped the question in casually. 'What's your interest Cliff?'

My throat felt dry as I formed the question in my mind; I eased the feeling with gin. 'What about the son, he around?'

'Baudin has two sons I think, depends which one you mean. Come on Cliff, what's it about?'

The professional note in his voice warned me to cover up. Rose was still a journalist, still a news-monger even if he was now a politician's errand boy. The last thing Lady C would have wanted was for everyone to be reading about her long-lost grandson before she'd met him herself.

'Baudin's just a small part of something else Tom,' I said. 'How's your job here working out?'

He told me at some length. I hated to hear it; it was all excuses, excuses for changing a real but uncomfortable job for an unreal one. I only half-listened and kept an eye out for Billie Harris and the secretary. I finished my drink. Rose had got through the beer and he went off for refills. I wandered down towards the pool in which there were now only two people — a man and a woman treading water and talking conspiratorially down at the deep end. The party had moved off towards a section of the lawn where a couple of portable barbecues were going full-blast. I stared down at the pool; in the fading light the water looked like slowly rippling green ink. I turned around to look for Jeeves and bumped into a woman who'd appeared behind me. I apologised and had to look her straight in the eye to do it; she was nearly as tall as me and held her head up. She looked arrogant.

'It's all right,' she said. 'I should have coughed or something. I wanted to talk to you.'

'Why?'

'I haven't seen you at one of these do's before for one thing and you were with Rose for another.'

'Is that interesting?'

'It could be. I watch his minister.'

'So you're a journo. What do you know about this Baudin character?'

She smiled and the arrogance fell away. 'Me first — got any dirt?'

'Tons, but not on Tom's master — sorry.'

'Oh well, worth a try.' She leaned closer. 'You've got a hard look to you now I come to notice. Are you a cop?'

'No, private detective.'

The smile again. I was starting to like her. 'But you're not sniffing around Crowley?'

'If that's Tom's boss, no. Why not pump Tom a bit?'

'He's pissed,' she said. 'He's over there with a whole box of cans.' She pointed towards the shadows. I tried to steer her over to the drinks table without doing anything as obvious as taking her arm or dragging her by the hair. She was wearing a dark blue dress with a red tie around the neck like a sailor's. She had dark, short hair and long, slim legs ending in white, high-heeled sandals. Her eyes were dark and slightly slanted in a wide, high cheek-boned face. We reached the table and she asked for scotch and ice. I made it and put two drops of gin into a glass of tonic.

I gave her the drink. 'Cliff Hardy,' I said. 'Who're you?'

'Kay Fletcher. What brings you here, I suppose you're from Sydney?'

There was a wistfulness in her voice that gained her another hundred or so points with me.

'Sydney, right. What's the party for?'

'Oh it's all about some deal he's pulled off, a mine of some kind I think. The government's put up some money, that's why the politicos are here.'

'And the likes of you and Rose.'

'I had nothing better to do.'

'That's hard to believe.'

'Thanks, but it's true. I went through all the possible men in this place in the first year, I don't feel like starting on the rest.'

It wasn't an invitation and it wasn't a put-down. I judged that she was ready to be interested in me if I could be interesting — fair enough. I was on a job, though, and despite myself I looked up to the house for the secretary. I saw him out by the wall looking over the guests who were gathered around the burning meat.

'Look Kay, I'm on a job.' I pointed out the big dark man. 'I have to see him and talk to Baudin, it shouldn't take long. Will you be around?'

She looked at her watch, a big one made for telling the time. 'I'll give you an hour,' she said, 'maybe a bit more.'

I touched her arm, which made me want to do more touching, and went up to the house. The secretary loomed up over me like a medieval knight surveying invaders from his castle wall.

'Mr Baudin will see you.'

I vaulted over the wall, showing off for the girl, and was sorry immediately. The knight seemed not to notice and strode off across the flagstones to the house. As I went in through the French windows it occurred to me that it was strange for Baudin to be still living in the same place thirty years later, given that he'd come up so far in the world. Not that it wasn't a pretty fair shack; the carpet was thick and the paintings on the walls weren't prints. The secretary showed me into a smallish room that had a bar against one wall and some books opposite. There were four big, velvet-covered armchairs. There were two men in the chairs. One was small and wizened with whispy grey hair around his bald skull. The top of his head was baby pink, incongruous beside the ancient, lined flesh on his face. He was wearing a cream shirt, cream trousers and white shoes, like the Wimbledon heroes of long ago. The other man had on a lightweight suit with the jacket open to show his soft, spreading belly. His face was pale and puffy. He was thirtyish.

14

Sir Galahad said my name softly and went away. The old man had my card in one hand. In the other was a glass with liquid in it the colour of very weak tea — at a guess it was the weakest of whisky and water.

'Good evening, Mr Hardy.' He lifted the card a millimetre into the air as if it weighed a ton. 'I am Nicholas Baudin. May I ask what you wish to see me about?' His voice was faint and fell away on the word endings.

Before I could answer the other man put in his oar.

'Don't be foolish father, what could you possibly have to say to someone like this?' There was a sneer in his voice but some apprehension also; he leaned over and peered at the card. 'A private detective who knows Rose and that slut Kay Fletcher. This is obviously some kind of newspaper muck-raking.'

'This is my son, Keir,' Baudin said. 'This is his house.'

'It used to be yours,' I said for no reason.

Keir took another drink. 'Researching the family Hardy? Won't do you any good. There are no skeletons in our cupboard.'

The skin on the old man's face tightened, his hand shook as he took a sip but he didn't say anything. I was feeling out of my depth; here were two people very much on edge and all I'd done was present my card.

'My father is ill as you can probably see — he mustn't be upset.'

There wasn't a lot of conviction in his voice and still some provocation. It crossed my mind that he wouldn't worry if Dad did get a bit upset. I decided I didn't like Keir. I addressed myself to the old man.

'I'll try not to upset you, Mr Baudin. I'm making enquiries about your adopted son but there's nothing sinister in it.'

'Warwick!' Keir almost shouted the word and I could feel his apprehension and aggression go up a hundred points.

I said 'My client . . .' and stopped. The pace had been too

hot for me to think out in advance how to approach this moment. And I hadn't expected it to come up so soon. How do you prise your way into the secret vault of adoption? Except that this wasn't an ordinary adoption. That gave me some leverage. Keir's obvious disaffection could be useful too, if I could play it right.

'We're waiting, Hardy,' Keir purred. 'Your client . . .'

'I can't give you the name of course,' I said, knowing how lame it sounded, 'but my client believes that your adopted son is properly part of her family. She wants to establish the connection; she's old, it's important to her.'

'I was always curious about Warwick's genes,' Nicholas Baudin said.

This galvanised Keir. He slurped down his drink and his previously carefully modulated voice went up into a squeak.

'Who are these people? Who?'

'I'm sorry, I can't tell you that at this stage. There are a lot of threads to tie up. This could be a false lead, if it's not you'll get all the details in time.'

'Thanks very much.' Keir again. He got up and stood as tall as he could — about five foot six. 'This is preposterous. I won't have it. I'm going to call Rogers and have this character thrown out. It's an original line, I'll say that for it.' He moved up to his father's chair keeping well away from me, still standing. He noticed that his glass was empty and went across to the bar for more. He slammed the glass down on the bar and turned dramatically.

'Of course! This is Warwick's idea! Come on father, this is some sort of hoax.' He took his drink across and stood protectively near the old man's chair. 'You're not a bad actor, Mr Hardy, you had me fooled. But I can't for the life of me see how Warwick would get anything out of this.'

'You're babbling,' I said. 'I've never met your brother.'

'Don't call him my brother.' The squeak was back. 'He forfeited that right years ago.'

'I'd like to hear about it.'

'Well you won't. Clear off.'

He was red in the face with anger and from the effort of keeping himself at his full height. I looked down at his feet and realised that I'd over-measured him; he wore built-up shoes that must have given him a couple of inches. Short men who want to impress should cultivate an icy mien or be jolly — I knew a few who did it successfully. I grinned at him.

'I'd say that was up to your father. I've told you the truth, as much of it as I can.'

The old man seemed to get the message. He pulled himself up in the chair and shoved his glass at Keir. 'Don't brawl Keir, it's not your forte. And for God's sake get me a decent drink, it's a crime to drown good whisky like this.'

The son snatched up the glass clumsily; his father could strip him of composure so quickly I almost felt sorry for him. Almost.

'Sit down, Mr Hardy.' The old boy pointed to the chair nearest him. 'Will you have a drink?'

'Thanks, no, I've got things to do tonight.' I took out my tobacco and held it up enquiringly.

'Go ahead.' He took the glass from Keir without acknowledgment; the drink was dark this time, neat scotch over ice. He drank some and settled back in his chair.

'That's better. Do you know the occasion for this gathering?'

I worked at the makings. 'Something to do with mining I heard.'

'That's right. A mine. It'll be operational in five years — I'll be dead.'

Keir made a noise that was hard to interpret, perhaps shock, perhaps dutiful protest. Baudin ignored it. So did I.

'I'm nearly eighty and that's the sort of thing I have to celebrate. What do you think of that?'

I had the cigarette going and took in a lungful. 'I don't know. You could celebrate being nearly eighty. A lot of people don't make it so far.'

His snort could have been amusement. His old eyes just looked old.

'There's something in what you say. Well, are you offering me something else to celebrate? Has my adopted son come into enormous wealth or a title?'

'No title. Some wealth I guess, if he's the man. Other considerations are more important. I'm concerned about the family.'

318

He drank again and smacked his lips. 'You should be. It pains me to say it of someone I raised, but if anything good is going to happen to Warwick it will be a colossal injustice. He's one of the most worthless people that ever lived.'

This pronouncement seemed to give Keir heart.

'He's rubbish,' he said. His father said nothing and his confidence went up. 'Father I simply can't believe this. He's snooping about something else.'

All that did was tell me that there was something else to snoop about. Baudin senior tilted his head at him and he subsided.

'Keir was born less than a year after we took Warwick. It was one of those cases. The two boys never got along.'

I nodded. 'His character isn't really my concern. I'd better come clean with you. I'm pretty sure he is the man I want. A physical similarity to other members of the family would help. Do you have a photograph of him?'

'No,' Keir snapped. 'We have nothing.'

Something in the way he said it made panic jump in me. 'You don't mean he's dead?' Then I remembered Keir's earlier remark.

The relief must have showed. 'This is important to you, Mr Hardy?' Baudin's face seemed to lose flesh with the effort of talking.

'Yes. Do you know where Warwick is now?'

I expelled smoke and waited for an answer. Keir supplied it from the middle of a smirk across his pasty face.

'No, we don't.'

Baudin *père* didn't contradict him. Instead he drank the rest of his whisky and set the glass down as if he'd lost interest in liquor forever.

'That boy was the trial of my life,' he said in his faint, falling tones. 'Everything else I touched turned out just right except . . . except Warwick. He was trouble from the start. Enormously gifted but a monster. He killed my wife. She loved him more than me, more than Keir. She called him her marvellous boy and he killed her with worry and shame.'

'What sort of trouble Mr Baudin?'

'Everything — cars, girls, drink, cheques. Everything.'

'Where was this?

'Everywhere. Here, Sydney, London, New York, Rome.'

Keir was loving it but he was a hypocrite to the core. 'Really father, is this wise? I don't trust this man an inch. His story is quite unbelievable. He's in this with Warwick, you can bet your life on it.'

'Bet my life,' the old man said dreamily. 'A good expression for the young. It doesn't carry much punch at my age. It might interest you to know, Keir, that I'd bet my life Mr Hardy here is telling the truth.'

'Why?' Keir said petulantly.

'God boy, you'd better sharpen up. If you can't judge character better than that you'll be on the dole before I'm cold. Have a look at the man for Christ's sake, does he look like a confidence trickster?'

'He's in a cheap trade,' Keir muttered.

'There!' the father said triumphantly. 'There! You accept that he's an enquiry agent. You're confused. You're believing what you want to believe.'

The unequal contest was starting to bore me. I wanted facts and leads, not a sparring match. All I had were impressions and hostilities; it would be hard to concoct a professional-looking report for Lady Catherine on what I had so far. The cigarette was a dead stub between my fingers.

'Let me get this straight, Mr Baudin. Your son is something of a black sheep, or was. But he's a grown man now. You mentioned gifts, what did you mean?'

'Everything again,' Baudin said slowly. 'He was brilliant at everything. God you should have seen him run . . . cricket . . . tennis . . . matriculated with honours . . .' He was weary. The whisky seemed to have hit him. His eyelids were flickering as if he were fighting to keep them up. Keir watched him intently and expertly and I realised that this was what he had on him — the staying power of fewer years on the clock.

'My father is tired, Hardy, and I have nothing to say to you.'

'When did you last see your brother?' I snapped.

'Three years ago.' Again, it came out too quickly; my firmest impression of this wispy young-old man was that he lied almost every time he opened his mouth. 'You have to go,' he said smugly.

There was no arguing with it, the old man was drooping. I put in a last desperate question.

'Mr Baudin, what was the last address you had for Warwick?'

'Sydney,' the old man whispered.

'He's wandering,' Keir said brightly. 'It was London, a slum in Islington. Don't make the trip, it wouldn't be worth it.'

'Why not?'

'Warwick is a drunk among other things. His last card was a drunken . . .' He stopped as if he was unhappy at giving this information away but I misinterpreted him. His pale face turned blotchy with anger and he seemed to be recalling nursery days. His voice went soft, almost babyish.

'I wouldn't put it past Warwick to dream up something like this. He hates me.' It was interesting psychologically but I needed facts.

'Have you got the card?' I said.

'What? No. I tore it up. Get out, get *out*!'

A light snore from the old man did the trick. Baudin senior was dead asleep in his chair. His hand rested an inch away from his glass which still held a few drops of whisky, just a few.

15

The sky had darkened and the party had thinned by the time I got outside. The secretary was hovering and he bustled back into the house when he saw me. I wondered which Baudin he served, Senior or Junior, or if he knew. Kay was sitting under a tree a little apart from the hard core drinkers. I walked over to her with that little pilot light of excitement burning.

'Did you get what you wanted?' She got up smoothly but didn't seem to mind my token help in the form of a hand on her arm. Her arm was cool and soft and I kept hold of it.

'I'm not sure,' I said. 'I'm a bit too tired to think about it right now. I'll worry about it later. Do you want another drink here or will we go somewhere else?'

'I'd like to eat. I'm starving.'

She went into the house and came out with a shoulder bag. We went down the drive past the remaining imported cars to my honest Falcon.

'No car?' I said.

'Cab — expenses.'

She untangled the crescents and circuits for me and steered me towards the city. Otherwise she was quiet and didn't volunteer much. I had to prompt her hard to find out that she worked two days a week at the university as a research assistant in Political Science and two days as a feature writer for *The Canberra Times*. She preferred the journalism but the two jobs complemented each other. We pulled into a big parking lot behind a department store and she stared out at the city lights.

'What's wrong?'

'I'm not used to talking about myself.'

'Okay I'll stop. One last question. What brought you to Canberra?'

'Marriage.'

We walked through the parking lot and down some streets and across a couple of pedestrian plazas. Canberra has scored a few points against the motor car in the centre of the city, but just a few. The closed-off roads with pot plants and painted barriers look as if they could be swept away easily enough if someone decided they should be. Kay led me to some steps that went down into a big, circular concrete cellar. There was enough light to see by and some kind of matting on the floor. The food was on a serve-yourself system. We got steaks and garlic rolls and salad on our plates and I got a couple of small carafes of white wine. There were about ten plain wooden tables which would seat a dozen people and the drill was to plonk yourself down wherever you pleased. I was surprised to see people choosing to sit near others, obviously strangers, rather than going off by themselves. Kay went over to where a hippie-looking couple were sitting: the woman, who wore a plaid poncho and jeans, was holding a baby on her knee. The man was dark-bearded and thin: they nodded as we sat down, pushed the pepper and salt along and went back to talking quietly about their kid. We started on the food.

'Good place,' I said.

She nodded and kept eating.

'Is there a no-talking rule?'

She shook her head and smiled. She had big white teeth and her smile was a fraction crooked. I looked at her hands — no rings. I drank the first glass of the cold wine fast and poured another — she did the same. Then we both smiled and touched glasses. She put down her knife and fork.

'Ask,' she said.

'It's a compliment really. What happened to the marriage?'

'It did what it was supposed to do.' She picked up her fork. 'Then it finished.'

'What was it supposed to do?'

She shrugged. 'Get him a PhD and a couple of books.' She didn't sound or look bitter, more amused. If it had scarred her she wasn't letting it show. Then she went back to eating and kept at it until all the food was gone. She wiped her plate with bread and put that down. We started on the second carafe.

'God I needed that. I ran out without eating this morning and I don't eat lunch. Sorry to be so incommunicative. I was just bloody hungry. Now, are you going to tell me what you're investigating?'

I suppose I'd known all along that I would and that I'd be needing her help. The wine and food and her company had relaxed me. Little things that had come out in the interview with the Baudins were floating around in my mind, coming to the surface and forming a pattern. Something about this girl, which was how I thought of her although she must have been in her mid-twenties, and something about the ease we felt with each other made me trust her and want to try out the pattern on her. So I told her. I gave her all the details as far as I could recall them and put it all in order as it had happened. She looked concerned when I got to the bit about being bashed, but more interested than concerned. I'd obviously survived to do more sleuthing and that was what mattered to her. To me too. It took some time and the wine was finished when I got to the end. The hippies had melted away into the night early on in my exposition.

Kay toyed with her empty glass. 'So you think Keir Baudin was lying. He knows more about his brother than he lets on?'

'Yeah, that's how it looks to me. He hates Warwick and he reinforces his father's disappointment with him. The old boy struck me as pretty tolerant so this Warwick must be a real bastard.'

'Mm, I've never heard of him, but I could ask a few people who might have. I could sniff around about Keir too, it sounds as if he's got things on his mind. Tomorrow.'

'Yeah, tomorrow.' I was tired but not too tired, the wine had done me good and I could feel the juices flowing. I stroked her arm, raising the fine, light hairs and smoothing them down again.

'That's nice,' she said. 'What's next Cliff?'

I laced my fingers through hers. 'I want to go back to my motel and go to bed with you. Then I want to get up at 4 a.m. and break into Keir Baudin's house with you keeping watch.' I took out my licence and put it on the table; the younger, smoother Hardy face mocked up at my battered mug. I wasn't sure why I'd put it there, unless it was some sort of personal commitment. But to what?

'That doesn't license you to break and enter.'

'No, rather the reverse. They come down hard if they catch you at anything fancy.'

'Ever been caught?'

I grinned. 'Yeah, once or twice. The trick is to come out smelling clean at the end — I've done that so far.'

She looked at me and the photograph and back to me. We were thinking the same thing — was there a story in it for her and under what terms? That accounted for some of her interest in me I knew, but how much? I thought bleakly of the house in Glebe with nothing waiting for me but the dust and yesterday's papers and realised that I didn't care about the percentages. If she was ten percent interested in me that was fine, twenty percent would be a jackpot. If we had an unspoken semi-professional relationship in the making what the hell did it matter? I squeezed her hand confidently.

'Come on, think about it on the way. If you're against it I'll just drive you home. Of course I'll have to tie you up with knots that'll hold you till dawn.'

She laughed. I paid the bill and we went out. The air was cool and we drew close as we walked. I put my arm around her and suddenly we were in a shop doorway kissing hard and fierce as if we'd invented it. I took her head in my hands and held it in close; she flicked her tongue into my mouth. We pressed together from knee to nose and I liked it, then we broke apart, both breathing hard.

'Yes then,' she said. 'Yes.'

I didn't say anything, just kept close to her all the way back to the car. I kissed her again before I started up and she let her long legs slide down in front of her. After a few minutes she fumbled beside her on the seat and came up with one of the bottles of Irish. I'd told her about Brain but not about the whisky.

'Do you drink this stuff much?'

'Not usually. It was to oil Brain's tongue. I hope he died easier for it.'

She glanced sharply at me and it occurred to me then that this was confirmation of a sort of what I'd told her. I hadn't thought until then that she might not have believed me — it was pretty weird for a pick-up story though.

She sat quietly with the bottle in her lap, then she said: 'We'll have a sip before we go to bed.'

The motel room was dingy and smelled of my washing but

it didn't matter. I could taste the sweet spirit in her mouth when we kissed and I pressed down on her and we connected. She thrust hard back up at me and dug her fingernails into my shoulders; we threw ourselves into it for a while and then she groaned and relaxed and I came hard and she hung onto me with her hands gentle now on my back.

We rolled apart and I reached for the telephone and booked the morning call. We pulled up a sheet and wrapped ourselves together and went to sleep. I woke up a bit later and disentangled; I put out the lights all but one and made a cigarette and looked at her while I smoked. She was lying curled up on her side; her face was hidden by the dark blob of hair; the sheet was down around her waist and her breasts were high set and pointed. Her skin was a faint amber colour like a faded summer tan or an early summer tan or an all-year tan. She slept still and quietly; I finished the cigarette, lay down, and curved in beside her.

Post coital sleep is deep and a few drops of wine and whisky help things along. I was well under when the light came on and the radio started blaring. Baudin's secretary or bodyguard or whatever he was stood near the bed. He had a big chrome-plated gun in his hand and although Kay was sitting up bare-breasted his eyes were only for me. He lifted the gun a fraction.

'Disgusting,' he said. 'You've only just met.' Kay pulled the sheet up, her eyes were wide and frightened and she looked at the gun as if she'd never seen one before.

'Then again,' he drawled, 'maybe you have met before. That's a thought.'

I pulled myself up and tried to get some balance and possible leverage in the bed. It's not a good place to launch an attack from.

'You better know what you're doing,' I said.

He smiled. He'd taken his tie off and he needed a shave which made him look even tougher. I searched my mind for his name — Reynolds? Rawson? Rogers, that was it, but it was one of those useless, irrelevant thoughts that come along at times like these. I should have been thinking about how to get his gun and put it down his throat.

'I know what I'm doing,' he said. 'I've come here to ask you a few questions. If I'm satisfied with the answers I go away. If I'm not people start getting hurt.'

'Ask away,' I said.

'Who are you working for?'

'No comment.'

'Where is Warwick Baudin?'

'I wish I knew.'

He sighed. He was a bit stagey in his role but still efficient. 'It looks like some pressure is needed.' He held the gun very steady, pointed it at my belly, and hit me on the ear with a short, hard left hand chop. He knew how to hit. I went back and heard a harsh ringing start up inside my head. He moved around the bed, reached down and grabbed one of Kay's breasts and twisted. She screamed and he slapped her hard, twice.

'You won't use the gun,' I said. 'Too much noise.'

He flexed the fingers of his hitting hand and pointed the pistol at my groin. 'You're wrong there. I've done it before. I really don't mind doing it, you know. A private detective and a journalist, dead in bed, who'd care?'

Kay covered herself again and massaged her breast. 'Cliff, I'm scared.'

'So you should be,' he said. 'That was just a start, the possibilities are endless.' She drew in a breath and Rogers moved a little closer to her.

'If you scream,' he said softly, 'I'll knock out a few of your teeth.'

My mind was racing trying to think why Keir Baudin had need of this animal. It had to be Keir; Rogers acted like an instrument — he was Keir's malevolence and cruelty put into action. He had good control but he seemed to like uttering the threats and inflicting petty violence a little too much to be first class at his trade.

'I'll ask you again Hardy — who and where?'

I said nothing.

'I think you're going to have to come along with me Miss Fletcher,' he said. 'Perhaps you'll be more reasonable.'

'Touch her again and I'll kill you.'

He gave a short laugh and reached for Kay's neck. I pushed

up off the bed and went for his wrist with both hands. I got it and twisted my whole weight against it; he yelled and dropped the gun but his recovery was quick. He hit me hard in the ribs as I came flailing to my feet naked and vulnerable. His eyes searched for the gun and I swung a roundhouse punch that got him high on the head and didn't hurt him much. He chopped at my neck and I took more of the weight of it than was comfortable. I hit him again, low down but it was too light to bother him. Then he spotted the gun and bent for it; I rushed him and jerked a knee up under his chin. He grunted, went down and got a hand to the gun but he was hurt; I took hold of his arm, twisted it round and broke it. The snapping sound was nearly as loud as his yell and I clapped my hand hard over his mouth. He sagged down with his good arm on the bed. Little moans ebbed from his mouth along with spittle.

Kay was sitting up with her knees drawn up protectively in front of her. She was looking at me but there was terror in her eyes and I knew that things wouldn't be quite the same between us again. I grabbed a handful of tissues and crammed them into Rogers' mouth, then I pulled off his jacket and wasn't gentle. Blood was seeping through the sleeve of his elegantly striped shirt. I ripped the sleeve from cuff to shoulder: the bone had broken a little above the elbow joint and a white splinter was showing through the skin which was discoloured. Rogers turned his head to look at the injury, his eyes wide in shock. I removed the tissues from his mouth.

'Hospital,' he croaked.

'Yeah.' I picked up the gun and put it on the bedside table before pulling on my pants. Kay crawled across the bed towards me and I put my arm around her and stroked her hair. I lowered the sheet; a big purple bruise spread around the nipple of her breast. The whisky bottle wasn't far away and I reached for it and took a swig. Kay shook her head when I offered it to her and I ignored the plea in Rogers' eyes.

'Get dressed, love,' I said. 'We're going visiting.'

'I need medical attention,' Rogers yelped.

'That's right,' I said. 'That's a nasty wound, gangrene's a

distinct possibility. You might bump it too. I'd say you could lose that arm.'

'Christ,' he moaned.

I got into my clothes; some of them were tangled with Kay's and we exchanged smiles as we sorted them out. I was dressed and just taking another slug of the whisky when the early morning call came through. We all jumped and Rogers' face contorted with the pain of the movement. I answered the call and then bent down close to his ear.

'Listen you bastard, you're taking us to Keir Baudin and you're going to be happy to do it. One wrong move from you and you can forget about your arm. Understand?'

He nodded.

'We don't have to break in now Cliff?' Kay's voice was shaky but she was pulling herself together fast. I considered persuading her not to come, or trying to, but decided against it. She'd had some of the pain and deserved some pleasure; I also thought it might be useful to have a member of the fourth estate along.

'Right,' I said. 'Change of plan. Are you up to it?'

'Yes.' She straightened her crumpled clothes and moved around towards me, taking care to keep well clear of Rogers. 'I'm worried about him though. That arm looks bad.'

It did, and Rogers was showing strain and the effects of shock. He probably didn't have very long before the injury would crumple him mentally and physically. I remembered his face when he hurt Kay though and I was all out of sympathy.

'He's a tough boy,' I said. 'He'll last until we do what we have to do, then I'll get him to a hospital. Come on, let's go.'

I put Rogers' gun, a business-like Harrison & Richardson Defender, in my jacket pocket and we went out as a threesome. A white Honda Civic was parked handily in the motel drive. Rogers stumbled and swore as we walked across the dark, quiet parking strip to the Falcon. I opened the back door and he scrambled in cradling his arm and muttering quietly. I asked Kay if she thought she could drive the Falcon.

'Drive anything,' she said.

I got in the back next to Rogers, pushing aside the clothes, tools and other junk I keep there. I got out the Defender, broke it and checked it. It was clean and fully loaded.

'Nice gun,' I said. Kay climbed into the driver's seat and tugged at the seat adjustment lever.

'Shit,' she said.

'Sorry love, it hasn't been moved in ten years, you'll just have to reach a bit.' She shuffled her feet and jiggled the gearshift.

'Not much,' she said. 'Give us the keys.'

After a few blocks Kay and the Falcon sorted out and she handled it well through the empty crescents and avenues. The dark blue of Rogers' stubble showed against his white face as if it had been applied with burnt cork; he winced and swore with the movement of the car and his hair was wet and matted from sweat.

'I could get an infection from this shit-heap,' he said.

'Could be,' I said. 'But for now just shut up and do what you're told if you don't want to drive that Honda with special fittings for the handicapped.'

Forrest was quiet and still under a bright moon; the road outside the Baudin house shone under the moon and street light like the centre court at White City. I told Kay to drive a little further to where some trees on the nature strip gave us some cover. She stopped and opened her door.

'I think you'd better stay here.'

'I'm coming,' she said sharply. 'You might need a witness.' She put her hand on the front of her dress and pressed. 'I'm involved, remember?'

I couldn't argue with that. I held the door open for Rogers and we made our way slowly back to the house. Rogers took a step on the path that led up to the front door but I jabbed him with my finger.

'Around the back,' I whispered.

'Why?' Kay was close but keeping clear of the pocket that held the gun.

'Who knows, this assassin here might have a mate. Did you see any signs of a dog when you were at the party?

She thought. 'No.'

'Me neither, but let's have a poke around.'

The only car at home was a nice, conservative white Volvo.

330

That probably meant Keir was on his own; Baudin senior wouldn't drive himself and I hadn't seen any cars out on the street that might belong to any extra muscle. We went around the back to where the memory of the party lingered on. One of the barbecues still emitted a dull glow and a few paper plates floated on the surface of the pool like pale lily pads. There'd been a clean-up; bottles and glasses had been collected and there was no food lying about but it looked as if the work had been interrupted.

'Okay,' I said. 'Let's go in the front door.'

'My arm feels stiff,' Rogers moaned.

'Good. Behave yourself and you'll be in hospital before dawn.'

'I'm cold,' he said.

We got back to the nice, moonlit path and walked up it to the flagstoned porch in front of the house. I took out the H&R and thumbed the catch back and forward a few times.

'Put that bloody thing away Cliff, please,' Kay said.

'It's just for show.'

I rang the bell twice and we waited until a light came on in the house. There were footsteps inside near the door and Keir's voice came through blearily.

'Who is it?'

I tapped Rogers' good elbow with the gun.

'Raymond Rogers.'

The door opened before the porch light came on which is always a mistake. I had my foot in the door while Keir was still focusing on Rogers' face.

'What . . .' he said.

'It's no time for the snappy dialogue Baudin,' I said. 'Your friend here didn't go about things in the right way.' I pushed him back into the house and shepherded Rogers and Kay through the door. Keir was wearing a paisley dressing gown over his pyjamas; without the built-up shoes he was gnome-like. I switched out the porch light which left us with the soft, expensive lighting in the hall. Rogers leaned against the wall and a trickle of blood ran down it towards the carpet. Kay stood with her back against the door. In the sailor-suit dress and with her face pale and eyes dark she looked like a tragic mime. The scene terrified Keir Baudin.

'Rogers,' he stammered, 'why are you . . .'

I made a backing motion with the gun and he backed. 'Anyone here?'

'My father.'

'Where?'

He shuffled along the carpet and pointed to a door near the end of the hallway. We trooped down and I opened the door quietly. There was a night light on and its beam was falling directly on the old man's lobster pink skull. He was lying on his back and snoring softly; his cream clothes were folded neatly over a chair and his teeth were in a glass.

I told Baudin we wanted the sitting room and he shuffled off obediently. The room was big with an elaborate ceiling rose, too many pictures on the walls and fussy furniture. Baudin was staring at Rogers as we sat down and he was licking his lips nervously. Kay went out and came back after a few minutes with a towel which she handed to Rogers; he dabbed at the blood and improvised a pillow for the arm. He didn't look at her or thank her.

'Let's make this fast,' I said to Baudin. 'Rogers made a mess of things, he assaulted Miss Fletcher and we could press charges against him and you. I don't think you'd like that.'

'No.'

'Also he's in danger of losing his arm. The quicker you tell me things the quicker he gets treatment.'

'He means it,' Rogers whispered. 'He means it, Mr Baudin.'

'Right,' I said. 'Now what's your problem, why all this aggravation?'

'Well, Warwick . . .' He stopped and it took a moan from Rogers to start him again but after that it came out fairly steadily. Warwick was blackmailing him. He'd lied about the last communication he'd had from him, now he produced it — a note scrawled on a postcard which was unstamped so it must have come in an envelope. It was undated:

Keir,

This will be the last time I ask you for money, I swear it. I'm on to something big but I need a decent appearance. $1,500 will do. Send it c/- Honey 10a Clark Street Darlinghurst. Last time I promise. When I get the money

I'll send your stuff back.

The note wasn't signed. I felt a surge of excitement at this nasty bit of work, but the timing was all-important.

'When did you get this?' Baudin looked relieved to get a question he could answer.

'A year ago, or a bit less.'

'Did you pay him?'

'Yes.'

'What did he have on you?'

The relief subsided, this was harder. He looked down at his tiny blue-veined feet. 'Sexual things,' he muttered.

I thought about it and didn't like it much. Sending Rogers was an over-reaction even if he thought I was in collusion with Warwick; there had to be something more. I brought my hand up to rub my face and realised I was still holding the gun. Baudin jumped at the movement and shrank back in his chair.

'Christ you're jumpy. You're hiding something. Did he send you whatever it was, this . . . stuff he talks about?'

'No. He was always a cheat and a liar.'

'And you're an upright man, I suppose.' I was feeling weary and out of ideas. I looked across at Kay who moved her shoulders in a sort of shrug. Suddenly I was angry, furious at the little creep and his thug who'd made me act like a sadist. I felt dirty and cheap and had to take it out somehow.

'Why did you send Rogers after us?'

'I told you,' Baudin said. 'I thought you and Warwick . . .'

'Crap! I want the real reason.'

Baudin just stared at me and I forced myself to smile and relax in the chair.

'All right,' I said. 'We'll just sit here until I get it. That okay with you Raymond?'

'Jesus,' Rogers croaked. 'Mr Baudin, this arm's on fire. Talk to him, for God's sake. I've got to get help.' Baudin said nothing and Rogers screamed: 'Talk to him!' Kay had the look I'd seen on her face when I'd clobbered Rogers. She was on my side but scared of me too. I felt I was losing the grip and getting dirtier.

'You talk to me,' I said to Rogers. 'Give me a clue, I'm easily satisfied.'

'Indonesia,' Rogers said. 'Indonesian oil, he's . . .'

'Rogers, don't . . .'

'You shut up!' I waved at Baudin with the gun hand. 'What about Indonesia? Give us a bit more.'

Kay was leaning forward in her chair, professionally alert. Rogers wet his lips and his eyes bulged with the effort of talking.

'He's cleaning up money for them, using his father's companies. He thought you might be on to him. I don't know much about it, I swear. It's a lot of money. Jesus God my arm!'

I stood up and beckoned to Kay. 'We're leaving,' I said to Baudin. 'Mucking around with Indonesian Colonels is about your style. I don't give a damn. But if you've lied to me about your brother I'll come back and see you. You'd better get him to hospital.'

Kay and I walked out and I put the revolver back in my pocket along with Warwick Baudin's note. I could feel the nervous energy in Kay as she walked beside me, her shoulder and head nearly on a level with mine. She was steady and keen and I suddenly wished that I was on my own, that I could just get in the car and drive off. By myself. I was reminded of why I always tried to work alone — because I'd never learned to trust anyone but myself. We got in the car and I sat on the passenger side tense and mistrusting and not wanting to be that way. She reached for me but sensed my mood and drew back.

'Do you want me to drive?'

'Yes.' I wanted to shout *No. Go away!* But I didn't, I was hoping the feeling would pass. My head ached where I'd been hit and the lack of sleep was getting to me. I found the other bottle of whisky, pulled the cap off and took a drink. She started the engine; I cradled the bottle in my lap and waited for the liquor to do me some good.

'Cliff, what's wrong?'

I didn't answer. How could I tell her I didn't trust her? How could I say I don't trust you to keep quiet about this juicy story. I said nothing and took another drink. She drove well but her fingers were tightening on the wheel and she was going too fast. I thought of the fights I'd had in cars with

Cyn, fights so bad I'd crashed my fist down on her leg so that she wept with pain and rage but kept driving, fights so bad she'd ripped levers and buttons off the dashboard and kicked out the windshield. And I thought that my distrustfulness must have contributed to those battles. I forced myself to reach over and touch her arm gently.

'Pull over Kay, pull in here.'

She looked at me suspiciously but she did it. I held her close to me, tight and warm; she resisted for a minute and then let go and we got as close together as we could in the front seat of an old Falcon. We stayed like that for a while, saying things that I don't remember except that they meant we were going to be good to each other. We eased apart and she drove again; I didn't drink any more whisky and I put the H&R Defender under the seat. It was still dark at the motel and we got inside and took our clothes off and went to bed. She fell asleep almost straight away with her head on my shoulder. I lay awake with my mind working, listening to a branch knocking against the window, but not for long.

16

The room was very light when I woke up and Kay was still sleeping beside me; her back was towards me and she was curled up in a tangle of sheets. I stroked her shoulder.

'Hey, it's morning.'

'Jesus,' she muttered from the huddle, 'what day is it?'

I had to think. 'Sunday.'

She curled tighter. 'Thank God.'

I pulled gently at the sheets and she pulled back and soon we were making love, starting gently and ending up in a hard, bucking rhythm. The bed was a ruin and it was nearly midday when we reached the motel coffee shop.

She ate appreciatively again and picked up toast crumbs from her plate with a moistened finger.

'You'll be heading back to Sydney then, to follow this up?'

'Yes, but not quite yet. You said you could ask around about the Baudins, can you do that today — Sunday?'

'Yeah, no problem. What do you want exactly?'

'Anything. I'd be hoping for something on Warwick's cock-ups — cars, girls and cheques they said. Something might have made the papers. He was a jock too, there could be a photo.'

I paused and chose the words carefully. 'There's a story in the Indonesian business. I suppose you'd be interested in that?'

'Mm, I'd have to wait until you've cleared all this up, wouldn't I?'

'Probably, but you never know. A bit of press could be useful at some stage. That's happened before.'

She nodded and finished her coffee. I made a cigarette and she pulled a face.

'What?'

'You shouldn't smoke.'

'I know.' I lit the cigarette, drew hard on it and blew the smoke away from her. 'It's a strange case this. It looks to be plain sailing except that there's someone trying to get in on it.

I have to assume they're trying to stop me reaching the . . .'

'Foundling?'

'He's hardly that. It sounds as if he had the best of everything.'

'Aren't you scared?'

'No. I can't see a lot of violence in this — Brain could have had a thin skull, and I only got a tap. It's one of the things that puzzles me.'

'If Warwick is the lost grandson, maybe someone knows that and has an interest in him not turning up.'

'Yeah, but why not just put him out of the picture — why mess about with the bit players like me?'

'Maybe the person doesn't want Warwick to prosper but can't bring himself to kill him, or can't afford to.'

'Keir you mean?'

'Yes.'

'Maybe. I have to find out who benefits most from things staying just as they are. I've got someone working on that.'

She went quiet and I finished my cigarette and picked up the bill. She shifted in her seat, the broad, almost Tartar face was clouded and she spoke nervously, without her usual crispness:

'D'you worry about the morality of this, Cliff?'

I went on guard. 'What morality's that?'

'Don't snarl, I mean about digging back like this, uncovering all these things, splitting people up.'

'It doesn't bother me,' I said but I knew I was lying. It did bother me but I couldn't help it. Shallow graves got uncovered, secrets were divulged, liars were found out — it happened all the time and I was just an agent, just a lever. Sometimes there were happy endings. Sometimes. She looked down and I thought *Oh Christ, more trouble*. But when she lifted her head all seemed well. She gave me the crooked smile and rooted in her bag for a pen and paper. Our hands touched when she handed the paper across and the contact was still good. We were both skirmishing I felt, both mistrustful, but hoping. It could have been worse.

'Phone me at the paper in a couple of hours,' she said. 'No. In one hour, I should have something by then.'

'Okay, what're you doing tonight?'

'Depends,' she said and got to her feet. 'Depends on a lot of things.' She waved and walked breezily out of the place. I watched her go in the crumpled dress, slim back and long legs and the evening shoes that looked oddly pathetic in the daylight. I sat and thought and the Chatterton case and Kay got all tangled up in my mind until I didn't know what I was asking questions about or what answers I wanted to find.

I rinsed my shirt again, shaved rough again and took a dip in the pool. The chlorine was fresh and sharp and the water was cold: I swam hard, lap after lap, and showered and put on the clean shirt and felt good. Then I called the number Kay had given me; her voice was brisk and efficient on the phone but there was warmth in it too. She sounded pleased with herself.

'Warwick Baudin sounds like a real rat,' she said.

'What does he do — rape old ladies?'

'I wouldn't be surprised. He was in all sorts of trouble. He crashed a few cars that weren't his.'

'Yeah, I heard about that. High spirits maybe.'

'No, there's a nasty streak to him. There's a story that he sold drugs here, not just grass, and made money at it. Then there was a bust and he got off. The word was that he informed on the others. He left Canberra soon after that. Oh yes, he assaulted his father in public once but it was hushed up.'

'Choice. Anything on Keir?'

'Not much. He sounds like the dullest man alive. He went to school and university here, undistinguished at both. Then he went to work for his Dad. He's sort of never left home.'

'He's been overseas I bet.'

'Yes, he used to travel with his Mum and Dad. It's been a bit of a joke, his closeness to them.'

'It's a cynical world. You said "used to".'

'Right. He's made a couple of trips to Indonesia in the last two years.'

'Aha. Anything on Warwick's sporting triumphs?'

'Oh Christ yes, tons. He went to half a dozen schools around here, he was always getting expelled, but he cleaned up at sport — running, swimming, throwing things, kicking things — the lot. It grieves me to say it, but he was bright as well; he got distinctions in his last year at school.' She paused: 'Yes, here it is — maths, economics, modern history, Italian. He only got a credit for English.'

'Tough. Went on to uni did he?'

'Yes, he did two years of Law. He won the iron man in his first year. Do you know what that is?'

'No.'

'It's a race. They run about five miles I think and have to eat things and drink a lot of grog throughout. They get disqualified if they vomit. Warwick holds the record.'

'Charming. How'd he go at Law?'

'Tapering off a bit but he got through the first year well enough — the drug bust came in the middle of the second year.'

'I see. Well that's terrific work, love, anything else?'

'Yes, you said you wanted photos, well I'm told there are two in *The Canberra Times*.' She gave the dates. 'I can't get a look at the file copies on Sunday. You'll have to go to the National Library. It's open today. You know where it is?'

'By the lake?'

'Right.'

'Tickets needed?'

'No, it's a public utility. You have full rights as a citizen.'

Then her voice changed and the brisk and businesslike tone took over completely. 'Phone me when you're finished,' she said.

'Look Kay, don't stand back so far. I'll come and get you at five. Okay?'

She said it was. I paid a bit on account at the motel; the money was running low but I had the receipts and Lady Catherine was getting value. I felt uppish; the tried and tested procedures were working. I had leads to follow.

Driving across the bridge in Canberra is a very low-key experience: the lake looks and is artificial, placid and blue with no debris. The bridge spans it easily. It all feels planned and controlled and easy, soft. The National Library is a cream and pink copy of the Acropolis on the sculptured shores of the lake. It's surrounded on three sides by car parks; cars were bullocked up on footpaths and dividing strips and parking tickets flapped on their windshields like bunting. I squeezed into a semi-legal space, grabbed a pad and pen and headed for the portals.

A gaggle of tourists was gasping at the stained glass windows and bronze work; another batch was inspecting a pottery exhibition on the mezzanine floor. I got directions from a succession of attendants and finished up in an airless room in front of a microfilm reader. The PhD students were scratching on cards, scratching themselves, yawning and chewing gum. I stabbed at the automatic button; months of life, marriage, death and world events flashed in front of my eyes and the students frowned as they crept, inch by inch, frame by frame, through their papers.

The Canberra Times is a broadsheet which meant that I had to adjust the machine often to scan the whole page. I got distracted by the headlines and stories at the beginning of the seventies. The rot had set into the Government, the ministers' speeches were getting sillier by the day and the Opposition was just sitting pat, trying to sound sensible and waiting for its finest hour. A tide was flowing — a three year tide. I found the first picture of Warwick Baudin in an issue for November 1968. He'd competed at the inter-school sports and won all three sprint races and the long jump; he was standing straight and tall in a track suit sucking on a can of soft drink. It was like an advertisement: he had a big, open face with a lot of curly dark hair. He looked sure of himself — so would I if I had a 48.4 440 to my credit. The best I could manage was 52 seconds. But Warwick, the boy wonder of the track, had slid a long way in two years. The next picture, in October 1971, was on the front of a Saturday paper. The crash had occurred on the Cotter Road — two sports cars. One driver was dead, a girl passenger was seriously injured and the other driver was standing unhurt in the photograph by the side of the road. A headlight had hit him full in the face, washing it stark white. They weren't ideal conditions to be photographed in, but Warwick's face looked much fuller, almost bloated, and his body was bulky inside the casual clothes. There was talk of charges — driving under the influence, manslaughter — it was a bad business. Staring at the frank, unstudied picture I tried to see a resemblance to the old man who'd handed down the savage sentences in court, or to the softened lines of the face that looked down from the wall in Rushcutters Bay. It was there all right, but oddly stronger in the younger face. Making all allowances for the circumstances, in the later pictures Baudin's face showed traces of a hesitancy or self-doubt which had never troubled Sir Clive.

I printed out a few copies of the pictures, made some notes and handed the reels back to an attendant who gave me a tired, sceptical smile. The whole operation had taken less than an hour and I hadn't used a single stick of gum. Outside the air was warm and still; I took a walk along the edge of the lake and tried to think about genetics and blood tests and whether it could be proved that one person was the child of another. I had a feeling that you couldn't and all the tests could establish was that some people could not be the progenitors of others. Maybe it wouldn't come to that, maybe it wouldn't come to anything. It was still a paper chase, the pictures in my pocket were like a talisman but, for all I knew, the man himself could be manacled to a prison wall in Bangkok for heroin dealing.

Wandering around the big, grey complex of government buildings I tried to push the whole thing aside. The letter I'd got from Keir Baudin was calling me to Sydney, to Honey of Darlinghurst whoever she was, but Kay kept breaking in on my thoughts. Ailsa and I had been on and off lovers, a night here, a night there; I tried to think when I'd last slept two nights in succession with a woman — it was a long time ago.

17

It was a good night. I ran the Falcon through a car wash just to kill some time while waiting to pick up Kay. I felt young again, transported back to when cars and girls meant everything. We had a couple of drinks and ate in a restaurant that had once been an old house — we took our own wine and I wasn't the only man not wearing a tie. Around ten o'clock we were standing in one of the pedestrian malls and her hips were pressing into me and we were kissing like I was leaving for the front the next day.

We broke apart. 'Come to my place,' she said, 'I can't wear the same clothes three days in a row.'

I smoothed her hair. 'I often do.'

'That's because you're uncivilised, a predator.'

'You disapprove?'

'No.' She kissed me quickly. 'The world's full of desk-sitters who smell of shampoo and soap. You smell of . . .'

'Alcohol and sweat?'

'A bit, not too much.'

Her flat was in Ainslie, close to the centre of the city. It was the top half of a house which we reached down a sideway pushing through an overgrown garden. Inside the colours were cream and brown and there was a comfortable amount of untidiness. I automatically browsed through her books while she showered; there was a touch too much philosophy for my taste, but the novels were sound — Hemingway and Waugh, Keesey and Amis, a sprinkling of Hammett and Chandler. I was reading Fussell's *The Great War and Modern Memory* when she came out wearing a Chinese dressing gown. Her hair was wet and spiky and gave off a smell of apples. We kissed hard and leaned into each other, needing and giving support.

'Great book,' she said.

'Yeah.' Then we were kissing again and soon after that we were on a big low bed under a window. We satisfied the first, hard, need quickly and then lay close and talked and let a slow warmth creep over us. The second time was slower and I was conscious of the whole of her body and her experience; her slim, strong arms and the long legs that trapped and held me lightly. I lay there in the dim light listening to her breathing and then my breathing fell into synch with hers and I slept.

I woke at five o'clock and got up quietly. I dressed and was copying down the number of her phone when I heard her move in the bed.

'What are you doing?' She sat straight up and I could feel a wave of tension flow across to me. I leaned down and kissed her bare shoulder.

'I have to go Kay. I've got your number. I'll call you.'

She grabbed my hand. 'When?'

'Tonight and every night until this is fixed. Then I'll come back here.'

'When you've finished the job?'

'Yes.'

'Business first.'

I knew what she meant the way I'd always known what Cyn had meant — the missed meetings and the professional drinking and the sleep binges. She flopped back and curled up the way she had in the motel.

'Canberra specialises in quick affairs Cliff,' she said. 'I've had men propose to me over breakfast and fly to London at lunchtime.'

'I'll call you tonight at eight. I promise.'

'I hope so,' she whispered; she rolled over away from me, twisting the sheet around her.

I let myself out quietly and negotiated the sideway; the dew was heavy and the overhanging branches dripped on me as I pushed through them. It wasn't like walking away from a good, quick roll in the hay, it wasn't like that at all.

I made myself unpopular at the motel by hauling the manager out of bed and paying my bill. From the look he gave me I would've bet the first thing he did after I'd gone was check the towels. It was going to be a hot one in Canberra; the sky was a blank blue and a heat haze was forming over the mountains. The air was still cool but a west wind was promising to make it dry and gritty within an hour. I cruised through the quiet streets along with the dogs and joggers and gave my newly cleaned car its head when we reached the highway. The drive from Canberra to Sydney has got easier in the last few years. They've punched through some hills and by-passed some of the towns. A good drive in a good car can do it in under four hours. It took me nearly five.

I was dry and hungry when I reached Glebe. I collected the mail and newspapers and went into the house; dust drifted about in the beams of light and the cockroaches, blissfully undisturbed for a few days, ran for cover. I cleaned myself up and made a meal with limp things from the fridge and plenty of cold wine. The papers carried a lot about the economy, all lies, something about prison riots, mostly lies, and profound analyses of events in the Middle East. There was no mention of Henry Brain. Four bills almost cancelled out the Chatterton money and as far as I could remember there was nothing else coming in. I called my answering service and learned I'd had two callers — Cy Sackville and Verna Reid.

I phoned Sackville who told me not to get into any trouble for a few weeks because he was going to a conference in Athens and planned to trip around Europe for a bit afterwards.

'Who pays?' I asked.

'You do mate, the taxpayer. Now about this Chatterton business. I couldn't get a lot on Henry Brain. He was a barrister, a good one, and he got struck off for drunkenness in court. That's going back a bit; he never applied for reinstatement.'

'He stayed drunk.'

'There's a lesson in that for you,' Cy said primly. 'On the Chatterton estate I can't help you much. Young Booth didn't know who gets the dough, Dad hasn't told him. There are a few funny things about it though.'

'Like?'

'Well, the secrecy for one thing. Booth junior says it's unusual for Booth senior to be so close-mouthed. It might mean that the estate is tied up in some way. Also, someone else has been asking about it.'

'Who?'

'Booth doesn't remember his name, some bloke who scraped an acquaintance with him at a squash court. Big chap was all he said, looked as if he needed the exercise. That probably made Boothie feel smug — he's in great shape.' Cy himself is as thin as a stick of spaghetti which he eats in large quantities. He never exercises; he's a workaholic who burns the weight off by mixing ambition with performance.

'What did this big bloke say?'

'Not much I gather and Booth probably didn't give a lot away. He's with an old firm, a conservative one, and Boothie knows that he's not the brightest. He plays it pretty cagey.'

'When was this and are you sure that's all?'

'A couple of weeks ago it was. Only other thing Booth recalled was that mention was made of the old lady's companion — Miss Reece?'

'Reid.'

Cy grunted, he wasn't used to getting things wrong.

'D'you want to be filled in on all this Cy?'

'Not really. It's bound to be sordid and I'm trying to clear my head for the holiday. I've got a lot to do, I've got to check on Greek scuba gear and I'm thinking of buying a Citroen over there and shipping it back . . . what do you think?'

'Great idea,' I said. 'Give me the old one.'

'I've seen your car, you don't deserve a Citroen.'

He gave me the name of the man who would be filling in for him and a run-down on his prejudices — they seemed to cover everything I did and stood for. He sounded like the right man to brief the prosecution if I got into trouble.

After hanging up I went to the car and dug out my notes on the case and added a few more facts. I sat and thought; I had a cigarette and some more wine; I wrote Kay Fletcher's number in my book. When I couldn't stall any longer I rang the Chatterton number. Verna Reid's voice came over the wire like a chill Melbourne wind. She didn't seem to want to connect me with Lady C but I insisted and the line stayed live. While I was waiting I wondered whether Miss Reid was in line for the money, a heartbeat away from a fortune, and where her boyfriend and Richard Selby fitted into the picture.

The phone crackled. 'Mr Hardy, are you there?'

I said I was.

'I expected to hear from you sooner. Where have you been?'

'To the south coast and Canberra.'

'What have you learned?'

'Henry Brain is dead — you know that. Nurse Callaghan is dead too.'

A long sigh whispered through. 'So you have nothing to report?' Her voice was empty of any interest in the lives and deaths of Brain and Callaghan. She'd known them both but they meant nothing to her except as stepping-stones to what she wanted. It reminded me that the Chattertons were ruthless elitists, not humanitarians. There was no point in *caring* whether the old woman got what she wanted or not. It was a job.

'I didn't say that,' I said soothingly. 'I spoke to Brain before he died and I may have spoken to the doctor who delivered your grandson. I'm in the process of tracing that person now.'

'Who is he?' she said excitedly. 'Tell me about him.'

I stalled. 'I don't think that would be wise; he may not be the right man and it may not be possible to locate him.'

'I've never heard so many may nots. I hope you're not covering up a failure, Mr Hardy.'

That caustic arrogance in the voice made me want to slam the phone down but I took a breath and used the only weapon I had.

'I'll give you one more may not,' I said harshly. 'You may not like him when and if you meet him.'

'If he is the right man, Mr Hardy, he will have character, he will be fundamentally sound.' Her tone was less confident than the words. 'Perhaps you can tell me one more thing: since you are determined to play cat and mouse, has the man in question been brought up by . . . respectable people?'

It was easy to see what she was thinking. A man of thirty is fully formed or should be. She could do some polishing, and a bit of money spent properly could do wonders, but she couldn't make a judge's grandson out of a brickie's mate. I put the needle in by delaying the reply.

'Very respectable.'

'Thank you, that is good.' Her voice sounded younger, lighter, and I wondered if she was patting her iron grey hair. It would be interesting to see how she'd tackle the future heir if I could produce him. I tried to tell her about some of the obstacles I'd encountered but she'd turned off. I wanted to ask about her will and maybe I could have got an answer: I was the life-jacket of her hopes and this could be used to control her natural tendency to treat me as a chattel. But I didn't know who could be listening on other phones in the house, so I asked her for more money instead.

'Verna will attend to it,' she said. 'Press on Mr Hardy. When you have a definite result we will have another meeting. Goodbye.' She was playing it cautious again, I thought, and regretting the outburst of enthusiasm. The boy would just have to learn that Grandma didn't let it all hang out.

Miss Reid came back on the line and I told her that Lady C had given the OK for some money. She didn't question it, which might have meant that she'd been listening. I asked her for three days' fees and seventy-five dollars in expenses.

'Have you receipts for the expenses?'

'Some,' I said, 'bars and massage parlours don't issue them. I'll send you a list.'

'That won't be necessary,' she said crisply. 'I'm authorised to pay you. A cheque will be sent today.' She hung up.

I squinted out the window at the day which had turned grey and ambiguous. There was a broad, pale band of sunlight across the wall of my neighbour's house and a fine vapour was lifting off his elegant ferns. My own garden is low and scrubby and features plants renowned for their ability to withstand neglect. I locked up a couple of copies of the photographs of Warwick Baudin, pocketed a set, and left the house. Clark Street in Darlinghurst is narrow and dog-legged so that, at the bend, the high terrace houses seem to lean over it the way houses do in Europe. The traffic runs only one way and the street rises sharply at the end where it meets Oxford Street. It was the middle of a warm, still day and the air was heavy with motor fumes and dust. The street was cluttered with illegally parked cars and barefoot people in jeans and men in three-piece suits.

A girl was sitting in the fitful sun in front of number eight. She had on a yellow, Chinese-design, silk dressing gown which had fallen open to the waist; her breasts were pale and heavy with pink, spreading nipples. She was filing her nails and her tongue was caught between her teeth in concentration. She looked at me with just the merest flicker of interest, the way an old dog looks at an old bone. I put my hand on the gate of number ten.

'They won't be up yet,' she said in a heavy accent, Dutch or German, 'can I help you?'

'I want to see a girl named Honey,' I said. 'Am I at the right place?'

'Yah.' She stopped filing. The dressing gown slipped open around the narrow tie belt and I could see a swelling of white, soft belly and the top of a thatch of blonde pubic hair. 'She lives there but she is not a girl. Do you like it with old women?'

'Not really. Miss . . .?'

'Inge.' She shrugged, her plump breasts shook like blancmange. 'You're about thirty years too late then.' She laughed and loose flesh moved under her chin, on her chest and down her hairless white legs.

'Don't listen to her, dear.' The voice came from above our heads and I looked up. A woman was leaning over the rail on the upstairs balcony of number ten. Her hair was purple and she was wearing a purple dressing gown. He voice was low-pitched and the vowels were over-careful. 'Wait there dear, I'll be right down. Be careful of that sun Inge, you don't want to ruin your complexion.'

Acne scars pitted the blonde girl's face. She saw me noticing them, turned pink, and went back to filing her nails.

I opened the gate and approached the door of number ten. The house was an old two-storey terrace; the brickwork had been rendered over and marked to simulate sandstone blocks. It had had at least three earlier paint jobs and now it was a flaking, dusty green with the window trimmings picked out in yellow. There was an iron-framed garden chair on the porch and two pot-plants — the pots overflowed with cigarette ends.

The door opened and the woman in purple struck an

attitude in the doorway; she was tall and thin and used to making the most of her figure. She cocked one hand up on her hip and let the other drift out aristocratically towards me. I put one of the cards in it.

'That's me,' I said. 'Would your name be Honey?'

'That's right darling, I'm Honey Gully.' She peered at the card and the set smile faded. 'Trouble?' The careful control peeled away like the paint from her house and the word came out harsh and anxious.

'I don't think so, Miss Gully, can I come in?'

She hesitated. 'It's early, place is a mess.'

'I don't mind,' I said. 'It won't take long and I'll pay you for your time.'

She brought her face up to mine and squinted to focus on it. A network of lines around her eyes and mouth had flecks of make-up embedded in them. Her mouth was wide and just beginning to fall in; she could have been a beaten-up forty or a well preserved sixty. She drew back and her eyes relaxed into a pale blue myopic vagueness.

'I don't like this,' she said. 'I'm not paid for my time, what do you want?'

I bustled up close and forced her into the hallway. She gave way and I bustled some more and closed the door behind me. Her forward drifting tendril of a hand became a nervous thing that plucked at the neck of the velveteen dressing gown, drawing it higher and safer.

'Where's your room, Honey?'

Maybe she liked my honest face, maybe she thought that if I'd been going to hit her I'd have done it by now; she shrugged. 'Top of the stairs,' she said. 'On the right.'

'Let's get up there and talk.' I took hold of her upper arm and my fingers met around it; she had bones like a factory-bred chicken and skimpy flesh to match. I propelled her in front of me up the stairs; using my weight. The stair rail was draped over with female clothing and there was a smell of stale scent, sweat and cigarette smoke in the air.

Honey Gully's room was full of early afternoon light and the signs of her own creativity; silk-covered cushions were scattered about on the floor and the low bed and some tapestries of Oriental design showing sexually ambiguous figures in contorted positions, adorned the walls. There was a dressing table covered with the usual stuff, a heavy carved chest and a high bookshelf crammed with paperback and hard-cover books.

She shook free of me and glided into the room; dropping down onto a big cushion by the bed, she drew her knees up, the purple tented up into an elegant triangle.

'Well?'

My aggressiveness had subsided on the stairs and dropped away completely now. Somehow the room was pathetic as if it were the work of a frustrated artist or a woman playing at being a college girl. Standing awkwardly in the doorway I let her regain the initiative. The chin cupped in the hand and the incline of the head were probably perfected twenty years before at least, but the gesture still had charm and some freshness.

'Well, I don't think you're here for a screw, you don't look the type. If you want information on someone you're out of luck. I don't ask their names and I shut my ears if they try to tell me.' She put her palms over her ears and grinned mockingly. I grinned back and came into the room.

'You're quite a girl,' I said and meant it. 'You must have been beating the men off a few years back.'

'I still am, darling.' She tossed her head. 'You'd be surprised how many men like drooping tits.' She played with the catch on her gown. 'Care to see?'

'Not just now. I want to talk about someone who probably saw the whole show.'

'I told you, no names.'

'You can't pull that, Honey.' I tapped my pocket. 'I've got his picture. I can tell you this, you won't be getting him in trouble. If you can help me it's a stroke of luck all round.'

She sighed. 'I could use a few strokes myself — of luck that is.' Her own wit cheered her up. 'Let's have a look at him.'

'Better put your glasses on, Honey,' I said.

She stuck her hand under the big pillow on the bed and pulled out an embroidered, beaded case which she opened and took out a pair of glasses with fuse-wire thin gold frames. She hooked them on to her fine, experienced face where they looked stylish.

'They look good,' I said. I lowered myself onto one of the cushions and took out the photo-prints.

'Rubbish,' she said as I handed the prints over, 'they make me look like a hag, which I am.' But she was pleased just the same and disposed to co-operate. She looked carefully at the pictures for a long time, then pulled off her glasses and stared across the mile or so of space between us.

'They're not very good of him.'

My heart bumped. 'But you do know him?'

She leaned back, vamping: 'Many times, many times.'

I was too tense for it. 'Where is he now?' I rasped.

'Haven't a clue, ' she said cheerfully. 'Haven't seen him for ages.'

'Jesus! You don't know where he lived?'

'No dear, he never took me home to meet his Mum.'

18

I wasn't really let down; I hadn't expected him to be boarding there, but I'd hoped Honey would still be in touch with him. Still, a year isn't a long time, I thought. The trail was still warm compared to some I've followed and it was time to consolidate, get all I could on him, and look for the next doorway.

I made a cigarette while she fiddled with the pictures. Her face was hard and vain but there was humour in it and in the set of her lean body. She looked as if a shrug might always be her next movement. I blew smoke and put the match in a seashell ashtray.

'You must have liked this one, Honey?'

'Why d'you say that?' She went on fiddling nervously.

'Do you let all your clients use you as a mail drop?'

She looked up shrewdly. 'Know about that eh? Let me tell you, I was furious. It broke all my rules.'

'Like not knowing their names?'

'Well, that gets broken from time to time. No, I mean about getting involved, families and all that.'

'I get it. Something came from Canberra?'

'Canberra, yes.'

'Was that the last you saw of him, when he picked that up?'

'The very last. I wasn't sorry, he was no good.'

'In what way?'

'In every way — mean, selfish, rough . . .'

'He was violent?'

'I'll say. I thought he was going to eat me the first time. Look, this isn't embarrassing you?'

'No, I'm older than I look. Go on.'

'He really liked the old stuff, you know? Kinky for it.'

'Kinky in what way?'

'Just . . . very keen, very appreciative of me and I'm no picture. I've been through the mill and I've got the marks to prove it. He lapped it up.'

'Did he have much money?' I butted the cigarette in the seashell; the old tart fanned the smoke away from her face irritably and reached under her gown to scratch. I decided she was closer to sixty than forty.

'He didn't have much money,' she said slowly, 'but enough. Most of what he had must have gone on booze.'

'What did he drink?'

'Everything, but he never got really pissed. He was big, see? I mean really big,' she tapped the pictures. 'These don't show it. He must have been close to fifteen stone and getting heavier. I suppose he could carry a lot of grog.'

'All right, now let's try to pin it down a bit. When did this letter from Canberra come?'

'About a year ago, October or November last year. Look, what *is* all this . . .?'

'Tell you in a minute. Did he say what was in the letter or give you any idea of what he was doing?'

'Not a bloody clue. He came here two or three times a week for six months or so, we had a few drinks and we . . .' she waved at the bed. 'Sometimes he stayed the night, not often. He paid up and we didn't talk hardly at all. As often as not he was drunk when he lobbed in and he stayed drunk; he always brought grog with him.'

'What did he wear?'

'Why?'

'Might give me an idea of what he was doing or where he lived.'

'Yeah, I suppose it could. Let me see now.' She resumed the hand in chin position and seemed to be enjoying herself. Somehow she gave out a lot of warmth and I would have been enjoying her company if I hadn't been so tense about the information. 'I never saw him in a suit, that means he wasn't a professional man, right?'

I smiled. 'Right,' I said.

'He wore jeans and T shirts I think, jumper sometimes . . . boots I think.'

'Anything distinctive — tattoo, scar, jewellery?'

'No, nothing like that. Oh, he was very brown.'

'Suntanned?'

'Yeah, sort of.'

'But not really like a tan?'

'No, it was a yellowish colour and very even all over. He must have been a nudist.'

Something was beginning to come through, a faint buzz, a distant hum that promised a connection, a link. I closed my eyes and let the synapses tick before I asked the next question. She looked at me expectantly.

'Tell me, Honey, was this fifteen stone all fat?'

'Oh shit no, didn't I say? He's a muscle man, or he was. He was getting a bit flabby from the drink but he had muscles like this.' She lifted her arm and flexed it in the strongman-admiring-his-bicep pose.

I smiled at her and she smiled back and rotated her wrist; I could imagine the ounce of muscle sliding along under the skin.

'Where did you meet him Honey?' I said quietly.

'I picked him up outside the Spartacus Health Studio. Know it?'

'No.'

'Pitt Street, bottom end, it used to be a good spot in the old days. I was just going past this night, not really looking. Well, I'm not everyone's cup of tea, not any more. He was coming out and he was really something, Hercules you know? I must have looked at him right because he said something and there we were.'

I believed it, every word. It all hung together, the athletics, the adulation, the muscle-building, maybe the dissipation, too. And other things made sense. I was itching to get back to my notes, to tie things together with arrows and signs for *a* equals *b*. I was staring straight at Honey while doing this thinking and she became agitated, her blue-veined hands started fluttering and plucking at the frill on her cushion.

'Ah, you said you'd tell me about this,' she said hesitantly. 'It's not political is it? I don't want to know if it's political.'

'Why do you ask that?'

'Oh, Canberra and that.'

'No, it's not political. It's about old ladies looking for lost boys and rotten apples in barrels and people not getting what they deserve.'

She yawned, she was used to babblers. 'You said something about paying me,' she said.

354

'Do you know anything more about this guy, Honey? Anything at all? Did he have a car?' I was clutching, reaching for little confirmatory details that would bolster up the theory I was building.

'No, I never saw a car. Hey where're you going? What about the money?'

I got up and pulled out my wallet, released a twenty and five and let them flutter down onto the bed. She looked at them with disappointment shaping her eyebrows and pouting lips.

'I thought there'd be more.'

I reached down and patted the purple hair, partly out of curiosity. 'You've been a great help, Honey. Tell you what, if it all works out I'll buy you a present. What d'you need?'

'A facelift.'

I thought of other faces, faces changed by time and booze and distress. My most recent picture of Warwick Baudin was more than eight years old. I wondered if I'd know him.

'I'll see what I can do,' I said. 'Talking of faces, is Warwick recognisable from the pictures?' I bent and gently retrieved the prints.

She shrugged. 'I dunno. Warwick is it? It just said W on the letter. I recognised him but I'm good with faces — depends how good you are with faces.'

Fair enough. I patted the hair again, it was stiff with spray and dye and chemicals. 'I hope it all works out Honey, I'll be in touch.'

She muttered something I didn't catch and I left the room and went down the stairs and out of the house. The sun had broken through again and the day was bright and glaring but Inge wasn't on her chair any more. Honey Gully didn't come out on her balcony to wave me goodbye — all the good whores were indoors waiting for the day to end.

19

My theory was built on hints and mortared up with guesses and intuitive leaps. I worked on it as I plodded through the steamy heat towards my car. Richard Selby looked to be at the bottom of it; I assumed he was Henry Brain's benefactor, the one who had set the works in motion and had followed up by talking to young Booth, the lawyer. He had a stake in it, his wife and kids were in line for the Chatterton money or threatened with the cold shoulder. He had a lot to lose but the question was — how had he got into the game? The obvious answer was in response to something dropped from Henry Brain's wagging, alcoholic tongue.

The car was a sweat-box; I wound the windows down and drove along with the other perspiring prisoners down past the park to lower Pitt Street. I parked a few blocks from the station, stuck the .38 in my pants and hit the street. The place was listed in the book and I reached it in a couple of minutes. There were two windows above an army disposals store; one said Spartacus and the other said Health Studio in big, freshly painted letters. I went up a narrow staircase and met the same words again, this time on two plate glass doors. Smaller letters said that the manager of the establishment was Leonidas Green. I went into a small room formed by six-foot-high movable partitions. A girl was sitting at a desk reading a magazine, smoking and drinking coffee from a polystyrene cup. Her yellow hair fell down from a centre part that ran like a white scar along her skull. She looked up and gave me a fifty carat smile with capped teeth, red lips and eyes like jewelled spiders.

'Good afternoon sir,' she breathed, 'are you interested in building your body?'

'Not really, I need a new one.'

She smiled at lower voltage. She was wearing a sleeveless dress the colour of her hair and an even, sun-lamp tan; she drew on her cigarette and showed me her profile when she blew the smoke away. Her voice was phoney-American.

'How can I help you?'

'Is Mr Green around?'

'He's very busy. If you could tell me your business.'

I gave her a card. 'A few questions, no trouble.'

'I'll see.' She got up and came sashaying around the desk on three-inch heels.

'I'll see, too,' I said and went through the gap in the partitions with her.

We went into a gleaming room about sixty feet long by thirty wide. The polished boards gleamed, chrome barbells and other equipment gleamed, but the gleamingest things of all were the mirrors that ran around all four walls. There was even a mirror on the back of the partition that formed the reception room. They ran from floor level up to the height of a tall man and after taking a few steps into the room I felt as though I was surrounded. The girl swayed over to where three men were throwing a medicine ball around. They stood about ten feet apart at the points of a triangle and they were heaving the big ball hard, mixing up low and high throws. We stood back and watched for a minute and when one of the players missed his catch the girl stepped forward.

'Mr Green, there's a gentleman to see you.'

The shortest man in the group, a chunky guy with crisp curling grey hair, jerked his head around impatiently.

'Not now Ronnie, tell him to come back later.'

I moved around Ronnie and stepped up to him. He was about five ten and four feet across the shoulders; muscles bulged everywhere under his black singlet. He was middle-aged but the skin on his face was tight and smooth. The other two were carbon copies — six-footers with waved hair and vacant expressions. Their muscles looked to be trying to burst out of their singlets and shorts and run away to start life on their own.

'Let's make it now,' I said. 'It won't take a minute and then you can go back to playing ball.'

The Adonis on the left suddenly flicked the medicine ball at me, I moved aside and it hit Ronnie in the stomach. She collapsed and coffee from her cup flew everywhere and her cigarette dropped onto a canvas mat. Green swooped on the butt and snarled at the ball-thrower.

'You fuck-wit Kurt, go and get a mop.'

The other man helped Ronnie up; her spider eyes blazed and she shook off his hand. Green was holding the smoking butt between two fingers as if it were a dead mouse.

'I've told you not to smoke in here Ronnie,' he said. 'Go away, I'll talk to you later.' He passed the cigarette to her and bent down again to pick up my card which the girl had dropped. He read the card and clapped his hand to his forehead theatrically.

'Oh my God, what do you want?' He eyed me professionally and noticed the bulge. 'Keep the gun where it is will you? I've got some sensitive people here, they're likely to faint at the sight of a gun.'

Kurt was back with a mop soaking up the spilt coffee. The other he-man had wandered off towards a wall. He picked up a small bar-bell and began moving it one-handed from waist level to shoulder; he turned sideways and looked lovingly at the overblown muscles in his upper arm. I pulled out the photographs and gave them to Green.

'I'm looking for this man. Do you know him?'

He gave them a bored glance. 'Hard to tell, I don't think so.'

'Look again, it's important.'

'Just who do you think you are? I've said I don't recognise him.'

Raised voices and a flurry of movement took our attention to the end of the room.

Green groaned, 'Not again,' and hurried off towards the commotion. Kurt shouldered his mop and followed; his mate moved in front of the mirror like an entranced Narcissus. At the far end of the room, away from the windows, four men were gathered around two who were lying on a canvas mat. A big, fat character who was polishing one of the mirrors stopped work and turned to watch the others. The men on the floor were stripped to their athletic supports and they lay in a line with the soles of their feet touching.

'What's going on?' I asked Green.

'A bet,' he said grudgingly. He addressed one of the men on the mat. 'What is it this time Carl, five hundred?'

Carl put his hands out behind his head and took a grip on a

medicine ball. 'Seven fifty,' he grunted. Green shrugged. 'Fifty against,' he said.

'You're on Leo,' said one of the watchers, a tall, heavily muscled citizen with a widow's peak of slick black hair. Kurt and one of the other body-builders got their bets down and Carl's companion flipped himself up into a squatting position, still keeping his feet braced against Carl's.

'Carl's betting he can get the medicine ball up to where Saul can touch it and back above his head seven hundred and fifty times. It's murder on the laterals, want to bet?'

'No,' I said but despite myself I was interested. Carl looked to have the equipment for the job; his stomach was quilted with muscle and his neck and arms were grotesque storehouses of power.

The mirror cleaner had let the fluid dribble down the surface and there were bubbles of spittle beside his mouth which was slack and open; fat clustered around his neck and sat in a great roll around his waist under a stained T shirt. Apart from me he was the only man in the room without perfect muscle tone.

Carl came up in an easy, oiled movement with the medicine ball outstretched, Saul patted it and down he went and up, and down and up like a machine set to stamp out a thousand identical parts. After a hundred, great ropes of veins stood out in his neck and forehead and sweat ran in the clefts around his perfectly defined muscles. At two fifty his breath was coming in short gusts and I was betting mentally against him; everyone in the room was riveted except the mirror-gazer who kept on pumping and admiring the result. I glanced across and saw Ronnie, on tip-toe looking over the partition. A man came past her and up to Green but I was too interested in the contest to notice him: Carl had passed five hundred now and the spectators were counting, softly, rhythmically, five sixty-one, five sixty-two, sixty-three . . .

I saw a movement in the mirror and moved but I was too late to miss the punch altogether; Leonidas Green's fist took me under the ear and toppled me sideways. I fell sprawling over Carl and Saul and the rhythm was broken and the men started to swear. Green came at me again and I ducked and rolled over and was on my feet. I moved into him and hooked him in the stomach and it was like punching a tree. He came on and I kicked him in the knee. He buckled and I hit him flush on the nose. Carl and Saul were on their feet shoving at each other and yelling and one of the muscle men came at me with a short, chromium bar in his hand; I let him swing it and put the heel of my hand hard into his face when he was off balance — blood spattered from his nose over the mirror. For a measureless instant I saw it all in reflection — Carl and Saul wrestling, and another man on the floor with blood welling through his fingers and Green on his knees yelling for someone to take me out. Then I was spinning around, backing up to the glass and pulling one of the muscle men with me when something sailed over my shoulder and shattered the mirror. The glass showered us and big sections of the mirror split and felt like guillotine blades. The noise stopped the action and I got my gun out and pointed it at Green's gut.

'Tell them to give us room Green,' I panted, 'or I'll blow a hole in you. Tell them!'

Green waved his arms like a man signalling a plane in. 'Go away,' he moaned, 'go away. Oh Christ look at the place, what a mess.'

The fat man had melted away somewhere leaving his mirror clouded and streaky, another six-foot stretch of glass was blood spattered and broken pieces littered the floor. There was a deep gouge in the polished boards where the thrown bar-bell had landed after it hit the mirror. I wasn't feeling so good myself.

Green got up off his knees and I signalled him with the gun to move to a corner where there was a chair and a low bench. He moved and did some more arm waving.

'Leave us alone. Kurt, Carl, get this mess cleaned up and piss off. We're closed.'

He seemed to have the authority he needed and some to spare. Two of them picked up the man whose face I'd smashed and carried him like a baby. A section of the mirror swung out and led to a locker-room and storeroom evidently, because they came back with brooms and wet towels and got to work on the devastation.

Green plonked himself down on the bench and gave me and my gun an ugly look.

'Do you know what those mirrors cost?' he barked.

'I didn't throw it,' I said. 'I didn't want any trouble. Now I'm going to ask you again, do you know anything about the man in those pictures?'

He paused and looked keenly at me; his eyes seemed to be mocking me or maybe they were just hostile. 'I said I didn't know him,' he said deliberately.

I brought the gun up a few inches but he knew I wouldn't use it; we both knew it. He relaxed and I wondered if he was thinking about trying to take me, but there was a deep cut under his knee, bruised around the edges and dripping blood, and I didn't think he'd risk it.

'Why did you start all that?'

He shrugged. 'I don't like coppers of any kind.'

'Bullshit. Who was the guy who spoke to you when Carl hit the five hundred?'

The eyes mocked or were hostile again. 'Nobody. He was putting on a bet.'

I looked at the clean-up gang. 'Where is he now?'

'Didn't you see?' Green sneered. 'He got in the way of some of the glass, I imagine he's gone for stitches.'

I tried to bring the man's features back and up into focus but I couldn't. I hadn't bothered to look at him closely, I'd been too interested in the stupid medicine ball game. He was big and dark, I had that much, but nearly all of them were big and dark.

'What's his name?'

'I'm not going to tell you. What are you going to do — shoot me?' He laughed and ran his hand over the grey hair.

'There's a racket here,' I said. 'I can smell it.'

'No racket here, my friend, I make men into the men they want to be. That's all.' He started to stand up and let out a gasp when the weight fell on his injured leg. He slumped down onto the bench. 'You've cost me money. I wouldn't come around here again if I was you.' He drew in a breath and yelled, 'Ronnie!'

The girl stuck her head around the partition, she saw the gun and pulled back out of sight.

Green yelled again. 'Ronnie, get me the first aid box . . . and bring a hand-out over here.'

She came teetering across the boards as the clean-up finished. Her eyes were big and frightened and her expensive top teeth were chewing on her ripe lower lip. She was carrying a white case about the size of a shoe-box and a piece of foolscap-sized, buff-coloured paper fluttered in her hand.

Green stuck out his leg. 'Clean this up, Ronnie.' He took the paper from her, folded it down the middle and handed it to me.

'This is a legitimate business, probably more legitimate than yours. Have this in exchange for your crummy card.'

I put the gun away and took the paper, feeling bad. It had the name of the joint printed stylishly across the top with a photo of Green striking a pose beside it. I put it in my pocket and got up. I had nothing more to say. I felt that if I threatened to shoot out all his mirrors Green would still laugh at me. I was preoccupied with the thought that Warwick Baudin and my bonus and everything else that mattered might have passed within touching distance of me. Green swore when Ronnie started in on his wound and I felt a little better about it all.

I unshipped the .38 when I passed Ronnie's desk and watched for vengeful lurkers on the stairs but there was no one. The disposals store bristled with bayonets and knives and there was a gun-shop next to that; the place was high on weapons and low on intelligence and I included myself in that. I bought coffee and some aspirin in the next block and sat rubbing the sore spot near my ear and wondering about my next move. I pulled out the Spartacus Studio's blurb and looked it over: Leonidas had his name in about ten times and there were testimonials to the efficacy of his courses from satisfied Mr Victorias and Mr Queenslands. A name near the bottom of the screed took my eye — the supplier of weight-lifting and gymnasium equipment to the studio was Richard Selby.

20

I was doing it all by reflex now, bouncing from point to point and not initiating anything, but that's the way things break sometimes and I had the feeling that my bounces were taking me closer to the nerve centre of whatever the hell was going on. Selby's firm was listed — the Titan Gymnasium Equipment Co. Its factory and office were in St Peters, a short drive, but a hot, bustly one in four o'clock traffic. I dragged myself back to the car and broke all the rules about drug use by swigging some of the Irish whisky before I started and smoking a cigarette as I drove.

I passed the dark, satanic chimneys that landmark St Peters and started threading through the streets that are a mixture of light-industry, factories and terrace houses. Selby's place was a big, red-brick structure with a flat face sitting flush with the pavement. It had big roller doors at either end and a glass-panelled door in the middle. The word Titan was written across the front, the letters being composed of strokes in the shape of barbells.

I sat in my car watching the place, smoking, and wondering how to tackle Selby. Maybe I could strongarm him into telling me what he knew about Brain and Bettina's child and Warwick Baudin and maybe I couldn't. Maybe he didn't know or someone else was using him. It was a tangled skein with the deaths of Brain and Callaghan as knots and the lost Chatterton at the end of the string. I was musing, stalling like this when two men came out of the centre door. The shorter man, wearing a yellow blazer and tan slacks, was Selby. His face was brick red in the sunlight and his oiled, black locks glistened. The other man was a few inches taller and very broad; he was wearing a fawn suit and his face was partly swathed in fresh, white bandages. I watched them talking for a while and then had to gulp for air; I realised that I'd been holding my breath. They talked intently for a few minutes and then Selby clapped the other on the arm and went back into the building. The man with the bandages stood for a moment squinting against the sun; I strained my eyes at him willing him to be the man I wanted but I couldn't be sure. He was about six foot two and his hair was dark but his features were disguised by the wrappings. His clothes were good without being hand-made; he looked fit but a bit on the heavy side: it was possible.

He walked over to a blue Datsun and got in it by bending the right places at the right time. I tagged along trying to feel confident that I had the fish in the net, but full of doubt. He stopped in Newtown for a paper and had his car checked right around; wherever he was going he wasn't in a hurry. His next stop was at Victoria Park where he sat on a bench and read the paper. Then he smoked a cigarette. I did the same fifty yards away sitting in my car with the beginnings of a bladder problem. He strolled across to a telephone booth, not far enough from his car to give me time to do anything about my bladder, and did some nattering. Then another cigarette, then some tie-straightening and comb work in the side mirror and he was ready to go.

The traffic had thinned out in Broadway and we took it nice and easy and turned right into Park Street. After the two soapy shaves in Canberra I'd stood back a bit with the razor and my face was blue and bristling. I'd talked to whores and he-men and had taken one smart tap from a man who knew how to dish it out. We were heading up towards the Cross and I wasn't in condition for a disco or blackjack den, but on reflection neither was the man in the Datsun. He looked in need of a good meal and some loving kindness; that made me think of Kay and my promise to ring her. I had almost two hours in hand.

We by-passed the Cross and went through Rushcutters Bay where the Stadium used to be — where the crowds came to see the men punching each other for the fame and the money until there was no fame and no money in it any more. And nobody wore hats any more the way all those men did and no one would ever smoke again the way they did, so guiltlessly. Now there were pricey boats tossing on the water; there were waiting lists for those moorings and people scanned the death notices hoping for a name to appear so that they could move up in the queue and tuck their own little fifty thousand dollar dream up near Sir Ian's and Sir Abraham's.

We climbed and took some turns and suddenly I knew where I was — right, slap-dab in millionaires' row and the Datsun was turning into Lady Catherine's drive and I was going past with things dropping into place in my mind like snooker balls being run into the pockets. The man driving the Datsun into the Chatterton residence had been driving it out when I'd last come calling, and that little blue car was the self-same one that had been parked on Nurse Callaghan's land the night I got my skull dented.

I waited an hour, getting more impatient and uncomfortable by the minute. I took in a little more whisky and a little more tobacco. A few expensive cars purred past and I prayed that the cops would be far away keeping the lower classes in order where they belonged — in that street the Falcon stuck out like a clown at a funeral. I kept low and was considering risking my aim into an empty beer can when the Datsun came out of the drive. I hung well back and let him pick up a couple of other cars as we headed back to the city. He drove fast and well, moving between the lanes and judging the lights; Warwick Baudin had had some car trouble, I'd been told, but that didn't mean he wasn't a good driver.

He turned into Macquarie Street and headed down towards the water. I got close, closer than is classical and confirmed that there was a woman in the car beside the driver. The impression I got was of thinness — Verna Reid. It looked as though they were headed for the Opera House which was good because I could get a parking place there and bad because there were a dozen different places they could go. I stayed close and parked a few cars behind them. He was gallant with the car door and his arm and Miss Reid hung on tight; she would have had her head on his shoulder if she could, but she'd have had to jump to get it there. They ambled on towards the billowing sails, the box offices and the Bollinger '71. I followed, gunless, innocent and with a bursting bladder.

They turned a few heads as they promenaded. You don't see a six-foot-three Hercules with his face in bandages boulevading with a handsome eagle-faced woman every day. I kept back in case Verna looked around and tried to blend in with the tourists and the lookers and the buyers. They hung over the rail watching the ferries pull in and out and the plastic bottles bobbing in the water for a while and then made their way around to the restaurant. I felt like cheering; if they only had the soup and salad it'd still give me time for a piss. I hung around for a minute to make sure they were settled and then set off in search of a facility. That was when I saw him or sensed him. The first rule in following people is not to make any sudden movements; you can pick up a quick movement even when it's outside your field of vision — an atavistic instinct maybe. As I turned around to go down the steps from the restaurant I caught a disturbance of the landscape behind me and to my left. I hopped down the steps and turned the first corner and put the antennae up: there were a few strollers and purposeful walkers about and there was someone following me.

He was still there when I went into the toilet and still there when I came out. I wandered about, getting the lie of the land and waiting for a few evening shadows to fall. The lights of the city and the expensive suburbs across the harbour started to do their job and the water turned from a soft blue to green and then to a flinty grey. The revellers went to their revels and I walked to the end of the point and ducked in flat to the wall around a corner. He came on. His feet were quiet but I thought I could hear the rasp of his breath and I fancied I could smell him. When he came around the corner I slammed my fist into his gut and twisted his arm like an elastic band. I rushed him over to the rail, thumped his back into it and bent him. Albie Logan looked up at me with big, round, frightened eyes like a frog about to give its life for science.

'Well, well,' I said nastily, 'it's Mrs Logan's boy Albert. Now just what would you be doing here?'

He didn't answer so I took him off the rail an inch or two and put him back on it hard. He yelped.

'Turn it up Slim, you're breaking me back.'

I did it again. 'Why are you following me, Albie?'

'I wasn't,' he said and then he yelped again as I bounced his spine off the rail.

'Why?'

'I was . . . hired to,' he gasped.

'You're lousy at it. Who hired you?'

'I dunno his name.'

I looked around. We were alone on the concrete peninsula. Albie was wearing a suit and tie and I yanked the tie off and pulled the handkerchief out of his breast pocket.

'Can you swim Albie?'

'Not good,' he stammered.

'Tell you what I'm going to do. If you don't speak up and answer every question I ask you to my satisfaction, I'm going to tie you up with this,' I showed him the tie, 'and stuff this in your gob and drop you over here. You're a dealer — who'd give a fuck?'

He turned his head to look at the water; it was dark with an ugly, metallic sheen.

'Okay, okay, give me some air.'

I eased back a bit. 'Who?' I said.

'The same guy you're following.'

That jolted me. 'What's his name?'

'Russell James, or so he tells me.'

'You said you didn't know Miss Reid had a boyfriend.'

'I didn't. I couldn't believe it when I saw them together tonight.'

I was confused, but it felt like the confusion that comes before clarity.

'When did James ask you to follow me?'

'Couple of days ago, after you'd come to my dump. I looked but you weren't around. I picked you up today.'

I tightened my grip because I was angry at my own carelessness. 'Do you do much of this Albie? Following people?'

'Easy,' he gasped. 'Not usually.'

'How long have you known James? Customer is he?'

'Sort of. Known him a couple of years but he only started buying a while back.'

'He doesn't look the type. How long back?'

' 'Bout a year. There's all sorts of people on drugs, Slim.'

'I told you not to call me that,' I snarled. 'Where'd you meet him?'

'Pub in the Cross.'

'Jesus. The Noble Briton?'

'I think so, yeah, how'd you know?'

'I guessed. Do you drink there often?'

He hesitated. 'No, well . . .'

I bent him over the rail a bit more. 'You're not off the hook yet, Albie. I want it all. If you make me happy I'll let you go on another one of your train trips and you can come back with a suitcase of shit. If you don't you're history. Now, you were saying?'

'Well, I really met him in this whorehouse in Darlinghurst. We sort of got talking and went for a drink to the Briton. I saw him on and off at Honey's, ah . . .'

'I know Honey,' I said. 'Go on.'

'He spent some dough, drinks and that. And he helped me to move a few things, you know. Then he started buying, if you ask me it was for someone else.'

'Who?'

'I dunno.' I twisted. 'I dunno. Shit, easy!'

'What did you talk about, you and James? Did he ask you about your old job with the Chattertons?'

'Yeah, I suppose he did. Yeah we talked about that.'

'What does he do?'

'He never told me.'

'You didn't ask?'

'No, look I was pissed half the time, or high.'

'What does he buy?'

'Fuckin' near anything — grass, speed, coke sometimes. Mostly speed and downers. He bought a big load when I seen him last.'

'You told him about my visit?'

'Yeah, well I was feeling pretty pissed off. I was just talking and then he put it on me to follow you. He said we could get you in the shit. He was gonna pay me.' He looked down at the water again. 'I'm sorry,' he gulped.

'You should be.' I heard sounds, voices, feet on the stones, and judged that people would be coming out of the cinema for a smoke. I moved Albie away from the rail keeping a strong grip on his arm and walked him down towards the car park. He was shaking and his colour was bad. We walked down between the ranks of cars and I backed him up against a VW Kombi van in a shadow.

'Have a smoke, Albie.'

He got out his cigarettes and lit up. The flame jumped around his hand and his eyes were pin-pointed with fear or drug need or both. He blew the smoke towards me and quickly fanned it away with his hand.

'Albie, this is a rough game you're in. Two people are dead before their time and your mate with the bandages hit me over the head from behind a few nights ago. So I'm not happy with him and I'm not happy about a dirty little creep like you following me around.'

He drew nervously on his cigarette and didn't say anything.

'Now you are a lucky man,' I went on, 'because you are fat and short and I don't feel like belting you. I suggest you go on an interstate run tomorrow and then take your holidays or something. If I hear you're in Sydney I'll make a couple of phone calls and you'll be out of a job and the narc squad'll be picking your teeth for you. Clear?'

'Sure, sure.'

I shovelled the tie and handkerchief into the front of his coat. 'Piss off, Albie.'

He sidled along, keeping his back to the van until he was clear of it and then he took off fast towards the comforting lights of the Quay. I made a cigarette and smoked it slowly while I pieced things together — Henry Brain, the Noble Briton, Russell James (as he called himself), Honey Gully, Richard Selby and Verna Reid, all interlocked in a pattern of calculation and deception. It looked as if Brain had run into Baudin in the Cross, noticed his powerful resemblance to the Chattertons, and spilled some of the story to him. Baudin could have known Selby through the Spartacus Studio and together they could have sent Brain up to Lady C to gauge her reaction. Getting nothing they switched to working through Verna Reid in some way. It fitted a lot of the facts; Russell James told Verna Reid he was a property developer; Keir's $1,500 could have been used to finance that, either for real or as a front. Whatever the tactic my turning up must have thrown them into a spin — exit Brain and Callaghan. It had holes in it: if James *was* Baudin why didn't he just declare himself and claim the loot? But there was a possible explanation for that — Lady Catherine's wish to find the grandson might be a secret she'd confided only to me. Selby's involvement could be complex, he could be in collusion with Reid and James or be playing another angle — in the normal course of things his wife was in line for a big slice of the pie anyway. Then there was the mystery of the Chatterton will, there could be something in that which necessitated a waiting game.

I finished the cigarette and looked out across the water in a mood of mild self-congratulation. I checked back over my reconstruction and didn't find anything too inconvenient although the Chatterton heir's character was looking blacker every minute. I walked quickly back to the restaurant and suddenly I was breaking all my own rules, moving hastily and obtrusively for cover at the foot of the steps — under a harsh neon light the big man with the bandaged face and his dark-eyed friend were stepping it out towards their car.

21

Verna Reid and Russell James were quarrelling; they kept well apart and their heads jerked as they snapped and snarled. Watching them, I dodged about on the other side of the road like a boxer trying to stay out of trouble on the ropes. James slipped quickly into his mildly aggressive driving style. The Toyota took the corners with practised ease and pulled familiarly up into Richard and Bettina Selby's driveway. I skulked on for a hundred yards before killing the lights, putting the keys under the seat, arming myself and heading up the street to do some genuine, in the field, sleuthing.

No front gate, no alert dog in the front yard, no kids' toys to trip over. I padded up past the Toyota; the Honda Accord was missing but a Chev was there instead. Lights were on in the back of the house and there was a soft, green glow from the pool which looked cool, inviting and uncomplicated. A heavy thumping, like a fist beating on tin, caused me to duck down into the shadows near the garage. I poked my head around the corner and saw the man in the fawn suit knocking his knuckles on the back door.

'Richard!' His voice was high and urgent. 'Richard, where the hell are you?'

Where indeed? It hadn't looked like a chance call and I'd expected to find them cosy over a beer with their ties loosened.

He kept on knocking and nothing kept happening, then he started to swear rather nastily and display a considerable bad temper by kicking the door. The gun was biting into my gut and I was getting cramped in the squatting position; I uncoiled cautiously and inched along trying to get a better view of the man assaulting the door. It all happened very fast — a car door slammed and I spun around and then something hit me in the stomach very hard. It bent me over and I had an impression of a wide, light shape near me and then my upper right arm was stinging like hell and I was throwing a long punch that went on and on to nowhere.

I was only a quarter of a man or less after that: the two of them dragged me into the house. I couldn't move but I could hear all right.

'She's away with the kids,' Selby said.

My head bumped against something as the other man spoke.

'Easy,' Selby grunted. 'Albie phoned, I was ready for this bastard half an hour ago.'

Albie, I thought. *Rotten little Albie, fucking Albie* . . .

They let me down roughly onto carpet that felt like marble.

'How long'll he be out?'

'It varies,' Selby said. 'That stuff puts some people under for hours and others hardly go out at all. Let's have a look at him.'

The smart thing seemed to be one of the susceptible; I let my eyelids drop and my head loll. I felt hands grab bits of my face and then I was on the carpet slab again.

I didn't have to act too hard: I was lying still but felt as if I was swimming and there was a roaring in my head like an eternal wave breaking over me. I heard snatches of their conversation through the foam.

'What are we going to *do* with this character?'

'You were supposed to find out tonight,' Selby said.

Then Verna Reid chipped in: 'He tried but I just don't *know*! She's kept it all to herself.'

I snuck a look through a shuttered eye; they were in armchairs but tense and nervous. Verna Reid was wearing her basic black which suited her fierce, hostile mood. Selby was wearing jeans and a white shirt, his face was scarlet above the snowy cloth. He was drinking what looked like scotch and the other man clinked bottles and ice and made himself something, too. I was parched and hearing a howling wind now along with the boom of the surf. I was slipping under and coming up, hearing words and missing some, and I was suddenly cold from my scalp to my big toes.

'We have to settle it,' Selby was saying. 'Is he up at the river?'

'Should be by now. But what if . . .'

'It's all ifs. We have to make a move, we have to find out.'

'What about him?'

The roaring and booming blotted out the rest of it and I felt them take hold of me again and move me. I summoned up everything and tried to fight them but for all the difference it made I might have been a butterfly. They dragged me easily with their weight-lifters' strength and they didn't care when parts of me hit things. I didn't care much either. I wanted to sleep, to curl up in a ball and sleep, and then I remembered Kay and that I hadn't called her and I heaved and strained at them and said uncomplimentary words that felt like stones in my mouth. They must have bumped me into something then or hit me because it all slid away; the noises stopped and I tobogganed down into darkness and silence.

Coming to was like being born — I struggled down a long, dark tunnel, not wanting to get to the end but not in control of what was happening. I was pushed and pulled towards a circle of light which grew bigger and bigger until it filled my whole field of vision and blinded me. I felt as if I'd been folded in half and put in a box. In fact I was sitting with my knees drawn up to my chin: I tried to lower my legs but they only got half way before they bumped into something. I shook my head and forced my eyes open and saw a wall; I felt a wall behind me and a hard surface under me. I was in a shower stall, my hands were tied behind me and my feet were strapped together at the ankles. Pains like cramps were shooting through me and my throat was as dry as a chalk duster. At first I thought the light tapping I could hear was inside my head but I found it was a steady drip from the shower rose. The drop fell about a foot in front of me but I couldn't lean far enough forward to get my tongue out to it — my whole body was thirsty. It was torture.

I had no idea of the time, lights were on in the room but I couldn't see a window. It could have been midnight or midday. I wasted some time cursing myself for carelessness and incompetence, and wasted some breath by shouting for help. Then I calmed down and became more practical: I listened, the house was dead quiet. I pulled at the cord holding my ankles and at whatever was around my wrists — nothing gave. I looked around as best I could but the stall was tiled and smooth, there was nothing to cut with or rub against. So I shouted again and choked and was sick all over my legs and everything was just that much worse. I tried kicking at the wall but the thing was built solid and I only succeeded in sending jarring pains shooting up into my crutch. I tried to roll and found that my wrists were tied to something firm — no rolling.

It was hard. The thirst and the cramps and the smell were bad but the feeling of helplessness was destructive. It washed over me in waves making me rave and struggle and then leaving me defeated, almost indifferent. The drug was still working; I blanked out a few times. I had bursts of cold anger and mushy self-pity; I did no clear thinking. I was in one of the indifferent stages when I heard the noises — a door opened far away, there were footsteps and other indeterminate sounds. I hardly cared, or thought I was imagining it. I smiled and felt the caked vomit on my face crack — ho hum. Then the noises were closer and then they were going away with a final sound to them. They were real. I shouted and thumped my feet on the wall; I howled like a wolf.

High heels rang on the tiles and the shower curtain jerked aside: Bettina Selby stood there, the most wonderful person in the world, a goddess, a saint.

'Jesus Christ,' she breathed.

I croaked up at her: 'Water, and get a knife.'

An hour later I was sitting in her kitchen with a third cup of coffee and wearing one of her husband's shirts. I was shaved, fairly clean and if not quite back to normal at least I could remember what normal felt like. Bettina had been fast and cool with the necessaries. She told me that she'd planned to stay a week with a friend but had come back for something she'd forgotten — the thought of a week in the shower stall made my guts turn over. I drank coffee and made a cigarette; I hadn't explained one damn thing to her and it was time. She was wearing an off the shoulder dress in a floral print and big wedge heels and looked good enough to eat. It was 11 a.m. on Tuesday, she told me, as she poured herself a hefty brandy. I accepted a slug of the same in my coffee.

'So, Mr Kennedy, was it?'

'Hardy,' I said. 'That was all a line. What did your husband say after our fracas?'

'Business trouble. But it's not is it?'

'No. It's family trouble, I'm working for your mother — I'm a private detective.'

She'd seen me flatten her husband and she'd found me trussed up like a chicken and covered in vomit. She knew I'd lied to her once; she drank some brandy and looked interested but sceptical. I got out the photoprints, unfolded them and passed them across. She took a quick look.

'A boy and a man,' she said. 'Not bad looking. So what?'

'That's your son, Betty.'

'Don't call me that,' she snapped, and then the message reached her and she pulled hard on her drink.

'Ridiculous.'

'It's true. He's thirty-one years old. Take another look, he's the dead spit of your Dad.'

She looked, looked hard and nodded slowly. Her knuckles were white around the glass and beads of sweat broke out along her hairline. She reached for the bottle.

'Take it easy,' I said. 'Try and face it. This should interest you, it's a change from booze and bad husbands.'

She smiled and that strength and intelligence that made her arresting shaped the planes of her face.

'I really gave you the business the other day didn't I?'

'You weren't yourself. I suppose you can guess what this's all about now?'

'Some of it. The old battle-axe wants to find him,' she tapped the pictures, 'and cut him in.'

'I think she intends to give him the lot.'

Her eyes opened and she took a thoughtful, not desperate, sip of her drink. 'How would you know that?'

'It's a guess really. There seems to be something strange about your father's will, or maybe your mother's. Your hubby's had a good sniff at that. Miss Reid is out for herself and there's someone else in there looking for an angle.'

She touched the pictures again. 'Him?'

'Could be.'

I told her everything then, more or less the way it had happened. She took Henry Brain's demise without a blink and cried a bit over Nurse Callaghan. She asked me what I knew about her son.

'Nothing good,' I said. 'He was a star athlete and pretty bright but he got lost somewhere. There was no serious score against him before all this that I know of, but he might have killed the old people. It's tricky.'

'I can see that. You want to deliver him all clean and shiny.'

'That doesn't look very likely now. Happy endings are hard to come by but you never know. Have you got a place on the river?'

'Yes, I mean . . .'

'Come on, it's out in the open, you've got to see it through now.'

She looked stubborn and we both drank some more and kicked it around for a while. She confirmed that her husband was keenly interested in her mother's property and had big plans for using it. I told her that it looked as if her husband was trying to get control of it one way or another — through her, or Verna Reid or the grandson.

'That's the way he thinks,' she said, 'he likes to cover all the angles.'

'He's doing all right isn't he?' I let my eyes drift around the gadget-laden kitchen.

'Yes, but he's ambitious, he wants to be big.'

'Why?'

She shrugged. 'Don't know, something to do I suppose. He's not interested in me or the girls. What's your next move, Mr Hardy?' She looked at the bottle and I had the feeling that she was the sort of boozer who rewarded herself with a drink before she tackled anything hard just in case she didn't make it. I moved the brandy out of reach.

'I'm going after them, it's time to break up their little game, get the thing running my way. Where's this river place?'

She looked at me with her mother's eyes, calculating.

'Would you like to go to bed with me?'

'Sure. Some other time.' I thought of Kay again as soon as I spoke. I was fifteen hours late with my call; I felt impatient, eager to get the Chatterton case wrapped up, anxious to get on with what might be called my life.

She sighed. 'I thought you might say that. I'll take you to

the river. If you don't let me come you can go to hell. It'd take you a while to find out where it is.'

True, I thought, and she might be useful. It was a hell of a situation, impossible to lay down rules for. I was going up against two men I didn't know. It was important that one of them didn't get hurt. To take the wife and maybe-mother along could be a good move, she could anticipate how Selby might behave. Or it could be a recipe for disaster.

'Are there any guns in the place?'

'Yes, a couple.'

Great. They already had one of mine, I assumed, and there was the drug angle to think about. Who was using the stuff — Selby, Baudin, both of them?

'Maybe we should get the police,' Bettina said.

That decided me. The police were out, the last thing Lady C wanted was the prying eye of officialdom — there'd be no bonus for Hardy in that event.

'No police,' I said. 'Let's keep it in the family. You can come but you do exactly as I say. Right?'

'All right. D'you want to go now? I'll change.'

I nodded. She got up with the grace I'd noticed before — when she wasn't drunk or traumatised she moved like a dancer. When she'd gone I grabbed a phone and dialled Kay's home number; it rang and rang hopelessly. I hung up feeling numb and empty, also resentful — the Chattertons with their dynastic ambitions and hang-ups and middle class boredoms were a pain in the arse. I felt like a mercenary, disaffected but with no other side to switch to. I was in the mood for Baudin and Selby, guns and all.

Bettina came back wearing jeans and a white Indian shirt; her hair was pulled back and tied and her make-up was subdued. She carried a big leather shoulder bag and looked ready for action.

I picked up my tobacco and other things while she waited; I was still stiff and my arm hurt where the syringe had gone in; otherwise I was in fair shape.

'Is there much grass up there?' I asked her.

'Plenty, why?'

I grabbed the brandy bottle. 'We'll take this for snakebite.'

22

I got my other gun, the Colt, from the Falcon. It's an illegal gun but a good one. We took the Honda north. The Selbys' weekender was at Wisemans Ferry, Bettina told me, but that's all she'd say. She drove well; there wasn't a lot of traffic but there were a few curly spots and she put the Honda through them with style. As we went I tried to reconstruct what I'd heard while the drug was working on me, but I was aware of gaps. 'Up the river' was clear and the intention to come to some decision about things, but not much more than that. I had a feeling that another person was involved — Leonidas Green? Albie Logan? I hoped it was Albie.

Bettina was quiet for a while, concentrating on her driving, and then she started spewing questions at me — about her mother, Henry Brain, Blackman's Bay. I had a sense of someone pent-up and thirsty for self-knowledge. One thing was clear, she knew that this was a crisis in her life and that the old round of booze and parties and battles with her husband over trivialities was over. I asked her what she'd do with the Chatterton estate if it came to her.

'I'd like to set up somewhere in the country,' she said. 'A farm, you know? Horses . . . it'd be good for the girls and might straighten me out. I don't suppose it'll happen.'

'Hard to say. It's your son she's lining up for the dough.'

'He could hardly be expected to care about me, I only saw him once.'

I shrugged. 'He might be tickled pink to meet his Mum.'

'That isn't funny,' she snarled.

'Sorry, just trying to keep it bright.'

She slammed the Honda through a corner using gears and engine, no brake. 'Are you ever serious, Hardy?'

'Nup, I meet too many crooks and liars to be serious.'

She sighed. 'I think you carry on like that because you're nervous and don't know what to do.'

'That's what I said.'

We left the highway and began the descent to the river which is big and bold the way rivers ought to be. The Hawkesbury is tidal, salt-water a good way up and has lots of sharks in it — there are also fashionable islands and a prison farm island where they send fashionable offenders like defaulting solicitors. We crept down the road to Wisemans Ferry — the place has been going for about 150 years but still consists of only a few stores and petrol pump. She turned left before the run down to the township and we bounced along a couple of hundred yards of track before she stopped and set the handbrake. We were on a steep hill running down to the river.

'We're close,' she said.

I looked out across the river to the rugged cliff face on the other side; we were only about ninety kilometres from Sydney but it wasn't too hard to imagine an Aborigine sneaking along that cliff hoping to spear his lunch. I tried to remember all the guff in the instruction manuals they'd thrown at us in Malaya: study the topography, high points, cover, look for exits — it all mattered, but what counted in the end was luck and guts.

'Where's the house?'

She pointed down to where two tin roofs glinted in the sun through a canopy of gum leaves.

'Down there, the house back from the road.'

There was a proprietorial note in her voice and I squinted to get the layout clear. One of the houses did sit a few yards further back from the road and apparently such details counted up here; me, I'd have called it the one with the fibro cement painted white rather than green.

She watched me nervously while I checked the Colt and attended to the basics, like tucking my trousers into my socks and making sure I wasn't going to lose a shoe heel at a crucial moment.

'What are you going to do?'

'First, make sure I don't get hurt, second try not to hurt anyone else. Try to give them a hell of a fright if I can. Anyone likely to be home next door?'

'No, they're real weekenders.'

'Okay, where would the cars be?'

'On the other side. We're sort of near the back here.'

'Can you show me the way in and let me get a look at the cars as well?'

She nodded. Her lips were tight and she'd lost a bit of her high colour but she looked determined rather than afraid.

'Let's go. Remember our deal — you do what you're told.'

I reached over, took out the keys and dropped them into the door pocket; we got out and I motioned at her not to slam the door. We walked down the road a bit and then took a rabbit track off into the trees. It was steep and Bettina steadied herself expertly on the slim-trunked gums as we went down.

The back fence of the Selbys' lot was three strands of barbed wire strung on half a dozen rough posts. The words of the old World War I song rang through my mind — 'hanging on the old barbed wire' — nasty stuff, anti-people. The scrub came up to within a foot of the fence and afforded cover along its length. I pulled Bettina down.

'The cars?'

She pointed and set off, bent double, towards the other side of the lot; for a big woman, past her youth, she bent well. I followed and grabbed her arm.

'You're enjoying this,' I said.

'Yes.' Her breathing was hard and short — exertion and excitement.

'I hope you don't tear your slacks on the wire.'

'Fuck you.'

Through the feathery leaves I could see the cars parked beside the house — the Chev and the blue Toyota. The house was well maintained, good roof and guttering, fresh paint. I focused on a window and could see a moving shape inside.

'Richard,' Bettina whispered.

'What's he doing?'

'Preparing food by the look of it — that's the kitchen.'

'This is as good a time as any,' I said in Bettina's ear. 'I'm going in the front and try to catch them with their faces full of food. Give me fifteen minutes and come on in if you don't hear more than one shot.'

'What if I do hear shooting?'

'Is there a town cop?'

'I think so, yes, there is.'

'Get him and anyone else useful you can find.'

'Good luck,' she said, then she giggled: 'Wish I had my camera.'

Christ, I thought, that's all I need, candid shots of Hardy creeping about in the scrub, gun at the ready. The idea relieved some of the tension though: it was a tricky situation going up against armed men I didn't know, but it wasn't full-scale war. I moved down the side of the lot towards the front. Beside the house and fifteen feet away was a thick screen of trees: a bird hovered and then dropped in a long, streaking dive behind them. I was snapping, scraping and tearing things as I moved, but I was doing the best I could. I worked down to the cars which had their windows open and the keys in the ignition — the way people leave cars in the country. I put the keys in my pocket.

The Selbys' cottage was as simple and unpretentious as their suburban house was the opposite. It was a square fibro bungalow set up on brick piers with a deck running along the front. It was also hemmed in with trees so that I had cover up to the deck. I never saw a weekender yet with a decent lock on the door and this was no exception; the man who taught me could have opened it with his thumbnail. I used the stiff plastic and the lock slid in; I held it there, eased the door open, and then freed the lock slowly and without a sound.

The interior was painted cream and there was sea-grass matting on the floor; a door at the end of the passage led to the rooms at the back of the bungalow and, as I stood looking at it, it opened. The man with the bandages and sticking plaster on his face came through and turned his head back to say something in the direction he'd come from and then he became aware of me and his jaw dropped.

I lifted the Colt and put a shot into the wall about a foot above his head; the sound was like thunder in the enclosed space and he stood rock still. I bustled up and stuck the gun in his ribs.

'Hey,' he said weakly, 'hey.'

'Back up. Get back in there.'

He went like a lamb all the way back to where Richard Selby and Verna Reid were sitting. Selby was lifting a glass of beer to his mouth, the woman yelled and he dropped it; the beer went into his lap and the glass shattered on the floor. I prodded the tall man again.

'Sit down.'

He did. He'd recovered from the shock and was starting to look me over carefully. His hands were big and thick around the knuckles and joints. He flexed them and shuffled his feet.

'Don't try any of that Bruce Lee stuff,' I told him, 'I owe you a bit and I'd be glad to get even.'

Selby looked up from mopping his pants. 'This is overdue, Hardy. It's time we had a talk.'

I gave him a hard look. They'd have called him Red Richard back in Norman days and admired him for a fine figure of a man. There was lard on him to my eyes and I thought I could see some pink scalp in places through the carefully arranged black locks.

'I owe you something, too, for that nice work in the garage,' I said, 'and I'm a vindictive man. Don't go smooth on me Selby, I can tie you into one murder, maybe two, and I will if that's the way you want to play it.'

Verna Reid's face was tight with malice. She looked at Selby with contempt. 'I told you we'd have to kill him.'

It wasn't clear whether he was talking to me or the woman but anyway Selby said: 'I don't know what you're talking about.' It carried about as much conviction as the warning on a cigarette packet and I let it pass.

The boy with the bandages was more direct. 'How did you get loose?' he asked. His voice was deep and educated.

'You'll see,' I said. I jerked the gun at him. 'Now you are going to take those bandages off.'

Alarm leapt into the voice. 'Why?'

'Just do it.'

'No! Russell no!' Verna Reid sounded as if she'd heard someone threaten to knock a leg off the Venus de Milo.

James touched the bandages and looked nervously at Selby. 'I can't!'

I grinned and raised an eyebrow at him, his voice wasn't as deep now or as educated.

'I can't, I've got bad cuts, that mirror at the gym — they'll scar.'

'Sonny boy you can end up like Quasimodo for all I care. I'm going to see your face now one way or another. If I have to do it myself I won't be gentle.'

He looked appealingly at Selby who shrugged. 'You better do it Russ,' he said.

'I'll need scissors.' He stood up quickly and pushed his chair back; he was dangerous, a nice mover and with enormous strength packed in the wide shoulders and arms. I needed to defuse him and quickly: I moved up closer raising the gun and then smacked him across the cheek with my left hand. He screamed and I thumped him on the shoulder with the gun.

'Sit down and start unwrapping!'

He lifted his hand to his face and then let it drop. 'I can't.'

The bandages covered most of the upper part of his face leaving good sized slits for his eyes and going down around his chin. I grabbed an end of plaster and yanked. He screamed again and I pulled the tape free and held it in front of his eye slits.

'Do it, or it'll be like that all the way.'

He reached up and began fumbling for the ends of the plaster strips. I felt like wincing as he worked them slowly off the surface of the bandage; tears jumped into his eyes and all the fight seemed to have gone out of him. I took time out to look at Selby who was playing with a bread roll on his plate. He looked puzzled, as if he wanted to say something but wasn't sure what language to speak in. It was a mistake to be distracted — James came at me suddenly, coiling up off the chair like a big cat, his hands out, stiff and deadly. He looked good but he was just a little slow; I side-stepped and swept the flat of the gun against the side of his face and he went down clutching and making tight little agonised grunts.

'I told you not to be silly,' I said. 'Get up.'

He lifted himself up into the chair and his trembling hands worked at the wrappings. Selby didn't say anything in any language, didn't move. It took James five minutes and blood started to seep out pretty soon; Verna Reid sobbed quietly. Blood was flowing freely down his face when he eased off the last bandage but his features were plain. He wasn't Warwick Baudin — nothing like him.

23

Disappointment hit me like an electric shock; I gaped and felt unsteady on my feet. Bettina Selby's voice cut through the accumulated tension.

'It's not him.' She stepped in from the passage and her husband's eyes moved between us both as he got the connection.

'Not who?' Blood ran down Russell James' face and spotted his cream silk shirt.

'Yes, who?' Selby got up and took a couple of steps out from the table. I moved and brought the Colt up to cover him but I was hopelessly unprepared. I'd let the gun drop while I'd watched the bandages come off and now I wasn't sure enough where it was pointing; now there was an extra person in the room and one of the others was moving. These are excuses for the fact that I ended up with my back to a door which had opened. I knew that when I felt something hard and sharp bite into my neck.

'Put the gun down, Hardy,' Selby said smugly, 'or he'll blow your head off.'

I let the gun drop and turned slowly. The man holding the shotgun was nearly as tall as the one dabbing at his bloodied face. He had an enormous ballooning belly and three chins. His face still wore the idiot grin I'd seen in the health studio when he was cleaning a mirror but the light was better and my eyes were ready to see whatever there was to see — under the fat and behind the grin and the vacant, crazy eyes was Warwick Baudin.

He still wore the battered T shirt, he had old sandshoes on his feet and his jeans were unfastened at the waist to give extra room to his vast gut.

The room was dead quiet. Having made his entrance, the fat man didn't seem to know what to do next; he looked at Selby and James who appeared to be as scared as I was.

'I heard the noise,' he said. His voice was slow and thick as if his tongue was too big for his mouth. He was in a bad way, his hair was lank and greasy and his skin pale and puffy. There was dirt in the folds of flesh on his neck and his pale grey eyes were bleary and rimmed with scum. He didn't look much like a Chatterton now.

'Nothing to worry about,' I said quietly and I put out a tentative hand towards the shot gun.

He threw back his head and let out a high, giggling laugh, but the double barrel stayed where it would cut me in half. Selby who'd nominated himself master of ceremonies a minute ago had lost his confidence; he moved back behind the table and looked as if he'd have liked to crawl under it.

'He's ripped out of his mind,' James said. He looked down at my Colt on the floor which was closer to him than me.

'Easy,' I said, 'he could blast us both. This isn't worth dying for.'

It was a crazy situation, like being bailed up against a wall by a child with a bazooka. Bettina and Verna Reid seemed almost uninterested, reserving all their attention, packed with malice, for each other. With an effort I called the old training into play and looked at his hands; in contrast to the rest of him they were clean and well maintained. It was a nice, sleuthly point but not of much use just now. Then I noticed something else and my breath started to come a little easier: only one of the hammers on the old gun was cocked and his finger was on the wrong trigger. That gave me all the time in the world.

Baudin turned his head a fraction to look at Bettina. 'Who's she?' he said thickly.

I moved fast and punched his upper left arm and swooped on his right wrist with my other hand. The barrels swung down to the floor and his finger clawed convulsively: the gun roared and pellets sprayed up at us from the floor. I wrenched the shotgun free and dug Baudin hard with it in the belly. He went down with a grunt. I bent for my gun and then I was holding all the aces again. Also I was one of the three people not bleeding: Baudin had taken some pellets in the legs, Selby in the shoulder and James had both hands over his face and was moaning quietly. It was a bad day for James.

Bettina got busy. She dumped her bag and helped her

husband and James into chairs. Baudin was shuffling back towards the wall and I let him get there and prop himself against it. I told Bettina to get some water and look for something to use as a bandage. I stood by the window and made and lit a cigarette. I wanted a drink. Bettina came back with a basin and a bottle of disinfectant and a shirt. She ripped and dabbed and swabbed and the wounded bore it stoically. Baudin had a few pellets embedded in the pudgy flesh of his right leg; Selby was only nicked; Russell James had taken a pellet in the face — it had ploughed up his cheek and veered off along the side of his head before reaching the eye. Lucky.

When she'd finished ministering, Bettina picked up her bag, opened it and pulled out the brandy. She cocked an eye at me and I nodded. She came back from the kitchen with five glasses and poured a generous slug into each. I hooked up a chair and sat in it with the shotgun across my lap and the handgun on the edge of the table. No one had spoken for some time and the grunters and moaners had fallen silent.

'All right,' I said. 'All this is nasty but nothing fatal. I think it's time we sorted this mess out.'

I looked across at Baudin who was staring down at his glass; he picked it up and drained it straight off. I motioned to Bettina to pour him another and he did the same again. He seemed uninterested in the proceedings, just keen to get as much alcohol inside him as was allowed.

I drank some brandy. 'What have you got to say Russ?'

He sipped his drink and didn't answer.

'No, well you wouldn't want to say too much because you're the boy who's really in trouble.'

'Why?' There was a whining tone in his voice now and all the polish had rubbed off him.

'Henry Brain, the old man in Darlinghurst. You hit him. He died.'

'I didn't hit him. We struggled and he fell.'

'You sure as hell didn't send for a doctor. Look, maybe you're telling the truth. There'll be a medical report that might bear you out but either way you look bad — hitting or struggling, what's the difference. It depends how we play it. Have you got a record?'

'A bit, not much,' he said sullenly.

'But you see my point don't you? My client carries a fair bit of weight still and I want to keep her happy. I might leave you out if I get co-operation.' I drank some more brandy and looked down at the sad fat man with the empty glass on the floor. 'He's the grandson, right?'

'Don't tell him, Russell,' Verna Reid barked, 'don't tell him a thing.'

James looked down at Baudin who was playing with the glass in his big, meaty hands.

'We think so,' he said slowly. 'It was all Richard's idea.'

Selby opened his mouth to say something but I waved my glass at him and he shut it.

'The way I see it,' I said, 'is that Brain spotted fatty here and blabbed something to you about his long-lost son. He told you that he'd been married to Mr Justice Chatterton's daughter and you knew Selby here was married to her now and you thought he might be interested.'

James nodded and put down half his brandy. Bettina looked interested and hadn't touched her drink yet.

'That's right,' James said. 'Richard took over then. We . . . he sent old Henry up to pressure the old lady but he made a mess of it. Then Henry dropped out of sight for a while, Richard had given him some money. Then the Judge died. We didn't know what to do after that. Then Richard . . .' He stopped and took a nervous sip of his drink.

'Richard came up with the idea of you latching onto Miss Reid,' I said. 'Dirty trick.'

Verna Reid's face lost its boldness, her hands flew up and fluttered like the wings of a bird beating against bars. 'I thought you . . .' she said, 'I thought that we . . .'

'Charades, Verna,' I said. 'All charades. Do you know what Lady Catherine planned to do with the estate?'

'Not really, she's mad. One time she told me she'd leave it to me, another time she said she'd leave me nothing. She hinted that there was someone else, I knew she didn't mean *her*.' She shot a look at Bettina who was nursing her drink and leaning forward as if she was watching a good play.

'Just what did you have in mind then, Miss Reid?' Bettina purred.

She didn't answer; she looked at James who was staring

down into his glass and at Selby who avoided her eyes. She seemed to know that she'd reached the end of things — a relationship, prospects, a job. Her eyes were empty and dull.

'I slaved for that old bitch. The wages are a joke. She was always promising things, promising. Well, the place is pretty run down and she hasn't got any money to speak of. The way things were going she'd have had to sell it sometime.'

'I get it,' I said. 'You could help that process along a bit and Russell here could do himself a bit of good when the place came up for sale.'

'Yes,' she said softly.

'What about Booth, the lawyer?' Bettina said angrily. 'He should have been able to protect her, he was my father's friend.'

'He's an old fogey,' Verna Reid said. 'She had him completely bluffed.' The tears that had flowed when I was heavying James had left streaks down her face and they got wet again as fresh tears started. 'It would have worked, it would have. And then this fool had to play around with this grandson idea.' Selby poured himself some more brandy and said nothing.

'They had the grandson idea first,' I said. 'You were just a supporting act. They kept both ideas running and couldn't decide which one to back. You're a tough nut Miss Reid, you put James on to me and he tailed me down the coast.' The words mortified me. Being tailed twice by amateurs and not picking it up is bad for the ego. I said: 'What about the old lady?' to James and some of the anger in my voice was for myself.

James jerked and held his hands out, palms up as if to ward me off. 'I didn't touch her, I swear it. I got scared and came back to talk to Richard and then you were all over the place. We didn't know what to do.'

Selby had finished his drink and he reached across and took the bottle again. 'Good on you, Russ,' he said, 'you always did drop your bundle. Well Hardy, what are you going to do about it?'

I was suddenly very angry, disgusted with them and part of the disgust was because there was nothing much I could do about them if I wanted to bring things out right for me. But I felt unclean just being in the same room as them. I suddenly wished I was in old Sir Clive's shoes and had the power to send the whole crew of them to the slammer for a long, long time. But I kept my voice flat and unemotional. 'You could go up on a series of conspiracy charges apart from Brain's manslaughter. And there's the drug angle. I could tie you in with Albie and put you right out of business. Health studios, weight-lifting, see what I mean?'

Selby looked glum. Bettina was showing no interest in him at all and I had the feeling that he'd be a back number pretty soon. She was sipping her drink, not desperately, and looking curiously at Baudin.

'That brings us up to him.' I inclined my head at Baudin. 'What drugs is he on? Don't tell me you don't know about that, James. Albie says different.'

'Speed, lots of pills, Mogadon, Largactyl, you know. Plenty of grog as well. He's a hopeless case.'

'You helped him along. Does he know anything about this? Does he know who he is?'

'I don't think so. He was on the skids when old Henry saw him. We tried to smarten him up at one stage, Richard had some idea of using him some way, but it fell through. He's been pretty well out of it since then.'

'Bit of a Svengali are you, Dicky?' I said to Selby.

Selby pulled cigarettes out of his shirt pocket and lit up, struggling for nonchalance. 'I'm not saying a word until I speak to my lawyer.'

'Lawyer!' I had to laugh. 'You haven't got a prayer there, Dicky boy. When he hears who you've been up against your lawyer'll take his holidays.'

'Christ,' Selby said. He puffed hard on his cigarette and looked at Bettina. She studied him as if she was making plans to have him mounted. He looked very uneasy but he still had a bit of fight in him. He pointed to Baudin on the floor.

'That's your son, Bettina dear, the one you never told me about. What d'you think of him?'

Bettina didn't take her eyes of his flushed, angry face.

'You always were pathetic, Richard,' she said evenly. 'I never knew anything you planned to come out right and you're still at it. If you think I'm going to break down you've got another thing coming. Henry Brain was a slug — he's no loss, by the way, Hardy. Being pregnant to him was like having a belly full of maggots. I just got it over with and tried to get on with my life. I thought about the child a bit at first, but it was all tied up with Henry. I wanted to forget about all that and I did. I'm sorry for him, that's all.'

Selby shook his head wildly and James gave a thin, bitter smile and winced when the movement hurt his face. He seemed to have accepted the new turn of events. The trouble was, the shape of those events had to be determined by me and I was confused. I had some ethical questions to sort out. I broke the shotgun open, took out the shell and leaned the gun against the wall. That seemed like an appropriate move towards finding a civilised solution. Among the living I had five people to consider — myself, Baudin-Chatterton, Lady C, Bettina and Dr Osborn. There were Brain and the nurse to consider, too; slamming the door on James, Reid and Selby wouldn't do them any good and maybe there was a nice irony in Henry Brain's son inheriting the Chatterton estate. As for Gertrude Callaghan, perhaps her memory would best be served by the proper preservation of the doctor's records. I could help with that.

Bettina finished her drink and rapped the glass on the table.

'Deep thoughts, Hardy — problems?'

'I think I've got them sorted out. What about you?'

She looked at Selby. 'I'm going to divorce him. Will he go to jail?'

'I don't think so, I think he should go back to his business and concentrate on supporting you and the kids.'

'So do I.'

She jerked her head at James. 'What about him?'

'He should be in a cage but bringing it all out will do more harm than good. I can sew him up in a drugs charge and that should keep him quiet. Besides,' I looked at James' cut and bruised face, 'he isn't going to be so pretty any more. Miss Reid here is going to resign her post, aren't you?'

She nodded; she was passive now, which was an unnatural state for her. I wondered how long she'd stay that way. I had a feeling that she would bounce back but there was nothing I could do about it.

That left the grandson and heir, the question was how much of a man was left in him after the drugs and the booze, given that he hadn't been such promising material to start with.

'Can you help him, Hardy?' Bettina said softly.

'I have to. He's worth money to me and a bit to a lady in Darlinghurst who needs it.' I spoke directly to him for the first time. 'You remember Honey don't you, Warwick?'

He looked at me for what seemed like an hour and then he nodded slowly.

'Sure you do. Great days. I'll give it a try. I'll need a doctor and some time. I can't give him to grandma like this.'

'Goodbye money,' Bettina said grimly.

'Maybe not. It looks as if you and yours were out of the picture anyway. Maybe you can get round her if she's doting on your son. You can try if you feel like it. Anyway, you'll have Richard here with his nose to the grindstone.'

'It's a nice thought,' she said.

Warwick Baudin started to shake, flesh wobbled on his big frame as his shoulders heaved convulsively. He lowered his head and big, fat tears fell on the floor.

Bettina moved over and put her arm across his shoulders, 'There,' she said, 'there, there.'

24

I located my Smith & Wesson in a kitchen drawer and collected up the few things Warwick Baudin had in the house. When we left, James and Selby were sitting at the table with fresh cans of beer open. They were both snappy dressers and somehow snappy dressers look all the worse when they're knocked about. These two were — they were bloodied and bowed. They were looking at each other and not liking what they saw. Verna Reid was staring out the window like someone with a lot to think over. I tossed the two sets of car keys onto the table and left them to it.

We bundled Baudin into the Honda and took the dusty trail away from Wisemans Ferry. I locked the back doors but Baudin didn't seem to have any fight in him which was just as well — he was a big lad. He fell asleep when we reached the highway and snored all the way back to Sydney.

Bettina didn't say much. At my prompting she blocked in an odd fact or two about Selby. I got a picture of a man who thought big but didn't have the ability to carry out his plans. At first she said she'd take him for every penny but she softened almost straightaway.

'Hell, I haven't been much fun to live with,' she said. 'I might go easy on him, there's the girls to consider.' She looked at her watch as she drove. 'Tell you one thing, I haven't been this sober this late in the day for a long time. Do you think that's a good sign?'

'Could be,' I said. I felt she was warming up towards something more intimate and I didn't feel up to handling it just then. I had too much on my hands with the drug-soaked man in the back seat and the nagging worry that I'd let Kay Fletcher down. Bettina saw I was preoccupied and left me alone. We reached her place late in the afternoon. She kissed me briefly and helped me shift Baudin over to my car. He was like a child just learning to walk. I wondered how he'd got up to Wisemans Ferry and what the hell he'd taken when he got there. We rolled him into the Falcon.

'When do you plan to present him?' Bettina said.

'About a month from now.'

'I'll be in touch, it should be interesting.' She peered in through the dirty window at the wreck of her thirty-one-year-old son. She shook her head, gave me a wave and set off towards her nasty house, her plain children and her problems.

I took him home to Glebe and put him in my spare bed, then I called my friend Ian Sangster who has a couple of medical degrees and an adventurous spirit. When Sangster arrived I gave him an outline of the problems — Baudin's history, the drugs, the manipulation, and turned him loose. Then I made a drink and rolled some cigarettes and picked up the telephone. There was no answer at Kay's flat. I called a journalist I knew in Canberra and he asked around and found that Kay had gone to Indonesia on assignment for the paper. She hadn't left any message for me. I was thinking about that and smoking one of the cigarettes when I got a call from Lady Catherine's residence. The caller was a Mrs McMahon who said she'd been hired for three days as a replacement for Verna Reid. Lady Catherine was ready to retire for the night and had instructed Mrs Mac to ring me for a progress report. It looked as if Verna had been giving herself a little elbow room. I told the woman that I'd report in half an hour and got the name of the hiring agency she worked for. Her assignment was going to run for a little more than three days.

I went through to the back of the house where Sangster was sitting in the kitchen with his long, mournful face drooping into a big glass of my scotch.

'That's a gunshot wound, Cliff,' he said. 'Should be reported.'

'Hunting accident.' I got some scotch for myself. 'The rabbits were jumping over a barbed wire fence and he tried to do the same. Happens all the time.'

He shook his head and drank. Sangster has a drinking problem but no money problem, so maybe it's not a problem.

'Your friend's in a bad way.' He pulled out a little notebook and began checking items. 'High blood pressure, furred tongue, dull reflexes, sugar in urine, obese, erratic pulse. He's really been hitting it.'

'Or being hit,' I said. 'I think he's been pilled up and down and round about by other people for the last year or so. I doubt he's made an independent move in that time.'

He grunted. 'So what do you want to know? You want information from him, is that right?' Sangster disapproves of my business which he calls a trade. I call his a racket.

'Wrong,' I said. 'First, is he going to be all right in the short term? I mean what's he been on?'

'Heavy amphetamine-alcohol mixture. He's disoriented, dependant, pretty paranoic too, I'd say. But yes, he's not going to die. If he went on the way he's been going I'd give him two years at the most.'

'He's stopping,' I said. 'He's going off everything and turning himself into a model citizen. He's going to wear a suit and read the *Financial Review*.'

He held out his empty glass. 'You're going to work this miracle, are you Cliff?'

'That's right.' I got two more drinks. Mine would put me well down the track but it was a drinking sort of night. 'What are the problems, would you say?'

'First, an incentive to be rehabilitated. It's a boring process I'm told. What's in it for him?'

'Money,' I said.

He drank reflectively. 'That should help. He's been going this way for a year you say?'

I nodded.

'Well, you'll have to watch him night and day. You might get him to try, he might really want to kick it, but he'll get pulled back and if he slips too far too often you're gone. A twenty-four hour vigil, seven days a week. How long have you got?'

'I need results in a month.'

He shook his head. 'You'll have to get him really keen. What did he do before he started blowing his mind?'

'Not much.'

'Be uphill work then. Tell you another thing, you might have to subdue him, he's a big bastard. Reckon you can handle him?'

'I don't know, we'll see. Will I need anything — drugs, medicine?'

He drained his glass and got up. He stands six four and looking up at him made me look at the ceiling which was festooned with cobwebs. The house had a rundown, seedy feel and there hadn't been a good solid laugh or a relaxed moment in it for a long time. Now it was to be a drying-out clinic and a jail and there'd be more ghosts and shadows and pain.

'You don't need drugs,' Sangster, 'just luck. You look pretty beat, Cliff. You should get some sleep. I gave him a shot and he's out for twelve hours. After that you'll have to be on your toes.'

I thanked him and let him out. Upstairs my meal-ticket and my bonus was sleeping. I felt drained, let-down, as is usual when a case has been resolved, but the feeling was exacerbated by the uncertainty about Kay. Women. That set me to thinking about how to play it with the old woman, how to stop her coming over in her wheelchair until the parcel was ready for delivery. A version of the truth seemed like the best ploy as it so often is.

I rang the ranch and gave Mrs McMahon a little low-key Hardy charm. It turned out she hadn't liked Miss Reid very much on their one meeting and had found signs of neglect in the treatment of Lady C. She was against neglect. She seemed pleased at my suggestion that she might be needed for some time and more pleased at the advice to pack Verna Reid's things and install them somewhere near the front. She passed me on to the widow.

'Mr Hardy?' That autocratic voice came on the line with a questioning note in it that was not really questioning. She knew the answers, or all the answers that mattered, except one.

'Have you found him Mr Hardy?'
'Yes.'

The silence was more expressive than words — dreams were fulfilled, hopes were given reality, life was full of promise as it should be.

'Are you certain?' No fakes tolerated.
'Yes, I think you'll be satisfied on that score. I can

document it pretty well, also the physical resemblance is strong — or will be.'

'Will be, will be?' she shrilled. 'What on earth does that mean?'

'He's had a pretty bad time. He's going to need a month's rest and some treatment. He's ill.'

'Nonsense. I must see him. Now!'

It got to me, the simple, blind command, trampling on the wounded, rough-riding over the lower ranks. I was coiled up tight and my temper snapped.

'Listen to me,' I snarled into the phone. 'He's been out in the real world doing dirty things with some dirty people. He's hurt and he needs help. I'll tell you this, he's more like Henry Brain than a Chatterton right now.'

The silence again; I could imagine her struggling against the impulse to strike down a subordinate, knowing that she was a crippled old lady locked up in a big house and that what she most wanted in the world couldn't quite be bought, not outright.

'Could you be more specific, Mr Hardy, about my grandson's condition,' she said at last, 'and about your plans?'

I wanted to say, he's simple-minded from Mogadon and liquor and he looks like a Sumo wrestler, but what good would it have done? She could probably have summoned up enough doctors and lawyers to get her hands on Baudin there and then if she had a mind to. It was probably then that I admitted to myself that I was interested in the problem of renovating Warwick Baudin. In my business I saw so many people putting themselves into his sort of nose-dive, I even gave them a nudge when I had to. It would be interesting to try to pull someone out of it. Gently, gently was the way with her ladyship.

'There is a drug problem, Lady Catherine,' I said quietly, 'and the question of rebuilding his self-confidence.' I thought that'd reach her. No Chatterton ever liked to be without a full measure of *that*.

'You can provide this care, Mr Hardy? Surely a doctor . . .'

Why didn't I just turn him over to her? What did I care how he handled it or what she thought of him? Maybe it was that first picture, with the record-breaking 440 just behind him and the whole world ahead. Maybe it was the wish to do a good, neat job and tie the package with ribbon. Maybe it was something else . . .

'I'll have a doctor helping me,' I said. 'He needs close attention from someone expert in watching people. A wrong move and he might take off and we'd have the same sorry business all over again.'

She didn't like it but she came around. She gave me a month and agreed to meet expenses and pay me a salary. We didn't discuss the bonus but I had the impression that it was still in the offing. Towards the end of the conversation she started to lose faith and seemed about to exercise her God-given right to change her mind. She was subtle about it though, referring to her health and suggesting that she didn't have long to go. I thought she probably had a month and told her so.

'You are impertinent, Mr Hardy,' she said. 'You have your month and not a day more. It will be almost Christmas.'

It was hard to think of the snoring slob upstairs as a present but, if that was how she wanted it, it was okay with me.

'How do you get on with Mrs McMahon?'

'Oh, a charming person, quite marvellous. But I suppose Verna will be back soon.'

'She won't be back,' I said. 'She was part of the nastiness. She was part of a plan to keep your grandson's identity hidden.'

This was enough to consign her to the fourth circle of outer darkness. 'I see,' she said icily; like all autocrats she valued loyalty.

'How're the memoirs going?' I asked, to needle her.

'Oh, quite well.'

This would be the end of them I thought, and I'd probably done the public a service there. Since I had her on the defensive I gave her one last thrust.

'You might care to contact your daughter, Lady Catherine.'

'Bettina?' Her voice was sharp and anxious. 'What has she got to do with this?'

'She can vouch for what I say. She's met her son.'

I left her to think that one over, spoke to Mrs McMahon again about money matters, and rang off. I was tired and not as drunk as I intended to be. While I changed that I thought about Warwick Baudin and Lady C and wondered whether I'd done either of them a favour. He could prove as big a headache for her as he had for his wise old foster father. On the other hand, despite her protestations, she could keep him waiting for his money for a long while yet. Maybe they deserved each other.

25

It started badly early the next morning. I came up slowly out of a foggy, boozy sleep to hear something crashing on the stairs. When I got out there he was lying at the bottom of the stairs with his limbs at all angles like a crashed hang-glider. He was unconscious but breathing steadily. I propped him up a bit and made coffee. His eyes were flickering open when I came back.

'Who the hell are you?' he said in that same, thickened, tongue-tied voice.

'The name's Hardy. Have some coffee.' I handed him the mug and he looked at it indifferently.

'Shit, I've got a head,' he mumbled. 'Got anything stronger?'

'Not for you boy. You're on the wagon.'

He sneered at me and drank some of the scalding coffee without seeming to notice how hot it was. All he had on was a pair of underpants and I looked him over appraisingly. The remnants of his athlete's physique were still there, buried under the fat. There were signs that his muscles weren't too far gone and he'd scrub up fairly well with the fat sweated off. His face was ghastly though, heavy bearded, scummy and bluish pale. I was glad I hadn't yielded to Lady Catherine's wish to see him. I doubt she'd have accepted him as the genuine article. He saw me assessing him and sneered some more.

'Hardy means fuck-all to me,' he growled. 'I never heard of you. I'm going.' He started to struggle up and I pushed him down easily using my left hand.

'Finish your coffee,' I said, 'I've got a few things to tell you.'

It took a while to get the message through to him and I had to push him around a few times to keep him listening. He was getting jumpier as the time passed. But eventually he got the picture. I got him a dressing gown and after a whole pot of coffee and my refusal to lace it with anything he was a quivering mess but very, very interested in his prospects. He told me about his long road to perdition and I was willing to listen. He'd had European and South-East Asian adventures and was deep in trouble with the narcs and the drug heavies when he'd run into Russell James and Selby. After that it was a bit of a blur. He'd been blackmailing his foster brother for years over a sexual matter and he put one last bite on him to finance a big buy. That came unstuck and so did he. I got pieces of the story over the next few days but it boiled down to a total dependance on James and the drugs he supplied.

I put his clothes in the wash and turned the bathroom and my shaving gear over to him. Then I took all the grog in the house — wine and beer in the fridge, scotch and brandy in a cupboard — and emptied it down the sink. My tobacco was lying around and I threw it in the rubbish. It was going to be tough all round and there was no sense in taking half-measures.

Tough is what it was. He was keen enough to become one of the pampered rich and he took my word that his best move was to present himself to the old lady in tip-top shape. It was easier to say than do; his dependence on the drugs and the booze was deep and the withdrawal was like a slow roasting over a fire. I'll say this for him, he tried. He fought the screaming pains and the chills and the black despair until he wept with the effort. Sangster was right, I had to watch him. After a week, in a phase of confidence, he slipped away from me and got a bottle. When I found him in the park he'd drunk the lot and was sleeping peacefully under a tree. I over-reacted: I took him to a Turkish bath and sweated him unmercifully, then I walked him and then I ran him. I was suffering myself; I hadn't had a drink or a cigarette for a week and I'd lost a lot of sleep and I was mean.

Strangely, it turned out to be the right thing to do. He was losing weight fast after the first ten days and his jeans were getting loose around his waist. We went to get some clothes which I could charge to Lady C and his eye was taken by some jogging gear. The shoes and shorts lay around the house for a few days while we drank coffee and watched television and screamed silently at each other. I could feel the resistance building in him; it was partly a false confidence based on a few days' clean living, partly an attraction to the degraded addict's life where there are no responsibilities and a thousand excuses. The novelty of rehabilitation was wearing off when he read a newspaper article about a hop-step-and jumper who'd cleared the metric equivalent of fifty-seven feet.

'I did fifty-two myself, once,' he said.

'Bullshit.'

'It's true. I could do a twenty-two foot long jump any day of the week and I tried the triple jump a few times and wasn't bad. One day in practice I put it all together and I did a fifty-two-footer dead, wind-assisted.'

I thought of my own triple-jumps into the rough school sand-pits — well short of fifty feet as my high jumps had been below six feet. My running was better and I looked at his brand new track shoes and felt a stirring, a nostalgia for jock-straps and starting blocks.

'I knew you were a runner, what was your best hundred?'

'Nine point six.'

'Wind-assisted?'

'No. I did a 440 in 48.4 once.'

'I know.' I dug out the photoprint and showed it to him. He turned it over and over in his hands and looked down sadly at his gut.

'God,' he said. 'They were good days.'

'What happened?'

He shrugged. 'I don't know. There was a lot of pressure to keep starring and there was that little shit Keir around the place. We were too different, I never felt right about my family. I was interested in the Law course and I did all right the first year, then the grog and the girls got to me. I had *hundreds* of girls . . .' He looked down again at his ruined figure. 'I haven't had one for a long time now.'

One thing led to another and within a few days we were out running around Glebe in the early morning and evening. It was slow, lumbering stuff at first for both of us, but we built it up. We kept up the steam baths and he went in for massage — Lady Catherine's boy wasn't going to come cheap. The weight dropped off him because he went onto a diet as well — I only followed him part of the way there. My own weight went down and I felt I'd kicked the tobacco habit after a couple of weeks. But I was promising myself a bottle of Chivas Regal when all this was through.

I got hooked on it and was pleased to see my stomach flatten and the wind get longer, but some of my weight loss was due to stress. I was nursemaid, trainer and jailer and I was deeply worried about Kay Fletcher. I toyed with the idea of going down to Canberra but I'd have had to take Baudin along and that seemed like a very bad idea.

So I worried. But we kept at it, partly because I had too much invested in a successful outcome by now, partly because the processes had acquired a momentum and interest of their own. It was childish certainly; we raised the number of laps and the distance we'd run, we lifted the number and rate of the sit-ups and press-ups. He was competitive to his back teeth and I'm a bit the same way going back to schooldays when I occasionally won things against the more talented by sheer dint of effort.

We competed. We went down to the University track and started running set distances against each other and against the clock. I beat him at first over his favoured 440 and on up to a mile. Then he ran an 880 in 2.35 and beat me by ten yards. He was standing there, cocky again, as I came past the post.

'Licked you,' he said. He was breathing easily, not as easily as he pretended but pretty good — better than me.

I remembered that I didn't like him, that he'd rolled cars and scarred girls, pushed drugs and informed on his mates. I'd lost sight of this in the competition — that's what competing does, it makes you insensitive to anything but yourself so that you could tolerate Jack the Ripper out there on the track.

'So you should,' I said. 'You're ten years younger than me. I need a handicap — a yard a year.'

His self-satisfied face went sullen. The features were clearer now that the fat had dropped off; he was still fleshy and probably always would be, a comfortable life and he'd need the best tailoring available, but you'd have to have been blind not to see the resemblance to Bettina and her late Dad. It was there in the high colour and the 'up yours' look in the eyes and efficient way they had of moving their bulk around.

'You're on,' he said. 'Ten yards, tomorrow.' He turned away and I gestured at his back. He slid into some loosening up exercises and I creaked off towards the showers feeling old and resentful and used-up.

He gave me the ten yards the next day and beat me going away. After nearly four weeks he could beat me at every distance and although he'd never be spring-heeled Jack again he was doing good jumps. I could still out-swim him but if we'd kept on he'd probably have taken care of that, too.

A few days before the month was up Cy Sackville rang.

'I've got news for you Cliff.'

'Don't tell me,' I said. 'You've bought a Greek island and you want me for head of security.'

'Shut up, I'm busy. I've got a mountain of work.'

'Great tan though.'

'Cliff,' he sighed, 'I'll say this once. Old Booth died, young Booth has seen all the papers.'

'Tell me.'

'The late Sir Clive's residence can't be sold. It can be used to produce income to cover expenses but if anyone tries to sell it the Imperial Legal Society has an option to buy at a nominal price. How do you like it?'

I thought about it for one or two seconds. 'I love it.'

'So glad. I'll send a bill.'

Twenty-four hours from D Day I phoned Mrs McMahon and made the arrangements. She told me that Verna Reid had picked up her traps and departed, also that a Mr Booth had been in touch with Lady Catherine.

'How did she take that?' I asked.

'Oh, very well, she seemed very relieved. I gather there's not much money, though.'

'Aah,' I said.

'But there is a cheque here for your fee — Mr Booth spoke very highly of you.'

'Mrs McMahon,' I said, 'I'm looking forward to meeting you.'

Baudin went to bed early and I settled down with my notes on the case and the bottle I'd bought to celebrate. I drank and pushed bits of paper around in front of me. Baudin Senior had arranged his birth registration nicely and some doctor and some government clerk had got a little spending money. A mere push of the pen could transform him into a Chatterton who could sow his seed in some suitable girl and produce a line of Managing Directors and hostesses with exquisite taste. To hell with them. I drank some more. By a roundabout route I'd found out that that cops weren't interested in the demise of Henry Brain. An old drunk, dead in a toilet — why should they care? His room was ransacked but anyone of his fellow knights of the bottle could have done that. To hell with them, too.

I had the level of the scotch well down when Baudin came into the room in his pyjamas. He looked at the bottle and sneered at me.

'On the piss again, Hardy? What, no cigarette?' He was smug but his eyes were full of pain and a terrible question. I poured myself out a big one and took a drink.

'How d'you feel about tomorrow. Nervous?'

He shrugged. 'Why should I be?' He watched me drinking like a lizard watches a fly. 'It'll be all right.' He stretched and yawned and for a second I thought he was going to ask for a drink. I don't think I'd have known what to do if he had. But he just stood there, six-foot-two of ego, all in pretty good shape.

'What will you do when you're all set up?' I asked.

'I think I'll finish the Law course.'

I had to laugh at that. I could see him in his after-shave and three piece suit, dealing. I laughed some more and drank.

'What's funny?'

'Nothing. Be sure to look up Honey Gully, won't you? She'd love to see you.'

He gave me a look that told me he hated me for what I knew about him. He was already living the role of Chatterton and Hardy was cast as an enemy. He marched out of the room and I got on with my bottle.

26

I delivered him on a fine, sparkling morning two days before Christmas. He was freshly shaved and barbered and he had a good tan. He had on a beige safari suit and everything that matched. He still had flab on him and there was a muddiness about his eyes, but you had to look very closely to see it. His teeth were good.

Mrs McMahon met us at the door; she was a middle-sized, middle-aged woman with grey hair and a restful face. She was grateful to me the way people sometimes are to those who help them get jobs they like.

I introduced Baudin-Chatterton and they looked each other over warily. He hadn't yet acquired that particular way of looking through servants but I was sure he'd pick it up. We went into the house and started on the great trek.

'How do you get along with her ladyship?' I asked.

Mrs McMahon smiled. 'She's wilful, but she has her soft spots.'

'I suppose your predecessor found that, too.'

She stopped dead in her tracks. 'That woman! I can't begin to tell you the things she did. The things she paid for and didn't pay for, it was a scandal.' We got moving again. 'Did you know she drank?' she said.

Touchy ground I thought. 'Well, perhaps . . .'

'Dreadfully, bottles everywhere.'

'Dreadful,' I agreed. 'But I expect you've sorted things out.'

'Oh yes,' she glanced at the heir who was avoiding a bare patch in the carpet. 'Mr Booth has been very helpful and things are on a very sound footing now.'

Lady Catherine Chatterton was waiting in state in the room I'd had an audience in the last time. There was colour in her cheeks and her white hair was waved softly. Her dress was new, a brown silk affair with white lace and it suited her. She looked as good as an old lady could.

I made the introductions; he bowed over her hand, a little

eighteenth century I thought, but it went down well enough.

'Thank you, Mr Hardy, my deepest thanks,' she said dismissively.

'How's Bettina?' I said.

She let it go. 'If you would be good enough to leave the young man and I alone? Mrs McMahon will see to the arrangements.'

He was sitting on the edge of a silk upholstered chair taking an intelligent interest in the paintings. He gave me one of his winning athlete's smiles and then looked away. For all his smooth appearance he still looked like trouble and it'd be her trouble and the thought came to me that he might be vengeance for all those small, frightened men the Judge had bullied in the dock. It wasn't a bad thought and I took it out of the room with me.

Mrs McMahon was waiting outside and we walked amiably along to the office. She handed over the cheque with a motherly smile. I looked at it. Five thousand dollars.

'A lot of money,' I said. 'Can she afford it?'

'I believe you've earned it. She can just afford it. There will have to be economies.'

'You like her, don't you?'

'Yes, she trusts me and I trust her.'

'Don't,' I said. 'She'll wipe her feet on your face if he tells her to.'

I left the house and walked down the path to my car. The lawn was ragged and weeds dominated the flower beds. I looked around but there was no sign of Rusty.

I paid the cheque in, drew out five hundred dollars and mailed it to Honey Gully. Then I packed a bag and headed for Canberra. My first call was at Kay's flat; it seemed to be occupied — no milk bottles or papers lying about, clean windows. My mouth felt dry and I felt flushed and edgy when I walked into the reporters' room at *The Canberra Times*. Kay was sitting behind a desk, hammering a typewriter. She had a pencil stuck in her mouth and her concentration was total. I watched her for a minute and then she shook her hair back and looked up; her eyes went wide and the pencil dropped. She caught it deftly and put it down on the desk as I walked over.

'Hello,' I said.

'Hi Cliff.'

'Busy?'

'Mmm, fairly.'

'What's the story?'

'You know, dirty Indonesian money and how to clean it.'

'You were supposed to clear that with me.'

'You were supposed to ring me.'

'I got tied up, Kay,' I smiled. 'I mean that literally, I called as soon as I could.'

'Well, it didn't matter. I started work on this straight away. The paper sent me to Indonesia. Just got back.'

'Yeah, I heard. Terrific tan.' It was true, she was wearing a green dress with white trim; her tan was TV commercial standard and she looked cool, clean and lovely. I was trying to hold my feelings in neutral but they wouldn't stay there. I wanted to touch her very badly. She moved her hand across the desk a little towards me, it was like a negotiating party advancing under a white flag. I reached down and put my hand lightly over hers.

'Let's go out for a drink,' I said.

'I thought you'd say that.'

We went back to the downstairs place of course and talked and drank there for a couple of hours. She had the goods on Keir Baudin all right and I had no reason to stop her exposing him, even if I could. I felt a bit sorry for the old man, though. I told her how the Chatterton case had developed and she expressed a polite interest. The fact was that she was committed to her story and the career advance it was probably going to bring her. I struggled with the knowledge that she didn't need me.

'You look better,' she said, 'fitter and you're not smoking. You'll be better at the job.'

'Yeah, we'll both be better at our jobs.'

She went back to work and we met again later. We ate, drank and made love and she went on with her work. I stayed in the flat and read her books and walked around Canberra seeing how the taxpayers' money was spent. The city's grass and gardens were drying out and would soon be yellow under the summer sun. After a few days I had a strong yen for a beach and I tried to persuade Kay to come to the coast with me but she was too involved in her story. We spent an evening together in which we couldn't find any common ground. Truth was, I was in Sydney and she was in Indonesia and we both knew it. I went back to Sydney to wait for work. Her articles on the Indonesian connection were run in all the capital city papers; the next time I saw her name in print she was writing about crime and politics — in New York City.

WHITE MEAT

I'd seen him a couple of times on the flat at Randwick racecourse — six foot four and eighteen stone of expensive suiting and barbering with jewellery and shoe leather to match. I'd given him some of my money and he'd put it in a bag. I hadn't liked him much but it's hard to like people you lose money to. I suppose we'd exchanged twenty words, not more, on the course, so I was surprised when he rang me at the office.

He was lucky to catch me. I had an appointment that afternoon and had called in to check the mail on a whim — private detecting is slow in the winter and I wasn't expecting any notes in invisible ink or bundles of currency. Turned out it wasn't just luck. I thought briefly about ignoring the phone but couldn't do it.

"Hardy?" The voice was rich, pickled in Courvoisier. "Ted Tarelton, I've got a little job for you."

"Good, I'm free. Tomorrow do you?"

"Today'll do me. Now!"

He could take my money but not my pride.

"Sorry Mr Tarelton, I can't make it, I've got an appointment."

"I know, with Tickener in Newtown. I heard. That's why I called you, you can kill two birds with one stone. Get over here first, you've got time."

I hung onto the receiver and thought. Tickener had called an hour ago asking me to meet him. He didn't say why and he'd been secretive about the whole thing. But Big Ted knew. Interesting.

"All right. Where's 'here'?"

"Paddington. Armstrong Street. Number ten. Make it quick."

He hung up. We hadn't discussed fees or anything like that but then that wouldn't be Ted's style. Eighty dollars a day would be a flea bite to him and my expenses wouldn't come up to his cigar bill. We also

411

hadn't discussed the job but I'd never heard that Ted was a villain so he probably didn't want me to kill anyone. Maybe he'd lost a horse.

I could have walked to Paddo at a pinch and it would have been good for me. Also the car wasn't going too well and it would have been good for it. To hell with doing good. I drove. Armstrong Street was long and curvy and you could see Rushcutters Bay along most of its length if you stood on tiptoe — that meant the view would be fine from the balconies. And balconies there were plenty of. Almost every house in the street had been restored to its former glory with glistening black iron lace standing out against the virgin white paint jobs. The gardens in front were deep for terraces and there was enough bamboo in them to build a *kampong*. Number ten was really numbers ten to twelve; Ted had belted down a three storey palace like his own to give himself some garage space. Two great roller doors faced the street beside his garden like giant sightless eyes. Say two hundred thousand all up.

I parked the Falcon between an Alfa with some dust on it and a spotless Volvo and went up to wipe my feet on the mat of number ten. The gate swung open in a way you could never get them to in Glebe where I live, but I thought I could see a small chip out of one of the ornamental tiles on the steps. The bell was a black button set inside several concentric rings of highly polished brass. I pushed it and something deep and tuneful sounded inside. While I waited I picked lint off my corduroy coat and brushed down the pants that almost matched. A quick rub of the desert boots against the back of the pants legs and I was ready.

The heavy panelled door was opened by one of those women who give me short breath and sweaty palms. She was thirtyish, about five feet ten inches tall and she wore a denim slacks suit over a white polo neck skivvy. Her hair was black and it hung over her shoulders, framing a long olive face with a proper arrangement of dark eyes, strong nose and wide mouth. Her lip gloss was plum-coloured like her eye shadow. If she was carrying an extra pound or two it didn't look as if it'd get in the way.

"I'm Madeline Tarelton," she said. "You must be Mr Hardy."

"That's right, Madeline Tarelton. I don't suppose you're his niece, going spare?"

She smiled understandingly. "Wife. Come in."

I followed her down a hundred yards of polished cedar planking in which the nail marks were black the way they always are — something to do with chemical reaction between the metal and the wood I suppose. I'm sure it's no problem. A cedar staircase ascended to the stars on the left before we reached a living room with an acre of Persian carpet on the floor and several tons of brass weapons and shields on the walls. Ted Tarelton was sitting on a silk upholstered chair reading a form guide and making sure that his cigar ash hit the enamelled dish at his side. He raised an arm in greeting, which I could understand, given the effort it would have taken to lift the whole carcase. He pointed to another chair done out in flowered silk and I sat down. Madeline murmured something about drinks and moved off with a rustling of denim and a light tapping of high cork heels.

"You met Madeline," Tarelton asserted. "Married her two years ago. She fixed up the house."

I nodded and rolled a cigarette and waited.

Tarelton folded the form guide this way and that and put it down on the chair beside him. He picked up his cigar from the tray and took a long pull on it. I lit my smoke and breathed some of it in and out and waited. After some tapping of cigar on dish and fiddling with the form guide Tarelton looked directly at me.

"I want you to find my daughter."

"OK," I said. "Is she in Newtown?"

Tarelton gave me a sideways look to see if I was kidding him. He decided I wasn't and displayed some of his intelligence.

"Oh that. No mystery. I rang one of my mates on *The News* to get a line on a good private man. He heard Tickener talking to you and told me about it. I remembered you from the track."

I nodded. "Newtown?"

He put three big fingers into a pocket of his tweed waistcoat and pulled out a card. He flicked it across to me with the practised gesture of a card player. It had been white but was white no longer, closer to grey. It hadn't been folded but it hadn't been pressed inside the family Bible either. The words "Sammy Trueman's Gymnasium" were printed across the card and an address and a phone number were in the opposite lower corners.

"I found this in with some of Noni's stuff," Tarelton said. "It seemed out of . . ."

"Character?"

"Yeah. Out of character. That's after this James bloke tells me she's missing."

"Hold on." I drew on the cigarette and wondered if I'd heard right when I thought drinks had been mentioned. "Let's get it clear. You've got a daughter named Noni and she's missing. How old is she? How long's she been gone?"

"Twenty-five. Been gone a week, I think."

"Who's James?"

"Saul James. An actor she . . . lives with."

"She's on with him?"

"Yeah. In a funny way, seems to me."

"Tell me about it."

"Well, Noni's my girl from my first marriage. Her mother died eight, ten years ago. I didn't see her for most of her young life but she came to me when Ingrid died. Finished school and started acting. That's when she met this James. She moved out and set up with him a couple of years ago. I only see her from time to time. I pay a lot of her bills though."

The cork heels came clicking again and Madeline's husky voice broke in.

"Too many."

"Yeah, well, she's my kid and I can afford it."

Mrs Tarelton was carrying a tray with three tall tinkling glasses on it. They were amber and had little bubbles rising through the liquid. Looked for all the world like Scotch and soda to me. I accepted one and looked at the gargoyle clock on the mantel — eleven o'clock, quite late.

Tarelton sipped his drink and then put it on the arm of the chair beside him. Madeline frowned so he lifted it up and held it close to his body like an undischarged grenade.

"Well, I got this bill to do with Noni's car and I phoned James because I wanted to talk to her about it. Hell of a lot of money. She wasn't there. James said she was with us but we never saw her at all around then."

414

"How often did you see her?"

"Once in a blue moon," Madeline chipped in. "When she wanted money."

Tarelton sighed. "Right. Turned out James thought she came over to stay with us regularly, every month. That's what she told him and he believed it. You'd reckon he'd ring or make contact some way but he says he never did. He sounds like a silly prick to me."

"Don't be coarse Ted."

"Well he does. What sort of man lets a girl go tripping off for a week a month and doesn't check on her? Bloody idiot."

I didn't want to be coarse but I had to agree, it sounded odd. A lot of things could go on in a week a month over a couple of years.

"When did you speak to James?"

"A week ago — no, four days — and she'd been gone for a few days then."

"Tried him again?"

"This morning. Nothing."

"All right. What about the card?"

"She left a bundle of clothes here for some reason on her last fleeting visit," said Madeline acidly. "Ted looked through them and found the card."

"It's rough country," I said and reminded myself of just how rough by taking a long swallow of the drink. Not too much of that brand in Newtown. "Did James know anything about this connection?" I licked a fingernail against the card.

"Yeah, strangely enough he did. He said she'd mentioned a boxer a couple of times, guy named Ricky. It was some sort of joke with them apparently. I don't get it."

"I think I do." Madeline moved off her chair to stand in the middle of the room between her husband and me. She stood well and Tarelton seemed to get uncomfortable from just looking at her; he started fidgetting again and crossed and uncrossed his legs. I couldn't blame him.

"I think Noni and James had an understanding," she said, "— what's called a sophisticated relationship, if you know what I mean."

"I think so," I agreed. "It's going to make her hellish hard to find. Too many trails to follow."

Ted decided to take offence; he had to do something. "That's crap," he barked. "Noni's a bit wild but . . ."

"You wouldn't know, Ted," said Madeline. "Let Hardy here find it all out."

The bookie sat back in his silk chair, picked up his Scotch and downed half of it. "Right, right," he muttered. He was half a foot taller than her and twice her weight but she had him on toast. I finished my drink and stood up.

"Could I see this bundle of clothes?"

"Why?" Tarelton growled.

"Just to form an impression. I'll need a photograph too."

Mrs Tarelton set her barely touched drink down on a coaster on a darkwood table. "Come upstairs. She has a room, her things are there."

I followed her up the stairs to the second storey. The shag pile was so deep I felt I needed snowshoes. Her jacket came down just below her waist and I had an almost irrepressible desire to slide my hand into the pocket stretched tight across her left buttock. I fought it down. We went into a room at the back of the house which looked down onto a leafy garden. There was a low narrow bed and a few bits of pricey furniture. Otherwise it was a rather bare room, not welcoming to anyone.

Madeline opened a couple of drawers to show me an array of female clothing. I ran an eye over it. Expensive stuff, not hippy — dressy. She opened a built-in cupboard and reached down a cardboard box. She flipped a few things inside it over and came up with a six by eight glossy photograph. It showed a girl in her early twenties standing in a street. The passers-by were washed out and the girl dominated the scene. She was shown full-length and looked to be tall with a high waist and long legs. It was hard to tell because she was wearing an enveloping cloak over a long dress.

"Some kind of publicity shot," said Madeline. "Good likeness though."

I looked closely into the picture. There was no sign of Ted's fleshy features in the face. This was a tight, bony structure with high cheekbones and a Slavic look. A strand of what looked like blonde hair was draped across the face.

416

Madeline drummed her fingers impatiently on the chest of drawers as I examined the picture.

"You'll know her if you see her," she said tartly.

"You don't like her?"

"She leeches on Ted. Doesn't give a . . . damn for him. Still, you'd better find her. He's in a state about it."

We went downstairs. Tarelton had finished his drink and the cigar was dead in the tray beside him. He was reading the form guide again. I told him my fee and he brushed the matter aside. Then I told him I needed a retainer and he reached back to his hip pocket. He stopped the action and produced the wallet from the breast pocket of his jacket. It bulged and he detached four fifty dollar notes from it without a thought. He handed them to me.

"This do?"

"Yeah."

"Get on it, eh? Newtown, I don't get down there much these days."

You wouldn't, I thought. You're a long way from the SP book in the lane beside the pub and the sly-grog joint at the weekend. You're in the silk department but the price is high.

"I'll be in touch," I said.

Madeline walked me to the door and I smelt some kind of apple fragrance on her as she moved. She opened the door and was bathed in a beam of ruby light from the stained glass pane above it. She knew it too. She always stood just there when the light was like that. I said goodbye and headed for the torn leather and faded duco and the clutch that slipped.

I met Harry Tickener outside Trueman's gym in Newtown. We crossed the street and had a beer in the bloodhouse opposite while we waited for Trueman to open the place up for the afternoon loungers. Tickener had put on a bit of weight since I'd first met him a year ago on the Gutteridge case, and I ribbed him about it. It didn't worry him.

"I've been living better since I got off the errands and into the real stories. Even got an expense account of sorts."

I put my money back in my pocket and let him pay for the drinks. We sipped the beer and he told me about the offer he'd had from another paper which he turned down. I told him about a few of the less dull jobs I'd had recently. Private detecting is mostly about missing people who may or may not turn up, guarding people and money and putting asunder those whom God hath joined together. I'd been doing a bit less of the latter lately which suited me fine although I never knew when I'd have to go back to it as my mainstay. The new divorce laws were cutting down on the old *in flagrante delicto* stuff somewhat, but there were always people around nasty enough to want it that way.

A clock above the bar, old enough to be the missing link with the sundial, struck two and we let the barman take our glasses away and mop up our puddles. Outside a fine rain was falling and we turned our collars up and dashed for the doorway across the street.

"Why did you bring me out in this?" I asked him. "I was drinking at home, you could have come over."

"You said you were interested in fighters," he sniffed. A drop of moisture that wasn't rain hung off the end of his long, thin nose.

"You're getting a cold Harry, you shouldn't be out. Yeah, I was interested in fighters, when there were some."

Tickener blotted his nose with a tissue. "There's one here, I want to get your opinion on him."

"Why? And why the hush-hush?"

"Might put some money on him next time he's up, might do a story on him."

"Well, your security's lousy and I thought you were above all that now, the sports page?"

I told him about Tarelton's grapevine but he shrugged it off.

"I like to keep my hand in. Come up and have a look at him."

We went up three flights in a building which had probably served a dozen different purposes since it was built in the middle of the last century. There were signs that it had been a stables on the lower level with living quarters above and it had been a sweatshop factory and a rooming house at different times and probably a brothel. Now the ground floor was a dry-cleaning plant, the second floor accommodated a dental technician and a small instant printing joint that looked dodgy. The top floor was taken up by Sammy Trueman's gym.

The room was about a hundred feet square and neon lit because the grimy, cob-webbed windows let in practically no light. A bank of lockers stood along one wall and a partitioned-off section contained a changing room, a toilet block and Trueman's office. The ring was in the middle of the room on a metre-high platform. The canvas was stained with sweat and blood. Incongruously the ropes were new, bright yellow, and the padding over the hooks and post tops was pillar-box red. In one corner a battered heavy bag hung from a hook in the ceiling and a punching ball on a stand stood a little to the left. The light bag in the opposite corner was red and shiny like a tropical fruit.

A big man, thick in the waist and shoulders, with a neck like a bull and frizzy white hair on his head and arms, came out of the changing room, plodded up to the bag and began pounding it. He danced a heavy one-two, one-two on the thin canvas mat. The noise was like a tattoo on a snare drum played a bit slow. Sweat started to roll down his pink shoulders and seemed to trigger off all the latent odours in the place. A stink of liniment, resin and cigarette smoke blended in the air, asserted itself and then faded to become an atmospheric background. A dark-skinned youth limped out, took a rope off a peg and started skipping; he had one slightly withered leg and he was clumsy on every second swing.

Sammy Trueman had been a useful lightweight in the years after the war when that division was in the doldrums. He held the Australian title for a short time and lost it to someone whose name I forget. It doesn't matter because Jack Hassen came along soon after and cleaned them all up. Sammy kept enough of his dough to get a long lease on the gym. He kept the equipment in reasonable shape and he'd trained a few boys who did alright without ever making headlines.

He came shuffling towards us as we came through the door into the gym. He was wearing shoes, old grey trousers and a V-necked sweater the same colour. The top of a mat of grizzled chest hair showed over the V. Below that the sweater ballooned out like a yacht's spinnaker in a high wind. Sammy was hog-fat, as the old-time fight writers used to say. He looked nearly twenty stone, double his old fighting weight. But then it had been a quarter of a century since Sammy had been in the ring and since then he'd spent more time with the bottle than the heavy bag.

"Harry — Cliff boy," he wheezed. "Good to see youse. Come to look over the new Dave Sands."

I shook his hand. "I guess so. I saw the last three."

Sammy's wheezing changed to a note that suggested he might be laughing. He thumped Tickener on the arm. "No way to talk is it Harry? This boy's the goods, eh?"

"Could be Sammy, could be. I hope so anyway, the fight game's in the shits at the moment."

"You never said a truer word," Trueman said sadly. He didn't add that it was mis-match merchants and dive-dealers like him who'd helped it to get that way.

"It's wet enough outside, Sammy," I grunted. "Don't get your sawdust damp. Let's have a look at your boy."

"You're a hard man Cliff, but OK, stick around, you'll really see something." He turned around ponderously and waddled off to the changing room. A tall thin young man came out of the door before he got there and Trueman grabbed his arm.

"Get your gear on, Sandy," Trueman spluttered, "you're going three with Jacko."

The youth nodded but darted a few looks around him as if he was looking for a place to hide. He walked across to a locker, pulled out tape, gloves and protective devices for above and below the belt, and went through the door after Trueman.

Tickener and I walked across and sat down in canvas chairs with steel frames in a row of ten lined up beside the ring. As we did so two men came into the gym. They were both dark, Mediterranean-looking, with the same cut to their clothes. They shook water off their hats, peeled off their coats and sat down in the chairs at the other end of the row. One of them, more burly and swarthy than the other, shot six inches of gleaming white shirt cuff and looked at his watch. Tickener pulled out his Camels and started one without offering the pack to me — he knew what I thought of them.

"Fuckin' depressing place," he said.

"Always was. Think this boy'll make a difference?"

"He just might. Here he comes, take a look."

Trueman came out along with a young Aborigine who had to lean down from his six feet to hear what the fat trainer was saying. He was wearing old boxing boots, baggy shorts and a torn singlet — not a gymnasium cowboy then. Trueman broke off when he noticed the Latins in the chairs. He gave them a quick nod and muttered something to his fighter. The boy put his sparring helmet on over a thick crop of bushy hair. With the hair covered he looked a bit like Dave Sands whom I'd seen once — the night he'd knocked Chubb Keith out cold in the fourteenth round. Four months later Sands was dead, his chest crushed in a truck smash. This kid had the same neat, handsome head, massive shoulders and those spindly Aboriginal legs that never seem to give out. Trueman led him across to where Tickener and I were sitting.

"Jacko Moody," he belched through the words. "Scuse me. Jacko, this is Cliff Hardy and Harry Tickener."

"Gidday," he said, "pleased to meet you." His voice was young but gruff. He looked about seventeen or eighteen, a hundred and sixty pounds or so and as tough as teak. We shook hands. Moody did a little jig. He was raring to go and made me conscious of my beery breath, tobacco-stained fingers and short wind. Still, I didn't have to be that fit. Taking and handing out beatings was only incidental to my work.

The thin lad called Sandy had togged up and was standing about lackadaisically in the ring. Moody climbed through the ropes and leaned back against one of the supports while Trueman taped and gloved his hands. The trainer squeezed a dirty towel out in a bucket of grimy water and hung it over the lower strand of rope near Moody's corner. No-one was attending Sandy but he was probably better off.

"Orright Jacko, Sandy, let's see what youse can do. I want a lot of punches, not too much steam in 'em, but mix it a bit if you feels like it. Bit of a show for the gentlemen, eh?"

Trueman hit the gong mounted at the base of the ring support and the boys moved forward towards the centre of the canvas square. I knew Moody was something special when I missed seeing his first punch. He put a hard straight left into Sandy's face and a right rip into his ribs before the white boy got set, and that was the pattern of the round. Sandy wasn't unskilled and he wasn't slow, Moody was just immeasurably better in all departments and he hit clean and often and tied Sandy up in knots. They broke out of a clinch of Sandy's making at the end of the round; Sandy's chest was heaving but the Aborigine hadn't raised a sweat.

It was much the same in the second session except that Moody stepped up the pace a little and made Sandy look worse. But he still hadn't thrown or taken a really hard punch and if they can't do that they can't do anything. The fighters took their rest, shaped up again and Trueman suddenly yelled at Sandy to have a go. He bullocked forward and got a good short right up under the Aborigine's guard onto his chin. Moody moved his head back a fraction to take some of the force out of it and to bring Sandy in, then he stopped him short with a straight left and brought over a right hook. The fair boy's arms flopped to his sides, his knees buckled and he went down, disintegrating like a demolished chimney tower. Moody stepped back, instinctively seeking the neutral corner then he moved towards Sandy.

"Leave him, Jacko," Trueman roared. "Don't spoil a good punch. Go and have a shower."

Moody nodded, banged his gloves together and took off his helmet. He vaulted over the ropes and danced off to the dressing room. Sandy sat up groggily and Trueman wiped his face with the dirty towel; the boy swore and pushed it aside.

"You're orright Sandy, you had a go, done your best. I'll fix you up later." Trueman thumped the sitting boxer on the back and got out of the ring. Blood suffused his face from the effort of bending and it was a full minute before he got together enough asthmatic wind to speak.

"Great eh? What did I tell youse? Bit of work on the killer instinct and he'll be ready."

"Is that why you wouldn't let him help the other boy?" Tickener asked.

"Yeah. He's got to get tougher, enjoy seeing 'em down."

"Bullshit," I said.

Trueman was about to reply when a noise over by the door stopped him. The big pink man who'd been pounding the bag the whole time was barring the way to a man trying to get into the room.

"Let me in, get out of my way." His voice was high and thin. "I don't want to make trouble, I just want to see Ricky." He struggled against the immovable flab and muscle in front of him, then he yelped when he caught a smack in the mouth delivered at about one tenth of the bruiser's force. I got up as the big man was manoeuvring the intruder into a position where he could get a good swing at him.

"Sick of you," Pinky grunted.

"Sling him out Tiny," Trueman yelled.

I grabbed the big, fair arm and pulled it down.

"Better not Tiny Pinky," I said. "You could go for assault." I tightened my grip but he could still have broken it easily. Confusion spread across his flat, piggy face and he looked across at Trueman.

"Fuck off," the trainer said to the intruder. "I'm sick of people coming around looking for that bum. Fuck off, Ricky's not here. You're upsetting my boys."

Tiny let go of him and the man straightened his clothes. He was on the small side with brown hair, regular features and a rather glossy, artificial look to him. His voice was stagey, clearer than necessary.

"Just tell me where he lives then, and I won't bother you."

"Dunno," Trueman growled. "Piss off. Tiny, get back to the bag."

The gorilla moved away and the newcomer turned to go.

"Just a minute," I said. I went over and put my foot down on Trueman's instep. "Where's Ricky live?"

"I said I dunno," he gasped.

I bore down a little. "Where, Sammy?"

Pain screwed up his eyes and cut his voice down to a reedy whisper.

"Albermarle Street, Redfern, 145." I lifted my foot. "Shit Cliff, what's it to you. Look, what do you think of my boy? Good?"

I beckoned to Tickener who got up and moved to the door with me.

"He's great Sammy. I hope he's got some brains left when you're finished with him. He won't have anything else."

Trueman staggered to a chair, sat down and started massaging his foot. Tiny sank his fist into the heavy bag. The boy with the withered leg tapped the light bag. Sandy sat on the canvas rubbing his chin. The Latin gentlemen hadn't moved. We went out.

3

He was leaning against a wall lighting a cigarette when Harry and I came out of the gym. Again, there was something exaggerated about the way he did it, the way he cupped his hands and flipped the spent match down the stairs. He was good-looking in an old-fashioned, Leslie Howard sort of way, and he turned a boyish smile on us.

"Thanks very much. That ape could've hurt me." He put a hand up to his face to make sure it was all there just the way he'd left it.

"Forget it," I said. "Gymnasiums aren't places to barge into shouting names. You're Saul James, right?"

He looked pleased and trotted along abreast of me as I started down the stairs after Harry.

"That's right. You've seen me on TV?"

"No, I only watch TV when I'm sick. Big Ted Tarelton told me about you."

It deflated him. He said nothing more while we went down the stairs and he seemed to take a great interest in the end of his cigarette when we stopped in the doorway.

"I know about Noni." I said. "We better have a talk about it. Drink?"

He nodded. Tickener wanted to talk about Moody and so did I but it looked like work would come first. He tagged along when I suggested the pub across the road. We made the dash through the rain again.

"Let me get them," James said. Harry and I didn't kick. We sat down at an ancient table; I rolled a cigarette and Tickener got a Camel going. We watched cynically while James got served. He was slim and he wore a waisted suede coat to accentuate the fact. They'd eat him alive in Redfern. He couldn't even get himself served in a Newtown pub. He tried waving his money and clearing his throat and the barman ignored him until he was good and ready. James was red in the face when he got back to us, but we watched with polite interest as he lowered three double Scotches onto the scarred beer-ringed boards. He sat down.

"Cheers."

We drank a bit. I studied his face. It was mostly full of conceit to my eyes but there were some signs of something else in it. Maybe it was character, maybe worry. He had tried to get into Trueman's after all.

I introduced Tickener and told James that he was a reporter. The actor looked interested and asked what branch of reporting Harry was in. When he was told he lost interest. He transferred his attention to me.

"And what do you do?"

I told him. "I would have had to see you soon anyway," I said, "I take it you'll co-operate with me?"

He nodded.

"Give me the story."

He told me that he'd met the girl two years before when she had a small part in a play he was in. They set up house with an understanding that there were no ties. The girl went off for a week once a month and she claimed to spend this time with her father. James said he didn't check.

"That seems odd," I said.

He shrugged and drank some of his Scotch. "That was the deal."

"Did you go off too?"

He looked smug. "Occasionally."

I was liking him less by the minute and wanted to get the interview over. Tickener looked bored. He finished his drink.

"Look Cliff, I've got to go. What did you think of Moody?"

"He's good, give him a bit of time."

"Yeah. He's fighting soon, I'll get you a ticket."

I thanked him. The reporter nodded to James and thanked him for the drink. He wrapped his big tweed overcoat around him and bustled out of the pub. For no good reason it crossed my mind that I knew nothing about Harry's sex life.

"Can you remember that address?" I asked James.

"Yes." He recited it back.

"What do you know about this Ricky?"

"Almost nothing. He's an Aborigine, but not dark I gather." He said it quickly as if it made a difference. "Noni met him when she was doing a TV film, he was an extra."

"How old is he?"

"Young." He hated saying it. "About eighteen."

"Why do you bring his name up?"

He shrugged. "I don't know. She's disappeared, I just thought . . ."

I got it. It was like that, never far below the surface in silvertails like him. I pulled out the street photo of the girl and showed it to him. He confirmed that it was a good likeness. I grilled him a bit on other contacts the girl might have had but he had the idea of the black stuck in his mind and had nothing else to suggest. He offered to buy another drink but I refused. I didn't want to be obligated to him.

"Has Mr Tarelton hired you?"

I said he had.

"That means I can't?"

"That's right."

"I would if I could. I want her back."

I believed him. It was the only plus about him I could see.

"I'll keep in touch with you. Where do I reach you?"

"The Capitol theatre, I'm rehearsing a new play. I'll be practically living there for the next few weeks."

"Carrying on, eh?"

He looked at me sharply. "I have to, work's scarce, even for me."

The Scotch he'd bought me suddenly tasted thin and sour. I put the glass down and reached for my tobacco packet. He offered me a filtertip.

"No thanks. What do you know about the girl, her background and friends?"

"Not much." He lit up himself and held the match for me. Nice manners, but my foot itched. "You've met the father, I haven't. I know her mother died some years back. She went to a private school on the north shore . . . I'd remember the name if I heard it. Friends? None that I know of, she doesn't make friends easily. She used . . ."

"What? What were you going to say?"

He took a deep draw on the cigarette. "I was going to say she used my friends. Funny expression but I suppose that's what I meant."

She was sounding more and more like someone who should stay lost. It's often like that. Nice poor people get lost and nobody gives a damn. Someone rich and nasty goes missing and there's a stampede. But I had to know a little more about her than I did.

"Did she have any money?"

"No, only what she earned, which wasn't much. Her father paid some bills when she got stuck but he didn't give her money. She was very bitter about that."

"Ted looked like a soft touch as far as she was concerned, why didn't he see her right?"

"A stepmother I believe?"

"Right. That fits. And you're surprised to find that she had connections down here?"

He raised a theatrical eyebrow and spoke through tobacco smoke. "Very."

I couldn't take any more. I got up, put out my cigarette and tossed off the drink. He did the same then stood looking helpless. I gave him a nod and walked out of the pub.

My car was parked a block away; I ran through the rain, risking instant paraplegia on the wet pavement. I pulled the Falcon's door open and sat down in a pool of water that had come in through the gap between the window and the frame. I swore and turned the key viciously. The answer was a choked whirring noise that indicated water where water didn't ought to be. I leaned my head forward on the steering wheel and sighed. It was a bad start to a job and I felt like giving it up and getting a taxi over to Ailsa's place and having a few drinks and getting into bed with her for twenty-four hours or till the rain stopped. But Ailsa was on a Pacific tour, looking in on her investments. I'd refused a free ride and had to stick with what I had.

I got out of the car and stood proudly in the rain until a taxi condescended to stop for me.

4

Redfern is like an untidily shaped ink blot to the east of downtown Sydney. It's one of those places that look worst around the edges where it's bordered by factories with stained, peeling walls and rows of old terraces with rusting wrought-iron and gap-toothed skew-whiff paling fences. A couple of high-rise monsters in the middle help to make Redfern's population density one of the highest in Australia. The taxi took me past tiny houses with flapping galvanised iron roofs, shops presenting blank, defeated faces to the streets and pubs full of Aborigines and Islanders drinking their dole money, improving their snooker and resenting Whitey like hell.

The house in Albermarle Street was a big sandstock terrace that had once been a prosperous townhouse but was now given over to flatettes and single rooms. I held the taxi outside for a minute while I tucked Tarelton's fifties down under my sole inside the sock. I paid off the driver, scooted through the rain, pushed open the gate and went up the steps to the door. There was no bell and the knocker had rusted solid and immovable on its hinge. Heavy metal music was blaring inside and I waited for a break in the monotonous riffs before knocking. I knocked and the music went down from ear damage level to loud. I heard feet in the passage and the door was opened by a black giant. He was wearing flared jeans and an open weave singlet; his shoulders blotted out all the light behind him and the fist he had wrapped around the door handle could have done sleight of hand tricks with a football.

"Yup?" He left his mouth open to show fifty or so pearly white tombstones inside his pink cavern of a mouth.

"Ricky Simmonds live here?"

"Who wants to know?"

"My name's Tickener, I'm a sports writer for *The News*. I want to talk to Ricky about boxing; I hear he's a mate of Jacko Moody?"

His laugh sounded like a chain saw going through knotty yellow box.

"You've got it arse-up mate, I'm the one who knows Jacko, comes from Burnt Bridge, same as me."

"Where Dave Sands came from?"

"S'right, we're all related. Look, come in outa the rain if you wanna talk about it."

I did. We walked down the narrow passageway through to a small living room. The giant stuck his hand out.

"Ted Williams," he said. "How you goin'. Beer?"

His hand was hard but he didn't put any muscle into the handshake. Closer up and in the light he looked well under seven feet and probably didn't weigh more than seventeen stone. He was a bit soft in the middle, not much, just a friendly amount. He was one of those big men who never have to get to their feet in anger in their lives. There were no fighting marks on him. I said yes to the beer and sat down in an armchair between the TV set and the stereo equipment. Williams had turned the volume right down and the record was spinning around on the turntable making angry, soft scratching noises as if the musicians were furiously struggling to be heard. A refrigerator opened and closed in the kitchen, there were two popping noises and Williams ambled back with two king-size cans of Tooheys Draught in his left hand. I took one and he dropped down into a chair opposite. He took a long pull on the can then leaned forward, stretched out a hand and plucked the arm of the stereo player off the disc with the delicacy of a scientist extracting snake venom. I said "Cheers" and drank some beer.

"Yeah. Now, what d' you want to know about Jacko?"

"How old is he?"

"Eighteen."

"How many fights has he had?"

"Ten or eleven, prelims, won 'em all."

"Knockouts?"

"Mostly. Look, Sammy Trueman coulda told you all this."

"Yeah, I don't like Trueman, that's why I want to see Ricky."

"I don't get you."

"He trains there doesn't he?"

"Sort of. Ricky had two fights and lost 'em both."

"What's wrong with him?"

The laugh ripped out again. "Nothing mate, just this," he held up the beer can, "and this." He made a ring with his left thumb and forefinger and stuck the little finger of his other hand through it. He didn't let go of the can. I laughed.

"I see. Well, he's probably better off sticking to that. I wanted to have a word with him about Trueman, whether he's right for Jacko, you know. He might be too good for Trueman. Do you know where I can find him right now?"

He lost interest a bit and took a minute before answering me. He used the time to suck the rest of the beer in the can out in one long gurgle and crush the aluminium tube as if it was cardboard. He flipped it across the room at a beer carton. He missed.

"Anything in it for me?" His black pupils were stark against the cloudy whites, his lids fluttered down a bit and I was conscious that it hadn't been his first beer of the afternoon.

"Tickets to Jacko's next fight?"

He sparked up. "That'll do me. How do I get 'em?"

"I'll leave them for you the day before at the front desk in at the paper, King Street, know it?"

"Yeah, good. OK, I'm not exactly sure where Ricky is but I know he went down to La Perouse. You'll find him down there if you ask around. Can't miss the car — big black Chevie, a Biscayne with white stripes on the bonnet."

I asked him whether Ricky had gone down there on his own and when he went.

"What's today, Monday? He went early last week. Monday or Tuesday. Not on his own, he had that white chick Noni with him."

He seemed to be about to speak again and I finished my beer and let him have the silence.

"Funny thing, Ricky's a popular boy just now, you're the second bloke been asking for him."

"Who else?"

"Don't know, didn't see him. Freddy, he lives here too, he saw him and told me."

"Oh yeah. White man was he?"

"Yeah, old guy, real pale."

I nodded and stood up. I held the beer can in my hand and Williams pointed to the carton. I tossed the can in and thanked him. When I left the room he was putting the arm back on the record; an ear-splitting guitar chord, distorted by the wah-wah pedal, tore into me as I reached the front door. I put the wood between me and the sound and went down the steps to the street.

The rain had stopped and the grey sky had thin, pale blue rents in it. I stood outside the house and a young Aborigine in a faded green track-suit came jogging down the street sticking out his hands in jabs and hooks. He went through the gate and bounded up the steps. I walked down the street towards a phone booth. A green Fiat pulled out from the kerb on the opposite side of the road and took off up the hill in a smooth effortless glide. The driver looked vaguely familar in the quick glance I got at him but I dismissed the possibility. The only person I knew who could afford that car was Ailsa and she drove other things. I called the NRMA, gave them the location of my car and took a taxi back there. In the cab I prised Tarelton's money out of my sock. Some of it was mine already.

The blue van was pulled up beside the Falcon and the guy in overalls had his head under the bonnet when I arrived in the cab. I waited while he did what I could have done except that for fifteen bucks a year I reckon I should keep my hands clean. He pulled himself out, took a look at my membership tag and told me to start the car. It kicked first time, he slammed the bonnet down and waved. I gave him a thumbs-up and crept out into the five o'clock rush.

To get to La Perouse you stay on Anzac Avenue all the way passing through the suburbs that blossomed there after the first war. The old permanent building societies and friendly societies lent the money to fill up this part of Sydney and its red brick uniformity is their monument. The streams of cars moved sluggishly along the wet road between the traffic lights in congested fits and starts. I battled along in the middle lane letting the wild men barrel past me on the right and staying out of the way of the geriatrics and rabbits on the left.

The traffic thinned out as the road swung down towards Botany Bay. Long Bay jail loomed on the left. I'd spent a few unpleasant weeks there on remand and didn't want to be reminded of it. I speeded up for the last slide down to La Perouse. The place is named after the French explorer who spent a few weeks there in 1788 before going off to get himself eaten somewhere in the Pacific. It might have been a clean, pretty spot in his time but it isn't pretty now. Botany Bay is polluted to hell. On bad days the sea has a dark, oily sheen and the few scraps of beach are grey and faded as if leached of colour by the hand of man. The foreshore has been mostly swallowed by roads and is dotted around with drab municipal buildings that wear a low-grade military look. I drove around the streets of La Perouse for a while getting the feel of the place. There were a lot of overgrown gardens and falling-down fences and houses that needed paint jobs badly. The rain had cleared out to sea; a purplish grey cloud lay out over the coast like a deep bruise in the sky and the landscape was bathed in a yellowish translucent glow.

I drove down past the kiosk and the pit where the snake man does his weekend show and stopped the car by a rail above the narrow beach. I got out, rolled a cigarette and watched a young Aborigine throwing a boomerang out over the water. The weapon left his hand shoulder-high, climbed steeply about ten yards away from him and moved off in a high air-cleaving circle. It made its banked turn fifty yards out and spun back slowing down until he plucked it out of the air like Young Griffo catching flies. He threw three or four times and each throw was perfect. I finished the cigarette and scrambled down the path to the beach. He saw and heard but ignored me until I was close.

"Nice throwing."

"Thanks, wanna try?"

Boomerang throwing is something all Australians think they can do by instinct. I knew better.

"No, haven't been here long enough."

He grinned. "It's easy, show you." His thin brown arm snapped out like Jacko Moody's straight left and the boomerang seemed to be grafted onto his hand. He lifted the arm and threw in a short, chopping motion that launched the boomerang off in a skipping, dancing spin; it arced out and came back humming like a model plane. I ducked and he threw his hand up. The wood slapped home with a

433

crack that rang out over the water and bounced off the old island fort a hundred yards offshore.

My knee joints creaked as I lifted myself up.

"You'd have won if they'd banned guns."

"Yeah, some hope."

He swung around and fronted me. He was nearly as tall as me but rail-thin. His thick lips were bluish and he breathed heavily through them like a runner at the end of a race. His nose was a flattened ruin. He shifted his feet and flexed his thin sloping shoulders. He was twitching with bottled-up energy. I pulled out the makings, began a cigarette I didn't want and offered him the packet.

"Thanks." The slim fingers with their tulip pink nails made a smoke as thin as a Mexican bandit's cigarillo. I got out matches and we lit up.

"Know a bloke named Ricky Simmonds?"

"Yeah."

"Know where I can find him?"

"Might. Why d'you wanna know?"

"I'm looking for his bird, Noni. Know her?"

"Yeah. You a cop?"

"Private enquiry. I just want to locate her, nothing heavy."

He smiled, reached out and patted me on the chest — the hand hit metal and leather.

"What's that for then? Rabbits?"

"You never know. Look all I want to do is get a line on this Noni, report back to her old man and pocket a few bucks. I'm not looking for trouble."

"No trouble for Ricky?"

"None, why?"

His mouth split open in a wide grin that showed white teeth stained around the edges by tobacco and a fine network of white scars around his eyes. I realised suddenly that he wasn't young at all, he was closer to forty than twenty.

"Nothing. We're related, and trouble follows Ricky. Who told you he was down here?"

"Ted Williams." I explained the way of it, he listened, not very interested except when I said I'd seen Moody spar.

434

"What'd you think of him?"

"Terrific. Too good for Sammy Trueman."

"That's what I reckon." He grinned again and the scars showed like badges of rank on the dark face. "He's a bastard, Sammy. Rooked me rotten. You interested in fighters?"

I said I was.

"Maybe you seen me. Jimmy Sunday."

"Jimmy Sunday. Yes I did. You had a great go against Booni Jack. Draw wasn't it?"

"Yeah. I fought two draws with Booni, Melbourne and Brisbane. Bloody hard man Booni."

"You weren't bad yourself."

He sucked on the last inch of his cigarette and flicked the stub away. He expelled the smoke with his wheezy fighter's breath and did another little shuffle on the spot. He was wearing only a thin football sweater over a singlet and the wind coming off the water was sharp. I shivered inside my layers of cloth.

"Why don't we go and have a drink," I suggested, "while you make up your mind whether you're going to talk to me."

He slapped the boomerang in his palm. "Orright." He lifted his arm and sent the boomerang off again. I moved away and watched it swing up into the pallid, darkening sky. It came back about knee high and he jumped neatly over it and let it land a few feet behind him.

"Nice one." I picked it up. "You're good. Where'd you learn, Burnt Bridge?"

"How'd you know?"

"A guess. Fighter country." I tossed the boomerang over to him and we walked towards the path up the low cliff. He asked my name and I told him. He nodded. We reached the car and I got in.

"Bit of a bomb," he said as I turned the key a few times till the motor caught.

"Yeah. I hear Ricky's got a Chev."

He grunted. He disapproved of the Chev.

"Where to?" I asked as the engine was ticking over.

He named a pub and directed me through the streets. We went through a smart section on into the low-grade housing with the overgrown privet hedges and the bungalows wearing defeated looks like

435

the faces of old men in a dole queue. I parked outside a pub that looked nearly old enough for La Perouse to have had a few *vins* in. Like all the best pubs it occupied a corner block and had a balcony running around two sides above the street. The timbers were lifting on its walls and the wrought iron was pitted and blasted by the salt air. It was dark now and the rain had started again. The light flooding out through the windows of the public bar had a soft, amber glow like the beer itself.

Jimmy Sunday pushed open the door which had "Public Bar" etched into the frosted glass. The room was quiet, the after-work drinkers had gone and the evening regulars hadn't come in yet. Two old Aborigines were sitting over their middies and a game of cards in one corner and in the narrow space between the short section of the L-shaped bar an intense quiet game of darts was in progress. One of the players was dark, the other two were young white men with the long, greasy hair and leather jackets of bikies. The painted circle, flanked by ancient, cracked black boards, was flooded with light from a naked bulb mounted above it.

We moved up to the bar. Spilt beer had lifted strips from its rubberised surface and the draining trays were rusted around the edges. We both put one foot on the rail and an elbow on the streaked surface in a ritual that means absolutely nothing. The barman looked like a football player gone to seed. Flesh hung off his face and shirtsleeved arms and his belly kept him well back from his work.

"Two middies," I told him. "Old?"

Sunday nodded. The barman pulled them, his thick fingers were puffy and mottled like supermarket sausages but they did the job neatly. I slid five dollars across to him, he made the change and I left it on the bar. We drank some beer. I asked Sunday if this was his local. He said it was and borrowed the makings from me. He rolled a cigarette, lit it and expelled the smoke in a thin stream through the next mouthful of beer.

"Made up your mind yet?"

"Not yet," he grunted. He looked at the money on the bar, reached into his pocket and pulled out some change. He signalled to the barman and spread the money out on the bar. The fullback pulled two more, the sausage fingers flicked out the right money with the delicacy of a croupier. I looked around the room. The greasy cards flipped over noiselessly, the darts bit into the pig bristle with soft pops like reports from a silenced pistol.

I finished my drink and pulled the second one across. "Thanks." I lifted the glass and drank. Sunday did the same.

"You'll do," he said. "At least you're not a bloody sociologist. They come down here with some weird fuckin' stories."

"How do you know I'm not?"

He grinned. "They never let a man buy them a drink. This the dinkum story, about Ricky and the girl?"

"Yes, any reason why it shouldn't be?"

"Two. Ricky's had trouble with the pigs before, I wouldn't want to put him in the shit."

"And . . .?"

"Someone else's been asking."

"Little white guy, oldish?"

"That's right, who is he?"

"I don't know. I heard of him up in town. He could mean trouble but I'm not part of it. I just want to find the girl, she's a free agent as far as I'm concerned."

"Fair enough. I reckon Ricky'd be at his auntie's. If he's not she'll know where he is. He moves around a bit, could have gone up to Macleay even. Anyway, try his auntie, Mrs Sharkey, she's on the corner opposite the bakery. You go left up beside the pub and it's one street along on the other side. Want me to come?"

"No, I'll be right. Thanks, see you around."

"Yeah, right." We each scooped our change off the bar. He picked up his beer and wandered over to sit with the old card players. They gave him a nod and took sips from their glasses, acknowledging his presence in the ritualised way of drinkers everywhere, but the sips were small because those beers had to last.

I walked out of the pub, crossed the road and used the public toilet. The hum of an aeroplane landing at Mascot filled the night air, which was moist, with a faint chemical tang. The area is ringed about with industrial plants of different kinds; tongues of fire shoot out from them like ignited gases from the escape valves of Hell. I walked over to my car, opened the door and dropped into the seat. I knew at once that something was wrong. There was something missing and something was there that shouldn't have been. I put the key in the ignition in a reflex action and then jet engines roared in my ears and an oil refinery exploded in my skull. Cascades of sparks and glowing concentric circles flared and died.

5

The hand shaking my shoulder seemed to be rattling the vertebrae like dice. I lifted my head off the stem of the steering column and blood dripped down into my eyes. As I came up out of the gloom I remembered what had been wrong — Sunday's boomerang wasn't on the seat where he'd left it.

"You all right mate?" Sunday was trying to steady me and get a look at the back of my head as I swayed about in the seat. I put both hands on the wheel.

"Think so." My voice was a squeak, the beer rose from my belly and burnt my throat. I choked it down. "Did you see anyone? How long have I been out?"

"Dunno. I had another drink then I remembered I'd left me boomerang in your car. Thought I'd catch you up at Sharkey's. Came out and saw the car was still here. Didn't see no-one though."

I put my hand up and felt the back of my head; the hair was clammy and matted. I pressed down and located the cut, it didn't quite run from my forehead to the nape of my neck and it wasn't six inches wide, but it'd do. Sunday eased me back against the seat and fumbled around in the car. He straightened up and leaned resignedly against the open door.

"Fuckin' gone. Best one I had."

"Don't worry, he probably threw it away — it'll come back."

He groaned. "Jokes. I should leave you here."

"Why don't you?"

"Couldn't have you on me conscience. If you can't have two beers and get into your car without getting done there's no hope for you. Come round to Sharkey's and get cleaned up."

I remembered that that was where I had been going and there seemed no good reason not to go now. I nodded and every hair on my head turned to a needle and dug in. I eased myself across and Sunday got in behind the wheel, started the car and drove up past the pub. We stopped in front of a house on a corner block. The street light lit up a rusty gate. The fence pickets started a few feet off from the gate on one side and marched off irregularly with many missing from the ranks. The house was a wide, double-fronted weatherboard. A wooden porch ran across the front of it behind two beds of healthy, waist-high weeds.

I pushed the car door open and swung my feet out onto the ground. Sunday came around and helped me through the gate and up the path. He lowered me onto the arm of a derelict sofa standing beside the front door and rapped his knuckles on the weatherboards.

I looked up and light flared painfully into my eyes from the glass pane above the door. The door opened and a girl stood there holding open the tattered fly wire screen door. She looked about seventeen, she was tall, slim and flat-breasted, in jeans and a tight, high-waisted sweater. Tears were making silver streaks down her coffee-coloured face. My brain was still reacting to the blow and for a crazy second I was convinced that she was crying for me. But she wasn't; she couldn't see me. She pushed the screen door wide open and lurched forward onto Sunday's chest. He caught her, put his arms around her tentatively and tried to keep his head clear of hers.

"What's the matter Penny?" He jerked his head out of the way of her thrashing frizzy mop and looked down at me, puzzled. The girl sobbed and couldn't make it on her first attempt to speak. Then she got it out.

"It's Ricky," she wailed. "He's dead."

Sunday took her full weight and let her head fall on his shoulder. Her voice came through muffled and incoherent but I thought I caught the word "Noni." The rough horsehair springing through the ripped fabric stuck into me through my clothes and I wriggled. The girl caught the noise and movement. She jerked free of Sunday.

"Who's that?" she hissed.

"Take it easy Penny, it's just a bloke been in a fight. I brought him here to tidy up. Let's go inside. Jesus . . . Ricky. He wasn't twenty."

He pushed the girl in ahead of him and I followed them through. We went down a short passage and into a small living room, part of which had been partitioned off to make another bedroom. An enormously fat black woman was sitting in an armchair. Her breasts rested comfortably in her lap and grief had twisted her face out of shape. She looked like a perpetual smiler and the lamentation had forced an unaccustomed arrangement of her features. A thin man with a grooved, teak-coloured face was sitting at the table cutting his fingernails with a penknife. The sight of the thin, sharp blade slicing into the pink cartilage curdled my blood. His face was an older male version of the girl's — thin with high cheekbones and a perfect symmetry between the thick lips and the flared nostrils. But his hair was an iron-grey crop whereas the girl's was brushed out into an Afro frizz.

Sunday went over to the woman and put his arm around her. He spoke softly to her. She rocked slowly back and forth and I realised that she was chanting the Lord's prayer. I stood feeling useless, like something inedible cast up on an island of starving men. Sunday detached himself from the woman and beckoned me across the room. I went and stood near him across the table from the man. The girl threw herself down in a chair and sobbed quietly.

"Where is everybody Rupe?" Sunday asked. "Thing like this, people should be around."

The man sliced a thin, curling paring from his nail and didn't answer.

"Uncle Rupe," Sunday said urgently, "snap out of it and tell us what happened."

The man looked up. His eyes travelled across Sunday's face and came to rest on mine.

"Who the fuck's this?" he said softly.

I was conscious of my appearance and irrelevance. I put my hand on Sunday's arm. "It's a bad time for me to be here. I'll push off."

Sunday snaked out his hand and hooked me back. "No, hang around Hardy, we might need some help here." He tapped his pockets and then held out a hand for the makings. I handed them over and he dropped the packet on the table.

"He's a mate, see Rupe? Have a smoke and let's hear about it."

Rupe drew a deep breath and reached for the packet. He teased some tobacco and rubbed it on his palm.

"OK Jim. Bit of a shock." His voice was slow and harsh like a file on metal. He gave me another look, pulled out a cigarette paper and rolled his smoke.

"Not much to tell, Jim. Copper come around here about an hour ago and said they'd found a body on the rocks at Bare Island. He was a bit of a mess but they reckoned it was Ricky from the clothes. Young Clivie went with them . . ."

"Them?" Sunday interjected.

"Noni was with the copper."

"Where is she now?" I blurted out the words unintentionally, knowing it was a mistake as I did so. They distanced me from the people in the room, cancelling out the spark of good will and arousing suspicion. I was asking about my own when one of theirs was hardly cold.

Rupe stared at Jimmy before deliberately crushing out his half-smoked cigarette. "Who is this bugger Jim? I'm not sure I want him around."

Sunday glared at me. I felt his approval dropping in notches like a mechanical jack. There was no warmth in his voice when he spoke.

"Yeah, well, he's looking for Noni. Her father hired him."

Rupe looked at me as if deciding whether to spit. After a time he shrugged and reached for more tobacco.

"Keep lookin' then. She pissed off, don't know where."

"What were Noni and Ricky doing down here?"

"Hanging around, same as usual."

"Anything unusual happen today, Mr Sharkey?"

The courtesy didn't noticeably soften him. Maybe he just felt better dealing directly with questions relating to Ricky's death.

"Yes — Ricky seemed excited today, but I don't know why."

"A letter, telegram?"

He looked across at the woman who stopped praying and was taking an interest. She shook her head.

"No."

"Was the girl excited too?"

"Hard to tell with her, she just tagged along with Ricky. She didn't seem no different today."

442

"I'm sorry for all the questions. Just one more. What did Ricky and Noni do down here, really?"

"They talked to people."

"What about?"

He shook his head and relit the cigarette which had gone out while we were talking. I'd run out of questions and answers.

"I'm sorry about Ricky," I said to the room in general.

"Yeah," Sunday grunted. "Maybe."

The girl had stopped sobbing and was looking at me with an expression I couldn't fathom. I was conscious again of the mess I looked, but that wasn't what was on her mind.

"You came down here looking for Ricky did you?" she said.

I turned to her. "In a way . . ."

"Is that a gun you're wearing?"

My coat was open and the shoulder strap was showing. I adjusted it. it.

"Yes."

"You were too late gubb, someone else got him first."

"What's that?" Sunday snapped at her.

"Ricky was shot." Her voice started to break then she gathered it up again and went on hard and cold. "By a shotgun, in the face and the chest, close up."

Sunday swore and the woman started praying again. Sunday led me off to the kitchen. I started to apologise for the tactless remark but he brushed the words aside. He ripped a piece from a greyish sheet hanging over a chair and handed it to me. I ran some water in the sink, wet the cloth and mopped at the back of my head. The cloth reddened up and got sticky. I wrung it out and mopped a bit more. I washed my hands and flicked the water off into the sink. I put the cloth in the kitchen tidy. Sunday watched, saying nothing. Up on the wall behind him was a photograph of Dave Sands, a newspaper shot of him wearing a championship belt, blown up to poster size. His dark, handsome face looked angry, as if he was thinking that being the champion didn't mean a damn thing.

"Sorry I upset your uncle," I said.

"S'all right, you've got a job to do."

443

"Is he Ricky's father or what?"

"Uncle, real close, his mother's brother. What are you going to do now?"

"See the cops, see the body."

We shook hands. We had some sort of understanding but it was pretty fragile. I walked out through the living room. Rupe was sitting at the table smoking, the woman was sitting like stone in her chair. The girl had gone. They ignored me and I went down the passage and out the front door.

I was more cautious about getting into the car than before but the girl sitting in it wasn't trying to hide. She was huddled against the window on the passenger side. I got in and settled down beside her about three feet away. White men have to be careful about sitting in cars with black girls in this part of the city and one gun under my coat and another under the dash didn't make me feel any safer.

She asked me my name and I told her.

"I knew that white bitch would get him into trouble." Her voice was thin and bitter.

"What did they talk to people about down here, Ricky and Noni?"

She looked at me. In the dim street light her eyes gleamed dark and cold.

"Are you going to look for whoever killed him?"

"It might turn out that way."

"Let me know when it does, I might help you."

I started to say something but she raged at me.

"Look, they fucked, got off, got pissed. She liked gang bangs, Ricky said. He was teasing me. Jesus."

She started to cry again; her thin shoulders shook and her breath shuddered in and out with a thin, reedy sound like papers being shuffled. I wanted to reach over and comfort her but it was the wrong move at the wrong time. I felt for my tobacco and remembered that I'd left it inside the house.

"What was Ricky to you Penny?"

"Nothing, worse luck." The childish expression seemed to stop the crying. "He was wrapped in Noni. She came down here from Paddo or wherever the fuck she lives and I wouldn't see him . . ." She pulled herself up in the seat until her back was ramrod straight. In that

444

position there was just a suggestion of swellings under her sweater. In profile there was a slight heaviness to her face that suggested strength and stubbornness. She swung her head around, the heaviness disappeared but the strength was still there.

"Take me to Bare Island, I want to see Ricky."

Her voice was steady with no note of hysteria in it and I couldn't think of any reason not to do as she said. She didn't look like someone who had to ask permission to go out at night. I started the car and drove off. I took a quick look at her. She was staring out the window as the familiar places whipped past in the dark but the look on her face made me think that she was about ready to leave La Perouse.

6

Bare Island is connected to the rest of Australia by a hundred yards of old wooden causeway over a rocky deep water channel. A wind off the ice cap was blowing in all directions at once and whipping up the spray from the water and blending it in with the drizzle when I drove down to the foreshore. I rummaged in the back of the car and found a yellow plastic slicker for me and an ancient, mouldering duffel coat which I gave to Penny. We coated up and ran to the police truck parked near the beginning of the causeway. Two cops were sitting in the truck and I pounded on the glass of the driver's window as we flattened ourselves against the side trying to get some shelter. The window came down and the occupant swore as some rain whipped into his face.

"What the bloody hell do you want?"

I'd seen his face down at police headquarters on one of my not infrequent and ill-starred trips down there. I dug deep for the name that went with it.

"Evening Mr Courtenay," I said. "Nice night?"

"Yeah great, who're you?"

"Hardy, private enquiries, I've seen you down at Brisbane Street."

"Yeah? Who do you know there?"

"Grant Evans."

It wasn't a bad name to throw around just then. Grant had recently got a promotion and men on the way up sometimes take others up with them. Courtenay wasn't unimpressed, as the writers say. I thought I'd better move in on him quickly.

"This is Penny Sharkey," I said, guessing. "She's a relative of the dead boy."

The other cop leaned across and looked out. "I can see that."

"Shut up Balt," Courtenay snapped.

I looked at Balt. The collar on his gabardine overcoat was turned up and some wisps of straw-coloured hair stuck out from under his hat. His head was long and his eyes were as pale as an arctic night. When the migrant rush from Europe got going after the war we called them all "Balts" wherever they came from, but this one looked like the genuine article.

"What's your interest, Hardy?" Courtenay asked.

"I'm on a missing persons case — girl. She was last seen with Simmonds. I hear she was on the spot but isn't around now. Thought I'd come and have a look here and ask you about the girl."

"Did you now?" Balt rasped. "What about *her*?" He jerked a thumb at Penny. His hostility was undisguised and probably stemmed from trouble he'd had himself as a migrant. Race prejudice has a pecking order and the Aborigines get no-one to peck. Balt seemed to be the wrong man on the wrong job, or perhaps the cops thought he was just right for it.

"I thought she might be able to help," I said mildly. "She saw Simmonds this afternoon, might spot something important now."

It was lame, I knew it, Courtenay knew it, Balt didn't even listen.

"Who's your client?" he rapped out. "Who're you looking for?"

"Ease up, Balt," Courtenay soothed him. He looked down at the girl who was huddled inside the duffel coat. The talk had washed over her like a wave of nothing. The water drops in her hair glistened in the light from the inside of the truck. She looked stoical and immovable, able to outlast us all.

"I heard he was on the rocks. Still there?"

Courtenay nodded. "Down on the rocks outside the wall. The place is a fort. You know it?"

"No."

"Well, it's a fort like I say, with these high walls around it. Built to fight off the Japs."

"Russians," Penny said suddenly.

"Alright, Russians. Anyway Simmonds was shot somewhere up on the island and fell down to the rocks. Ended up in a sitting position. He's still there. We need some pictures."

"Who found him?"

"Girl. She called us, went around to the house. Then she shot through. She your misser?"

"Yes. Can we take a look out there?"

"If you like. He's not pretty. No face to speak of."

Penny turned away, her nails scratched the smooth surface of the truck as she reached out for support. I moved closer and put my arm around her. Balt's sneer was a hiss of stinking gas in the dark.

"Let's go," she said.

"Who's out there?" I asked Courtenay.

"Foster, forensic guy, photographer, stretcher boys on the way. Tell Foster I OK'd you."

"Right." We crouched ready to move off into the rain which seemed to be easing a little.

"You might remember the co-operation when you see Evans," Courtenay muttered, trying to keep the sound from travelling to Balt.

Penny sprinted off into the drizzle. We dodged the posts that prevented vehicles driving onto the causeway and started across. The visibility was poor and we had to watch our footing; the wooden handrail and the planking were twisted as though the island had tried to wrench itself free of the continent. There was an oasis of light down under where the causeway ended at a gate that stood up like a stand of spears. We struggled down some steps to where two men stood in stiff formation near a dark shape on the ground. A roughly rigged-up floodlight on a six foot high stand threw shadows around and caught flecks of spray and drizzle in the air. One of the men was wearing a white boiler suit and heavy rubber gloves, the other was fiddling with one of the cameras slung around his neck. The dark crumpled heap against the pitted cement wall looked like something that had been screwed up and thrown away. One of his legs stuck straight out and the other was tucked up under him at a crazy angle. His face was a sagging collapsed hole. He was wearing a light khaki jacket and denims. The left side of the jacket was an oozing dark stain. Penny looked down at him, a shiver ran through her and I could feel her trembling across the distance between us. Then she turned away and leaned her back against the wall. She stared ahead of her, across the water to La Perouse and beyond.

"How do you read it?" I asked Foster.

He pointed up. "He got it up there and fell down. Got the head shot I mean."

448

"And then?"

"Can't be sure, but I think he was propped up and shot in the chest."

"To finish him off?"

He shrugged. "Could be."

"When was this?"

"Sometime this afternoon. Look, who're you?" I'd wondered when he was going to ask. I told him that Courtenay had given me the nod. He looked happier, as if he'd done his duty as a policeman. The cameraman suddenly let off a flash. We all jumped.

"Sorry," he said sheepishly.

I asked Foster what was on the body and he told me "nothing remarkable". I bent down to get a closer look at the corpse. The belt was fastened about two holes too loose and one of the laces on the canvas sneakers was untied. This could have been the result of the body being searched and I was going to ask Foster about it when the stretcher bearers arrived. They came down the steps and we all stood aside. They lifted the body onto the stretcher, covered it with a dark blanket and secured the load with broad straps. The procedure finished off the process of the elimination of a person that had begun with the first shotgun shell.

The drizzle had stopped. We watched the men in their pale blue uniforms carry the stretcher up the steps and back along the causeway. On the bridge, with the long, flat burden betwen them, they looked like a strange monster, low backed, with a high, pale rump and head.

The cameraman assembled his gear and unhinged the stand. I thanked Foster for his co-operation then the girl and I started back to the land — where this had all started and where the reasons for it lay. Her high-heeled boots thudded on the wooden planking and I glanced down at them; they gave her an extra three inches; without them she would only have been medium tall. Lost in the duffel coat, she looked small and young, and I wondered about what having your dream man shot to death when you were seventeen did to you. It couldn't be good.

Courtenay and Balt and the ambulance had gone. The car for the photographer and forensic man was parked a little further on and it

449

made me think of Ricky's Biscayne, the car you couldn't miss. Where it was and how it had got there would be important. I'd have to get Grant Evans' help on that. We got back into my car and she huddled in the corner again.

"Home?"

She snorted. "If you can call it that."

"They your parents?"

"No."

"Is your name Sharkey?"

"Is now."

I started the car and drove back through the wet, empty streets. The pubs were still open, letting out a fitful light and a trickle of people. I pulled up in front of the house. The girl shrugged out of the duffel coat and folded it before putting it on the back seat. She opened the door.

"Just a minute," I said. "You can help me."

She raised her eyebrows, theatrically bored and sceptical.

"How?"

"What did Ricky and Noni talk about down here, what did they do?"

"Why should I tell you?"

"You want Ricky's killer caught."

"I know who killed him."

"The girl, you mean?"

"Yes."

"I doubt it."

"You would. What would you do if it turned out to be true?"

"I'd let it be that way."

She sneered. "Why?"

I was getting tired of the conversation and let some impatience come into my voice. "I'm not a crusader and I've cooked the books in my time, but I let the facts alone unless there's very good reason not to. I can't think of any reason to do differently in this case."

She turned her head and studied me through the gloom. The inside of the car smelled damp and old; it didn't reek of high-priced corruption or the sweet smell of success.

"All right Mr Cliff Hardy," she said slowly. "Maybe you're telling the truth. I can't tell you much anyway. All I know is that Ricky's father was a crim and he dropped out of sight about twelve years ago. No-one knows what happened to him. For the last couple of years Ricky has been driving people mad around here with questions about his father. I don't know what he's found out." She let the sentence hang there.

"That's interesting, but not much help. There's something else you can tell me?"

"Yes. It's just a feeling. I went around with Ricky a bit and saw him talking to people. I got the feeling he wasn't only interested in his father. He seemed to be almost looking for someone else as well."

"Can you make it clearer?"

"Not really, it was just a feeling. He seemed to stare at people, men, who couldn't have known his father because they were too young. Men his own age, you know?"

I nodded and stored the information away. It could mean something but I felt tired, my head hurt and I remembered that I hadn't had a drink for too many hours.

"Thanks, I'll think about it. Tell me about the girl."

"Noni?"

"Yes. What's she like?"

She clenched her hands in her lap to stop them from flying about like angry birds. When she spoke her voice was full of malice with a note of fear. Maybe she believed Noni had actually killed the boy.

"She's a blonde, thin, a bitch and a bloodsucker. She acts freaked-out, you know? But she's really ice-cool. Know what we call her down here?"

I shook my head.

"White meat," she hissed. She opened the door and started to get out of the car.

"See you Penny," I said.

"Not here you won't."

She slammed the door and moved off. I watched her go through the collapsed gate and up the overgrown path. She was an elegant parcel of brains, bone and muscle wrapped up in hate. Seventeen. I drove away.

451

7

I had two fast Scotches in a pub in Kensington and bought a half bottle for company, so I was feeling better when I parked in the lane beside the Capitol theatre. The Capitol is a grimy old matron on the outside; it hasn't had a face-lift for a good many years and the layers of old posters splattered over its walls seemed to mark its age like the rings in tree trunks. The posters for Saul James' musical were up now covering over last year's spectacular and greatest shows on earth long forgotten.

A chink of light showed through the door at the side of the building. I pushed the door open and went up a flight of stairs that ascended nearly as steeply as a ladder. I moved slowly, smelling unfamiliar odours, not the usual urine and garbage smells you get on dimly lit stairwells, but something richer, more exotic. The stairs ended at a corridor that had rooms going off it on both sides. One of the rooms was showing a light and I could hear soft voices. I paused outside and placed the odour, a combination of perfume and the sweet herbal smell of marijuana smoke. The door at the end of the passage opened out onto a backstage area behind a massive green velvet curtain. A few props, a coffee table, some chairs, a bookcase and a wheelchair, were scattered around. Against the wall, on the floor, was a big tape deck flanked by two king-size speakers and connected by a heavy cable to a power point that bristled with double adaptors. I could hear voices through the curtain and I stepped forward to where its two sections met.

"It has to go in there," I heard a woman's voice say. "If you move it it'll be out of place and you'll cut it later. I know you bastards."

"We won't Liz." a high voice, wheedling. "I swear to you darling that the song stays in, whatever happens."

"What do you mean?" Her voice rose to a near-shriek and I took a peek through the curtains. She was wearing body paint and a spangled

G-string; her nipples, showing through the paint and tinsel, looked naked and obscene. She was lean and sinewy like a stockwhip and she was stalking up and down in nervous, gliding strides. Saul James, wearing jeans and a striped, matelot-style T-shirt, was sitting on a turned-around chair. Another man squatted on the stage. His fat thighs bulged in brown corduroy and his body was heavy and gross inside a flowered Hawaiian shirt.

"It's an essential song Liz," James said quietly. "It won't be cut, it can't be. You do it superbly."

The woman stopped prancing. James' mild tone seemed to calm her down and I was interested to see that he had some authority when operating professionally. She moved smoothly up to the actor and stood in front of him, her breasts almost touching his chest.

"Alright Saul," she purred. "I'll take your word for it, and if the song doesn't stay in I'll hold *him* responsible." She pointed to fatty who got creakingly to his feet. The stage lights were dim but I could see the flesh shaking on his red face.

"Now that's not fair sweetie, I . . ."

"Don't call me sweetie, you slob," she snapped. "Half of those fancy boys of yours can't sing for shit and you know it."

She turned and marched off the stage to the right as if she'd just delivered the last line in the first act. The fat man pulled out a flowered handkerchief and wiped his face.

"Nerves," he said. "Jitters, highly strung. It'll be alright."

James nodded. He seemed to have lost interest in the scene and its implications very quickly. I opened the curtain and walked forward. The fat man stared at me.

"More trouble," he said.

"Why do you say that?" I asked.

"Your face, your eyes. You want money. You're going to threaten me."

"You need to watch your guilty conscience, sport. I don't care if you're the Woolloomooloo flasher and keep an unlicensed dog. I want to talk to Mr James here."

James looked at me. His face was pale and more Leslie Howard-like than ever; he looked as if Scarlet O'Hara had just given him the latest piece of bad news.

"Have you found her?"

"No. But I've been close. We have to talk some more. Here?"

James glanced across at the fat man who was looking on with interest. He seemed to be enjoying James' distress.

"Lost her again have you Jamie?" he said maliciously. "I do hope you find her. This gentleman looks . . . capable."

"Just shut up Clyde or I might sic him on to you."

"Charmed I'm sure."

I didn't like being their verbal plaything and said more roughly than I needed: "The talk, James. Where?"

He swung off the chair and walked through the curtains without giving Clyde a glance. I followed him down the passage and into one of the rooms on the right. He turned on the light which showed the room to be pretty bare apart from a cupboard, a make-up table in front of a mirror and coffee-making things on a card table. There was a chair in front of the make-up table and I hooked it out and sat down. James looked at me, then went out of the room and came back with another chair. I rolled a cigarette and lit it. James tried to let go one of his boyish smiles but it came out thin and strained as if only half the required voltage was available. He got up and shook the jug, it responded and he plugged it in.

"Coffee?"

I shook my head. I was wondering how to play him. I needed more information on the girl. Maybe he had it, maybe he didn't. I didn't want to tell him too much, possibly out of sheer habit, but I must have looked worse than I felt.

"What happened to you?" He spooned instant coffee into a mug and added boiling water. He held up the other mug. "Sure?"

"I'm sure."

He shrugged elaborately and anger flared in me.

"Listen, I've been bashed and seen a man dead on the seashore while you've been poncing about on the stage. I'm not in the mood for games."

His eyes looked moist and he spoke softly. "Sorry."

He was a deal too sensitive and raw in the nerve endings for my comfort. He wasn't a kid. Late twenties probably. I remembered how well he'd handled the scene on the stage and wondered whether his personality was completely professional. His private role looked to be a bit beyond him and he seemed to need to set up a particular emotional atmosphere in order to operate. I didn't want to play along and he wasn't employing me, but somehow I'd begun to feel responsible for him and the feeling irritated me.

He sipped his coffee and tried again. "You said you'd come close to Noni. What did you mean?"

I gave him a version of the events of the past couple of hours. He looked concerned when I mentioned the strip off my scalp and he flinched when I gave him a watered-down account of Penny's remarks about his girlfriend. He looked concerned again when I told him that I'd turned up at a murder scene and couldn't avoid telling the cops exactly why sooner or later. I'd protect Ted Tarelton's private affairs as long as I could but the pressure was on me now to find the girl quickly. I needed to know everything about her, particularly where she might have gone.

He caressed his coffee mug and took a long time in answering.

"Well, one thing. Noni has a drug habit."

"Hard drugs?"

"Yes. She handles it pretty well most of the time, not always."

"That's great." I suddenly felt old and weary, running up again against that problem which symbolised the generation gap for me. He misinterpreted my action.

"You aren't going to give up are you?"

"No, I'm not going to give up but it's not going to be easy. I must know where she's likely to run when she's in trouble. That fat queen out there implied she'd taken off before. Where to?"

James was shaking his head and opening his mouth to speak when the door flew open.

"I resent that," Clyde squeaked. "I belong to a noble brotherhood which roughnecks like you wouldn't begin to understand." His plump face creased into a plummy smile. "But I understand all about little Noni. Jamie here barely knows her name."

"Shut up Clyde," said James. "You don't know a thing about her."

"Oh yes I do." Clyde sang the words in a near falsetto. "Are you a policeman?"

I told him who I was and what I was doing. James protested but

Clyde hushed him and I didn't back him. Clyde rested his chin in the palm of his left hand and sat that elbow in the other hand.

"Little Noni now, she's a *naughty* girl. You wouldn't believe the things she does and the people she does them with."

"Maybe I would," I growled. "I'm just back from her hang-out in La Perouse."

"Ooh yes, loves the *noiros* does our Noni, the blacker the better."

I shot a look at James. He was nursing his empty coffee mug, just taking it. Clyde was enjoying himself immensely.

"Why do you take it Jamie? What do you want now?"

"I want her back with me."

Clyde cackled. James sounded defeated, beaten hollow by something he couldn't understand. I understood it in part. My ex-wife Cyn had affected me the same way. I kept crawling back, signing cheques, waiting up till dawn and hoping everything would come right. It never did and I felt sure it wouldn't for James. But no-one else can tell you that and you can only see the end when you get there on your own. Still, I didn't want any part of Clyde's baiting game. I stood up with my coat open and let him see the gun.

"Cut out the crap. Tell me something useful or piss off."

He recoiled and his jowls shook. The plummy malicious smile dropped away.

"Newcastle," he muttered. "She lived in Newcastle and she knows the heroin scene there."

"This true?" I asked James.

He shrugged.

"It is, it is!" Clyde squealed, "and she has an uncle there named . . . Ted or something."

"Bert," said James wearily. "Bert, and he's in Macleay not Newcastle. I remember now, she lived up there when she was young."

Clyde looked deflated at James' knowledge. He changed posture and waved his hands about as if he was trying to think of an exit line. He didn't find one and I jerked my chin at him. He went out and left the door open. I closed it and noticed for the first time a photograph pinned to the back of the door. It was a glossy postcard-size print with the Capitol theatre showing behind a woman. She was wearing denim shorts that looked like cut-down jeans with enough material whittled away to show the beginnings of the cheeks of her buttocks. She had on a blouse rucked up and tied under her breasts, striped socks pulled up calf-high and high-heeled sandals. In the black and white picture her hair looked as fair as a wheatfield and the set of her body dared you to touch her. Anyone with the juices still running would want to.

I put my hand on the door knob and pulled the door open. James started in his chair.

"Where are you going?"

"Newcastle, first off."

"Now?"

I had no one waiting up for me and the paper boy stayed his arm if he saw one uncollected on my doorstep.

"Why not?" I said.

8

A private detective leads a throw-away life for much of the time. Some men in the game overplay this by sleeping on couches in their offices and never changing their underwear. I don't go so far; I've got a house in Glebe with reasonably civilised fittings and I sleep in a bed more nights than not. But some cases don't let you go to bed on them and this was looking like just such a one. The Tarelton girl was running from one piece of trouble to another and there was no time for packing the matching pigskin luggage. I didn't have too much to go on except that she and the car would stand out in Macleay like Gunsynd in the Black Stump Cup. She could become detached from the car but it would take a lot of work to tone down her eye-turning image and she was probably too vain to do so. Half the people I'd met that day seemed to come from Macleay or thereabouts and the place was fixing itself in my mind as a destination, a source and an answer.

I made two calls from a box outside the theatre. The first got me a sleepy-sounding Madeline Tarelton who said nothing while I gave her a sketch of events. She refused to wake Ted and wouldn't or couldn't confirm that Noni had an uncle up north. Just on spec I asked her what name the girl went by.

"Rouble, Noni Rouble."

"Professional name?"

"No, her mother's. She took it back when she broke up with Ted."

"When was all this?"

"Years ago. Look Mr Hardy, this is scarcely the time . . . you should have got all this information from Ted this morning. Do you know your job or don't you?"

"Sometimes I wonder," I said. "I agree with you. Just an outline will do. Noni didn't live with your husband for how long?"

"Oh most of her childhood."

"Where did she live?"

"Somewhere north. Really Mr Hardy . . ."

I apologised again, told her I was going north and called off.

The second call was to police headquarters in the hope that Grant Evans was on duty. He was and not too happy about it. He wasn't working on the Simmonds killing but had heard the talk about it; so far the cops had nothing but questions.

"Like what?" I asked.

"Like who was the blonde and what was that snooper Hardy doing on the scene?"

"And like, where's the kid's car?"

"Yeah. Can you help a little on some of these points? Hate to press you."

"Quite all right. Maybe soon. Thanks Grant." I hung up in the middle of a curse from him and it occurred to me that most of our telephone conversations ended like that. Lucky we were friends.

I drove through the city and over the Harbour bridge. Theatregoers clogged the roads and the drizzle had started in again making for slides, swearing and crumpled mudguards. I crawled along like a link in a slowly moving chain and failed in every attempt to jump a light and get a run. On the north side the traffic moved faster and I could have got into top gear. Instead I pulled into a garage for petrol and a check on the oil and water. I used the lavatory and the smell of the greasy food in the place's snack bar reminded me that I hadn't eaten for ten hours. I bought a hamburger and a carton of chips and ate them as I drove. The Falcon groaned a bit under the unaccustomed load of the full tank, but nothing dropped off and when I'd made it to the beginning of the tollway I felt confident that she'd go the distance.

Since they put the tollway in, the drive to Newcastle is easy. The only danger in driving it at night is falling asleep at the wheel. I warded this off by taking quiet slugs from the Scotch bottle, letting the liquor jolt me but not taking enough to get me drunk. My head was aching and the whisky was good for that, too. I should have been asleep in bed. Instead I was driving a tollway at night and drinking whisky. Mother wouldn't approve. Father wouldn't approve. But then Father never did approve. Funny thoughts. Maybe I was drunk. A few cars passed me but neither the Falcon nor I was feeling competitive and we couldn't have done much about it anyway. The road was slippery and I swayed about a bit and got bored by the dark, indeterminate shapes whipping by. I wished I had a radio. I wished I had new tyres, but I stayed loyal — I didn't wish I had a new car.

Like all big cities, Newcastle emits a glow which you pick up a few miles out. It's composed of neon glare, factory smoke and the small glimmers of a hundred thousand light globes and television screens. There's a good measure of the day's wastes drifting about as well; Newcastle is like Sydney, you can taste it about as soon as you can see it. I felt the grittiness of the air and its load of rubber and gas between my teeth as I began the descent from the hills towards the city.

Newcastle sprawls about like a drunken whore: it trickles off towards the coalfields in one direction, climbs up into the hill country in another and slides down to the sea on the east. The beach is a surprise; a fair-sized slice of white sand in front of a reasonable stretch of water for humans to swim in. It's like a reward to the city's inhabitants for putting up with so much else that is appalling. I hadn't been there for five years but the bird's eye view I got of it from the highway suggested that it was much the same, only worse. The long flat approach from the south is a ribbon of used car yards, take-away food stands and decaying wooden houses. A string of motels five miles out from town invite you to stop over, miss the city and push on to the clean country up ahead. I pulled into one of them, the Sundowner, which had a "Vacancy" sign with the second "a" flickering fitfully on and off.

A middle-aged blonde woman with big bouncing breasts under a black polo neck sweater was behind the desk in the office. She ran an experienced eye over my clothes and wasn't too happy. Also I wasn't carrying luggage and they never like that. She sneaked a look past me at the Falcon and wasn't impressed by that, either. Luckily I wasn't planning to stay. She probably would have made me pay in advance and leave a deposit. I reached into my pocket for the photograph of Noni and laid it on the desk in front of her impressive mammaries. I opened my wallet, letting her see the fifties in it and took out my operator's licence which I put down next to the picture.

"Ever see her?" I asked.

She looked at it for a hundredth of a second. "Sure."

I was so surprised I had to ask her again. It isn't usually that easy. My puritanical soul told me it *shouldn't* be that easy. But I'd heard her right.

"Anyone along here'd know her." There was a tone in her voice that was hard to interpret, maybe amusement. I looked at her and noticed her colossal double chin. She smiled and the chin tensed up a bit. "That's Noni Rouble. Haven't seen her for years."

"How is it you know her then?"

She asked me why I was asking and I told her some lies. She looked closely at the photograph of me on the licence, the one taken three years back and in a good light. She wasn't too happy about it so I eased a five dollar note out of the wallet and let it sit on top to get some air.

"I suppose it's alright," she said, eyeing the money. "Noni was an R and R girl around here — oh, seven or eight years back."

"R and R girl?"

"Right. Not to put too fine a point on it, she slept around with the American soldiers. You know, the ones on leave from Vietnam. She stayed here a couple of times. She stayed all up and down this strip." She waved her hand at the road.

"Somebody had to do it I suppose," I said.

"Yes." She shrugged and her heavy bosom lifted and subsided like a swell on the sea. "Nothing to do with me."

The thought crossed my mind that she was just the right age to have done the same thing when the Yanks were here in World War Two and to resent the passage of time.

"You didn't like her?"

"No."

"Why not?"

"Too flash, she made you feel she was doing you a favour shacking up in your place."

"I see. Well my information is she's headed this way. You wouldn't know where she'd go?"

She sighed, the way hotel keepers do when the beds aren't full and the overheads are going up all the time. She reached out a meaty hand, knocked about from cleaning rooms and wrinkled around the three rings on her fingers. The fingers closed over the money.

461

"I haven't seen her, but if Noni's back in Newcastle she's at one of two places."

I waited.

"If she's flush she'll be at the Regal in the city."

I thought about it. "I don't think she's flush but I'll check it out anyway. What if she's not?"

"She'll be at Lorraine's boarding house, Fourth Street. It's a brothel."

"Literally?"

She looked puzzled.

"I mean is it really a brothel?"

"Oh no, not strictly speaking, not any more. Probably was once. I mean it's a dump, you can flop there for a dollar a night, single or double."

"Sounds choice."

She chuckled. "Right. Lorraine's got one rule."

"What's that?"

"No blacks."

I grunted and asked to use her phone. She pushed it across the desk to me and I reached into my jacket pocket, took out a pen knife and sawed through the cable.

"Hey!" she yelped and banged one of her big red hands down on the desk.

"You can splice it," I said. "Give you something to do in the wee small hours."

"You bastard. I could go out and phone."

"You won't. You don't care that much."

She grinned and picked up the cut ends of the cord. "You're right. Give Noni a belting for me." She rubbed the ends together. "Hey, there's no electricity in this is there?" I told her there wasn't.

Outside the Falcon was clicking and squeaking as it cooled down after the long drive. It started under protest and I had to coax it out onto the road. I joined in the thin stream of traffic, mostly trucks, heading for the city. The drizzle had stopped and the clouds had peeled back leaving Newcastle squatting sullenly in a pool of moonlight. It opened its mouth and sucked me in.

9

The Regal Hotel is in the middle of the city and it dominates the scene on the skyline and at ground level. The building is a tower with black and white facades alternating each storey so that it looks like a giant pile of draughts. I parked outside and made my usual mistake of trying to push open the self-opening doors. This leaves you with a hand held out impotently in front of you and gives the desk staff an initial advantage. Under the lobby lights my boots looked more scuffed and my denims more wrinkled than they did normally. The girl behind the desk was lacquered and painted like a Barbie doll; her fingernails were purple talons and her mouth was a moist, ripe plum. I marched up to the desk and looked straight and hard into her eyes. She blinked and lost a fraction of the sartorial advantage. Her greeting was an incline of the head. No "Yes sir". That would have been a total defeat. I took out my licence card and the photograph of Noni and held them at her eye level, one in each hand.

"I'm a private detective on a missing persons case. Nothing sordid. I want to know if this woman is registered here."

Her eyes moved lazily across my offerings. She might have been short of sleep or her lids might have been tired from heaving the enormous false lashes up and down. Her lips parted and tiny fissures appeared in the make-up beside her mouth. She was got-up to be looked at, not to talk.

"I can't disclose any information about our guests." She spoke as if she was reading the words off an idiot card pasted to my forehead.

"I'm not asking for any information. Just yes or no. If you say yes I'll ask the manager and go through all the proper channels. If you say no I'll be on my way."

The impossible lashes fluttered up and she looked at the picture.

"No, then."

"Thanks." I put the card and the photograph away. Her face fell back into its fixed repose as if I had never caused it to move. I bounced away across the carpet and remembered not to try to open the door. Along to the left of the entrance a concrete ramp sloped down under the building. I went down into a dimly lit half-acre car park; there were a few score cars parked in rows. I walked quickly up and down the aisles between the cars — no Chev Biscayne.

I had a map of Newcastle in the car and checked it for Fourth Street. It runs through a housing estate near the northern edges of the suburbs up into the coastal ranges. It was a thirty-minute drive from the Regal to Lorraine's boarding house but in terms of class and cash they were a million miles apart. The boarding house was a two-storey wooden job with peeling paint and a collapsed front balcony on the top level. There was about two acres of land around it and, as far as I could judge in the moonlight, what wasn't covered by blackberries and bracken was serving as a motor car cemetery. A driveway at the side of the house was a shadowless black hole. The road ran steeply past the building and there were empty paddocks opposite it. Lorraine's was flanked by cheap brick bungalows on either side, but there were vacant lots up and down the street as if parts of it had been blighted and made unfit for human habitation.

I cruised up the street and parked at the top of the hill about fifty yards beyond the house. The steel works was belching out white smoke and laying down a background hum a couple of miles away towards the water. A few headlights flicked along the roads below but Fourth Street was empty and silent. I checked the Smith & Wesson. The drizzle started again as I eased open the passenger side door and slipped out onto the road.

The gravel road was slushy under my feet as I moved up to the black tunnel beside the house. Bushes overgrew the driveway, their straggling ends whipped clean by cars brushing past them. The ground's surface changed abruptly and I bent down to examine it. Deep fresh ruts were etched into the earth in an arc that curved around to a clear patch in front of the house. The ruts ended in a shallow ditch where the wheels of a vehicle had spun before getting a grip on the damp ground. Someone had left here in a hurry not so long ago. I moved up into the tunnel; blackness closed around me like a cloak and I bumped into the rear end of a car when I was about half way along the side of the house. I ran my hand across its boot which seemed to be about as wide as a bus. I put out a hand for the tail fin and the cold chrome rose up just where it should — a Chev Biscayne if ever I felt one.

I unshipped the pistol and held it stiffly in front of me like a divining rod. I skirted the car and felt my way along the weatherboards to the back of the house. A dim yellow light seeped out through a window and another thin block of it outlined a partly opened door. I kept my back pressed against the rippled wooden walls and scraped along to the door. I couldn't hear anything except the droning of the steelworks and the tight hiss of my own breathing. A fly wire screen that looked as if a large dog had gone through it flapped open. I eased it away with the toe of my boot and pushed the door in. It swung easily, creaking a little, and gave me a view of several square feet of greasy green lino. I stepped into the room and my foot skidded in a dark patch just inside the doorway.

A woman was sitting on the floor with her back against a set of built-in cupboards. Her head lolled crazily to one side and a dark trickle of blood had seeped down from her mouth over her chin and onto the bodice of her cheap chain store dress. She was a thin, yellow woman with lank black hair and a scraggy neck with dirt in the creases. A vein in her forehead was throbbing and her flat chest was rising and falling in millimetres. I opened a door which let on to a long passage running towards the front of the house. The light barely penetrated six feet of its length but it seemed to be empty. I closed the door and bent over the woman. Her breath, what there was of it, was coming out in little erratic gasps and each one smelled more of stale gin than the last. I looked around the room. The bench tops were littered with bottles of sauce, food-encrusted plates and empty beer bottles. An electric toaster had one of its sides down like a drawbridge; crumbs were scattered around it and a fly was trapped in a smear of butter across its top. The mess — jars of jam, brimful ashtrays and slimy cutlery — flowed across the benches and into the sink. The detritus leaped across to the laminex kitchen table which carried a number of grimy glasses, pools of liquid and a two-thirds empty bottle of Gilbeys gin.

I put the gun on the table and hooked my hands under the woman's shoulders. She was a dead weight like a sack of grain. I dragged her across the room, kicked one of the chairs out from under the table and dumped her into it. She didn't move except that her head slumped across the other side. I pushed her hair aside. There was a long jagged tear near her ear and a deep oozing cut on her mouth, the sort of wound the foresight and backsight of a pistol make across a face. There was a lot of blood on her face and on the floor but there didn't seem to be any other injury to her and this one wasn't fatal. The dishtowel on the sink gave off a stomach-turning smell but I ran water on it, screwed it out and dabbed at the blood. She flinched as the water went into the cuts and her eyes flickered open. I pressed the wet cloth against her forehead. Her head tried to slide away to the right but I held it steady. Her eyes opened into dark slits and stared fixedly at the bottle on the table.

"Are you Lorraine?" I asked.

She nodded. The action must have sent waves of pain through her because she shuddered and slid lower on the chair. I hoisted her up.

"Water?"

She made a sound that could have meant yes, so I rinsed one of the dirty glasses, half filled it and held it to her lips. She sipped a thimbleful then shook her head. On a close look her Chinese ancestry was apparent. Her eyes were jet black and sloped a bit and although there was practically no flesh on her face the bone structure was broad and oriental. She picked up the damp dishcloth from where I'd dropped it in her lap and mopped at the slash beside her mouth.

"Did Noni do this to you?"

Her mouth twisted into a grin, the movement brought flesh blood out of the cut and she checked it.

"Not likely," she croaked. "I can handle Noni any day."

"Who then?"

"Guy with her. Dunno his name."

"What happened?"

"They got here late this arvo — no, a bit later. Noni said she wanted to stay the night, her and him. I said alright and gave them the room. Then they went out for a while, came back with the booze."

She nodded at the bottle on the table and immediately regretted it. I gave her another sip of water. She held on to the glass and some colour came back into her face making it grey like old, stained china. I waited.

"I made them something to eat, we had a few drinks, friendly like. Then the bloke started to talk about him and me swapping cars. I've got a Holden ute — bomb, but it goes. I said alright. I thought he was joking. I asked him to throw in the rest of the gin. He said OK and to give him the keys. I thought he was joking. When I wouldn't he smashed me."

"With a pistol."

"Yeah. Big bastard."

"The man?"

"No, the gun."

"What did he look like? What did the girl call him?"

She handed me the glass. "Get me a drink and a smoke and tell me who the hell you are and I might say some more."

I tipped the rest of the water in the glass into the sink and poured in a slug of gin. I looked around for something to put in it but she snapped her fingers and held out her hand.

"Put that much in again and give it here."

I did and rolled her a cigarette. I lit it and she drew it down half an inch and pulled the smoke deep into her lungs.

"Thanks, that's better. Now, who're you?"

I told her the story quickly, suggesting that the man travelling with Noni had probably killed Ricky Simmonds.

"Jesus," she said when I'd finished, "I was lucky; he might've done me."

"That's right. Will you answer my questions?"

"Yeah, what were they?"

I repeated them and she drank some gin and smoked while she thought it over.

"I can't remember that she called him anything," she said at last. "They weren't getting on too well seemed to me. You know Noni?"

I shook my head and produced the photograph.

"That's her, the slut. Well, the bloke's not big, about five foot six or seven, not more. He's thin but sort of flabby thin, you know?"

I said I didn't know.

"Well, there's not much meat on him but what there is looks sort of soft. His chest's sort of slid down to his gut. Can't make it no clearer. Gimme another smoke."

I got out the makings and started to roll one but she reached over impatiently and took the packet away. Her fingernails were black-rimmed and the thin skin on her hands was stretched tight like the fabric on a model plane. She made a fat cigarette and twisted the ends.

"Anything else about him?"

"You mean clothes and that?"

"Anything."

"He had an old suit on, blue with a sort of checked shirt under it, like tartan. Looked a bit funny with the suit. He was real pale, like he's been in hospital. Oh, and his ears stuck out, like this." She fanned her ears out from under her lank, greasy hair.

"What did they talk about? Did they say where they were going?"

"Let's think." She put a black fingernail through the black hair and scratched. "He didn't say much but Noni blabbed a bit. She was pissed and I reckon she was taking something else as well. You know?"

"I know. What did she say?"

"Well, I went out to do somethin' and I heard her say, when I was coming back, that it was a long time ago and he should forget it and it was only money."

"What did he say?"

"Told her to shut up. Then she said something about Macleay and he told her to shut up again. Listen, did they take the car?"

"Was it parked out front?"

"Yes."

"They took it."

"Fuck 'em. They leave the big one?"

"The Chev? Yes."

Her thin, ratty eyebrows went up. "Is that a fact? Reckon I can keep it?"

I thought of Ricky Simmonds, slumped down dead in a ditch around a fort built to repel invaders of an already invaded land. Crouched over like an Aboriginal warrior buried with all ceremony as in the time before horses and guns and arsenic and venereal disease.

His car had been his shield and his weapon and now it was discarded beside a house where black men were banned by a yellow woman. Australia.

A man in a dressing gown and three days of stubble came through the passage door before I could answer about the car. He shuffled into the kitchen and stopped short when he saw the gin.

"Piss off, Darby," Lorraine said sharply.

The man looked at her with bleary eyes that sagged down into deep pouches about his cheekbones. With the eyes and the stubble and the grizzled grey hair poking through the top of the dressing gown he looked like a tired old owl who'd lost his way.

"Go on Lorraine," he whined. "Just a small one."

She shrugged and nodded at me. I poured some gin and handed him the glass; he didn't seem to notice me, just lifted his hand and let the liquor slide down his throat. His neck convulsed once and he set the glass down carefully on the table. He let it sit for a few seconds, then tilted it again and got a few drops on his tongue.

"Right, piss off," Lorraine snapped.

He pulled the dressing gown around him and dragged himself out of the room. I looked at the woman.

"A bum," she said. "Probably came out to piss in the sink. Now, about that car?"

"Not up to me. Give me the details on the ute."

She did, the number and colour and a description of the frame mounted over the tray. I picked up my gun from the bench and tucked it away. I nodded to her and headed for the door. She ignored me, her hand snaked out for the gin bottle and she wasn't worried about her glass.

Outside the drizzle was steady and the ground was slippery underfoot. I walked slowly along the side of the house and pulled open the driver's side of the Chevvy. The interior light came on. A profusion of wires and fuses spilled out over the floor like a heap of multi-coloured guts.

10

I was tired and Macleay was three hours away by road if I didn't kill myself by falling asleep at the wheel. It was three a.m. and I needed some sleep badly. I drove to Newcastle airport and bought a seat on the flight leaving for Macleay, Coffs Harbour and points north at six a.m. I parked my car in the airport lot and locked it after taking out the duffel coat and the whisky. I wrapped the .38 in a scarf and stuffed it into the coat pocket. The bottle went into the other pocket. I found the dimmest corner of the passenger lounge, stretched out on the seat and took a long pull at the whisky. It hit hard and started to close down some departments in my mind. I pulled the coat over my legs and went to sleep.

Three hours later I was awake with stiff joints, a headache and a vile taste in my mouth. The lounge canteen wasn't open this early so I went into the toilet and swilled water around in my mouth and lapped it into my face. The black-bristled dial that looked back at me from the mirror was red-eyed and pale-skinned.

"You look terrible," I said to it and it insulted me right back.

There were a few people standing around in the drafty lounge. There was a sleek guy in a suit carrying a steel-rimmed briefcase and a girl in overalls and a fringed shawl straddling a big New Guinea-style string bag who looked aggressively at me when I glanced at her. A clutch of kids swarmed around a woman in black who had the long-suffering, my-reward-is-not-of-this-world look of an Italian matron. A young man with a thin aquiline face like a Spanish gypsy was reading a paper and seemed to be taking some trouble to ignore me as I walked through to the seat allocation desk. The clerk ripped leaves out of the ticket and when I looked around again the gypsy had gone and left his paper behind. I went over and picked it up. It was the *Newcastle Herald* of three days before.

More people turned up and about twenty of us got on the plane. We took off dead on time and ran straight into a headwind which we battled for the whole trip. The dark widow fed sweets to the children like a conveyor belt. The executive type took papers out of his briefcase and worked on them with a gold ballpoint pen. The girl in the overalls dug a paperback copy of *The Golden Notebook* out of her bag and didn't lift her head from it the whole way. I looked down across the wing of the plane as the central coast of New South Wales slipped past beneath us. The mountains and valleys were wrapped in swirling blue mist and the ground, when it showed through, was a patchwork of brown and green and white like camouflage. I rubbed my hand across my face and promised myself a shave and some breakfast in Macleay. The eight hour sleep in a soft bed would have to wait.

The plane bucked about on the descent but the weather up here, a few degrees north of Sydney, was clear and the moist wind blowing across the little runway was warm. The terminal was a fibro-cement affair with a galvanised iron roof, the whole structure sitting up on yard-high brick piers. We trooped across the tarmac, went up some rickety wooden steps and into the arrivals lounge which was also the departure lounge and the cargo despatch. I had all my luggage in my pockets so I went through the building and out into the real world before anyone else. The executive was hot on my tail but I caught the first taxi going. The driver seemed half asleep when I got into the cab and he stayed that way. We ran out of the airport standing area and along a road that was only wide enough for one car to drive on the metal; the gravel beside the road was washed thin and runnels threatened to undermine the surfaced section. I sat in the back seat and rolled a cigarette for want of anything else to do. The rainforest grew close to the road on either side and screened out everything else, only the occasional track running in, showing deep caterpillar treads, betrayed the logging going on inside that would eventually thin the forest away to nothing.

After a few miles the straggling houses and half-hearted fences that mark the outskirts of all Australian country towns appeared and then we crossed a bridge over a river and houses stood side by side and we were in the main street of Macleay. The shopkeepers were out, splashing water over the dusty footpaths and sweeping the night's rubbish into the gutters. On both sides of the street most of the shops had iron awnings which covered the whole depth of the footpath. A couple of gnarled old jacaranda trees buckled the bitumen and the streetscape was dominated by two pubs on either side of the road. Rusted tin signs on their sides advertised brands of beer long since defunct and both buildings boasted acres of trellis work, painted white, around the balconies which ran across the front and along one side. The Commercial Hotel had a sign out front promising breakfast for non-residents. I paid the cab fare and went in.

I wolfed down the mediocre breakfast of chops and eggs and put a little character in the thin instant coffee by adding some whisky. An old biddy eating crumpets at another table and dabbing at her thin, bloodless lips with a lace handkerchief caught me at it. I stared defiantly at her and was surprised when she gave me a tolerant smile. When I crossed the room to pay the bill I noticed the patchwork of blue veins under the powder on her nose. I'd made her day. She probably didn't start till ten.

Barber shops are getting thin on the ground everywhere, but they're hanging on better in Macleay than most places. There were three in the main street. I chose the cleanest and sat down to think while the artist went to work. The coolness of the lather on my face was nice and the razorman's total silence was soothing but they didn't change anything. I was still just chasing people, following thin leads and not understanding the pattern of things. I tried to tell myself this was flexible, open thinking, but I wasn't convinced. I refused a hair trim, gave a good-sized tip and got the address of Bert's garage. He said I could walk it from there so I walked.

The garage was set on a narrow block with the pumps right on the street in the style of the 1920s. The workshop needed a coat of paint and the bowsers hadn't yet been changed over to decimal currency. The alarm cable didn't work when I trod on it and an old dog lying in the sun between the air hose and a rusted watering can that seemed to serve as the radiator water supply didn't even scratch himself as I walked past him.

I went up to the workshop and peered inside. An old Holden was up on jacks in the middle of the floor which was littered with tools, car parts and other equipment. A battered work bench was in the same condition. I called out and nothing happened. Another yell and a door opened at the back of the shed and a man came through it carrying a teapot and an enamel mug. He moved carefully, picking his way through the litter like an actor obeying chalk marks on a stage. He had been tall but had lost inches from years of bending over cars. He wore thongs, old grey flannel trousers and a brown cardigan over his bare chest. His grey felt hat had been all the rage when Don Bradman was a boy. I moved forward into the shed and heard a growl behind me. The dog was bristled up and baring its teeth six inches from my ankle.

"Easy Josh," the man said. "Back off boy."

I let the shiver run its way down my back and legs and stood still. The dog growled again then jogged off to the shade of the petrol bowsers.

"Is your name Bert?" I asked.

He moved closer and took a good look at me. It was impossible to judge his reaction. The nose was a bit purple and the face hadn't been shaved today, yesterday or the day before. The smell coming off him was strong — motor oil, tobacco and underarm. I dropped back a fraction.

"What if it is?"

"Got a niece, Noni?"

"Yeah, you a cop?"

"You expect one?"

"Where Noni's concerned, yes." He beckoned me further into the workshop and peered over my shoulder as I came in.

"What's wrong?" I said, turning to look out towards the street.

"Nothing." He poured tea into the mug and sipped it. "Just looking. Abo hanging around earlier." He blew steam off the tea. "Sorry I can't offer you a cup, only got the one mug. A cop you said."

"No, I didn't. Don't worry about the tea."

He looked at me over the rim of the mug. His eyes were pale blue dots amid a mass of wrinkles and puckered flesh.

"If you're not a cop what are you? Bookie's mate?"

He was off on a new tack and sketching in areas of Noni's past life. She was probably in trouble with the Commissioner of Taxation and hadn't renewed her driver's licence.

473

"Noni's missing," I said evasively.

He shrugged and finished his tea in a long gulp. He began patting his pockets in the age-old manner of the tobacco cadger. I handed him my packet, papers and matches. A cigarette took shape between his fingers; he didn't look at what he was doing as if that was against the rules. He lit up and handed the makings back.

"Thanks, son." His voice was friendly, almost wheedling but there was a guarded, semi-hostile undertone to it.

I let my eyes wander about the shed and spotted something in a far corner. He saw me looking.

"When did you last see Noni?" I asked.

"Years ago."

I sauntered over to the rear of the shop and kicked at a tarpaulin-covered lump on the ground. It clanged and I eased the tarp away to show a cage of silver-frosted bars, the frame from Lorraine's ute. I started to turn back and stopped when I saw that he'd moved across to the work bench. He fumbled behind him and his arm swept around but he was much too slow and I ducked to let the heavy spanner fly over my head and crash into the metal frame. I moved in on him fast and crushed him back against the bench. He wasn't as old as he looked and he was quite strong but he had no confidence. He pushed against me briefly but I pulled him forward and then slammed his spine back against the bench and the fight went out of him. I slapped the side of his face lightly.

"Why'd you try that old-timer? What's it to you?"

He didn't answer so I slapped him again. I don't like hitting people older than me, but then there's a lot of things I do that I don't like.

"Come on! What's it to you?"

Still no answer. I hit him two jolting slaps. His face blotched suddenly and took on an unhealthy rubicund glow.

"You'll have a heart attack," I said. "Natural causes." I pulled my hand back for another slap. He wriggled a bit but wasn't really trying; his breath was coming in short, wheezy spasms like an emphysema case in the last stages.

"OK, OK," he gasped, "you're right, me ticker'll give out. I'm too old for this. I can't take this many frights so quick."

"Noni's bloke?"

"Yes. Shit, what a hard case. He dumped the frame and took some plates off a wreck out the back."

"You let him?"

"He showed me the gun. That was enough for me."

"Where did they go?"

An impulse to lie and a touch of fear came into his face. The fear won.

"Gone to see Trixie Baker."

"Who's she?"

"Woman in Macleay. She was in on some trouble Noni had a few years ago. Good few years now."

"Tell me about it. Sit down."

He sat on the bench and watched me while I made a cigarette. I got it going and put the makings away.

"You're a sick man," I told him. "It's bad for you. Let's hear the story."

But I'd somehow lost the initiative. Perhaps he saw in my eyes that I wouldn't push him into a heart attack or maybe he just didn't care. He swore at me and told me nothing. I raised my voice and then thought of the dog outside the shed but he didn't give the dog a whistle. He shut up and didn't do anything, just put up a total defence of silence. Then I took another look at the Holden, it was an FX in the last stages of restoration. Repeated cutting and polishing had brought the duco up to a mirror finish and the chrome gleamed in the dim light like sterling silver. I pulled open a door and glanced at the upholstery; it was leather, flawless and luxuriant. Bert watched me as I circled the car. I came back to him.

"Just two questions Bert."

Silence.

"Where does Trixie Baker live?"

Nothing.

"Tell me about the Abo?"

More nothing.

I swooped down and picked up a gallon tin which had fluid of some kind splashing about in it. I smelled it. Petrol. I pulled out my matches, jumped over to the car and held the tin and the matches up near the driver's window.

"Hate to do it Bert." I put the can on the car roof and struck a match. He jumped up and his mottled face was pale and working.

"No, wait . . ."

The passion was in his face and the truth would be in his mouth. I dropped the match and scuffed it out. The words came flooding out of him like extinguisher foam.

"Trixie's got a farm, ten miles north. Sallygate road, first farm past the bridge, you can't miss it. I don't know what the old trouble was, I don't honest."

I believed him.

"The Abo?"

"Young bloke, tall, caught him in here early this morning. Scared the living shit out of me."

"Was this before or after Noni was here?"

"After."

"What was he doing?"

"Sleeping, back there." He pointed to a heap of bags half-hidden by the side panel of a car at the back of the shed.

"Why so scared? Just a drunk or something."

"Not him. No fear. Stone sober."

"What did you do?"

"Told him to shoot through and he did, but like he was going anyway, you know?"

I put the can down and stuck the matches back in my pocket. I couldn't waste any more time on Bert. Noni and her companion weren't too far ahead. I asked him how far and he told me they'd left about four hours ago. He didn't seem to object to the extra question. I rolled him a cigarette and lit it for him. He inhaled gratefully.

"Thanks Bert," I said: "You've been a great help. Now, you're going to drive me out to Trixie's. You drop me there and forget the whole thing. OK?"

He protested but I overrode him. We went around the FX and out the back door to where an ordinary-looking Valiant was parked. Bert climbed in and started it up and it didn't sound so ordinary. He'd modified it in ways that I couldn't understand which had turned it into a high performance car. He explained this to me in taciturn grunts as we drove; cars were at the moral centre of his life and he was

476

prepared to talk about them as about nothing else. I listened to his technical explanations in silence, thinking. Noni and the man had pushed hard to get this far and it seemed logical that it would be the last port of call but I had no idea what it added up to.

The driving seemed to relax Bert; he looked better somehow at the wheel, more physically in charge of himself and any nervousness he betrayed could easily be put down to uncertainty about my behaviour or that of the man with the gun. I put just one question to him on the drive and the answer was no, he'd never seen the gunman before.

Ten miles out from Macleay we passed over a wooden bridge and the metal road changed to dirt. Bert drove in second gear for a hundred yards and stopped where the road took a right-hand bend.

"Trixie's place is just around this corner." He jutted his bristled chin in the direction he meant. "If I was you I'd take it easy. That bloke with Noni looked jumpy and mean to me." His eyes opened as he saw me pull the .38 out of the coat pocket. "Jesus! You too. You said I just had to drop you here." His hand was on the gear stick, ready to move.

"That's right." I opened the door and stepped out. "You wouldn't be the sort of man to go to the police telling tales would you Bert?"

"Not me."

"One thing interests me. You don't seem concerned about the girl. She's your niece isn't she?"

"Not really. I was married to her mother's sister once. She doesn't mean anything to me."

I nodded and stepped back. He put the car in gear, U-turned neatly and drove off. I held the gun under the coat and moved along the side of the road. She didn't mean anything to me either, but here I was with a loaded gun going up against another loaded gun and not a friend in sight. I had the negative, defeated feeling that I wouldn't like to die up here, in all this lush vegetation and so far from home. I fought it down and turned the bend.

The farmhouse was set back about a hundred yards from the road at the end of a dusty drive. Some straggly gums grew along one side of the track and I came up through these to within spitting distance of the house. It fell short of colonial elegance by a long way, being basically a one-pitch wooden shack that had been added to by side and back skillions. What paint was on it was white. There were wheelmarks on the drive but no car in front of the house where the drive ended. I skirted around the house, keeping under the windows and close to the walls. No car. Behind the house, about fifty yards back was a big iron shed. A road ran up to it from the eastern boundary of the farm. There was no cover between the house and the shed so I dropped the coat, took a grip on the gun and ran, weaving and keeping low.

I made it in creditable time and circled the shed. Plenty of wheel marks, old and new, but no car. The shed's sliding door was half open and I went in. There were a couple of long trestle tables and lots of wire netting racks suspended about head high from the roof. Over in one corner there were a dozen or so big green plastic garbage bags, bulging full. I went over and untied the top of one. There was enough grass inside to turn on every head between Bermagui and Byron Bay.

I worked my way carefully back to the front of the house. There was no bell and to use the knocker I would have had to step inside because the door was standing open inside a fly wire screen. I rattled the screen and waited. A fly battled against the wire trying to get out. I let it out and went in myself. The house had the low hum — made up of refrigerator motor, dripping taps and the ghosts of voices — that all empty houses have. I walked through the nondescript rooms and passages on the way to the kitchen which was poky and dark with blinds drawn and flies buzzing. The buzzing was loudest over in a corner near a walk-in pantry.

A foot and half of a leg in a pale beige stocking were sticking out of the pantry. I went across and crouched down. A woman was lying with one leg extended and the other tucked up under her. One side of her face was a dark, crumpled ruin. Flies were gathering around the dried blood. Her features were reconstructable from the undamaged side — thin mouth and high forehead. She wore a severe blue linen dress that looked expensive. As I reached for her wrist I heard a noise behind me and I turned bringing the gun up but I was too slow and the business end of a thin-bladed knife was tickling my ear while the gun was still pointing nowhere.

"Drop the gun."

Two men with swarthy complexions, Italianate suits and stockinged feet were standing over me. They looked strange in the neat suits and socks but I didn't feel like laughing. One of them, the taller, said something in Italian and his mate moved back out of the kitchen. He returned with their shoes and they slipped them on, the taller guy still holding the knife close to my head. My joints were creaking and I made to straighten up and felt the knife go into the ear flesh a fraction. I sank back.

The Italians had the build of men who knew how to move and what to do when they got there. Ideas of taking them were out of the question. They conferred in Italian and weren't talking about *pasta*. I pointed at the woman.

"She's dead," I said stupidly.

They didn't even look at her. The knife artist retracted the blade with a click and while I was listening to it the other one stepped forward gracefully and clouted me on the side of the head with something thick and black and hard. I slid down and then he hit me again and a bright flare of pain went through my skull and spread and took away the light.

11

I woke up inside a small gloomy room with points of light stabbing in through the roof. The floor was rough planking with heavy metal strips binding it down. The light was about the same as in a cinema just before they start showing the ads. The room was drafty. It was also moving. My head throbbed viciously when I moved and I dropped back down on the pile of sacking and carpet scraps where I'd been thrown. I closed my eyes and let myself adjust slowly to the surroundings. When the headache had settled down into sync with the noise of the engine and the wheels I admitted to myself that I was in the back of a small enclosed truck. I crawled and lurched about the cabin checking the walls and rear doors. Tight as a drum. Through a chink in the floor I could see the road rushing past at a steady pace, but there's no way to tell from moving bitumen which way you're headed. I pounded on the wall near the driving end of the truck and got no response. I was locked in as safe as the crown jewels and nobody was going to do a thing about it. I wadded up the packing, put my head down and drifted off to sleep.

I dreamed I was crushing rocks on the Long Bay rock pile and then I got over the wall and made it down to La Perouse. The crowd around the snake pit was immense; it flowed over the road and up the grassy slope towards the houses on the hill. I pushed my way through the throng which was mainly made up of blacks until I got to the fence. The pit was full of snakes of all sizes and hues writhing about and rearing up to strike at the audience. Penny was in the middle of the pit with a python coiled about her and she was screaming for help. I was trying to get over the fence and the people around me were laughing because a big black snake was waving its head in front of me, darting at me and holding me back. I yelled something and woke up drenched with sweat and clutching at the empty air.

I sat in the truck while it cruised along for what seemed like ten hours. My watch had stopped at eleven a.m. and if there's any way to tell the time from inside a closed truck I don't know it. The traffic noise picked up at one point indicating that we were passing through a town. I heard the rattle of a train a bit later — that still put us anywhere on the east coast. I was edgy from tobacco withdrawal and almost hallucinating from the effects of two hard blows on the head within twenty-four hours. Also I was scared; there were a few bodies in shallow graves, courtesy of the grass producers and I didn't want to join them. I tried to quell the fear and kill the time by sorting out the parts of the case so far.

Noni was on the run, maybe semi-unwilling, with an unidentified man who was prone to violent solutions of his problems. What they were running to was a mystery. A woman named Trixie Baker was involved, fatally as it turned out. There was something in Noni's past that connected her to the live man and the dead woman and I wouldn't begin to unravel the affair until that secret was yielded up. I gave it away at that point and concentrated on my thirst. I thought about exactly what sort of drink I'd like to have in what circumstances and settled for a middy of old with a double Teacher's on the side. The saloon bar of the Imperial Lion with Ailsa along for company would be nice. I went to sleep again.

The truck stopped suddenly and threw me against the wall. I swore and struggled to get up, then the doors opened and a blaze of electric light flooded and blinded me. I crawled to the edge of the tray and stopped there like a rabbit transfixed by a spotlight. I heard a snigger and then an accented voice told me to get down. I dropped off the end of the truck and my knees buckled when I hit the ground. I heard the snigger again and thought it would make a good target for a fist if I ever felt strong enough again to make one.

My eyes adjusted to the light and I took in that I was in a warehouse of some sort. The ceiling was high and the floor was hard cement. Two hundred-watt bulbs hung down close to my face like lit-up heads in nooses. Four men were standing near a new green Fiat sedan parked beside the truck. I'd seen three of them before, the two who'd taken me in Macleay and the one in the camelhair overcoat. He'd been in Trueman's watching the Moody workout. The fourth man was dressed the same way as the others in a suit with highly polished shoes. He had a frizz of dark curly hair around a bald top. I didn't know him.

The one in the two-hundred-dollar coat spoke with a guttural voice in an accent that was almost stage Italian.

"Mr Hardy, you're putting me to a lotta trouble. Why you sticking your nose in my business?"

"What business would that be?"

"You're smart, an investigator," he drew the word out ironically, "you think it out."

"You're the olive oil king," I said. "You're going to rough me up for using peanut oil to fry my chips."

One of the Macleay boys stepped forward and slammed me in the gut. I felt the breakfast of God knows how long ago rise in my gorge. I straightened up.

"I don't know what your business is Mr . . . ?"

He laughed. "That's better. No jokes. Coluzzi. You were at the gym watching the black, Moody. You go to see Ted Williams, you see Sunday in La Perouse, then you go to Macleay."

"I went to the toilet in between."

He struggled to keep his hands and feet still. "I told you no jokes. Why you hanging around these people?"

"What's it to you?" I was puzzled that he hadn't mentioned the marijuana. He was prepared to use muscle on me but not to go all the way. He was talking to me for some reason rather than having me kicked into paraplegia — that gave me some leverage but it was hard to judge how much. I snapped my fingers.

"I've got it, you're the boomerang king . . ."

The knuckle man moved again but I was ready for him this time. He swung his foot and I went down, got hold of it, lifted, twisted and flipped. His arms flailed and he went over and belted his head into the bumper of the truck. He groaned, rolled over and lay still. His mate exposed a knife but Coluzzi motioned him to stop.

"My business is fighters, Mr Hardy . . . one of my businesses. I'm interested in the black fighters. I want to put them in against my boys, the Italian boys. We would get terrific houses no? A lot of money to make."

"Honest fights?"

He spread his hands apologetically. "We see. Maybe. You could do yourself some good."

"How?"

"First, you tell me who you working for and what's the angle."

Some light dawned. Coluzzi figured he had competition and he wanted to know more about it. He was a shrewd guy who wanted to sew the whole thing up neatly before he put any time and money into it. Maybe he did have competition. In any case my skin seemed to depend on him continuing to think so.

"Did you have me bashed outside a pub in La Perouse?"

"No."

"You had someone watching me in Newcastle?"

"Sure."

The man I'd thrown was on his feet again looking very pale around the edges. The man with the blade was looking anxious to have a go and the priestly character was very quiet and still. If I was going to get out of this without any more of the physical stuff this was the time to talk.

"I heard a whisper that something like this could be on," I said.

"Yeah? Who from?"

"Tickener, the reporter. I don't know his sources."

"What you snooping around for — Redfern, Macleay, La Perouse, the black belt?"

The priest sniggered and Coluzzi spoke sharply to him in Italian. At a guess he was telling him to shut up or he'd do something unpleasant to him that would cramp his style with the ladies. Coluzzi repeated the question angrily.

"I'm looking into it for Harry," I improvised. "I haven't got on to much yet but I've got no axes to grind. I could keep you informed. I've been in the middle so far, copping it from both sides. Maybe it's time for me to come off the fence."

"How do you mean?"

"I got bashed in La Perouse as I said. My guess is that was your opposition."

Coluzzi scratched his jaw and turned aside to talk to the bald man. The bruisers stood flapping their ears and I listened to the flow of

Italian, catching a word here and there but not making much sense of it. The bald man did most of the talking and Coluzzi did a lot of nodding. He swung back to me.

"Adio's got a good question. If you help me and I get ridda this opposition you talk about and you talk to the reporter, where does that leave me?"

It was a good question. I looked at Adio with respect and he gave me a tight, sardonic smile. I took out my wallet and showed him the money in it. Twenty-three dollars.

"I've got about twice that much in the bank. I could use some more. You don't pay tax on money you win on fights."

He didn't look convinced but the money argument was intelligible to him.

"What about Tickener?"

"He doesn't own me. There'd be one condition though."

"What?"

I looked at the two enforcers in their padded shouldered suits and narrow crocodile skin shoes. They looked well fed, they were probably pampered by their women and generous to a fault with their kids. In Coluzzi's service, though, they were vicious thugs and their indifference to the dead woman in Macleay suggested that they'd done worse things than hit people on the head. I pointed to the taller man.

"Give me a free swing at him with the blackjack."

Coluzzi laughed gutturally and rapped out some more Italian. The other two men smiled, the tall one didn't smile. His face lost a few shades of colour and his mouth twitched as Coluzzi dipped into his mate's pocket and lifted out the blackjack. I gathered that the tall man's name was Carlo. Carlo stood stock still and ground his teeth together. He seemed to be setting his bones and gristle and tensing his flesh against the cruel bite of the cosh.

I tossed it in my hand; a short, palm-sized hard rubber grip with about six inches of whippy, lead-loaded rubber attached. Carlo screwed up his eyes and swayed just a little. I pulled back my arm and stretched out my other hand to touch him on the left ear. He flinched a fraction. I swung hard at his head and let the blackjack go just before my hand got in range; it sailed over his shoulder and crashed against the tin wall. Carlo sagged slightly at the knees. His face was dead white and his eyes were hard with hate. I slapped him lightly on the face and let out a harsh laugh that didn't sound as nervous as I felt.

Coluzzi echoed the laugh with more feeling. Some of the tension evaporated and I asked him for a cigarette. He snapped his fingers and a packet of king size Chesterfields was produced. I took one and Carlo's off-sider lit it. I sucked the smoke deep and expelled it in a long stream, it floated up and hung like ectoplasm in the harsh light. A few more vigorous bursts of Italian between Coluzzi and Adio settled it. Coluzzi came forward and looked hard into my face; he was a few inches shorter than me and had to tilt his head up to do it. The skin stretched over his jaw and pulled taut around his neck. I saw for the first time that he was old, wrinkled by age but without a spare ounce of flesh on him. He looked like a Corsican bandit, hardened by years of sun and rain, good for a fight until the day he died.

"Alright Mr Hardy," he said, "you're on. I want to know what you find out. Everything."

"How do I reach you?"

He reached into his waistcoat pocket and pulled out a card; Adio produced a gold pen and he scribbled a number on the back of it. He handed the card to me. On it was printed "Aldo Coluzzi, Merchant," and an address in the city. He hadn't mentioned the marijuana. I wondered why but wasn't about to raise the question now. The less said about that the better. Coluzzi looked pleased with himself and rubbed his hands together.

"So, Mr Hardy, she's arranged. We understand each other. Now you show a little trust and take another ride in the truck."

I was expecting tricks, double-crosses, anything, but this looked a little too obvious.

"Why?"

"You don't know where you are. I want it that way."

He sealed it by handing me my gun. Then he turned away and he and Adio got into the Fiat. There was no question of argument. Carlo and the other hood had an unsatisfied look about them that I wasn't anxious to test. I climbed up into the back of the truck. Its doors closed. I heard a heavy sliding door being opened and then we were bumping over a rough surface for a while before getting onto a road. I checked the pistol — empty breech, empty clip. We drove fast for what felt like an hour and then cruised to a stop. The doors swung open and the lights of the night flickered outside.

"Out," said Carlo.

I got down and stood uselessly in the middle of a small lane running between two high factory walls. The Italians didn't speak. They shepherded me over to the left-hand wall and motioned me to press my face into it. I did and waited for the sap or the kidney punch. Nothing happened. They got back into the truck and drove off. I didn't even get the licence number. I turned around and stood with my back against the wall and waited until the sweat running down my chest reached body temperature. I started walking and found that I was in Annandale, quite handy to home. I hailed a taxi and was there in a few minutes.

I used a key I kept hidden under a half brick behind a pot plant to get inside the house and smelled the familiar odours, even if a bit stale. From habit I'd picked up the newspaper and taken it with me. A glance at the date reminded me that I had no idea of the time. It was two a.m. This whole thing had started a bare forty hours ago and I'd already covered a lot of territory for Tarelton's money. But there are no prizes for that. As of now the trail was cold. It was time for some brain work. For that I needed help. I found some stale tobacco in the house and rolled a couple of cigarettes. I got a flagon of wine and a soda syphon out of the refrigerator and sat down with an ashtray and a glass. After finishing the cigarettes and lowering the level of the wine considerably the pattern of things still eluded me. I seemed to have two different problems on my hands.

One was Coluzzi and the fight game. Well that was nasty with the knives and all, but there was nothing much in it for me. I'd have to discuss aspects of that with Harry Tickener. And I still worried about the marijuana farm. Maybe there was some connection between Coluzzi and the mess Noni Rouble was in. That had two sides to it — a black and a white — and I was sure they were connected. There was something up there in Macleay, some time back and involving money, only money. A pale, flabby, violent man had been told to forget about it. I didn't think he would. I was beginning to get a feeling for what that money trouble might be, and I didn't think it concerned a map to Lasseter's lost reef.

That was as close as I got to clarity. I thought about the list of great black fighters who'd come out of the game with nothing to show for their scarred eyes and broken hands and slurred speech. I thought of Jimmy Sunday and Penny Sharkey, and I thought about Harry Tickener again.

I finished the drink and went upstairs. I got out of my pants and shoes and sweater and sprawled on the bed pulling a blanket over me. The light was on but it didn't bother me a bit.

12

The telephone woke me. I caught sight of the clock as I rolled over to grab the receiver — six-thirty a.m. I put my head back on the pillow and tried to unscramble reality and dreams. I grunted into the mouthpiece and it sputtered back at me like a firecracker. I sat up.

"Easy, easy. James?"

More sputtering and incoherence on the other side of the wire.

"Stop it," I yelled. "Shut up, take a breath and give it to me clearly."

A pause, a long one, then the actor's voice came through, still with a note of panic but under control.

"Noni's been kidnapped. I've just got a note."

"At six-thirty?"

"I couldn't sleep, I was up early and found the note taped to the door."

"What does it say?"

I heard a rustle over the line and then James' voice, shaky, reading.

"We have got the girl. Five thousand dollars gets her back."

"Is that all?"

"Yes."

It didn't figure. Ted Tarelton could raise twenty times that. Why hit James? My silence made him panicky again and he almost stammered, asking if I was still there. I said I was.

"What should I do?"

"Can you raise it?"

"The money? Yes, just."

"Will you?"

"Yes of course, of course."

"Stay put. I'll be right over."

I hung up on him, jumped up and took a quick shower. I was

pulling on some clothes when the phone rang again. I made a bet with myself and won. Madeline Tarelton.

"Mr Hardy? Just a minute. My husband wants to speak to you."

I heard a click, waited and then Ted's rich voice came in.

"Hardy? My girl's been snatched."

"I know. You got a note?"

"Yes, how . . . ?"

I told him how and asked him to read out the note. It was the same as James' except that it asked for a hundred thousand dollars and said a contact would be made at five p.m. the following day. Ted's voice vibrated a bit and the idea occurred to me that he'd be on the Courvoisier a bit earlier today. I promised him I'd be over as soon as I'd seen James. He wasn't too happy about that, claiming an employer's rights but I soothed him. He seemed impressed that James had said he'd raise the five thousand, as if it was a bride price. I suppose it was, in a way. My cool competence was dented a bit by having to ask Ted for James' address. I'd forgotten that I didn't have it, but he gave it to me without seeming to take it amiss.

My perfectly good car was sitting in the Newcastle airport parking lot and it was raining again. I got a taxi to James' place in Darlinghurst. It was a terrace house with a door that let straight out onto the street. It was painted white and had some new iron on the roof but it hadn't been made over into anybody's dream. A yellow Mini with a cracked rear window, taped up, was parked outside. I knocked at the door and James opened it with a buzzing electric shaver in his hand. Half his face was shaven and half not. He looked terrible. He ushered me in and started to gabble. I reached out and clicked off the shaver. That shut him up.

"Let's see the note," I said.

He went out to the kitchen and I followed him. The house wore the same look all the way through, pleasant enough but as if no-one cared. He pointed to a piece of paper on the table and I picked it up. The words he'd read out were printed across a cheap piece of notepaper in capitals. A black ballpoint pen had done the writing and there were no idiosyncrasies in it that I could see. Across the back of the paper, which had been folded in three, was a strip of cellulose tape. James resumed his shaving, wandering about the little room stroking his jaw. He was wearing drill slacks and an orange-coloured thing I think is called a shaving coat. He would. I waited until he'd finished shaving and turned the motor off, then I told him about Tarelton's note. He ran his hand over his smooth face and frowned where he found a missed spot. I pushed the shaver out of reach and leaned on him.

"How soon can you get the money?"

"Today. I'd have to see my family's lawyer, but I'm sure it can be arranged."

"Good. Do it. Don't tell anyone else." I started for the passage but he came after me and caught me by the arm.

"God, don't just walk out. What do you think of it? What's going to happen?"

"I don't know," I growled. "I'll talk to some people, then we'll play it the best way we can."

"It all seems so strange — I mean for this to happen so long after she disappeared. It seems — I don't know — oddly managed."

"You're the theatre man," I said.

I brushed him off and left the house saying I'd call him at the theatre when things had been decided. I caught a taxi to Armstrong Street and wondered why I'd replied the way I had to his last remark. I didn't know. Maybe just to be rude.

Madeline Tarelton opened the door again. She was wearing a lime green trouser suit today and nothing about her had deteriorated since I'd seen her last. She seemed to be bearing up under the strain and her voice was edged with contempt when she spoke.

"Ted's still in bed. He'll see you there."

"Where's the room?"

"Upstairs, in front."

I went up. The room was big with two glass-panelled doors letting out onto a balcony. The water was visible through them, shining dull and grey under the thick white sky. In bed Ted was not nearly as impressive as he was when up and around and properly togged up. The skin around his jaw sagged, his rumpled hair looked thin and his body under the bedclothes was lumpy and powerless. The room had pale candy striped wallpaper and a deep pile carpet; it was too fussy and frilled, with fringed lampshades and a brocade bedcover, for my taste and Ted looked uncomfortable in it. I sat on a bentwood chair cushioned with satin while Ted folded up the newspaper and pulled himself straighter in the bed.

"Bad business this, Hardy," he said. "Fair knocked me. I took a bit of a turn. Crook heart." He placed his hand over his chest. I nodded.

"Got the note?"

He produced it from the breast pocket of his puce pajamas and handed it over. Identical to James' except for the extra information.

"I was up early. Meeting on today at Randwick. I went for the papers and there it was, stuck to the door. Madeline had to bloody nearly carry me back here."

The experience had swept away his usual bluster; I couldn't tell whether he was most upset by the kidnapping of his daughter or the reminder of his own mortality, but it was obviously the right time to pressure him a bit.

"You can raise the money?" I asked.

"Easy. Reckon I should?"

"Yes. But there's something weird about this. It doesn't smell right."

"How do you mean?" he said listlessly.

"Could the girl be shaking you down?"

Colour flooded his face and he looked about to sound off at me which he undoubtedly would have done if he'd been feeling his usual, successful self. Now he flopped back against the pillows and fidgeted with the quilt.

"Possible, I suppose," he said lamely. "Is that your theory?"

"I haven't got a theory, just a feeling. It's a strange one. I never heard of two ransoms being asked before. Complicates things. Not that they're not messy enough already."

"Madeline told me you'd rung the other night. By complicated you mean about the Abo? What's happened since then?"

I gave him an outline leaving Coluzzi out and not going into details about Noni's reputation in Newcastle. He couldn't help on that score; he'd practically lost all touch with the girl from the time his wife had left to when Noni turned up motherless. Ted's instincts, bred in the SP game and sly grogging, were to avoid the police, so he fell in with my suggestion that we keep the police out of it for the time. I had a feeling, which I was backing, that the girl wasn't in danger. But the cops wanted to talk to her in connection with Simmonds' death and if they started poking around and stirring things up it could all turn sour and Noni might suddenly become dispensable. I gave Ted the gist of this and he agreed to raise the money and wait for the contact.

"I think that's just plain stupid," Madeline Tarelton said from the doorway. She came in carrying a glass of water and some pills on a tray. She set them down on the bed and gestured at her husband to take them. He did. I pocketed the note and got up from my chair.

"Just a minute," Madeline said quickly. "This is insane, you must go to the police."

"I don't think so," I said. "And your husband agrees with me."

She snorted. "You're playing games. I have my doubts about you Mr Hardy. This is a mistake."

"Keep out of it Madeline," Ted said sharply. Maybe the pills had done him some good. Madeline swung round on him, surprised, but he cut her off.

"You don't give a damn about the girl, she's nothing to you. Alright, fair enough, but she's my daughter and I want her back safe. We'll do it Hardy's way."

"That's not fair!" Her composure was disturbed which looked like a rare event. "That girl is a menace, the dregs, she . . ."

"Shut up!" Ted roared. His face turned purple.

"Don't shout, you'll have another attack."

I left them to it and went down the stairs and out of the house.

I pulled up the hood of the light, plastic parka I was wearing and walked through the drizzle to Oxford Street where I caught a bus to the city. On the bus I read yesterday's paper. Simmonds' death got a small notice on page four in between an item on rail fares going up and the birth of an elephant at the zoo. The police appealed to the blonde woman who'd found the body to come forward. The Chev Biscayne was described. The woman and the car were the police's only lines of investigation. I couldn't imagine the La Perouse blacks identifying Noni to the police, however much they disliked her, but some back-tracking by the cops could turn her name up soon and then the heat would be on me.

I got off the bus outside *The News* building and bought the morning paper. There was nothing more on Simmonds but the discovery of an injured woman on her farm near Macleay got a mention. The woman was in a critical condition in Macleay hospital and police were anxious to interview a tall dark man wearing light-coloured clothes and carrying a dark coat. If they were any good it wasn't going to take the local police long to trace that man from his taxi to his breakfast to his shave. I'd used the name Colin Hocking for the plane ticket but a quick scout about at Newcastle would turn my car up and then I could expect visitors. On the sporting page there was a preview of the fight coming up between Jacko Moody and Tony Rosso. It would be the first main event for them both. They had good, rather similar records, but Moody had KO'd two men whom Rosso had only decisioned and he was favoured to win. It reminded me that I had to get tickets from Harry Tickener for Ted Williams.

The News building is a standard glass, concrete and plastic tower which creates a canyon without and neuroses within. The lobby was hung about with glossy blow-ups of press photographs that showed politicians with beer bellies and worn-out smiles, football players spattered with mud and fashion models of unbearable thinness. I went up to the fourth floor where Harry shares some cramped office space with thirty other reporters. They steal each other's cigarettes and listen to each other's phone conversations. I wound through the desks and wastepaper bins. Harry's typewriter was blasting.

"Hallo Cliff — hang on a second." He pushed a lock of his thin yellow hair back and stabbed at his keyboard with long, tobacco-stained fingers; three of them.

"Carry on exposing," I said. I sat down in the hard chair drawn up in front of the desk and rolled a cigarette. The old tobacco had tasted bad enough last night; this morning it was disgusting. Tickener stopped pounding and stretched both hands up in the air. Nothing creaked, he was still young.

"What can I do for you Cliff?"

"Two things; tickets to the Moody fight — a pair. OK?"

"Yeah, no trouble. You coming with me?"

"I hope so. I've got something on but it should be worked out by then, one way or another. Remember the guy we met at Trueman's?"

493

"Oh yeah, the actor. His bird was missing. Flushed her?"

"Not yet. Now the other favour."

He looked quickly down at his typewriter, picked up a pencil and made a note on the copy.

"Are you sure you've got the time Harry? I'd hate to throw your schedule out."

He looked embarrassed. "Shit. Sorry Cliff. It's this piece on Moody. I want to get it right."

"Read A. J. Liebling. Who's your top crime man?"

"Garth Green."

"Good memory? Knows the files?"

"Steel trap."

"Will you introduce me to him?"

"Sure, when?"

"Now."

He looked relieved and jumped up from his chair.

"Steady," I said. "Are you sure he'll be in?"

"He'll be in." Tickener came around the desk. "He works till two p.m. and drinks till two a.m. Let's go."

I followed him. There were a few people walking about in the corridor and a small clutch of reporters was grouped talking in a doorway. They parted like the waters when a six-foot girl with close-cropped red hair walked through the door. She was wearing boots, a long dark skirt and a tight-fitting jacket and she carried her head like a Queen. She had a high, proud nose and big dark eyes in a face as pale as a lily. I gaped with the journos but Harry seemed not to notice her and kept on his way. I wondered about Harry. He knocked on a door which had stuck to it a file card with the name garth green typed on it in lower case.

Tickener pushed the door open and I went in after him. A big man in shirtsleeves with heavy striped braces was sitting in a swivel chair looking out the window. With his grizzled balding head and meaty arms he looked like a cop which probably helped him in his calling. Looking out the window was probably a good idea for a crime reporter too. As sure as hell there'd be some of it going on out there. He turned slowly round to face us.

"Hello boy wonder," he said.

Harry laughed a little more heartily than he needed to. "Garth, this is Cliff Hardy, he . . ."

"Private man, I know." He leaned forward to shake hands. "Glad to meet you." I trusted him with my hand and he gave it back to me undamaged.

"Hardy's on a case Garth, and he could use some help. I thought you might have something for him. OK?"

Green waved at him and pulled a cigar out of his shirt pocket.

"I've got a piece on the run," Tickener went on. "I'll just get back to it."

Green waved again and Harry gave me a nod before he scampered off.

"Good bloke, Harry," Green said. He lit the cigar. "Doing well too. What can I do for you? Who do you want the shit on?"

"Not like that. It's criminal history I'm after."

"Why don't you ask your mate Evans?"

"You're well informed."

"Good memory," he grunted. "Read Harry's stuff on the Costello case. You've got the right contact there. Evans is an honest cop."

"That's right and so I can't use him right now. I'm in a bit too deep and there's things I'd rather not say."

He grinned; his big, boozy face broke up into amiable creases and more grizzled grey hair poked out of his nostrils. "I get like that myself sometimes. Let's hear it. I'll help if I can."

I reached over and stubbed out my cigarette in the half tobacco tin he used for an ashtray. "It's pretty general. What do you know about crimes, solved and unsolved, up around Macleay way?"

"A bit — when are we talking about?"

"Twelve years ago, maybe longer."

He leaned back, took a drag on the cigar, sucked the smoke in and blew it at the ceiling. The action brought on a coughing fit which left him red in the face and clutching the edge of his desk. "I've tried everything . . . fucking pipes . . . these things." He waved the cigar. "All the same, I have to do the drawback. All I want to do is smoke fifty plain Turf a day like I used to."

"Why don't you?"

"Too scared." He put the cigar down; a thin column of smoke rose up from it like an Apache signal. "Macleay . . . not too hard to name the big one, bank job in . . . sixty-six."

"What happened?"

"Two men did a Commonwealth bank on a Friday. Took away fifty thousand dollars."

"Never caught?"

"Not a sign."

"The money?"

"Never found. The bank put up a big reward but heard nothing."

"That's strange. Did you cover it yourself?"

Green picked up the cigar again. There was a faint curl of smoke coming from the end and he sucked it into life, blowing out an enormous cloud. He looked at it virtuously. "Yeah. I went up there and looked around. Thought I might get onto something and make a big man of myself. Nothing doing. It was a pretty amateurish job. They got away on foot. Dead lucky."

"How did the cops figure it?"

"Same as me, two roughies who got lucky. The cops dragged in everyone they could think of but got nowhere. I wrote a piece on it . . . hang on."

He lumbered over to a battered filing cabinet under the window. He pulled out a drawer and riffled through the folders standing up inside it. He took one out and back to the desk where he opened it and leafed through some foolscap sheets with news cuttings pasted to them.

"Yeah, here it is." He handed the sheet across to me and I ran my eye over the columns of newsprint. It was a straight recital of the facts including a description of the bandits who'd worn stocking masks and carried sawn-off shotguns. I pushed the sheet back across the desk. Green fiddled with his cigar and looked at the wall over my head. His eyes screwed up and he let out a tired sigh. His first drink was still a good way off.

"Yes?" I said.

"I remember now, there was a whisper about it. They were trying to fit someone up with it, a standover man with some local form."

He butted his cigar and a smell that would soon be a vile reek started to sneak across the desk towards me. I thought that it might help his anti-drawback campaign if he smoked better cigars. I was about to say so when he started drumming his fingers on the desk.

"I'm slipping," he grumbled. "Can't remember his name. Look Hardy, I'm rambling. This of interest to you, this the one?"

"It could be — missing money sounds right. What about the standover man?"

"The name's gone but he went up for rape in Newcastle, young kid. He got ten years."

I heard something click inside my head like a combination lock tumbler coming into place. I sat up sharply. Green looked amusedly at my reaction.

"That's right, they didn't have anything much on him for the Macleay job as I recall, just something about the company he kept. The cops were just as happy to do him on the rape charge. It was open and shut." He leered at me and I winced at the joke. He laughed. "Now you look interested."

"I am. I see a connection. How can I get some dope on this rape case?"

"I thought you were interested in lost money."

"Yes, and lost women. Let me get it straight before I go off half-cocked. What was that about the company he kept, the rapist?"

"Jesus Hardy, it's twelve years ago. I might be confusing it with something else." He picked up the sheets of paper, aligned them and tucked them back in the folder. Handling the relics of the time gave him assurance. "I think it was just that this bloke, whoever he was, used to hang about with an Abo up Macleay way."

"So what? There's lots of them up there."

"That's right but you didn't read the story very thoroughly did you?" He handed it back to me and I read it word by word. One of the tellers said that one of the bandits looked dark under the mask, like an Aborigine. The thing was coming together now. I passed the cutting back.

"Pretty thin."

"That's what I said," Green barked. "Macleay's a racist hole; was then anyway, probably still is. It wasn't much to go on but it was the only whiff the coppers had." He blew a kiss at the wall. "But it died on them."

I leaned forward, excited. "I'm sorry to press you, but the names are important, is there any way to get on to them?"

"Sally Fitch would be your best bet. Get at it from the rape angle. What she doesn't know about criminal fucking isn't worth knowing. I'll take you along."

We left the room and he moved along the corridor in that light, fast way that some big men can. He must have weighed sixteen stone and no-one got in his way. He nodded to people and I kept an eye out for the crew-cut redhead but she didn't show. Green poked his head through a door then went in and I followed. It was another thirty-desk room with a good deal of noise and screwed up paper. Green ushered me across to a corner where a pot plant, a hat stand and a filing cabinet sheltered one desk a bit from the hurly-burly. He introduced me to the woman behind the desk; they ribbed each other about their drinking, smoking and other vices. Green shook my hand again and went away.

Sally Fitch was a lean blonde in her thirties. Her hair was rather faded and she showed signs of wear and tear; there was a scar running down the left side of her face that she covered with make-up. She was a good-looking woman, nonetheless. She lit a cigarette and looked me over with steady green eyes that wouldn't be surprised at anything, not even if I leaped up that minute and threw myself out the window.

"What can I tell you that Garth can't, Mr Hardy?" she asked. "Like those virtuous private eyes I can say I don't do divorce work."

I laughed. "I do when I can get it. It's getting rarer."

Her eyebrows went up. "Divorce is?"

"No, the dirty work those virtuous private eyes say 'I don't do' to."

She tapped ash off her cigarette and pushed it about in the glass ashtray. "Good thing too. Mine was as dirty as you'd hope to see. Well then, what?"

"I want to know all you can tell me about a rape case in Newcastle around 1966 or '67 — all the names, all the details. I don't have time to look up the papers and my guess is it wouldn't have made the papers anyway."

"Why?"

"If I'm on the right track, the girl involved would have been a juvenile, very much so."

She drew on her cigarette and let the smoke trickle out through her nostrils, an unusual thing for a woman to do. On her it looked amusing and I grinned. She didn't notice. She scribbled "1967" and "Newcastle" on a blotter in front of her and drew lines around it. She embellished the lines, producing an ornate, curly doodle, then she got up and pulled a drawer out of her filing cabinet. Two drawers and some vivid swearing later she lifted out a thin manilla folder. A glossy photograph slipped out and I bent to pick it up.

"Hold on!" She came around the desk and retrieved the picture. "I don't just hand this stuff out willy-nilly." She smiled and softened her voice. "Anyway, don't steal my thunder."

I nodded and waited while she looked through the papers. There wasn't much to it and it didn't take her long. She closed the file and looked up.

"I think this is the one you want. The girl was fifteen, Newcastle, May 1967. It was a bit out of the ordinary; the girl knew the man who raped her. She knew the woman he lived with better. And the girl reported the rape to the police herself. There was a short piece, no details, in the Newcastle paper. No reporting on the trial, that's the law."

"Yes. You've got the names though?"

"Uh-huh. The girl was Naomi Rouble, the man was Joseph Berrigan. The woman he lived with was Patricia Baker."

I nodded. "That's it. It makes sense in a crazy way. What about the photo?"

"The girl. It was taken when she came out of the police station — suppressed of course." She slid it across the desk. The hair was wild and dishevelled, the eyes were puffy from crying and it was eleven long years ago, but the face was unmistakably that of Noni Tarelton.

13

By the time I'd thanked Sally Fitch, looked in on Tickener and cleared the building (no sight of the redhead), it was midday. The streets were crowded with people doing their lunchtime shopping and gawking. George Street was a solid wall of bodies coming the other way and I gave up the battle and ducked into a pub to drink my lunch and do some thinking. I had a steak with the wine and turned the case over in my mind. A constant stream of smooth-voiced chatter from the businessmen pushing out their waistcoats with expense account lunches didn't help, but then there wasn't much to think about. Noni Rouble-Tarelton was on the run with a man who'd raped her eleven years before. He'd killed one person since getting out of jail and savagely beaten two more, both women. Now it looked like he was a blackmailer. There were still questions on all this but a few answers were coming in; the bank robbery and fifty thousand dollars was part of it. On the ethical side was the question of when to let the police in. That troubled me. It always does.

I walked up George Street through the thinning ranks as the slaves went back to work. The rain had cleared away and a pale sunlight was dappling the footpaths and glinting on the oil slicks on the road. I hailed a cruising cab and said I wanted to go to La Perouse. The cabbie was a chunky, greying veteran who looked as if he'd been born behind a steering wheel. He was reluctant about the trip.

"It'll cost you."

"La Perouse," I repeated. "You could get lucky."

He grunted and dropped the flag. He was sour at the possibility of having to drive back to town without a fare, but every profession has its perils. I settled back and endured his company. The traffic was light and we made good time. Long Bay didn't look too bad in the sunlight, especially with the new outside walls. Inside them it was a different matter. I directed the driver through La Perouse's neglected streets and we found the pub where I'd drunk with Jimmy Sunday. I tipped the driver and he forced out some thanks before slamming the door harder than he needed to.

A dark woman was behind the bar. She was sitting on a stool smoking and reading a magazine. Apart from her the bar was empty. I went up and laid a five dollar note on the counter and ordered a middy. She pulled it.

"Jimmy Sunday around?" I asked before she could get her hand on the money. She drew on her cigarette and expelled smoke over my head.

"Might be."

"Will you have one yourself?"

"Tah." She flicked out a glass and slid it under the gin bottle in a smooth, practised movement. I waited while she splashed tonic into the glass, dropped in some ice and made change from the five. She took a sip of the drink and sighed appreciatively.

"You know Jimmy?" she said.

"A bit. I was drinking with him here the night before last. Thought I'd run into him again."

"What's your name?"

I told her. She drank some gin and pulled on the cigarette, it burned down to the filter and she dropped it at her feet. She was a big woman wearing a blouse and jeans. A packet of cigarettes was in the top pocket of the blouse resting on the shelf of her big, stiffly brassiered bosom. She pulled out the cigarettes and got another one going.

"Jimmy's around. Could give 'im a ring if you like."

"Thanks." I drank some beer while she went off to the telephone at the far end of the bar. I wandered over to the wall and looked at the sporting photographs that are a part of the decor of all genuine Australian pubs, symbolising some mystic connection between athleticism and alcohol. The pictures were mostly of racehorses, stretched out near the winning post and standing in the victory ring with flowers around their necks. One of the winning jockeys was an Aborigine but none of the proud owners was anything but true-blue Caucasian. There was a collection of boxing pictures and a cartoonist's attempt at capturing the mystique of the Sands brothers:

Dave, Alfie, Clem, George and Russell stood in a ring with their gloved hands clasped above their heads in the fighter's victory salute. There was a close-up of dark little Elley Bennett landing one of his famous knockout punches on "Mustard" Coleman and another of Bobby Sinn, face wrinkled with concentration, picking off a bewildered Jimmy Carruthers with a classic straight left.

I turned when I heard the door to the bar slapping shut. I suppose I'd expected Sunday and had arranged my face in a grin but it slid away when I saw who'd come in and what they were doing. Ted Williams was slamming home the top bolt on the door. His companion was making shoo-ing gestures at the barmaid. She ducked under the bar and went out through a back door. I heard a key turn in its lock. Williams' mate was an Aborigine, very dark and not young. He couldn't have been more than five-foot-six tall but he must have weighed fifteen stone. He had massive shoulders and a chest like a grizzly bear. He was wearing thongs, jeans and an outsize black T-shirt; his black, wavy hair was slicked down with water as if he'd got out of the shower in a hurry. Williams hadn't changed a bit which meant that he was still a black Goliath. The only difference was that he'd left his smile in Redfern. I opened my mouth to say something but Williams cut me off.

"You said your name was Tickener mate. Now it's Hardy. We don't like gubbs who hang around bullshitting us, do we Tommy?"

The bulldozer shook his head and shuffled forward a few inches.

"No suh, wese don't."

I tried to smile but the joke wasn't for me and my mouth was desert dry. I backed off towards the bar with my near-empty glass in my hand. I wished it was a gun. I wished I were somewhere else. Tommy looked me up and down and came forward again, this time with the light, balletic step of a trained fighter. His massive arms swung loose at his sides and he turned them over like a man cranking a car engine. The bar top ground hard into my spine and there was nowhere else to go.

"Who're you?" I croaked. "I was expecting Jimmy Sunday."

He grinned and slammed one fist into a palm.

"Jimmy's busy," he growled, "I come to take care of you meself."

"You know Jimmy?" I was desperate, using Sunday's name as a talisman.

He moved closer and from the way he moved I could tell that he wasn't planning to waste any more breath on words. It wasn't a negotiable situation. I wished I had Carlo's blackjack. The glass in my hand felt as useless as a yo-yo. His eyes under heavy bushy brows were focused on my hands and feet the way every bar-room heavyweight knows to do. To hell with the look in the eyes — if you know your business that's going to be fear. I slid along the bar just to stop myself from freezing up and to give him a moving target. But I had to stop somewhere and I did so where the bar met the wall. I let him get within punching distance and made a shaping-up gesture with about as much threat in it as a pas-de-deux. His punch came in hard and fast but he was a little bound up by fat and I leaned away from it. He lost balance for a fraction of a second and I clipped him on the ear as hard as I could while on the retreat. If I thought that'd win me a little respect I was wrong; he rushed at me like a bull crowding a matador into a *barrio*. He half-caught me but I twisted free and ground my elbow into the same ear. It didn't seem to bother him; he circled with his arms outstretched and seemed to cut off half the room.

I backed away and cornered myself again over by the table where the elders had been playing cards. I stumbled against a chair and he came forward and threw a right at my belly. He was more than half a foot shorter than me and the punch was straight and full-forced. I rode back from it a bit but it knocked wind out of me and jellied my legs. He came on and I cocked my right for a haymaker to the head. He couldn't have cared less and kept coming. I braced myself and swung my foot short and hard up into his crotch. He doubled over. He'd expected a fancy fist fight and I didn't give him a chance to correct his mistake. I shuffled fast and delivered the foot again to the same spot. He started to crumble and I bunched my fingers and drove into his fleshy neck below the ear. I felt the muscle under the skin resist and then the knuckle bit into the veins and cartilage. He dropped in a heap and crashed his head on a table edge on the way down. As he fell, the breath wheezed out of him and I had a flash of memory about the sound. It was like the noise I'd heard in the car in the split second before my head caved in.

Williams hadn't moved from the door. I eased my way out from the table and went across to the bar. I reached over it and pulled up a schooner glass which I filled with beer from the tap-gun the woman had left lying on the rusty tray. I took a deep drink and waited for my heart to settle back to a normal pace. Tommy was lying with his feet drawn up to his bulging belly. I set the glass down next to him. His eyes were open and he was concentrating everything he had on his pain. His dark skin had a yellowish tinge and some veins had broken in the whites of his eyes making them a murky pink. The harsh breath was coming regularly but with enormous effort. I was safe from him for at least ten minutes. A sound behind me made me turn as the barmaid came through her door at the back of the bar. She stared down at the man on the floor and then up at me with a new respect.

"Jesus," she breathed. "What did you hit him with?"

"This." I held up my fist which was swollen from the neck-punch and bleeding around the knuckles from the earlier tap.

"Jesus, do you know who that is?"

I looked at him again and tried to imagine him years younger and without the fat, as a chunky welterweight perhaps. But I couldn't place him.

"No. Fighter was he?"

"That's Tommy Jerome," Williams said quietly.

I let out my breath in a whistle and felt back for the support of the bar. The jelly feeling had come back into my legs and I suddenly felt very, very tired. Tommy Jerome had killed two men in the ring and had beaten others so savagely that he'd run out of opponents. He was number one contender for the Australian welter and middleweight titles for a couple of years but he never got a shot at the titles because no fight manager wanted his meal ticket wrecked that badly. The championships changed hands a couple of times while Jerome sat there at number one. I'd read that he'd gone to England and lost a few fights there which could have only one explanation. That was ten or more years ago and he'd gone to seed badly. Still, I was glad I hadn't known who he was before I hit him.

"I got lucky," I said to the barmaid. "He thought I'd fight fair."

"Lucky? Fair or unfair, you're lucky to still have teeth." She lit a cigarette and looked across at Williams. If it was a challenge he wasn't taking it up. There'd been enough talking, now I had to get something done. I reached for my change on the bar and detached two dollars. I went around the bar and made her a gin and tonic and pulled a middy for Williams. I gave them the drinks and dropped the money on the till. There was a rattle at the locked door but we ignored it. Neither Williams nor the barmaid was happy with the situation but they seemed to have run out of ideas. They took the drinks.

"Right. Now I want Jimmy Sunday. Where is he?"

They drank but didn't answer.

"Look," I said to Williams. "I gave you a wrong name. OK, I'm sorry but I had reasons. Get Sunday here and you'll see what I mean." I jerked my thumb at Jerome who was lying crumpled and still. "What do I have to do, eat his kidney fat?"

"I'll get Jimmy for you." The barmaid moved off to the phone.

"Where is he?"

"Sharkey's."

"Call him."

She did. A voice came on the line and I grabbed the phone. Sunday didn't sound surprised to hear me and said he'd come straight down to the pub. The barmaid had picked up a cloth and begun polishing glasses. She was humming "Get me to the church on time". I went over and slid down the door bolt and opened the door. Sunday was jogging easily down the street and I stood back with the door open and waved him in. The barmaid flicked some money out of my change and pulled a beer. She slid it along the counter to Sunday who grabbed it and went over to look at Jerome. He'd straightened up a bit and was trying to prop his back against the wall. He made it and massaged his crotch with both hands. A vein was throbbing hard in his forehead and there were bubbles of saliva at the corner of his mouth. I stepped quietly across and handed him the two-thirds-full schooner. He wrapped a big, dark hand around it and lifted it to his mouth.

"This is the guy who bashed me the other night," I said to Sunday. "He came back for a second go and got careless." I took Sunday by the arm and steered him to a chair. I got the makings out, made a cigarette and put the tobacco on the table like a peace offering. "Now, you tell me what's going on around here," I waved to indicate the room and the world outside, "and I'll tell you what's going on in here." I rapped my bleeding knuckles against the side of my head.

Sunday looked at my fist and took a long pull on his beer. "Silly bastard Tommy," he said. "I told him you were alright."

"You're a fuckin' Uncle Tom, Jimmy," Jerome rasped out from his position against the wall. "Always were."

"Will you knock it off," I snarled. "Jimmy, can you tell me what all this heavy stuff is in aid of?"

Sunday mused for a second, then lifted his hand. "Sadie, four beers and a drink for yourself. You've got a say in this. Come on over here." He reached into his pocket. The barmaid got the drinks and carried them over on a tin tray. She asked Jerome if he could get up.

"Yeah, if I have to." He pulled himself up from the wall and eased his bulk into a chair. I reached down for the schooner and put it on the table. He drained it in a gulp. He still hadn't spoken to me. Sadie distributed the drinks and Sunday rolled a cigarette from my makings.

"Ever heard of a bloke named Coluzzi?" he asked me.

"Heard of him and met him," I said.

"Doesn't surprise me one bit," Jerome muttered. Sadie hushed him. "Let him talk."

Sunday drew in smoke and gagged on it. "Shit, this stuff's terrible. Well, this Coluzzi's trying to take over the fights. Reckons he can get boxing back on TV. Whole thing's been very quiet lately."

"Yes," I said, "since that Yank was killed."

Sunday nodded. "Right, well we're all for more fights, but we hear this dago wants to set it up all his way."

"He told me he wanted to match Italians and Aborigines. Good for the gate."

"Yeah," Jerome snorted, "how many do you reckon the Kooris'd win?"

"He was vague on that point," I admitted.

"I'll bet he was," Sadie spat. "I've got a son, he's just starting in clubs, they tell me he's good."

Jerome and Sunday nodded solemnly.

"I hate bloody boxing," Sadie went on. "I reckon it's ruined more good men than anything except the war. Still, my Chris's dead keen on it and I want him to get a fair go. He'll have to lose more'n he'll win if this Coluzzi gets hold of it."

"It's nothin' new," Jerome said bitterly. "Everyone has to throw a few on the way up . . . used to, anyway. I threw 'em on the way down."

"That's right Tommy," Sunday said soothingly. "That's why it's got to change, especially now."

"Jacko Moody," I said.

They nodded and everyone drank. It was like a salute but not a cheerful one.

"Jacko's a champion for sure," Sunday said. "You'd agree with that?"

"With luck and good management, yes."

"He's fucked before he starts if Coluzzi gets him," Jerome said.

"He hasn't got a contract has he? He's barely out of the prelims."

"He's barely out of the bush too," Sunday spoke slowly. "He's got a sort of contract with Trueman, he signed something. He was so anxious to get into the game he did what Trueman told him. He doesn't know exactly what he agreed to. What's sure is that Trueman's in with Coluzzi and he'll do a deal on Jacko if the money's right."

"So will this bastard," Jerome grunted.

I slammed my glass onto the table top. "Well let's talk about that! What brought you down on me Jerome?"

Jerome knocked back some of his beer and scowled at me across the table. Physically he was almost a monster but his brain appeared to be working well enough. He held up thick fingers with enormously broad nails as he made the points.

"You were at Trueman's gym when Coluzzi was there and you stopped a row. You lied about who you were to Ted here and one of Coluzzi's boys escorted you out of Redfern. Then you fuckin' come down here pokin' around and looking for Ricky. I didn't trust him either. That was enough for me. You admit you know Coluzzi."

"I can explain it," I said, "but it's a long story and not much of it is to do with what we're talking about now."

"Double bloody Dutch," Jerome growled.

"Easy Tommy," Sunday said, "I told you this Hardy was alright, you didn't need to bash him."

"You wouldn't take me like that again Hardy."

"I know I wouldn't Jerome. But if we can get over all that we could do something useful about this fight business." I could feel the racial disharmony mounting and the need for some practical, immediate proposal to deflate it. I'd been ready to sell Coluzzi out the minute I was sure I could get away from him alive. This was a bit earlier than I'd have chosen and it was hard work dealing with a hot-head like Jerome. Sunday was in better control of himself though and I felt I could work something out with him.

"We can do our own planning," Jerome said.

"Sure you can, but could you get Coluzzi and his mob in a particular place at a particular time?"

"No way," Sadie put in. "Those dagoes are dead scared of our boys. They carry guns, too."

"OK, OK," Sunday said impatiently. "We'd have trouble getting close enough to Coluzzi to smell the garlic. What's your idea?"

"I'll look into Trueman's connections with Coluzzi and if there's anything in that I'll give it to Tickener. He'll screw them in the paper. And I'll set up a meeting with Coluzzi and have Jerome and a few others along, that should be fun."

"It sounds a bit fancy to me," Jerome said.

"Yeah, it's fancier than hitting people over the head with boomerangs, but where did that ever get anyone?"

Sadie laughed. "Drink up and I'll shout. I reckon it sounds alright. Jimmy?"

Sunday and I drained our glasses. Sadie and Williams did the same. Sadie put them on the tin tray.

"I'm on," Sunday said quietly. "Ted?"

"Me too. I'll go and see Jacko and word him up a bit. He's a nervy bastard Jacko and he's worried about this Rosso."

"Why?" I asked. "He can beat him."

"I reckon, but he says Trueman's teaching him some trick or something." Williams' voice trailed off vaguely.

"Sounds fishy," Sunday muttered. "Jacko wouldn't need any tricks to take the Italian."

Sadie came back with the drinks. Jerome grabbed his and downed it in two swallows.

"It'll be the death of you Tommy," Sadie said.

Jerome wiped his mouth. "Yeah, what a pity. Well, I gotta go."

With a little imagination I could include myself in the farewell. I decided to and to follow it up.

"Before you go, can you tell me why you don't trust Ricky Simmonds?"

"Don't?"

"Slip of the tongue. Didn't, then?"

Jerome looked at our faces in turn and let his eyes rest on mine. Then he shook his head. "I'm not talking personal about one of ours to you Hardy. You might be alright like Jimmy says — we'll see." Pain shot through him and he winced as he stood up. He kept himself straight though and walked out of the pub. The door slammed behind him and Sunday let out a long, relieved breath.

"It's lucky you're a good talker Hardy," he said. "Wouldn't have fancied your chances in a re-match."

"You're so right." We drank and didn't say anything for a few minutes. The door opened and two men came in brushing water off their clothes and swearing about the weather. Sadie got up and went behind the bar to serve them. I could hear the swish of tyres on the road outside. The fine day had caved in, the way it can in Sydney, in a few minutes, without warning.

14

I signalled to Sadie for another round. "This'll do me," I said. "I've got things on tonight, I can't be pissed."

Sunday nodded, then he tapped himself on the forehead.

"Got a message for you. Forgot with all this boxin' business going on. From Penny. She wanted to get in touch with you. Reckoned she saw Noni."

"Where?"

"I dunno. Not around here. Penny moved out the other night and went into town somewhere. She phoned me and wanted to talk to you. She'd forgotten your last name. I said you'd be in the book. Are you?"

I didn't answer. Sadie came with the beer and I drank automatically although thirst had long since been defeated. It sounded odd, help from an unexpected quarter at this stage of the game. Again I got the feeling that events were being stage-managed, directed from on high but why and by whom I didn't know. Noni on the loose fitted in with the feeling I had that she wasn't in direct danger, but the further involvement of Penny I hadn't anticipated. Images of the two girls, black and white, formed in my mind. The black girl, young and clean, nursing a corroding hate of the white girl with the murky past. Sunday snapped his fingers in front of my face.

"Hey! Hey Hardy! You there man?"

I came out of it. "Yes. Just thinking. Did she say where she'd seen her? Noni?"

"No, we didn't chat. Seemed like it was just then, this morning about ten, but that was just a feeling. Listen, you've got to take it easy with Penny, Hardy."

"What do you mean?"

He drank some beer and pulled on his thin cigarette. It burned fiercely and unevenly down one side and he flicked the ash off into a

510

beer puddle. Williams was sitting massive and still beside him. I thought I had never seen a man so passive but it was a menacing passivity, like a reservoir of emotion, dammed up, able to be burst.

"Penny's got a lot of guts, you know?" Sunday said jerkily. "She's real determined. Anything she wants she goes after and nothin' stops her. Some people down here say she's a bit cracked."

"I could see she was out of the ordinary. Why cracked though?"

He leaned back in his chair and expelled smoke through the battered gristle and bone that had once been a nose. My feeling was that Sunday saw himself as a leader, a wise and respected man, and was building up that role little by little every day. That was the way it was done and one mistake could ruin it all. He knew me for what I was, a functionary, a weapon of white society and he wanted to keep me trained on my own kind, but he needed to reveal a little of what he knew to hold me that way.

"Down here there's three kinds, much the same as up in town. There's the ones that don't give shit. Just get pissed, do what they have to do and die. There's the whingers and bludgers who moan about bein' black and disadvantaged and do fuck all about it. Then there's the goers who try to change things, don't piss their brains away, don't whinge."

"You're a goer?"

"Bloody oath I am. Penny is too, but in a different way. She's a bit of a loner, reckoned she wouldn't take any government money. Make it on her own then hit the whites for everything she could, that was her idea. She was starting to study law. Get the idea?"

"I think so. Why do you talk as if this was all in the past?"

"Well, that's the trouble. She used to go on with all this stuff, get people's backs up too, but a lot knew she was talking sense. Then she fell for Ricky . . . bad — you know? And Ricky's nothing special, bit of a no-hoper like his Dad. Penny reckoned she could reform him but he didn't pay any attention, and people laughed at her then. I mean Ricky just didn't fit in with Penny's ideas about life. That made Penny crazy on the subject of Noni. You probably saw that yourself?"

"Yes."

"She's been heard to say she'd kill her."

I let out a breath. "That'd be all we need. I better call my answering

511

service to see if she's left a message." I was pretty sure there'd be no message. What Penny wouldn't trust to Sunday she wouldn't leave with an impersonal recorded voice. I got up to go to the phone and something Sunday had said came through the channels again. I leaned over him resting my hands on the table.

"Don't take this wrong, it's all in confidence, but what did you say about Ricky's father?"

"Said he was a bit of a no-hoper. Right Ted?"

Williams nodded and there was something collusive in that nod. I had the feeling that whatever information I got about Ricky's father, it wouldn't be the whole story.

"He did some time," Sunday went on. "Small stuff. He's dead now."

"Sure of that?"

"Must be. Vanished years ago." He opened his hands.

"Were he and Ricky close?"

Sunday sighed and I knew I was pushing it. "No," he said.

"How was that?"

"Dunno. Ricky's old man went off him when he was a nipper. Happens."

"Not often."

Sunday shrugged.

"Have you ever heard of a man called Joseph Berrigan?"

"No." He enveloped the word in smoke.

"You don't seem sure."

"It rings a bell. Can't place it though. Something to do with Ricky."

I shook my head. "Jesus, this is getting complicated." I went over to the bar phone and rang my service but there was no message. I got money out and reckoned up with Sadie. The bar was starting to fill up and my fighting hand was throbbing and the beer had made my thinking thick and sluggish. I felt that one more piece of information might make the pattern clear to me, might explain why a girl was running with a man who'd raped her. And fifty thousand dollars was a lot of money to be still missing. Age would not weary it nor the years condemn.

"What's this about, Hardy? Where's Noni?"

"Kidnapped, Jimmy, that's the way it looks anyway."

Sunday traced a design in the spilt beer. "Always thought it was wrong, Noni and Ricky and that. What's her chances, Hardy?"

"I don't know. Is there anything you can think of that might help?"

"You don't think one of us done it do you?" Williams said gruffly.

"No, but there's missing pieces everywhere. Ricky, he's a real mystery."

"Why?" Sunday snapped. "Flash young bloke, bad boxer, good fucker who liked white meat."

"So I've heard. What was wrong with his boxing? Ted here said it was too much bed not enough sleep."

"Not altogether," Sunday said. "That was part of it. You see him fight Ted?"

"No. Just in training, sparring."

"Yeah, well he was fast enough, his legs were alright and he was game but his left was no good, stiff like. He was in a car crash when he was young, got spiked through here." He indicated the left side of his chest.

He seemed about to say something more but he stopped himself. I was aware again of their suspicion of me. They held back as a matter of experience and pride. Pride is a hard quality to deal with in an investigation — it holds secrets and distorts facts.

"One last thing Jimmy," I said slowly. "Where do you put Ricky in that list of yours?"

"Ricky doesn't go on a bloody list," Williams said harshly. His emergence from passivity gave his words unusual force. "Rick was different, he had . . . power."

"Power," I said.

"Yeah, some people say he was a bit mad after that accident." He was sorry as soon as the words were out and ended lamely. "He wasn't mad, he had power."

I nodded and knew I had all I was going to get. Sunday gave me the Sharkeys' telephone number and I said I'd be in touch. Williams grunted goodbye without committing himself.

The rain was a fine mist, veiling the buildings and traffic. I hunched my shoulders against it and ran for a bus stop. After a half hour wait I caught a passing taxi. The alcohol, the tension and the fresh air had done strange things to my brain. I felt I had two heads: one of them was thinking about Sunday, Coluzzi, Moody and boxing; the other about Noni, Berrigan, blackmail and bank robbery. I tried to switch off the first head as we ripped along the freeway back to the second head's problems.

15

It was close to five o'clock when the taxi dropped me in St Peters Street. I skipped through the rain and used my key on the door of my office building. The other tenants had cleared out for the day. Trade was bad. I went up to my office, picked up the mail from the floor and settled down behind my desk. The one cheque in the collection was small enough to remind me that I had to get some more money from Tarelton. The bills could wait. I dropped them into a drawer. A fat, colourful envelope offered me the chance to win a split-level home north of Townsville with a stud farm, Mercedes sedan and power boat thrown in. I looked at the pictures; nice, pretty house, pretty horses, pretty beach. I fished out five dollars and started to fill in the ticket blanks, then I noticed that it said "No cash. Cheques or money orders only". I screwed the stuff up and dropped it in the waste bin. Then the phone rang.

"Cliff? Grant Evans."

I dragged my hand wearily across my face. "Shit, don't tell me the building's surrounded and there's no escape."

"Knock off the bullshit. I thought you were going to report in?"

"Who said that?"

"That was my understanding."

"You misunderstood, mate."

"Like that, is it? Look, this is not time for games Cliff. This thing is hotting up."

I made a non-committal noise and he went on.

"You're on the scene up Macleay way, we hear. You get around all the best murders don't you?"

"She's not dead."

"Bloody near it. I suppose you saw the grass?"

"Is *that* what it was?"

"Lot of it Cliff, and there's an enquiry on."

"I know."

"Do you know two Italians, one tall one short?"

"Yeah, Primo Carnera and Carlo Ponti."

"Terrific Cliff, you're a ball of style and you've told all the jokes. Now I'm going to tell one. Heard the one about the private detective who lost his licence for withholding information from the police?"

"No."

"Yeah, he's a bus conductor, makes a hundred and fifty bucks a week and gets to wear a nice green uniform. Meets a lot of people and travels all over town."

"Sounds nice."

"He misses the glamour. Listen Cliff, I'm serious. We're under real pressure to look good with these enquiries on. I'm appealing to your better nature."

"I can't tell you anything yet Grant. Give me twenty-four hours, maybe thirty."

"No."

"You have to. You owe me."

There was a silence, then he said: "I owe you one. Are you calling it in?"

"I have to Grant."

"OK." He paused. "Thirty hours."

"Thanks. And one thing — where's Simmonds' body?"

"Just around the corner from you, cock. Glebe morgue."

He hung up. The line buzzed emptily and I put the receiver down. I swivelled around on my chair and looked out the window at the city. The light was just about gone and the buildings were drained of colour. They were all grey, and it didn't matter whether they were insurance offices or churches, they were just shapes. The tops of the park trees were waving in the wind like dark, threatening tentacles. It was a good night to be with someone you knew well, in a place you liked with some good food and wine. The air in the office smelled old and stale as if it had been packaged and put there and was due for a change.

I called Saul James at home and got no answer. They pulled him out of a rehearsal at the theatre and he told me that he'd have the money tomorrow. I said I'd collect it. Madeline Tarelton answered the phone again and said that Ted was out. He'd left a message for me that the money would be ready by noon tomorrow. I told her I'd be around to wait for the call. She seemed to want to talk but I wasn't in the mood.

"What will you do between now and then?" she asked. There might have been a hint of invitation in that, but I didn't want to know, not then.

"Investigate the living tonight. Tomorrow morning I'm going to look at a dead black man. A shotgun took his face away."

It chilled her and she rang off. I left the building.

I caught a bus back to Glebe and had it to myself for most of the way. I got off near the pub, bought wine, and walked the rest of the distance. Harry Soames next door had guests. That meant they would smoke a lot of grass and sit around listening to music through headphones. Soames had installed headphones in the bathroom, in the garden. I didn't know what sort of music he listened to any more and that suited me fine. I went into the house, drank wine, showered, drank wine, cooked an omelette and drank more wine. By nine o'clock I was as ready to break the law as I'd ever be.

I had on sneakers, dark jeans and sweater and a denim jacket. The wine glow lasted through the bus ride to the university and the tramp across the campus into Newtown. It lasted while I waited for the stragglers to leave the pub across from Trueman's gym and there was just enough of it left for steady hands and quiet feet as I skeleton-keyed the lock to the old building. I went up the stairs by the thin beam of a pencil torch and the keys took me through the door into the gym as if I owned the place. It wasn't my first burglary or my tenth, but I was nervous. There aren't any faithful bobbies on the beat checking the doors and windows these days, especially in Newtown, but unusual lights or noises can still draw attention and I had no excuses. Trueman hated my guts and if I was caught at this he'd play it for all it was worth.

The gym smelled of the day's sweat and smoke as I sneakered through to the office. The door wasn't locked. Sammy wouldn't keep any money here and that accounted for the absence of burglar alarms too. Sammy had had a little celebration it seemed; a Scotch bottle stood empty on the battered pine desk and beer cans and plastic cups were strewn around. The room had a heavy, rich odour produced by liquor, tobacco and human bodies. The party mess only added to what was already a mess. Trueman kept papers on spikes, in drawers, on top of chairs and on the floor. Pictures of past fighters were Sellotaped to the walls and papers were slid in behind them; letters were stuck between the pages of racing guides and bills and receipts bristled from the pocket of an old raincoat hanging on the back of the office door. It looked so unsystematic as to be burglar proof. I wasted minutes flicking through the relics of Sammy's past failures and found nothing more recent than a picture of Tony Mundine captioned wishfully "The next cruiserweight King".

I sat in Sammy's chair and thought as well as my noisy heart would let me. Maybe there was nothing here. Maybe I'd have to try Trueman's house. That would be a very different proposition; Sammy had a few boys from the country living with him always and I didn't fancy padding about in the dark in a house full of fighters. Ted Tarelton had a lot of money and I'd probably be covered for the bridge work and jaw wiring, but they say it alters the shape of the face and I was fairly content with the face I had. I fiddled with it now the way you do when you're thinking hard; moved sections of it about and pulled bits of it. There was no way of getting inside Sammy's mind to crack his system and that was a disgusting thought anyway. Its whole area was probably occupied by beer, boxing and bathing beauties. That led me alliteratively to books and to the one example of the animal in the office — a half-dead copy of Ray Mitchell's *The Fighting Sands* and that led me to Jacko Moody's contract. Or copies of it.

They were carbons, folded down the centre and tucked inside the book which was lying on top of Medibank forms. The contract tied Moody up for two years and was due to expire in a month. It was the standard thing; Trueman collected expenses and fees out of Moody's purses and had sole rights to OK and veto matches. It was hard to see what the fighter himself could have been getting out of his penny-ante preliminary earnings. It was legal and binding as far as I could tell but the expiry date made Trueman vulnerable. That is, if another contract hadn't been signed. With Coluzzi's schemes still in the planning stage that seemed unlikely. I took one of the copies and put it in my pocket.

I was straightening the papers when a noise out in the gym made me freeze. I clicked off the light and the tiny noise sounded like a gunshot. Four steps took me over to the door which I'd left open and I peered out into the darkness of the big, pungent room. I could hear feet shuffling on the floor and harsh, stifled breathing. I slid out of the office and along the nearest wall. No weapons came to hand and the torch was slim, elegant and useless. There was a muttered curse in the darkness and a floundering, stumbling noise and I used the cover of it to make it across to the locker bay. I pressed myself back against the cold metal and ran a hand across the top of the set of lockers feeling for a weapon. Nothing . . . just dust. I was fighting against a shattering sneeze when the light over the ring came on.

A man was standing in the middle of the ring holding his hands up above his head. As a picture of athletic triumph it was spoiled by the bottle in his hand. He kept one hand raised, brought the other, the one holding the bottle, down and took a long, gargling drink. He walked carefully over to the red corner and set the bottle down on the stool. Then he moved back to centre ring and began to shadow-box. He was as drunk as an owl and his movements were a broken, unco-ordinated parody of the boxer's grace. He blundered into the ropes, fell and crawled across to the stool. The sleeve of his coat had come down across his hand; it was a cast-off coat, a derro coat, and he fought for what seemed like minutes to get clear of it and to get hold of the bottle. He made it and took a quick slug. He pulled himself up by the ropes and struck the attitude of a fight announcer. He mimed pulling a microphone down from the roof.

"Ladeez an' gennlemen," he bellowed, "fifteen roun's of boxing, for the lightweight champeenship of th' world. In th' red corner," he pointed to the bottle, "at nine stone nine pounds, Taffy . . . Taffy Thomas." He flung out his arm, lost balance and collapsed to the floor. He tried to pull himself up again but thought better of it. He crawled to the corner again and used the bottle. It fell from his hand onto the apron of the ring and off to the floor. He pitched forward, rested his head on his arms and went to sleep. I came across to look at him; the ear showing was cauliflowered and his body was pear-shaped and dumpy inside the formless coat. I'd never seen him fight but I'd heard about him. It wasn't that long ago.

I doused the light and left the gym.

It was after midnight when I got home. The house next door was dark and quiet; no-one around to spot Raffles sneaking back with His Lordship's silver. I'd forgotten to check the mailbox earlier and I reached into it now and pulled out an airletter. I read it over a cigarette and a glass of wine. Ailsa was in Samoa and missing me; I was in Sydney and missing her and Samoa. I distributed the papers I'd taken from Trueman's office among the pages of the three volumes of Bertrand Russell's autobiography. Cyn had bought me the books, one by one, as they'd come out, and written inscriptions in them. I didn't read the inscriptions. There was dust on the books and I opened and closed them hard, blew on them and put them back on the shelves. I didn't spend enough time at home to get around to dusting bookshelves. There were probably silverfish too, maybe mice. It would be a good house for mice, nice and quiet with just the occasional scrap of food around. I went upstairs to bed, quietly, so as not to disturb my mice.

The city morgue is in the basement of a low, long building the colour of dried blood. The building houses the Coroner's Court and the Forensic Medicine division; the live people go in the front off Parramatta Road, the dead ones go in the back off Arundel Street.

The desk attendant was thin and hatchet-faced. He wore a narrow black tie, a brilliantly white shirt and an even whiter coat. I showed him my licence and told him my business and he didn't like any of it. His voice was a thin bleat: "I haven't the requisite authority to show cadavers to members of the public."

"I don't want to see your whole collection — just one."

"The rule applies."

"I'm investigating his death."

"Not officially, and you have no proof of that."

I needed a name. Not Evans. He wouldn't bail me out of this. I reached around in my mind and came up with it.

"Dr Foster, the police forensic man will OK it," I said. "Call him and see."

It was bluff and weak as a politician's promise but it did the trick. He didn't want to bother the brass.

"Very well. Take this down those stairs and show the man at the door." He scribbled the time, date and three initials on a card and pointed to a set of stairs descending into the bowels of the earth. I went down three flights. It got cooler and the tiles got bleaker and my steps rang sharply in the still, clinical air.

The man at the door was the exact opposite of his counterpart upstairs. He was red-faced and cheerful, over-weight and scruffy around the neck and lapels. He took the card and stuffed it into the torn pocket of his coat.

"Through here mate," he chirped. "Keep your breakfast down won't you."

I said I would and followed him through a set of heavy perspex doors. The room reminded me of a changing room at a swimming pool. It had a concrete floor and mirrors at either end. It was white-tiled with a green strip around it at shoulder height for a touch of gaiety. The fluorescent light was harsh and instead of the swimming pool's smell of chlorine and sweat this place reeked of formaldehyde. There were steel handles sticking out of the walls, waist high at six-foot intervals. We stood in the centre of the room by a bench that had straps attached to it and a shallow basin mounted beside it. A gutter ran from the basin to a channel in the floor. The attendant asked me who I wanted to see as if he was in charge of a theatre dressing room. I told him.

"Ah yes," he crooned, "black beauty." His voice was still chirpy and his step was jaunty. I expected him to break into a dance routine.

He went over to the far wall, pulled on a handle and a seven-foot long, three-foot wide tray slid out soundlessly.

The attendant twitched the calico sheet aside. The naked body was pale under the harsh light, scarcely darker than a suntanned European, but it was the same colour all over. I looked down at the corpse but it wasn't like looking at a person. There was no face. The mangled head had been sprayed with something which had made it a dark, featureless blob. I leaned over and looked closely at the left side of the chest. The flesh had been burned and shattered by the shotgun blast. Bone and other matter obtruded from the hundreds of small wounds which added up to a massive injury. The attendant looked at me oddly.

"Something?" he asked.

I straightened up. "I wanted to see whether he had a scar on his chest, here."

"It should be on the report. Oh, I see what you mean. I'll get the report anyway. Finished?"

I said I was. He slid the tray back and we left the room. In the cubicle at the foot of the stairs a couple of rows of clipboards with papers affixed hung on hooks. He reached one down and scanned the top page.

"Male Aboriginal, aged . . . about twenty-five years . . . ah . . . no, . . . scar on leg . . ." He flipped the page. "Autopsy . . . massive haemorrhage . . ."

"Any mention of an old chest wound?"

"Ah . . . no, but then you wouldn't expect it, would you, not with that lot."

I said I supposed not and thanked him for his help. He gave me a cheery smile and ducked back into his cubicle. I had my foot on the first step when he stuck his head out.

"Here, take your card back. The old chap who came to see him nearly left his here too."

I went back and took the card.

"What old chap?"

"Old Abo. Down here . . . let's see . . . yesterday. Had a police pass. Relative of some kind. He just took one quick look and left. They're superstitious about the dead aren't they?"

"Yeah. So am I. About this man." I described Rupert Sharkey to the attendant but he shook his head.

"No, nothing like that. This man was short and stocky . . . an' older than what you're saying."

"What was the name on the card?"

"I don't remember. He'll have it up at the desk."

I thanked him again and went up. Hatchet-face looked displeased to see me but showed off his efficiency by producing the black man's police pass within seconds. It carried the name Percy White and an address in Redfern. I handed my card in and left the place puzzled, unenlightened — but alive.

I celebrated my condition with a beer in the Forest Lodge hotel up the street from the house of the dead. I bought tobacco and smoked a few cigarettes and let the fumes of liquor and weed take away the stink of death.

Half-way through the second beer I called Sharkeys' number in La Perouse. Sunday was there and I filled him in with what I had on Moody's contract with Trueman. He said Williams had seen Moody and warned him not to sign anything further and the fighter had agreed. Nothing more had been heard from Penny. I asked Sunday about Percy White but he'd never heard of him. As far as he knew, and that was pretty far, Simmonds had no such relative. The description I had could fit a hundred men in La Perouse alone. I asked him if Ricky Simmonds had a scar on his left leg. He laughed.

"I never knew an Aborigine who didn't — falls, burns, sores, insect bites, you should see me."

I grunted something and rang off. I finished the beer, left the pub and walked across to the university library. A quick check of an old city directory told me that the address "Percy White" had given in Redfern didn't exist.

This heavy detecting took me until midday. I bought some Vogel bread sandwiches outside the library and stretched out on the lawn that overlooks Victoria park. The buildings around the quadrangle loomed up behind me, solid and gothic and echoing to the footsteps of the learned. The neophytes gathered on the lawn giving me, an outsider, a wide berth. Almost to a man and a woman they wore jeans, forbidden dress at university back in the days when I'd played briefly at the experience. Otherwise nothing much had changed; the sexes basically grouped apart with only a few of the stars from each side coming into collision. But the lawn lunch-eaters weren't representative. Behind closed pub doors and in smoky studies the drinkers and hairy politicians gathered to plot the overthrow of society within the next semester. The deadly swots were still in the library and the smooth-talking professionals who would control this place and most others like it in a few years, were debating, or running the tennis club or sipping sherry somewhere with their masters. I ate the sandwiches and watched a pair of tight-jeaned women parade slowly across my field of vision. Their breasts jogged gently under linen shirts, their bottoms rode high and tight and their legs seemed to go on forever. I sighed, got up and brushed grass off my clothes. I was sweating. It was a fine day. Maybe I was too warmly dressed.

17

I caught a taxi to Paddington and was met at the door by a flushed and anxious-looking Madeline. She had a couple of dresses over her arm and there were shoes on the floor in the passage behind her.

"Leaving?" I asked.

She bit her lip. The white chunky teeth went into the moist purple lip and sent a sexual shiver through me. She saw my reaction and it didn't throw her one degree off course.

"I am if you must know. Ted's impossible. All that money for that worthless slut . . . the police . . ."

"She's his daughter."

"Maybe — if her mother was anything like her who could say?"

It was nothing to me except that men being left by their wives are apt to act irrationally and Ted couldn't afford to. I said so and she spun away and started to gather up shoes. I came a couple of steps into the passage and tried to keep my mind off the yard of deadly stocking she was showing under a white crepe dress. She saw me looking, straightened up and smoothed the dress down. My mouth went dry.

"You haven't the time," she said softly. "Ted got a call half an hour ago. He was to wait for another call at his office. He's there now with the money — off you run, Mr Hardy."

"Where's the office?" I croaked. She walked off down the hall; she'd spent hours on the walk and it was worth every minute. She came back with a card and I took it.

"Don't leave," I said. "See it through. You're being childish. See how it looks after we get the girl back."

She threw the dresses down and burst into tears. She dumped the shoes and ran off down the hall.

Well done Hardy. Terrific work. So subtle. I closed the door quietly and backed out to the gate. A white Celica was parked outside the house with some clothes on the back seat. The key was in the ignition and Madeline's perfume was in the air. I slid in behind the wheel, started the car and drove off towards the city. I didn't like the new twist. It had an amateur feel. It's easier to watch a house than a city building, easier to spot reinforcements. Then I swore at myself for not scouting Armstrong Street. If there had been a look-out he'd have got the message loud and clear. Maybe it wasn't an amateur play after all.

Ted's office was in a tower block across from Hyde Park. The Celica had a sticker on it that let me drive into the car park under the tower and almost got a salute from the attendant. Ted's suite of offices had a lot of shag pile carpet, stained wood and tinted glass. Here he was Tarelton Enterprises and looking like he could spare a hundred grand, but you can never tell.

An ash blonde stopped pecking at her typewriter and showed me into Ted's lair. The carpet was deeper and the wood more highly polished than outside; there was an interesting-looking bar at the end of the room and that's where Ted was standing. He greeted me and dropped ice into a second glass and built two Scotches. He walked back to his quarter-acre desk and set the glasses down carefully; it wasn't his first drink and it wasn't his second. He waved me to a chair; I picked up the Scotch and sat down — it was a drink to sit down with.

"Got the money?" I asked.

"Sure." He reached down, missed his aim and had to steady himself on the desk. He pulled up a black, metal-bound attache case. "Wanna see it?" He was aping confidence and assurance but it was a bad act.

I nodded. He sprung the locks and pushed the case across the desk. The money lay in neat rows held by the case's straps. It looked what it was — a hell of a lot of cash.

Ted said the call was due at four o'clock and we were twenty minutes short of that. I drank and looked at my employer. He seemed to have shrunk inside his clothes; the expensive tailoring hung on him indifferently and his patterned, Establishment tie was askew. Normally Ted had a high colour — the product of good health, good times and good brandy. Today he was pale with a couple of vivid spots. Bristles that had survived a shaky shave outcropped on the pale skin. His hand shook as he scrabbled a cigar out of a box on the desk. I rolled and lit a cigarette. We drank and my nerves started to twang in the silence.

"I pinched your wife's car," I said. "I think she was planning on leaving. Why don't you ring her?"

"You a bloody marriage counsellor now?"

"Just an idea. You're going to need help through this."

Panic leaped through the liquor and into his eyes. "Why? You don't think they'll . . . they won't kill her?" He looked at the money.

"You can't tell. I don't think so, but it might not be easy getting her back."

"You're saying she's in with them? I told you that's crap. I don't want to hear any more of that."

"Mr Tarelton," I said wearily, "this is nice Scotch but this isn't a nice job. You don't know your daughter, you don't know the first thing about her. I've found out things about her that'd make your hair curl. That's my job. I rake muck and mostly I keep it to myself when I can. Sometimes I can't and this looks like one of those times. Please don't tell me what you don't want to hear. It doesn't help." I'd started to raise my voice. Now I dropped it back to as comfortable a tone as I could manage. "I think it would be a good idea if you called your wife."

He was in no shape to fight. He drained his glass and took a long pull on the cigar. "Alright, alright, you know your business. Jesus, I thought I knew about strain but there's nothing to touch this."

He was getting gabby and I had no use just then for the full story of his life. I pointed at the phone and he picked it up and dialled. He held it to his ear for a minute then slammed it down.

"Engaged," he snarled. "At least she's still there. That blasts your theory . . ."

The intercom buzzed. "I said no calls," Ted barked. He flicked the switch. "No calls till four!" The black box spoke back: "I'm sorry Mr Tarelton, it's your wife on the line, she sounds upset."

"Put her through." Tarelton picked up the receiver and swung half-away from me. He suddenly jerked upright in his chair.

"What!" His voice broke and he stammered, "What? What?"

I mouthed at him to play the call through and he flicked switches clumsily. Madeline Tarelton's voice cut harshly into the room, its elocution-lesson tones pared away by fear.

"Ted, Ted," she gasped, "there's a man here with a gun." Her voice was cut off by a short scream and Tarelton yelped into the phone. "Madeline, Madeline, what does he want? Do what he says."

There was a pause and she spoke again, fighting for control. "He just wants me to tell you to do as you're told." The line went dead. Tarelton looked at the receiver in his hand. He was clutching it as if he could squeeze more information from it. I got up and took it away from him. Then I picked up his glass, went to the bar and made him another drink; he had another phone call to get through and he wasn't going to do it without help. I went back and he took the glass.

"What does it mean?"

"They're making sure. It doesn't change anything."

He sensed my uncertainty and turned his cornered frustration on me.

"It's your fault, you took her car, she'd have been . . ."

"Where? Would you rather that? It's not true anyway. They'd have moved when they were ready. She'll be alright. Shut up and let me think."

He bridled. "Don't . . ."

I flapped a hand at him and he subsided, then the box spoke again.

"A call for you sir. It's just past four o'clock."

"Thank you," Tarelton said weakly. "Put it through please."

"Pay-out time, Ted." The voice was male, not rough, not educated. Australian, not foreign. Tarelton croaked something indistinct.

"The money Tarelton. Have you got it?"

"I've got it. It's here. Let me talk to Noni and if you harm my wife I'll . . ."

"Shut up and listen. The girl's alright. You'll see her tonight. I don't know nothing about your wife. Who's helping you with this — a lawyer, a friend or what?"

"Nobody. You said . . . "

"Don't give me that. You'd have someone. He there with you now?"

"Yes."

528

"What's he look like? Describe him."

Tarelton looked unseeingly at me. His colour was bad and he was working at his shirt collar with one finger.

"Tell him," I said.

"He's tall and dark . . . thin," Tarelton said desperately. "Thin . . ."

"Yeah, I caught that. How old?"

"Late thirties."

"What's he wearing?"

"Dark trousers, grey pullover, light blue . . ." he searched for the word. I gave it to him: "Parka."

"Blue parka."

"What the fuck's that?"

"A sort of jacket. Look, can't we settle this reasonably? Just let my wife go and . . ."

"I told you, I don't know a bloody thing about your wife, now shut up! Send this character with the money to Elkington park in Balmain at six o'clock sharp. Got it?"

"Yes."

"Before he goes tell him to ring Saul James — here's the number . . ." He gave it in a firm confident voice. "Just tell James he's acting for Tarelton. He'll know what to do. Oh, one last thing. Tell your man to go to the park by taxi. That's it."

"But . . ."

"But nothing. Do as you're told and the girl'll be alright. Slip up and I'll cut her bloody throat."

He broke the connection. Sweat was pouring down Tarelton's face which had settled into creases and lines that aged him ten years. He reached for his drink and gulped it.

"Take it easy," I said. "You don't look well. You could have a long wait and you can't keep sucking that stuff down the whole time — you'll crack up."

"You're right," he pushed the glass away as if he meant it. "What do I do next?"

"Call your wife."

He did. The phone must have been snatched up the second it sounded. Their voices over-rode each other and a great gust of relief filled the room.

"He's gone Ted. He just walked out a minute ago."

"He didn't hurt you?"

"No, he didn't touch me, not really. I couldn't have stood it, either." There was a note of horror in her voice of a kind I'd heard before so I wasn't surprised when she said: "He was black, Ted. An Aborigine."

"Shit," Tarelton said.

"Ask her if he was stocky, middle-aged or older, carrying weight."

He did and she said it was an accurate description. I thought of "Percy White" holding his gun on a flower of white womanhood in the hundred-thousand-dollar house. It was a bizarre, cinematic image, unreal, but it had been real enough to terrify those comfortable people through to the marrow. It had been totally effective in securing Tarelton's consent to the kidnapper's terms, but the man on the line had affected to know nothing about it. He was either very tough, a good actor or telling the truth. Either way it was confusing. Tarelton found it so too. He promised his wife that he'd be home within the hour and she rang off. Apparently her thoughts of leaving home had been dispelled. Tarelton stroked his jaw as if to reassure himself that the old familiar truths were still intact.

"What's with the Abos, Hardy? I don't get it."

I picked up the bag and started for the door, then I noticed that I had an inch of Scotch in my glass and I came back and drained it.

"I told you, Noni ran in rough company. This is part of it but I don't know how it all ties together yet. I've got some ideas but this comes first." I held up the bag. "Marked the money?"

"Yeah," he looked ashamed. "That is, I've got a list of the numbers."

"That'll do," I said. "I'll be in touch as soon as I know anything." He nodded and I went out. I was in the car park before I remembered that I hadn't asked if I could use the Celica. Neither had I asked for more money but I was carrying more than I'd ever seen in one go in my life and it hadn't seemed like the right time.

18

The Celica took me to Darlinghurst in five minutes. I parked outside James' house and rang the bell. James opened the door and ushered me in. I could hear voices.

"Television," James said apologetically. Maybe he thought I was one of those people who disapprove of tele-viewing in the daytime. Maybe I was. We went through to the kitchen. He was wearing the same sort of clothes I'd seen him in before; soft shades and fabrics to match his character. His hair had recently been combed when wet and I noticed that it was receding a little at the forehead. I slung the briefcase down on the table.

"What's that?"

"Ted Tarelton's hundred grand. Got your share?"

He blinked at the harshness of my voice. "Yes, here." He pointed to a blue airline bag on the floor.

"Got a list of the numbers?"

He looked surprised. "No, why?"

"So the money can be traced after the pick-up."

He arranged his face virtuously. "I don't care about the money."

I grunted. "Up to you. Got anything to drink?"

"Vodka. In the kitchen."

"I'll fix it," I said. "Want one?"

"Yes, I suppose so, thanks." He slumped in his chair and lit a cigarette. I went out to the kitchen and got the bottle. Smirnoff. Actors always drink vodka. Maybe it makes them feel like Raskolnikov or maybe they just don't like people to smell booze on their breaths. I poured two hefty slugs, chopped bits off a lemon and dumped some ice into the glasses. To my mind the recipe should then read: "Pour down the sink and open a bottle of Scotch" but it was no time to be choosy. I went back into the living room and handed one of

the drinks to James. The second he touched it the phone rang and he
dropped the glass. The liquor splashed onto the rug and spread about
in drops and rivulets like runaway quicksilver. He bent to recover the
glass.

"Answer it!"

He stumbled across the room and snatched up the receiver. His face
was drained of colour and his knuckles were tight and blanched where
he clenched the phone. He opened his mouth to speak and was cut off
by a quick, staccato flow of sound across the wire. He nodded once,
looked up at me and said:

"Yes, yes, he's here."

More nodding, then: "The rotunda . . . towards the water. Yes, I'll
tell him. Taxi, yes . . . Look, is Noni . . ."

I heard the click from across the room. Decisive man with a
telephone, this character. James put the instrument down slowly as if
he was still obeying orders issuing from it.

"You're to leave the money . . ." he began.

"In the rotunda and walk towards the water. Yeah, I gathered that."

"Don't bite my head off."

"Sorry," I said grudgingly. "It's just that I don't like this set-up. It
stinks of double-cross for one thing and there's a phoney feel to it."

He flushed angrily. "What do you mean phoney? Kidnap, ransom."
His anger dropped suddenly away as if he was incapable of holding
any strong emotion for long. A dull stupefied look on his face made
me wonder whether there was any centre to his character at all under
the histrionic shell. He went on lamely: "Do you mean it's all too,
well, dramatic to be real?"

"Not exactly." I couldn't tell him what I meant. I didn't really
know myself. I'd been on the sidelines in one kidnapping that had
ended the worst way a couple of years back and I'd talked to men
who'd been involved in others. I remembered, and had got from
participants, a sense of desperation and urgency that wasn't here now.
Still, the terms were clear and so was my responsibility.

"What do you think will happen?"

"I know what you're hoping for," I said tightly. "You're hoping I'll
drop the money and that your girl will come walking out of the mist

and I'll bring her back and you'll live happily ever after."

His face twisted into a grimace that was part self-pity, part something else.

"You think I'm soft don't you?"

"It doesn't matter what I think. I'm trying to tell you that kidnapping almost never works out sweetly. Someone nearly always gets hurt and people get changed by the experience. Some people begrudge the ransom money for the rest of their lives."

"I've told you, I'm not worried about the money."

"Maybe not. That's not the point. You're not listening to me. Get ready for something rough. If all I hear about this girl is true you're in for a bad time whatever shape she comes out of this in."

The half-hearted anger came back in the form of a pink flush.

"What the hell do you mean by that?"

If I'd thought he was working some kind of deal on the case, some tax dodge or any one of the hundred or so reasons people have for setting these things up, I would have tried to break him with the information I had on the girl's past. But I didn't think that; he'd accepted a lot of things about her that would have sent most people off in the other direction, fast, and his concern for her seemed genuine, if immature. This was no time for self-discovery. I suspected that the events of the next few hours would stamp him as perpetually young or force him to grow up fast.

"Never mind," I said. "I've got to go."

He looked alarmed. "You'll be too early."

I juggled the car keys in my hand and reached for the briefcase and the bag. James moved quickly across to block me.

I brushed him aside roughly. "Look, there are no rules in this game no matter what they say on telly. It's a game of chance. You can't tell what's the right thing to do and what's not. But I'll tell you two things I'm not going to do. One, I'm not going to walk into a park in Balmain after dark carrying a hundred and five thousand bucks without having a look around first. And two, I'm not going to leave myself stranded there with no transport. Sit down. Look, I'll drive to Balmain, scout around and then get a taxi. Got it? Have another drink. Have a couple."

He looked relieved. "Sorry. I didn't mean to tell you your business."

"You've got a right," I said more gently. "It's your girl and your money." He started to speak and I held up my hand. "I know, I know, you don't care about the money. I've got to go. I'll call you when I know something."

Thick dark clouds had blotted out the fine afternoon and heavy rain was falling when I climbed into the Celica and stowed the money on the back seat. A strong wind was whipping the rain around and the spray from other cars cut down the visibility. I crept through the city and picked up speed over the Glebe Island bridge where the lighting was good and the roads were clear. I reached Terry Street half an hour before the appointed time, parked the car in a lane and worked up to the edge of the park using what cover I could. The wind bit in through the light parka and the thought of leaving that much money in the car nagged at me. The .38 inside the jacket where I'd slashed the pocket and reinforced the lining was heavy but a comfort. It was slow to get at it but it was there.

The park runs down from the road to the water and ends in a narrow peninsula with steep, rocky sides. It's bounded by a residential street on one side and by the Dawn Fraser pool and some gardens on the other. The park is about six hundred yards deep and is sixty or seventy yards wide at its broadest point. The rotunda sits in the middle like a salt dish on a table. I hadn't seen it for years but I remembered its vandalised wall linings and smashed fittings and it was unlikely to have changed. I moved up from the street to a point behind a toilet block at the edge of the park and peered into the gloom.

Nothing was moving except one of a pair of swings which creaked like a door in a Gothic mansion. The slides and turnabout were weird, inter-stellar shapes against the harbour mist and drops of water splattered down on me from the ancient Moreton Bay figs. I waited and watched for ten minutes then eased back down to the street. I went back to the car, got in and wrote down the serial numbers of the money in Saul James' bag, then I transferred Tarelton's cash to the soft bag. I walked up to Darling Street holding the bag and trying to feel confident. A taxi U-turned at my whistle and pulled up beside me, splashing water on my legs.

The driver pushed open the front passenger door. "Sorry mate. Where to?"

I got in and took out a two-dollar note. "Around the block and drop me at the entrance to the park. It's a two-dollar ride."

He looked at me quickly, the Sydneysider's suspicion of parks and perverts showing in his eyes but he shrugged and slipped the car into gear.

"You're the boss."

He did the circuit in second and I tried to push an unwanted image from my mind — it was a picture I'd seen of ex-President Gerald Ford looking bulky and unsure in a bullet-proof vest.

I paid off the cab outside the arched sandstone entrance to the park. The pistol butt was cold and hard in my right hand and the plastic handle of the bag was slimy in my left as I went down the short flight of stone steps.

My rubber soles squelched on the wet path as the darkness of the park closed around me. I stared hard ahead of me and around but there was nothing moving that shouldn't have been. The path sloped down slightly to the basin occupied by the rotunda. I could sense eyes on me and the wind seemed to be carrying the sound of harsh breathing and the smell of fear. I went up the steps to the rotunda. It hadn't changed, except to be even more dilapidated. A crazy network of slats hung down from the roof and one of its brick pillars was now a pile of rubble spilling out towards the centre of the concrete floor. A pool of water about six feet across and a few inches deep gleamed in the middle of the circular space. I set the bag down in the centre of it and straightened up slowly.

"Very funny mate." The voice was harsh and thin like a fingernail across a blackboard. "Take the hand out of the jacket and keep it in sight."

I did what he said. The voice seemed to be coming from the front of the rotunda, low down, beneath my eye level. There was a gap between the floor and the railing with plenty of space to see and to shoot through. I held my hands out wide and empty.

"OK. Out you go and walk down to the water. Don't look back or it'll be the last thing you do."

The voice, still harsh and tight, was steady and sounded as if it meant what it said. This was the part I didn't like. I backed out, walked around the side of the structure and started down to the harbour. I thought I might have a chance at him when I'd moved down a bit because it was too dark for good shooting and there was some cover beside the path. The idea died when I heard the voice again. It was much closer. He'd moved around and stood at the top of the path, positioned where he had me in a shooting gallery for a hundred yards, targeted against the lights where the peninsula begins to narrow down. He said "Keep going" and I did, concentrating on getting to the lights without any bullets in my hide. I'd gone about forty feet when I heard a noise like a scuffle behind me and I instinctively dropped down. A muffled shout and a sharp crack and a bullet whined off the concrete ahead of me and to one side. I pulled the gun out and started to crawl to a tree. A bullet thudded into the trunk I was headed for and I twisted round and fired back at the rotunda, aiming low. For no reason I could think of I shouted a word:

"Berrigan!"

The response was a hissing curse. A shape loomed up at the centre of the rotunda, a dark menacing shape that flashed fire at me. I felt leaves and dirt kick up into my face and I fired again and there was a scream and metal rang on concrete.

I rolled off the path and crawled behind a tree. I screwed up my eyes and strained them through the darkness but I couldn't see any movement up ahead of me. The park had swallowed up the sound of the shots and the whisper of the trees and the wash of the sea took over again and restored the quiet, normal rhythms of the night.

I got to my feet and approached the rotunda, keeping off the path and using the trees for cover. Moon and park light gleamed on metal. I looked down at the big gun and left it where it lay. I hoisted myself up over the railing and came into the circle from the rear. A man was lying on his back in the middle of the pool of water. Water had splashed out all around from the impact of his fall and a section of the pool was nearly dry where the water had seeped into the man's clothes. I put my fingers on his wrist and waited to hear the blood pumping through, but there would never be long enough to wait. He was dead. There was no sign of the airline bag. I lit a match and held it up to make sure. The flickering light caught and danced over his face; the skin was stretched tight over the sharp, hawkish cheekbones. Bony, bat-winged ears stuck out from his close-cropped skull. The coat of his suit had come open and exposed his tiny bony chest covered by a woollen shirt. I struck another match and bent over him. The shirt front was a sodden, oozing mess that glistened thick and oily in the match-light.

I walked up to the road feeling only marginally like a member of the human race. Each killing of another person diminishes your share in the common feeling that unites civilised people and my stocks were running low. Military service is supposed not to count in this process but for me it did. As I walked I realised that my hand was clenched tight around the butt of the Smith & Wesson and I recalled other pistols I'd fired at other men in this city and other guns, all shapes and sizes, growing hot in my hands as I pumped bullets at human flesh. Small soldiers, their hats festooned with jungle camouflage, danced before my eyes and I sweated as freely as I had back in those Malayan jungles.

I found a phone booth and called Ted Tarelton and told him what had happened. I couldn't tell him anything about the girl except that I'd have to report the whole thing to the police now and her name would come out. He accepted it better than I expected. He didn't try to talk me out of it and I wondered what he felt now about the girl. His wife had answered the phone and handed it straight to him without comment; even over the impersonal wire I could sense their reconciliation and maybe that's what mattered most. The money certainly didn't matter a damn. With Saul James it was harder; he showered me with abuse and almost broke down. When he recovered he put one question coldly:

"She's dead, isn't she Hardy?"

I still didn't think so and that's what I said but it made no impression on him. He hung up on me. They had one thing in common — neither of them cared a hoot how many men I shot to death.

The Balmain police station is tucked up next to the town hall like a bedmate. I parked the Celica outside, went in and asked for the duty officer. A uniformed constable with pimples asked my name, inspected my licence and wanted to know what it was about. I told him briefly and he showed me through to a cold, cream-painted room with a table and two chairs. I sat down, rolled a cigarette and waited. I stuck my head out of the door to ask for coffee but there was no-one to ask. I memorised the cracks on the walls and the cobwebs hanging from the roof. I took my gun out and put it on the table in front of me. I swore at it and the little black hole at the end of its muzzle stared me down. I put it away.

After fifteen minutes the door opened and two men came into the room. One of them was the new style of copper with a modish, broad-lapelled suit, collar-length hair and a Zapata moustache. His type imagines it can efface itself at a rock concert but it always sticks out like a bull's balls and never gets offered a joint. The other man was cast in the traditional mould; his face was shaped by grog and collisions with fists and the cut of his hair and clothes owed nothing to vanity. He spoke with the rasping whisper that comes from years of hushed conversations in pubs and stilted evidence-giving in court.

The young one stationed himself by the door, the other swung his leg up and perched on the end of the table across from me. His eyes dropped to my trousers and stayed there. I noticed for the first time that they were smeared with blood. For no reason my reaction to this inspection was cheek.

"You better go down to the park. Someone might take him home as a souvenir."

The older man turned around to grin at his mate.

"Pathetic isn't it? Give them an investigator's licence and they all think they have to be smart." The younger cop nodded on cue. The veteran settled himself more comfortably on the table.

"Oh, I'm sorry, Mr Hardy, I'm forgetting my manners. My name is Carlton, Sergeant Jim Carlton and this is Sergeant Tobin."

I said nothing and re-lit my cigarette, which had gone out.

"Yes, well, now that we're all introduced I think we'd better get on." Carlton's voice was friendly in a dangerous way. I prepared myself for the boot that would knock the chair from under me or the slap that would send the cigarette flying, but nothing like that happened. Carlton went on, showing his great weaknes; he loved to talk. I relaxed.

"You know I really dislike men in your game Hardy — I always imagine they've got beautiful, rich mistresses and good ins with high-up coppers. I know it's not true. I know you're all seedy little losers scratching a living around the divorce courts. The reality makes me happy but the image gets up my nose, know what I mean?"

I grinned at him. "You're an intellectual. Eloquent too. I'm sorry to disappoint you."

"You don't," he said. "You're just right. You haven't got two bob and you're up to your balls in trouble."

"You could be right Carlton," I said. "Why don't you pick up the phone and talk it over with Grant Evans? He'll be interested."

Tobin looked alarmed. "Evans?" The modish moustache twitched. "He's alright, Evans. Jim, what d'you think?"

Carlton sighed and rubbed his hand over his bristled face. He'd seen it too often before — influence, names, interference. He looked resigned, then angry. He banged his fist on the table.

"'Alright, you know a Chief Inspector. Big deal, he can't cover you for this."

"I don't need cover. I just have to tell you what happened and I'm willing to do that."

"How nice," Carlton sneered. "Talk away."

"Don't be silly. I've been through this before. You take a statement now, stenographer and all, with my solicitor present, or we go down to the park in a friendly way and I'll tell you about it. I don't know the derro scene in Balmain too well, but I imagine you could have some bad cases of alcoholic freak-out if you let corpses lie around in the parks."

"Stop being clever Hardy. We've checked out the park, the body's being taken care of. I want to hear what you've got to say."

He was throwing his cards away and the younger man could see it. He levered himself off the wall and came forward to lay a hand on Carlton's shoulder.

"Easy Jim," he said. "Let's play by the book. We're getting nowhere."

Carlton shook the hand off irritably like a dog shedding water. The difference in their ages and the sameness of their rank was eating at him like a cancer. He bulled up from the table and jerked a thumb at me in a gesture that was meant to be tough but lacked all authority.

"OK Hardy, we'll play it your way. Guys like you and your tame Chief Inspector make me sick."

I got up slowly and watched him stalk out of the room. He was probably an honest cop and that couldn't be any easier in Balmain than elsewhere. The honest ones were edgy and this sometimes prompted them to behave like the dishonest ones. It's an old trade. Tobin let him go and waved me through the door.

"Have you got rich, beautiful mistresses too, Hardy?" he asked as I passed him.

I grinned. "Just the one."

We went out into the night and got into a police car. The uniformed man at the wheel gunned the motor and U-turned violently, throwing Tobin almost into Carlton's lap. The older man swore and pushed him away. The night had thickened and the rain was falling steadily. Carlton stared gloomily out of the window and refused a cigarette from Tobin. I took one and he lit it with a nice-looking gas lighter. Three puffs and we were at the park. We piled out of the car and the driver pulled police issue slickers from the boot. We trudged down towards the rotunda like a set of spies, all distrusting each other and caught in a ritual over which we had no control.

Two heavily built cops were sheltering in the rotunda. One of them stamped out a cigarette as we approached and his companion plodded out into the rain.

Carlton marched up to the body and looked down at it. The corpse had about as much emotional impact on him as a pound of potatoes.

"Let's see your gun," he grunted.

I handed it over and he sniffed it. He fiddled with it for a minute and seemed unfamiliar with its mechanism.

"We'll hear the excuses later. You shot him. Where from?"

I retraced my movements up the path and pointed to the approximate spot. "I shot *at* him," I said.

"One shot?"

"Two."

"Why?"

"He was shooting at me."

"How awful." He prowled around the path and the body and I heard him cursing the rain and the wind. Tobin came forward and squinted back down the path to the shadowy structure.

"Pretty good shot," he said, "given the conditions. What was the angle?"

"I was flat on my belly and I was shit-scared."

"Yeah, I would be too." He squared his shoulders and marched back to the rotunda. I leaned against a tree with my shoulders hunched against the rain. I heard muttered voices and then one of the cops scurried up the path to the road. Tobin came out of the gloom and joined me under the tree.

"You've got a licence for the .38?"

I told him I had.

He drew in a deep breath and raised his cigarette to his lips. It had gone out in the rain. I looked at the damp butt between my fingers and we threw them away simultaneously.

"There must be quite a story to this Mr Hardy."

"Why so?"

"The dead man isn't holding a gun and there's no other gun around that we can see."

19

It took more than two hours of questions, coffee, cigarettes and hot tempers to get it all sorted out at the station. Carlton and Tobin went through their version of the heavy-soft routine, but their hearts weren't in it. They didn't like me, they didn't like me dealing with kidnappers and they particularly didn't like me doing it in Balmain. But they didn't think I'd criminally killed Berrigan. I told them who he was and how he was connected with Noni Tarelton. I told them about the Baker woman in Macleay but I didn't make the connections for them, I just had to clear myself on that count. Tobin tried to tie it all together.

"This Berrigan was a nutter, right? He was still hung up on the girl and he killed the Abo who was screwing her. Then he went to Macleay after the money but he didn't get it. He bashed the Baker woman, then he dreamed up the idea of getting some cash by ransoming the girl. Maybe the girl was in on it — yeah that'd explain it."

I was tired and would have agreed to anything but he didn't need the encouragement. Carlton was sneering at him from across the room and that was enough to spur him on.

"It looks bad for the girl," he continued. "It looks as if she was in on the whole thing and then double-crossed Berrigan. She scooted with the money."

He was the original wrap-it-up-and-post-it boy. The theory had some merit; I was pretty sure I'd seen two figures at least in the park and the gun and the money couldn't have flown away. There were things I didn't like about it though: I wasn't sure that the relationship between Berrigan and Noni would have permitted this development. I wasn't sure the girl would have been cool enough to pick up the money and gun and fade into the night. It looked full of holes, but perhaps I just didn't want to look failure squarely in the face as I'd have to do if I accepted Tobin's scenario. Ted Tarelton and Saul James were out a hundred and five thousand dollars and still no girl. I was out a few hundred myself. If I'd belonged to a professional association of private detectives I'd have deserved drumming out. Carlton broke in on my musing.

"That the way you see it Hardy?" The sneer was still on his face. It was also in his voice.

"Yeah. I suppose so." I hadn't told them about Coluzzi or the blacks or Noni's drug habit. They were little private pieces of worry that didn't need airing. Still, it didn't say much for Tobin's power of mind that he didn't ask how I'd got back from Newcastle or how I'd been spending my time. Mentally, I threw his theory out the window.

"Right," said Tobin. The word came out smugly. He turned to Carlton and waved him in like a football coach calling a reserve off the bench. "Jim, how do you see Hardy's position now?"

Carlton looked as sour as a green lemon. The look he shot at Tobin suggested that if the younger man ever got an inch out of line Carlton would pour it straight into the official ear sooner than he could spit. The enmity between them explained the unworkability of the team; Carlton too sour to be imaginative, Tobin too ambitious to be careful. It was a brilliant sadistic pairing and had to mean something within the police set-up. Not my problem.

Carlton glared at me. Cigarette ash had fallen on his waistcoat and his dark stubble was shadowing his cheeks and doubling his chin. He didn't look spruce and he knew it. He knew that I knew it. Tobin, elegantly arranged against the wall, looked fresh and bright. He got out a cigarette and lit it with a snap of that fancy lighter.

"I still don't like you Hardy," Carlton grated. "Your type shouldn't be running around with licensed guns. You're a menace."

I let it pass. It was just guff, old, stale, defeated air. He took out a notebook and began checking off items.

"One, failing to give information concerning a felony — the Simmonds killing. Two, failing to report a felony — the Baker woman. Three, conspiracy in a felony — this ransom balls-up."

"I'm illegally parked outside the station, too," I said.

Tobin grinned. He'd contrived to do all the smart talking himself and left the silly, hack stuff to his partner. Suddenly I felt vaguely sorry for Carlton and a sharp dislike for Tobin. But I had to stick with the strength. I shrugged and squashed out a cigarette I hadn't wanted when I'd made it.

"Book me on it then. I'll call Cy Sackville and we can all go home to bed."

Carlton dusted off his hands to release some aggression and worked his heavy body off the table. "Get out Hardy. Piss off."

I held out my hand as I got to my feet. "Give me my gun back."

He shook his head. "No way. It's evidence for an enquiry. I might get you delicensed yet. Why? Do you need it to get from here to your cute little cottage?"

"You never know. I lead a dangerous life. That all then?"

Carlton ignored the question and left the room. Tobin barred my way with a stiff arm across the door.

"Aah, you might mention to Evans that you got a fair shake here."

He was the second cop to ask me for the same favour in forty-eight hours. It made me feel like a pimp for a venereal whore. I brushed the arm down.

"I might," I said.

At least he didn't thank me. I walked out of the station, got in the car and headed for where there would be consolations — cold, wet and alcoholic.

It was close to ten-thirty when I got home. I left the car in the street rather than do the fancy backing and filling it takes to get into the courtyard. The bushes and shrubs whose names I don't know were heavy with water and I got some of it on me as I brushed past them. A voice hissed my name from the shadows near the front door. I crouched and slapped my hand to where the gun should have been, then let it drop uselessly to my side. I was a sitting target, caught in the glow from the street light and my stomach lurched with the knowledge. Then she stepped out of the shadows, slender as a wand even wrapped up in a donkey coat.

"Mr Hardy, it's Penny Sharkey."

She moved into the light and her finely-shaped head picked up a sort of aura. She was wet and breathing heavily; I should have heard that from the path, but it wasn't my night for professional standards.

My initial feelings were completely erotic. Extreme tiredness can do that to you. I wanted to hurry inside with her and let everything go to hell except sex. The fantasy lasted perhaps a tenth of a second before the veneers of civilisation and notions of professional conduct and God knows what other inhibitions crowded it out. I took hold of her arm and I could feel her shaking. I hung on hard, got the key in the lock and opened the door. She stumbled ahead of me into the passage and threw her hand up over her face when I turned on the light. I clutched her harder, perhaps out of a fear that she'd run away, perhaps from lust. She wrenched her arm back and I felt the pain shoot along and affect her voice.

"You're hurting me!"

I said I was sorry and let her go. I went past her into the house turning on lights and leaving her to follow me if she wanted to. I opened the refrigerator and got out some wine.

"Drink?"

"Yes, thanks."

I poured the drink and set it down on the table. I didn't look at her too closely. I was conscious of the slenderness of my hold on her and she was the only tangible thing I had left of the Noni Tarelton case. If she was part of it at all. Suddenly I was sure that she was. She stood in the middle of the kitchen dripping water on the floor from the soaked nap of her coat. I sat down at the table.

"Take your coat off, Penny, and sit down. I'm sorry I hurt your arm, I've had a rough night and I'm not thinking too straight." I mustered up a smile from somewhere and made unbuttoning motions with my hands. She undid the coat, slipped out of it and dropped it over a chair. A stream of water ran off it and made a pool on the floor. She sat down and drank three inches of wine in one steady pull. The tiny breasts pushed up under her white skivvy and I tried to distract myself with the wine. I drained my glass and poured some more. I held the flagon up enquiringly.

"No, this'll do." She sipped the stuff as if it had a name and an age.

"Why are you here, Penny? What's going on? Sunday told me you wanted to contact me."

She curled her hands around the glass and wouldn't look at me.

"I saw Noni. Just by accident. In Balmain. I tried to tell you."

"Why didn't you call again?"

"I couldn't. They left the cafe. I rang Jimmy while they were eating."

"What were you doing in Balmain?"

"I got a job there, in a solicitor's office. I started yesterday. I won't have the job now, I haven't been in today."

"Why?"

"I've been looking for you, waiting for you."

"Why me?"

"I want to see Noni in a box. You said you'd let things work out the way they had to. Noni's with a man who'll kill her. I'm sure of it."

I described Berrigan and she nodded vigorously. "Yes, that's him!"

"Tell me what happened."

"I was in this cafe having coffee and reading the paper. I was hidden by the paper when they came in. They sat down a couple of tables away and ordered food. I could just hear what they were saying."

"Which was?"

"They were having an argument, about plans or something. His plans and her plans. And about money. I couldn't catch the details."

"Then what did you do?"

"I tried to get you through Jimmy. I got a bit closer to them when I came back. I was wearing these big shades and Noni didn't look at me. She wouldn't recognise me easily anyway. She hasn't seen me often enough."

"What did you hear this time? Where was this by the way?"

She named an all-night cafe in Darling Street. "I heard him say that if it all went alright they'd have the money anyway. She was saying they'd missed the money or something like that."

I drank wine and thought about the story. It sounded alright, a bit too pat perhaps but she'd had time to get it straight. It fitted the facts as far as I knew them but it didn't lead anywhere.

"Anything else?"

She drank some more of the wine, a little nervously I thought. She stood up, went across to the coat on the chair and dipped into a pocket. She came up with some filter cigarettes and I lit one for her. She puffed at it and fiddled with the spent match.

"I know where he . . . where they're going after the plan is finished, whatever that is." She drew in smoke and expelled it through her finely-shaped dark brown lips. The hand holding the cigarette was shaking and she was staring at my face as if willing me to do what she wanted, including, maybe, believe her.

I tried to keep anxiety out of my voice. "Where would that be Penny?"

"I'll tell you if you promise to take me with you and let me in on whatever happens."

I shook my head. "No, it could be rough. Besides, I'd have to search you for concealed weapons."

"Nothing like that," she said fiercely, "I promise. I just want to be there. I could help."

I was sure she wasn't telling me the whole truth, but I could only guess what she'd left out. I was sure that she didn't know of Berrigan's death. That meant we'd both be heading into a tricky situation with only partial knowledge of the background facts. That sounded like a recipe for misunderstandings and disaster. But in the plan that was slowly forming in my head she could certainly be a help. In fact, the more I thought about it, she was indispensable. I couldn't take her on without checking her story though. That done, I could risk it. I had to, anyway.

"Alright, I'll take you. Where?"

"Macleay. I know where in Macleay, too, but I'll tell you that when we get there."

I grinned. "You're like an old pro. Fair enough, I'll check the flights." I got up and started to move out of the kitchen. "Got any money?" I said over my shoulder.

The airline informed me there was a flight north at seven-thirty a.m. I booked two seats. When I got back Penny had tipped the contents of a small embroidered purse over the table and had arranged things in piles. The money didn't amount to much of a pile. "Twenty three dollars, thirty eight cents," she said quietly.

"I've got about a hundred. We'll need more. I'll have to go out tonight and get some."

"Don't go out." I looked up, surprised at the different note in her voice. She was pushing her hair back with both hands. Her figure was lean and flat but definitely female. I felt the juices flowing again and she came around the table to where I'd sat down. She leaned over and pushed the wine away, then she bent and kissed me on the lips. She tasted fresh and salty like a clean stretch of sea on a clear day. I hooked my arm up around her neck and pressed her head down for another kiss, a long one. I felt my tiredness drop away. I felt eighteen years old and I wanted her. I stood up and put my arms around her. She was slim and firm like a young tree. It seemed as if my arms could go around her twice and I was feeling younger by the minute. I was hard and breathing fast and she was pressing her hips forward at me and then suddenly it felt all wrong. I was twice her age and a few years more and she was alien and strange. The bones of her back felt fragile under my hands and I felt clumsy and old. I eased her away.

"It's not a good idea," I croaked.

She looked incredulously at me. "You want to, you're hard as a rock."

"I know, but I don't go to bed with teenagers. It doesn't mean I don't want to."

"Bullshit." She embraced herself, crossing her arms, and pulled off her skivvy. Her tight trousers had a silky sheen and they shimmered as she slipped out of them and let them slide to the floor. I watched her thumb down her pants and the hard, spare lines of her brown body cut off my breath. She squeezed her minuscule breasts together with the spread fingers of one hand.

"Come on, I like you." Her teeth shone in her beautiful dark face but her eyes were as hard as agate. I was suddenly aware that she was giving a performance, a good but cold one and I resisted the knowledge but it took over and gripped me. I reached for the wine.

"No," I said hoarsely. "Come back in five years."

She laughed a bit unsteadily. "Don't be silly. Where's your bed?"

"Upstairs, front."

She whipped around and I heard her feet dancing up the stairs. Carefully carrying a full glass of wine I followed. She'd turned on a lamp in the bedroom and was bending to pull back the cover. In the lamp glow she looked like an Egyptian maiden of infinite grace performing some domestic task. She slid into the bed except for one thin bare arm which she arranged outside the covers and alongside her. She lifted the arm and let it fall.

"Get in."

She'd have tempted Gandhi and I knew that if I moved an inch towards the bed I was done for. I raised the glass and drank some.

"Go to sleep. If it's any consolation to you I'm going to get drunk."

I started back to the stairs. She was laughing when I reached them but the sound stopped very soon.

I didn't get drunk. Not then. I let myself quietly out of the house and caught a taxi back to Balmain. The all-night cafe was fighting the darkness with a pale, flickering neon sign and droning, toneless canned music. I pushed the door open and went in to the smells of burnt bread and over-fried oil. There were about ten tables in the place and solitary men sat at three of them. One of the men had his head on his arms and the other two weren't far off it. A heavily built man wearing a large white apron came from the back of the place when the door slammed behind me. He went behind the counter and leaned forward over the espresso machine. His hair was black and curly above a round olive face. The thought crossed my mind that he was the same nationality as Coluzzi, but that's where the resemblance to that predator ended. This was a soft, comfortable man.

"Yes? You want something sir?"

I asked for coffee and got out a five-dollar note. He pushed the cup over to me and I gave him the money.

"You can keep the change for a little information."

He held his fingers poised over the keys of the cash register like a typist waiting for her nails to dry.

"Information?"

"Nothing dangerous. Were you working here yesterday morning?"

"Sure, I own the place. I'm here all the time."

I handed him the picture of Noni Tarelton. He looked at it and shrugged.

"Maybe. Lots of girls like that around here."

Balmain, it's the only place to live. I described Berrigan to him and he nodded so hard his chins wobbled.

"Sure, sure, I remember now. Ears like this." He fanned his ears out the way Lorraine had; it must have happened to Berrigan all his life and it was a bad thing for a criminal to be so recognizable. He should have tried another trade.

"That's him. What did they do?"

"They had breakfast — eggs and toast and coffee."

"Did you hear them talking?"

"No, too busy."

"OK. Now this is the important part. Who else was here?"

He laughed with the rich, high notes of the Italian tenor. The guy slumped at the table jerked up and looked around, then his head fell back.

"I couldn't tell you Mister, the place was full. It's my busy time like I said."

"I appreciate that, but you should remember this one — a black girl, young, very good-looking."

"Ah, the blackies, sure I remember them."

"Blacks? Did you say blacks?"

"Yeah. The girl, must be the one you mean, and a man, youngish fella, a tough guy."

I felt the excitement rise up inside me. He pushed my coffee cup forward on the counter.

"It's getting cold."

"Forget it," I said, more sharply than I meant to. He look offended and I picked up the cup and took a sip. "Terrific. Tell me about the girl and the man, what did they do?"

"Are you the police?"

"No, private enquiries. Look. I showed him the licence and drew another five out of my wallet.

"Is it about dope?" he said quickly. "I hate dope, sloppy people, dirty . . ."

"So do I. Yes dope's part of it. Just tell me about the girl and the man." To encourage him I finished the coffee. He pulled out a packet of Gitane filters and offered them to me. I refused and he shook one out and lit it; the acrid smoke overwhelmed the cooking smells and gave the place a conspiratorial, secretive atmosphere. I fiddled with the note, folding it and tapping it on the counter.

It got to him and he screwed up his eyes against the smoke, visibly searching his memory. "The man was here first, yeah, that's right. He had just had coffee, over there." He pointed to the deepest, darkest corner of the cafe. Then he thumped himself on the head and his curls bounced. "No, no, I've got it wrong. The girl, the blonde, and the man with the ears came in first. They sat here." He indicated a table near the door. "I didn't see the black come in. He must have come in the side door. It's open at the busy time." The cafe had a lane running beside it and a door let out onto the lane. I nodded and he went on: "He was just there, the toughie, in there where I said. I remember because he paid me when I brought his coffee. That's not usual, you know?"

I knew, I said. "What about the dark girl?"

"She didn't stay, didn't buy anything. The blonde and the man with her paid and went, then the young guy went after them. The girl came in the front — they were all going out the side, see? She just went straight through after them. She came back later and had coffee . . . yeah, I think it was her."

"You've got a good memory."

"I sing, opera you know? I have to remember the words and the movements. You like opera?"

I hate it. "Yes," I said. I gave him the other five and he tucked it away in his apron.

"Thanks, I'll buy a lottery ticket. The big one, you know?"

"Yeah, good luck."

"It's bad luck for those people, isn't it?"

"Why do you say that?"

"Don't get me wrong , it's nothing personal, but I got a sense, you know? You're a bad luck man and the chair told me anyway. The one with the ears, he sat in the bad luck chair."

"What's that?"

"Don't let this get around, eh? But there's a chair in this place that's unlucky. People sit in it and they have bad luck. A friend of mine, his daughter died, and a woman I know, she got hit by a bus, right out there." He pointed out into the street. I took a last look around the cafe. Nobody had moved. Nothing had changed. It was just a little bit later and the air was a little bit staler. And for the men at the tables the park was just so much nearer.

"Why don't you move the chair?" I said.

"I do, every day. It's over there now." He waved his hand with the cigarette in it to the far wall. "You think I'm superstitious?"

I shrugged. "I don't know, could be. Why don't you try an experiment?"

He looked interested. "Like what?"

"Try the chair on someone you don't like."

"There's no one I don't like that much."

"You're lucky. I've got to go. Thanks for the help. Goodnight."

"Goodnight Mr Hardy."

He was quick. I grinned at him and went out.

The house was quiet when I got home. The bedroom let out a soft glow and Penny's coat and clothes were still in the kitchen. I tossed the clothes onto a chair and fought down the impulse to go upstairs. I needed help in the fight so I rooted around and found a bottle of rum, half-full. I got out ice and chopped up lemons and settled down in the front room with the bottle and the fixings. I worked steadily through the liquor and started on *Flashman* for the third time. I remember reading "Possibly there has been a greater shambles in the history of warfare than our withdrawal from Kabul . . ." and taking another drink of the rum and thinking what a shambles the Tarelton case was in and then nothing more. The couch was big enough and soft enough and I was drunk enough. I slept.

20

When I woke up Penny was standing over me with a cup of something emitting steam in her hand. I groaned and pulled myself up on the couch. I took the cup and sipped it. Instant coffee. Not the worst thing for my head just then but not the best. I ungummed my eyelids a second time, enough to see that Penny had put her clothes back on. Not that it mattered. I was in no condition to take her up on her offer of the night before if she should repeat it. Her hair was damp from the shower and her skin shone like polished copper.

"You look terrible," she said.

"Thanks. What's the time?"

"Six-thirty. The taxi's due at seven. You've got time for a shower."

"Thanks again." I set the coffee down on the arm of the couch and swung my feet off it. My head rang like a J. Arthur Rank gong. I headed unsteadily for the shower. The water helped a bit. I felt better still after a shave and ready for a drink after I'd dressed. In the kitchen Penny was sinking a big white tooth into a piece of toast. I shuddered when she offered me some and got the white wine out of the fridge. When a tall glass of riesling and soda was fizzing in my hand I felt well enough to compliment her.

"Don't work in offices. Go on television, advertise things, make yourself some money."

"I might," she said and knocked back half a pint of orange juice.

Carrying the drink with me I went from place to place collecting things. I packed a cassette tape recorder and a pair of binoculars into an overnight bag. An old credit card Ailsa's firm had issued me and not cancelled went into my wallet and an unlicensed Colt automatic went into the lining of the parka where the .38 had been. She had her coat on and the glasses and plates and cups were rinsed and stacked when the taxi honked outside. We went out of the house into a neutral and uncertain dawn.

We preserved silence on the drive to Mascot. The airport preliminaries weren't any more complicated than usual and I still had a few dollars left after buying tickets, papers and magazines. Unlike most people, Penny was easy to travel with; she was there when she was needed and not in the way when she wasn't. We got looks, usual I suppose for couples of mixed colour; half curiosity, half hostility. Penny noticed me glowering at the lookers.

"Don't worry," she said, taking my arm, "your lot have been staring at us since you got here."

Flying was a novelty for her and she enjoyed the rituals of it all. I sat in my seat and obeyed orders slavishly out of some dark belief that this would keep me safe. When we were airborne Penny stared out of the window at the few flashes of green and brown that showed through that high-flying fog. We were half a hundred people flying blind, trusting our lives to a few fuses and valves. I tried to concentrate on the papers but couldn't. Penny read in a desultory fashion for a while and then I felt her go tense beside me. I sneaked a look across and she was gnawing her lip.

"What's wrong?"

"I'm frightened."

"Of flying?"

"No." She waved strong men's traumas away with one thin hand. "No, of course not. It's nothing, flying. I thought it would be more exciting. It must be boring after the first time."

I nodded. "Well then . . . ?"

"All this. How's it going to end? You haven't even told me what's happening."

"You're holding out on me, too."

"Where they're going? I told you I'll tell you in Macleay." She glanced around the cabin. "I suppose I can tell you now. We're not going anywhere else."

"It can wait," I said sharply. "I think I know anyway. No, you're holding back something else, but I'm not going to press you. In fact I'll tell you things and not ask for anything from you. OK?"

"Why?" she said warily.

"I have reasons. Partly because I have to. I want you to do

something for me and it won't make sense unless you know what's going on."

I filled her in on some of the details — on the ransoms for Noni and who paid them and how the police were in on the whole thing now. I didn't tell her about Berrigan's death or about "Percy White". She'd heard a little about Coluzzi and the fight game from friends. I expanded on that a bit and kept away from the subject of Ricky Simmonds until I mentioned Trixie Baker. Penny looked interested in the name.

"I've heard of her," she said, "from Ricky I think. Doesn't she have a farm or something?"

"That's right, just out of Macleay. Ricky talked about her?"

The smooth brown skin on her forehead wrinkled. "I think so, once when he was a bit drunk, not so much about her as about someone who worked for her, one of us."

"An Aborigine?"

She snorted. "I don't mean a Hottentot."

"OK, OK, keep your hair on. What did he say about this person of your own race?"

She looked at me to decide whether to take offence or not but I'd arranged my face in its most winning shape and she let it pass.

"I told you Ricky always seemed to be looking for someone. Well I asked him about it this time, when he was full and he said 'I'm sure that was him, at Trixie Baker's' or something like that. I didn't push him, it didn't make sense to me. Does it mean anything to you?"

"I think so. Ricky was looking for his father, I reckon. I think his father and Berrigan robbed a bank in Macleay in 1966. Berrigan was connected with Trixie Baker, maybe Ricky's father was too. Perhaps Ricky got a lead on him but couldn't clinch it. Anyway, this is where you come in — I have to ask the Baker woman some questions and I haven't got a chance in a million of getting in to see her."

"Why?"

"The police already dislike me for leaving the scene of the crime — her bashing that is. I did, but I had no choice. That's sort of been squared now in a way, but I'll still be very unpopular around Macleay."

"What do you want me to do?"

"Done any acting?"

"A bit, street theatre, black theatre stuff."

"That'll do — this is a cinch for you. I'm going to get hold of a hospital cleaner's uniform. Dressed in that you should be able to sneak around the hospital and find Trixie Baker. It can't be a big place. I want you to take this in," I tapped the bag with the tape recorder inside, "and ask her some questions. The right answers will sort this mess out. Will you do it?"

She seemed about to ask a question, an important question, but she bit it back.

"Yes," she said quickly, "of course I will."

"There's another thing. Is there anyone in Kempsey, one of you I mean, who'd know all about the Aborigines in the area — who's who and when and where?"

She didn't have to think. "Yes, Charley Gurney, he was initiated, he's old, a clever man. That means . . ."

"I know what it means. I've read Elkin. Would you take me to see him?"

She nodded. "Anything else?"

"That's all for now, except to warn you that you're in for a rough time. I expect all this to sort out, but I don't expect it'll come out neat and pretty."

She shrugged. "We'll see."

"Yeah." I picked up her hand. In my yellowed, scarred claw it looked like a soft, brown orchid. "I'm sorry as hell I had to refuse you last night, I didn't want to."

"You were right I think, but I'm sorry too."

I put her hand back on the seat rest. "It's better we didn't because we're on opposite sides in this even if you do help me. I want to get Noni Tarelton back home to her rich Dad in one piece and you're not going to stop me. I'll flatten you if you try."

She looked quickly at me. I wasn't smiling and neither was she. It was a risky declaration because the help she would be giving me would be substantial and things could get into a hell of a mess without it. Maybe they would anyway. She had a right to know the rules I was playing by but I hoped it wouldn't come to an outright conflict between us. She had strength and guts and would fight hard. Also there was something between us, a connection, part sexual, part temperamental. It would be a nasty falling-out if it happened.

The plane swayed around like a mast in a high wind on the last hour of the flight and Penny didn't seem quite so blasé about flying. I didn't enjoy it myself and then I had to face a moment of tension when I presented the out-of-date credit card at the car hire desk. It passed muster and there was a white Datsun waiting for us in the company bay outside the airport building. The air was warm and dusty. A haze in the sky suggested that the day would get a lot warmer. I unlocked the driver's door and threw the bag into the back seat. Penny stood by the passenger door sneering at me as if I was some inferior and unpleasant exhibit at a zoo. I didn't like that look. I settled myself in the seat and turned on the air-conditioning. She tapped on the window. I wound it down.

"Yes?" I said.

"Let me *in*, Hardy."

"A girl like you wouldn't ride in a big, fat, Nip capitalist car like this would she? Take a bus, I'll meet you behind the pub."

Her eyes blazed at me and I could hear her breath coming in short, hard bursts.

"Let me *in*!"

I flicked the door open, she got in and sat down hard staring straight in front of her. It was a bad start.

"Don't be so touchy," she said.

"I'm sorry. Look, we need a car for this job. They're all rubbish, they're all too expensive and they fall apart too soon, but we need one and this'll do. Alright?"

"Yes," her voice was tight and small.

I swung the beast out of the car park. I wanted to tell her to get ready for some lying and shooting, but I didn't know how.

We drove in silence along the dusty roads into Macleay. I hadn't liked being there the last time and I didn't expect this time to be any better. Penny sat with her arms wrapped tightly around her thin body as if trying to physically contain her resentments. The car handled well, a bit squashy and soft compared with the Falcon, but it would be fast if that was needed. The air conditioning worked, cooled me down

557

and smoothed the edges off my temper. Penny took her coat off and threw it on the back seat. We exchanged small smiles as she did so. She hit the radio button and got some country and western music which she turned down very low.

I drove into Macleay and cruised slowly past Bert's garage. Penny looked out at the place with the rough-painted sign hanging over the bowsers and nodded. "You *did* know where they were going."

"Yeah. The thing is, are they still there?" The garage looked closed although it was after ten a.m. and a piece of cardboard with something written on it was hanging on the handle of the office door. I drove past again and could see at least two cars parked in the alley beside the garage. I found a phone booth and located Bert's number in the directory. I called it. The phone rang twice, then it was answered by the voice I'd heard telephonically at Ted Tarelton's. I asked for Bert and was told he was sick. I asked when his place would be open again and the voice said "tomorrow". He hung up.

The way to the hospital was signposted and the building couldn't have been anything else; it was like hospitals everywhere, all clean lines, light and airy, set in lawns and trying not to look like a place where people died. We parked in the visitors' area and Penny got out of the car. "Wait here," she told me.

I did as I was told. I rolled a cigarette and fiddled with the tape recorder. It seemed to be working alright, drawing power from the batteries and responding to all buttons. I smoked and waited while the morning heated up. Sweat was soaking into my collar when Penny got back. She climbed in and unrolled a bundle.

"Chic, isn't it?"

She held up a pale green, front-buttoning, belted dress with yellow piping.

"Terrific. Your size?"

"Close enough. We'll have to go back to town, I'll need a scarf and some sneakers."

We drove back to the shopping centre and bought the things and a pillow case and a plastic bucket. On the way back I showed her how the tape recorder worked. She nodded, wrapped the machine in the pillow case and put it in the bucket. She changed clothes in the back of the car and left her platform soles, slacks and top on the back seat with her coat. I drove to the service entrance of the hospital and let her out. She stood beside the car while I told her what I wanted to learn from Trixie Baker. I gave her two hours and she didn't argue about it. She pointed to a park bench near a small copse artfully contrived by the landscape gardener.

"There, in two hours." The sheer confidence in her voice made me look at her carefully. She'd moved into the role already, her shoulders were slumped and she carried the bucket as if she'd forgotten it was there. The uniform and the scarf and the sneakers toned her down. She'd pass as a menial as long as nobody got a good look at her fierce, alert face and beautifully tended nails. She slouched across to the heavy plastic doors of the service entrance and slipped through.

I drove slowly back into town, turning the next steps over in my mind, looking for snags and dangers. There were dozens of both. It took me nearly half an hour to pick my spot from which to watch Bert's garage. Behind the building and across a narrow lane was a shop that had been burnt out. The blackened brick shell still stood and an iron staircase took me up to the second storey which was intact apart from many missing floorboards. Crouched by the back window I could get a good view through the binoculars of the back doors and windows of the garage.

It was hot, boring work. I didn't want to send smoke up into the still air in case the watched were also watching and I hadn't brought the Esky and the chilled beer with me. For a while nothing happened and as my eyes adjusted to the light and the shadows and shapes I began to be aware of a fine mist drifting out from one of the windows. Coming from a motor garage that could mean only one thing — spray painting. This was confirmed when a man wearing overalls came out into the yard pushing painter's goggles up onto his head. He was short and stocky and dark — very dark.

He took a few deep breaths and some more mist came floating out of the open door behind him. Then he ducked back into the garage and came back a minute later with a welder's torch. He gave it a few experimental blasts and took it back inside. The set-up wasn't too hard to figure and I had to admire it. You've got a hundred thousand or so dollars in ready money but it might be marked. You've got cops in Sydney and Newcastle looking for you. And you're black. So what do you do? Fix up a truck, really fix it up with bars and secret compartments and a new spray job and take to the roads. Get out into the bush where you can camp, spend the money carefully, spinning it out, while the heat dies down. You can come out in Perth or Darwin or wherever the hell you please. Not bad. It was a pity to disturb it but I had to. Fixing a truck in the way I imagined they'd be fixing it would take time and that was what I needed.

I watched for another hour but nothing changed. I fiddled with the adjustment mechanisms of the glasses, trying to get a clearer focus on an oil drum near the back door of the garage. Something about that drum disturbed me, but it was in shadow and I couldn't pick out any details. I backed away from the window and went down the staircase and out to the car. My shirt was a wringing wet rag when I got there and I took it off and draped it over the hot roof of the car while I rolled and smoked a cigarette. The shirt was hot and stiff after a couple of minutes. I put it back on and drove to the hospital.

Penny was waiting on the seat when I drove up. She ran across to the car and threw the bucket savagely into the back.

"Easy," I said. Then I noticed that she was carrying the tape recorder. I took it from her and settled it gently on the seat. "How did it go?"

"No trouble," she said tightly. She got into the back seat and began changing her clothes. I resisted the temptation to watch her in the rear vision mirror. She stuffed the uniform, sneakers and scarf into the bucket and clambered over into the front seat. She put the tape recorder on her lap and patted it.

"Want to hear it?"

"Not now. How's Trixie Baker?"

"Bad. I don't think she wants to live."

"Upset about all this?" I nodded at the machine.

"Not really. I think she's a bit relieved it's all come out."

"How about you?"

"Doesn't change anything for me. What have you been doing?"

"Watching the garage. They'll be there till night time I reckon. We've got time to see the clever man, how do we find him?"

"Stop the first boong we see and ask." I looked quickly at her. The hospital encounter had got to her and the tough indifference was a pose. Her features were all drawn tight and there was tension in every line of her body. The bitter remark was hard to interpret. I had too little experience of her moods, but she was seething inside, fighting some deep battle in which her pride and her colour and her loyalties were all taking a hand.

21

We picked up some sandwiches in town and Penny talked briefly to an Aboriginal girl in the shop while she was waiting for the food. I lurked in the car. About fifty pairs of male eyes followed her as she trotted across to where I was parked. She got in and handed me a paper bag.

"Thanks. Got the address?"

"Yes, and directions. You'd better get moving. It's out of town a fair way."

We ate as I drove. I wanted a drink badly and said so.

"You'll have to pick up some grog for the old man anyway," she said. I could hear the disapproval in her voice. Drink for her was synonymous with broken heads and blood or maudlin sentimentality that wasn't the same thing as love. Nothing to show for the rent money but a reeking breath. I'd seen it too but managed to overcome the prejudice. I stopped at a pub on the outskirts of the town and bought a dozen bottles of beer. I cracked one and swigged it as I followed Penny's directions. Her voice, as she gave them, was muted with contempt.

We got clear of the streets and houses and passed through a strip of forest and a patch of fifty-acre farmlets. The road got dusty and narrow and when a couple of vehicles came from the other direction I had to put the bottle down and steer cautiously. We went over a hill and crossed a bridge across a sluggish creek. Around the bend a small weatherboard cottage appeared. Its front gate was about three feet back from the side of the road. I swung the car down a rutted track that ran along beside the house. An ancient Holden ute was parked under a lean-to at the end of the track. Rusted car bodies and unidentifiable bits of ironware lay around like corpses. A thick bush grew all over the place; it straggled up the peeling walls of the house and ran around the front and tackled the decrepit verandah.

We got out of the car and Penny put her hand on my shoulder.

"Let me do the talking. I'll have to introduce myself and that'll take a while."

"What about the beer?"

"Leave it in the car for the moment. Tobacco will do for now."

We went around to the front of the house. The verandah boards creaked under my weight but held. Penny knocked on the door. The house wore a guarded, cautious air with curtains drawn across the narrow windows and a blind pulled down over the glass pane in the door. Penny knocked again and we heard shuffling footsteps inside. The blind flew up and an old, thin Aborigine looked at us through the glass. His deep-set eyes ran over Penny and then pierced into my face. I had to look away. His eyes were like lasers searing through to the back of my skull. He released the door catch and pulled the door inwards.

"Gidday. Come in." His voice was like the rest of him, smoky dark and seamed with experience. He wore grey trousers and a white shirt pressed into razor sharp creases. Veins and sinews stood out in his arms like a network of thin ropes. The verandah and the floor of the house were on a level. So were his eyes and mine. That made him six feet and half an inch tall. I wondered if I would still measure that in my seventies. He ushered us through to a small sitting room occupied by a threadbare couch and some old padded chairs, a scrubbed pine table and a glass-fronted case. Penny and I sat on the couch and he lowered himself into one of the chairs; his feet were bare so he was taller than me. His hair was thick and grey, waving over his neat skull like a finely worked helmet. I searched my memory for the face his reminded me of and got it — Robert Graves. He had the same beaky nose and sunken eyes, old as time.

Penny set about introducing herself. It involved references to Auntie this and Auntie that and towns in this part of New South Wales and gatherings held over the past twenty years. Gurney nodded and smiled at the familiar names. While this was going on I looked around the room; the case held photographs, elaborately framed, and sporting trophies. There was a picture of the Queen on the wall above the fireplace. Penny finished talking and the old man leaned back in his chair and beamed at her with what looked like a full set of genuine teeth.

"Well, I'm pleased to meet you girlie. I never knew your dad but I heard of him. Who's your friend?"

I got up and leaned forward, sticking my hand out. "Cliff Hardy, Mr Gurney. Glad to know you."

We shook. His hand was as hard as iron and a joint of his little finger was missing.

"Hardy, eh? What's your game Cliff?"

I told him and rolled a cigarette while I spoke. I offered him the makings and he took them.

"Thanks. How can I help you?"

"Penny here tells me that you know all there is to know about the Aboriginal people in this district."

"S'right. Lived here all me life, never been to Sydney even. I was put through up by Burnt Bridge in 1919."

"Initiated? Can't be many around like you."

"I'm the last one." He got his cigarette going and pierced me through again with those eyes. "What do you want me to tell you?"

"All you can about Albie Simmonds."

"Albie in trouble?"

I nodded.

"What sort of trouble?"

"Bad. Kidnapping. Gun trouble."

"Why should I help you. You huntin' him?"

"Not exactly. I want the girl he took. If I know certain things maybe I can stop more people from being killed. Two men're dead already."

"Albie kill 'em?"

"I don't know. I don't think so. That's one of the things I've got to find out."

He leaned back and blew smoke at the roof. There wasn't an ounce of spare flesh on him; his belly was flat and the skin around his throat and jaw stretched smooth and tight. He had authority. If he'd said no and told me to leave I'd have gone. He was that sort of man.

I felt as if he was putting me through some kind of test only I didn't know the rules and the proper way to conduct myself. I sat there and tried to look honest and strong. He looked at me so long I thought he was going into a trance. Then he came out of it and nodded sharply.

"All right." He took a draw on the cigarette. "I can tell you a bit about Albie. Mind you, he's had a few names in his time. Not too many people know him as Albie Simmonds."

"Percy White?"

"That's one. Terrible man for the grog Albie, that's no secret."

"That reminds me, I've got some beer in the car, would you like some?"

"Too right."

"I'll get it," Penny said. She left the room. Gurney watched her appreciatively. So did I. I wondered if he lived alone. There was no sign of a woman's touch in the room we were in.

"Where d'you want me to start?"

"Just tell me about Albie, from the beginning."

"Yeah, well, Albie wasn't a bad lad. Too much grog around the family always, but that wasn't his fault. He got into bad company and a fair bit of trouble with the coppers. Small stuff though."

"Is he a full blood Aborigine?"

"Pretty nearly. Like me. Why do you ask?"

"His boy, Ricky, wasn't very dark, I just wondered . . . what about the mother?" He looked at me again, as if he was testing the quality, the very grain of me. "Nellie? Half and half," he said slowly.

"I see. Go on Mr Gurney."

"Albie moved around a bit . . . up here . . . Sydney. Couldn't settle. Nellie just had the one kid, Ricky, and she died young. The boy went to people in Sydney."

"Did Albie see much of his son?"

"No."

"Why not?"

"That's something you'd have to ask him."

"Fair enough. Did Albie work for Trixie Baker?"

"Sort of — aah good girl!" Penny came back into the room with a tray. Two open beer bottles were on it and three glasses. She poured a glass for the old man and half a glass for herself. I filled a glass and we all said cheers and drank. The beer was warmer than it should be but still not bad. Gurney sighed and emptied the glass in three long gulps. He filled it again and watched the head rise and settle.

"Where was I? Albie and Trixie, yeah. You couldn't say Albie worked for her, he was a mess then, drinking fierce. He was calling himself Carter then — this is a few years ago."

"Why all the names?"

"Police trouble I s'pose. We all knew who he was but the whites around didn't. It's a bit like that up here."

"Do you know if his son got in touch with him at that time?"

"He tried."

"What happened?"

"Albie ducked him, went bush."

"Why?"

"I'm not sayin'. Personal to them."

"I suppose you won't tell me about Albie's relationship with Trixie Baker either?"

"That's right. Sorry. I haven't been much help. I will say this, you seem to know a thing or two about Albie and the boy."

"Not enough."

"You know some. It's dangerous. I'd keep out of it if I was you."

"I can't." I finished the beer and got up. Penny had hardly touched hers and she didn't give it a glance now. She shook hands with Gurney and he and I exchanged nods. I'd intruded too far on a matter that excluded whites or should, in his view. It was too delicate to be trusted to me with my clumsy, money-motivated ways. He'd decided that and exercised just as much of his authority as he needed to keep the knowledge from me. He knew that I'd go on, that he couldn't stop me. He accepted that, but he didn't want to shake my hand again.

"Thanks for the beer," he grunted.

I said something polite and we trooped down the passage and out into the raw sunlight.

"Not very helpful," Penny said as we walked to the car.

"Could have been worse. I got some things out of it by implication."

"Trixie Baker told me she and Albie Simmonds were lovers. It's on the tape."

I nodded. "I thought so."

We got in the car and I noticed that three of the beer bottles were still on the seat. I pointed to them.

"That was for him."

"Not good for him."

"I know what he'd say to that. Has he got a wife by the way?"

She grinned. "I heard he has three."

We drove off and Penny yawned a couple of times and knuckled her eyes. I pulled over under a tree and stopped.

"Have a sleep if you want to. I'm going to listen to the tape."

She nodded, took her coat with her out of the car and settled herself on the grass using it as a pillow. I made a cigarette and lifted the top off one of the beer bottles. The liquid frothed out and the stuff left behind was warm but I sipped at it anyway. I pushed the "play" button.

PENNY: "Mrs Baker, can you hear me?"

VOICE: "Yes, I can hear you, who're you?"

PENNY: "My name is Sharkey, Penny Sharkey. You don't know me, but I know who hit you — Berrigan."

BAKER: "How do you know that, I never told . . ."

PENNY: "I'm working with a man who knows all about it. He wants to fix Berrigan, will you help?"

BAKER: "I dunno, Berrigan . . . he might come back . . ."

PENNY: "Hardy says he won't. He guarantees it."

BAKER: "Hardy? Never heard of him. What is he, a cop?"

PENNY: "He's a private detective . . ."

BAKER: "Shit, no, nothing doing . . ."

PENNY: "I trust him."

BAKER: "Well, good for you . . . Something about you. Can't see with all these bloody bandages. What are you, a darkie?"

PENNY: "I'm an Aborigine, yes."

BAKER: "I like Abos, good people. I had a good man once. (Cackling laugh). Could be one of your tribe — Albie Simmonds, know him?"

PENNY: "I knew Ricky, his son."

BAKER: "That right? Well, well." (Laughter) "Yeah, well that's another story. What's in this for you girlie?"

PENNY: "I want Noni."

BAKER: "How's that?"

PENNY: "Noni Tarelton. She's with Berrigan now. I hope he kills her. Anyway, she's up to her neck in this. She'll go to jail if I have anything to do with it."

BAKER: "Now you're talking! That slut Noni. Tarelton you call her? She was Rouble when she was fucking everything in sight round here. You reckon this Hardy's good, he'll get Berrigan?"

PENNY: "I'm sure of it, but he needs to know the story to put the pressure on. I don't really understand it myself Mrs Baker, I just have to ask you some things."

BAKER: "All right, ask away."

PENNY: 'You've answered one — you and Albie Simmonds were lovers?"

BAKER: "Yeah, when he was off the grog."

PENNY: "Hardy said to ask you about the bank job, Simmonds and Berrigan, Noni and the money."

BAKER: (Laughter) "Shit, he does know a thing or two. Smart bugger is he? Alright, this is it. Joey and Albie did the job. Fifty thousand they got. Nearly killed them. Well, me and Joey weren't getting on so well, on account of me and Albie, see? They gave me the money, but Joey got real rough one night and I decided to do him. I got Noni to get off with him and charge him with rape. I paid her a hundred dollars." (Laughter) "Funny thing, I never had to pay her all of it because she got put away for moral danger, you know?"

PENNY: "Yes."

BAKER: "Well, Joey got sent away. Albie went to see him. They'd been mates for years, and I don't know what Joey told him, like, but Albie wasn't never the same again. He went on the grog like you've never seen. He took his boy to Sydney. Nellie, the mother, she was dead by this time, and he stayed down himself a while. He came back from time to time but he was never much good. Nice bloke though, Albie. What's his son like?"

PENNY: "Bit wild."

BAKER: "Yeah? Albie was quiet, real quiet, drunk or sober."

I stopped the machine, re-wound the tape and played the last two passages again to make sure I had it right. Then I let the tape run on.

PENNY: "What about the money?"

BAKER: "I moved it, got about thirty thousand for it. I sat on it for a while, then I got the farm and started to set up . . . you know about that?"

PENNY: "No."

BAKER: "Doesn't matter then. Oh shit, this pain in the side of me head, I can't stand it."

PENNY: "Are they giving you something for it?"

BAKER: "Yeah, doesn't help though. I reckon I've got something bad. Growth or something. They won't listen, nobody'll listen . . ."

PENNY: "Why did you stay here? You must have known Berrigan would come back."

BAKER: "Yes, I did. Well, I've got some money put away. I was going to give it to him, it'd be his share of the job nearly. And there's big money coming. Was, anyway, before this. But I hadn't reckoned on him looking up the girl and finding out it was me set him up, see? It's a long time ago but he was wild, crazy. When I didn't have the whole fifty grand to give him he went off his head. Noni just watched while he worked on me. Christ it hurt, still hurts . . . Well, that's it, that's what your man wanted to know?"

PENNY: "I suppose so. Is there . . . anything else?"

BAKER: "No. That's enough isn't it? Jesus what a mess. He wouldn't let me explain. I wonder if Albie seen him?"

PENNY: "Do you think he might have Mrs Baker?"

BAKER: "Ah, I dunno. Albie was up here not long ago. He was talking about Joey and his boy. Pissed, though. Didn't make much sense."

PENNY: "I'll have to go. Don't worry Mrs Baker, I'm sure nothing will happen to you."

BAKER: "Good luck to you girlie, you're game. I'm not worried . . . doesn't matter . . . I'm not going to leave here alive anyway."

22

I woke Penny up and we got on the road again. I was tired and edgy from the heat and the travelling and the unravelling of people's private lives. And this was just the beginning; the real sortings-out were ahead. I smoked and the tobacco tasted like old spinach. Penny looked at me as I swore and threw the butt away.

"What's the matter?" she said. "Is the tape alright?"

"The tape's fine. I feel lousy."

She looked and smelled fresh. The breeze was in her afro mop and there wasn't a drop of sweat on her.

"Too much beer," she said shortly. "Have you thought what you're going to do next?" She clicked her tongue. "I can't see how that tape will help you."

I wasn't quite sure myself. It had confirmed things I'd sensed, things about a quiet, dark man who'd dumped his son, parted ways with another man and gone to pieces. Twelve years ago. If I was going up against a talking situation the more I knew the better. Trouble was, it might be a shooting situation. I was afraid of that; I didn't trust Penny not to do something independent and dangerous under those conditions. I considered calling in the cops but rejected the idea quickly. To do that would up the chances of shooting starting. That is, if the cops didn't just run me straight out of town. Macleay cops would feel about an armed private detective wandering about with an Aboriginal girl calling in on the hospital and the black citizens, like they would about a drop in pay. I didn't say anything. I thought and sulked and drove.

It was nearly four when we got back into town; long shadows were starting to drape themselves over the streets and the air had cooled. The sky was like a sheet of pale blue silk stretched over the frame of the world. It would be a good night for taking a walk, or going to a drive-in or doing almost anything other than what I had to do. I drove up the back street and stopped by the derelict shop.

"We watch for a minute from there," I told Penny.

"Then what?"

"I'll phone the place and start bargaining."

"For Noni," she sneered.

"Right. Come on."

The street was empty. A factory faced the shop from across the road and nothing seemed to be going on there. I grabbed the binoculars and got out of the car. Penny followed me as I picked my way through the rubble of the shop's ground level. I took a quick look at the back of the garage before going up the staircase and what I saw made me stop in my tracks. Penny bumped into me and swore.

"Shut up," I hissed. "I don't like this."

"What?"

"See that car, the yellow one?"

The yellow Mini was parked at the back of the garage. I could see the tape holding the rear window together. I'd seen the car before — in the street outside Saul James' terrace house in Darlinghurst.

"I see the Mini. So what?"

"It belongs to Noni's boyfriend, actor named James. He's the last person I need around just now."

"Isn't that nice?" she purred, "Noni's boyfriend. Tough character is he?"

I laughed. "Just the reverse. Soft as mush."

"Is he in on it, the kidnapping?"

"I can't see how." I considered it. "No, no chance. He's blundered into it somehow and it screws it all up."

"How?"

"He's a potential hostage for one thing, and if he was thinking of coming up here he might have told someone else. He might have told Tarelton. The army could be on the way."

"Your precious Noni could get hurt," she crooned.

I lost my temper and rounded on her. "Drop it Penny! This is serious, I've got bad feelings about what's going on in there. It's not just Noni who might get killed. Another man's dead anyway."

"Who? There was panic in her voice." What are you talking about, who's dead?"

I got myself under control and felt disgust at my outburst, but it was too late to play secrets. "It's time to come clean Penny, to stop the games. I'll tell you something you don't know. Berrigan's not in there. He's dead. He was shot in a park in Balmain the other night. I know because I was there, in fact the police think I did it. Now I'll tell you something you *think* I don't know. Ricky Simmonds is in that garage."

I heard the quick intake of her breath and felt her stiffen beside me.

"How did you know?" she said softly.

"I wasn't sure until I checked at the cafe. You saw Noni and Berrigan alright. You also saw Ricky. I didn't think you'd go through all this just for revenge on Noni. Ricky's your obsession — which is worse luck for you."

"Why?"

"Remember you told me he seemed to be looking for someone, a young man?"

"Yes."

"He was looking for his father. That's alright, nothing wrong with that. But who do you think it was who got shot at Bare Island? Who do you think shot him and why?"

She was silent and another voice cut in from behind us.

"Don't let it worry you Penny."

We turned together, he held the rifle steadily on the centre of my chest and it wasn't far away, not a fraction of a second away. My gun was in the car, light years away, the binoculars were on the staircase where I'd put them when I spotted James' car. He was standing with his feet nicely spaced in a clear spot. I was off balance on a pile of rubble.

Penny stirred beside me. The rifle didn't waver but his voice was sharp and menacing.

"Easy Pen, easy. I don't want to hurt you."

"But you will if you have to," I said.

"That's right mister. I got nothing to lose now. I been waiting for you. Saw you last time — who are you anyway?"

"Let's go inside and talk about it." I tried to get balance and a better foothold but I was kidding myself. There's something about a couple of feet of rifle barrel and the black hole at the end that stiffens your muscles and throws your hand-eye co-ordination to hell. I just stood there. All I could do was talk.

"We have to go inside," I said. "You can't shoot us here. How's James? How's Bert?"

He ignored the remarks and made his decision.

"Go out through the back door and up to the fence. I swear I'll blow your head open if you try anything. Sorry Pen, you too."

We went. The yard at the back of the shop was a rubbish heap — bottles and deadly missiles by the hundred — but I believed he'd do what he said and I tried to look as innocent as a man on a golf course. The back fence was missing palings and there were plenty of places for a person to step through it.

"That's far enough," Ricky snapped. "Perce!"

He yelled the name again and the man I'd seen before came out the door carrying a sawn-off shotgun, double-barrelled. The stock had been cut back too and was wound around with black insulation tape. It wasn't for rabbits.

"Get through. You first, Pen. Nice and easy."

Penny slipped through and I bent and followed her. This brought me to within a few feet of the man with the shotgun. He was fiftyish and every day of it showed in his face which was lined and creased like an old boxing glove. His body was thick, still strong-looking but with the mark of thousands of measures of alcohol on it. His hands seemed to be shaking slightly and that was even more frightening than Ricky's steely strength. I shot a look at James' car. It was dusty and travel-stained; its bright cheerful yellow was dimmed but still incongruous in the surroundings. I wondered what had brought the owner here and how he was coping; how his stagey manners were standing up to the real-life situation.

I half turned and spoke to Ricky who'd come through the fence with the rifle still nicely poised for use. I nodded at the car.

"Why's he here?"

"Christ knows." It was the first indication that he wasn't in total control, with everything figured out. Maybe that was a good sign, maybe not. I told myself it was. Perce moved aside and we went out of the fading sunlight into the near night of the workshop. Before we went inside I saw close-up what had disturbed me during my earlier, apparently incompetent, surveillance. By the door there was a cut-down oil drum with a crank handle sticking out of it. A cloud of flies buzzed around the metal shaft and the top of the drum.

I wasn't prepared for her; I'd chased her up and down the coast and looked at her picture and talked to a dozen people about her, but I still wasn't ready for the impact of her. She was taller than I expected, leaning against Bert's workbench, and somehow more vivid. Her hair was a dark blonde tangle and she had one of the most passionate faces I'd ever seen. The high cheekbones were startling and the mouth was a wide, sensual slash. Her face was pale with the imprint of tension and lack of sleep. Her eyes were dark, shadowed pools. She was wearing a white dress, street-length and cut very low in front. It was spattered all over with something dark and I thought I knew why the flies were gathering outside. She took a few steps towards us as we came into the garage and her movements were like something from an adolescent's daydream. I could understand the depth of Penny's hate and the quality of Madeline Tarelton's feeling about Noni. She wasn't a woman's woman.

If she was a man's woman she certainly wasn't Saul James'. He sat on a chair a few feet away from Noni. He had on his usual beige outfit and his beige look. The girl washed him out completely; his eyes were fixed on her as she moved, but you had the feeling that he could disembowel himself there and then and she wouldn't notice.

"Well, well, well. Little Penny the La Perouse picaninny." Her voice was husky, edged with tiredness and maybe fear, maybe something else. "I always said you'd end up with a nice white man. Who's your handsome friend?"

The remark semed to be directed at Ricky as much as Penny and I didn't like that one bit. She was pure trouble. Penny glared at her but didn't speak. I broke the silence.

"Hello Noni. Hello James. Everything under control?"

James raised haunted eyes and looked at me.

"No, it's not." He pointed to the younger dark man. "He's going to kill us."

I studied Ricky in detail for the first time. He was several shades lighter than Perce, hardly darker than a Latin. His face wasn't heavily influenced by Aboriginal ancestry either. It was craggy rather than

574

fleshy and his ears stuck out a bit. A few gloved fists had hit and moved it around but hadn't diminished the intelligence and character in it. Not that it was a nice face. It was a dangerous face and it scared me more than a little. He wasn't tall, I had that on him, but right then I'd have traded a few inches for my Smith & Wesson.

"I don't think so." I tried to make my voice sound calm and confident although my throat was dry and my tongue felt like a bit of old rope. "He only kills when he has to and there's no point in killing any more people. Three's enough. Where's Bert?"

Noni let out a high laugh that cracked and ran down to a sob. "Ricky didn't kill *him* — I did." Her eyes flew off to the shadows near the front door, past the truck which stood near the middle of the floor, over the pit. Ricky didn't say anything or move, he just kept that rifle steady. I went over and looked down at the shapeless heap on the floor. I twitched back the hessian covering. Bert's heart wouldn't trouble him any more. Nothing would. The side of his head was caved in; a dark, soggy-looking mass like molten chocolate covered it from above the ear to the collar of his shirt. It hadn't been done with just one blow of the crank handle, or two.

Penny shot me a look that could have been triumph, then the impact of the whole thing reached her.

"Who did Ricky kill?" she said softly.

"The boy at Bare Island, to give him the cover for this big play." I waved my hand to take in all of us, including Bert, and the truck. "Only it's gone a bit sour, eh Ricky?" I turned to look at the older man.

"How about you Albie, who have you killed today?"

He put the shotgun down, leaning it on the running board of the truck which was an old Bedford, and began to roll a cigarette from makings he kept in a tin. He glanced across at Ricky.

"Might have ta be you," he growled.

Ricky looked puzzled, glanced at the man smoking and then stared at him as if trying to find answers to a hundred questions in his face. Noni was standing by the bench, only a few feet from me now, and running her hand over the smooth, artificial surface of the airline bag. The money bag.

"You'll never spend it Noni," I said quietly, "not now."

"Shut up," Ricky snapped. "Fuckin' shut up. You can't tell the bloody future. We'll spend it, we'll go . . ."

"You won't go anywhere, even if you got this rig fixed up." I pointed at the Bedford. "You're blown. There's half a dozen people in Sydney know about you now. How far do you think you'd get, you and her? You'd have to live in a cave, what good would money be then?"

Ricky was looking agitated. He shifted the weight of the rifle in his hands and looked speculatively at me. It was dodgy talking to him like that. If he felt too hopeless about his prospects he might feel like going out in a welter of blood. Why not? I wanted him desperate, off balance, but not crazy desperate. I had to offer him something.

"I suppose you might get away somehow. Up north you could get a boat perhaps. Risky as all hell . . ."

Ricky clutched at it. "We'll make it. Shit, there's boats leaving Australia all the time. We'll make it."

"I don't understand any of this," James wailed, "not a word. Noni, you can't go off with this . . . killer. I love you, you're mine . . ."

The words must have sounded ludicrous, even to him. Noni let out a hoot of derision. She spun around and advanced on James waggling a finger in his face.

"Poor Saulie," she crooned, "poor baby Saul."

It didn't throw James, he must have been used to it.

"You're sick Noni," he said sharply. He'd said it before — maybe it had worked. Not this time. She broke into a crazy, jerky dance.

"Ricky, oh Ricky baby," she sang, "we'll go to Thailand, we've got enough money there for a thousand fixes, ten thousand fixes, big fixes, lovely fixes."

James put out his hand as if to steady her, help her down from her perch, but she slapped at him, skittered away. She slammed into the side of the truck and crumpled, sliding down to the oily garage floor. James moved towards her but Ricky's rifle came up sharply.

"Leave 'er," he rapped out.

James stopped and looked helplessly at me. I shook my head gently.

"She doesn't understand," I said. "She thinks she's in it with him but she isn't. He's got no use for her."

"I still don't understand all this," James said. He seemed less pathetic, sensing that his nursemaid role might have a little longer to play. That'd be enough for him. I looked across at Penny but it didn't seem to make any difference to her. She was looking at Ricky in a way that chilled me. It evoked a memory and I placed it. She was looking at him the way she'd looked at the corpse at Bare Island. For her, he was dead already. That was a pity, but probably sound judgement. I just wanted to be sure that he didn't take any of us with him on his second exit. James, frail reed that he was, looked like my only certain ally. Some knowledge might steady him. Besides, I had only one card to play and I had to prepare the game so that it would count decisively.

"Since we're all here, more or less, and nobody's going anywhere until night time, I might as well tell it the way I see it." I raised my eyebrows at Ricky. "OK, Ricky, you're the one with the gun and the money?"

"Watch him Rick, he's a smartarse," Perce said. "I'm going to finish off the wiring." He started to get into the truck. The Bedford had been spray-painted grey and bars had been welded onto the front of it. A light metal frame had been welded up over the tray and I could see a couple of petrol drums on the tray just behind the cab. A tarpaulin that looked big enough to fit over the frame was lying on the floor beside the truck.

"I've got a couple of bottles in my car Albie," I said. "Be a bit warm but . . ."

He got down and looked at Ricky. "Jeez, Rick, I could use a drink."

"No," said Ricky. "Why do you keep calling him Albie mister?"

"That's his name, Albie Simmonds."

"Percy White's my name, smartarse."

"You can call yourself Joh Bjelke-Petersen for all I care, but your name's Albie Simmonds and you robbed a bank in 1966 with Joseph Berrigan."

"I knew it," Ricky said softly. "I knew you was him."

"It's bullshit," Albie muttered. "I didn't know Berrigan."

"He ever let Berrigan get a look at him Ricky?" I asked.

"No, no he kept right out of the way."

"Berrigan would have known him, even after all this time. There's a woman in the hospital here that knows who he is."

Albie's sullen face showed some interest.

"You see 'er? How is she?"

"I didn't see her, the girl did."

He turned towards Penny, the shotgun forgotten, the rifle forgotten, everything forgotten but the woman. I was seven feet from the shotgun. I'd have to step over Noni who was slumped down by the running board. I looked at Ricky. He was angry and puzzled but he wasn't careless. I'd never make it.

"I saw her," Penny said. "She isn't well. She was badly hurt but she thinks there's something else wrong with her. From the look of her she could be right. I'm sorry."

He shook his head and climbed into the truck.

"How long Perce?" Ricky asked.

"Coupla minutes."

Not long, not long enough. Noni pulled herself up and limped over to the bench. A handbag was lying beside the airline bag and she reached into it and pulled out cigarettes. When she had one lit she struggled to regain the arrogance that was ninety-nine per cent of her style. It was a real struggle and she didn't quite make it.

"What's that about Ricky and me?" she said shakily. "What would you know about it? Who the fuck are you anyway?"

"He's a private detective, Noni," James put in.

"Don't tell me you hired him, baby? Not to get little me back?" She tossed her head and puffed smoke. She was still trying.

"No, not me, your father."

"Him. Fuck him."

Oh Ted, how much sharper than a serpent's tooth it is.

"He cares about you, Noni," I said quickly. "With the trouble you're in he's your only hope. Ricky'll drop you off at Oodnadatta crossing."

"No, he wouldn't," she said wildly. "He wouldn't."

"He's been planning to from the word go. Look, I'll tell you how it is. Ricky was looking for his father. Some kids who get dumped are like that, can't think of anything else." Albie quietly got out of the truck and stood listening. Ricky made no move to interrupt me so I went on.

"He found out a bit, got a line on his father and Berrigan and the bank job. Then he met you and found out that you were connected with that Macleay scene. I think he probably had the kidnap idea planned first but I can't be sure. When Berrigan contacted you Ricky saw it as a chance for the bank money if it was still around. He killed the boy at Bare Island to give himself a cover. God knows where he found him, and he stuck close to you and Berrigan, up here and back. When there was nothing doing on the bank money he hit on the idea of Berrigan fronting for the kidnap. You put Berrigan up to it, Noni, at Ricky's suggestion. It worked, more or less, and he killed Berrigan. I know I didn't because I fired low — ballistics will prove that — but Ricky didn't care. He reckoned he had enough red herrings dragging around to get clear."

"What about his father, how does he come in?" Penny asked quietly.

"He'd kept out of Ricky's way for years, then he heard that Ricky'd been killed. He checked at the morgue and knew it wasn't him. My guess is that he came in on it just because he thought Ricky would make a balls-up of it — which he has."

Penny started to cry quietly and Ricky looked at her amazed. For the first time the rifle wasn't ready for instant use. I was encouraged. This seemed to be the right tack.

"You had it alright there mate," I said, "but maybe it's not your fault, maybe it's inherited."

He swung the rifle on me, but carelessly. I could see the black hole wavering and his eyes weren't any steadier. "What the fuck do you mean?"

"Albie, Perce, whatever you want to call him, he denies he's your father, right?"

"Yeah, but . . ."

"Let me finish. Did you know he was on with the Baker woman, the one Berrigan bashed?"

"No. So what?"

"After Berrigan went to jail for raping Noni, so it was thought, Albie here and Berrigan had a meeting and a bad falling-out."

"So? Berrigan found out Perce was fucking his woman."

"No, other way round."

"I don't get it." The rifle was all over the place. Soon . . . soon.

579

"Albie isn't your father. Berrigan told him who was."

Ricky shook his head. He took one hand off the rifle and brushed it over his face as if it was covered with cobwebs.

"No. No . . ."

"Right. You killed your father in the park Ricky."

Now! I jumped him and nearly made it. I pushed at the rifle and swung my foot at his crotch but he was strong and young. He went back and fended me off with a sweeping lift of the rifle. It caught me in the mouth and I went down. Everybody had moved — Albie bent for the shotgun and his foot caught it and he fumbled, getting it near the trigger guard — he was bent over it and he took both barrels in the face. His face disappeared and blood erupted as the gun's roar was still filling the garage.

Ricky took in the full horror of the man collapsing, faceless, and he made a leap for the cab of the truck. Noni screamed his name, snatched up the bag and clawed her way into the truck. Ricky had the thing started and revving and he drove it straight through the doors. The truck went thump thump as it passed over Bert and the doors splintered like matchwood. Then there was a big empty space where the truck had been and Penny was frozen like a statue. Blood had rained on her, drenched her.

23

I got up and went past Penny, out the back door and through the fence and the shop. The Datsun started like a dream and I swung it around in the quiet street and headed off after the throbbing, roaring truck. I scrabbled on the seat beside me and got the gun out of the parka as I drove. I put it on the floor on the passenger side. That way I'd have to think for a second or so before I could use it. The gun made me feel better. It shouldn't have but it did.

We were in a wide street and the Bedford was bucketing along ahead of me scattering the few cars around in front of it. They pulled over to the sides of the road haphazardly and I had to drive dodgem style to avoid them. A man jumped out of his car and made flagging motions. Maybe he wanted to make a citizen's arrest, make a hero of himself. I cursed him through some broken teeth with all the foul vocabulary I had picked up from school, army, pub and married bliss. He jumped clear. A quick look in the rear vision showed me what I should have expected — a yellow Mini burning along behind me just close enough to be a nuisance.

The truck was blowing thick, rich, blue smoke but going well, heading west, into the sun. We thrashed past the houses and the shops and the factories where people were pursuing their legitimate and illegitimate ends. We slewed around the corners and I could see the petrol drums bouncing just slightly on the tray of the truck; they were anchored well enough and were giving the Bedford stability. It had a big, strong engine for pulling loads and now it was just pulling Ricky, Noni, a hundred and five thousand dollars and the fuel. I could catch it, but Ricky drove like an angel and I couldn't pass him. We left the wide, sealed road and got onto a thin ribbon of bitumen flanked by ten feet of gravel on each side. The wheel base of the truck could hold the bitumen but Ricky moved off and on it just enough to throw up a screen of dust and slow me down.

The road started to climb and wind and I could get a look ahead as far as a hundred yards; the sides of the road were baked clay now and Ricky threw up less dust. Twice vehicles came from the other direction and Ricky barrelled straight at them, forcing them off the road. For a minute I thought the shape I could see up ahead of us was just another citizen, then the Bedford picked up speed and seemed to be driven with some mad purpose. I strained my eyes and was able to make out the distinctive shape of a police wagon. Ricky drove straight at it but the wagon veered off the road onto some cleared space and I could see the driver fighting to turn the thing as the Bedford rocketed by.

I braked and the cop was back on the road and giving the wagon all he had. It was probably the most excitement he'd had in years. The pace picked up and I stayed a bit back of the police vehicle, letting him do the work. James stayed back of me. The cop was pushing Ricky to the limit and I caught a glimpse of the Bedford swaying as she went round a bend, then we were on a long, straight stretch, climbing hard.

The grey truck dipped on one side and started to go into a slide. Ricky fought it and stopped the thing from turning over but he went into a sideways spin that took him off the road and ran the front of the truck into a clay embankment. I braked and stopped fifty yards short of the truck. The police wagon shot past and the driver plastered rubber on the road getting it to stop. Two cops jumped out and started to run the thirty yards or so back to the truck. I heard a sharp crack and they stopped, turned and raced back to the wagon. I got out of the car after grabbing the Colt and saw Ricky on the running board sighting along his rifle. With a shriek a bullet whipped off the hood of the wagon.

One of the cops rested a rifle on the mudguard of the wagon and opened up. A window shattered in the cab and Noni climbed down and started to run back towards me. She dropped the airline bag in the first stride and half-turned back for it. I screamed at her to keep coming and sprinted towards her. I reached her and thumped her hard onto the road. We were twenty yards from the truck when a bullet went into the petrol drums. A thousand heavy guns went off and a fiery wind blew over our heads. My eyeballs were scorched when I raised my head to take a look — the Bedford was a dark, ghostly shape inside a bright, dancing ball of yellow and orange fire.

James was standing beside his car and I lifted Noni up and half-carried her back to him. She collapsed into his arms and started to cry into his shoulder. He lowered her into the car seat and crouched by her, stroking her hair and murmuring in her ear. I started to walk towards the cops when one of them dropped to one knee, brought up a pistol and pointed it at me.

"Drop the gun," he yelled.

I looked at my hand, the Colt was still in it. I dropped it and came on.

Petrol had leaked from the truck and the ground around it was a pool of fire, somewhere in the middle of which was the money. Pity. One of the cops was inside the wagon frantically using the radio; the other held his gun shakily on me while I talked. He let me show him my documents but he was too nervous to take in much of what I said. I tried to keep out of direct line of the pistol while reinforcements arrived. What had happened on the road was going to take some explaining. Other things would take even more explaining. It was going to be a long night.

24

It was. They bundled us into police cars and took us into town. I told them about the garage and who Noni and James were. They let Noni clean herself up a bit but she needed much more than a bath, she needed a lot of expensive medical treatment. I hoped she wouldn't talk too much but she let James protect her and she scarcely said a word. With luck, I thought, I'd be able to get her out of this and back to her father fairly clean. Maybe that wasn't letting all the cards show but I recalled what someone had once said to some cops: "Until you guys own your own souls you don't own mine. Until you guys can be trusted every time and always, in all times and conditions, to seek the truth and find it and let the chips fall where they may — until that time comes, I have the right to listen to my conscience, and protect my client the best way I can."

That's how I felt. The cops sure as hell didn't seem too concerned about an incinerated black man and another the same colour with no head to speak of. That's how I thought I'd play it, but Penny threw a spanner into the works, or tried to.

They picked her up in the garage. When she came to see us in the police building she'd washed the blood off and was wearing some kind of policewoman's smock. They'd told her about Ricky. It didn't seem to touch her. Then she told me that she'd given the cops who came for her something to take with them and be careful of the fingerprints — a crank handle. Her eyes glittered maliciously when she told me this. Noni was within hearing but it was wasted on her. She was burying herself in James' warm solicitude, a good beginning for the attitude she'd have to take up when all Ted's money started working for her.

It was very complicated and I didn't help by refusing to tell them anything until the lawyers got there. Cy Sackville came up the next day and some smoothie Ted got to handle Noni's part in it. Sackville spoke for James, too, but he was pretty much in the clear. The cops didn't like it one bit. There was nothing in it for them but trouble. They tried to stick me with various things from conspiracy down to dangerous driving, but their hearts weren't in it and Sackville brushed them aside. Penny they didn't even hold and she stayed for a few days with relations in town, then she left without contacting me.

The lawyer took Noni back to Sydney and I never saw her again. I heard later from Cy that Ted's lawyers had headed off any charges connected with Bert's death. The crank handle held her fingerprints alright but she claimed that Bert had tried to rape her. If his body had been in the state it was when I saw it, the coroner might have wondered how many blows with a crank handle to the head it took to prevent a rape, but the truck wheels had passed over Bert's head, front and back, making a mess that no-one could interpret. I was pretty sure she'd been in on the kidnap idea with Ricky, but there was no way of proving it and it wasn't in my interest anyway.

I saw a fair bit of Saul James in the few days I spent in Macleay straightening things out. After they pried him loose from Noni he seemed to have no direction, no purpose and sort of attached himself to me. I asked him about his part in the play.

"Gone," he said wryly. "The understudy was too good, he filled in on the first rehearsal I missed and now he's got the part."

"Tough."

He shrugged. "I wonder what will happen to Noni?"

"Overseas trip if I know Ted. She's no loss to you James."

He looked hurt.

"At least there's one consolation. It didn't cost you any money."

"I thought the money was burnt?"

"It was, but I wrote down the serial numbers of your share, you'll get it all back."

He looked at me as if I'd betrayed him instead of saved him five thousand dollars. I'd denied him his little bit of martyrdom.

I finally got clear of the cops and of James. I flew back to Newcastle, played games with some more cops and got my car out of their clutches. Someone had washed it by mistake while it was impounded and it was with pride that I drove it back to Sydney.

That took me back to the let-down that follows cases like this one. I mooched into the office and screwed up circulars and paid a few bills in anticipation of Ted Tarelton's cheque. I sat around at home reading novels and writing a report on the case. My .38 came back from the Balmain police. Berrigan's case closed. I heard from Grant Evans that the Macleay cops were glad to have the bank robbery off their books. They hadn't revealed any of this pleasure to me.

Three days went by like this, slowly and with little ends of the Tarelton case being tied up. Ailsa's return was imminent — there was that at least to look forward to. I was at home in the middle of the day in the middle of the week when the phone rang. I put my book down and looked at it reluctantly. I answered it reluctantly. My stomach lurched when I heard the voice on the other end. For a fraction of a second I thought it was Ricky Simmonds.

"Hardy?"

"Yes. Jimmy Sunday?"

"Right. You sorted it out — Ricky and Noni and that?"

"You could say that. It's over anyway. Who told you?"

"Penny."

"Oh, how's she?"

"Alright. You see Jacko's fight with Rosso's coming up on Friday?"

I hadn't seen; I'd pushed the whole Aboriginal-Italian business away into a corner of my mind, a worry corner but a corner. I associated it with the Tarelton business and that was cleared up. Besides, no-one would pay me for interfering in Coluzzi's plans. I was a mercenary wasn't I? That reminded me, Ted Tarelton hadn't paid my account yet.

"Umm," I said.

"We're ready to move."

"What does that mean?"

"Trueman's been at Jacko, you know, hinting he might have to take a dive. Jacko's played it smart, let Sammy think he'll co-operate. Probably will, not for sure, you know? He's not stupid, Jacko."

"I never thought he was," I grunted. "Where does that get you?"

"Coluzzi's got a bundle on Rosso. Too much to lay off."

I felt relieved. Well done. "Good, you've got him then, provided Moody can win."

"Oh, he'll win. Shit, you should see him, sharp and hard, he'll kill him. He scared me when I saw him sparring, he's that good."

Sunday knew what he was talking about. I respected his judgement in matters pugilistic, but he was undercutting my relief. Why was he telling me this?

"That's great Jimmy. I'll be there, I'll see you. Tell Ted Williams I'll get the tickets I promised him."

"Hold on Hardy, we need your help. We want Coluzzi's balls, not just his money."

"Oh?"

"Fuckin' right. He's for it and you're going to set him up for us. You can contact him can't you?"

I said I could. I didn't want to, but I could.

"OK. Tomorrow night at Trueman's."

"What do I tell him?"

"Tell him the niggers are organising and they want some of the action. Make him think he can tie up the Moody-Rosso fight. That'll bring him."

"What are you going to do?"

"Kick the living shit out of him."

I suddenly felt insecure, old, in need of a rest. "Look, have you gone into this? I mean Coluzzi's a professional, they don't leave things to chance."

"We've been tailing his heavies for days. We've got 'em all pinned. Jacko'll be safe. There'll be a small party going on in Newtown tomorrow night too. Just a small do -- a few cops might feel like coming along though."

That was persuasive. They obviously meant business and weren't going to let me off. "OK, I'll contact Coluzzi and get back to you. You'll have plenty of people along? Those Italians aren't soft."

"Don't worry. Tell him nine o'clock."

I hung up, made a cigarette, got a drink and thought about it. Siding with Sunday against Coluzzi was like backing the Apaches against the cavalry, but something was working inside me. I could have ducked it, could have pretended that Coluzzi wouldn't buy it, got out of it some way. But I thought of the two men dead in the unfriendly town up north and the girl who'd seen too much pain and blood at seventeen. They hadn't taken a trick in the whole mess. Noni was on her way to London, or wherever, and I was due a big cheque. I hunted around for the card, found it in some unwashed clothes and called Coluzzi.

I got a female Italian voice on the other end and then a long, long wait. When Coluzzi finally came on the line his voice was soft and guarded.

"I've been wondering about you Mr Hardy, what do you know?"

"Hello Coluzzi. I've been out of town, up north with the black people."

"So?"

"Maybe you've got problems, maybe not. The Aborigines are organising themselves a bit. I don't think they'd be too keen on your idea of fights between blacks and Italians, not the way you see it anyway. They'd like to see their boys coming out on top once in a while, or twice in a while."

He didn't say anything, forcing me to go on.

"I've met their top man, Jimmy Sunday. He wants to talk to you about a deal."

"What deal? I don't need a deal. Why should I meet him?"

"Well, I'm just passing this on you understand? He says he can arrange the result of the Moody-Rosso fight. That's to show his good faith."

There was a pause while he considered it. When he spoke again it was with all the straightforwardness of Lucrezia Borgia inviting you to dinner.

"That's interesting, very interesting. Maybe I better meet these people. Where and when?"

I told him. He didn't sound happy but I said that was all I'd been given. He said he'd be there and rang off.

It left me edgy, without diversion. Ailsa wasn't due in until the next day. A postcard told me that. The rest of the mail was just waiting to be waste paper and I obliged it. I wished I'd asked Sunday about guns. I hoped there wouldn't be any guns. I wished Penny would come to see me but I knew she wouldn't. I wished the fight would be called off; I read the last couple of days' news reports on the fighters. They were both in great shape, both going to win, according to their trainers, both going to be world's champions. Moody had made the better impression in training. He was comfortably favoured to win. Coluzzi must have got good odds on his money. I called a man I knew and got fifty dollars to win thirty-five on Moody. Then I worried. What if Coluzzi knew the man I knew? What if the man I knew told Coluzzi? I drank and smoked and worried. Then I thought the hell with it. I'm a private detective, I'm tough. I can be stupid if I want to be.

I called Harry Tickener and we insulted each other for as long as we could stand it. He had tickets for the fight and was going himself. He agreed to leave two for Ted Williams at the paper and to meet me at the club with two for me.

"Ailsa?" he asked.

"I hope so."

"Good. I expect to have company too."

"That's nice. Do I know her?"

"Your name's never come up."

"OK, be mysterious. I'll see you there."

"You won't be able to miss us."

That was a good exit line. I wondered what it meant. Harry sounded happy. Good. If Harry could be happy maybe we could all be happy.

25

Twenty hours later I was happy. Ailsa flew in around eleven and we went straight back to her place and to bed. We got out of bed an hour later for something to eat and drink and then back again. After that session I smoked and we picked up the pieces. Her tan told the story of where she'd been and she filled me in on the progress of her interests in the Pacific. The picture amounted to good news and more good news. I told her I was glad about it and she scrutinised me for the irony in such remarks that usually sparks off our fights. It wasn't there. The heart had grown fonder. I told her about the Tarelton case and promised I'd take her out to dinner when I got the cheque.

"Oh that reminds me," I said. "I'm taking you out tomorrow night if you're free."

"Good, where?"

"The boxing."

"Ugh, no thanks — horrible."

"Harry Tickener'll be there."

"Harry's nice but still, no."

"I think he's got a girlfriend."

"Really, that's interesting. Who?"

"I don't know, and if you don't come tomorrow night I'll make sure you never find out. I'll break it up and you'll never know."

She yawned. "Who cares."

"I gather you're not coming?"

"Right. Come and see me afterwards."

We wasted the afternoon a bit more and I left. I went home and played with my pistols for a while; I cleaned them and loaded them and checked their actions. Then I wrapped them up and put them away. I'd bought some cut price Scotch and I sampled it just to see whether it was a bargain. Not bad. Quite smooth. Of course the first drink can be misleading so I had a second. I thought I detected a metallic taste so I had a third. I was mistaken about the metallic taste. It was good smooth whisky that needed drinking without any judgemental attitudes in view. I had a fourth in a calm, purely objective frame of mind.

I ate something and showered and dressed myself in the clothes I'd worn to break into Sammy's gym some nights before. I took the papers I'd removed then from the hiding place and stuck them in my pocket. I thought again about the guns and compromised by putting the Colt into the clip in the car. The Celica had gone back to the Tareltons soon after my arrival back in Sydney. I had a mind-flash image of Madeline Tarelton as I climbed into the Falcon. An unscrupulous, despicable person would ring her up some time and find out just how much her husband didn't understand her. But an unscrupulous, despicable person wouldn't be driving to Newtown for a show-down between ethnic minorities, and he wouldn't be haunted by the eyes of a dark girl standing stock-still while blood rained on her.

I was nervous and early, much too early. I drove into town and down to the Rocks to kill time. The Opera House billowed up like bedsheets in a high wind. North Sydney was canopied by purplish cloud, but the sky to the east was a pale powder blue. The stratosphere was in two moods like me; my satisfaction at the conclusion of the Tarelton case, messy though it was, was tempered by the threat of the events ahead. I parked and wandered up through the city which gradually emptied around me. By eight o'clock there was only a thin line of traffic made up of people snapping up the last parking spots for their night on the town. Nine-tenths of the city was asleep and the remaining tenth was only fitfully awake in those oases of light where celluloid was spinning, liquor was flowing and there was money to be made. I went back to my clean car and drove to Newtown.

I parked half a mile from the gym and walked through the streets. Any one of the couple of black people I passed could have been Sunday's confederates, or none of them. It seemed to me that Coluzzi was a brave man to agree to a meeting in this territory. I'd have insisted on neutral ground. The thought bothered me as I walked along. Coluzzi was totally professional to all appearances and this was a bad move. I scouted around the gym looking for signs of trouble but everything was as quiet as a synagogue on Sunday. I walked back to my car and took out the gun. The door to the building was open and I took the stairs as quietly as I could. On the stars the stale smell of tobacco smoke and the reek of sweat blended into a threat of mustard gas. The place whispered of tension and danger. It was a good place not to be.

I pushed open the door to the gym. The bulb over the ring was glowing, making a sickly greyish patch of light in the centre of the room. My feelings of threat and danger became more intense; I felt as if I were walking into an ambush prepared especially for me. Still, I went. I took a couple of steps into the room and strained my eyes at the darkness that hung in every corner. There were no sounds, no movements. I looked again at the ring, this time with eyes that had grown used to the gloom. What I'd taken for shadow at first glance now didn't look like shadow any more. It had shape and bulk but it was very still. I moved quickly across to the ring and climbed through the ropes.

Jimmy Sunday lay there with his eyes open, staring up into the bulb the way no living eyes could. He was wearing a polo-neck sweater and jeans. The rolled neck of the sweater was soaked with blood and blood had seeped through and run in a trickle across the canvas floor. I crouched beside him feeling sad and sick and furious with myself. Every instinct should have told me that Sunday would be out-matched coming up against Coluzzi. I had know that, but I'd let myself be persuaded otherwise because I was being easy on myself. I'd dramatised my own self-sacrifice of siding with the Aborigines and ignored the objective facts — that they didn't have a chance. I had the resources to do something about it, I had the cop contacts, or I could have headed Coluzzi off somehow. But I hadn't and this was the result.

Death does different things to different faces. I'd seen my father dead and ready for departure in a funeral parlour; his skin was painted, a thing unimaginable in life. He looked like a waxworks dummy and my mother just said "It isn't him" and we went away. She didn't even cry.

Death in the raw, violent death, is different again; I'd seen the evil stamped like a stencil mark across some dead faces and innocence blooming on others. In death Jimmy Sunday looked younger than he had in life and I was reminded that I'd thought him young when I'd first seen him at a distance. The scars from boxing and boozing and living had been almost erased and his brown skin was smooth and taut. Somehow that made it worse. I closed his eyes and went away. There was nothing else to do, not there.

I left the gym and walked back to my car with my shoulders hunched and the pistol tucked into my waistband. I felt an urge to use it on Coluzzi or one of his apes but at the same time I recognised that as the immature and useless impulse it was. When I got home I had a drink and poured another, then I called the Sharkey number. When Rupe came to the phone he was nervous. When I identified myself he was hostile. I told him that Sunday was dead and asked if he had any family. There was a silence before he spoke.

"Yeah, sort of. A woman and a kid, not his, but same thing."

"Did you know about the plan to move against the Italians?"

"A bit, not much. I wasn't gonna be in on it. Too fuckin' old. But I heard Jimmy was gonna give the word at lunchtime today, but no-one seen him since last night. Where'd you see him?"

I told him and he said he'd send someone over there.

"Who done him?" he asked.

"I can't prove it Mr Sharkey."

"Ah, what the fuck does it matter. You got anything else to say?"

"No. Just that I'm sorry."

His answer was the sharp click of the connection being broken. That did wonders for me. I sank some liquor and poured some more. The glass suddenly felt as heavy as lead, full of reproach. I set it down and started working through my little red book of telephone numbers. My first call was to Grant Evans. The second, back to me, was from a policeman in Macleay. My next call was to a security organisation in the city. I followed that with a call to Major Ian Mahony who was head of the security firm that guarded Macleay hospital. I had to give him references in the constabulary and the military. They seemed to satisfy him and I got an interview arranged with him for the following morning, in Macleay. I poured the liquor back into the bottle and went grimly off to bed to prepare myself for my busy day.

My last conscious thought was that I had put the finger on Jimmy Sunday for Coluzzi.

26

Busy is right. The radio alarm woke me at six o'clock. I came swarming up out of a dream in which I'd been fighting a ring full of people with my bare fists. I must have set my jaw resolutely in the dream because it was aching like fury when I got out of bed. I made coffee and swilled down aspirin and caffeine tablets. The coffee was stale, this case had dragged on and I'd neglected my domestic necessities. I promised myself some fresh coffee and clean sheets when I'd done what I had to do. I had a shower and let the water play on my injuries, a split scalp and battered knuckles, both beginning to heal. I had lost two teeth, knocked out clean, and another was very loose. That wasn't such a bad score except that I was still waiting for the cheque to justify them. Today, I'd be on my own time, the way to go out of business someone once told me.

I drove to the airport through a clear, mild morning. The traffic seemed to acknowledge the clemency of the day by parting in front of me and staying back to allow me through. As before, there was no crush for the flight to parts north. I handed in Penny's unused return ticket and my unused Newcastle to Sydney section plus some cash and got a return ticket to Macleay. I had no luggage, no guns, no hand grenades, just my bright, sharp wits and my tarnished old soul. I bought the papers and a copy of *Ragtime* and boarded the plane. The papers told me everything that was going on in the country around that time which was nothing; *Ragtime* gripped and held me like a new lover and I didn't lift my face from it for the whole trip. I knew what I was going to do in Macleay. I didn't have to think about it any more.

I got a taxi into town and arrived at Major Mahony's office punctually at nine-thirty which was just as well. Mahony was a Britisher in his fifties. His face spoke of hot parade grounds and long

595

nights over the bottle in the mess. He was bulky behind his mahogany desk. Pink scalp showed through thinning silver hair but he still had a few good, bullying years in him.

"You come well recommended, Mr Hardy," he barked, "but you ask a lot. Convince me."

It was an old tactic and the only way to confront it was head-on.

"What do you think of drugs Major — hemp smoking and things like that?"

He glared over the pipe he was stuffing, a big black job that looked fit to roast a quarter pound of shag.

"Hate it. Degenerate. Catch any of my people at it and out they go."

"Precisely. That's why I'm here. If you co-operate with me it'll help to close down a drug-growing and distribution point in this part of the country."

He grunted and puffed at the pipe.

"Hemp you said?"

"Hemp certainly, but you know where that leads."

"Do I not. I was in the Middle East for long enough — people lolling about, pansies . . ." He broke off choked, I suspected, by his excitement, but he coughed as though the tobacco smoke had caught in his throat. I followed up quickly.

"All I need is access to the woman, ten minutes alone with her, then the services of a stenographer for a few minutes."

"Sick woman, Mr Hardy, very sick. I checked with the hospital this morning. She's dying."

"Does she know?"

"Yes, they told her. She insisted on knowing. Does that alter your plans?"

"No." I could have added "on the contrary" if I'd intended to be perfectly frank with him, but I didn't.

"I suppose it can't do any harm considering the circumstances," he mused. "The woman might be glad to perform a last service." He looked at me enquiringly.

"I think she will." I hated myself for indulging him in his pompous humbug, but I had no choice.

"Very well then." He picked up a pencil and scribbled a note.

"Take that to the operations desk outside and you'll get what you want."

I stood up and assumed as respectful an attitude as I could without saluting. I don't think he'd have minded if I had saluted.

"Thank you Major. Great help." We shook hands. He managed to turn the gesture into a condescension for him and a privilege for me.

I went out to the office where all the work was done and handed in the note. A tired-looking man with red-rimmed eyes lifted a phone and spoke briefly into it. I looked around the room. There must have been ten or more telephones and the walls were covered with maps of Newcastle and Macleay and other towns in the area with red-headed drawing pins sticking in them. I waited five minutes before a young woman in a white blouse and blue skirt came into the room. The weary man nodded at me and she walked across and stuck her hand out.

"I'm Pam Henderson. Mr Hardy is it?"

I shook the hand and said it was. She picked up a notebook from one desk and slid a portable typewriter out from the cupboard. She was all business. Her hair was drawn back and well pinned. She wouldn't waste a second of a working day fussing with it. She collected a set of keys from a hook by the door and we went out to a car yard behind the office building. She got behind the wheel of a big Valiant station wagon and had the car out of the yard and heading down the street while I was still fastening the safety belt. She parked in a reserved bay outside the hospital and marched up the front steps with me trotting along behind her. She was just what I needed; if I'd had an assistant like her I could have sat in my office and thought up wisecracks. I could just turn up for the denouement and make sure the client had the name right for the cheque.

The hospital reception desk stayed her for maybe five minutes and the ward sister for about three, then we were inside Trixie Baker's room. I summoned all my courage and spoke to my companion.

"I won't need you for a few minutes Miss Henderson. Please wait outside close by."

She spun on her heel and went out. I breathed a sigh of relief and approached the bed. Neither the appearance of the Baker woman when I'd found her at the farm, nor the desiccated voice on the tape had prepared me for the head on the pillow. Flesh had fallen away from her bones and she looked mummified. I couldn't remember what colour her hair had been when I first saw her, but it was white now, snow white. Her eyes were open but they were filmed over with pain, or perhaps morphine. I hoped it was the latter.

"Mrs Baker," I said softly. "Mrs Baker, how are you feeling?"

The pale eyes widened a little and the creases beside them deepened.

"Bloody awful, but not for long. Who're you? Doctor?

"No, I'm a detective. My name's Hardy. You've heard of me."

"I have, from the darkie. I seem to be able to remember everything just now. Too much really, too much. What do you want detective?"

"Some help, Mrs Baker. Some help for Albie Simmonds in a way."

The smile that spread across her ravaged face was almost sweet.

"Oh Albie. He was a dear, Albie. How is he?"

"I'm afraid he's dead Mrs Baker. He was shot. A friend of his is dead too and that's where I need your help."

The information didn't trouble her. Somehow she'd acquired some strength in her last hours. I felt guilty about manipulating her.

"Are you a religious woman Mrs Baker?" I asked.

She let out a short, breathless version of the cackle I'd heard on the tape.

"No, no, not a bit. Wish I was, then I could think I'd be seein' Albie soon, couldn't I?"

"I suppose so."

"But it's bullshit. Things are so bad, so rotten, there couldn't be a God, not a nice one like they say. Why anyway?"

I explained to her. It took some time and I had to repeat myself. She kept slipping away into some state that telescoped the last fifty years of her life. Things I said triggered memories and resentments and she lived through some scenes the meaning and content of which only she could know. It was her way of facing death and I couldn't deny it her. In the end she agreed to do what I asked. I called Henderson in and she took down the statement in shorthand, typed it up there and then and Trixie signed two copies.

I took the pen from her skeletal fingers and stepped back from the bed. Her hand fluttered on the coverlet and I bent down to hear what she said. Her voice was very faint.

"All gone now, eh? Albie, Joe Berrigan, me soon. What about Noni? What happened to her?"

"She missed out on all the trouble. She's got problems though, she's on drugs."

"She'll be alright. She'll die old and rich."

It sounded like wisdom and I treated it as such, nodding and saying something in assent. A soft sigh came from her and her eyelids came down. I jerked up alarmed and Henderson glided up to the bed. She took the stick-thin wrist in her strong brown hand and laid fingers across it. After a few seconds she put the arm down and raised her fingers to her lips. We went quietly out of the room.

"She's asleep but it can't be long," Henderson said professionally.

"Are you trained?"

"Five years, army nurse."

"Your typing looks alright, too."

"Business school. Graduated first-class."

"You should be doing more with it."

"Are you making me an offer?"

I backed away physically and verbally. She'd be running things within a week, telling me what jobs to take and how I could increase my fees.

"No, sorry, I'm in a very small way of business."

She sniffed and drove me to the airport. It wasn't the worst of my rides out of Macleay but it wasn't the best either.

I read *Ragtime* in the waiting lounge and finished it on the plane. I kept it with me to give to Ailsa. On arrival in Sydney I went to Cy Sackville's office, talked to him for a while and left the papers plus several others I signed myself. Cy wasn't wearing the suit I'd seen in Macleay, in fact I'd never seen the suit before. Cy probably had more suits than I had fillings. Still, I liked him and promised to pay him before Christmas. He waved the promise aside which was probably wise.

I left, taking note of how to furnish an office with taste and style. There were only two problems: one, I'd never be able to afford it and two, if by some chance I ever could, this decor would be out of fashion. Difficulties . . . difficulties . . . On the drive home I considered what I'd done. The papers I left with Sackville were sworn statements by Patricia Baker, widow of Macleay, made in the belief that she did not have long to live, that Aldo Coluzzi was her partner in the marijuana-growing business, supplying capital and arranging distribution. Two other men, Carlo and Adio, surnames unknown, were mentioned as agents.

It wasn't much. It probably wouldn't even stick, but the papers would go in to the Drugs Enquiry Commission that was sitting just then and it wouldn't do Coluzzi any good. He'd get a mention in the press with luck and there'd be some investigation of his business affairs. I calculated that there should be something in there for auditors and tax men to chew on. At the most there might be a deportation order in it. I'd settle for that.

As for fat Sammy Trueman, he was going to lose money and the best fighter he'd ever had.

27

Prizefighting is in the doldrums, of course. I can remember when the big stadiums in Melbourne, Sydney and Brisbane did a roaring trade a couple of nights a week and stories on fighters pushed the politicians off the pages of the newspapers. That's all finished; the big stadiums are closed and pulled down mostly and the big crowds assemble for football and to see androgynous pop stars who are millionaires at eighteen and dead of drugs by twenty-five.

The Moody-Rosso fight was being put on at a League's club in the eastern suburbs, a great barn of a place designed to park as many cars as possible and accommodate as many bars and poker machines as possible. Living near it must be hell. The club had put on a good front for the fight; there was a big red banner with the fighters' names on it draped over the main entrance and a few old-time pugs were on hand to lend colour. Still, nothing could disguise the fact that the place had been designed for a softer generation. This place smelled of money. The stadiums smelled of sweat and piss.

I parked the Falcon and went up the steps into a lobby furnished in what might have been Elizabeth Taylor's taste when she was a girl. It was all scarlet and gold and the mirrors seemed to me to have a slimming effect. Most of the members thronging through to lose their money could use it. I scouted around for Tickener but he wasn't there. I was, as usual, neurotically early. Passages led off from the lobby to bars and entertainment rooms which were off-limits to non-members.

There was a bank of poker machines standing by one wall and I shook out some change and started dropping it in and pulling the lever. The machine devoured the money like a Venus fly trap taking nourishment. I turned around and almost had to grab the lever again for support. Tickener was walking towards me and beside him was

601

the six foot redhead I'd seen at the newspaper building. They came up and I summoned the strength to move away from the machine. The reporter's face wore a half-moon grin; I could have sworn he'd grown an inch or two. That still left him a few inches short of the redhead.

"Cliff, this is Toni Blake. Toni, Cliff Hardy."

I admired her. She was wearing black harem trousers with gold high-heeled shoes and some sort of beaded, lacy top; the slim arms, completely bare, were creamy, not one of your freckled redheads. I tried to keep my eyes off the cropped hair and treat her like a normal human being.

"Hello," I said. It sounded weak so I said it again. Then it sounded stupid so I gave up.

"Going to be a good crowd Cliff," Tickener said heartily. He was enjoying my reaction, as he had every right to. I'd taken the mickey out of him more times than was fair. The girl took hold of Tickener's arm enthusiastically, the way you handle a good bottle of Scotch.

"Let's go in and get a drink," she said thrillingly, "the auditorium's this way."

Harry kept up manfully and I tagged along, trying to get my mind off her swaying, queenly gait. I failed. Harry flashed the tickets and we went into a room a couple of hundred feet square with bars along three walls. It was filled with rows of metal chairs and the boxing ring was set up on a three-foot-high stage in the middle of the floor. The place would have held about 3000 people which, even with tickets at five to ten bucks each, doesn't amount to much of a gate. There were television rights though; the crew had set their gear up around the ring and heavy cables snaked across the auditorium floor. A couple of hundred people were already there, some sitting down but mostly crowded around the bars. I saw big Ted Williams over in a corner with Rupert Sharkey. They both held schooners of beer and looked depressed. I nodded at them and they returned the nod guardedly. I wanted to go over and talk to them, tell them what I'd arranged for Coluzzi, but I didn't. It wouldn't have helped. There were a fair number of Aborigines in the crowd, maybe a quarter of the people were dark, and this proportion held as the room filled up.

People parted in front of Toni and we walked down what was virtually an aisle to the bar.

"My shout," I said. "Toni, what will you have?"

"Triple Scotch," she said. "I'll have just the one drink all night."

"Harry?"

"Beer," Tickener said. "Middy."

"You'll have to give that up if you're going to hang around with me," the girl said. "It makes you fat and gassy in bed."

"Scotch," said Tickener.

"Three triple Scotches."

We took the drinks over to our seats which were in the ten-dollar section with a clear view and just far enough back to keep your neck comfortable. Tickener asked me about Ailsa.

"Wouldn't come," I said. "She doesn't like the fights."

"I love them," Toni said.

"Why?"

"They're exciting, primitive."

"What about the blood?"

"I don't mind that."

Oh Harry, I thought, you've got your work cut out here.

"What do you report on?" I asked her.

"Politics mostly."

That figured.

The lights went down and an announcer as wide as he was tall pulled over a boom mike and started his spiel. I glanced across. Tickener and Toni were holding hands. There was a rush through the doors and a lot of foot noise as people took their seats. The announcer heaved himself out of the ring and the first of the two preliminary bouts started. The four-rounder was between a pale, crop-headed boy with heavy shoulders and a thin Aborigine whose arms seemed to hang to his knees. Their styles were completely different and didn't mix. The crew-cut was a rusher and flailer and the dark boy was a fancy stepper with a neat straight left. They did no damage to each other and the fight was a draw. Two white men came up for the six-rounder, a heavily tattooed six-footer and a chunky guy who assumed a crouch while the referee was giving his instructions. This fight was over in five seconds; the tattooed man tried a left lead and the croucher came up under it and clouted him with a right he'd brought up off the floor with him. The tattooed man folded like a butterfly's wings and the big body sank gently to the floor. The referee raised the arm that had done the damage without bothering to count over the fallen one.

That brought Rosso and Moody out early. I realised that I'd nearly finished my drink. Tickener and Toni were whispering and had barely touched theirs. The seat beside me stayed empty until the announcement of the main event began, then I was aware of a huge bulk beside me and a cracked, hissing voice.

"Gidday Hardy, can I use this? Can't see a fuckin' thing from back there."

"Hello Jerome. Sure, it's vacant. My woman wouldn't come." I don't know why I said that but Jerome laughed.

"Mine neither. Reckons she seen enough fights when I was at it. Cunt of a game."

Toni caught the word and glanced across sharply. I made muted introductions and a wave of beer breath swept across us as Jerome responded. He had a glass in his fist and raised it as an ex-welterweight champion took his bow.

"Woulda killed him," he said.

Under the savage glare of the TV lights Rosso looked ugly, dark hair fuzzed on his arms and shoulders like fur on an animal and his skin was mottled. He wasn't tall, about five nine, a real natural middleweight with terrific strength in his arms and thighs. He looked as if he could go all night. Moody looked better. His skin was glossy under the lights and he was better proportioned with the meat and muscle better distributed. If I'd been his manager I'd have been a bit concerned about him. He looked as if he might grow into a light-heavyweight, the disaster division where there's no money to be made unless you're wasting to get in against middleweights or giving away pounds to heavies. But he looked good tonight.

The announcer didn't hold the action up too long. He tried a joke in Italian which got booed by a section of the crowd and then he gave it up and waddled away. The referee was Tony Bourke, a better than useful lightweight in his day. Trueman crouched in Moody's corner, whispering in the fighter's ear. He mimed a low punch and combination and the young Aborigine nodded. He clamped his teeth around the mouthguard and jumped up off his stool. I heard a sharp intake of breath from Toni as Moody skipped across the ring. But the Italian started the business by rushing Moody into the ropes and trying a clubbing left which Moody took on the glove.

The Aborigine had no trouble in ducking under Rosso's follow-up right swing and propping him with a straight left as he moved back into open space. That was the pattern of the round; the shorter man rushed in, bullocked his opponent to the ropes and tried to smash him with short, clubbing punches. Moody jabbed him. Moody took the points for the round but there was something a bit supercilious about his style; his shots stung the Italian and made him look clumsy, but they didn't hurt or frighten him or sap the strength in his body.

Rosso's handler had smooth silver hair like Rossano Brazzi and a ring with a big, bright stone in it glittered on his finger as he waved and jabbed in the air in front of his fighter. Trueman and someone who looked like the dark boy with the withered leg worked quietly and efficiently on Jacko and there was little conversation in the corner.

In the next two rounds Rosso tried to cut Moody off and slam into him in confined sections of the ring. He managed to hem him in a few times but he couldn't do much when he got there. Moody tied him up quickly and Bourke broke them and the Aborigine was off again, not dancing exactly, just moving in and out quickly and precisely and scoring with long lefts. His timing was good but not perfect. Rosso caught him with a few heavy body swings that had more power than they should have, given Moody's evasive abilities and speed. But the Italian was way behind on points when they came out for the fifth.

It wasn't a good round for Jacko. He seemed to have tired a bit and looked apprehensive. I couldn't help wondering if the fix was in, somehow. Moody took a couple of punches he should have slipped easily and Rosso roughed him up badly in a clinch. The crowd noise went up a couple of notches. The Italians felt that their boy was getting on top and the Aborigines weren't happy at all. No-one was neutral and the change of fortunes in the fight affected everyone. I could hear the rustle of money as bets were put on and laid off.

Moody looked a little distressed in his corner after the round but Trueman's style hadn't changed at all. The sixth started out much the same as the last round with Rosso aggressive and clumsily effective. Rosso brushed Moody's left lead aside as if it was a cobweb and slammed in a hard clean right to the mid-section. Moody felt it and responded with a cuffing, playful-looking left to the side of the head. Rosso ignored that and bored in to land a short, jolting right near the Aborigine's heart. There was a commotion behind me and I turned to see Ted Williams on his feet with beer slopping out of a schooner.

"Do him for Sunday!" he roared.

The punch or the shout transformed Moody. Maybe it was both. He seemed to settle into a firmer stance and loom over the Italian at the same time. He swayed out of reach of Rosso's next swing and speared a hard left into his face. He followed that with a crisp right; it was the quickest punch combination of the night and Rosso faltered. He missed with a roundhouse drive at Moody's head and Jacko came in shifting his weight slightly and sliding into position for the perfect punch — his whole body flowed in behind a short right that took Rosso on the chin and destroyed him. Moody's shoulder hardly moved and the punch wouldn't have travelled a foot. Rosso's knees sagged and he collapsed like a ruptured bag of cement. The darkness was in and wrapping around him before he hit the canvas.

It was the sort of end-of-fight you read about, rather than see, maybe like when Dawson finished Patrick or Burns knocked out O'Neill Bell. Everyone was standing up shouting and people were turning to each other asking if they'd seen it. Toni towered up there, her eyes like saucers staring at the ring. I could feel the excitement in Tickener beside me. Jerome, on the other side, was hustling. He brushed men aside to get to others and I caught a flash of his brown fist in the air, full of money.

I'd made money too but it was that kind of moment when money doesn't mean anything. I'd invested a lot of emotional capital in the events leading up to this and the moment was sweet. I finished my drink and felt the euphoria of the blacks around me catching hold and sweeping me up. My face creased into a smile and I was standing there foolishly taking in the scene like a stoned-out hippie. Suddenly the euphoria washed away and the alcohol warmth inside me died.

Five rows away Penny was standing beside a tall Aborigine. She was wearing a flame-red dress of some satiny material that touched a fetishistic nerve inside me like a dentist's drill going into tooth pulp. A poplin trench coat was floating out around her shoulders; it was too big for her; someone else's coat, and her eyes were shining and the flash of her white, chunky teeth was a stark, erotic signal. She moved her head a fraction, saw me, and looked straight through me. I stood still, empty and cold, and the fellow-feeling I'd had with the blacks around me ebbed away and I was back where I'd been before — alien, excluded and hostile.

Jerome said something to me and I grunted in reply. I started to move off and found Tickener by my elbow.

"Great fight, Cliff," he bubbled.

"Wonderful," Toni said.

"I don't know," I said blankly. "I think Sands would have been home sooner."

A while later I was driving to Mosman to see Ailsa, but I didn't expect the visit to be a good one. My head was too full of the images of women: wild ones, rushing to the edge; ambitious ones with their toe-holds on the ladder of preferment; old ones with their greed and the need for security showing in their eyes, and young ones with the illusions being scrubbed off their faces by the long days and nights.